FISH AND CHIPS TODAY, CHIPS & FISSION TOMORROW

'WE WANT BREAD AND ROSES TOO.'

'CHWARAE TEG I'R SIANEL!'

NUCLEAR WASTE DO NOT OPEN THE YEAR 20

ARIANS LL RIES E!

UNITY IS STRENGTH

'WE WANT BREAD AND ROSES TOO.'

TEN MILLION STARS ARE

'CHWARAE TEG I'R SIANEL!'

BURNING

PROLETARIANS OF ALL COUNTRIES UNITE!

NUCLEAR WASTE – DO NOT OPEN 'TILL THE YEAR 200,078!

'WE WANT BREAD AND ROSES TOO.'

'CHWA TEG SIAN

UNIG EB

PROLETARIANS OF ALL COUNTRIES UNITE!

UNITY IS STRENGTH

'WE WANT BREAD AND ROSES TOO.'

YR UNIG ATEB

PROLETARIANS OF ALL COUNTRIES UNITE!

FISH AND CHIPS TODAY, CHIPS & FISSION TOMORROW

'WE BREA ROSE

ANEL MRAEG

UNITY IS STRENGTH

SAFE? SO WAS THE TITANIC!

SIANEL GYMRAEG

SIANEL GYMRAE

LETARIANS OF ALL OUNTRIES UNITE!

UN STR

TEN MILLION STARS
ARE
BURNING

JOHN OSMOND

Gomer

First published in 2018 by Gomer Press,
Llandysul, Ceredigion SA44 4JL

ISBN 978 1 78562 249 6

A CIP record for this title is available from the British Library.

© John Osmond, 2018

John Osmond asserts his moral right under the
Copyright, Designs and Patents Act, 1988
to be identified as author of this work.

This book is published with the financial support of the
Welsh Books Council.

Printed and bound in Wales at
Gomer Press, Llandysul, Ceredigion
www.gomer.co.uk

Ten million stars are burning
Above the plains tonight,
But one man's dream is greater
To set the world alight.

Idris Davies, *Gwalia Deserta*

For
Morwenna Gwenan Haf

CONTENTS

PART III

Principal Characters

Owen James, *journalist*
Gwilym, *Owen's father*
Anna, *Owen's wife*
William, *Anna's father*
Sylvia, *Anna's mother*
Mari Môn Hughes, *artist and Owen's lover*
Robin, *journalist and Owen's friend*
Steve Evans, journalist and Owen's friend

Rhiannon Jones-Davies, *student and Cymdeithas yr Iaith Gymraeg activist*
Rev Penry Jones-Davies, *Rhiannon's father*
Gertrude, *Rhiannon's mother*
Ioan Rhys Thomas, *Rhiannon's boyfriend*
Siobhan Cunninghame, *Rhiannon's friend*
Branwen Thomas, *Rhiannon's friend and Cymdeithas yr Iaith Gymraeg activist*

~

Phil Williams, *professor of astrophysics at the University of Wales, Aberystwyth; Chairman and later Vice President of Plaid Cymru*

Leo Abse, *MP for Pontypool*
George Thomas, *MP for Cardiff West*
Donald Anderson, *MP for Swansea East*
Neil Kinnock, *MP for Bedwellty*
Barry Moore, *agent to Neil Kinnock*

John Tripp, *poet*

John Ormond, *poet and television producer, friend of John Tripp*

Peter Finch, *poet and friend of John Tripp*

Nigel Jenkins, *poet and friend of John Tripp*

Cyril Hodges, *poet and friend of John Tripp*

Leopold Kohr, *professor of economics and Rhiannon's tutor at the University of Wales, Aberystwyth*

Alwyn Rees, *director of the extra mural department at the University of Wales, Aberystwyth, and friend of Leopold Kohr*

Saunders Lewis, *playwright, academic, political philosopher, and founder of Plaid Cymru*

Raymond Williams, *professor of drama at Cambridge University, novelist and political thinker*

Gerard Morgan-Grenville, *businessman and founder of The Centre for Alternative Technology, Machynlleth*

Gwynfor Evans, *MP for Carmarthen, President of Plaid Cymru*

Dafydd Wigley, *MP for Caernarfon*

Dafydd Elis-Thomas, *MP for Meirionnydd*

Dafydd Williams, *general secretary, Plaid Cymru*

Geraint Talfan Davies, *assistant editor, Western Mail*

Duncan Gardiner, *editor, Western Mail*

John Humphries, *news editor, Western Mail*

Aneurin Rhys Hughes, *an official with the European Commission's General Secretariat*

Gwyn Morgan, *chef de cabinet to George Thomson, European Commissioner for regional policy*

Hywel Ceri Jones, *head of the department of education and youth policy, European Commission*

John Mackintosh, *Labour MP for Berwick and East Lothian and professor of politics at Edinburgh University*

Stephen Maxwell, *press officer, Scottish National Party*

Emrys Jones, *secretary, Wales Labour Party*

Ray Powell, *chairman, Wales Labour Party*

Jack Brooks, *leader of South Glamorgan County Council, member of the Wales Labur Party Executive*

George Wright, *secretary, Wales TUC*

- Other personalities that appear or are referred to, are listed in the *Biographical Notes* appendix.

Cwar y Gigfran
March 1979

'It's over there.'

Owen's gaze followed the line of Robin's arm pointing across the Caerfanell Valley, high in the Brecon Beacons.

'Can't you see it?'

Owen stared, but all he could make out was a steep slope of rock, grass, bracken and snow below the ridge on the far side of the valley.

It's about a hundred feet below Cwar y Gigfran,' Robin shouted against the wind. 'You'd know it as Raven's Ridge. To the left, can't you see?'

Then he saw the crash site. At first it looked like just another litter of grey scree. But now he could make out the jagged, twisted aluminium, the remains of the Wellington bomber that had crashed in 1942, thirty-six years before.

'They wouldn't have stood a chance,' Robin said.

The five Canadian aircrew had been on a training flight from their base near Stratford-upon-Avon. It was a dark night with thick cloud. They should have been flying at 10,000 feet. It was thought they descended below the cloud level to try and fix their position. Either that, or ice built up on the aircraft's wings, forcing it to lose height.

'They probably had no idea they were flying over the Brecon Beacons,' Owen thought, trying to imagine the scene. He had flown himself, in the RAF air squadron at university. He knew all too well the suppressed panic of not being in control of your aircraft. He felt again the rawness of the oxygen mask against his face, the reek of fuel mixed with cordite, the heaving of the cockpit, the queasiness, the looseness of the joystick in his hand.

The aircraft must have clipped Craig y Fan Ddu at just the

point where they were standing. Another fifty feet and it would have cleared Cwar y Gigfran and crash-landed on the upward slope of Waun Rydd above. They might have survived. Instead, the sudden loud impact of metal and wood driving into rock. The explosion, the engulfing flame… instant oblivion.

Owen shuddered and stepped closer to the edge of the ridge. He peered down into the Caerfanell Valley and the stream rushing far below. Beneath his feet ice made the path slippery. Snow had drifted and covered much of the moorland that stretched toward the peaks of Corn Ddu and Pen-y-Fan. The two friends turned, and pressed on into the wind as the temperature dropped.

* * *

It had been much warmer earlier when they tackled the first steep ascent, following the waterfalls of Nant Bwrefwr to the crest of Craig y Fan Ddu. As they climbed, the summits of the Black Mountains appeared to the east. Owen caught sight of the Sugar Loaf mountain above Abergavenny about ten miles distant. It had been a hard winter and three weeks into March there was no sign of spring. But the weather was clear. There were high cirrus clouds, and despite the wind it was a good day for walking.

Owen and Robin, both journalists, had been heavily involved in the devolution referendum that had been held on St David's Day a few weeks earlier. For them the outcome was a disaster. They had invested time and emotional energy into charting a new direction. Yet all their hopes had been shattered. It was not so much that the proposals for an elected Assembly were rejected. Rather, it was the scale of the defeat. The vote was four-to-one, with every part of Wales heavily against. It had put paid to the Assembly for at least a generation. Patrick Hannan, the BBC's political correspondent, had pronounced the end of Welsh politics.

Owen thought back to the last weeks of the campaign. It had been conducted in the grip of winter. A rash of public sector strikes had relegated devolution to the inside pages of the newspapers. There had been an atmosphere of hostility to the Labour government that was ostensibly campaigning for a Yes vote. The reality, of course, was that Labour's Welsh MPs and their constituency parties were hopelessly divided. Indeed, the strongest campaign against the Assembly had been led by Labour activists.

Owen had an abiding memory of driving into the car park of Transport House in Cardiff to attend a press conference. As he was climbing the steps at the rear of the building he noticed Hubert Morgan, the party's assistant general secretary, walking through the underground part of the car park. He was clutching a large box which he threw into a skip. Afterwards, on his way out, Owen looked inside. It contained thousands of *Labour Says Yes* leaflets.

Owen had delivered a fair few leaflets himself. He remembered crunching his way through ice and snow one night along Heol Llanishen Fach, a long road that divided a housing estate in the north of Cardiff. The yellow glare of the street lamps lit up the falling snow. A woman came running after him and thrust a leaflet back in his hand.

'We don't want this rubbish,' she said.

At the *Western Mail* he had received a telephone call from Ioan Bowen Rees, chief executive of Gwynedd County Council. Owen asked how the campaign was going in the north.

'We haven't enough people in key positions,' Bowen Rees told him. 'We don't have opinion formers on the ground.'

An editorial in the *South Wales Echo* had listed the names of sixty of Wales' leading writers who had declared their support for the Assembly. 'There now!' the *Echo* declared. 'You are impressed by those names, and each one is so well-known to you!'

Another day Owen was driving near the headquarters of the Wales for the Assembly campaign, a shop front in Cardiff's Lower Cathedral Road. He was surprised to see the organiser, Raymond Edwards, a retired schools' inspector, walking along carrying a large brown suitcase. A few days after the vote Owen noticed the suitcase lying on the floor of the office. Inside were hundreds of letters. He opened a few of them and found cheques and offers of support. Edwards had run the office virtually single-handed and during the last weeks of the campaign he had been overwhelmed by the volume of mail.

Owen had driven one of the campaign's leading speakers, Dai Francis, the retired general secretary of the South Wales Miners, to numerous meetings across south Wales. As they were returning to Cardiff late one night, they discussed the likely outcome. Owen voiced pessimism.

'You're probably right this time,' Francis replied. 'But don't worry, boy, our day will come.'

When the campaign committee met for a post-mortem Owen relayed this story. It drew an exasperated response from Gwilym Prys-Davies, special adviser to the Secretary of State for Wales John Morris. A solicitor, he had been a member of the republican movement when at university in Aberystwyth in the 1940s. Later he had joined Labour as the best vehicle to promote Welsh aspirations.

'Our day, as you put it, may come,' he said bitterly. 'But you're young. It'll be too late for my generation.'

* * *

As they moved further along the ridge, the outline of the Beacons grew larger. At first they had appeared low on the horizon. But now their glacier-cut profiles, sharpened by the snow, rose higher in the sky. They reached the headwaters of the Caerfanell and the cwm below them narrowed. Crossing the stream where a waterfall fell precipitously they traversed another few miles along Graig Fan Las ridge until they reached the head of the valley. A little further on they came to the northern edge of the long Beacons escarpment and turned sharply right. The path headed uphill through peat hags, cut through by wide gullies. The going was difficult. They repeatedly slipped into the channels, waist-high in snow. But eventually the ground levelled as they climbed the Waun Rydd moorland plateau.

Breathless, they stopped and gazed at the wide horizons that encircled them. Pen-y-Fan rose, majestic at their back. Llangorse lake shimmered in the lowlands ahead with the snow-covered Black Mountains beyond. Below them to the north was Brecon itself, with ranges of blue-grey hills flowing away in the distance.

They discovered a small cairn at the highest point. Robin signalled that they should continue walking onwards to the escarpment's edge where another cairn stood, a large beehive-like structure, the height of a man.

'Carn Pica,' he said.

Owen slipped in the snow as he followed him on to a more clearly marked path.

'What does the name mean?'

'I'm not sure. Refers to something sharp or pointed, maybe the land here or even the cairn itself. Pia is also short for magpie in Welsh. But if it's that, I can't think why. The only birds I've seen round here are crows, ravens and the odd buzzard.'

They sat out of the wind on a ledge at the foot of the cairn. Far below to their right they saw a glimpse of Talybont lake between the hills. On the other side was Craig Pwllfa, an amphitheatre of stone carved out of the hillside by a retreating glacier. In between the land fell steeply to the Usk Valley.

'This must be one of those points where the three Wales meet,' Robin said after a while.

'Three Wales?'

'I was in Aberystwyth a few weeks ago and met with some researchers. They're doing a survey on the referendum, a kind of extended opinion poll. They're trying to get at the way people feel about being Welsh, that kind of thing.'

'And?'

Well, obviously, they haven't got all their results in yet, or at least I don't suppose they've analysed them fully. But they're working on this Three Wales hypothesis.'

'Meaning?'

'That there are three different kinds of Wales.'

Robin took off his gloves and pulled a water bottle from his rucksack. He took a long drink.

'They reckon there are three distinct areas which have different outlooks. When you think about it, it's pretty obvious really. First, there's the north and west, the heartland as far as the language goes. Then there's the Valleys, the coalfield essentially.'

'And the third?'

'All the rest.'

Robin pointed at the valley below.

'They call that British Wales, the eastern marches along the border, together with Cardiff, the southern coast and Pembrokeshire.'

'You say they're doing this research at Aberystwyth.'

'Yes, the university, the politics department.'

'So if this and the rest you said are British Wales, what do they call the Valleys?'

'Oh, they're calling it Welsh Wales.'

'Welsh Wales?'

'Yes, because it's where people are most likely to describe themselves as Welsh even though they don't speak the language. More people in the Valleys were born there than anywhere else in Wales.'

'And what are they calling the first area, the north and west?'

'Y Fro Gymraeg, the language heartland.'

'So what are the differences exactly?'

'Political mainly, but cultural as well. The Valleys, Welsh Wales, that's where Labour is dominant. Y Fro Gymraeg is where Plaid Cymru wins, or has a chance of winning.'

'And the rest?'

'British Wales, the Tories have the edge there.'

'Well, I can see the distinction I suppose. But they all voted No in the referendum.'

* * *

Making their way back, they traced the edge of the Waun Rydd plateau, round Gwaiciau'r Cwm with its precipitous drop to woodlands below. Then they turned northwards once more, following the path until they reached Cwar y Gigfran.

Robin pointed to the crash site about a hundred feet below, with its twisted metal now clearly visible. 'You're right I suppose, about the referendum, despite the differences.'

'You mean about our unity in defeat,' Owen said.

'That's a good way of putting it. But there wasn't much unity in the campaign was there? It was everybody against everybody else.'

'How do you overcome that?'

'I don't know. Leo Abse was especially vicious.'

'About the language,' Owen agreed. 'Absolutely. No one challenged him.'

'He went on about a Welsh-speaking bureaucratic élite that would dominate the Assembly.'

'Complete nonsense, of course.'

'Yes, but it touched a nerve, didn't it? He said that giving one language superiority over another - and it was Welsh he was getting at - that's what the Nazis practised.'

'He goes on about language fanatics. *Fascists* he calls them.'

'And a lot else besides.'

They clambered down a steep path to the crash site. There were two piles of metal. Most were small twisted pieces, parts of the frame of the fuselage. One large piece looked as though it came from a wing. A long, rusted tube might have been part of the landing gear.

'The debris was scattered across a wide area but it's been gathered here where the impact happened,' Robin said. 'One of the engines rolled down to the bottom of the gulley by the stream and it's still there. They took the other to an aircraft museum near Shrewsbury.'

Owen picked up a small piece of the aluminium.

'It all looks terribly vulnerable.'

'I suppose it does. They covered the metal framework with wooden panelling and doped linen. It looks a bit primitive, you're right. But in fact, as a structure it was quite rigid and immensely strong. Even when bits of the fuselage were burnt or blown away, they could still fly.'

'Not when they hit a hillside.'

Owen studied a small stone memorial covered with red artificial poppies pasted to wooden sticks. A metal plaque bore the names: Flight Sergeant John Kemp, Pilot, age 21; Flight Sergeant Edward Mittel, Observer, age 22; Sergeant Harold Beatty, Gunner, age 28; Sergeant James Hayes, Gunner, age 22; Sergeant Kenneth Yuill, Observer, age 30.

He thought how he had grown up in the shadow of the war

in which these young men had died. He had played at being a soldier. His comic books had been full of the battles. Every year on Remembrance Day he had marched behind a Union Jack through Haverfordwest in his scout's uniform. Even today, the television and cinemas were full of images of that time when Britain stood alone.

'The thing is, Robin, most people in Wales think they're British.'

'They still feel Welsh.'

'Yes, but if we're going to know what makes them tick, we're going to have to understand what makes them feel British as well.'

'How, exactly?'

'We're going to have to work out what Britain means to them, especially when it comes down to politics and the way they're represented.'

PART I

Aberystwyth
October 1973

The smoke-filled bar of the Belle Vue hotel was alive with noisy debate. Carrying a couple of pints, Owen James brushed past a girl with long red hair, arm-in-arm with a man in a white shirt. He was waving a cigarette at a group of onlookers.

'It's always the same,' he shouted above the noise. 'They just want you to go along with what they've decided in advance.'

'They don't know what to think about Europe, that's the truth,' a bearded man in front of him interrupted.

'All this Common Market business is doing is changing one set of dictators for another,' the man in the white shirt told him.

'No, no, it's not like that at all,' the bearded man said, peering through the cigarette smoke. 'Wales is part of Europe, always has been, since Roman times.'

'Load of rubbish.'

'No, no! It'll mean the end of Britain. That's what it's about. Britain will dissolve into the Common Market.'

Owen stopped to listen. Some thought Europe stood for centralisation. Others said it could be made to fit Welsh aspirations. Only last week the party had been represented at a meeting in Paris, attended by delegations from Flanders, the Basque Country, Brittany and Alsace. It had been agreed to establish an office in Brussels. The party's chairman Phil Williams had been bitterly attacked for taking part. Nevertheless, he had won a standing ovation for his speech.

Across the room Robin gestured to a free seat. Owen squeezed between him and Cynog Dafis, an intense, sharp-featured man. He always looked a bit haunted, Owen felt.

'What do you think of the Common Market?' Owen asked him.

'It's split the Labour Party so it can't be all bad.'

Robin laughed and leaned forward, about to add something when he was stopped by an argument across the table. In front of them a pasty-faced man had a more immediate concern.

'Without the language Wales would just be like the Lake District, or maybe Cornwall.'

Owen recognised the man as coming from Port Talbot. He was tempted to ask how many Welsh-speaking people lived there. Instead, he said, 'It's a funny kind of nationalist party that seems intent on disowning two-thirds of the people of its country.'

'That's not the point,' the man answered, flicking a dank length of hair from his eyes. 'The point is what do we want? What are we aiming for?'

'Well?'

'We should be seeking a Welsh-speaking Wales. That means having a different attitude towards Welsh and English.'

'What do you mean a different attitude? You mean to English-speakers. But that's most of the Welsh.'

'If it wasn't for the language we'd be completely absorbed. We'd be some sort of West Britain. What does Wales mean for English-speakers anyhow? Rugby, Gren cartoons in the *Echo*, Prince Charles and the Investiture? Any real sense of Welshness is bound up with the language. Without it we'd just become English.'

'But all you're doing is dividing us,' Owen objected. 'In my book anybody can be Welsh who chooses to be and, I suppose, is prepared to take the consequences.'

Robin leant forward.

'What was it that Irish guy said? Conor Cruise O'Brien I think it was? Being Irish is not a question of blood, birth or even language. It's about being involved in the Irish situation and usually being mauled by it.'

'It's not that simple,' Cynog Dafis intervened, pausing to sip from a rapidly diminishing glass. 'You can't just factor the language out of things. It's fundamental.'

'Well, of course the language is important,' Robin said. 'That's why I came back to Wales. But you can't base a political movement on a language.'

'If I may say, coming from the south, you simply have no idea of the crisis we're facing.'

'I'm from the north actually.'

'All the same, the language is under threat as never before. And that's despite years of campaigning.'

Dafis sat upright, taut as a spring. He turned to Owen.

'It's the first language for many of us here. There's been a retreat, but until recently we thought that somehow it was reversible.'

'But instead?'

'Instead the decline is accelerating. Look at the mass of English people moving into places like Ceredigion. There's a critical failure to integrate. Schools where the predominance of Welsh was only recently taken for granted are rapidly being anglicised. It applies to whole villages as well.'

He stood up, drained his glass and placed it on the table.

'Maybe it will force a response. The fact that it's all happening so fast could provide a catalyst. It's out in the open now.'

As he was leaving he turned to Owen again.

'You should look at what J.R. has to say – J.R Jones, I mean. But, of course, you can't, he writes in Welsh. How did he put it? Something like, there's only one experience worse than being exiled, of being torn by the roots from your country. And that's having your country leave you. That's irreversible. If your country leaves you, if your language dies, that's forever.'

'How can it be my language, if I don't speak it?' Owen asked.

'It's just as much your language. It's our nation's heritage.

And it's being sucked away from us, as though by a consuming, swallowing wind, into the hands and the possession of another country.'

* * *

Owen and Robin left the smoke-filled warmth of the bar to take some air along Aberystwyth's rain-lashed promenade. A gusting wind blew dark, billowing clouds across a full moon. Storm-driven waves broke over the promenade steps, spraying the hotels, boarding houses and student accommodation that lined the seafront.

'Cynog's a difficult man,' Owen said. 'Unbending.'

'Maybe, but there's something about him, don't you think? He's one of those people you can rely on. You sense he has to force himself to do things. He's not a natural campaigner. But there's a quiet, steely centre there.'

They walked on for a while in silence until Robin stopped and turned to Owen.

'He's right, I think, when he says no language can survive without a territory where it's used in everyday life.'

The two men lent on the railings that lined the promenade and looked at the swirling waters below. The incoming waves pounded the stones and shingle on the beach while the undertow dragged them back in a loud roar. Robin turned and, leaning back against the railing, lit a cigarette, shielding his face with his hand against the wind.

'It's much the same as saying there's little point in having our own parliament if we've already lost the language.'

'You mean it wouldn't be worth having without the language.'

'I suppose you could say that.'

They began walking again and Owen pulled his jacket tighter against the wind.

'I can see how you, as a Welsh-speaker, might think that. But I don't feel it. I didn't even know the language existed until I was well into my teens.'

They gazed out to sea in silence for a while.

'It's true what you were saying in there though,' Robin said at last. 'It's a bit of a contradiction for a nationalist party to operate on the basis that most of their nation's population don't really belong.'

'Exactly. Banging on about the language just makes people cross.'

'But what makes English-speakers feel Welsh?'

'It's the question Plaid should be asking.'

'You're unlikely to get any answers in there.'

At this point they reached the end of the promenade. Constitution Hill loomed above them, lost in the darkness of the clouds. Robin kicked the bar of the railings that marked the end of the walkway.

'Supposed to bring you luck with the girls,' he said, before heading off to his room in the Marine Hotel.

'See you in the morning,' Owen called after him.

They were sharing a car back to Cardiff.

* * *

Owen turned back to the Belle Vue. It was gone midnight. Yawning, he pushed through the swing doors and was immediately accosted by a genial man with a mischievous smile and a strong Gwynedd accent.

'Owen! Where've you been man? Come and have a drink.'

'I'm off to bed.'

'Don't be *twp*. It's kicking off in there, I can tell you.'

Known as Alun Gwallt – he was a hairdresser in Pwllheli – he grabbed Owen's arm and pushed open a door leading to the bar from the hotel's reception area. It seemed even more crowded than before. A group singing 'Cwm Rhondda' added to the already deafening background noise.

'What'll it be?'

'Scotch.'

Around them the singing rose to a crescendo and then a lull, until at the far end of the room two men began a slow rendition of 'Myfanwy'. Others joined in, engulfing the conversations in the bar with the swelling sound.

Owen followed Alun and found himself next to Phil Williams.

'Wales, you know, is just the right size,' he was saying. 'I remember the first time I flew from Cardiff to Dublin. I was hopping from one side of the plane to the other like a little boy. It was a perfect day to pick out the landmarks. Ponty market, Cadair Arthur, Llyn y Fan – and then under Tro'r Gwcw I could see Pantcilwrach where my parents were staying.'

Phil stopped for a moment to take a drink. Then he laughed.

'I could even see my mother in a field. Yet at the same moment I could scan the whole of Wales from Eryri in the north to the coast of Pembrokeshire. That moment has always symbolised Wales for me – large enough to fill the horizon, but small enough to recognise every human being.'

As he was speaking another sound cut across. It was the girl with red hair. She was standing on a chair and singing 'Ar Lan y Môr', about a love deepening beside the sea. To Owen, she appeared like some apparition. Her voice, a clear contralto, rose effortlessly and seemed to settle above the hubbub, hushing the noise around the bar. The purity of the sound made him feel as though time was suspended, held still.

'Who's that?' he whispered, sipping his Scotch.

'Rhiannon Jones-Davies,' Alun Gwallt answered. 'From Anglesey, I think, but in Aber now, at the university.'

Then the impromptu choir around the girl joined in, and her boyfriend lifted her off the chair. Conversations resumed, rising from a murmur to a flood. Owen turned to Williams who was still talking in his animated fashion. As well as being a leading figure in the party he was a professor of astrophysics, an expert on the solar winds of the upper atmosphere. Owen thought him among the most remarkable men he had met.

'Wales is certainly the right size if you live in Aberystwyth,' he was saying. 'It's possible to finish work here at six, have supper at home and still enjoy an hour's legal drinking time in a pub anywhere you like in Wales.'

'You've tested it out, have you?' Owen asked.

'I reckon I've been on every A and B road in the country,' Phil answered without a pause.

'Anyway, what are you going to do about the Common Market?'

'Putting your journalist's hat on again, I see.'

'Not sure how to take it off any more.'

Phil grinned. Owen gave a wry smile as he sipped his Scotch, but he didn't let the question go.

'This European thing is a problem for Plaid, don't you think? They're right, aren't they, those who are saying we're just replacing one large state with a much bigger one? From the frying pan into the fire.'

Phil shook his head.

'We should welcome the European dimension. Gives us more room for manoeuvre. But it should be a much larger number of units than the present nine.'

'How many?'

'Oh, as many as fifty, I would say, including those that were represented last week in Paris. But others, too, like Bavaria in Germany, Corsica, Scotland of course, and territories like Catalunya in Spain if it were to join.'

'Do you think it will?'

'Certainly, once Franco's days are over. We see these nations and regions as our allies. But from Britain's point of view, or rather England's I should say, the other members of the Common Market are competitors.'

Phil leaned forward, as if through sheer proximity he could convince Owen.

'Listen. Yann Fouéré calls it *L'Europe aux Cent Drapeaux*, the Europe of a Hundred Flags. It's a... a federalist vision. There's no future in the balancing act between the large powers – Britain, France, Germany and the rest.'

He paused for a moment's thought, before continuing.

'Left to themselves, all common markets produce a polarisation between rich and poor. In France everything is centralised on Paris. Southern Italy is seeing its population drain to the north. London is the magnet in Britain.'

Owen aimed a sceptical eyebrow. 'And you reckon your Europe of the hundred flags would change all that.'

'Absolutely. The system Fouéré advocates gives full rein to our Welsh identity, our sovereignty at the Welsh level you could say. But it also recognises what we share in common as part of Europe. It's about breaking down the nation-state, getting rid of the outdated concept of Britain and Britishness.'

'Seems a bit improbable to me.'

Phil threw him a mischievous grin.

'Everything about Plaid Cymru is improbable. But hang around long enough and who knows?'

Llanddona

October 1973

The following afternoon Rhiannon boarded a bus to take her the four-hour journey from Aberystwyth to Bangor. Her father Penry Jones-Davies, a retired Presbyterian minister, would meet her at the bus station and take her across the Menai Straits to their home in Llanddona, a hamlet on Anglesey's east coast.

An only child, Rhiannon missed her parents and the small cottage on the water's edge that her mother Gertrude had inherited. It was a fortunate inheritance. Throughout his ministry her father's meagre income had been supplemented by free accommodation in the manses of the churches he had served. However, on retirement he had no property to call his own save for Tŷ Mawr Llan.

The name belied its size. It was built in the style of a Welsh long house, with half its length made up of a barn that had once held cattle. It was small, comprising a kitchen, bathroom and and living room, with two bedrooms in the eaves above. Since their retirement, Rhiannon's parents had fashioned a lean-to extension with high windows on the seaward end which Gertrude had made into a lounge. However, it faced the driving gales that came off the Irish Sea and, without a constantly fed fire, was uninhabitable in winter.

Rhiannon knew every stone of the building. Now, as the Crosville bus wound its way through Bow Street towards Machynlleth, she imagined herself in bed in the loft, listening to the constant murmur of the sea and the rustling of the shingle dragged back from the shore by the undercurrents, the abiding sound of her childhood.

Rhiannon pulled her duffle coat round her as the bus sped northwards. Her thoughts returned to the previous night in the

Belle Vue, and she shivered involuntarily at the memory of her performance in the packed lounge bar. How had she done it? She hadn't sung like that since her eisteddfod days.

As the strains of the male voices subsided Ioan had picked her up, swung her on that chair and cried, 'Give us a song Rhi, go on love.'

And before she knew it, she was caught by the exhortations and warmth of those around her. Almost without thinking she had closed her eyes and, barely conscious of the sudden quietness in the bar, had begun to sing, from deep inside her as she had been taught so long ago at school. As always when a song went well, she had felt herself almost physically lifted by the notes flowing effortlessly through her body.

And at the end, as the others took the song Ioan lifted her again, crushing her to him.

'I knew you could sing, *cariad*, but not like that.'

Rhiannon had flushed, searched for her glass and returned to singing with the others, following the lead of the men around her.

'Ioan,' she thought to herself now. 'Ioan Rhys Thomas.'

She was attracted to him, to be sure. Who would not be? With his curly black hair already flecked with grey, and his brown eyes that held a direct, unembarrassed gaze. His voice was a lilting bass baritone that enfolded the listener into an effortless intimacy. He was tactile in that easy Valleys way, a hand invariably reaching out to the elbow or shoulder of his listener.

'Watch out for him,' one of her friends had murmured. 'Lady's man for sure, string of women he has.'

They had met in the bar of the Coopers Arms – Y Cŵps – the student pub at the bottom of Penglais Hill from where the university and National Library stared out at Cardigan Bay. He was studying for a PhD he told her, on the history of the south Wales miners.

'I'm focusing on the 1926 strike, what led up to it, what came out of it. Both my dad and grandad went down the pit.'

It was Ioan who had persuaded her to attend the conference in the King's Hall on the seafront. She had stood at the back during the Saturday afternoon and watched as he took part in a confused debate on the Common Market. 'Free movement of capital is their lodestar,' he had shouted. 'Building up the capitalist system at the expense of the workers.' He had continued in this vein, pouring out words like *class*, *struggle* and *solidarity* that bobbed about on a streaming flow until, finally, he was ruled out of time, and then out of order.

Rhiannon was unmoved. She was too intellectually self-aware and critical to be swayed. And, anyway, she disliked his constant references to the working class. She thought it sounded patronising. 'Who are the working class, anyhow?' she asked herself. 'What are they supposed to be like?' She thought about the hill farmers on their smallholdings around Llanddona, above Tŷ Mawr. They certainly worked with their hands, and had callouses to show for it. But she could hardly think of them as working class. They were too individual for that. They were neighbours and friends. The faces who had looked out for her when, as a small girl, she was walking the fields. The voices that called out her name, asking after her mam and dad.

She had helped them herd cows at milking time. She could remember placing her head against their soft-furred sides, inhaling the warm smell of dung and hay as she pulled on their udders and saw the milk squirting into the bucket below. Sometimes a gift of eggs, turnips or potatoes, even the occasional chicken would be left at the front door of Tŷ Mawr. They were an acknowledgement of Penry's help in drafting a letter to a bank manager, a solicitor, or to the county hall in Llangefni about some planning matter.

'They're just people,' Rhiannon thought to herself. 'They're not *working class*. But maybe it's different in Ioan's Valleys in the south.'

She reached into her bag and pulled out a small powder compact case. Unclipping it, she stared closely into the mirror. Normally she would see a wide, generous face, surrounded by flowing red hair, with deep-set blue eyes above a gently curved nose and sharply defined cheekbones. But now she saw a pinched, wan expression. It was the early hours before she and Ioan had stumbled out of the Belle Vue on to Marine Terrace. Rhiannon rented a bedsit in a terraced house in Prospect Street a short distance away. On the steps outside Ioan had caught her again in an embrace. He kissed her, and she had felt his tongue tasting of tobacco.

His voice was husky with alcohol.

'Let's go up.'

Rhiannon pushed him back.

'No, no, it's late. I've got a lot on tomorrow.'

Ioan recoiled, unused to such a rebuff.

'Well, see you tomorrow night?'

'No, I'm away home.'

'Monday, then.'

'I'll be late.'

'Tuesday?'

'Yes, well… yes, OK.'

'The Cŵps, nine o'clock... for a drink.'

After a chaste peck on her cheek, he lurched back up Prospect Street towards his own bedsit closer to the seafront.

Rhiannon wasn't at all sure whether Ioan Thomas was a good idea. She'd had a boyfriend in Bangor. He was from Denbigh, in the same year as her, also studying history. Dafydd

Evans had been hesitant, unused to girls, but useful to tag along with to social events in the union. He had been part of the background of Rhiannon's student life.

But Ioan was altogether different. She found his easy-going urgency overwhelming. She worried that, like other men she had observed, he regarded women as a kind of possession, to be taken up, used and then discarded as the mood changed. Rhiannon did not want to think of herself as a someone's possession, unless of course it was Dada's, but then that was different. She thought of girlfriends at school and also some in college, who talked endlessly about getting married, having children. Boyfriends were just a vehicle for their plans. Some were already married with babies.

'Perhaps I'll never get married,' Rhiannon thought. 'Perhaps I'll never *want* to get married. Perhaps I'll end up as a spinster teaching in a school or some musty old college.'

* * *

As her bus passed through Tre Taliesin and Eglwys Fach Rhiannon caught a glimpse of the Dovey estuary and its far shore flickering through the tree-lined road. When they pulled into Machynlleth, she suddenly felt glad she was going home, even if only for a fleeting visit. Her early years had been spent in Llanelli where her father had ministered in his last full-time church before retiring. But the family would always spend their summers at Tŷ Mawr, where Rhiannon was free to roam the fields and wander the shoreline.

Penry had retired when she was ten years old. Rhiannon had spent a year at the village school before attending Ysgol David Hughes, six miles away in Menai Bridge. Tŷ Mawr's isolation added to the intimacy of the couple and their only child who had been born late on in their marriage. Indeed, when she was small many people had assumed Penry and Gertrude were her grandparents.

There were compensations. If not precocious, Rhiannon had always been mature for her years, confident, outgoing, and used to the cut and thrust of arguments with her father. She often disagreed with him, especially about his politics. He was a pacifist, and a socialist, preaching both in a forthright way to his congregations, often to their discomfort. Many chapelgoers believed religion and politics should not be mixed. For Penry, Christianity and socialism were two sides of the same coin and led logically to pacifism. He preached all three with a theatrical intensity that invariably divided his congregations. Nevertheless, he still received invitations. Indeed, he was in constant demand from churches across the north of Wales.

Penry's socialism was rooted in the southern Valleys. Born in Maerdy, a mining village at the head of Rhondda Fach, he was the youngest of ten children. His father David had also been a Presbyterian minister, but of a sterner and more unbending nature. Penry was only three when his mother died, worn down by years of childrearing and poverty. Her husband was left bereft and brought in a sixteen-year-old girl from a nearby terrace to help look after the children. However, her presence caused consternation amongst the church elders. They scented a scandal and voted their minister out of his living. Eventually he found his way to a new calling in Barry, on the coast.

There Penry grew up until, aged fifteen he had escaped by persuading the army he was a year older and eligible to join as a boy soldier. After three years his father's influence enabled him to be accepted into the Presbyterian theological college in Trefecca. Later the denomination sponsored him to study at university, first in Cardiff and then Aberystwyth.

Rhiannon inherited her father's determination and stubbornness together with his drive, indeed his need to have a cause commanding single-minded devotion. In Penry's case it was Christian socialism; in Rhiannon's it was the Welsh language. A clash between the two was inevitable. At university in Bangor Rhiannon had studied history and Welsh literature, and become a member of Cymdeithas yr Iaith Gymraeg. Now she was studying for a Masters in the Department of International Politics at Aberystwyth, following a course in African de-colonisation. She had discovered an interest in the Algerian war of independence in the 1950s and the life and work of the revolutionary Frantz Fanon. She saw many parallels with the situation in Wales, or what she thought was the situation.

* * *

The bus halted for a break in Dolgellau and Rhiannon bought a cup of tea from the station café, on the verge of closure this late Sunday afternoon. Returning to her seat she opened a biography of Fanon she had borrowed from the university library. It told her Fanon considered that all theoretical ideas about politics grew out of action: 'All of Fanon's most original ideas were the result of his own life.'

'That's exactly it,' she thought. 'In our case it's Cymdeithas's willingness to take direct action that has created what we stand for. It's a bit like growing up. You become who you are by what you do, the choices you make. Who knows where things will lead? At the start I had no thought of studying for another degree. But then I found Fanon and now I'm in Aberystwyth. It's the same with Cymdeithas. One thing has led to another. First the demand for bilingual forms, then road signs, now a television channel.'

Rhiannon looked unseeing through the window, deep in thought. 'By taking action, we have developed what we believe.'

She was drawn to Fanon's insights into the colonial

relationships. He was born in the French colony of Martinique in the West Indies in 1925. His upbringing was relatively well off – his father was a customs inspector and his mother owned a hardware store in downtown Fort-de-France. At first this background led him to strive to assimilate into white French culture. But later, after leaving Martinique, aged 18, to fight with the Free French forces in the last days of World War II, and then studying medicine and psychiatry in Lyon, he adopted a radically different position. His direct encounters with French racism forced him to explore the impact of colonisation. He concluded that speaking French meant accepting the collective consciousness of the French.

'And that consciousness identifies blackness with evil and sin,' Rhiannon told herself, as she continued to read: 'We use language as another means of dominating colonial areas.'

'Could the same be said of Wales?' she wondered.

> It has always been made clear in Europe and the colonies that the native cannot rule himself because he does not speak a civilised tongue. The Caribbean black is only considered part of the human species as he becomes fluent in a purer form of French, English or Spanish....

Rhiannon immediately saw parallels, for instance how English was assumed to be the language of the courts. 'It takes determination, and a good deal of trouble, to insist on using Welsh,' she told herself.

By now her bus had climbed the steep road north of Dolgellau through Coed-y-Brenin and Ganllwyd, and was picking up speed along the old Roman road in a straight line towards Trawsfynydd. In the gathering dusk Rhiannon could see the outline of the nuclear power station. On the horizon to her left were the jagged peaks of Rhinog Fawr, and northwards the outline of the Snowdon range.

As it grew dark Rhiannon dozed, and was only jerked awake when the bus juddered to a halt in Porthmadog. There was another short break before it set off again, sending her to sleep once more as it pressed northwards towards Caernarfon and beyond.

* * *

In Bangor Penry was waiting for her, leaning against his car, pipe in hand. He pressed his other arm around Rhiannon as she embraced him. 'We've missed you, *cariad*,' he murmured as she inhaled the familiar tang of his old coat – tobacco, peat from their fire, and oil from his 1965 Rover 2000.

'How's Mam?'

'Fine and waiting for you.'

Penry threw her bag on to the back seat. They drove out of Bangor on the road that took them across the Telford suspension bridge into Menai Bridge and then back along the Straits to Beaumaris. From there it was a few miles inland and over the hill to Llanddona.

Though a commanding presence in the pulpit, Penry was small in stature, barely able to peer over the top of the steering wheel of his car. Smoke from his pipe further obscured his view and, as often before, Rhiannon wondered how he managed to avoid accidents, let alone find his way. Removing his pipe, he asked how she was getting along with her course.

'I've been really lucky with my supervisor. He's an amazing man, only arrived at the university this year. He's called Leopold Kohr, an economics professor, though I can't imagine anyone less like an economist.'

'Oh?'

'Well he's really funny to start with, and so charming. He lives around the corner from me. The other day he invited a few of us to his house for coffee.'

'Go on.'

'Well, for him Aberystwyth is a perfectly sized town. Living where he does, in Baker Street, which may as well be my street as it's only a stone's throw away, he says he can get anything he wants by just walking a few yards. He doesn't need a fridge because over the road there's a small shop that sells most of what he needs. Not far away is an off licence so he doesn't need a wine cellar. He said he didn't need a library either because just up the hill there's the most important library in Wales. And, of course, he doesn't need a car.'

'How's that?'

Rhiannon laughed.

'Because, as he put it, he can achieve more on foot, which costs nothing, than by car, which costs a lot and which he could not use except to leave town.'

'Where's he from, this professor?'

'He came to Aber from the University of Puerto Rico, but originally he's from Austria. He was born in a tiny village, Oberndorf near Salzburg, you know the place where 'Silent Night' was composed. His father was a doctor there. He told us a really funny story about him. He's full of stories.'

'Well?'

'A patient came to the surgery complaining that he had measles and his father, the doctor, said "Enjoy it! Because if you don't enjoy it you've still got measles."'

'Sounds a peculiar economics professor to me.'

Rhiannon laughed again.

'You'll think he is even more peculiar when I tell you he's an ardent supporter of Plaid.'

Penry grunted. He was less than fond of Welsh nationalism.

'How did that come about? An Austrian from the University of Puerto Rico?'

'He's some sort of specialist in small nations. And he's a great friend of Gwynfor Evans, apparently. He's written a wonderful book which came out a few years ago that I've started reading. It's called *Is Wales Viable.*'

'Depends what you mean by viable,' Penry grunted again. 'And as for that Gwynfor Evans, he's no socialist. When he was on Carmarthenshire County Council, I heard it said he always travelled by train first class on expenses.'

'Oh Dada, don't be silly.'

Penry drove the car through the small lanes at the centre of Llanddona and headed down the steep hill to the beach.

'At the beginning of term, I was at a reception in the department and this woman, a county type, came up to Professor Kohr. "Leopold," she said in a haughty voice, "Your piddling small countries can't even provide poor people with *bathrooms!*" And do you know what he said? "Madam, in Salzburg, which is part of a small nation, even the *horses* have been provided with bathrooms."'

Despite himself Penry laughed as he steered his car through Tŷ Mawr's narrow gateway into a small drive. At the doorway of the cottage Gertrude, a tea towel in hand, was waiting. But before getting out of the car, Rhiannon couldn't resist continuing the story.

'Do you know what this woman replied? She said that the professor may well have come from Salzburg but that its main time of glory was when it was part of an enormous empire – the Austro-Hungarian Empire. So it was not a small nation at all.'

'What did he say to that?'

'"Ha hah!" he said. "It was a ramshackle empire! It didn't do much damage to the many small states that it was supposed to rule. It didn't try to suppress their languages, nor their cultures, nor interfere with their trade. They just went on as though it didn't exist.'"

'What are you two talking about?' Gertrude demanded. 'Come on in, for goodness sake. It's cold out here.'

Inside, she and Rhiannon embraced. Gertrude held her daughter's shoulders and stared at her.

'Are you getting enough to eat? You're certainly not getting enough sleep by the look of things. Anyway, supper's nearly ready.'

And with that she bustled into the kitchen, leaving Rhiannon and Penry to settle in front of the fire. There was silence for a while, only broken by the sonorous ticking of the grandfather clock. Rhiannon drew her knees up to her chest and, grasping her arms around them, said, 'It's nice to be home, even if it's only for a night.'

Gertrude had prepared roast ham, creamed mashed potatoes finished in the oven, salad, beetroot and homemade chutney. 'But, as ever, only water to drink,' Rhiannon thought.

'Have you heard from that boy you knew at Bangor?' Gertrude asked. 'Dafydd wasn't it? A nice lad I thought.' They continued chatting in this vein while they did the washing up.

Rhiannon wondered whether she should bring up the subject of Ioan. She knew her mother would be intensely interested, but she thought better of it. There would be too many questions which she would be unable or unwilling to answer. She wondered again, why it was she was so reserved with her mother. 'With Dada, it's different,' she thought. 'We just talk about everything.' But with her mother she was always afraid of setting off a train of worries. 'And Mam hardly ever talks about herself, about what's going on in her own life.' Rhiannon involuntarily felt herself stiffen, but then relaxed as she listened to her mother carry on talking about some neighbours and their children.

Afterwards, they returned to the living room with tea to listen to the news on the radio. Then the chess set was brought out and Penry and Rhiannon renewed a rivalry that had lasted for as long as she could remember.

Before going to bed, she stepped out of the cottage and wandered down to the water's edge and a high tide. It was a cold, clear night. Clouds scudded across a near full moon. In the distance, gulls called mournfully as they drifted on a wind following the ocean currents.

Rhiannon knelt down to feel the pebbles at her feet, finding one that was thin, smooth, and round. She stood and weighed it in her hand. Then she crouched and skimmed the stone hard across the flat, gently heaving sea. Gratifyingly, it made a dozen skips before disappearing into the blackness. Hunching down on the beach once more Rhiannon stared out at the water. Her mind went back to what she had been thinking earlier in the day. Would she become a teacher in a school or a lecturer in some college? Maybe she would do something completely different.

'Whatever happens, this'll be where I end up,' she decided.

* * *

The next morning was bright and the tide far out. After breakfast father and daughter put on their coats and walked across the wide sands of Red Wharf Bay. A keen wind gusted grains of sand to knee level and flecks of foam scudded across the beach. Rhiannon was always amazed how large the sky looked when the tide had retreated. Leaning into the wind, she put her arm through Penry's and the two walked companionably in silence.

Eventually, Penry asked her about her course and how she was managing. Rhiannon began to answer but then interrupted herself.

'Dada, there's something I must tell you. I've joined the Cymdeithas yr Iaith cell in Aberystwyth and we're planning to take part in the television campaign.'

Penry grunted with displeasure, as she knew he would, but she pressed on.

'I'm not sure what it's going to involve but it will be direct action of some kind – you know the kind of thing we get up to. But you're not to worry, and you mustn't let Mam worry either. In fact, it's probably best not to tell her. I'll be fine. I'll be with friends, and people who've done this kind of thing before.'

'Oh *cariad*, must you get involved? At any rate, shouldn't your studies come first?'

'Dada, we've had this argument before. There's no point going into it all again.'

'When is all this going to happen?'

'I don't know. Maybe not until next year. We'll be told when we're needed. The Senate decides those things.'

'What you're talking about, I suppose, is non-violent direct action. But you know that's playing with words. Certainly that's what most fair-minded folk would say, me amongst them.'

'Dada, we believe fundamentally in non-violence. You know that. *The Welsh language is not worth one drop of innocent blood* is what we say. Violence of that sort would undermine the whole moral strength of our movement. But that's not the same as saying the Welsh language isn't worth breaking the law for, and the destruction of property, when that's justified. It's been the mainstay of our campaigns since the beginning. It's the reason we've had what success we've had. It's only the use of illegal methods that's achieved anything.'

'But what do you mean by *justified*?'

'Well, Ffred Ffransis set it out in his court case in *Yr Wyddgrug* back in '71. Breaking the law and the destruction of property is only justified when all other means have been tried and failed – for instance, the repeated requests for forms in Welsh that have been refused. As for the television campaign, the current broadcasting system is in effect a form of oppression against the language, against the very personality of the Welsh people. It would be quite wrong to use violence against the broadcasters themselves.'

Rhiannon hesitated for a moment.

'But it's right to destroy their equipment, their property if you like, their tools of oppression.'

Penry stopped and looked seriously at his daughter.

'That may be. It's a clever distinction in moral terms. The problem is where do you draw the line? What if you're in the middle of doing something, perhaps in a broadcasting studio, at night I presume, after you've broken in, and you're disturbed, maybe by a security guard? What do you do when he moves to stop you, as he must?'

Penry fiddled with his pipe in a distracted way, and looked worriedly at his daughter.

'What happens then? In situations like that things can easily get out of hand. And you'd be the ones who started it. You'd be the ones who created the circumstances where violence could break out.'

'Well, if we were surprised in that way we simply wouldn't resist. And as for non-violent direct action we didn't invent it. It has a long history. You know that. Your pacifist hero Donald Soper supported it in the campaign against nuclear weapons.'

'Donald was campaigning against weapons of mass destruction, which is a quite different order of things.'

'There is a connection, Dada.'

Rhiannon extracted her arm from Penry's but at the same time took his hand before continuing, as if doing so might persuade him.

'Certainly, I would agree with Donald Soper that using

non-violent direct action to try and halt the production of nuclear weapons is justified. But what is happening to the Welsh language is a form of mass destruction as well. Don't you see? Welsh is not just a means of communication. It's part of our soul, part of our very humanity. Without it, would we still be Welsh?'

'Are you saying that all those thousands of people in the south who don't have the language aren't Welsh?'

'No, of course not, but the language is part of what makes them who they are, even if they don't realise it, the fact that Welsh is still a living language.'

Rhiannon pulled on Penry's arm causing them to stop walking.

'Dada, you go on in your sermons about the materialist culture that is flooding into our lives. Welsh is part of our defence against it, surely you can see that? If Welsh were to die out, then part of us would die as well. All we would have left would be the shallowness of an Anglo-American anti-culture – a mishmash of capitalist values and linguistic oppression.'

'Well, I agree with you about that at least.'

Penry shook his head and put his pipe in his mouth. But feeling the wind, he returned it to his pocket.

'We'd better go back, or we'll be late for your mam's lunch.'

Llangadog
October 1973

The next day, at the exact moment Rhiannon was boarding a bus back to Aberystwyth, Owen James was standing on Platform 3 of Cardiff's main railway station. He was waiting for a train to arrive from London. On it were three embargoed copies of the report. With some difficulty David Rosser, the *Western Mail's* political editor, had persuaded the Press Office at Number 10 to allow him four advance copies of the bulky document, one for himself and three for head office.

On the phone to Owen, a testiness had entered his voice.

'Why do you need three copies?'

'One for myself, one for the editor and the other for the leader writer.'

Owen failed to point out that he would probably be writing the editorial himself and that the editor would certainly not wish to read such a long report. In fact, only two copies were to find their way into the offices of the *Western Mail*. Later that day Owen was planning to place the third into the hands of Plaid Cymru's leader Gwynfor Evans. His victory in the 1966 Carmarthen by-election had been one reason for the creation of the Commission on the Constitution. At Westminster Prime Minister Harold Wilson resorted to a classic delaying tactic in response to this vexatious revolt in Labour's heartlands – he set up a Royal Commission on the Constitution. Although announced in the autumn of 1968, the Commission had not begun work until the following spring and its deliberations took the best part of three years. Publication, much trailed in an expectant press in Wales and Scotland, not least by Owen himself in numerous speculative articles, was then delayed for more than a year.

As the train approached Owen had little idea what to expect. Rosser had only told him that he had slipped the guard a five-pound note with instructions that he should hand the package over on the production of some means of identification. Owen duly presented his driving licence and received a bulky brown paper package, trussed in gaffer tape. He retreated to a seat away from the passengers streaming off the train and tore at the edges of the parcel. Inside were six documents. He saw that the main report was accompanied by a *Memorandum of Dissent*, almost as bulky. Each was bound by silk string, rather like a lawyer's brief, and stamped in blue with an embargo until 1am on Wednesday.

Owen leafed through the reports, one running to 579 pages and the other to 221. 'Where's the summary?' he asked himself and, finding none, glanced through the chapter headings of the main report. There were twelve parts and thirty-four chapters, with separate ones devoted to Wales, Scotland and England. He sped to the summary of conclusions at the end. He found 220 paragraphs.

'Nightmare,' he muttered and flicked back to a few pages from the end.

> Our preferred schemes all provide for the establishment of Scottish and Welsh assemblies directly elected by the single transferable vote system of proportional representation for a fixed term of four years... For Scotland eight of us, and for Wales six of us, favour a scheme of legislative devolution...

'Who are the six?' Owen wondered. He found a footnote indicating that they were all from Wales, Scotland and Northern Ireland. The recommendations of the eight English commissioners all fell short in various ways. Some wanted executive devolution for Wales, others an advisory council. The two signatories to the Minority Report were both from the north of England and they wanted nothing unless it would be the same across the whole of the UK.

'Dog's breakfast,' Owen muttered to himself as he rose and hurried out of the station. 'But more than we expected, really.'

Heading to the *Western Mail* a short walk away, he stopped by his car, a grey Volkswagen Beetle with an *Ynni Niwclear NA!* sticker emblazoned across the back window, and threw one copy of the report on the back seat.

* * *

Owen ran up the office stairs and paused by a small windowless room inhabited by the assistant editor, Geraint Talfan Davies. His uncle, Sir Alun Talfan Davies, was a leading QC and one of the report's Welsh commissioners. Poking his head through the door Owen passed over a copy and said, 'Alun's on side, calling for a legislative assembly, but otherwise they're pretty much all over the place. The recommendations splinter into any number of options. There's whatever you want.'

Geraint seized the bulky documents and started looking through them.

'We've known all along they wouldn't be unanimous. They've been split on how to handle Scotland and Wales. Douglas Houghton resigned from the Commission back in January, you remember. I think he felt it was getting a bit out of hand.'

'How do you mean?'

'I've been writing a backgrounder on how the Commission got started – in the wake of Gwynfor and Carmarthen and all that – and how the evidence sessions underlined the nationalist pressure.'

Geraint's contacts had given him direct access to Lord Crowther, the Commission's first chairman with whom he had some revealing conversations. He found him a strange fellow, bald and inoffensive-looking but sharp as a razor. He had been a journalist himself, rising to become chairman of *The Economist*.

'Crowther said that what had impressed him more than anything else during the evdence sessions in Cardiff was the force of nationalism in Wales.'

'More than in Scotland?'

'Yes, that was my first reaction as well. So I pressed him, and he said that in a surprising sense nationalism existed in Wales whereas it didn't exist in Scotland.'

'That sounds odd.'

'Well, he said that as far as he could see the difference was that while the Scots wanted to do things, the Welsh simply wanted to be, to exist as it were. To be recognised anyway. Intriguing thought, don't you think?'

Geraint studied the report, marking a few paragraphs with his pen. Then he looked up.

'Tell you what, come back in an hour or so when I've had a chance to go through this in more detail. We'll decide how to handle it then. I'll need to brief the editorial conference. We're going to have to increase the pagination for Wednesday, I think.'

*   *   *

Owen continued along a corridor framed by panelled interior windows behind which were the offices of the editors of the *Western Mail* and *South Wales Echo*. Beyond them was the cuttings library and, turning right, he passed the Features

Department before walking into a large open plan office that housed the news rooms of the two papers. He ignored the throb of conversations and ringing phones. Years of working for newspapers had inured him to this background noise. When he had first started as a junior reporter he was astonished how those around him could pick out commands and queries directed specifically to them from a news desk half a cricket pitch away. And they would only respond to the ringing of their own telephone. Now, as Owen sat at his desk to study the report, he, too, was oblivious of the sounds around him.

Looking again at the chapter headings, his eye was caught by a section entitled *The Welsh People*. It described how a land that within living memory had been made up of small communities, most of them naturally Welsh-speaking, was now buckling under the onslaught of modernity. Few miners now walked to their pits. Instead, they travelled by car or bus to distant workings, or to factories and trading estates. In the rural areas, small farms were amalgamating and there was an increasing influx of retired people from England. The main road and rail communications connected Wales with England rather than linking the north and south of the country. Radio and television were another anglicising influence. Nevertheless, the report struck an upbeat note.

> As one moves eastward and southward through Wales, the 'Welshness' of the people, though it undergoes subtle change, persists. Despite divisions and gradations, there remains a strong sense of Welsh identity, a different way of looking at things and a distinct feeling that the needs and interests of people in Wales must be considered separately from those of people elsewhere in the United Kingdom.

Owen detected the hand of the two Welsh Commissioners behind this description, Alun Talfan Davies and Ben Bowen Thomas, former permanent secretary to the Welsh department of the Ministry of Education. He reckoned they were also responsible for a later section on the nature of Welsh nationalism.

> It seems that, for a good many people in Wales, the distinctive Welsh culture and language has come to assume the degree of importance which is attached to the idea of Scottish sovereignty in the minds of people in Scotland. It is interesting to speculate how far this recent revival of interest in Welsh culture is the answer of a sensitive people to the pressures and disappointments of modern society. Whatever its inspiration, it is an important present-day phenomenon which must be taken into account in any consideration of government reform in Wales.

As he underlined these words, Owen was interrupted by the ringing of his phone. Immediately he heard his wife Anna, a note of panic rising in her voice.

'Owen, is that you? He's here already.'

'Give him a cup of tea or something. I'll be along soon. But I've got to speak with Geraint first. Tell him I've got the report. I shouldn't be more than half-an-hour.'

As he put the phone down, it rang again. This time it was Barry Jones, a university politics lecturer who had undertaken research for the Commission. He was also a member of several Labour policy groups and a key contact.

'Is it out yet?' he asked.

'It's published on Wednesday, but I've got a copy.'

'And?'

'It's more radical than we thought. The Welsh and Scots

commissioners have come out for legislative assemblies for Wales and Scotland, in effect Home Rule, but nothing for England. One group of the English commissioners is willing to concede executive assemblies for Wales and Scotland. A smaller number have opted for advisory councils. And two – Lord Crowther-Hunt and Professor Alan Peacock, an economics professor at York I think – have produced a Memorandum of Dissent. They're arguing for executive devolution across the whole of the UK, including England.'

Barry Jones whistled.

'That'll take some swallowing. Looks as though they've split between regionalists and nationalists.'

'What do you think the reaction will be?'

'The recommendation on legislative powers will come as a bit of a bombshell. That would mean parliaments in Edinburgh and Cardiff. If that happened there'd have to be a reduction in Scottish and Welsh MPs at Westminster, eventually anyway.'

'How will the government play it, do you think?'

'A lot of the MPs will want to kick it into the long grass.'

'I can see that, but I reckon there's going to a head of steam behind it. Look, I've got to dash. I'll ring you tomorrow.'

Replacing the phone Owen collected his things. As he stuffed them into a battered duffle bag it occurred to him that *Bombshell for Labour* would be the headline on his reaction story. Clutching the report, he paused at the news desk.

'Hang on a moment,' the deputy news editor said into the phone he was holding. Then he placed his hand over the mouthpiece, so his conversation with Owen couldn't be heard.

'I'm taking this home to read.'

'OK, see you in the morning.'

On his way out, Owen stopped in the doorway of the assistant editor's office. There was hardly room to stand let alone sit down.

'You're right,' Talfan Davies said. 'They're all over the place.'

'Legislative powers will come as a surprise, especially for Labour.'

'Yes, but the main point is that all of them, all thirteen members, are united that at least there should be an Assembly or elected council of some sort, even if it's just advisory. That's the line, I think. It's a start, at any rate.'

Geraint turned over a few pages of the report, then looked up at Owen.

'Tell you what, I'll write the front page and the editorial. You do the detail inside, reaction and analysis. I'll get on to graphics to see if we can knock up some panels. You know, mug shots of which members support which options, that kind of thing. OK?'

'Fine. Trust you, as ever, to see the positive.'

* * *

Driving home, Owen reflected on the events that had led to this moment. He had first spoken to Gwynfor Evans over breakfast at Plaid Cymru's annual conference in Rhyl a year before, not long after he had joined the *Western Mail*. Their conversation had turned into an interrogation about his roots. Informed they were in Pembrokeshire Gwynfor immediately launched into a meditation on medieval Welsh history. He gave Owen a lecture on leadership, as exemplified by one of his heroes, the Lord Rhys. Through the middle decades of the twelfth century, Rhys had fought a war against Henry II to secure overlordship of the lands between the rivers Dyfi and Teifi.

'Rhys is a striking example of the importance of leadership in our history,' Gwynfor enthused. 'Like his father Gruffydd ap Rhys and grandfather Rhys ap Tewdwr, he was a leader of heroic stature. If he had accepted the status quo as inevitable, if he had thought it impossible to withstand the huge Norman power, then Wales wouldn't exist today.'

Owen had been tempted to ask if Gwynfor saw himself as a modern-day Lord Rhys. But then he realised that the comparison could hardly be made. Gwynfor was such a soft-spoken, self-effacing man. It was true he could lay claim to be one of the longest serving political leaders in the world. He had been president of Plaid Cymru since 1945. And he had the bearing of a leader, tall with a distinguished sweep of grey hair. All the same his demeanour was more of a preacher than a politician.

Their next meeting had been shortly after the New Year when, on a cold January day, Owen had driven across the Brecon Beacons to Llangadog to interview him for a series of profiles he was writing.

'I immediately thought of including you because of what you were telling me about Lord Rhys,' he had said. Like most politicians, Gwynfor was not immune to flattery, and needed little encouragement to hold forth on a long litany of heroes. He was working on a history of Wales.

Seated in his study, surrounded by bookshelves, Gwynfor seemed at his most contented. A log fire kept away the afternoon cold as they sipped tea and chatted. The door creaked slightly ajar as a collie sheepdog crept in.

'He only understands Welsh,' Gwynfor said before providing Owen with a survey of the political scene. 'I reckon we've a chance of winning four or five seats at the next general election.'

'How do you remain so optimistic?' Owen asked.

'Oh, there's no alternative.'

There was a pause and then, for some unaccountable reason – looking back he could never understand why he chose that moment – Owen suddenly said, 'You know, I'd like to be of some help if I could work out how.'

Gwynfor stood up to pour some more tea.

'What you're doing on the paper, giving us coverage on all these issues, is of great importance. Not long ago there was someone else sitting where you are now and he asked me the same question.'

'Oh, who?'

'I'd better not name him. As a Labour councillor he was best off staying where he was. He could do far more good for the national movement by working from within, as it were, from inside the Labour Party. The same applies to you, in a different kind of way. From your vantage point you could give us the story behind the stories. You could be an extra pair of ears and eyes in Cardiff. I've a number of people around Wales who keep me in touch in this way.'

And so it was that most Sunday evenings, usually after Gwynfor had attended chapel, Owen would receive a phone call and he would settle down to a conversation about the latest moves being played across the chess board of Welsh politics.

There was more. Gwynfor asked him to prepare some policy papers. Following one he put together on the likely contents of the forthcoming report of the Commission on the Constitution, Gwynfor invited him back to Llangadog for a Saturday evening's discussion. When he arrived, Owen found himself part of a small group of advisers, only a few of whom he'd previously met. Among them was an alarmed Phil Williams who, when Owen entered, looked askance at Plaid's general secretary Dafydd Williams.

'For goodness sake, what's a *Western Mail* journalist doing here?' he hissed.

'Not to worry. He's one of Gwynfor's latest recruits,' Dafydd whispered back.

That was in June. In July Owen attended a two-day meeting in Aberystwyth when the same group, with a few others in attendance, discussed in a more detailed way Plaid's response to the Commission's anticipated recommendations. There was tension between two views. Phil argued that if Plaid compromised on independence it would set the movement back decades. Others, led by Gwynfor, insisted the party should recognise that, whatever its powers, an institution directly elected on an all-Wales basis would be a huge advance.

'We've never had such an opportunity as we have now,' he said.

This argument won the day in the debate at the Aberystwyth conference in October. Now, two days later, Owen drew up outside his terraced house in Cardiff's Gabalfa suburb, bearing the long-awaited report.

Inside, Gwynfor sat perched on the edge of a settee, cup of tea in hand.

'Anna and I have been enjoying an interesting conversation', he began but, catching sight of the bundle in Owen's hand, interrupted himself.

'Is that it?'

Owen passed the two volumes across and Gwynfor held them for a moment.

'Five years, we've waited.'

Then he looked questioningly at Owen.

'It's not unanimous. We knew that of course. But the Welsh and Scottish commissioners have come out for a legislative Assembly, which is more than we could have hoped for.'

'It'll give us a platform. I must go away and absorb this.'

As he went through the door he said to Owen, 'Anna's been telling me you're planning to learn Welsh. That's good news. Better, really, than this.'

St John's Wood
November 1973

On a November evening, after a vote in the House of Commons, Leo Abse joined a crowd gathering in the Members' Lobby. Despite his short stature he moved easily through the throng. He possessed a strong and unmistakable presence, even though his pompadoured hair barely reached the shoulders of most of the men around him. He was hated by some, feared by others, but generally respected.

The MPs were very different from when he had entered the Commons sixteen years earlier. The ex-Colonels and former naval officers in the Tory ranks were much less in evidence. In their place were ad-men and public relations directors. On the Labour side, trade unionists were losing ground to lecturers from red brick universities, dressed like perpetual undergraduates. As Abse was fond of saying, where the black coat and striped trousers had once been the MP's uniform, sparing him the burden of sartorial choice, he was now trapped, wanting but fearing flamboyance, and yet hating anonymity.

Abse himself firmly resisted this trend. His suits were well cut and often colourful. He had become famous for wearing particularly extravagant eighteenth century-style waistcoats on Budget days, created by his designer wife, complete with a dress coat, a gold chained pocket watch, cane, gloves and a black felt hat. This exhibitionism was more than self-indulgence. It entailed a shrewd calculation that, once the public had focused on his attire they would be readier to listen to what he had to say.

It was also a self-conscious act of defiance against some of his Tory enemies who, as he saw it, took a patronising view that finery was for them while socialists should wear cloth caps. He extended the same principle to food and wine, and his three homes. He possessed a five-bedroomed detached house in St John's Wood near Regent's Park, an Edwardian villa in affluent Cyncoed in Cardiff, and a holiday retreat in Nugola on the Tuscany coast.

When Abse became an MP he was already a well-established lawyer with his own practice. This, together with his wealth and confidence, gave him a much-valued independence as well as inevitable unpopularity. He never sought office, acknowledging that party discipline was not for him. Instead, as a backbencher he pursued a wide range of progressive changes, from abolition of the death penalty to reform of the laws affecting abortion, suicide, adoption and divorce. He was famous above all for promoting the legalisation of homosexual relationships.

'You love Parliament,' he once told Michael Foot. 'I use it'.

Amidst the milling MPs in the Lobby Abse suddenly found himself confronted by one of his oldest friends, the shadow secretary of state for Wales.

'Leo! I've been looking for you,' cried George Thomas. 'I wanted to give you this, it's long overdue.'

With that he thrust a thick brown envelope into Abse's hand, pressed his arm tightly, murmured 'Thank you Leo', and moved quickly away, as if unwilling to open a painful wound.

* * *

George Thomas was a secret homosexual, and because of it his political career had always hovered on the edge of catastrophe. Leo Abse had first met him in 1938 when he was a twenty-one-year-old candidate for the Cardiff ward where Thomas was an elementary schoolmaster. Over the years their paths had frequently crossed, especially after Thomas became an MP in the city at the 1945 election. By then Leo was a councillor and chairman of the Cardiff Labour Party. They often shared political platforms, sometimes on street corners, sometimes in packed halls. When Leo married, it was George who acted as witness in the synagogue. And when he was sworn in as a newly-elected MP in the Commons, it was with George by his side that he took the oath of allegiance.

Through all this time Abse was aware of his friend's predilection. He was understanding rather than censorious, though it was never discussed. It was this that cemented their friendship and not the crucial interventions Abse made at the moments of crisis that inevitably came Thomas's way. Sometimes they involved blackmail. On one occasion, after hearing George's distraught account, Abse insisted on dealing directly with the young Cardiff criminal into whose hands he had fallen. Abse was a prosecuting solicitor and his reputation in Cardiff's underworld stood him in good stead in dealing with the blackmailer. The man was put in no doubt that, unless he desisted, Abse was certain to carry out his threat to put him behind bars for at least ten years.

During the decade-long campaign that preceded his 1967 Sexual Offences Act, Abse was in frequent contact with lobbies seeking to end the criminalising of homosexuality. It was through them he learned that George was visiting a cinema in Westminster where groping under cover of darkness was common. He warned him against his lack of discretion and, alarmed at his friend's knowledge, George took heed. But later, while he was still a backbench MP, he sought out Leo for an £800 loan. The large amount was disturbing. Leo urged George to let him intervene directly, but to no avail. George insisted that the sum – to pay for a ticket and resettlement to take the extortioner to Australia – would put an end to the affair. Leo relented.

He had thought deeply about his friend's sexuality and

concluded the explanation lay in his early life in the Rhondda. Thomas's violent, alcoholic and bigamist father had regularly beat up his wife and children. Abse had long believed in the illuminating power of psychoanalysis, not least in explaining the motives and behaviour of politicians. Indeed, he had recently written a book on the subject, naming many politicians in Westminster as examples, so adding to his widespread unpopularity.

In George Thomas's case he thought of the Oedipal drama that has to be worked through by all children in relation to their parents. However, for Thomas the fantasies that accompany a little boy's desire to protect the mother and to dethrone the tyrannous father, were realities and not imaginings. Every Saturday night, after the pubs in Tonypandy had closed the father, his wages spent, returned to make the home a hell, as mother and young children vainly tried to contain the violence unleashed against them. Relief only came when the father left to join the army, never to return. However, by that time the mother and her favourite child were bound together in an unshakeable defensive alliance.

And so it remained into George's adult life. His mother Emma Jane was beside him on every platform and in every social gathering. She featured in all his conversations and election addresses. In Wales she was widely adopted as a symbol of an idealised Mam – caring, concerned, and forgiving. Leo divined, accurately, that George's widely publicised relationship with his mother contributed much to the affection in which he was held and indeed, the charisma he gathered about him.

There was a further aspect which attracted Leo's empathy. While George's father was a Welsh-speaker, his mother was not. Her father had emigrated from Hampshire to Tonypandy and, finding only Welsh was spoken in religious services, defiantly established the first English-speaking Methodist chapel in the area. With such a background, George was certainly not prepared to have himself or his beloved mother defined as a second-class citizen, disqualified by language from full status in the community. To Leo's satisfaction, he constantly vented the full force of his resentment against such presumptions, especially when he sensed they came from a nationalist direction.

Even more than George, Abse was dismissive of what he saw as the xenophobic tendencies of Welsh nationalism. Instead, he espoused the internationalism of the south Wales Labour movement. This was accompanied by an intense feeling of locality produced by the comparative isolation of Valley villages and townships. In his youth in the 1930s, Abse had been inspired by Communist leaders like Arthur Horner, president of the South Wales Miners, and the Rhondda novelist Lewis Jones. Their allegiance was to their locality and the world. As Abse often declared, 'Nationalist flag-waving, whether Russian, English or Welsh, was an anathema to them.'

Later that evening, when he had reached home and poured himself a glass of Chianti, he opened the envelope that George had given him and counted the notes. They came to £620, short by £180.

'Typical of George,' he said to himself. 'Hopeless with money.'

* * *

A few days later Leo and his wife Marjorie were entertaining guests, among them MPs from opposing parties. They were the Conservative Norman St John-Stevas, just promoted as minister of state for the arts in the Department of Education and Science that was headed by Margaret Thatcher, and the Liberal leader Jeremy Thorpe and his fiancée Marion, the concert pianist and divorced Countess of Harewood. He had much in common with both men. They shared his enthusiasm for flamboyant dress and liberal causes. St John-Stevas had been a co-sponsor of his sexual offences legislation. They were amusing, eager for gossip and generally good company. Moreover, they were fertile subjects for Abse's continuing study of the neuroses and obsessions of his fellow politicians.

His spacious dining room was sparsely furnished, creating an uncluttered and confident feel, creating a sense of escape from the claustrophobia of Westminster. An unframed portrait of a scarlet-robed Persian ruler hung on the wall behind Leo's chair at the head of the table. It was the only picture in the room. A touch of exoticism was added by two majolica bowls set on an elaborate Mozambique chest positioned alongside.

Before dinner champagne had been served with crostini, chopped liver pâté with thyme, onion, anchovy and capers fried in virgin oil and served on crisp fried bread. The main meal was a tribute to Leo's love of Italy. It started with tomatoes stuffed with basil and saffron rice bound with egg, dipped in flour, and then dropped in hot olive oil. The roasted Vitello veal followed, the juices flavoured with rosemary, garlic and Marsala wine. Accompanying green beans had a sauce made from tomatoes that had simmered in oil, garlic and basil. The food was accompanied by a young Montecarlo Bianco and a garnet-coloured Gattinara Abse had brought back from Lucca, near his holiday home in northern Tuscany. The cheeses were soft Gorgonzola, pecorino di Siena, Parmigiano dolci, and some hard Sardinians.

As ever with his dinner parties, Leo set out to stimulate an amusing flow of conversation. On this occasion the talk ranged widely, embracing the likelihood of a referendum on the Common Market, the Yom Kippur war and its aftermath, the mounting oil crisis, and the economic difficulties that were crowding around Edward Heath's government.

'Heath reminds me of a plum pudding,' Thorpe remarked. 'The trouble is that no one around him knows how to light the brandy.'

Abse chuckled.

'It's fascinating that he once revealed he has a secret wish, a frustrated desire if you will, to run a hotel.'

'Yes, I've heard that.'

'It gives you a rare glimpse of his fantasy world. The hotel-keeper greets his guests with an ever-present bonhomie, rather like Heath's fixed smile. He's charming, pleasant, correct but distant. And of course, all who come soon go, like ships that pass in the night.'

'Yes, yes, exactly so.'

Abse warmed to his theme.

'Not for our prime minister the dream of a home, wife and family. Only the impersonal hotel over which he presides and where undemanding transitory acquaintances, but not real relationships, are formed. His fate is to hug himself, as we so often see him doing on the front bench in the Commons. At the piano or organ, it is his pleasure to play alone.'

Anxious to change the subject, St John-Stevas lighted on one he correctly predicted would provoke his host.

'I see Leo that your bilingual signs are finally coming to Wales.'

'They're certainly not *my* bilingual signs, as you put it, nor those of my constituents in Pontypool. Every day English-speaking Welshmen will be compelled to look at signs they do not understand, look at television they do not understand and listen to the radio in a language they do not understand. All this has resulted from the tactlessness and pressures of a minority.'

Majorie emerged from the kitchen bearing more wine. Hearing the conversation was turning to Wales, she sought to intervene, cutting Leo off in mid-flow. Nevetheless, he held the attention of his guests, including Jeremy Thorpe who pursued the exchange.

'Surely we need to respect the wishes of minorities?'

'The majority also have rights,' Abse countered. 'In Gwent, we will find ourselves greeted twice when we arrive in our own county. People who cannot understand the language in the place where they live get irritated and vexed. They do not like to feel that they are being treated like strangers in their own land. Every road sign will be a propaganda exercise.'

'I hear people are turning their aerials towards the Mendips and away from the Principality because of the amount of Welsh on television,' St John-Stevas said.

'Because a small, obsessive and persistent group has brought pressure to bear.'

'But Leo, what is so problematic about bilingual signs?' Thorpe protested. 'After all, they're a common sight throughout the world.'

'It's because the language question in Wales has been deliberately politicised by Plaid Cymru and its followers in the Welsh Language Society. The sit-ins, the attacks upon television transmitters, the fanatics with their mock heroics... they're turning the Welsh language into a political football.'

'Surely some of your forebears were Welsh-speakers,' St John-Stevas said. 'You once told me your mother was from west Wales. Isn't there a cultural loss?'

'Well, you're right to the extent that the history of my family reflects a general Welsh experience. My elderly mother was born in Ystalyfera and she will be eighty-four this month. She still falls into her doubtlessly colloquial Welsh when the lady who cooks for her comes into the house. But I was born in Cardiff and, along with the overwhelming majority of its citizens — and those of my Pontypool constituency — can do little more than sing 'Land of my Fathers' inadequately in Welsh.'

'But attitudes are changing,' Thorpe said.

'It's true that the way of thinking which created the sad and catastrophic decline in Welsh began to change in the post-war years. Many people who had lost the language realised that we would be impoverished if we allowed it to peter out completely. That's why we agreed to the Welsh Language Act in the Commons in 1967.'

'Giving Welsh equal validity, as I recall,' St John-Stevas said.

'Exactly so, but now the language zealots are perverting that effort of reconciliation. The lobbying and demonstrations have been pushed to the utmost limits. There has descended a deluge, a torrent even, of Welsh forms upon English-speaking Welshmen for whom, regrettably, they are meaningless.'

'What harm can there be in a few bilingual forms?' Thorpe asked.

Abse's voice rose, becoming heated.

'We see them as a defiant act of political propaganda rather than an attempt to resuscitate the language. So instead of there being a relaxed attitude to the language, it is now unhappily a matter of bitter controversy.'

There was an embarrassed lull in the conversation following this peroration. But as Marjorie began setting out the dinner's final course, a fresh fruit salad sprinkled with an orange and brandy liqueur, the mood swiftly changed. The conversation moved on to more congenial matters.

Pontcanna
November 1973

The thirty young Cymdeithas yr Iaith activists met at the top end of Cathedral Road on Llandaff Fields, not far from the television studios of the commercial broadcaster HTV. It was a Friday evening and there was an autumnal chill to the air. Looking around Rhiannon guessed they were all students. Certainly the half-a-dozen from the Aberystwyth cell who had accompanied her on the bus to Cardiff were. She knew a few more from her time at Bangor University. Others were from Swansea and Cardiff. But most had come from Carmarthen where they were studying at the teacher training college.

Rhiannon only had a general idea of what was intended. That was deliberate, to prevent advance warning of the demonstration. All she had been told was to expect to be in Cardiff for much of the weekend. The group formed a line and moved off the common on to a pathway alongside a terrace of cottages. Word was passed that they should give the appearance of being an invited audience to a studio broadcast.

'But one that intends staying for a bit longer than the programme,' joked someone behind Rhiannon.

Not for the first time that day a tremor of nervousness passed through her. Now it deepened into a rush of panic.

'You don't have to do this,' she thought. 'You could step out of this line. Just leave and let them go.'

All the same she carried on, pushed by the momentum of the group.

'Is it your first time, too?' whispered a girl close to her. Rhiannon saw it was Branwen Thomas, another postgraduate student at Aberystwyth with whom she had chatted on the bus.

They turned a corner, filed through a wide unguarded gate

into the television complex. In no time Rhiannon could see that at the head of the column a long-haired youth was pushing through the swing doors of the entrance to the main building.

They were moving faster now. Once inside Rhiannon looked round, expecting some kind of opposition. Surely there would be a figure of authority? But she could see no one.

She followed the line blindly down a corridor, then up a staircase.

'How do they know where they're going?'

The line bunched and she stumbled into the person in front. They were crammed into a narrow corridor. Then they were moving again, but shuffling slowly. Rhiannon passed through a double-door and her arm was seized.

'Quick!' a voice hissed in her ear.

She was pulled into a dimly lit cavernous space.

'We've got to secure the doors. Find some furniture, anything.'

Rhiannon looked around. A ladder was leaning against the high wall. She ran and grabbed it. Other hands helped her. They wedged it across a doorway, blocking the main entrance to Studio Three.

* * *

Aled Vaughan, HTV's director of programmes, was sitting down to dinner in his Llandaff home when the telephone rang.

'How many did you say?'

He put his half-drunk glass of red wine down, took hold of his jacket and quickly left the house.

His main worry was the equipment, particularly the colour cameras that were worth more than £100,000. A Welsh-speaker himself, he sympathised with the language campaigners. Admired them, even. He used to believe that it was inevitable that the language would eventually die out. But now he thought it might live, a prospect that was down to these young people and their campaign. They had changed the climate of opinion and given the culture a new status. Certainly, he shared their wish for more airtime for the Welsh language.

'What reasonable person wouldn't?' he said to himself as he steered his car out of the driveway. 'They've made the making of Welsh language programmes a legitimate occupation and not a comic pastime.'

All the same, he thought their methods divisive and their objectives wildly impractical. They wanted a dedicated, independent Welsh language channel. But who would pay for it? Wales was already the most expensive area in Britain to cover with the transmitters necessary to provide a colour service. There were too many hills, and too many people living in valleys. HTV's Welsh service was only possible because it was cross-subsidised by its operation in the West of England, and also because it was part of the wider ITV network across Britain. Some argued that HTV should join with the BBC in Wales to create a distinctive channel. But how could you merge a publicly-funded station with one that operated in the open market? And even if it could be afforded, a single Welsh service would create a monopoly.

These were the endlessly repeated arguments that ran once more through his mind as he drove the few miles to the studio in Pontcanna. He thought an opportunity might come with the imminent creation of a fourth channel across Britain. The BBC already had two channels. He himself had argued that ITV should be given the fourth channel, and in Wales it should be used to expand the provision of a Welsh language service. But it was the politicians who would have to be persuaded. And a bunch of misguided youngsters threatening to wreck a television studio was no help in trying to convince them.

'How did they get in?' he demanded when he reached the reception desk.

'We thought they were coming to take part in a recording,' a bewildered security man answered. 'They looked harmless enough. We had no idea …'

'Shall we call the police?' another asked.

'Oh heavens no, we don't want to make martyrs out of them. Get Studio Three on the internal intercom for me.'

He was passed a phone and for five minutes spoke intensely, in Welsh. Passing it back he said, 'Look, I've done a deal. We'll just leave them there, at least overnight, and we'll allow them access to the toilets outside. In return they've promised not to damage the equipment.'

* * *

Inside Studio Three there was a cheer when the arrangement was announced. Rhiannon noticed that a youth with dark hair flopping over his eyes had been the one to take the phone. He had also led the way into the studio.

'What's his name?' she asked Branwen who had moved to stand next to her.

'Arfon, Arfon Jones I think, from somewhere in the Llŷn.'

Rhiannon suddenly remembered him, from when she was at Bangor. Intense, quiet, he had kept himself to himself. 'Can't be more than nineteen or twenty,' she thought.

Now he raised his hand to quell the cheers and stepping on to a platform alongside a camera, began to speak.

'We're not against the mass media. We're not looking to live in a world without television. All we want is to ensure that it doesn't destroy us.'

There were shouts of agreement, but he held his hand up again. Rhiannon thought this was a completely different Arfon

Jones to the one she had known. He pointed to a monitor and his voice rose.

'We want to see a face on that screen and hear a voice from that box which are a mirror of ourselves. Isn't that the true function of the mass media? To express fully the culture of a people?'

More cheers accompanied these questions.

'But when I look at the television, it shows me nothing of where I'm from. What it shows are the lives of a totally different people. To me, HTV and the BBC are Big Brother, as George Orwell described them, omnipresent, omnipotent, even omniscient – if that isn't a blasphemy. In Wales it's as if there must be no language except the language of Big Brother, no other way of living except that shown by Big Bother. And Big Brother is always with you. He is always there in the corner of your room speaking to you, mesmerising you into conformity.'

Arfon Jones stopped for a moment, and stared around the dimly-lit television studio. His voice slowed, becoming more persuasive.

'We're not asking for the moon. We're just asking for our own television channel. And we're tired of being fobbed off with excuses.'

There were more shouts of agreement. Jones spoke over the interruption.

'Let the policy-makers beware. Let the producers of conformity and mass mediocrity beware. This issue is dynamite. On it rests the life and death of a people. Faced with death, people become desperate. Who knows how fiercely they will oppose this death? Who knows at what price they will sell their lives?'

With that he jumped off the raised platform and was enveloped in the arms of his fellow conspirators. Listening,

Rhiannon felt a border had been crossed. There was no going back.

*   *   *

Less than a mile away, oblivious of the demonstration in HTV's studios, Owen James was in the back bar of the Conway pub. He was sharing a pint with a group of journalists, teachers, and other regulars, including the poet John Tripp. Owen had got to know him as a fellow contributor to *Nails*, an irreverent arts programme broadcast once a month by HTV. They were charged with coming up with the quirky ideas that were its hallmark. The team were known as the Epilogue Men since *Nails* was scheduled close to midnight, in the final slot before the weather forecast.

'I was born in Bargoed in 1927 and I want to know why,' Tripp declared in an angry, mocking tone, holding his pint of beer at a precarious angle. A man of boyish candour, he was something of a showman, with a mordant wit. He had striking looks, a hooked nose above a studied moustache, glittering eyes, and a wave of distinguished white hair that belied his lack of a comfortable living. On the left lapel of his jacket he wore the broken rifle badge of the War Resisters International. It added to his actor's pose.

'Why do you want to know, John?' Owen queried.

Tripp raised his pint theatrically so that those around him stepped back, fearing it would spill.

'We come here through no fault of our own. Nobody consulted me about being born, did they? There were no instructions. I'm just the result of a bit of fun my parents had.'

He had said this many times before. As ever it produced a ripple of laughter. Indeed, it was undoubtedly borrowed from another writer. Tripp hoarded phrases like a magpie. 'None of us is going to get out of this alive,' was another. It appealed to him because it chimed with his generally fatalistic outlook on life.

'I think we have to discover our purpose, our vocation if you like,' Owen said.

'I don't believe we're put on this earth for any reason we can fathom,' Tripp contradicted him. 'I have a certain talent and I use it to the best of my ability. Money doesn't come into it. Nothing comes into it except saying what I think and feel about the mess we're in, about Wales, the absence of God, the futility of our lives.'

'So, why does it matter what you say?'

'A poet is one of the few people who can speak with any authenticity.'

Tripp had settled back in Cardiff a few years earlier after two decades in a hectic blur in London, scratching a living as a copywriter, then a freelance journalist, and finally as a publicity officer in the Indonesian embassy. He now lived with his elderly father in a rundown bungalow in Whitchurch, spending lonely days working on his papers and poetry, interspersed with raucous evenings on the town.

He often wondered why he had returned to Wales. The death of his mother was a turning point. Then the literary awakening in the mid-1960s inspired a new focus. 'I had to come back to Wales to find a voice, to find something worthwhile to write about,' he said on one occasion.

Yet he realised he was an odd sort of patriot. Brought up in Cardiff, he had no Welsh and was only now, in his middle years, acquiring a knowledge of his country's history and literature.

'Could I possibly be some kind of exiled, demoted mercenary clinging to a lost Anglo-Welsh fort in Glamorgan?' he had written.

At another time, when asked what Wales meant to him,

he replied, 'Oh, I don't know, the landscape, Pembrokeshire, Tongwynlais up the road, the clubs of Ebbw Vale, a visit to Senghenydd, a drizzling, drunken Saturday with good old boys in Merthyr.'

Drizzle, rain and mist were a constant feature of John Tripp's imagination. 'There is a downpour, always, as the carriages inch into Newport,' he had written in the title poem of his first anthology *Diesel to Yesterday*. 'On the terrace I hitch up my duffle against blowing rain,' he recorded as he waited for a package holiday jet to land at Rhoose airport close to Barry. The rain fell, too, as he stood watching the demolition of his father's blacksmith forge in Tongwynlais. 'We walk home in the rain, away from forty years of his life.' Rainfall was the essential accompaniment to the decay and desolation that he saw around him. In his imagination it was a contrast to sunnier yesterdays, centuries ago when the Welsh controlled their own destiny.

Now, as he reached for his third pint of the evening, he was railing against the rootless, philistine, and materialistic culture of his native city.

'It makes me sad rather than angry. All they watch on the telly is *Coronation Street*. All they see on the streets is Wimpy and Coca-Cola. It's beer, bingo and the betting shop.'

'Oh, come on John,' Owen said, 'it's not as bad as all that.'

'I kid you not, and this is a true story. A visitor from Bala asked a girl in the Cardiff railway station paper shop whether she had a copy of *Barn*.'

Tripp glanced at the circle round him.

'For those of you not privy to the language of heaven the title means *Opinion*. But do you know what the girl replied?'

Owen primed him, 'What did she say John?'

'"What's that? A farming magazine?"'

Tripp continued through the laughter.

'And when you get off a train at Cardiff there aren't many

clues as to where you've washed up, are there? I've seen more than one visitor look bewildered as he waited for a cab – perhaps he thought he was in Newcastle.'

'It's got some way to go before it's a real capital city,' Owen conceded.

'Take where I live, Whitchurch. It's a kind of frontier, a buffer zone. It's nothing much really, a sad coffin of the Tory-Macmillan culture of meretricious hollowness. Life is dull there, the doomsville of conversation, the inhabitants having little interest in Wales except the rugby.'

'Why do you live there then, John?' a fellow drinker queried.

''Cos of the old man, I guess. But really, in Whitchurch life is too banal and humdrum to accommodate thoughts of calamity in any shape or form.'

'Is there nothing about Cardiff you like?' Owen asked.

'Oh yes, for sure, there's a prickly affection, despite the occasional feeling that one is a bit of a misplaced person. There's an element of the seedy about Cardiff, and where there's seediness there are usually characters. They can be raw material for a writer, you know.'

Tripp took a pull at his pint and rubbed a hand across his moustache, removing flecks of foam.

'Take the Hayes, where the winos gather. They share a kind of brotherhood of the leaky boot and the meths bottle, and the defeated look in the eye... but sometimes you can catch a fragment of good dialogue.'

*   *   *

Little more than a stone's throw away, the protesters in HTV's Studio Three settled down for a long night, quietly talking in small groups scattered across the floor. Rhiannon gravitated towards one from Aberystwyth, becoming involved in a conversation they were having.

'I agree with Emyr Llewelyn,' Branwen Thomas was saying. 'We have to have an area of Wales where the language is secure, where it is used on an everyday basis, in the shops and pubs.'

'You mean his Adfer idea,' Rhiannon said, moving to sit next to her.

'Yes, in the west and the north. There can be no question of bilingualism in those areas.'

'You're right. Wherever there's bilingualism, Welsh always loses out,' another said. 'People say a few words in Welsh at the start and then revert to English, to accommodate the English speakers. We've all been in situations like that.'

'We have to have a space like you say, otherwise the language will just die out,' a third added.

'That's right,' another said. 'It's only when people live their lives through the language, only then can it retain its energy and inventiveness, its power to adapt and change.'

'Of course, I see all that,' Rhiannon sighed. 'But we can't abandon the English-speaking areas.'

Branwen, who had been lying on the floor sat up.

'Emyr Llew got it right. After we've built a fortress in the west, we will go out to restore the language to the land from which it has been disinherited. That's what he said.'

'Doesn't sound all that practical,' a voice behind them said.

'We have different policies for the Welsh-speaking and English-speaking areas,' Branwen answered, turning round to catch the eye of the person who had objected. 'We want an English language channel for Wales as well as a Welsh one.'

'It's a tactical thing I suppose,' Rhiannon reflected. 'I can see the point of concentrating on the Welsh-speaking areas. But if we were to lose sight of the rest of Wales that would lead to disaster. And there is tremendous growth going on there, the

Welsh schools and so on. We must win new ground as well as defend what we have.'

A few others in the group joined the debate, batting arguments back and forth between them. Rhiannon leaned forward, arms crossed around her propped-up knees. She was suddenly tired but unwilling to leave the flow of ideas. The conversation carried her, as on an outgoing tide, long into the night.

* * *

Empty glass in hand, John Tripp looked into the front bar of the Conway pub. It was quieter there, inhabited by locals including, as Tripp anticipated, his friend and fellow poet John Ormond. Wandering in he announced himself with a cunning smile.

'Taking dictation from the Muse again, I see.'

'Ah, John, good to see you,' Ormond said. 'It's a drink you're after, no doubt.'

'And some sense as well.'

'If you'll listen.'

Ormond made for the bar. Theirs was an unlikely friendship. In contrast to Tripp's bombastic presence, Ormond was a private man. His poetry avoided commitment, favouring a contemplative gaze on life's predicaments. Where Tripp felt impelled to collide noisily with what he saw as a recalcitrant, reluctant Wales, Ormond wrestled to find the words to describe more personalised, internal contradictions.

Tripp's was a chaotic lifestyle. He had no job and existed close to the edge of poverty. Ormond was a successful television producer with a luminous record of documentary films. He was a settled family man with a comfortable home, wife and children. He had studied English and Philosophy at Swansea University. On the other hand, Tripp had little formal education. Instead, he had matured through the army and the finishing school of journalism.

Despite this they had much in common. Both had to wait until middle age before discovering their poetic voice. In his youth Ormond had been eclipsed by the pyrotechnics of Dylan Thomas. When he was in his early twenties his fellow Swansea poet Vernon Watkins had advised him not to publish anything more until he was gone thirty, advice he had taken to heart. In Tripp's case, he had to wait until his forties before he found a subject he could address. Both believed in art as a democratic intent that was the finest expression of collective social life. Both recognised in one another the essential otherness, and indeed loneliness of the artist. As Ormond returned from the bar, drinks in hand, their conversation slipped back into well-worn grooves.

'I like your technique,' Tripp said. 'The way you bring conflicting phrases together to create a spark, like *Wild calm, calm chaos*.'

'Paradox is at the heart of it,' Ormond told him. 'One of the Greek philosophers, Heraclitus I think it was, said the way up is also the way down. The staircase is the essence of the idea that each thing contains the notion of its opposite. *Life's miraculous poise between light and dark*, was the way Vernon Watkins put it.'

Tripp leant back in his chair.

'I reckon we turn to poetry to bring some order out of chaos. We're trying to sellotape together a baffling multiplicity of fragments.'

He paused to take a sip from his glass.

'But for me it also has to be about the here and now, and that inevitably means the past as well. If you don't have a sense of your history, it's like walking without your shadow.'

'You're trapped by your subject, John. You rattle on about the death of Llywelyn ap Gruffudd, Owain Glyndŵr, the succession of military defeats, the Act of Union, Penyberth.'

'I was reading with a group at the Mermaid Theatre in London a while back, and a woman in the audience made the same point. She asked, "Why do you go on and on about the past?" And I said, "Because we can't forget about it, madam."'

'Your metaphors constantly go on about frontiers, border castles, the burden of the language and the fact you don't speak it. But real poetry comes out of your own experience, John, the ambiguities you feel.'

'Maybe you're right. But there's always brooding history at the back of what's happening. It's when the historical and the personal truly engage that I fire on all cylinders.'

'What I ask of a poem is that, first and foremost, it should be a good poem,' Ormond demurred. 'That is to say, an excellent poem in my use of the English language. If there is any particular Welshness to it, that can look after itself.'

Provoked, Tripp leant forward, pushing his pint to one side.

'But you've got to decide. That's what I think. You have to make a conscious choice to get inside the frame of your country's history. You've got to give up your own point of view to an extent. To find yourself you have to get in touch with the nation's past.'

Ormond disagreed.

'You're attracted to nationalist politics because it allows you to wallow in sentimentality about the country. You go on about your romantic concepts of history in the hope they'll tell you about our future. You have a kind of gloomy longing for an imagined Wales of the past. It doesn't exist, never has, and never will.'

Tripp argued back, a hand sweeping up in a half-emphatic, half-accusatory gesture.

'We have to discover a thread of continuity. That's what

I think. I mean, discover the layers of Wales that are buried beneath the present.'

Ormond was silent for a while.

'We each have to go our own way, I guess,' he said finally. 'I'm not so concerned about making sense of things in the way you seem to be. For me it's a mistake to set out to write a poem in support of some particular line. But for you, politics springs from the heart. What is it that you really want, John? What are you looking for?'

Tripp cast his eyes upward for a moment, as if looking for rain.

'I don't know. A benevolent country I suppose.'

* * *

The following morning, just after nine o'clock the occupation of HTV's Studio Three came to an end.

'They look worn out, like a bunch of teenagers after a night on the town,' a security man said as the Cymdeithas yr Iaith activists straggled out of the building.

'Some night out,' said another.

'More like a night in,' answered the first, laughing.

Rhiannon was tired, cold, emotionally drawn, but also exhilarated, feeling that a blow had been struck. She felt more strongly part of the movement, more confident. She realised that the protest had been largely symbolic, a preliminary outing for untried activists. All the same it made the front page of that day's *Western Mail*.

She slept during most of journey on the bus back to Aberystwyth. As they neared the town she wakened and stared out of the window at the darkening countryside. Branwen Thomas slipped into the seat beside her.

'They're planning something in London and looking for volunteers,' she said. 'I've said I'll go.'

Into Rhiannon's mind crept the words uttered by Arfon Jones the previous evening in the heat of their occupation. *This issue is dynamite. On it rests the life and death of a people...*

'I'll go, too,' she said.

Rhydyfelin
November 1973

'This is going on forever,' George Thomas told Owen. 'I'll keep our place here if you run to the end of the corridor and see if their queue is as long as ours.'

It was an early evening and they were waiting for a table in the Members Dining Room in the House of Commons. There were two restaurants about twenty yards apart, and as bidden, Owen discovered there was a free table in the other one.

'Come on then,' George said, bending to pick up his briefcase. As he did so Enoch Powell, who was standing behind them, stepped forward and wagged his finger under Thomas's nose.

'Hah ha! There you have it George, the free market at work.'

At first Thomas was flustered, but quickly recovered.

'You're a card, Enoch, I'll give you that.'

Owen had discovered a fortuitous connection with the shadow secretary of state for Wales through his Uncle Jack. Although now retired, during the 1940s and 1950s he had run the Harlingford Hotel, near Russell Square. George Thomas had made it his London base during his early years as an MP and still regarded Jack as part of his extended family. So when Owen arrived at the *Western Mail*, it was a small favour for Jack to phone George and ask him to do what he could for his nephew.

Owen was in Westminster to cover for the paper's political editor who was on holiday. He was intent on making full use of his connection with George Thomas who had become secretary of state for Wales in the last years of the Wilson government in the late 1960s. He had continued to shadow the role after Labour lost the 1970 election. Now he was looking forward to resuming the full ministerial position, assuming of course that

Labour won the next election. This was expected sometime in the following year, during 1974.

That afternoon Welsh Labour MPs had met to consider their response to the report of the Commission on the Constitution. Owen was keen to have a first-hand account.

'How did it go?'

'Herding cats,' George replied, swallowing a forkful of House of Commons cottage pie. He pushed a piece of paper across the table. 'Here, have a copy of the press statement. Gives the impression we're as one, doesn't it?'

Owen read the opening sentence. 'It says you were unanimous.'

'Nothing could be further from the truth. What we have is the lowest common denominator. It goes on to say that we support an elected council with executive powers. But people like Cledwyn Hughes, Elystan Morgan and John Morris want to go much further. To all intent and purposes, they want a parliament.'

George sighed, and then dug his fork savagely into his pie.

'As for Wil Edwards and Tom Ellis, they simply fan the flames of nationalism at every opportunity. But a lot of us, people like Neil Kinnock and Leo Abse, and myself come to that, would prefer to have nothing to do with the whole thing.'

'But it's been party policy for the best part of a decade.'

George shook his head.

'I know, I know. We've been led by the nose by the nationalists. What I resent most of all is that it's our own nationalists who've been doing the leading.'

'But don't you think, George, that the Commission proposals are a logical extension to what we've already got? I mean the Welsh Office, the Quangos and all the rest.'

'I know the arguments and they're hard to refute. The worst

thing we ever did was set up the Welsh Office. It opened the floodgates for nationalism.'

'Really? But you were secretary of state in the last Labour government. Didn't you see the benefits for Wales of having a voice at the top table?'

'Well, there is some truth in that.'

George sipped his tea. He was a teetotaller, or claimed to be.

'Gives us a platform, undoubtedly. But the Welsh Office was an artificial creation you know. When I went there I soon discovered that its main preoccupation is to look for issues we can say are specifically Welsh.'

Owen looked again at the press statement. It welcomed the Commission's rejection of the nationalists' prescription of separation, Liberal notions of federalism, and the Conservative adherence to large numbers of undemocratic, nominated bodies.

'It's all very well to reject the policies of the other parties. But it's going to be hard to get people enthusiastic about something that sounds like just another tier of local government.'

'What you need to understand, Owen, is that there is no way we can accept any policy that hints at a reduction of Welsh MPs at Westminster.'

George took a large cigar out of his pocket and lit it with a match. Sending a cloud of smoke across the restaurant, he leant back in his chair and adopted the tone he'd used as a schoolteacher, before entering Parliament.

'If we went down the road of a legislative council or Assembly or whatever it's going to be called, then it would inevitably take us in that direction. Wales is over represented in the House as it is.'

'So the real story is that the Welsh Labour Group is split.'

'Don't quote me. You know the form, sources close to and so on. We'll have to hope that the whole thing goes away. Certainly,

I can't see it featuring in our election manifesto. And a good thing too.'

'But as shadow secretary of state you'll have to have a position on this, won't you?' It says here...'

Owen picked up the press release once more, and read its final sentence out loud, 'The Group welcomed an Assembly with real powers as the best means of exercising greater democratic control over the distinctive features of Welsh life.'

'Yes, yes, as I say that's the lowest common denominator.'

Thomas leant forward, picked up his teacup and, still holding his cigar, reached out to grasp Owen's arm with his other hand.

'Now then my boy, you can be of help. I've got to make a speech at the university in Aberystwyth. That could be an opportunity. Why don't you draft me some notes?'

* * *

A few weeks later Owen was driving in a misty afternoon rain along the Ceredigion coast road northwards to Aberystwyth. On the seat alongside him was the speech George Thomas was giving to a student audience that evening. Owen had to concede it was a disappointment. He had put a lot of work into preparing his memorandum. It had run to six closely-typed pages, emphasising the history of the Welsh Office and the fact that Labour's Assembly policy had been proposed a year before Gwynfor Evans' by-election in Carmarthen in 1966. He gave a detailed analysis of the £260 million a year spent by over fifty unelected nominated bodies. Finally, he provided an outline of the arguments made by those on the Commission on the Constitution who favoured legislative powers, in the hope of persuading George to be a bit more adventurous.

However, and as he had suspected would happen, only the

statistics about nominated bodies had found their way into George's speech. There was a grudging acknowledgement of the case for an elected council. Otherwise, the main thrust was a defence of the role of Welsh MPs at Westminster. Only at this point did the speech come to life.

It was inconceivable that Wales should be given 'a proper parliament', was the way George put it. 'That way would lead to the complete separation of Wales from the United Kingdom. Only a few fanatics in Wales want this catastrophe to come upon us.'

Owen was about to call on one of those fanatics. He had decided it was time to highlight Phil Williams' role in Plaid Cymru as a figure at the other end of the spectrum from George Thomas. After all, he had led for the party when it had given evidence to the Commission on the Constitution.

Driving into Rhydyfelin, a village a few miles south of Aberystwyth, Owen turned right into a small, winding lane that led to the house. It was an extended stone cottage set against a steep hillside with sweeping views over the valley below. Phil was waiting for him in a large, untidy kitchen, heated by a wood stove set in an archway in a corner of the room.

'Welcome to where the work gets done. On your way to Aber?'

Owen explained he was covering George Thomas's speech.

'Yes, I heard he was coming. Doubt if he's got much constructive to say, least of all about us.' He imitated Thomas's Rhondda accent. 'Nothing good will ever come from those Welsh nationalists.'

'What was it that made you into one? Bargoed was hardly a breeding ground for Plaid Cymru.'

'You're right about that. Before I went to Cambridge I had a completely distorted view of the Blaid. I went up in 1957. In those days I thought of the party, if I thought much about it at all, as full of short, furtive men dressed in nightgowns and attending eisteddfodau. They refused to speak English and crept out after dark to paint slogans.'

Owen laughed.

'What changed, then?'

'Well, in Cambridge I found myself sharing rooms with a member of Plaid and that was the basis for a fierce argument that went on for two years, day and night.'

'It took two years to persuade you?'

'I was in the Labour Party at the time. But then came the 1959 general election. I was at home in Caerphilly, doing my totally unnecessary bit for Labour, and suddenly – out of the blue – here was a nationalist candidate who shattered my prejudices.'

'In Caerphilly?'

'Yes, John Howell. He was brought up in Pakistan, didn't speak Welsh, and had worked in the aerospace industry in California.'

'Not your identikit Plaid candidate then.'

'Quite. I was now more than halfway to joining and, then, when I read Plaid's manifesto I became a member.'

'How old were you went you went to university?'

'Just seventeen.'

'Cambridge must have felt a bit of a change.'

Phil poured some tea.

'I'd hardly been to England before. Bargoed was a mining town and I went to the local school where most of my friends were children of coal miners or steel workers.'

'A bit different from you I would say.'

'Well, yes, I came from a large extended family, a clan if you like. There were a few miners to be sure, but mainly farmers, teachers and milkmen, one professor of physics, three ministers, three publicans, six or seven doctors, a grocer, a baker, a stationmaster and one high ranking United Nations official.'

Owen laughed again.

'That's quite a mix.'

'I suppose it was. All the same it seemed perfectly natural that we were all part of the same family and kept in close contact, especially at weddings and funerals. But then, when I went to Cambridge I made a big discovery.'

'What was that?'

'That England was different, totally different. Wales had a clan system, England had a class system.'

'How do you mean?'

'Well, just look at the statistics. When I was a student only five per cent of kids went to private schools. But about sixty per cent of the students in Oxford and Cambridge came from those private schools. And about eighty per cent of the top echelon of the civil service was recruited from graduates who had attended those private schools and went on to Oxford or Cambridge.'

'So you discovered the English class system.'

'Yes, but more importantly you might say, I discovered the other side of the English class system. There I was, my face covered in pimples, and like every other student I was given a *gyp* – a college servant who cleaned my shoes, made my bed, washed my dishes, and laid a fire.'

Phil shook his head.

'Extraordinary, when you think about it. That man had served in the RAF in the war, stationed in St Athan – but he was expected to call every student *Sir*. He was on the other side of the English class divide.'

Passing a refreshed mug of tea across to Owen, Phil warmed to his theme.

'In fact, you could say this wasn't even a true class system – it was more of a caste system, with a small and clearly defined ruling élite passing on power and influence from one generation to another...'

'The ruling class.'

'Absolutely. But not just a ruling class, a ruling élite with their own way of speaking, their own schools, their own health service, their own separate way of life.'

'Quite different from Bargoed, then.'

'Totally different, don't you think? In Wales we belong in a different way. It's family ties that matter. We all belong to a family. We say, "Oh, yes, I'm belonging to him" and we don't understand why the English smile, we don't realise that you can't say that in English.'

'I see what you mean. We have a stronger sense of place in Wales as well. It's as though place trumps class.'

Phil walked across the room and stared out of the window.

'There's no doubt as you say, that we *belong* to the place where we grew up - *y filltir sgwâr*, the square mile. We ask people, "Where are you from?" But for the English, the upper class English anyway, the ruling class, that's an odd question. They don't come from anywhere, really. They just come from the upper class.'

* * *

After attending George's lecture in the Old College on the seafront, Owen made his way to the Cŵps, where Phil had told him he would be playing saxophone with his jazz trio. Walking into the bar, a soft flowing sound greeted him, punctuated with occasional impulsive shrieks. Through a haze of smoke at the far end he saw Phil, accompanied by piano and drums. In a world of his own he was oblivious to the buzz of conversation around him.

Owen ordered a beer and took in the scene, leaning with his

back to the bar. Halfway down the room he caught sight of a man seated against the wall alongside the red-haired girl who had so captivated him at the Plaid conference. He made his way towards them, found a stool and placed his pint on the table between them.

'I saw you at the George Thomas lecture. What did you make of it?'

'Can't say I was overwhelmed,' the man said. '*Underwhelmed* would be a better word.'

'Well, for George that's about as good as it gets, on devolution anyway.' Owen extended his hand. 'I'm Owen, by the way. Owen James. Work for the *Western Mail.*'

'You're a reporter?'

'That's right.'

Owen looked across at the girl who, he saw, was watching him closely. Ioan introduced himself and then Rhiannon. Owen reached out his hand and she took it, in a soft firm grip.

'I couldn't help noticing you that night in the Belle Vue. You've got an amazing voice.'

Rhiannon flushed and elbowed Ioan in the ribs.

'It was his fault. He lifted me on that chair, you know, and when I got there I felt I had no choice. Bit like an eisteddfod at school...'

'You studying here in Aber?'

'International Politics, I'm doing an MA. Are you reporting on the George Thomas speech? I couldn't make out whether he was for or against this Assembly business.'

'Well, really he's against it, but he's the shadow secretary of state and as its party policy he has to be for it.'

Ioan snorted.

'Typical. Can't see they've got a policy, on that or anything much else.'

'He called it a parish pump parliament,' Rhiannon said. 'That's what I heard him say.'

'What he was getting at was that even a law-making Assembly would still be a local institution. It would still be run by Westminster, financed anyway, so there'd be a lot of duplication.'

'But wouldn't whatever it was he was arguing for, an executive Assembly, be run by Westminster even more?'

'You're right, except that an executive Assembly couldn't pass legislation, so it wouldn't be a threat to Welsh Labour MPs in London. That's what George is most worried about, that their numbers might be cut. But it's a good question. It sums up the quandary they're in.'

'Nothing will happen anyway unless Plaid starts getting its act together and wins a few seats,' Ioan said. 'That's the only thing that concerns them in the Valleys, their seats.'

As he was talking, Owen noticed that Phil had placed his saxophone in its stand and was making his way towards them. He had a pint of what looked like lemonade in his hand.

'You made it then.'

'I wouldn't have missed your playing,' Owen told him. 'Rather sets you apart from the run-of-the-mill politician, I'd say.'

'He's doing something on me for the *Western Mail*,' Phil said apologetically, looking at Rhiannon. Then he turned to Ioan, 'Haven't I seen you around? At the Plaid conference a few weeks ago?'

Ioan grinned.

'You stopped me when I was in full flight on the Common Market, don't you remember? I was just about to come up with a killer fact, though I can't think what it was now.'

'It was a good debate.'

'The Common Market's just a capitalist club.'

'That's true, but there are opportunities you know. Gives us a chance to put Wales on the map.'

'Putting us on a par with the Basques and the Bretons, I suppose.'

'It's much more than that.'

Phil had been standing but now he pulled out a stool and, placing his glass on the table, sat down. He leant forward, holding his hands together.

'The way I see it is this...'

He stopped, struggling to find words for what he wanted to say.

'Look, I'm a scientist and science is probably the most international of all activities. My research has given me a chance to work in a whole range of countries with a lot of different people. I was totting it up the other day. Since coming to Aberystwyth I have written joint papers with Americans and Russians, a man from France and one from Poland, with Norwegians and Swedes, with Finnish-speaking Finns and Swedish-speaking Finns, with two Indians and one Pakistani, with Scots, Irish, English and, of course, with Welshmen as well. I've written joint papers with Catholics, Protestants, Muslims, Jews, Sikhs, Marxists and agnostics. The result of it all is that I now see Wales as a part of Europe and not just as a small fringe of Britain.'

'That's all very interesting,' Ioan told him. 'But at the end of the day the Common Market is still a capitalist club for the big countries.'

Phil half rose from his stool, barely suppressing his eagerness.

'Paul-Henri Spaak, you know one of the founders of the European Community. Well, he said there were only two kinds of state in Europe, small states and small states that haven't yet realised they're small.'

Owen laughed, but Phil was in full flow.

'Seriously though, in the future, certainly by the next century, there'll be huge opportunities for countries with a population of less than ten million people.'

'And that would include us, I suppose,' Owen said.

'Absolutely, countries I've lived in like Norway, Sweden and Finland, and other countries, too, like Denmark, Ireland, the Netherlands, Switzerland and Austria. They're already the most successful countries in the world today. They have the highest standard of living, the best welfare services. Wales would be a natural addition to that list.'

'That would be brilliant if it was true,' Rhiannon said. 'But how does all that fit with the powers that seem so dominant in the world? I mean America, the Soviet Union, China I suppose, and now the Common Market.'

'Well there's a natural role for those major power blocs, as you say. They all have populations over 200 million. But, don't you see, there's no long-term, independent role for the in-between countries, those that have around 50 million people, the ones that don't realise they're small.'

'How can a country with a population of 50 million be small?' Ioan queried.

'But don't you see, on its own Britain is too small to have its own car industry, or an independent aircraft industry. It's too small to have an independent space industry, too small to build mainframe computers, and certainly too small to have an independent nuclear deterrent.'

Owen interrupted.

'I suppose you're really talking about England.'

'Well yes, it is a small nation the way the world is going. But as Spaak said, it just doesn't realise it.'

'Hard to think of England as a small nation when you put it alongside Wales,' Rhiannon said.

'At a stretch I suppose it's a medium-sized nation,' Phil

answered. 'At the same time it finds it difficult, impossible really, to behave as even a medium-sized nation. It's trapped by its history. It can't escape from the memory of the time when it really was the world's number-one power.'

'But you think that some time soon it'll have to face up to the reality of its position.'

'Exactly, events are catching up with it.'

The Havens
December 1973

Anna and Owen were spending Christmas with Owen's father, on the shores of St Brides Bay in Pembrokeshire. Gwilym had moved into the terraced cottage in Little Haven the previous year after his wife Mary had died. They had been living in Haverfordwest since before the war. For Gwilym the move was a retreat to happier years when his two sons, Owen and Rees, were small. On summer weekends they would drive the six miles to the seaside village and picnic on the beach.

Gwilym was bereft when his wife had died so unexpectedly from an aggressive cancer. He had been retired for a year from his job with the National Provincial Bank and they were planning to take regular holidays by train to cities across Europe, especially to Italy where he had fought in the war. Now all these plans had vanished. Gwilym found he could not bear wandering alone around the large semi-detached house on the edge of the town.

'I know people say you shouldn't do anything in a hurry,' he'd explained to Owen, 'but I can't stay here.'

It was Owen who suggested he might look for somewhere on the coast.

'Think about it, Dad, you won't have to get in the car to take the dog on the beach or walk the cliffs.'

So over the summer of the previous year, they had driven the length of the north Pembrokeshire coast, from St Dogmaels to Dale, before finally they found the place in Little Haven. A short distance from the beach, the terrace of cottages had been built for fishermen a century before. Now many of them were holiday homes. However, Gwilym's had been occupied by locals, latterly an elderly widow, and was little altered. The front door opened straight out on to a narrow pavement, but the back was more extensive. The living room and scullery had been knocked into one and had a black range with an open fire. The room faced southwards on to a large narrow garden that ended in the mill race stream that flowed to the sea. A conservatory lined one wall to the side. Behind was a wooden shed that Gwilym had extended, adding a wood-burning stove for heating in the winter. Here he spent hours at his lathe, fashioning and polishing wooden plates, bowls, and candlesticks, which the craft shop in the village had begun selling.

Gwilym was watching Anna in the kitchen preparing their Christmas Eve supper. He regarded her as the daughter he had never had. She and Owen had arrived from Cardiff earlier in the day, stopping off to shop in Haverfordwest. She was kneading pastry for a steak and kidney pie.

'It's good to see you settling in so well,' she said. 'It feels as though you've been here ten years, not one, and Ben certainly looks at home.'

Gwilym leant down to pat the head of his black and white border collie stretched out before the range.

'He likes his walks on the beach. But it's good to have people in the place all the same.'

'How are you finding Little Haven in the winter?'

Gwilym lit his pipe.

'There's a surprisingly large number of people here over the winter months. The back bar of the Castle is usually full of an evening. The only thing is you can't get any television reception in this dip. But there's talk of raising an aerial on the hill and piping it down.'

They spoke companionably in this vein for a while, waiting for Owen to return with driftwood from the beach. Observing Anna at work reminded Gwilym of his wife, whom he had so often watched performing similar tasks. She was very like Mary.

Little more than five-foot tall with long dark hair, the young woman's eyes lit up when she smiled. And when she laughed, which was often, it was with a throaty, infectious chuckle that seemed to lighten whatever surroundings she was in.

'That's a cwtshy girl you've found there,' Gwilym had told Owen when he brought her home for the first time. 'Mind you take care of her.'

That had been a year before Owen's mother died. They met in Bristol, where he'd been at university. He had returned to stay for a weekend with friends with whom he had shared a flat in the student quarter in Clifton. Unlike him, they had been unable to part with university life when their degree courses had come to an end. While Owen had gone north to begin his journalistic career, they had continued their student existence. Pete pursued a desultory further degree and Greg worked in an antiques and second hand furniture business. Hankering after their lifestyle, every few months Owen was drawn back to his old haunts.

It was at a party in their place that he had met Anna. She was one of a group of student nurses who rented a large first-storey flat in Victoria Square. Owen was immediately drawn to her lively warmth. She thought him a bit serious. He discovered she came from Grosmont, a village on the Welsh border between Hereford and Abergavenny, where her father was the vicar. Though, as she put it, 'You'd hardly say he was conventional.'

The noise and loud music did not allow them to talk a great deal. But it was enough for her to agree that he could meet her when he was next in Bristol, in a fortnight's time.

From then on, every other weekend Owen made the long, seven-hour drive south, across the Pennines, through the streets of Manchester, down the Welsh border to Gloucester, and then Bristol. He would start at seven or eight o'clock after a day's work, and arrive exhausted in the early hours. Most of

Saturday morning they would spend in bed. They would have breakfast sprawled across the floor, reading the papers. Later, in the afternoon they'd go for a walk or shop in Clifton. In the evening they might go to a cinema, but usually preferred to curl up in front of the gas fire in Anna's room watching television.

Owen had never felt more settled in a relationship. Although Anna was a student, she was really working her passage towards a job. Somehow that made it different from the on-off affairs he'd had with girls in his own student days. Beneath Anna's bubbly exterior he found a calm oasis, an authority to which he deferred. Anna decided she liked Owen's earnestness, his ambition to be a writer, his passion for debating political matters, and his search for commitment. She thought he was a bit like her father, especially in his tendency to drift off into dreamy self-absorption. Certainly she had never met anyone close to her age who seemed so complicated and, as she put it to herself, so 'deep'.

They had married in the church at Grosmont. Looking back in later years Owen realised that his father's insistence he make 'an honest woman of her' had precipitated his proposal. Yet at the time it felt natural enough. The wedding took place on a hot summer's day in a marquee on the vicarage lawn. Anna's two older brothers and younger sister joined forces to make it an uproarious occasion. Owen observed that Anna's mother, like her daughter, managed to stay calm throughout the ceremony. Her father just beamed. In contrast, Owen's relatives were uncertain how to respond to such a display of boisterous family interaction. If his mother had still been alive, it might have been different.

*   *   *

Christmas Day was bright and cold and the tide out by mid-morning when, muffled in coats and scarves against a keen wind, Owen, Anna and Gwilym ventured on to the beach. Ramsey Island beyond St David's was shaped clear on the horizon and halfway across the bay the usual coastal tankers were anchored, waiting for a berth in Milford Haven. Ben had discovered a stick which Owen hurled into the sea. The dog splashed in after it, jumping over the waves, oblivious to the freezing water. They walked over Settlands and then across Broad Haven as far as Lion Rock where they lingered, watching the wind pick up foam from the incoming tide, driving it over the sand.

'It's time we headed back,' Anna said eventually. 'I'll need to see to the dinner. You two go for a pint if you like.'

The Castle was full of people from Haverfordwest and further afield, and some spilled outside despite the cold. Owen and his father found a couple of seats close to a blazing fire. Owen asked after his older brother who long ago had moved to Essex to teach in a large comprehensive school.

'He's with Beth's family up in Norfolk. He phoned me the other evening. They and the kids are all fine.'

Filling his pipe, he looked closely at Owen.

'I often wonder how you two turned out so differently. There's Rees now, just happy enough with his wife, kids and his job. And then here you are, all caught up with this politics business, chasing after some romantic notion of Wales.'

Owen stiffened, becoming defensive.

'It's what my job is about. I need to follow what's happening.'

'It's more than just a job with you, Owen.'

'I suppose it is.'

'Yes, well, remember, you've got Anna to think about. She's a rare girl, that one.'

After lunch the next day Owen drove Anna to Haverfordwest to catch a train to Cardiff. She was working night shifts at the hospital during the coming week.

'There's really no point in your coming back. I'll be asleep most of the day anyway. Best you stay and spend some time with your dad. I do worry about him being by himself down here, with just Ben for company.'

Later, in the gathering dusk Owen and his father took the dog for a walk along the cliff path above the village. Their way was lit by a near full moon, surprisingly bright so early in the winter's night. It rose between menacing clouds, but still cast a cold light across the darkening seascape. Lifted by the evening wind, gulls passed close to the cliff edge, gliding silently towards some unknown destination. Father and son walked through Blue Bell Wood to Borough Head where the lights of Newgale and Solva were visible. Out to sea regular flashes pulsed from the Smalls lighthouse. Gwilym stopped to stare as they sent shadows across the water.

'I never tire of this place you know. Every day is different. the weather, sea and land, they're always changing.'

'But you're alright here, Dad, by yourself for so much of the time?'

'I'd be by myself wherever I was. But it's not so bad. I'm getting to know more people in the village. You'd be surprised how much social life there is here, especially during the winter. There's a whist drive in the Castle on a Thursday evening.'

* * *

In the cottage Gwilym built up the fire with some logs and then busied himself making ham sandwiches, which he delivered to the fireside with a few bottles of beer. Owen was leafing through the latest volume of Michael Foot's biography of Aneurin Bevan which Anna had given him for Christmas. He was interested to see how Foot would deal with Bevan's renunciation of unilateral disarmament in his speech at the Labour conference in 1957.

It was obvious that his position was not the simple betrayal Owen had previously assumed. It was more nuanced and, Owen reflected, in some respects principled and courageous. He asked his father what he thought about Bevan.

'He was a great politician, there's no doubt about that. Where would we be without the health service?'

'No, no, I was wondering what you thought about his opposition to unilateral nuclear disarmament. You know, his speech about not sending him naked into the conference chamber and all that.'

'I'm sure he was right there. You've got to stand up for yourself you know, otherwise you get trampled on. The war taught us that, if nothing else.'

'It's not so straightforward as I thought. I always assumed it was because he decided they could never win an election if they kept to unilateralism. But if you read the whole speech you can see the complexities.'

'There's always those.'

Owen leafed through the book, lighting on a page.

'He explains it in a letter to Huw T. Edwards. Do you remember him? He was leader of the Transport and General Workers.'

'Aye, he was known as the unofficial prime minister of Wales.'

'Anyway, Huw T. must have written to Bevan about his speech, because Foot quotes his reply.'

Owen read it out.

> I do not regard the possession of the hydrogen bomb by Great Britain as making the slightest contribution to peace or our security, so the argument is not for, or against, Britain possessing the hydrogen bomb. My case is a little different. It rests upon the argument

that if we unilaterally reject the bomb, then we are at the same time rejecting all the alliances and obligations in which this country has become involved, either rightly or wrongly. We could not keep an alliance with countries possessing the bomb and yet repudiate it ourselves. When I spoke of Britain going naked into the conference chamber, I was not thinking of the bomb at all.

'It sounds a bit like playing with words to me,' Gwilym said. 'Seems to me you're either for it or against it.'

'No, don't you see? It's not so black and white. Everyone was asking at the conference and still is to this day, "Why did Bevan do it?" Michael Foot argues we should look at what he actually said.'

Gwilym threw some whitened driftwood on to the fire. It spluttered and burst into vigorous life, startling a somnolent Ben.

'That's the trouble with politics, things are rarely what they seem. Your mother thought a lot of Bevan, you know. We once heard him speak, in Haverfordwest at one of those elections after the war, '51 I think it was.'

'Gwynfor calls him a great, but deracinated politician.'

'Deracinated?'

'Yes, rootless, certainly so far as Wales is concerned.'

'You have to bring everything back to Wales, don't you? For the life of me I don't know where your fixation comes from.'

'Do you really want to know, Dad?'

'Go on.'

'Well, it started when I was at university. I've never told you but I had this extraordinary experience, a moment of revelation if you like. Anyway, looking back it feels like a turning point.'

'Which was?'

'It was on my birthday, my twentieth birthday. A Friday, I can remember it like yesterday, the 21st of October 1966.'

'Yes?'

'Well, I was walking down Queen's Road, opposite the University Wills Memorial Building, carrying two shopping bags full of stuff for the party we were organising that night, cans of beer mainly. Then, when I stopped by a newsagent I saw the *Bristol Evening Post*'s banner headline.'

'And?'

'It had just one word, Aberfan, in large capital letters.'

'Ah, I see.'

'Yes, well I had this reaction, extraordinary really. I put my bags down, picked up the paper, and started to cry.'

'Cry?'

'Yes, wept.'

'But why? You'd never been to Aberfan, had you?'

'No, that's what made it so unsettling. I couldn't understand it. I'd nothing to do with the place. Never been there. It was a terrible disaster, of course, a hundred and forty-four people killed by that tip, a hundred and sixteen of them small children. Disasters – earthquakes, famines, floods – happen all the time all over the world, don't they? But I'd never had a response like this to such a thing and for a long time I couldn't understand why.'

'So why was it, then?'

'I came to realise what had happened to those people had been done to them, from the outside – by the system, if you want to call it that, a malignant system.'

Gwilym looked at his son, and wondered what to say. He found it difficult to understand. In his own case, the event had washed over his head. It had been terrible, of course. Everyone had spoken of it for days. But he had thought of it as just another disaster.

'Most of us thought of it as an Act of God,' he said eventually.

'Act of God? Act of the National Coal Board more like! Act of a colonial system. I thought about it for a long time. Remember, I was studying philosophy. We were trained to think about things. I started to get really angry about it, but it was all so pointless. There was nothing I could do, was there? I kind of stored the whole thing in a corner of my mind and tried to forget about it, get on with other things.'

'Well, clearly you didn't forget about it.'

'No, I used to revisit that corner in my mind now and then. And all the emotions would come back, especially the anger. I just couldn't see a way through it, until one day I said to myself, "Do something about it, don't just get angry". That's when I became *fixated* with Wales, as you put it.'

Penarth
December 1973

It was already dark on the day after Boxing Day when Owen set off for Cardiff. By the time he drove through the Downs on the hill overlooking the city it was approaching ten o'clock. Then, on an impulse, instead of following the familiar streets to Gabalfa and home he swung right and headed to Penarth.

He came to the centre of the town and took several turns up to the headland with its views across the estuary. He parked the car and wandered down towards Kymin Park. Victorian terraced houses lined the landward side of the lane while the park with its dense foliage sloped away on the other. Near the middle of the terrace Owen stepped towards a wide door. Looking up he saw a light from the third floor casting a glow across the trees. He paused, raised his hand, hesitated, but then pressed the bell. Nothing. A few long moments passed. He pressed again and as he did so the door flung open.

'Owen! *Quelle surprise!* What brings you at this hour?'

Nevertheless, as she put the question she took hold of his arm and pulled him through the doorway. Then, pushing him against the wall, she shut the door and pressed her mouth gently to his.

* * *

They had met in the summer at a press launch for a David Jones exhibition in the National Museum. Mari glanced his way as he was passing, searching for a drink, and then later when he passed her again. Their eyes met and she held his gaze with an amused, mischievous smile.

'Get me another glass of red, why don't you?'

When he returned she had moved further along the gallery and was studying a series of watercolours. Owen pursued her through the crush of people and followed her eyes to an arresting image of the Crucifixion. It looked medieval in character. The cross dominated a terrain of conical hills, trees, a grazing horse and a small chapel. Along the wall were other images of the same landscape though none, he thought, as striking.

He passed her the glass, and she gave him another smile.

'The landscapes are so intense, overwhelming even, don't you think? My feeling is that until then, the mid-1920s that is, he had only been familiar with the flat lands of south-eastern England. But suddenly he was confronted with the hills of Wales. It had a big impact. *Land of enchantment*, he called it.'

She pointed at the picture which had caught his eye. It bore the lettering *Sanctus Christus de Capel-y-Ffin*.

'David finds extraordinary rhythms in his landscapes I always think. It's not just the hills, but the trees and the brooks. He makes it all so fluid.'

She pointed to a bird flying across the sky behind an image of Christ on the cross.

'The bird of hope. Look, there's Y Twmpa. It's the mountain across the Honddu valley from Eric Gill's settlement where David stayed. It appears in lots of his drawings and paintings from this period.'

'You seem to know a great deal about him.'

'Well, yes, David Jones is a particular interest of mine.'

She introduced herself as Mari Môn Hughes and laughed.

'Not my real name. Really I'm Mari Roberts from Ystalyfera, a Swansea Valley girl. I just married into the Môn Hughes.'

They were a north Wales family, she explained. Her husband John ran an estate and farming business outside Llanrwst, but she spent much of her time in the south. She had a house in Penarth.

'It just works better for us this way,' she said vaguely when Owen raised an eyebrow. 'And John has somewhere to stop off when he's on his way to London.' Then laughing again, she added, 'But of course, he could get the train directly from Llandudno, and I suppose he does most of the time.'

She was an artist herself, he discovered. She had trained at the Slade School in London and was working on an exhibition she was hoping to show in about a year's time. He also learnt that she had three children, a boy and twin girls, teenagers who were at boarding schools in England. She was less than Owen's height, but her flowing, pale Laura Ashley dress made her seem larger. People seemed to instinctively give way when she walked through the crowded reception. Curving dark hair framed her sharply cut features. It was a face that sought engagement rather than admiration. Owen found her direct, uninhibited manner unsettling. There was something enticing about the combination of her sharp, sceptical features and her ample form only partially hidden beneath her flowing dress.

'You could give me a lift home if you like,' she said towards the end of the evening, as if she was talking about the weather. 'I imagine you have a car.'

While she made coffee, Owen examined what he thought must be her paintings hung across the walls of the sparsely furnished lounge in her large terraced house. The high ceiling ensured there was plenty of space. The pictures were a great swirling mass of dense colour that seemed to merge land, sea and sky. Owen guessed they were meant to indicate landscapes but there was no telling what locations might have inspired them. In some he thought he detected an outline of cliffs or hills but generally there was nothing he could readily identify. He was so absorbed, he started as she entered the room bearing a tray.

'Your work?'

She laughed, a low peeling sound that invited accompaniment.

'You don't need to say anything. I'm just trying to capture light, the light off the land and sea.'

'The colours are, well, striking.'

She laughed again.

'There, you see, I said not to say anything.'

Owen sat on a cushion on the stripped pine floor.

'Tell me about David Jones. I know hardly anything about him.'

Mari sat on a rug opposite him folding her legs under her.

'Where to start? I think he's one of the most original artists of the century. There's no one quite like him. It's difficult to see the influences, though they are there, Eric Gill and so on.'

'So, essentially, he's English?'

'He wouldn't say that, even though he was born in England and his mother was English. No, he'd say he was British, but Welsh first and foremost, behind all of that.'

'How come?'

'Well, James, his father was Welsh and Welsh-speaking, though he moved to London long before David was born. But it was much more than that. It's the mythology and sense of a distant lineage that is defining for David. He sees the world from an ancient Celtic perspective, and in a way that is really imagined or invented... it seems so to me, anyway.'

'I'm not sure I follow.'

'He once told me about his father who was born in Holywell, around 1860 I think it was. That was hundreds of years after a battle that was fought there by Owain Gwynedd against the Normans. It was at Coleshill between Flint Sands and Halkin Mountain. Despite the centuries gap in time, David said the Welsh victory was supremely important for him in a direct personal sense.'

'How could that be?'

'The birth of his father in that place had enormous implications, don't you see? Owain Gwynedd's victory meant the recovery of a tract of land close to the present-day border. Until then, it had been in England's possession for well over three centuries.'

'So?'

'If that twelfth century recovery had not happened, then the area around Holywell, where David's father was born, what was known in those days as Tegeingl, the land between the River Clwyd and the Dee estuary, well all that would have remained English. The Welsh border would have been further to the west.'

'Ah, I see what you mean. His father would have been born in England.'

'And he would not have had any Welsh roots at all. David says the story demonstrates a truth that pervades his work, that history is not something in the past, it's the past living in the present.'

* * *

Mari Môn Hughes decided she liked Owen James. In fact, she liked him very much. She liked the way his dark features lightened when he smiled. She liked how his apparent journalistic worldliness concealed an eager enthusiasm. It was all too plain that Wales lay at the centre of his world. She liked him above all because underneath everything else, she divined a naive vulnerability. It brought out an unfamiliar feeling in her of warmth and motherliness. As he was leaving that first night she suggested he might drop by again one day, soon.

When he visited for lunch the following week they ate cheese with a baguette, olives and dried tomatoes and drank a bottle of red wine. Afterwards she suggested they take a walk along the promenade which was not far below the house.

It was a warm, late summer day. The tide was high and lapped against the promenade below the balustrade as they strolled past Penarth pier. The pale blue sky softened the mud-grey waters of the Bristol Channel. As they climbed the short stretch to the cliff walk beyond the promenade, Mari threaded her arm into Owen's and pulled him close.

When they came to the top of the rise she pointed to a shrivelled oak tree that grew at the edge of the cliff.

'See that? That's Sisley's tree.'

She explained it had been painted by the French Impressionist Alfred Sisley almost eighty years before when he visited Penarth. The painting had found its way to the Museum of Fine Art in Rheims.

'I've seen it there. It's a wonderful, glowing picture full of light. That tree – it's the same tree, it has exactly the same shape – is in the foreground. *The Cardiff Shipping Lane* it's called. The pier is at the edge of the painting, as you can see it now, and a platoon of small boats, headed by a paddle steamer are coming up the channel. They're enveloped in a misty, luminous orange light.'

She went on to extol the Impressionists, how they captured light in ways she herself attempted. The National Museum had a fine collection, one she spent a good deal of time studying. They included another of Sisley's that must have painted from near the same spot, a view along the coast to Lavernock Point.

Mari linked her arm to his once more and chuckled as they walked on.

'Sisley had a romantic time of it in Penarth. He stayed with his lover Eugenié Lescouezec in lodgings in Clive Place, just a few streets away from me. In fact, they got married while they were here, in the Cardiff Registry office.'

Once on the cliff top they crossed an open park until they reached hedgerows with the edge of the cliff on one side and fields on the other. Occasionally the bushes parted to allow them a clear view across the channel to the Somerset coast. They had gone about half-a-mile when Mari led Owen through a small gap in the hedge and briars. They emerged into a secluded cliff ledge with tall grass that had been flattened in places.

Mari knelt to the ground.

'It's me that's done the flattening. I come here a lot to sketch. It's an ideal spot, to capture the light where the sea meets the land and sky.'

She laughed.

'Ideal for other things, too.'

Lying on his elbows and chewing a stalk of grass Owen gazed across at Flat Holm and Steep Holm, two islands that split the ocean stream a few miles away.

'It feels as though if you reached out, you could touch them.'

'It's the high tide that makes them seem so close.'

Mari stroked the back of his head. Owen turned round, leant forward on his elbows and examined her quizzically.

'How did you get to know David Jones so well?'

'Why do you want to know?'

'It's interesting. I know you're an artist, but he's a completely different generation, isn't he? And has a totally different background. But you talk as though he's some kind of relative.'

'Well, I wrote a letter to *The Times*.'

Owen sat up.

'Letter?'

'Yes, about Tryweryn. It was in the late fifties when the whole controversy was taking off. My letter caught David's eye. In those days, if you got a letter in *The Times*, they printed your full address under it. Anyway he wrote to me, said how much he admired what I'd said and wondered if I might be interested in meeting him.'

'Bit forward, wasn't he?'

'Perhaps, but David didn't think in those terms. He was impulsive about that type of thing, hopelessly emotional and romantic. He invited me to lunch at the Paddington Hotel, and things just developed from there.'

'Developed?'

'I used to visit him quite often. He had a pokey bedsit in Harrow, on the ground floor of an apartment building overlooking a car park. He hated going out, you see, suffered from agoraphobia. I'd say that was a throwback to the First World War. In a way I think David found it natural to live in a room in that way. It was similar to a dugout in the trenches. But still he made the room beautiful for himself, with small treasures he had collected over the years.'

'There was a huge gap in your ages.'

Mari laughed.

'Only forty years. I was in my twenties, at art school. He was in his sixties by then. The whole thing was wearing at times, I'll admit. He was so intense, but he was mesmerising as well. And he had these romantic notions, especially about Wales and about me. He adored that I was a Welsh-speaker. He demanded that I wear black flowing cloaks, seeing me I think as some kind of throwback to a mythological Welsh past. It was all very odd. But I went along with it because he was so brilliant, charming as well, so vulnerable.'

'Vulnerable?'

'He was so needy, so unworldly. I used to do his laundry. He'd send me flowers at any opportunity, red roses on my birthday. I learnt later on that he even wanted to marry me. But it got a bit oppressive in the end.'

'He wanted to marry you?'

'Yes, it was Saunders who told me, Saunders Lewis…'

'How on earth?'

'Well he and David were great friends. They had a lot in

common, you see. Both of them had fought in the first war. Both were artists. Both had converted to Catholicism. They shared a passion for the Catholic Mass. David said it was the highest form of human expression. They had a lot in common as I say, and they corresponded a good deal. Anyway, on one occasion David asked me to have tea with him and Saunders in the Howells department store in Cardiff.'

'Really?' Owen was fascinated.

'There wasn't much to it, except it was a nice occasion, unremarkable in a lot of ways. We just chatted and I poured the tea. But much later Saunders told me that David had said he was thinking of asking me to marry him and wanted to know what he thought about it. Saunders, in his typical practical way, said that before venturing an opinion he should meet me. So that's how we ended up having tea together.'

'And?'

'Oh, Saunders told him I was far too young, and that was that.'

'What an extraordinary story. So that was that, was it?'

'Yes, though I still keep in touch with David. Mind you, he's far from well these days. He's in a nursing home.'

'And Saunders Lewis?'

'I got to know him quite well after that, see quite a bit of him as a matter of fact. He lives in Penarth you know. Would you like to meet him?'

* * *

One early evening a week later Mari led Owen up a short drive to the front door of a semi-detached house in lower Penarth and rang the doorbell. A diminutive figure appeared in the large doorway. Saunders Lewis had a forbidding thin face and high forehead with retreating, swept-back black hair and a long prominent nose that came close to a thinly pressed mouth. This creased into a smile as soon as he saw Mari.

'Well, well, come in, come,' he ordered, leading the way into a front room that was obviously his study. A long desk lined one wall and every available space was filled with books. Papers cluttered the floor. Despite the warm summer evening Lewis was wearing a suit and tie.

'Saunders, dear, this is the young man I was telling you about, the journalist on the *Western Mail*, Owen James.'

'Yes, yes, I know all about him, or rather I know what he writes in what they like to call our national newspaper.'

He snorted dismissively, but gave his hand to Owen. Then he busied himself moving a pile of papers from two chairs at one end of the room, allowing Mari and Owen to sit.

'Sit down, sit down, there's space somewhere.'

'Owen writes about politics, among other things.'

'I know. I've been reading his article about Phil Williams, profile I think they call it these days. Brilliant man, of course, in his field, but I don't go along with his brand of socialism.'

'But surely you are at one in wanting to create a Welsh state?' Owen asked hesitantly.

'It depends on what you mean by a Welsh state, as you put it. I am completely opposed to a state-dominated economy. And, of course, in Wales that could not be possible except that we remain a part of England. The present set-up is essential to it. On its own Wales couldn't have these state-run nationalised industries. Indeed, in that sense the Welsh Labour Party is more practical than the south Wales nationalist leaders like Phil Williams and Emrys Roberts.'

At this point he rose abruptly from his chair.

'I am forgetting myself,' he said and left the room hurriedly.

Owen grimaced and glanced questioningly at Mari who laughed.

'Don't worry, he obviously likes you.'

A few moments later Lewis returned with a tray bearing a bottle of wine and glasses which he passed to Mari and Owen.

'So what is it you want us to discuss?'

'Well, er… I'm interested to learn your views about a number of things,' Owen replied. 'To begin with the fact that you were born in England.'

'You're suggesting that because I was born in Liverpool I was in some sense born an exile from Wales?'

'Not exactly.'

'The idea is completely false. I don't know what the statistics are but I'm pretty sure there were round about a hundred thousand Welsh-speaking people in Liverpool during my boyhood. And I should say that at least half of those were Welsh-speakers who could barely manage a word of English. For instance, girls would come as maids to our house and to my aunt's house in Liverpool, from Anglesey and Caernarfonshire, absolutely monoglot Welsh girls. They would come with us to chapel for a few years, then they would get married and go back to Wales with just as little English as when they came to England. In Liverpool in my time there was a society as monoglot Welsh as any village in Anglesey.'

'North Wales Welsh is your natural tongue anyway,' Mari said.

'I should say Anglesey Welsh, more or less. It was my mother's and aunt's Welsh certainly.'

Lewis turned to Owen and refilled his glass which emboldened him to venture another question.

'I can see how natural it was for you to write in Welsh, but what would you say to today's generation? I mean, would you say that a writer today has a duty to stick to Welsh in the same way? It must be a temptation for many young writers to turn to English.'

'I don't know what I would say. I think one must say this – it isn't a matter of choice. For instance, I didn't choose to write in Welsh as you suggest. In fact, to begin with I intended to write in English. But when you look around, suddenly the thing gets hold of you, and you can't write in any other language.'

He got up as if to reach for book, but had second thoughts. Instead, he sat back in his chair, and pondered for a while.

'If a young writer is able to choose what language he is going to write in, Welsh or English, all I can say is that I'm dreadfully sorry for him, dreadfully sorry. Because I'm fairly certain that it is very exceptional for anyone to have mastered writing well in two languages. There may be a few exceptions where people have written masterpieces in two languages. I think there are a few exceptions. But they are so infrequent, they don't provide a model for anyone.'

This reply led Mari to explain to Owen that it was the theatre that had attracted Saunders' interest from the beginning. It was in drama that he had made his reputation.

Turning to Saunders she said, 'It must have been difficult that there was no professional theatre in Wales. It must have made you have doubts about writing plays in Welsh, whether it was worthwhile.'

'Yes, I have doubts, even today. It's painful to write plays that I know no one can act. It's extremely painful. I recognise that. But you see, it's at that point that I come face-to-face with this problem. The only kind of writing that appeals to me at all strongly, within creative writing, is drama. For one thing because, like every creative writer, I have an exceptional gift for telling lies. Every creative writer has it, so that surely the only way to tell the truth is to write a play. Your characters express every aspect of any event or any person. You can tell the truth in a play.'

Owen leant forward in his chair and took out a notebook, which drew a sharp look from Saunders.

'I wonder whether your success as a playwright partly compensates for the lack of success you've had as a politician?'

'Indeed, I have said that to myself. I had a desire, no small desire either, a very great desire in fact, to change the history of Wales – to change the whole course of her history, to make Welsh-speaking Wales something lively, strong and powerful, a part of the modern world. And I failed completely.'

'Completely?'

'I was rejected by everyone. I was rejected in every election in which I offered myself as a candidate. Every one of my ideas – I started with sociology, and the sociology of nationalism – every single one has been cast aside. That being so I had nothing to turn to, to express my vision, except writing the history of Welsh literature and writing plays.'

'Yes, but in the long run the politician's function is inimical to the artist's way of life,' Mari said. 'I think the best thing that happened was for you to abandon politics and enter the literary world.'

'Well, that may be so. I was warned once as a young man in Liverpool not to do anything except write, for I should be sure to fail at everything else. I was given that warning by a phrenologist. So it is possible that I should have been a failure anyway, if I had continued in politics. But the result is that you put into your writing what you have failed at in your life.'

Llwyngwern
January 1974

Looking around the house in downtown Aberystwyth, Leopold Kohr observed with satisfaction that his soirée to welcome in the New Year was going well. He beamed with pleasure. He was dressed in his habitual open-necked check shirt, cravat, a waistcoat with a chained pocket watch, corduroy trousers and sports jacket. The one problem was that the background noise interfered with his hearing aid. He had to continually adjust it in an effort to accurately gauge what his new friends were saying. They were part of an ever-widening network that extended across the globe.

Leaning against the sink in the kitchen was John Seymour, a doyen of self-sufficiency who had spent a lifetime roaming the world and was now famous for his writings about his smallholding in the Preseli hills. Through the open double doors into the dining room was the anthropologist and Welsh sage Alwyn Rees who had been so welcoming to him when he first arrived at the university. Kohr saw with approval that he was talking with Rhiannon Jones-Davies. A buzz of conversation floated from the front lounge and through the hallway.

Adjusting his hearing aid once more, and gesturing with the glass of red wine in his hand, Leopold took issue with a lecturer in his department who had described the university as provincial.

'When I moved here one of my former colleagues at Rutgers had the audacity to ask me about Aberystwyth's standards. "Are they very low?" he asked. "Yes," I replied, "about as low as in New Jersey."'

The group around him laughed. Even so the lecturer persisted.

'But surely there's a difference between a university like Aberystwyth and one like Harvard, say, or Oxford.'

'No, no, a university is a university wherever it is, whether in Vienna, Paris, Cambridge, Swansea, or Aberystwyth. It's not a matter of where they are located, but the universality of knowledge – hence the name university. The idea of a *provincial* university is a contradiction in terms. It must be either the one or the other. It cannot be both. It cannot be at the same time provincial and a university.'

'But it's also a question of reputation through achievement, wouldn't you say?'

'Not at all. As Gertrude Stein put it, "a rose is a rose is a rose". So, a university is a university is a university. Wherever it is located, it has the same corridors of power, the same student riots, the same faculty knifings.'

'Then why is so much prestige attached to Oxbridge and the Ivy League universities in the United States?' another person asked.

'This is a good question.'

Leopold gazed benevolently at the small group that had gathered to listen to the conversation.

'Certainly the universities you mention have prestige, but that has little to do with academic standards. Most of the lecturers in American and British universities are graduates of the prestige universities whose standards they must necessarily carry wherever they teach. If Oxbridge is great, so therefore must be Swansea. If Swansea is no good, neither can Oxbridge be either.'

'Then what is it that provides the Ivy-League and Oxbridge with the prestige they most certainly have?'

'Well, as the terms Ivy-League or red-brick universities indicate, it seems to have something to do with buildings, with architecture, heritage and age, above all with cities.'

Leopold leant back on his heels, adopting a lecturing mode.

'And so, if we look at the prestige universities, we find that in contrast to the suburban dispersal of the others, they are not only in the midst of the loveliest of cities, they are completely interwoven with the fullness of their life. Indeed, if you look at Cambridge or Princeton, they often are the cities. What would Cambridge be without its university, or Oxford for that matter?'

'Can you say that of Aberystwyth?' another guest asked, causing a ripple of laughter.

'But most certainly you can say the same of Aberystwyth. The town is the university. We have the Old College on the sea front.'

Leopold gestured with his hand through the window.

'We have the magnificent National Library and then the campus extending above with its splendid location on the hill and its outlook over the Irish Sea.'

He paused again, but this time for emphasis.

'Aberystwyth is certainly a prestige university. Just like Oxford and Cambridge it is surrounded by convivial and academic facilities – libraries, bookstores, inns, streets of leisurely business, squares of conversational companionship, and buildings of such exquisite architectural taste that they would attract the best, even if their academic quality were poor. But, precisely because of their architectural and convivial power of attraction that, of course, can never be the case.'

Leopold inspected his audience quizzically, as if daring his interlocutors to question him further. There was a hiatus as his guests struggled with the import of his message.

'Well, it's nice to hear that we're a prestige university,' the lecturer who had begun the discussion said eventually. 'Someone should tell the Welsh Office.'

'If only they had ears to hear,' said another.

'They'd think you were a crank,' a third told Leopold.

'Ha ha!' he cried delightedly in response. 'I have often been considered a crank. But it has not bothered me in the slightest, any more than it bothered my great friend Fritz Schumacher. As he once said, "After all, what is a crank? It is a tool that is cheap, small, efficient, economical and," he added with exquisite emphasis, "it makes revolutions."'

* * *

At the edge of the circle surrounding Leopold, Rhiannon had also been listening. As he brought his assault on the notion of a provincial university to a triumphant end, he caught her eye.

'Ah Rhiannon, I am so glad you have come. There is someone here, a great friend, you must meet.'

With that he clasped her elbow and steered her out of the kitchen, whispering with a chuckle, 'He's the great grandson of the last Duke of Buckingham. They say he was the richest man in England in his day.'

In the hallway Rhiannon came face-to-face with a tall, military looking man in his early forties, with short, swept-back, dark hair, a high-bridged nose and penetrating eyes.

'Gerard! I want you to meet Rhiannon, one of my favourite students.' With that he passed on to his front door to greet some new guests.

Rhiannon blushed at Leopold's reference and also in response to the direct, inquiring stare she received from this unusual stranger.

'Gerard Morgan-Grenville,' he said holding out his hand. 'And you? Rhiannon?'

'Jones-Davies. Professor Kohr is supervising my dissertation.'

'Dissertation?' Morgan-Grenville gave the beautiful young woman in front of him his undivided attention.

'I'm looking at anti-colonial movements in North Africa,

their struggles against France, especially in Morocco and Algeria.'

'I don't know much about the politics of those places, but I've spent some time in the northern Sahara.'

'Really? I should love to go there myself one day to do fieldwork, maybe if I can get my MA converted into a PhD.'

'You should go, definitely. It's an extraordinarily alluring place. I thought it was like being on the surface of the moon or on the bed of the ocean. It has a solitude and tranquillity impossible to find anywhere else – in my experience anyway. In the day time the sands stretch forever under a constant blue hemisphere. At night the stars are incredibly bright. Altogether, it's a spiritual experience.'

He stopped, suddenly embarrassed at speaking so openly. But Rhiannon encouraged him to continue.

'When were you there?'

'Oh, it was a few years ago now. I run an importing business with my brother. Our sales operation had expanded quite quickly and we decided we needed a team-building exercise. So we took everybody off in a couple of Land Rovers to an oasis called M'Hammid in southern Morocco, quite close to the Algerian border actually. It was quite an experience. None of us had been to the Sahara before.'

'And now? What brings you to Aberystwyth?'

'Well, apart from Leopold's hospitality...'

Gerard paused to allow some guests to move past, and then stepped into the front room, guiding Rhiannon towards a chaise longue in the bay window.

'The thing is it's hard to describe. I've bought a quarry, an old slate quarry. Or, rather, I've taken a lease on it, a hundred-year lease that is, which is as good as buying it, wouldn't you say?'

Rhiannon had no idea how to respond. This strange man

with his clipped English accent was one of the most surprising people she had encountered.

'Where is this quarry?'

'Oh, not far from here. Just beyond Machynlleth as a matter of fact, and it's pretty ideal for us. An amazing find, really.'

Rhiannon was puzzled and intrigued in equal measure.

'Ideal for what?'

Gerard smiled.

'Yes, well it's a bit of a convoluted story. You see a few years ago I began to become more and more uneasy about what we're doing to the environment. My mother brought me up to be strongly aware of the countryside. I also took to landscape painting and began to see how we were despoiling everything around us. I kept noticing the plastic bottles and containers being thrown into the hedgerows. Then I read Rachel Carson's *Silent Spring.*'

Gerard wondered how he could explain the experiences which had led to the venture on which he was about to embark. He took a different tack.

'I have this business, as I say, and it's quite successful, importing and selling all manner of household goods and luxuries. But I became uneasy about that, too. I started asking myself, where will this pattern of consumerism end? It's just take, take, take. How can we put things back? I mean, in a practical way. That's what concerns me.'

Rhiannon looked around the room, wondering whether their intense conversation was being observed.

'How does your slate quarry come into all this?'

'It's because I think we have to have a practical response to these questions. To cut a long story short, I took a sabbatical from work and went off to California.'

'California?'

'Yes, you see it was plainly the source of much of what I was getting into. I had introductions to some leading businessmen there and also a few politicians. Everybody I talked to acknowledged the threats to the environment. They all agreed that they must be tackled if the world is not to go into terminal decline.'

'So what did they think should be done about it?'

'There were divergent views. Some thought there could be a technical fix. Others argued we need a shift towards simpler lifestyles. But everybody agreed that change would be difficult, if not impossible, so long as the existing order continues. I mean consumerism, I suppose. But how can you stop it? After all, it's the engine that's driving employment, growth, wealth and all the rest of it. What government would want to tamper with that?'

Rhiannon had a feeling that, although he was talking about things far from her experience, he was all the same on a similar wavelength.

'I know what you mean about trying to persuade the government. But I still don't see how this quarry of yours fits in.'

'Well, after talking to these people for a while I became disillusioned, and quite a bit depressed. So, in desperation really, I started making contact with a number of communes that were springing up in the Santa Cruz mountains outside San Francisco.'

Rhiannon looked startled and Gerard laughed.

'I can see all this must seem a bit puzzling. Anyway, I hired a car and found a few of them, communes I mean. They were all different. Some seemed to embrace the need for organisation and hard work, to grow food and so on. Others just lived in rank squalor, and seemed devoid of any ideas or leadership. There were draft dodgers, a lot of unemployed university graduates, layabouts, kids who seemed to be living off their parents, artists of all kinds, people playing the guitar.'

'So?'

'It seemed to me they all had one thing in common.'

'Which was?'

'They were all passionately opposed to nuclear power. For them it represented all that was authoritarian and secret, and it was dangerous. Could be fatal in fact, to man and nature.'

'And without the nuclear power industry we wouldn't have nuclear weapons.'

'That's right, of course. But the thing that most impressed me was the way a few of these groups were trying to respond in practical terms. There was a lot of talk about alternative energy sources, but some were making primitive efforts to harness the wind and the sun to provide electricity. That's what impressed me most. I came home convinced that I had to do something practical in a similar way to demonstrate there was an alternative.

'So that's where the quarry comes in.'

'Exactly.'

'You want to use it as a place where you can try out your ideas.'

'That's right. But the problem was that I had no money, no staff, and to begin with no place to try them out either.'

'So what did you do?'

'I got in touch with Robert, my older half-brother. He's farmed for years in different places in Africa. He's retired now, living on the Kenyan coast at Malindi, has a reputation for being something of a recluse. In fact, I hardly knew him. But he inherited a lot of money. Anyway, I wrote to him and I got a letter by return, saying what I had in mind was a great idea and asking how much I wanted.'

'Goodness.'

'So I got the money, £20,000 as a matter of fact. Then I needed to find a place. Almost immediately I met this guy, Steve Boulter, an American specialist in alternative energy – wave, solar, wind and so on. I set him loose to find a site. And eventually, just a few months ago in fact, he came up with this place in Wales.'

'What an extraordinary story.'

'I tell you what. I have to go there tomorrow, to sort a few things out with the owners. Why don't you come and have a look at it? I'm staying at the Belle Vue. Come for an early lunch and we'll head out afterwards.'

* * *

At midday the next morning Rhiannon stepped cautiously into the Belle Vue. She had agonised over what to wear, eventually opting for warm black tights, a blue denim skirt just above her knees, and a polo shirt and jumper. She'd tied her hair back. Over her shoulder she carried a duffle bag with a coat and, as instructed, walking boots.

Peering into the bar she noticed Gerard was sitting near the window reading the Sunday papers. He looked up and gave her a welcoming smile.

'Drink? Mine's a gin and tonic. Will you have one?'

Rhiannon would have preferred a pint of lemonade and lime, but nodded in acquiescence. Gerard returned from the bar with the drinks and cleared the newspapers to make way.

'Leopold's party was up to standard, don't you think?

'How did you meet him?'

'Oh, through Fritz Schumacher. Over the past few years I've tracked down and spoken with anyone I could find who's had something to say about the environment. I got in touch with Barbara Ward after reading the report she prepared for the UN Stockholm summit a couple of years ago, *Only One Earth.*'

'A good title.'

'Then I met Barry Commoner when he was over here from the States to launch his book *The Closing Circle,* about what has gone wrong with our planetary housekeeping as he put it. That had a big influence. Then, of course, I met Teddy Goldsmith. You must read his book *Blueprint for Survival*.'

'How does Professor Kohr fit in with these people?' Rhiannon asked.

'What he is saying is fundamental and, by the way, highly original. You must get him to talk to you about his basic theory. He says that most, if not all our problems are related to size and I agree with him. Have you seen his book *The Breakdown of Nations*? Came out a while ago. What Leopold is saying is that we need to reduce the scale, the size of our problems if we are to have a chance of tackling them. Ahead of his time. It's what Fritz is saying as well.'

'Fritz?'

'Schumacher, yes, the economist, a great friend of Leopold's. He told me he got most of his ideas from him. Fritz says Leopold is an economist who puts economics in its place. He wrote somewhere that he is an artist, a historian, an adventurer who can walk with philosophers and kings.'

Gerard stopped for a moment, embarrassed by his exuberance. But he noticed that Rhiannon was listening intently.

'Fritz told me that men like Leopold are rare, and unrecognised in this age of specialists. In his view Leopold is, how do you say, a whole man. The way he put it was, "Whole men are unpopular with fragmentary men."'

Rhiannon's eyes widened.

'Have you seen Schumacher's own book *Small is Beautiful*? It's just come out, so I don't suppose you have. But I think it's really important. For one thing it provides the answer to the oil crisis we're going through. Fritz told me he actually got the title from Leopold. He finished the book in Aberystwyth, you know, in Leopold's house as a matter of fact. All Fritz has done really is apply Leopold's ideas to technology, what he calls intermediate technology. And that's what we're planning to use the quarry for, to make it a place where we can demonstrate alternative energy, wind power and all the rest.'

*   *   *

After lunch, as they were driving out of Aberystwyth through rain showers towards Machynlleth, Rhiannon thought about her diminutive supervisor, so charming, so amusing, and so modest. She'd no idea he moved in such a world of writers and thinkers. She looked across to Gerard who was pushing his Jaguar coupé down a gear as they approached a bend.

'Do you always drive so fast?'

'Do you think so?' Nevertheless, he slowed the car a little.

'Why did you choose this place? Isn't it a bit off the beaten track?'

'Planning.'

'Planning?'

'Yes, you have to get local authority planning permission for constructing anything, especially new buildings. Everywhere we looked proved difficult, impossible in fact, until we found this place. I was almost on the point of giving up.'

'How did you come across it?'

'Steve Boulter, the specialist in renewables I was telling you about, saw a small advert in *Country Life*.'

By now they had driven through Machynlleth and crossed the bridge over the River Dyfi with its warning signs threatening floods. Gerard swung a sharp right and drove a further two miles on the road towards Dolgellau. Then he slowed the car.

'It's along here somewhere. It's quite difficult to spot. We'll have to erect a sign. Probably need planning permission for that as well.'

They turned right, off the main road and entered a narrow

lane that led into what seemed a dense mass of greenery. Gerard drew the car to a stop, and wound his window down as he turned off the engine. There was a sudden, deep silence, broken only by the murmur of a stream. Above the lane a precipitous bank of slate rubble and vegetation rose to a line of trees.

'Better get our boots on,' Gerard said. 'Welcome to Llwyngwern slate quarry.'

The track up the steep hillside was covered with a wet tangle of brambles, wild rhododendron and bracken. After a few minutes climbing they reached a plateau and further on were the rearing walls of the old quarry itself. There were three ruined cottages and two derelict slate cutting sheds complete with rusted guillotines. Several flatbed rail trucks lay on their sides across the plateau and here and there were lengths of rail. Chunks of slate were scattered about, with drill holes where they had been exploded away from the rock face. Elsewhere were piles of half-finished or broken slabs of pigeon-grey slate. Rhododendrons, gorse bushes, and birch trees were growing in profusion, some with withered leaves still attached, even though autumn was long gone. Near the middle of the plateau was a small lake into which a stream flowed. Gerard and Rhiannon walked along the bed of an old railway that led from the cutting sheds to the lip of the plateau. They could see a vast heap of spoil spreading downwards toward the green valley below. Beyond were the tree covered slopes of Mynydd Du just inside the Gwynedd national park.

Gerard told Rhiannon the quarry had been founded in the early nineteenth century and that at its height it employed around one hundred and fifty men. 'Many of them lived with their families nearby in rather grim conditions,' he said. 'It's what's known as an accidental quarry.'

'Accidental?'

'Yes, that's what they called it. Unlike the other larger

quarries to the north that follow a main seam of slate, success here depended on working a fault and hitting a vein. The quarry was often on the verge of bankruptcy and changed hands many times.'

Gerard explained that the slate tended to be weak, making it unsuitable for roofing. Instead slabs were produced for window sills, fireplaces, and tombstones.

'I've heard it said that Llwyngwern slate was used in the building of the National Gallery in London. But after the First World War it gradually declined until only about a dozen or so men were left when it finally closed in 1951. That was not long after the owner was killed. He had been with a group of his men trying to open up a new chamber when a large piece of dislodged slate stone fell on him from high above.'

'How terrible.'

Gerard glanced at his watch.

'We'd better make tracks. We're already late for the appointment I've made with the present owners, John and Audrey Beaumont.'

* * *

It was to their farmhouse that they headed up a narrow track after clambering down the steep slope to the car. 'You see, we're hoping to get started in a few months,' Gerard told Rhiannon as he steered the car up the steep gradient to the farm near the top of the hill.

Audrey opened the door of the substantial stone-built house that overlooked the quarry. She gave Rhiannon a warm smile as they were introduced. Inside, John Beaumont shook Gerard's hand.

'I see you've got planning permission.'

'We were quite surprised actually. But I think the

123

Meirionnydd council felt we couldn't do much harm. We'd be out of sight – and out of mind – and probably wouldn't last very long anyway.'

'You've got permission to renovate the derelict buildings as well?'

'Yes, and to bring a few old caravans on to the space below once we've cleared it.'

'It's a pity to see it developed in a way,' Audrey told Rhiannon as she filled a kettle at the sink. 'I used to take the children there for picnics in the summer. They went swimming in the old reservoir. The boys wanted to turn the thing into a dinosaur theme park. I thought we might clear it and put up holiday chalets. But then Gerard came along and persuaded John.'

'How did he manage that?'

Overhearing the conversation John laughed.

'I remembered him from Eton.'

'It wasn't that,' Audrey corrected him as she set out some cups and saucers on the kitchen table. 'As it happens we didn't need a lot of persuading.'

She paused to pour the tea.

'You see, I'd been brought up in India and John and I lived in Africa for twenty years. We had next to nothing there, no electricity or running water. We had to do everything ourselves. We even had to make our own bricks when we came to build our home. John did all the plumbing and the electrics. So, I suppose you could say we're pretty alternative-minded ourselves.'

'I've been lucky with my vendors,' Gerard said.

'You most certainly have,' Audrey told him, passing Rhiannon a cup of tea. 'Not only did you find the one quarry in probably the whole of the UK where you could get planning permission for your wild scheme. You found a couple of ageing hippies willing to let you have it for a peppercorn rent as well.'

Wandsworth
January 1974

At Charing Cross station Owen searched for the entrance to the Northern line and a train that would take him to Clapham Common. From there it was a short distance to the home of James Griffiths, now in his eighties, and a man Owen revered as a pioneer of the Labour movement. He was interviewing him for a series of articles he was writing about the tenth anniversary of the founding of the Welsh Office.

He felt a little nervous visiting such an august figure from a time that now felt part of history. As Minister of National Insurance in the 1945 government, Griffiths had put in place one of the cornerstones of the welfare state. Even so he had never ceased to identify with his roots in the west Wales anthracite coalfield. In the 1950s he had ensured that a commitment to creating the position of a Welsh secretary of state with a seat in the Cabinet found its way into Labour's manifesto.

Owen was emboldened to pick up the phone to Griffiths following an exchange they had in the *Western Mail*. He had started it by claiming there was a lack of political debate because an overwhelming proportion of Welsh MPs came from just one party.

Griffiths had responded somewhat testily to the *Letters* page.

'This has always in my lifetime been true of Wales. When I joined the Labour Party in 1908 Wales had thirty-four Liberal MPs – and only one Labour and not a single Conservative. Surely Plaid Cymru does not contemplate denying the people of Wales the right to choose their own representatives – to whatever party they belong. The lesson of our times is that nationalism, like patriotism, is not enough.'

Stung by how, accurately, Griffiths had placed him in the

nationalist camp, Owen had countered with a further article suggesting that the first-past-the-post electoral system failed to reflect the diversity of views.

'There is every reason to believe, even from the voting figures of the 1970 election, that if Welsh people were given the opportunity to vote after a debate concentrated entirely on Welsh issues, it would result in a far more balanced representation of parties.'

* * *

When Owen arrived at Griffiths' bungalow in Wandsworth he was met by Winnie, a bird-like figure in a shawl.

'My husband's not at all well, you know, though he insisted on your coming. He does like to keep in touch with his young men, as he calls them.'

Owen advanced down a narrow hall and was shown to a room towards the rear. There he found James Griffiths sitting up in bed in worsted blue striped pyjamas and a red and gold dressing gown. Newspapers and books were strewn around the room. Griffiths' shrunken face emphasised his hooked Roman nose. Small wisps of hair strayed across his bald skull and his skin stretched across his cheek bones. But his eyes still gleamed as he gestured to the *Western Mail* lying at the end of the bed.

'I've been checking on the mischief you've been getting up to today.'

Then, turning to Winnie, he said, 'I'm sure this young fellow would like a cup of tea, don't you think? And a Welsh cake I've no doubt.'

As his wife left the room Griffiths pointed to a chair near the bed.

'So what do you want to talk to me about? I'm out of the run of things now you know.'

'Well, as I said on the phone, I'd like to talk about the Welsh Office, the discussions you had before it was set up.'

'The arguments, you mean.'

'And your life in the coalfield when you were young, how you became involvemed with the Labour movement in those days.'

Griffiths sank into the pillows that propped him up.

'I think more and more about those times...'

His eyes closed and Owen wondered whether he was drifting off to sleep. But suddenly he put out his arm and pulled at his dressing gown.

'See, I still bear the scars, the blue scars. And I've got the dust in my lungs, too, which is why you see me propped up in bed.'

'How old were you when you started in the mine?'

'I was thirteen when I left school and began as a collier's lad. That was in 1904. I worked underground until 1919 when the union sent me to the Central Labour College in London.'

'The anthracite field, wasn't it?'

'Aye, glo-carreg, the best coal in the world. It started at the head of the Afan Valley and then across the valleys of the Nedd, Dulais, Tawe, Aman, Gwendraeth and away to Pembrokeshire where it ran into the sea. I was born at the centre of it, in Betws. There were ten children in the family.'

Owen listened, fascinated, while Griffiths told of his time working in a small colliery near the village, known as Wythien Fach because of its narrow vein of coal. An older brother had sponsored him to become second boy to his mate, Shoni Cardi.

'Call from Mother at 5.45am. Don the Welsh blue flannel shirt and drawers, moleskin trousers and an old coat with big pockets sewn inside to hold the food box and water jack. Then on to the road to reach the pit-top by 6.15am.'

'Not much time for breakfast, then.'

'A piece of bread and dripping in my hand if I was lucky. Then it was down the slant and a halt for the Miners' Spell.

Mwgyn Gweld we called it in Welsh, time for the eyes to adjust to the darkness.'

This was the colliers' parliament, Griffiths explained, where the issues of the day were discussed, last Saturday's rugby match, last Sunday's sermon, the stubbornness of the masters, and, of course, the gossip of the village.

Owen asked what it was like underground.

'Well, the seam was two feet seven inches thick and the roadway, or stall as it was called, would measure three yards. There was a steep incline in the seam and this added to the burden of the collier's boy whose job was to gather the coal, cut by his mate, into the curling box and carry it to the tram.'

'And the days were long.'

'At that time it was from seven in the morning to half-past four in the afternoon. In the winter months we would only see daylight on Saturday afternoon, when we finished at 1pm, and on Sundays.'

* * *

Winnie came in the room bearing a tray with a pot of tea and some Welsh cakes.

'Don't you go wearing yourself out, now.'

'I've been telling the boy about the old days in Betws. He seems interested enough.'

Owen chose the moment to steer the conversation to new territory.

'I wanted to ask you about Bevan, what you thought of him. I've been reading about the speech he made at the 1957 conference on unilateral nuclear disarmament. Why did he change his mind, do you think?'

'Oh, Nye changed his mind on a lot of things at that time. He changed his mind on the secretary of state for Wales question, too. That was another thing, and it was quite decisive.'

'Why was he against it?'

'He said we were responding to nationalism, which he thought divided people. He often said how early on he realised that if we were to achieve our objectives we had to reach out from the valley, from the county, from Wales itself, and control the centre in London where the levers of power operated. He thought a Welsh Office would steer us away from the mainstream of British politics.'

'But you persuaded him.'

'He was changing his mind on a whole lot of things, as I say, becoming more pragmatic. He was always very supportive of our culture. I think he saw it as a bulwark against uniformity and standardisation, what he called the universal greyness of modern times. I think I persuaded him that what we were proposing should be seen in that light.'

'I see.'

'But we had interminable arguments, you know, when we were drawing up the 1959 manifesto. At the end of one meeting we were still arguing as we left the committee room in the House of Commons. In the corridor outside Nye turned to me and said, "You really want this thing, don't you."

'So I told him, "With all my heart and soul." And do you know what he answered?'

'Tell me.'

Griffiths chuckled but then broke into a fit of coughing.

'Well, you better bloody well have it then!'

'Sounds as if it might have been an emotional spasm of the kind he used to accuse his opponents in the party.'

Griffiths sat up.

'No, no, not at all. That was how he was. He could see it meant a lot to me. There was an innate generosity about him.'

Griffiths paused, before turning and grasping Owen's arm for a moment. 'Maybe he really was persuaded by the arguments I made. Certainly, I felt that at a later meeting we had with Gaitskell. He was chairing and summed up the options.'

'Which were?'

'A Royal Commission on Devolution, a Welsh Grand Committee in the House, or a minister for Welsh Affairs with a seat in the Cabinet. Gaitskell said he didn't mind which one we went for, but if it was to be the last then he said such a minister should have something to do, which was the way he put it.'

'What did Nye say to that?'

'Well, he was at his best then, clever and funny. He said the Royal Commission and Welsh Grand Committee ideas were useless. Said they were shadowboxing. Then he dealt with the idea that we might have a minister in the Cabinet but with no specific departmental responsibilities, such as over health and education and so on. "What would be the use of that?" he asked. "Was he just to travel around, listening to people, but with nothing to do?"'

'Even so there was still opposition?'

'There most certainly was. It was Ness Edwards, I think, who intervened to say that a secretary of state would perpetuate conflict between Wales and Westminster. Nye turned on him then, saying, "What do you mean by perpetuating conflict? What conflict can there be? The minister is there, the office is there and you have agreed to give him Cabinet rank. Where is the conflict when you decide on giving him something definite to do?"

'Then Ness had one last go. "Well, we should make him subject to other ministers", he said. "No, no, no," Nye retorted, "responsible to the Cabinet."'

Owen, busy making notes, looked up.

'So in the end, you think that once you had convinced him

of the idea, of having a minister in the Cabinet, he sided with the practical arguments around making the position work effectively?'

'Yes, of course. As I say, that's the way he was.'

* * *

Their conversation turned to the politics of the present day with the miners and Tory government locked in another wages dispute. Owen suggested that the government was trying to engineer an excuse to call an election.

'That's exactly right. Heath is negotiating in bad faith, spinning things out. Why doesn't he submit the miners' claim to arbitration, to an independent body? We would soon see whether the miners are justified or not.'

Griffiths reached for his tea and took a few sips, his hands shaking.

Owen hesitated, but then asked, 'I was intrigued by that letter of yours, to the *Western Mail*, the one in reply to my article, when you spoke about nationalism not being enough. What did you mean?'

'Simply that by itself nationalism or patriotism, or however you like to call it, will not answer the most important questions of getting social justice for our people, getting fair play for the miners.'

Griffiths paused but then continued, a little plaintively.

'I've been thinking a lot about that young leader Plaid has. Phil Williams, that's his name isn't it? He's a good socialist. It worries me that he isn't in the Labour Party. We need leaders like him. Why isn't he in Labour, do you think?'

Owen had no easy answer he could think of that would assuage Griffiths' concern.

'I suppose he must be convinced that socialism can be joined with nationalism in Wales.'

'That may be so. But you know what they say, a house divided cannot stand.'

There was little more to be said after that. It was obvious that Griffiths was tired. Owen collected his things.

'I much enjoyed our meeting. It was fascinating to hear your memories about your early days in the colliery.'

'I grew up with the coal industry in the years of its expansion.'

'A different era.'

'Yes, and now I'm saddened as the news comes, almost every week, of another mine closing.'

Griffiths' eyes closed as he gazed sightlessly to somewhere in the past.

'I'm filled with hiraeth, you know, for those days. The men I worked with as a boy, they were so rich in character.'

He lay slumped as if defeated, but after a moment brightened, and sitting straighter in his bed, called out to his wife.

'The lad's going, *cariad*, but before he does let's be having a dram.'

As if unbidden, Winnie brought in a tray with a bottle of Scotch malt whisky and three small glasses. James Griffiths, his hands still shaking, filled them to the brim.

'A toast,' he declared, raising his glass in which his pale waxened face was hazily reflected.

'Here's to the day when the last miner leaves the last pit.'

Butetown
January 1974

Poetry readings in Cardiff had once been stately affairs, held in hotels like the Angel and the Park or in the Reardon Smith Lecture Theatre alongside the National Museum. Poets in suits sat in line on upright chairs, revealing the tops of their socks and waiting their turn. Sometimes readings were heard first in Welsh, and then in translation. Evenings were often interminably long and it was gone ten o'clock before the oasis of a bar could be reached. They were hardly social occasions.

By the 1970s however, more convivial poems and pints were the norm, especially in the pubs of Cardiff docklands. One was now underway on a Friday evening in the Big Windsor in Butetown. It featured John Tripp and a couple of younger writers.

Nigel Jenkins was new on the scene, certainly to this Cardiff audience. Brought up on a farm on Gower he had left school at sixteen and worked as a reporter with papers in the Midlands before joining a travelling circus in America. Now he was studying literature and film at Essex University. His looks were those of a religious figure of the Orthodox persuasion. Black hair rolled and flowed from a parting at the top of his head to his shoulders. Much of his face was obscured by a beard and moustache. But his most striking feature was a mellifluous baritone voice, at once beguiling and hypnotic.

He was standing beneath a spotlight close to the bar on the Big Windsor's first floor. An audience of perhaps thirty young people, mainly students and aspiring writers, were listening intently as he read a poem about nostalgia and loss, recalling how as a child his mother had left rural Carmarthenshire for city life in Swansea.

She who has forgotten
remembers as if yesterday
the scythe they left rusting
in the arms of an apple,
the final bang on the door
on those sheep-bitten hills.

In Abertawe, in Swansea
There were killings to be made,
And they politely made theirs.

As time went on the family's diet had turned from brown to white bread, while in the attic dust gathered on an ancient harp. The men wore shiny shoes, the dung-filled farmyard left far behind.

It's autumn now, an evening
that ends in colour t.v.
and the washing of dishes.
I ask her, as I dry,
Beth yw 'spoon' yn Gymraeg?
Llwy, *she says,* llwy, dw i'n credu,
and she bites into an apple
that tastes like home.

There was a muted round of applause and a rise in the hum of conversation as Jenkins retrieved his pint glass, left the spotlight and found his seat. Peter Finch replaced him, another man with hair that reached his shoulders. He had attended the Glamorgan College of Technology, leaving at eighteen to work as a clerk with the city council. He was editor of the avant-garde *Second Aeon* poetry magazine. It had a tiny circulation but contributors from around the world. Recently, he had become manager of the Oriel gallery and bookshop in the city. He struck a lighter note.

> *To live in Wales,*
> *Is to be mumbled at*
> *By re-incarnations of Dylan Thomas*
> *In numerous diverse disguises.*

> *Is to be mown down*
> *By the same words*
> *At least six times a week.*

Laughter flowed across the room.

> *Is to be bored*
> *By Welsh visionaries*
> *With wild hair and grey suits.*

'Yes, you tell 'em boy,' John Tripp called out from the corner.

> *Is to be told of the incredible agony*
> *Of an exile that can be at most*
> *A day's travel away.*

'That's right,' Tripp interrupted again. 'Exactly right.'

The sentiments chimed with Tripp's jaundiced outlook on political commitment of all kinds, including nationalism, though his view of the Welsh variety edged on sentimentality. His criticism was invariably softened by what he regarded as its ineffectuality. He saw himself as having emerged from an earlier, romantic period. These days he had a baleful, sardonic view of Welsh prospects, coupled with a whimsical sarcasm.

Stubbing out his cigarette, he stepped towards the microphone to complete the evening's first session. Standing in the spotlight he struck a very different figure from the younger performers. In place of their leather jackets and jeans he wore slacks and a round-topped pale jersey. Short silver hair and the moustache below his imperious nose provided a sense of authority. His voice had less of a Welsh cadence and more of an officer clip that further commanded attention.

'This offering is called "Mission",' he announced by way of an unnecessary introduction. However, it induced relative silence across the bar. He began softly at first but his voice gathered strength as he bent to the task.

> I was eating my porridge one morning
> when I heard a whirring sound.
> I looked through the porthole and saw
> A large round object in a field.
> Through a trap-door came two small figures –
> green, with red bulbs lit up in their foreheads.
>
> I went out into the field.
> 'Good morning,' I said. 'Can I help you?'
> One of them had three pips on his shoulder,
>   And the other had two.
> 'Bore da,' said Three-Pip. 'Take us to your leader.'
>
> I got out the car and took them down to Penarth
> to see Saunders Lewis. He was in his dressing gown,
> eating a boiled egg and reading R.S. Thomas.

A wave of laughter engulfed the room causing Tripp to glance up from his papers but he pressed on.

'Yes?' he asked.
'Shwdwch chwi,' said Three-Pip. 'We'd like to help you.
    We believe in your cause. We dropped in on the way
    to Cuba.'

More laughter.

'That's all right,' said Saunders. 'As long as it's peaceful.'
'We can't guarantee that,' said Three-Pip.
    'We've got a cobalt ray that could wipe out London.'
'No, no,' said Saunders, 'don't even wipe out Cardiff.
    It's full of people. We'll sort it out ourselves.'
'Well,' said Three-Pip, 'we just thought we'd ask, before the
    Chinese come. We like to protect minorities.'
Saunders nodded: 'Diolch yn fawr,' he said,
and gave them a cup of tea,
and I drove them back to their object in the field.

Before they took off they gave me
a beautifully stitched Welsh flag, a pocket history of
    Wales,
a cobalt ray-gun, and a copy of the inter-galactic bible.

Whistles accompanied loud applause as Tripp ducked from
the spotlight. Acknowledging the approval with a wave of
his hand, he accepted a pint from an unknown benefactor
and retreated to the other side of the room to join the
younger poets.

Together they mulled over their drinks.

'A lot of your stuff leans in a nationalist direction,' Nigel
Jenkins said eventually. 'But it seems to me you don't really
think in those terms.'

'I never joined the Blaid. How can I put it? I suppose I'm

a commie. In fact, I did join the Communist Party once, in the early 1950s I think it was. I remained a member for quite a few years. That was the way I thought society should be run. I still do. I just stopped being a member – you know what poets are like – I probably let my subscriptions lapse.'

'So 1956 wasn't the reason?' Finch queried.

'Hungary, you mean? Oh no, I take a longer view than that. Or Czechoslovakia for that matter. When you consider the things that Britain and America have done… I hate capitalists. I hate greedy and property conscious people. The English coal-owners and so on. I don't like the governing instinct. I don't like power maniacs, and if that comes out, it comes out.'

Nigel Jenkins leant forward.

'But where does it come from, John?' I mean your background wouldn't account for it, would it? After all you were brought up in Whitchurch.'

'Cardiff, yes. My old man wasn't political in any conventional way. If anything he was old school monarchist. Fought in the first war and brings out the flag whenever there's a chance. My mother was a bit of a Tory, with a small t you could say. They certainly didn't think of themselves as working class. I guess lower-middle class. Decent people, all the same. Where I come from, why I'm so different? I don't know. And when it happened to me? I don't know that either. It could have happened very early on – the army probably.'

Nigel was surprised. 'You were in the army?'

'In 1945, at the end of the war. It was either that or be a Bevin Boy. If you were Welsh, if you lived in any of the coalfields, they gave you that option. I was only eighteen, but I had a clear idea of what the pits had done to my family, so I went into the army.'

'What was it like?' Finch asked.

'Well, those boys I was flung together with, Breconshire and Radnorshire farmhands plus a batch of hard cases from the reformatory at Quaker's Yard in Merthyr Vale, we all hated the army. We didn't know what the hell we were supposed to be there for. After all, the war was nearly over.'

Tripp stopped, and took a long pull from his pint.

'There was what I suppose you could call a kind of general anarchy. We were being knocked about by tough sergeants and establishment officers from Sussex. They'd all had enough of the war themselves.'

He halted again, reflecting.

'I suppose we began to think it wasn't good enough. In fact, we were anarchists. It took no sophisticated political shape, of course. It was a general revolt against the kind society we saw around us. I suppose I've never been the same since.'

'But you've obviously been influenced by the nationalist poets,' Jenkins persisted. 'People like R. Williams Parry and Gwenallt. You've written about them.'

'Yes, yes, I've celebrated those buggers because I felt a terrific link with them. I felt something in common. Idris Davies as well. All the same I've reservations about some Welsh language poets. Because they're safe within their language there can be a kind of complacency. They take it all for granted. Seems to me it's the Anglo-Welsh poets who are beating their breasts, who are worried about the country. It's the Anglo-Welsh, or some of us anyway, who are asking for the barricades.'

'I'll get us another pint,' Finch said.

*   *   *

A few hours later, some time after Nigel Jenkins had left to catch a late train to Swansea, Tripp and Finch stumbled out of the Big Windsor. In West Bute Street they stopped at a fish and chip shop and then made for the city centre and the bus station, swaying slightly.

Finch waved a chip in the direction of his mouth.

'Did you get anything at all out of the army, John?'

'Reckon it was the making of me. I grew up a lot, quite quickly really. Sex, of course, we were pretty well inhibited, buttoned up on that. It was a problem. We didn't know how to do it. But you learned, you know. The NAAFI women taught you. I wasn't a bad looking boy one will admit. My first rough lessons were behind the Nissen huts with the NAAFI girls. Splendid, I thought, this is rather good.'

Finch crunched the remains of his oily fish and chip papers between his fingers. With great accuracy, given the alcohol, he threw them into a waste paper basket. Attached to a lamp post, it had slid to the ground.

Tripp followed with the stub of his cigarette. This set the chip papers alight. The flames grew slowly but then more vigorously. The side of the plastic bin began to melt.

Finch tried to put out the fire with his shoe. He stamped on the chip papers and the melting edge of the bin where plastic was beginning to run. But his foot became stuck. The flames crept over his shoe. His trousers ignited.

'Bugger!' Finch cried.

He made a huge effort to extract his leg. He leant back, heaved and wrenched, to no avail.

Observing the impending disaster Tripp calmly unzipped his fly. Then, with an accompanying sigh of contentment, he proceeded to quench the flames.

'Can't have a leading member of the new generation of poets going up in smoke,' he said. 'Not yet, anyway.'

Sebastopol
January 1974

Owen was standing at the end of a long room on the first floor of the British Legion club in Sebastopol. Laid out for the annual dinner of the Pontypool constituency Labour Party, it was gradually filling up with mainly middle-aged men and their wives. Leo Abse had invited Denis Gane, the *Western Mail*'s deputy news editor with whom he had formed a close relationship when he was a reporter on the *Monmouthshire Free Press*.

But Gane had sent Owen instead. 'Do you good to see a bit of real Valleys politics for a change,' he said.

Abse quickly spotted Owen as he entered the room, bought him a drink and introduced him to Barry Moore, Labour agent in the neighbouring Bedwellty constituency. He was younger than most of the other men and Owen sensed a sharper edge to him. He told Owen that he lived in Pontllanfraith and used to work at the South Wales Switchgear factory in the town before winning a scholarship to Coleg Harlech. Now he was with the Workers' Education Association. He had stepped into the shoes of Neil Kinnock who had the job before becoming Bedwellty's MP.

Owen asked what it involved.

'Setting up classes on political and economic themes mainly, and linking up with Cardiff University to provide an adult education service for this part of the Valleys.'

'Bit different from working in a factory.'

Moore sipped his beer.

'You could say I'm a self-made intellectual. But seriously, we're reinventing Labour in this part of the world. Neil's driving it. Things used to be a bit moribund round here. The constituency party hardly met before he was elected. These days Neil insists on regular monthly meetings. Reports back and gets a debate going.'

By now the noise was rising. There were queues at the bar, and women were sitting in clusters at the long trestle tables that were covered with red paper tablecloths and white paper plates bearing bread rolls. Many of the men were former miners who worked in light industry, mainly the car component factories that had been attracted to Cwmbran New Town.

Owen followed Moore to the far end of the room and sat next to him, aware that the men opposite were studying him carefully.

'This is Owen James, from the *Western Mail*,' Barry said. 'Don't worry, Leo's invited him, so he's probably OK.'

'*Western Mail*'s no friend of ours,' a man facing him muttered, reaching for a bottle of wine.

'Don't take any notice of Les,' a man alongside said. 'He's forever going on, aren't you Les. Where're you from, son?'

'West Wales, Haverfordwest.'

'Welsh-speaking then, are you?'

'No, no, I'm from below the *Landsker*. We're known as the down-belows in Pembrokeshire.'

Owen coloured, wondering whether he should have used the phrase.

'How come this place got to be called Sebastopol?' he asked.

'No idea,' Barry said, looking round the table quizzically. 'Something to do with the Crimea was it?'

'It used to be called Panteg,' Les said. 'But you're right, they changed the name when news reached here of the fall of Sebastopol.'

'A great British victory,' Owen said.

'Doesn't mean we're not Welsh as well,' Les replied.

Just then the noise in the room lowered as a man at the far end of the room rose, tapping his wine glass with a pen.

'That's Paul Murphy, secretary of the party in Pontypool,' Barry whispered. 'Leo's right-hand man. Went to Oxford. Probably go far.'

'I'd just like to welcome everybody and thank you all for making it such a good crowd. Just as well, really. Leo here tells me there's going to be an election soon. So dig deep in your pockets, brothers, when we send round the raffle tickets.'

There was laughter and the conversation rose again as the first course, roast lamb with side vegetables and gravy, was served.

* * *

A while later Barry Moore turned to Owen, 'As Les was saying, we're Welsh, of course we are. But that's not the real question is it, despite all the column inches you devote to it in the *Western Mail*.'

'Well, we're Welsh and British, don't you think?'

'We're just as Welsh as anyone else. But you're asking the wrong question so, of course, you're getting the wrong answer.'

'I'm not sure what you mean.'

'The real question is not whether we're British, Welsh or anything else. The real question is whether the rich have a divine right to rule. What is important is our identity as working people.'

'I agree with that, but all the same...'

Barry Moore cut across him.

'The real question is whether we can develop enough confidence in ourselves as the working class to assert our rights. And in a democracy the working class have the majority, around here they do anyway.'

'Can't dispute that,' Owen agreed. 'But it's only part of it surely? The nub of it is what you said about confidence. Where do you get it from? I think our Welshness should give us it. But the way it's all mixed up with Britishness confuses the issue. It drains the confidence away.'

'The way I look at it the party is the main thing,' Barry insisted. 'Wales, your Wales anyway - whatever that is - is a diversion. What we need is proper control of the party. We need confidence in ourselves you're right, but we need confidence in our leaders as well. We've never really had that, except perhaps with the '45 government.'

'But why is that? Isn't it because of the dominance of a British way of thinking, over class as much as anything else?'

'The British way of thinking, as you put it, is not the point. The point is that the working class is always in danger of being exploited and it needs to be represented effectively.'

Owen thought for a moment before answering.

'You're wedded to Britain despite the fact that it's in decline, in crisis even.'

'Doesn't look that way from where I'm sitting.'

As their argument continued Owen reflected that for Barry Moore it was Britain that determined his outlook, whether about class or anything else. There was constant talk about the Welsh language being in decline but so, too, was Britain. All these relationships were confusing because no one seemed to share the same sense of what the words meant. Barry Moore was insisting he was Welsh, but that seemed to mean something completely different from the way Owen himself thought about it. 'Even more to someone from the Welsh-speaking areas,' he thought. 'In those places people think about themselves in a way that can't possibly be the case in the Valleys.'

After listening to Moore for a while he tried another tack.

'What would you say are the main supports, pillars if you like, of Britishness?'

'Don't know what you're getting at.'

'Well, I'd say they were deference, hierarchy and authority, all of which are central to the class system you talk about. They underpin the way the ruling class, what you call the rich, control things. It's what makes them think they have a divine right to rule.'

'I suppose there's something in that.'

'And they're all in retreat, don't you see? We were talking about the Crimea a moment ago. That's when there was the Charge of the Light Brigade, the gallant six hundred and all that. When would you say that attitudes changed from seeing it as being something heroic to just being plain daft?'

'No idea, when would you say?'

'It didn't happen overnight, of course, but over decades. I'd say attitudes changed somewhere between the the trenches in the First World War and when Harold Wilson gave the Beatles the OBE.'

Barry laughed.

'But it's a serious point,' Owen insisted. 'That kind of British authority has shifted don't you think? It's coming to an end. And it's leaving a vacuum.'

'Maybe you're right.'

'The unity that you speak of, based on class interests is simply not the same as it was. We need something else. I think it's significant that it was in the 1960s that Welsh politics first achieved any real prominence. That was when Welsh nationalism emerged as a political force.'

'All of that was just a diversion.'

Barry was becoming testy, provoked by the mention of nationalism. He put down his pint and turned directly to Owen.

'This Welsh identity you go on about, patriotism or whatever you want to call it, can't be denied, of course. But the danger comes when people put those sorts of feelings above their judgement, when patriotic pride becomes nationalism.'

'What's wrong with being proud of being Welsh?'

'I'm not denying we're Welsh, not for a moment, but that's simply a question of seeing ourselves as equal to the English, Scots, Irish or whoever. To say any more than that, to see it as the beginning and end of who we are politically as you're suggesting... well, that's just a distraction from the class struggle. It's quite dangerous actually.'

'I can see that we're not going to agree.'

'I think we need another drink.'

Barry rose and made his way towards the bar. Watching him go Owen was frustrated that he had obviously failed to persuade him. Nonetheless, he felt something had been clarified in the exchange.

* * *

By the time Barry returned, pints in hand, Leo Abse was speaking, standing at the top table and hurling imprecations at the government. He warned that, amidst the growing industrial unrest, an election was inevitable. Across the smoke-filled room, Owen could barely make out the diminutive figure, but his harsh incantation was clear and unmistakeable.

'The ball is over. With a breathtaking recklessness, this profligate and divisive government mocked at the need for social priorities and a just tax system. From 1971 they threw themselves into an orgy of a credit free-for-all which is now having such calamitous consequences.'

Abse flung out an arm for dramatic effect, before picking up on his theme.

'Heath's dream that the uncontrolled injection of credit into the national economy would mean more would be spent on the growth and modernisation of industry can now be seen by all to be a fantasy.'

Barry Moore leaned across to Owen. 'Heard all this before I expect?'

'Yes, I got the press release earlier. *MP warns of snap election over miners' dispute* will be the headline in tomorrow's paper.'

Abse was in full flight, appealing to the undoubted biblical background of his audience.

'And while the money lenders flourished British industry remained sluggish. The uncontrolled but expensive credit sucked in a flood of foreign cars and all manner of consumer durables that has pushed up our import bill. The resulting inflation has caused housing prices to escalate out of reach of what the ordinary family could hope to afford.'

A low murmur of assent filled the room, as Abse's voice reached a fresh pitch in persuasive power.

'Heath is engaged upon a gigantic confidence trick. He is now absurdly trying to shift responsibility for his folly wholly upon the mining communities. Yet, within the law, all the miners are doing is to seek to raise their living standards. And they are doing a job more hazardous and far less congenial than any other in the kingdom.'

There was another, louder murmur of approbation as Abse lowered his voice, making his audience strain to hear.

'Soon we will have an election on the issue. Will Heath succeed again in conning the nation? I do not think for one minute that this time he will succeed. Certainly not in our Valleys, and certainly not in Pontypool.'

Leo Abse sat down to sustained applause. Barry Moore turned to Owen, 'Heath is going to try and make the election a choice between who rules the country, him or the miners. And there'll be no difference in that argument whether the miners come from Durham, Derbyshire, or Dowlais.'

Then he pulled from an inside pocket of his jacket a newspaper cutting and Owen could see it was a story he himself had written a few days before, with the headline *First Labour MP calls for a legislative Assembly.*

'If this is the way things are going, there's going to be trouble,' Barry Moore muttered. 'John Morris said this, did he?' He reached for his glasses. 'It is not beyond our wit to fit the Welsh Assembly into the legislative process.'

'I spoke to him on the phone before he made that speech,' Owen said. 'What he meant, I think, is that you can't just give an elected Assembly a purely administrative role. It's bound to be involved in policy-making.'

'But that's well beyond what's been agreed. I can't see Neil or Leo accepting it and nor should they.'

Moore held the cutting up to the light and read aloud once more. 'John Morris agreed that a public impression had been created that Labour was for an executive assembly and Plaid Cymru was pressing for one with legislative powers. "To some extent I'm bridging that gap," he said.'

Moore folded the newspaper cutting and put it back in his pocket.

'John Morris may want to bridge the gap. But if he tries there's going to be trouble. We're not going to have this out before the election. But mark my words, just see what happens afterwards.'

Cadair Idris
January 1974

Rhiannon and Ioan picked Siobhan up from her bedsit overlooking Aberystwyth's promenade just before nine o'clock on a January Saturday. The weather was cold but bright. Rhiannon was pleased to see that her new friend was well equipped. She wore hiking boots and had a lined waterproof jacket strapped to her rucksack. They had agreed to spend the day climbing Cadair Idris, some thirty miles to the north, the most accessible mountain in the Snowdonia range.

Siobhan Cunninghame was some years older, but Rhiannon had immediately taken to her when they met at the start of term. She had a wicked sense of humour, a pealing laugh, and a sharp, irresistibly penetrating Belfast accent. Caught off-guard her strong features could look sullen and unattractive, but they gave her an unexpected warmth when she spoke. She had closely cropped black hair, invariably wore a combination of black shirts, cardigans and trousers, a black leather belt with a large silver clip, black leather boots and long swinging, circular silver earings. The combination had the intended effect of making her stand out.

Her father, a welder in Harland and Wolff's Belfast shipyard, had died when she was six years old, after which her mother had brought her up on her own. 'My Da was a Protestant so we lived in the Shankill,' she told Rhiannon. 'My surname says I'm Protestant, but my mother's a Catholic and insisted I have an Irish first name. She's loyal to the Gaelic rather than the British account of things, you might say. But it made survival a bit difficult.'

She had studied for her first degree, in English, at Queen's University in Belfast. During that time her mother had left to settle in Dublin, her home city. This provided an added incentive for Siobhan herself to look for somewhere else to pursue her postgraduate studies.

'I couldn't get out of Belfast fast enough, to tell you the truth. With the Troubles it was getting a bit oppressive. If you haven't lived there you can't imagine what it's like. I needed a change of scene, but I'll go back some day.'

Rhiannon was surprised to discover that Siobhan was quite religious.

'You can't be otherwise coming from the Six Counties, in outward observance anyway, especially if you're a Catholic, like me.'

'So you go to mass, confession and all that?'

'Oh, yes, I go through the motions. I don't know why, really. If you've been brought up where I'm from something just pins you to it. Maybe now I'm away from home I won't feel it, but it hasn't happened so far.'

In the car heading out of Aberystwyth they sat together in the back while Ioan drove. They talked about living in the town, the university and their tutors. Rhiannon asked Siobhan what she had in mind for her dissertation.

'I want to do something about writing in Northern Ireland. The way writers from the two traditions see Ulster and its connections with the rest of Ireland and Britain, that kind of thing.'

'I imagine you can get a lot of insights from that.'

'Yes, I'm especially interested when Catholic and Protestant writers interact with each other, though that's quite rare. But if you can tease it out you can get a glimpse of a new way of looking at things. I think so anyway.'

Siobhan took out a slim volume of poetry from her rucksack. 'I'm keen on this fellow, Seamus Heaney. Have you heard of him?'

Rhiannon shook her head.

'He has an interesting way of putting ideas across. You can tell from his name that he's a Catholic. But he's not direct about the Troubles, not at all really. He comes at it in an oblique kind of way.'

Siobhan leafed through the book, lighting on a page.

'Heaney was brought up on a farm near Derry, one of nine children. In this poem he describes how a neighbouring farmer, a Protestant, comes to visit. But he waits outside the door for the family to finish their rosary, before knocking ... which is quite extraordinary.'

And she began to speak the lines, softly so that Rhiannon strained to hear. She leant forward to catch sight of the page.

> *Then sometimes when the rosary was dragging*
> *mournfully on in the kitchen*
> *we would hear his step round the gable*
>
> *though not until after the litany*
> *would the knock come to the door*
> *and the casual whistle strike up*
>
> *on the doorstep. 'A right looking night,'*
> *he might say, 'I was dandering by*
> *and says I, I might as well call.*

Siobhan stopped reading, stared unseeing through the window for a moment, before turning to Rhiannon.

'It must be hard for you, not being from the north of Ireland to realise how poignant that is. I can't imagine something like that happening in the Shankill. But out in rural Derry, well there it must be different. And I reckon it tells you, Heaney is telling you anyway, things could be different.'

'What are you two wittering on about in the back,' Ioan called out, glancing at the two of them in his rear view mirror.

'Never you mind,' Rhiannon said.

'Women's things, is it?'

'And what would you know about them, Ioan Rhys Thomas?' Siobhan flashed back.

*   *   *

They turned off the road near the Minffordd Hotel on the southern side of Cadair Idris and pulled into a small car park which had a few scattered picnic tables. As the girls pulled on their jackets, Ioan took out a map and laid it on the table next to the car. He pointed out the path they would be following.

'It's the most difficult route but the most dramatic,' Rhiannon told Siobhan. 'I've climbed it before, with my dad about three or four years ago. Its steep and hard going at first but you get some spectacular views, depending on the weather of course.'

Ioan chuckled in his mischievous way.

'Difficult to tell what it's going to do, but the forecast is good, otherwise I wouldn't have brought you.'

Looking up they could see mist clinging to the side of the mountain high above, though the wind was pulling at it. They left the car park and walked along a tree-lined track that crossed the Afon Fawnog. After a short while they branched off to join a footpath heading directly upwards. Alongside them the Nant Cadair fell off the mountain with a gathering rush. They crossed it on a small wooden bridge and then climbed the path that wound its way steeply through a covering of trees. Even though it was well past autumn the woodland still contained a splash of colours from the few leaves still hanging on the trees, a combination of reds, browns, light greens, and yellows. Through it all the Nant Cadair cascaded relentlessly, its tumbling rocky waterfalls creating mists pierced by odd rays of the sun that caught the evaporating moisture in a series of flickering rainbows.

It took them nearly an hour to climb through the wood. At times the path was treacherous, muddy and slippery underfoot. When they reached the open valley Rhiannon was breathless. 'Let's stop for a bit, I've got a stitch.'

'I know what you mean,' Siobhan agreed. 'I'm not used to this type of walking, it's more like rock climbing.'

'You'd really know it if you were rock climbing,' Ioan said.

Nevertheless, they stopped for a while and gazed down at the valley below and the steep mountainside of Mynydd Dol-Ffanog opposite. At the bottom of the valley a few cars on the straight line of road looked like toys. Rhiannon pointed at the northward direction they were heading.

'The road takes you over to Cross Foxes and then Dolgellau. We'll be able to see the town on the other side when we reach the top. We're lucky it's turning out to be such a clear day.'

They resumed their climb. The path became less steep as it took them into the Nant Cadair hanging valley and the stream's source. In front of them was an imposing cliff face, shaped like one side of a pyramid with its point rising imperiously into the sky.

'Is that Cadair Idris?' Siobhan asked.

'It's part of the range,' Ioan told her. 'That's Craig Cwm Amarch. Pen y Gadair, the highest of the peaks, what most people think of as Cadair Idris, is beyond.'

'It means the top or literally the head of the chair,' Rhiannon explained. 'We have to clamber up the ridge to our left first, climb Craig Cwm Amarch the mountain in front of us, and then drop down into a col before making the final ascent.'

They continued climbing. The path followed the line of the stream, traversing a mixture of grass, bog, stones and scree.

Eventually it levelled out and they came within sight of the metallic azure of Llyn Cau. The small lake filled the bowl of the cwm whose sides towered steeply upwards. Rolling clouds concealed and occasionally revealed the peaks of the mountains.

'If we're lucky the mist will be gone by the time we reach the top,' Rhiannon said, pointing upwards.

Siobhan gestured towards the inside of the cwm.

'Is that what's meant to be Idris's chair?'

Rhiannon laughed.

'Oh no, Idris ap Gwyddno would have got a wet bottom sitting in that. His chair is on the other side, between Pen y Gadair, the summit which you can't see from here, Cyfrwy and Tyrau Mawr, two other peaks beyond.'

'Who was Idris anyway?'

'A mythical figure, said to be a warrior king of Meirionnydd from around the sixth century. He was known as Idris Gawr, Idris the giant, renowned as a philosopher, poet, and astronomer. The myth says he carved the mountain out as an armchair to gaze at the stars. Really, of course, these mountains were carved out by glaciers thousands of years ago.'

Rhiannon put her hand on one of a number of huge boulders they were passing.

'These were part of the debris left behind by the glacier when it retreated. But the story goes that they were stones that Idris shook out of his shoes when he was carving his chair.'

* * *

Leaving the lake, they climbed again, steeply to the left and upwards towards a rocky outpost that was the starting point for the ridge walk. It curved round Llyn Cau, taking in Craig Cwm Amarch. As they reached the ridge they were able to look down again to the valley floor where they had begun their ascent. Immediately below a lake loomed into view framed by mountains receding to the west.

'That's Talyllyn, another glacial lake,' Rhiannon said. 'Literally it means the end of the lake. Its proper Welsh name is Llyn Mwyngyll, though hardly anyone calls it that these days.'

'It's beautiful.'

'The Dysynni river flows out of it into Cardigan Bay which is not far from here. The valley is famous because of Mary Jones.'

'Who?'

'A girl who walked to Bala to buy a Bible. She's become a kind of folk heroine.'

'Is she a myth as well?'

'No, no, there are true accounts that have come down. She was born in the 1780s in Llanfihangel-y-Pennant, at the foot of Cadair Idris over the other side. She lived around there all of her life. Had six children. Kept bees.'

'Where do you get all these stories?'

'From my dad mostly. He uses the Mary Jones tale in one of his sermons – *Cadw fy ngham yn sicr fel yr addewaist* is the text he starts out with.'

'Which means?'

Rhiannon thought for a moment.

'I guess "Direct my footsteps according to your word", or perhaps "Order my footsteps…." It's from Psalm 119. Mary Jones lived at the height of Methodism you see, at the end of the eighteenth century. The Sunday Schools were where people like her learned to read. Her name became a symbol for the desire among common people to become literate so they could read the Bible.'

By now they were halfway along the ridge.

'Sounds a bit sentimental to me,' Ioan, who was bringing up the rear, shouted against the wind. 'The common people, as you call them, were just rough sheep farmers.'

Rhiannon, who had taken the lead, turned round.

'You've got to admit that they were dedicated to their religion. But they were so poor they often couldn't afford a Bible.'

They carried on walking. Then Rhiannon stopped again, this time turning to Siobhan.

'It took Mary six years to save the three shillings and sixpence she needed to buy a Bible. Can you believe that? The trouble was the nearest place to get one was Bala. So, aged sixteen, she walked the twenty-seven miles over these hills, barefoot as a matter of fact.'

'Barefoot?' Siobhan queried.

'Oh it was quite normal in those days. She had clogs, but carried them so they would look smart when she arrived. Her zeal is said to have inspired the Minister who sold her the Bible to found the British and Foreign Bible Society. That was Thomas Charles, a Calvinistic Methodist. The story goes he was so impressed with her fervour he gave her two extra Bibles, so she came away with three. One of them is in the National Library in Aberystwyth.'

'People were certainly passionate about their faith in those days,' Siobhan said.

'In Northern Ireland they still are, aren't they?' Ioan said.

'In the North religion is more about identity. There's quite a difference.'

* * *

They continued upwards along the ridge until they reached the top of Craig Cwm Amarch, revealing the summit of Cadair Idris beyond, in the distance across the col. A strong wind had risen and with it a fresh chill. Rhiannon and Siobhan searched in their rucksacks for their hats and gloves. Ioan already had his on. Only a few feet from their path was a vertical drop. Through a gap in the rocks a chimney fell hundreds of feet down to Llyn Cau. The lake was now a shade of green and blue, lit up by the sun with the wind whipping up flecks of white foam. Siobhan peered over the edge and drew back quickly, shuddering.

'I wouldn't like to be here if it was shrouded in mist,' she said.

'It can be dangerous if you're not careful,' Ioan told her. 'No mist on map, as they say.'

Rhiannon studied the lake far below.

'Legend has it that Llyn Cau is bottomless,' she said. '*Cau* is a wonderfully expressive word I always think. Generally, it means to enclose, for instance some land with a hedge or fence. Here I guess it means the enclosed lake, circled by the steep slopes. But it can also mean hollow, hollow ground that is, or even something hollow as in false logic. Perhaps it's a reference to the lake's supposedly infinite depths.'

'Your Welsh words carry a lot of meanings,' Siobhan said.

The remnants of mist had now completely blown from the mountain and Pen y Gadair rose majestically before them. But they felt the wind's chill again as they stumbled down the slope to reach the col at Craig Cau, again close to a vertical drop, hundreds of feet down to the lake. Then they started the last steep ascent to Pen y Gadair. They had to use their hands to pull themselves up the rock-strewn mountainside. It was hard going and bitterly cold. After about two hundred metres they paused for a breath, wedged between two large boulders.

Rhiannon drank some water from a bottle she was carrying and then handed it to Siobhan.

'I'm surprised it's not frozen solid,' she said.

'It's not far now. There's more boulders and scree for about half-a-mile and we're there.'

'Feels more like a couple of miles.'

They climbed slowly upwards and eventually caught sight of the Ordnance Survey trig point at the top, standing against the sky. Reaching the summit, they clung on to it and gazed about them. Ioan pointed to the north.

'We're lucky it's so clear. See, there, in the far distance, that's the Snowdon range and to the left the Rhinogydd above Harlech.'

He pointed again, this time to the west and a wide expanse of spreading white and yellow sand mixed with blue-grey sea.

'That's the Mawddach estuary. Beyond is Barmouth and beyond still is the Llŷn Peninsula.'

'What's the dark line crossing the sands?' Siobhan asked.

'That's the bridge that carries the Cambrian coast railway,' Rhiannon said. 'It's one of the longest wooden viaducts in Britain.'

They turned to see whale back mountains riding far to the south to the peaks of the Brecon Beacons. Turning again, to the north-east they saw the Berwyn range. Behind them was the sweep of Cardigan Bay and on the far horizon the Preseli hills.

'Can you see Ireland from here?' Siobhan asked.

'When it's really clear, but that's not very often,' Ioan told her.

He took a few steps back, searching in his rucksack for his binoculars. Looking up at the two women it occurred to him how striking they were. They had taken off their hats to let the gale-force wind blow through their hair. Siobhan was a diminutive figure in her black padded coat, with the wind pressing her short black hair closely to her skull. Rhiannon wore a red waterproof jacket, her long red hair streaming behind her.

'You look like a couple of Celtic nymphs,' he cried out to them.

Siobhan turned, a dark expression on her face that lifted as she laughed.

'More like a pair of leprechauns I'd say.'

Just below the summit was a low-slung stone shelter with a

corrugated iron roof. Inside, away from the wind, they sat on a cold stone ledge and unwrapped sandwiches.

'The views make you realise how mountainous Wales is,' Siobhan said after a while.

'Takes longer to travel from Bangor to Cardiff than from Bangor to London,' Ioan said.

'Makes it difficult, too, to get any unity across the country,' Rhiannon added.

'That's certainly the case,' Ioan agreed, fumbling with a packet of crisps. 'Most people in the south have never been to the north. I'm one of your rarities.'

He took a bite of his sandwich.

'For a lot of people where I come from Wales is just the south. It's the people between Swansea and Chepstow, stretching if you're lucky to take in Merthyr. Everything north of there is above the tree line.'

'It's one reason why we contantly refer to *North* and *South* Wales, giving them capital letters, as though they're separate countries,' Rhiannon told Siobhan who laughed.

'One of my teachers at school used to say that if you give words capital letters it's because you're afraid of them.'

* * *

It was cold in the hut and they didn't linger long. Instead, donning their rucksacks, they continued their ridge walk around the Cadair Idris heights, heading down a gentle slope towards the easternmost peak of Mynydd Moel. Behind them and to their left rose Cyfrwy, another peaked mountain above its own lake, Llyn y Gadair. Rhiannon told Siobhan that the mountain's name meant saddle.

For a while the path dropped below the line of the ridge, reducing the wind and obscuring their view. But soon they were climbing again to Mynydd Moel's less dramatic summit that marked the northern tip of the Cadair Idris range. From there views were still magnificent. Directly below was the town of Dolgellau and then the great sweep of the Mawddach estuary to the sea. The hills to the north gathered in waves and merged with a line of clouds that were advancing towards them.

They stood there for a while, leaning against the wind, reluctant to lose the vantage point the height gave them. But eventually they turned and began their descent. At first the slope was gentle and grassy but it soon steepened, with rocks and marshland making it slippery underfoot. The path reached a sheep fence and the angle of the slope steepened further with jutting rocks that gave the impression of an angular, crazy stairway. They stopped by a high stile that traversed the fence with the path continuing down on the other side. Following Rhiannon and Ioan over it, Siobhan paused at the top and glanced back. Craig Amarch, looming above Llyn Cau, was even more impressive from this vantage point, its triangular shape reaching high into the sky.

Rhiannon noticed her friend studying the mountain.

'We must be close to the spot that Richard Wilson stopped to sketch before painting his famous view of Cadair Idris.'

'Another of your people I know nothing about.'

'He was an eighteenth-century landscape painter from Montgomeryshire, but he made his name in London. Travelled to Italy as well. He was one of the first people to paint the Welsh landscape. His most famous paintings were of Snowdon but I think his one of Cadair Idris the best.'

Siobhan looked at her friend.

'You know Rhiannon, you're so steeped in Wales, the place, the history, the language and all the rest, it puzzles me why you haven't chosen something about it for your dissertation. Instead, you're chasing after your African revolutionary.'

'Frantz Fanon wasn't an African. He was black, of course, but he was French, by nationality anyway, from the Caribbean.'

'Makes him an even odder choice.'

'Not really. He spent the whole of his life trying to understand colonisation.'

'So that's the connection, is it?'

'There are parallels, with Ireland too, don't you think? But the main thing about him for me is that all his ideas came directly from his own experience. First, growing up in Martinique, and then in Algeria where he went as a doctor, actually a psychiatrist.'

'What about Fanon's position on violence?' Ioan objected. 'Can't see Gwynfor having much truck with that.'

'You're right so far as that goes,' Rhiannon answered. 'Wales is different. But still, it raises an important question. How far is violence inevitable in liberation struggles?'

'We know all about that in Ireland,' Siobhan said bitterly.

'In our campaign we've thought a lot about it as well,' Rhiannon told her, as they continued their descent. 'You should read our manifesto.'

'Cymdeithas yr Iaith make a distinction between violence against the person and violence against property,' Ioan explained. 'Most people don't understand it.'

'But the difference is crucially important,' Rhiannon said. 'It's interesting isn't it, the reason we separate the two things, I suppose the reason we're able to differentiate between them.'

'How do you mean?' Siobhan asked.

'Well, as you know there've been some pretty violent anti-colonial struggles in Ireland. But the Irish faced a lot of oppression from the English. We haven't had that kind of thing, not in the recent past anyway.'

'Wales is certainly different from Ireland.'

'These days yes,' Rhiannon agreed. 'But it wasn't always the case. Take the Normans. Their castles are everywhere you go. We've got six hundred of them. More than anywhere else in the world.'

'That's ancient history,' Ioan said. 'It's still not clear to me that Fanon was right about the armed struggle being inevitable as you put it.'

He stopped as he said this, removing his rucksack and taking off his waterproof.

'The wind is dropping.'

'You'll tempt it to start raining,' Rhiannon said, passing him her hat. 'As far as Fanon goes, you've got to take account of the realities.'

Ioan laughed, 'There's always those.'

'But seriously, the French occupation of its colonies in North Africa was based on sheer military strength. Resistance inevitably involved violence since that was the only language the French understood. Fanon says violence is imposed on the colonised by the colonisers.'

'You can't argue that Wales is a colony in anything like the same way,' Ioan objected.

'Not in the same way, I guess you're right. These days it's as if our minds are colonised, isn't it? It's as if we're colonising ourselves. How do we break out of that?'

PART II

Carmarthen
February 1974

It was a cold Friday afternoon in late February as Owen drove northwards out of Cardiff. Flakes of snow scattered against the windscreen of his ageing Volkswagen Beetle. Warmth from its heater competed with a blast of cold air from a hole in the floor below the dashboard. The rear engine chugged away, sounding like the outboard motor of a fishing boat.

Owen settled down in his seat, pulled his scarf and coat closer to his throat and peered into the gathering gloom of the winter afternoon. Soon the sides of Taff Vale made it gloomier as he passed through Rhydyfelin, Treforest and Pontypridd and then on through Cilfynydd, Treharris, Merthyr Vale, Aberfan, Troedyrhiw, and Pentrebach. In each of the small villages parked cars choked the road, slowing the traffic. It was more than an hour before he reached Merthyr. It took another twenty minutes to negotiate the town's early evening traffic, pass through Cefn-Coed-y-Cymmer, and reach the moorlands and the open road.

Owen had missed lunch in a scramble to finish a story for the following day's paper. He was cold, tired, and hungry, but nonetheless elated. It was less than a week before the general election and he had persuaded the new editor Duncan Gardiner, a genial Yorkshireman, to let him go north to cover the campaign in Anglesey. Dafydd Iwan was Plaid Cymru's candidate and Owen had argued that whether he won or not it was still a story.

Influenced by his Irish wife, Gardiner did not share his predecessor's overt hostility to nationalism. He was indifferent to, rather than prejudiced against, what he saw as the idiosyncrasies of Welsh politics. Moreover, he was inclined to encourage the enthusiasms of his reporters. Consequently, he held back from suggesting that an article about a leader of Cymdeithas yr Iaith standing in a safe Labour seat was hardly of the first importance in an election campaign dominated by whether the miners should be allowed to hold the government to ransom.

In the wake of the oil crisis, soaring energy costs and the three-day week, the miners were on strike for more pay. Meanwhile, the former Conservative minister Enoch Powell was urging his supporters to vote Labour in protest against Britain's entry into the European Economic Community. Set against these concerns Welsh preoccupations counted for little.

This was not Owen's view. He believed the election would herald a momentous, even historic, shift in Welsh politics. For the past three weeks he had been moving constantly across Wales absorbed in a series of localised contests involving clashes between personalities. He was sure they were symptomatic of fundamental shifts close to the surface that would soon erupt with unpredictable consequences. Labour was being challenged by markedly different opponents in different parts of the country.

*   *   *

As he traversed the Brecon Beacons Owen caught a glimpse of the snow-covered peaks of Pen-y-Fan and Corn Du. To the left a road skirted the hillside towards Hirwaun and Aberdare. A week ago he had spent two days there reporting on a contest in what should have been one of Labour's safest seats. However, Plaid Cymru had halved the majority in the 1970 election and now Glyn Owen, the loudest self-publicist Owen had ever come across, was leading its campaign. It was not difficult to find him. Stand on any of the roads that wound through the Cynon

Valley and it would not be long before a large white van with a loudspeaker thundering out Welsh rock music appeared.

'This is Glyn Owen, Plaid Cymru,' he announced through the noise. 'It's time for a change, brothers. The Labour Party is anti-working class. They've closed 48 pits and destroyed 37,000 mining jobs. What's the difference between a Labour Peer and a Tory Lord? You only see the Labour Party when they want to put a sticker in your window.'

He was a political barrow boy who led the opposition to Labour on both the local urban district council and the newly created Mid Glamorgan in its county hall in Cardiff. He made his living hawking drapery and soft furnishings from his van in markets across the Valleys, while simultaneously operating a street-side loan business. Owen wondered at the levels of interest he charged. But all was glossed over in bonhomie.

Glyn Owen brought his sales pitch from the streets into the political bear pit of the county hall, and was famed for physical dust-ups with his opponents. He was an unlikely Plaid leader, but feared by Labour across the Valleys. He had become committed to the nationalist cause during two years in the Merchant Navy when he had observed plenty of small countries successfully managing their own affairs. A bust of Keir Hardie stood on the television set in his terraced house in Cwmbach.

'I couldn't have fitted into the old Plaid Cymru,' he told Owen. 'It was full of poets, writers and ministers. But it's a socialist party now.'

Nevertheless, the Cynon Valley was likely to remain safe Labour territory. The opposite was true of Cardigan in the far west. There Owen found a contest completely different in tone. A stranger passing through would hardly notice that an election was underway, let alone one that was being keenly fought. It was as traditional a Liberal seat as it was possible to find, unless it was neighbouring Montgomeryshire, though that was generally more sharply fought by Conservatives. It was true that Labour had won Cardigan in the 1966 election and held on to it into the 1970s. But that was solely down to the personality and local roots and connections of the candidate, Elystan Morgan. As a farmer in Tregaron told Owen, 'If Elystan was a Liberal – and he's not so far from being one – he'd be in this seat for life.'

In fact, for many years Elystan Morgan had been a leading figure in Plaid Cymru. A protégé of Gwynfor Evans and predicted to be his likely successor, he had fought three elections for the party, twice in Wrexham and once in Meirionnydd, in 1964. Shortly afterwards, however, he had defected to Labour and was quickly selected to fight his native Cardigan seat. He argued that Labour was the only party capable of delivering a Parliament for Wales. Sceptics in Plaid Cymru bitterly resented what they saw as political opportunism. Even so, Elystan Morgan had won Cardigan in 1966 and in short order became a parliamentary secretary at the Home Office. It was a position he used to good effect in persuading Harold Wilson to establish the Commission on the Constitution in the wake of Gwynfor Evans' Carmarthen by-election.

Now, however, he faced stiff competition from the Liberals in the shape of a distant relative, Geraint Howells, a large, genial, quietly-spoken sheep farmer from Ponterwyd. Though less charismatic and articulate, Owen could see that Howells had a deep affinity with the Cardiganshire people. For the best part of a day they travelled the length of the constituency meeting voters in shops and on street corners.

Just off the main square in Aberaeron, Howells ran into a woman who embraced him awkwardly. It was obvious that she was an old girlfriend. However, as he got back into his car Howells brushed off the encounter. Instead, he explained there were three main requirements to be successful in Cardiganshire politics.

'Never openly contradict anybody,' he said. 'Never demonstrate intense feelings that might reveal extremism. And always ensure that the people who are not actually related to you have at least shaken you by the hand.'

A very different style of campaign was taking place in neighbouring Pembrokeshire, Owen's home county. Here the Conservatives had broken Labour's hold in 1970 and were now in a make-or-break fight to consolidate their position. Labour's loss had been a self-inflicted wound. Their long-standing MP Desmond Donnelly had first won the constituency in 1950. He described himself as an Englishman with an Irish name sitting for a Welsh seat. At first he had been a supporter of Aneurin Bevan, but then he shifted rightwards, from 'ultra left to ultra violet' as it was said.

Donnelly finally abandoned Labour in 1968 to form his own Democratic Party. Standing in Pembrokeshire in his new colours in 1970 he failed to win the seat but split the Labour vote. This gave victory to the Conservative candidate Nicholas Edwards, a London stockbroker. He had hardly expected to win, arriving late to his selection meeting to find he was the only candidate available, the others having withdrawn. So began a career that was to have a profound impact on Welsh political life.

Owen spent an afternoon in Edwards' company. They toured villages near Milford Haven in a Land Rover equipped with a powerful loudhailer. Whenever they reached the outskirts of a settlement Edwards took the microphone, his casual Home Counties drawl echoing against the houses.

'This is Nicholas Edwards, your Conservative candidate, calling!'

Owen wondered at the effect it might have as they passed through Freystrop, Johnston, Tiers Cross, Rosemarket, Lawrenny and Burton. In all of them Edwards pointed to new housing developments that were springing up.

'Look at them,' he said harshly. 'They're all owned by incomers, and they're all voting for me.'

Owen had never felt more depressed. At the end of the afternoon when Edwards dropped him off outside the County Hotel in Haverfordwest, he felt obliged to wish the candidate the best of luck.

'You don't mean that,' Edwards answered in his bluff, cheerful and forthright manner.

* * *

Owen had stopped off in Brecon to fill the petrol tank located in the front boot of his Volkswagen and grab a sandwich. Now he was driving in darkness over Mynydd Epynt towards Builth. The headlights lit up flurries of snow. A glance at his watch told him it was nearly seven o'clock.

'At this rate it'll be midnight before I reach the north,' he thought.

Three hours later, stiff and nearly frozen to his seat, he had driven through Dinas Mawddwy and was climbing a high pass with the Cadair Idris range rearing to his left. He wondered how much further he could go that night. Over the top he sped down hill to Dolgellau but still pressed on. Approaching Ganllwyd and passing the Tyn-y-Groes hotel, a sixteenth century coaching inn, his resolution faltered. He stopped the car, reversed and parked near the entrance.

Across the road he could hear the rushing waters of the Mawddach river. The black hills rose steeply to a night sky, clearing to reveal a host of stars. It was bitterly cold. Owen stamped his feet, took his bag and typewriter case from the back seat and made his way inside.

He was grateful to see a roaring log fire and to be told that a room was available. Ordering a pint and a bowl of cawl with cheese, he found a place in the snug close to the fire. As the warmth reached him Owen began to listen to the slow murmur of conversation that was coming from a group at the bar. He could understand enough to realise they were talking about the forthcoming election. But the language defeated him. Eventually he rose and, approaching slightly awkwardly, spoke in English.

'Couldn't help overhearing you were talking about the election. Which constituency are we in?'

'Meirionnydd.'

'Ah, how are things going here, do you think?'

'The money is on this new young fellow, Dafydd Elis-Thomas. It's going to be close, though.'

'He's Plaid Cymru, isn't that right?

'Yes, but Labour have been losing ground. Their candidate Wil Edwards is none too popular, not much of a constituency man anyway.'

Owen bought a round of drinks and continued chatting for a while. Then, glancing at his watch, he went to find a telephone. Before leaving Cardiff he had called in at the house to gather an overnight bag. He'd left a hurried note on the kitchen table telling Anna he was driving north and would call later. Now he found a phone under the stairs near the reception desk with a stool and a small table piled with tourist brochures. Owen squeezed in, dialled 100 for the operator and asked to reverse the charges. He heard Anna's voice, distant and anxious, agreeing to take the call.

'Owen! Is that you? Where are you?'

'I've found a pub, a bit north of Dolgellau.'

''I was worried.' A tremor sounded in Anna's voice. 'You hadn't called. What are you doing?'

'I persuaded Gardiner that we should be covering Plaid's

campaign in Anglesey. You know, where Dafydd Iwan is standing.'

'I'll be glad when it's all over.'

'But Anna, things are happening. I've just been having a conversation in the bar. They're saying that Plaid has a chance of getting in here.'

'Where?'

'In Meirionnydd. The candidate's a young guy, Dafydd Elis-Thomas. Haven't met him. Perhaps I should have. I'm beginning to think I should be covering the election here and not in Anglesey.'

'When will you be home?'

'I'm not sure. Probably the day after tomorrow. But I'll be late.'

'You're away such a lot. I hate this stupid election.'

Owen sighed and carded a hand through his hair.

'Things are beginning to shift. It's an important moment. I can feel it.'

There was a long silence at the other end and Owen wondered whether they had been cut off.

'Anna?'

'Yes, I'm still here. We'd better finish. The call will be expensive. Drive carefully, won't you?'

'Don't be silly.'

'I miss you.'

'I miss you, too. But I'll soon be home.'

Then the phone clicked and went dead. Owen stared at it for a while, before hanging up the receiver. Then he went to bed.

* * *

The next morning was bright and frosty. Owen set off early. The road was clear and he made good progress through

Penrhydeudraeth and Porthmadog. Driving into Penygroes he saw a group of Plaid canvassers, among them Dafydd Wigley, the party's Caernarfon candidate. Owen stopped the car and hurried after him.

'Owen! What on earth are you doing here?'

'Covering the election, but not in Caernarfon I'm afraid.'

'Perhaps you should be. Things are going well.'

'I see the Liberals have put up a last-minute candidate.'

'They're the joker in the pack in this election everywhere, don't you think? But they shouldn't bother us too much here.'

Wigley had no more time to spare. He was ushered forward by a team of followers with green and yellow rosettes pinned to their lapels. He waved as Owen shouted, 'Good luck.'

Driving northwards once more, Owen pondered at the chance encounter. He had met Dafydd Wigley on a number of occasions. Once had been at his home in Merthyr, where he was an executive with Hoover, a big employer in the town. Owen found him a natural leader, down to earth, with a crisp, highly organised approach to politics. Caernarfon was Plaid's main target seat in the election, yet the *Western Mail* had neglected it. Once again Owen thought that he should be spending time in a constituency other than Anglesey.

An hour later he was on the island and making for Holyhead to meet Labour's Cledwyn Hughes. The former secretary of state for Wales was welcoming but reserved. As chairman of the Parliamentary Labour Party, he remained a senior figure at Westminster. A man of short stature, bespectacled and slightly otherworldly, he looked as though he might have been a nonconformist Minister. Nonetheless, he was a canny operator, his political guile concealed by a somewhat avuncular exterior. They settled down over a coffee on a bench in the shop window of his temporary election headquarters.

'I'm surprised the *Western Mail* is interested in Anglesey. I suppose it's because Dafydd Iwan is standing.'

'Well, yes, that is a factor. You must think he is pursuing a vendetta after the road signs campaign when you were at the Welsh Office. And now he's standing against you here.'

'We're basically on the same side, you know. The only difference is our methods.'

'We're as much interested in how the election is playing out generally.'

'I think we'll get back in. People are worried about inflation, rising prices.'

'You don't see Welsh issues playing much of a role?'

'They're important, of course. They've been a focus of my political life, in many ways the main focus. But they're not uppermost in people's minds. As far as those sorts of issues go, I think what really matters is to have an MP they can trust. And, after all, I'm the only candidate who is from the island.'

Hughes was reluctant when Owen asked if he could accompany him canvassing.

'Is that really necessary?'

'It gives a feel of things, some colour.'

'Oh, very well.'

Owen followed Cledwyn into the street where they found his Morris Minor with a solitary Labour sticker in the back window. They drove to the edge of the town and stopped in a small terrace of houses that bore off from the main road, backing on to a housing estate. Cledwyn picked up a bundle of leaflets and set off. He knocked desultorily on a few doors before one was opened by a woman with a tea towel in her hand.

'Oh, Mr Hughes, how nice to see you. Would you like a cup of tea?'

'No, thank you very much. We have to get on. I'm just showing this young lad from Cardiff around Holyhead.'

'Oh, indeed.'She stared at Owen. 'And what brings you to this part of this world?'

'The election and how it's going in north Wales.'

'There you are,' Cledwyn interjected. 'Very nice to see you, Mrs Williams. Is Jim better?'

'Oh, yes, thank you. He's out of hospital.'

They continued down the terraced cottages for about twenty minutes until Cledwyn Hughes said, 'Well, I hope you've seen enough.'

Owen had. He was struck how Hughes never asked for a vote, never raised a political matter. But he always inquired after the families of the people he met, especially their children.

* * *

Owen caught up with Dafydd Iwan and a team of supporters leafleting in Newborough in the south-west of the island. They were advertising a public meeting being held in the village's Prichard Jones Institute that evening. Wearing a black leather jacket, Iwan had the air of a revolutionary, though this was an image he was keen to dispel. He was wary of Owen's interest, wishing to leave his folk-singing image behind him. Instead he was anxious to present the demeanour of a more mature politician. But it was not working. Children followed the leafleting team chanting his name, demanding stickers, and pointing to him as 'the man on the telly'.

In many ways Iwan was typical of his generation of Cymeithas yr Iaith actvists. He was a son of the manse, at Llanuwchlyn not far from the Tryweryn valley. He regarded its drowning by the Liverpool corporation as symbolic of the decline of Welsh as a community language. His cousin Emyr Llewelyn had been imprisoned for bombing the Tryweryn dam site. But Iwan's activism had taken a different course. Through his popular music, his recordings and television appearances, he had mobilised a generation and become an iconic leader in Cymdeithas's ranks.

Owen had interviewed him when his candidature had been announced six weeks earlier. He was in his brother's home in Bridgend, surrounded by his wife Marion and three young children. Owen heard how the Cymdeithas yr Iaith leader had been living with a year's suspended sentence hanging over him for defacing road signs.

Owen asked why he had decided to move into the political mainstream.

'It's time to move on,' he said. 'I'm thirty years old, and I've got a wife and kids and a mortgage.'

There was a feeling, too, that Plaid Cymru was losing its way. It was concentrating too much on economic policies at the expense of the language. Whether his campaign in Anglesey would yield dividends would test this argument. In 1970 Plaid had substantially increased its vote, though it still came third behind Labour and the Conservatives. The question now was whether it would hold on to this position or fall back.

The meeting that evening had a revivalist atmosphere. Around a hundred and fifty people crammed into the Institute and were rewarded by some sparkling speeches, not least from Iwan himself. He appealed unashamedly to nationalist sentiment rather than the finer points of any social or economic policies. Owen, who struggled to follow the Welsh, was impressed by the response that revealed a far from captive audience. Many of the questions were about the language. A sceptic queried the amount of money local authorities were contributing to the National Eisteddfod, describing it as 'jobs for the boys'. Iwan, a member of the Eisteddfod council, insisted the contributions helped the economy of the areas the festival visited from year to year.

'This talk about the language is all very well but what do you intend to do for Anglesey?' another questioner asked.

'Of course we need jobs. The future of the language depends on there being good quality jobs in the Welsh-speaking areas.'

Whether there would be a political realignment once a Welsh Assembly was established was another question. Iwan answered that Plaid Cymru would split three ways. Left wing elements would likely go one way, and the right wing another. That would leave a moderate core to continue nation-building, which he said was what the party was essentially about.

*   *   *

The election failed to produce a clear majority at Westminster. Overnight there was talk of a coalition. Meanwhile, the battle in Carmarthen continued as recount followed recount. It was clear the result might have an impact on the formation of the next government.

For twenty-four hours following the close of poll political eyes across the United Kingdom focused on Carmarthen. At the end of the first count, a little after 3am, the Labour candidate, Gwynoro Jones, was ahead of Gwynfor Evans by just ten votes, 17,205 to 17,195. A recount was immediately called and tension mounted.

Gwynoro, who had won the seat from Gwynfor in 1970, was on tenterhooks. He moved restlessly from one pile of voting papers to the next, often hovering at the table where the totals were displayed. Every now and then he went over to the returning officer to inspect the slips that had been spoiled. He would hold one up against the light, anxiously examining whether it was a vote for him. Cyril Hughes, Gwynfor Evans' agent, undertook the same task.

In a closely fought election, Plaid had by far the better

organisation. It had thirty-two party branches across the large constituency where none had existed twenty years before. A first canvass had been completed within a week of the election being called. However, the Gwendraeth and Amman valleys in the southern half of the seat were dominated by coal mining. There the miners' pay claim eclipsed other issues. Gwynoro, whose father was a carpenter at the Cynheidre colliery, had the stronger credentials.

For his part Gwynfor emphasised essentially moral themes. One of his leaflets referred to the importance of keeping Christian civilisation alive in Wales.

At 6.50am the third count put Gwynfor ahead by four votes. Labour's agent Ivor Morris immediately demanded a further recount. However, the tired and bleary-eyed clerks and count officials needed a break. The returning officer announced they would resume at 4pm that afternoon. Gwynfor went home to Llangadog for some sleep. By then it was clear that Britain would have a hung Parliament, the first since 1929.

The result of the fourth Carmarthen count was declared at 7.35pm. Labour was ahead of Plaid Cymru, but by just one vote.

Following a fifth count Labour was still ahead, but now by three votes. It was ten o'clock. Gwynfor came under intense pressure to demand a sixth count. There was talk of a handful of votes found in a rubbish bin. However, wiser counsels prevailed. One of Gwynfor's supporters, Wynne Samuel, clerk to Tenby's urban district council and a veteran nationalist, advised that it was far better to lose by three votes than win by the same margin. Another election would probably be held within a year. Then the momentum and public sympathy would be with Gwynfor. And so it proved. In the following October election, he garnered 23,325 votes, 3,440 ahead of Labour.

*   *   *

During the highs and lows of his count, Gwynfor had been fortified by news that Dafydd Wigley had won in Caernarfon and Dafydd Elis-Thomas in Meirionnnydd. Meanwhile, in Scotland the nationalists had taken seven seats. As Owen would later write, 'When you have spent forty years campaigning in what at times must have seemed a wilderness, a three-vote margin in your own election, two Plaid Cymru MPs elsewhere, and the probability of a nationalist balance of power at Westminster must be something of a miracle.'

He arranged to interview Gwynfor the following Sunday and reached Talar Wen, his home outside Llangadog, by mid morning. It seemed as though the election was still underway. Visitors arrived in a stream and the telephone rang endlessly. A telegram was delivered from the SNP President Robert MacIntyre: *Regret three tragic votes against the future of Wales, Scotland, and England.*

Owen carefully edged his way through the kitchen where Gwynfor's daughter Meinir and several other of his children were repainting campaign banners. They were to welcome home Meinir's husband, Cymdeithas yr Iaith leader Ffred Ffransis, after a nine-month gaol sentence.

Owen and Gwynfor retreated to the study, where large wall-length windows presented a fine view of the Tywi Valley beyond the trees that ringed the garden.

'We underestimated the rise in the Liberal vote,' Gwynfor began. 'Except for that we would have won easily. I suppose the same effect was everywhere, the impact of television.'

'But still, winning Caernarfon and Meirionnydd is a breakthrough,' Owen said. 'I sensed something was moving when I was in the north last weekend.'

'Indeed, and it's important in more ways than one. Dafydd Wigley's position in Parliament gives him a great advantage in the party, which is all to the good. There's been a massive shift in the leadership from the south to Gwynedd, not just as far as Westminster is concerned but even more in local government. I think Dafydd's position is now unassailable. Gwynedd will be setting the pace for years to come.'

'And yourself?'

'I don't know. The next few years are going to be important. I reckon I've got another decade in me to make a difference.'

Pontypridd
March 1974

'Our job is to blow a few deflating raspberries at the Welsh establishment,' John Tripp was saying. Leaning back in his chair in the back bar of the Conway pub in Pontcanna, he took a draught from his pint and wiped his mouth and moustache with the back of his hand. Facing him across the table were Owen James and Tom Davies, a freelance journalist working mainly in London. The three were the collective mind behind *Nails*, an abrasive and irreverent arts programme broadcast once a month by HTV.

Davies, son of a Pontypridd coal merchant, had started his career at the *Western Mail*, but swiftly made it to Fleet Street. He was the programme's anchorman, hard-boiled, cynical, a completely professional reporter.

Tripp warmed to his theme.

'They take the gaiety out of life, the black deacons who patrol the boundaries of acceptability.'

Owen laughed, but Tripp was not to be interrupted.

'Their rules about what passes for culture are bound up with respectablity. They stamp everything in sight with their mark of solemnity.'

'Too bloody right,' Tom Davies agreed. 'Take this character Bobi Jones. Brought up in Cardiff, proper English-speaking like, tidy you might say. Trouble is he learns Welsh at school and then goes off to Dublin and now Aberystwyth. Learns Welsh, he does, and then starts attacking his own people.'

'How do you mean?' Owen asked.

'Well, he says that Anglo-Welsh writing, in so far as it exists – can you beat that, in so far as it exists – is a perversion. Calls it a grunt – a grunt! Says it's an odour, rising out of a cultural wound. Talk about bloody pompous.'

'What's his point? That if we write in English it can't be Welsh writing?'

'Exactly. Says it's not Welsh at all.'

'What is it, then?' Owen asked again.

'He reckons that if all we were left with in Wales was writing in English, if say, the Welsh language had died out, then all that would remain would be a provincial form of English writing.'

'He wouldn't dismiss Australian writing in that way,' Tripp said. 'Or Canadian, or Nigerian for that matter.'

Tom stood up and collected their empty glasses.

'He thinks that if we write in English, we end up in some kind of no man's land.'

'Is it because we're immediately next door to England?' Owen wondered. 'Is that why he's saying that writing here is different from somewhere like Australia?'

'That would be to give him the benefit of the doubt.'

Tom went for more drinks.

'Maybe we could make something of this argument,' he said when he returned. 'Get this Bobi Jones character on, grill him.'

'He'd never agree,' Owen said. 'He'd know we'd string him up.'

Tripp put his pint on the table and leant forward, half a smile passing across his face.

'Why don't we just invent someone. A poet, say, who's been ignored by the Establishment, the Arts Council and the rest of them.'

'You can't interview a non-existent poet,' Tom said.

'What if he's died?' Tripp persisted. 'Yes, let's say it's the anniversary of his death and we're digging him up as it were, paying homage, giving him a voice and the exposure he never got in life.'

'Could be interesting.'

'Let's call him Viriamu Lewis.'

'Viriamu?' Owen queried.

'Yes, like Viriamu Jones,' Tripp said. 'The first boss of Cardiff University. They've got a statue of him. He was named after some missionary called Williams. He went to a south Pacific island where the natives corrupted his name to Viriamu. Got their own language. Erromanga it's called. They also ate him by all accounts, made him into a martyr.'

'What a great story,' said Tom Davies. 'Perhaps we should do something on him.'

Tripp was not to be diverted.

'Our Viriamu is Viriamu Lewis. For years he's lived alone in Pontypridd, in total obscurity. Never received a travel grant, writers' bursary, nothing at all. No invitations, lectures, or readings. Cruelly neglected, he was. Rejected by the great and the good. Died in poverty and despair.'

* * *

A chance encounter had sparked Tripp's idea. He'd been at the Chepstow races and won some money. In the bar, he'd run into a strange character. Small, stocky, bald, brown faced, and puffing a woodbine the man looked for all the world like a shrivelled walnut. Over a drink he confided he was an aspiring poet, trying to get published. He had paid a vanity press in Brighton to include a few of his poems in an anthology, but had yet to see the outcome.

Later they sat down at a small table where the man produced a notebook, with some of his poems. Tripp read through them and made encouraging noises. The poems were unremarkable but not dreadful, not much worse than many he had seen in small press poetry magazines. He gave the man the addresses of a couple of editors who might be interested, and they parted, never to meet again.

When Tripp thought of the man at the racecourse he also thought of his own predicament, his long periods of isolation trying to write in his Whitchurch wilderness. It also made him think of Idris Davies, another poet who in his time had failed to achieve recognition by the arbiters of the culture. To all intents and purposes, Viriamu Lewis was John Tripp himself, though he did not admit this to Gareth Jones, the *Nails* director, when they met in his Llandaff flat to discuss the idea.

In his early twenties and still a trainee, Jones was regarded as something of a rising star at HTV. A public school education, followed by Cambridge, had provided him with the easy confidence of someone well beyond his years. He had been brought up in London, but his family roots were in Ceredigion.

Over a bottle of Jameson's whiskey, Gareth Jones needed little persuasion. They discussed logistics. Jones suggested they use a dilapidated barn at the end of the garden behind the large Edwardian house in which he had his top floor flat. They could make it appear as the place where Viriamu Jones had spent his last days.

'We'll need to do a spot of filming in Pontypridd, though I guess we'll have some library footage.'

Gareth Jones dispatched Tripp to deliver a script.

* * *

A week later, the film crew decamped from HTV's Pontcanna studios for Pontypridd, picking up John Tripp in Whitchurch. It was a crisp, blue day that gave a bright clarity to the sides of the Taff valley. They found a spot in Ynysangharad Park with views of terraced housing clinging to the slopes behind the town. While the camera was being set up the director organised some practice runs. Tripp spoke as he walked towards the camera, stopped in front of it and then looked away into the distance as he finished.

After a few rehearsals, Tripp declared he was ready. He eyed the production assistant, dressed in a pink leather jacket, white shirt and tight blue jeans. She raised her clapperboard, snapped it together with a loud retort, and shouted, 'Viriamu! Take one!'

Tripp walked purposefully towards the camera.

> 'Viriamu Lewis, who was born here in Pontypridd and where he spent most of his life, was a man of his people and his time. He shared his people's experience of industrial decline, unemployment and, of course, poverty. But there was more, much more to it than that.'

He stopped and glanced upwards towards the hills, before resuming his walk.

> 'The people of these Valleys created the industrial revolution, a moment of worldwide enduring significance. They made the Valleys a crucible for the creation of the modern world. The coal extracted from places like this flowed through Cardiff's docks and fuelled the world's fleets.'

Tripp halted, turned, and looked directly into the lens.

> 'This continued for the best part of a century and culminated in the defeat of the General Strike of 1926. Then began the long decline that has continued through most of this century.'

Tripp paused, passed a hand across his mouth and then spoke in a more intimate, persuasive manner.

> 'But this does not mean the story of these Valleys is insignificant and only of local interest. And neither is the work of their great chronicler, Viriamu Lewis. Yet the way he has been ignored, both in life and death, may lead you to suspect that is the case.'

'Great, John,' Gareth cried. 'That'll do. We'll be calling you one-take Tripp before long.'

* * *

In Cardiff the film crew stopped for a coffee in Gareth Jones' flat. Later, they repaired to the crumbling barn in the garden below and fitted out a makeshift bed from boxes. They littered a table with papers, and found a few bookcases and a camping stove. These provided images for a commentary on the poet's background. The camera roamed about, picking up the residue of the poet's life, his manuscripts, books, pictures, cooking utensils, and the solitary bed.

Sunlight streaming through the broken windows, gave the interior a warm glow suggestive of a Mediterranean location. The camera shots were put together like a sequence of Impressionist paintings. Tripp found an ancient sepia photograph of his father Paul, as a young man, to stand in as an image of the poet. He held it as he sat on a stool in the middle of the barn.

Staring into the camera he continued to speak with the soft, confiding tone he had adopted previously.

> 'Those critics who have taken any notice of Viriamu have judged him a minor poet. They have damned

him with faint praise while always paying due reverence to his role as a spokesman for his people, the people of these Valleys. Of course, they do not question his sincerity. They could hardly do that. What they do question, however, is his felicity with language.'

Tripp stopped and waited for the camera to change position. Then, on Gareth's signal he turned on his stool.

'It's hard not to conclude that they do so because Viriamu wrote in English. They immediately move to the judgement that, because he uses the language, the cadences, and the dancing vowels of his people, he must necessarily be provincial. Some have accused him of being a regional poet. Others have even described him as pathetic. But as Viriamu himself put it...'

Here Tripp paused, lifted an unidentified thin booklet which in fact contained his own poems, and leafed through the pages.

> *Little gift for our native tongue*
> *has not left us speechless*
> *as we remind the governors that the governed*
> *have souls.*

Looking up he glared coldly at the camera,

'What, we are entitled to ask, is parochial or pathetic about that?'

Gareth Jones provided the film's finishing touch. The graphics people in the studio had prepared an authentic-looking blue-and-white memorial plaque. Stuck on to the barn wall with Blu Tack it stated simply, 'Viriamu Lewis, Craftsman in Letters, Lived Here'.

Tripp stood alongside it to deliver his closing lines.

> 'What, finally, does the life and work of Viriamu Lewis tell us? Simply this, it seems to me. The two so-called tribes of the Welsh, those who speak the ancient tongue and those who do not, are not separate races that, through a matter of chance or accident happen to be located in the same part of the earth's territory.'

Tripp raised a hand to touch the plaque, as though caressing it, looking intently at the camera as he did so.

> 'No. They are not different nationalities, such as you might describe the English- and French-speakers in the Canadian province of Québec. No! We are one people, sharing in our own peculiar way our own distinctive identity. Our consciousness may have been split by the oppression of past conquerors. Indeed, some political forces in our own times have continued to promote our schizophrenic tendencies. Viriamu knew who they were. But in the end our cultural and, yes, it needs to be said, our political solidarity can triumph. That is the great message and legacy of Viriamu Lewis.'

Tripp reached into his inside pocket, and took out a sheet of paper. He said this was his tribute, as one poet to another.

His art was blunt inside its shattering glove,
His spleen well thrust against a failure of heart.
He offered no quarter to the grubbing merchants of cant.

*   *   *

After the programme had been recorded and a couple of hours before it was due to be broadcast, Gareth Jones, Tom Davies, Owen and John Tripp gathered in the Pontcanna studio club for a drink. Wynford Vaughan-Thomas, the white-haired, ruddy-faced founder and director of HTV, joined them.

'What have you got going out?'

'Oh, we've done a piece on that Pontypridd poet, the late Viriamu Lewis,' Tripp said, without the trace of a smile.

'Ah yes,' said Wynford. 'He never had enough recognition, that one.'

Edinburgh
May 1974

Rhiannon boarded the train standing in Aberystwyth station just after six o'clock on a Friday evening. It would take more than four hours to reach Birmingham where she had booked a night sleeper for Edinburgh. The next day she was due to deliver a paper to a conference at the university's politics department.

She felt excited but nervous. It had all seemed so straightforward when she had first responded to a call for papers on the theme of language, identity and nationalism. John Mackintosh, the head of the department, had responded with an enthusiastic letter. From the letterhead Rhiannon saw he was not only a politics professor but also a Labour MP, for Berwick and East Lothian. He wrote warmly about her suggestion that the ideas of Frantz Fanon could add a new perspective on the identity dilemmas underlying the devolution debate. He had spent time at the University of Ibadan in Nigeria, and was familiar with Fanon's work.

'I think it's right that what is happening now in the developed world in places like Catalonia and Scotland should be viewed against the backcloth of the retreat from empire,' he wrote.

But now, as she settled in her seat, Rhiannon worried at the relevance of the paper she had prepared, about black identity in Martinique.

She glanced out of the window as the diesel train gathered pace eastwards towards the rising hills at the head of the Ystwyth valley. Soon it swung northwards following the coast. Rhiannon was familiar with this part of the journey, as far as the sands of the Dyfi estuary where the train turned eastwards once more, pausing at Machynlleth station. Then it sped into the gathering dusk and new territory for Rhiannon, passing through Cemmaes Road, Llanbrynmair, Caersws, and on through Newtown and Welshpool into England.

She extracted a file from her large handbag and spread its contents on to the table between the seats. Leafing through one of Fanon's books, she stopped at a paragraph she had underlined.

> Every colonised people – in other words, every people in whose soul an inferiority complex has been created by the death and burial of its local cultural originality – finds itself face-to-face with the language of the civilising nation; that is, with the culture of the mother country.

'Could we say England was the civilising nation in Wales?' Rhiannon pondered. 'Hardly.' But she read on, following the lines she had underscored with a red pen.

> The colonised is elevated above his jungle status in proportion to his adoption of the mother country's cultural standards. He becomes whiter as he renounces his blackness, his jungle.

This was to be a key text for her presentation. In her notes Rhiannon asked, 'Could we say that, by analogy, the more they adopt the English language, the more the Welsh become English?' Then she added, 'I'm not sure that such a question would be asked in Scotland, but it certainly can be in Wales.'

* * *

The sleeper that had begun its journey in Plymouth rolled slowly into Birmingham's New Street station at eleven o'clock.

Owen had boarded the train at Bristol Parkway a few hours earlier and now stared from the restaurant car at the dimly lit platform as the train jerked to a halt.

Yellow neon lights reflected back off a swirling mist, giving the few people waiting a ghostly appearance. Suddenly Owen thought he recognised a girl who was stepping aboard the train a few carriages down. He pulled down the nearest window and leaned out for a better view, but by then she had vanished. Without pausing to think he walked down the narrow passage that lined the sleeping compartments. Pushing through the doors that separated the carriages he walked on until, through an open doorway, he saw her. She was heaving a rucksack on to a top couchette and had her back to him.

'Rhiannon?'

She turned.

'Rhiannon Jones-Davies, isn't it?'

'Why, yes.'

Owen made a half-step involuntarily into the compartment as the train lurched to a start.

'We met a few months ago. In the Cŵps in Aberystwyth.'

'You're the journalist.'

'Yes, that's me, the *Western Mail*.'

'What? I mean why?'

'I'm off to Edinburgh for the weekend, for a conference, as a matter of fact.'

'Not at the university? The one being run by the politics department?'

'You as well? What a coincidence. Look, why don't you join me for a drink in the bar a few carriages back, I mean when you've sorted your things out.'

Rhiannon hesitated for a moment, then smiled.

'Well thank you, yes, I will. Just one drink mind. It's rather late.'

When she found him a few minutes later, Owen noticed that she had changed from jeans into a skirt and let her hair down.

'Will you have a Scotch or perhaps a glass of wine?'

'No, no,' Rhiannon laughed. 'A coffee would be fine.'

When he returned with the drinks, Owen saw she had taken the conference folder out of her handbag and he nodded towards it.

'I didn't notice your name.'

'I'm involved in the afternoon session *Voices of Identity*. There are two other speakers as well, postgraduates at Edinburgh I think, from Catalunya and Québec. And you?'

Owen placed their drinks on the table between them.

'I'm part of the *Devolution and Democracy* roundtable in the morning.'

Puzzled, Rhiannon looked at him.

'You're wondering how I got involved. Well, it was through John Mackintosh.'

'Professor Mackintosh.'

'Yes, I met him in Westminster. He's an MP as well, you know.'

'I did see that.'

'He liked some articles I had in the *Mail*, about the patronage state.'

'The patronage state?'

'It's one of the main arguments for devolution, the democratic argument if you like. All the appointed bodies. Well, as I say, John liked them, the articles that is. He asked me to speak about the whole thing. So here I am.'

Rhiannon sipped her coffee.

'Tell me about this - what do you call it?'

'Patronage state.'

'Yes.'

'Basically, it's an argument about the way we're governed - or rather, administered.'

'Aren't they the same?'

'Not altogether. The point I've been making is that, over the last hundred years or so, there's been a lot of change at the Wales level but the local administration has remained virtually unaltered.'

'You mean the local councils.'

'Yes.'

'But aren't they being reorganised now?'

'That's true, but in practice it won't alter much. Make things worse, in fact. They're reducing the number of authorities, changing the boundaries, but the functions will remain the same and there'll be no change to the way they're funded. In Wales, we're having eight new counties and thirty-seven districts, whereas before we had thirteen counties and one hundred and sixty-eight urban and district councils. So that will mean a big drop in the number of elected councillors, a reduction in democracy.'

'So where does your patronage state come in?'

'Well, as I say, the structure of government has remained more or less the same since the 1880s, but in that time society in Britain has changed dramatically. There's been urbanisation, for a start, with large increases in the size of our cities. Then there's been a massive growth in central government activity, the number of civil servants, the bureaucracy.'

'I still don't see.'

'These and a host of other changes – mass communication and television, for another thing – they've all changed the nature of administration. Local authorities, which managed quite well a hundred years ago, simply can't cope today. They don't have the resources. They've abandoned many of the services they used to be responsible for, like health, water, gas, electricity, forestry, tourism… the list goes on.'

'So who runs them?'

'The government in London, but crucially through appointed boards, agencies and committees. They operate mainly at the regional level in England and, of course, at the national level in Wales and Scotland. It's a largely unknown but very important layer of government. And because it's unknown it's unaccountable.'

'So this is the patronage state you're talking about.'

'Exactly. Some of them operate for Britain as a whole, but most of them are run regionally, as I say. So in Wales we have the hospital board, the gas and electricity boards, the tourist board, the water authority and the rest. I've researched it and reckon that altogether the Secretary of State for Wales makes around seven hundred appointments to about seventy-five appointed bodies.'

'Good heavens.'

'I'm having another drink. Would you like one? Scotch?'

'Yes, well alright, thanks.'

Owen returned from the bar to find Rhiannon with her elbows on the table, holding her chin with her hands studying him closely.

'So this patronage state, these appointed bodies you're talking about, is why we need devolution, the Welsh Assembly they're talking about.'

'It's the democratic argument. There are other reasons, too, more nationalist arguments. But democracy is the key, I think.'

Rhiannon smiled.

'Nationalist arguments?'

'Yes, you should know. Wales is a nation and so should control its own affairs, all that kind of thing. That's where it gets controversial, wouldn't you say?'

'So it's better to stick with democracy.'

'I think so.'

'But where's the passion?'

Rhiannon looked at her watch.

'Goodness, it's gone midnight. Soon there won't be any point in getting to bed.'

Owen laughed. 'Yes, well…'

Rhiannon stood up and downed her Scotch. As she was leaving, Owen reminded her that the train would arrive in Edinburgh at about six, but they didn't have to get off until eight.

'*Nos da*. Thanks for the drink.'

After she had gone, Owen sat alone for a while swilling the remains of his Scotch around his glass. He realised that he had asked Rhiannon nothing about her own presentation to the conference.

* * *

At just after eight o'clock they met on the platform of Waverley station. Unused to the rhythm of the train, neither had had a good night. They were woken when it stopped at Lancaster and Carlisle. Then at Carstairs junction at the edge of the Scottish Lowlands, there was clanking and shunting as the coaches were separated. Part of the train headed west to Glasgow, while the rest went on to Edinburgh. When the train finally stopped, some passengers immediately clambered out with much attendant disturbance. Owen and Rhiannon dozed fitfully amidst the noises of a railway station coming to life.

Neither had been to Edinburgh before. It was a blustery but blue day, which set off the high black-brown Regency buildings of the city. Out of the station they climbed the short hill to Princes Street, passing the Walter Scott monument. The writer's sculptured figure was enveloped by a toga and encased within Victorian Gothic arches reaching two hundred feet towards the sky.

'The biggest monument to any writer in the world, I've heard,' Rhiannon said.

'Typical of the Scots,' Owen muttered, unable to suppress a growing envy of the Scottish capital's fine architecture that loomed in every direction he looked. To their left the high ramparts of Edinburgh Castle completed a jagged skyline of buildings set against the hills behind, notably the extinct volcano that was Arthur's Seat. To their right was a line of four- and five-story Georgian housing blocks, part of Edinburgh's expensive shopping quarter. Immediately in front of them was the National Gallery, looking like a temple imported from Greece.

They walked along Princes Street for a while before heading back the way they had come. They passed the North British Hotel and turned on to the North Bridge that towered above Waverley station. Behind them was Calton Hill and its collection of Athenian-style monuments poking above the skyline. Owen pointed out the Royal High School with its imposing pillars.

'They say that could be the home of the Scottish Assembly.'

Rhiannon laughed.

'Where's the home of the Welsh Assembly likely to be?'

Crossing the North Bridge, they passed the offices of *The Scotsman*, a huge baronial style structure whose stonework plunged down to a street far below.

'It's not just the magnificence of the buildings, is it, but the way they seem to grow out of the landscape,' Rhiannon said.

A little further on was the university quarter, and they stopped at a café for coffee and a croissant. Afterwards they found the politics department just off George Square, housed in a modern office block that seemed diminished by the grandeur of the Victorian architecture that surrounded it. Inside they were directed to a room on the first floor where a buzz of conversation emanated from a gathering of about twenty people.

'More like a seminar than a conference,' Owen whispered to Rhiannon.

'Thank goodness,' she said, pressing an urn that produced what claimed to be coffee. At the head of a long table that took up most of the room, John Mackintosh was talking with a lanky, sandy-haired man in his mid-thirties who had a look of quizzical earnestness. Rhiannon passed a paper cup to Owen.

'Do you know who he is?'

Owen examined a sheet of paper he had picked up from the table.

'Stephen Maxwell, I think. The SNP's press officer it says here. Bit of an academic as well by all accounts, teaching and research roles in international politics at the LSE, and the University of Sussex as well as here.'

They moved to find a space at the far end of the table as Mackintosh was introducing him.

'Putting party politics to one side and sparing his blushes, Stephen is one of the most original and penetrating analysts of the contemporary scene. He's going to be talking about the historical basis for Scottish nationalism.'

Maxwell's style was quiet and tentative, but if anything, more authoritative for it. His soft Edinburgh accent invited consensus rather than confrontation. Nevertheless, he acknowledged his remarks would puzzle and offend many in his party.

'For most Scots, their nationality is mere sentimentality,' he said. 'It can't be the basis for a modern independence movement.'

Maxwell explained that the history of Scotland was quite different to the other submerged nations of Europe. Owen leant forward with interest and began taking notes. Looking up he realised that he had missed some of the argument. Maxwell was saying that unlike Wales and Ireland, Scotland had the strength to withstand the English military assault on her independence in the Middle Ages. However, that had merely disguised an underlying economic weakness. At some point a political union was inevitable. And when it came in 1707, following dynastic succession, the result was a disabling legacy for the nationalist movement that emerged in the twentieth century.

'Scotland's experience as a junior partner in imperial Britain virtually extinguished her sense of political identity,' Maxwell was saying. 'Her role as the industrial workshop of the world, her share in the international prestige which the English model of parliamentary government enjoyed in the nineteenth century, the career opportunities which the Empire offered to educated Scots... they all seemed to provide an unchallengeable retrospective justification for the surrender of Scotland's sovereignty.'

Owen thought this an extraordinary admission coming from an SNP spokesman. He leant across to Rhiannon.

'I can't imagine anyone in Plaid Cymru analysing our relationship with England like this.'

'But then our relationship has been completely different,' she whispered back.

Maxwell was now arguing that the social relations between the Scots and the English presented none of the obstacles to Scotland's assimilation that the Irish had encountered. Scots were seldom the target of English chauvinism. And unlike Irish immigrants, they shared the religion of their host community.

The Scots also differed from the Irish in escaping the stereotyping which fed the the racialism of the English response to mass Irish immigration. Not only that, the professional classes were strongly represented among Scots immigrants and, by virtue of their superior education, the Scottish working-class were also socially mobile immigrants. Industrialisation was another factor. Coinciding with the heyday of Empire, it created an area of common experience between Scots, English and Welsh which fed the growth of a united British labour movement.

Maxwell was approaching a conclusion and paused to consult his notes, with a wry smile.

'Some nationalists spend a lot of time wishing Scotland's history had been cast in a more melodramatic mould. If only Scotland had been the victim of English armed might as Ireland was. If only the Scots language and culture had been suppressed by the English as the Welsh language and culture were suppressed. If only Gaelic Scotland, crushed by Cumberland had been the whole of Scotland and not just one part of it at war both with itself and with Lowland Scotland.'

He stopped for a moment and placed his notes on the table.

'If only history had treated Scotland with less subtle cruelty, what a lion of a nation we might now be!'

He was rewarded by some low, ironic laughter around the table, making him pause before moving decisively on.

'Nationalism must build on reality. Scots have little cause to be grateful to English governments, but Westminster has not acted towards Scotland as a despotic colonial power. We may resent England, but we do not hate her. To the great majority of Scots, the English are not foreigners as Germans or French are foreigners. Most Scots think of themselves with little difficulty as both Scottish and British.'

There was a round of muted clapping and some fists drummed the large seminar table as he sat down. John Mackintosh rose to his feet.

'That was a powerful analysis. And I certainly agree wholeheartedly with your last point Stephen. But from a nationalist perspective, your account surely presents you with a dilemma. You say we must build on the reality of Scottish identity. If I heard you correctly, you were saying that the SNP cannot rely on historical grievances to build its case. What, then, is going to work for the nationalist cause?'

Maxwell stood to reply.

'When you look at events in Scotland over the past few generations, they lead you to only one conclusion. What we've experienced is a long, slow decline of manufacturing industry, a takeover of Scotland's firms and natural resources by foreign capital, and the demise of our locally-controlled private sector. Since the 1950s we've lost more than 150,000 manufacturing jobs.'

He took a sip of water from a glass in front of him.

'This long decline has destroyed the social and economic base for building an independence movement on the Scottish middle class, what you might call bourgeois nationalism.'

John Mackintosh raised a hand.

'I think what you're saying is right, but when I look at the SNP MPs in front of me in the House of Commons, they are virtually all from the Scottish middle class.'

'That's true, but if you look more closely you'll see they're overwhelmingly from the public sector middle class – that is to say, they all used to work in education, health and social services, and in local government.'

Maxwell hesitated for a moment, as if reconsidering his argument, but then continued in his measured, confident way.

'And it is true as well, that these groups have an economic interest in supporting the creation of a new political system that will insulate the Scottish public sector from London's spending cuts. But important as all that surely is, the public sector middle class is just too small a base on which to build a successful independence movement.'

'So where do you look?'

'There's only one place. We must look to the working class to supply the core of our vote. It offers the only possible base for a popular nationalism. The Upper Clyde campaign in 1971, and the swing of working-class support to the SNP in the last election suggests that it has retained at least some potential for radical action.'

'But aren't they the natural constituency of the Labour Party?' asked someone halfway along the table.

'Certainly, the Labour Party was born of a desire to challenge the class power structure. But that was three generations ago. Today it doesn't challenge. In fact, it actually sustains the existing class structure. Not only that, it's compliant with Scotland's subordinate role within the United Kingdom. It has failed hopelessly to exploit the new bargaining power which North Sea oil has given us.'

'It's still got the support of the unions,' someone else muttered.

'That's true, and it's also got a strong base in local government.'

Still standing, Maxwell leant forward and placed his hands on the edge of the table.

'But, and I think this is extremely significant, Scottish Labour has made no contribution to the recent strategic debates about the future of the Labour Party at Westminster. Indeed, I would go so far as to say that in the eighty years or so since the foundation of the Independent Labour Party by Keir Hardie, only two other Scottish personalities have made any contribution of note to the party's debates. One was John Wheatley in the 1920s and the other is John Mackintosh here, in our own day. But then John is something of a maverick, isn't he, even in his own party.'

And with that he sat down to some laughter, allowing the seminar to take a break for coffee.

*   *   *

Rhiannon had only ten minutes for her contribution later that afternoon. She began by quoting Frantz Fanon. 'To speak means above all to assume a culture, to support the weight of a civilisation.'

Language, she said, was pivotal in the formation of identity and in the relationship between peoples. For Fanon, speaking French meant an acceptance of the collective consciousness of the French. Rhiannon looked around the table, allowing a moment for the import of these words to sink in. Then, from memory, she spoke from notes she had made earlier.

'And that consciousness identifies blackness with evil and sin. So in an effort to escape the association of blackness with evil, the black man dons a white mask – hence the title of Fanon's first book *Black Skin, White Mask*.'

As she said this, she held up a copy of the book and turned it round to reveal the image of its author. Out of the back cover stared the intense features of a man whose eyes conveyed anxiety and a deep intelligence.

However, Rhiannon said she would be examining the work of another man, one who had taught Fanon. This was the poet Aimé Césaire, born in Martinique in 1913 and the most influential Caribbean writer of his generation. It was he who coined the term *négritude*, which gave its name to a literary movement in the 1930s. It was led by French-speaking black writers and intellectuals from France's colonies in Africa and the Caribbean.

She picked up her notes from the table.

'Négritude, Césaire said, and I quote, was "the simple recognition of the fact that one is black, the acceptance of this fact and of our destiny as blacks, of our history and culture".'

The interesting question, Rhiannon continued, was how Césaire and his fellow black writers dealt with the French language. Jean-Paul Sartre had raised this in an illuminating way. He had written that while struggling for their independence most ethnic minorities also passionately tried to revive their national languages. A striking example was Ireland.

'As Sartre puts it, to *be* Irish, one must also *think* Irish, which means above all: think *in* Irish,' Rhiannon said.

'And as he goes on to say, the specific traits of a society correspond exactly to the untranslatable locutions of its language.'

She looked up from her notes around the table to judge the reaction to what she had said. All she saw were expectant, but slightly bemused expressions.

'*Untranslatable locutions...* What did Sartre mean?'

Rhiannon allowed the question to hang in the air for a moment.

'Simply this, it seems to me. Because they did not share a common language, the black poets of the diaspora, in the French colonies, had to appropriate the language of the white coloniser in order to communicate their views.'

Rhiannon saw that Owen was watching her intently as she spoke.

'So where did that leave the emerging black writers in the 1930s and 1940s? Having been dispersed to the four corners of the earth by the slave trade, as I say black men had no common language. Instead they had to rely on the words of the oppressor's language.

'And, since words are ideas, when the negro declares in French that he rejects French culture, he accepts with one hand what he rejects with the other.'

Rhiannon hesitated slightly, before continuing.

'In fact, what he does is to set up the enemy's thinking-apparatus inside himself.'

She paused again, struck suddenly herself by the implications of her argument, some of which had evaded her until now. She placed her notes on the table, knowing exactly how she should continue.

'The black man does not express himself in a foreign language since he has been taught French or English from childhood. So he is perfectly at ease in everyday terms. However, Sartre tells us that when he thinks about his identity, his négritude, he will not use this direct language. He will not speak about his négritude in prose.'

Rhiannon looked up wondering if her audience appreciated the significance of what she was saying.

'Instead, frustrated by prose, he turns to the more abstract construct of poetry. Sartre describes poetry in this context as a dark room where words are knocking themselves about. In fact, he says they are quite mad. As he puts it, they are collisions in the air. He says, *They ignite each other with their fire and fall down.* We must understand this capacity for the poetic destruction of an alien language if we are to understand the black négritude poets. As Sartre says, *Since the oppressor is present in the very language that they speak, they will speak this language in order to destroy it.*

'And Césaire confirmed this rather abstract point in a more concrete way, it seems to me, in an interview he gave in the 1950s.'

Rhiannon reached for her papers and, picking one, she read it out.

> Whether I want to or not, as a poet I express myself in French, and clearly French literature has influenced me. But I want to emphasise very strongly that at the same time I have always strived to create a new language, one capable of communicating the African heritage. In other words, for me French was a tool that I wanted to use in developing a new means

of expression. I wanted to create an Antillean French, a black French that, while still being French, had a black character.

Owen thought Rhiannon's argument fascinating. He could see how her ideas could be applied directly to Wales, not so much to Welsh language writing, but to Welsh writing in English. In a similar way to the black writers, Welsh writers could convey Welsh experiences and identity through the medium of English by creating a Welsh English.

'Especially in poetry,' he thought.

But looking around the room, Owen could see that much of Rhiannon's audience either lacked interest or found the ideas too theoretical. He was glad for her sake when her presentation came to an end.

*   *   *

That evening John Mackintosh had booked the Calvados, a small French restaurant in the Royal Mile, for the seminar's speakers. Owen and Rhiannon were staying in university accommodation a half-an-hour's walk away and were a little late when they arrived. Mackintosh rose to greet them as they came through the door, asking them what they would like to drink.

When he returned from the bar he handed Rhiannon a glass of lager and said how much he liked her paper.

'Quite fascinating. In Wales, questions of identity always find their way back to language, do they not? It makes life difficult for you I think.'

'You have your own identity issues as well,' Owen said.

'Yes, but we're rather less complicated. Your nationalist MPs, for instance. I've talked a good deal with Gwynfor Evans and Dafydd Elis-Thomas. They're quite cerebral aren't they, especially when compared with the SNP.'

'We can't all be philosophers,' Stephen Maxwell said with a smile.

'No, no, but your lot are a bit blood-and-soil. You couldn't say that about Gwynfor Evans, such a gentle soul, and so charming.'

'I think you'll find there's steel beneath the soft surface,' Owen said.

'I dare say.'

A waiter appeared, interrupting the conversation. Mackintosh was a genial host, overseeing their orders with a constant stream of advice and suggestions. Owen thought he and Stephen Maxwell had a good deal in common. It occurred to him that they could be characters out of a John Buchan novel. As the waiter circled the table, Owen turned to Maxwell who was seated next to him.

'I was intrigued by your bracketing the professor with John Wheatley this morning.'

'No other Labour figure has contributed so much to the contemporary Scottish debate as John. For the media, he is the authoritative voice on Scottish developments.'

'You say the media.'

'Yes, elsewhere it seems to me he adopts a somewhat plaintive tone when he acknowledges the growing autonomy of the debate in Scotland.'

'You mean in the university?'

'And in the Commons as well. I think there's an ambivalence, the result of his enforced exile in London, I'd say.'

'But no one has a more consistent record of support for devolution.'

'That's certainly true, goes back to the 1950s. But his approach is essentially British. He sees it as part of a British-wide reform, including devolved structures for England and, of course, Wales.'

'But that's the essence of what devolution's about, surely?

'Yes, but don't you see, for John that involves denying Scottish nationalism the status of being a genuine nationalism.'

Owen was puzzled. 'I'm not sure I follow.'

'For John, Scottish nationalism is neo-nationalism and not what he would think of as *real* nationalism, of the kind you might find in colonial Africa for instance. For him, Scottish nationalism is just a response to worldwide problems Britain shares with other highly developed political systems. Of course, it has an edge, sharpened by a residual sense of Scottish identity.'

Rhiannon, who had been listening intently from the opposite side of the table, leant forward.

'So for you, it's his British outlook that's the problem?'

'In essence, yes. What blocks John's vision is his insistence that the Scots have a dual identity, that they are both Scots and British. And for him it's the British aspect that comes first, certainly as far as politics are concerned.'

Owen noticed that Mackintosh had heard the latter part of their exchange. Now he intervened.

'Look, there's no mystery to any of this. It's simply factually the case that since 1707, the Scots have operated inside a British political system. That may or may not be desirable, depending on your point of view, but it's a fact.'

'I think Stephen is saying it's a question of the priority you give to Britishness,' Rhiannon said.

Mackintosh gave her a warm smile.

'I don't see it as a matter of choice or even priority, as you put it. It's the same in Wales, surely? You see, you can be British for certain purposes and be Scottish for others. A Scotsman can belong to a Scottish regiment within the British army. He can play rugby for Scotland and for the British Lions. Are the Scottish universities part of a vertical pattern of Scottish education or are they part of a horizontal tier of UK higher education? The answer is that they are both.'

Stephen Maxwell leant back in his seat, and threaded his fingers together. Owen thought he seemed slightly amused by the argument. Now he leant forward again and addressed John Mackintosh directly.

'Your fixation on the duality of our identity, as you put it, is a residue of a rapidly wasting sense of British identity. If we examine Scottish cultural history, where is the British political identity you speak of? If such a hybrid as British culture ever existed, it was surely only in the nineteenth century in the thinking of such Anglo-Scottish figures as Macaulay, Carlyle and Ruskin.'

Mackintosh bridled for a moment, but then his customary charm and good humour got the better of him.

'You said a moment ago that, when I say that we Scots have a dual identity, I'm denying Scottish nationalism its status as a full or proper nationalism. But surely that's true in one obvious sense. Scotland has not been independent and therefore has simply not had that form of nationalism – the kind that arises in France or Germany. But you appear to be saying that a *full* or *proper* or *complete* nationalism can be discernible even when the institutional conditions do not exist.'

'Absolutely.'

'But historically that's not correct surely? You can't identify a single set of feelings or conditions or objectives which can be said to exist and that when they exist, there is a *genuine nationalism*. It varies from case to case. Sometimes national movements that lack a political or institutional expression base themselves on language, sometimes on race. Other times they just resort to a common historical experience. But in all these cases their nationalism is incomplete. To put it at its kindest, you might say that for them their nationalism is a work in progress.'

At this Mackintosh sat back in his chair, his posture radiating that he felt the argument settled. But Maxwell was intent on pursuing it.

'I think your position can be compared with Pierre Trudeau's confrontation with the Québec separatists.'

'Go on.'

'Like Trudeau, you represent a new reformist element. He believes that the Québecois should adapt themselves to the role of French-Canadians. You believe that Scots should do the same, adopt a dual identity and be Scots-British. As Trudeau sought to reform federal attitudes to accommodate Québec's non-separatist ambitions, so you've laboured to instruct English public opinion to what might be called the new Scottish realities.'

'Well?'

'Well, Trudeau began by patronising the Québec nationalists as narrow-minded chauvinists. Later he learned that they had as keen a sense as himself of the international context in which both Québec and Canada must operate. In just the same way, you once scorned the SNP as political kailyarders. But I think you've now come to see that we have a far more catholic view of Scotland's international links, even if we haven't been familiar faces at Königswinter.'

'Stephen, my most vivid memory of the last Königswinter conference was Margo MacDonald leading the singing of 'Flower of Scotland' late in the evening.'

At this the two men joined together in chuckling. But then Mackintosh continued, more seriously.

'Stephen, there are two ways one can feel Scottish and I have experienced both. One is to feel the resentment. I think you've felt it, too. Against the assumptions of superiority, so evident in the older English universities, in London media circles, and among Whitehall civil servants.'

'You're right about that. And the other way?'

'The other is to be confident that the best of what is done in Scotland and by Scots is as good as anything that those custodians of what they regard as proper standards can produce.'

'I certainly agree with that, as well.'

'I'm not arguing that the SNP are not entitled to fight for independence, not at all. Given sufficient depression of the British side of the dual nationality, and given sufficient stupidity on the part of UK politicians, you might win.'

Mackintosh grasped a bottle of red wine and, to soften what he was about to say, refilled Maxwell's glass.

'But I think you'll still have difficulty in pushing your support beyond a certain level. Too many Scots will be unwilling to let the British side of their consciousness go.'

'That may be,' Maxwell answered. 'But even if you're right in arguing for a British identity, that wouldn't necessarily guarantee the continued existence of the United Kingdom. Norway and Sweden have demonstrated that their national autonomy can co-exist with a common identity, even a common political identity – the Nordic Union and so forth.'

Mackintosh chuckled again.

'Now that's a much more nuanced position than I've heard you suggest before. Who knows, we may get there some day.'

After that the conversation lightened and went on late into the evening about more general, but less memorable things.

* * *

The following day Rhiannon and Owen caught a mid-morning train from Waverley station. Being a Sunday, the journey southwards was slow and tedious, but at least it would get them home before nightfall.

They spoke little to begin with, absorbed in the Scottish Sunday papers. There was no restaurant car but eventually, as the train approached Carlisle, a woman appeared pushing a trolley. Rhiannon bought two coffees and passed one to Owen.

'What did you make of it? she asked. 'The seminar, I mean.'

'I liked Stephen Maxwell's presentation. His take on Scottish history. Makes you realise how different the devolution business is for them.'

'Yes. It's all about their institutions, their legal system, their church, education and the rest.'

'Whereas for us?'

'I don't know. Our culture, I suppose.'

'You mean the Welsh language.'

'Basically, yes. For us, the crucial thing is to have *official* status. That's Cymdeithas yr Iaith's main aim.'

'But why? No one is stopping you speaking Welsh. Thousands do it every day. And it's growing in the schools, isn't it? It's a matter of choice, it seems to me. Take us, for instance. I mean Anna, my wife, and me.'

'Well?'

Owen hesitated.

'We're going to Welsh classes, for one thing. Then again when, if, we have children, we've agreed we'll send them to a Welsh school, *ysgol feithrin* and all that.'

'That's fine, and up to a point you're right. People have to make the choice, to be persuaded. They have to be convinced of the benefits. But don't you see, underpinning it all is the status of the language.'

'No, I don't see. What do you mean by status?'

'How it's regarded officially, by the government and in the courts.'

'How does that affect whether or not someone like me decides to send their kid to a Welsh school?'

'It all goes back to the Act of Union, between England and Wales in 1536.'

'Oh, come on, that's historical hokum. You'll be calling up the ghost of Owain Glyndŵr next.'

'No, no, it's a reality, it still affects how things are. Anyway, it wasn't an Act of Union. Calling it that makes it sound as if it was some kind of agreement.'

'What was it, then?'

'It was an Act of Incorporation. That's what it said, if you look at the wording in the Act. In fact, it was an act of subjugation. From then on anyone who wanted an official position had to speak English. It was a body blow to the language.'

Rhiannon stiffened and stopped to take a sip of her coffee. Owen looked at her anew.

'It was a long time ago,' he said. 'Surely it can't mean that much today?'

'Oh, but it can. It abolished any distinctive governmental or administrative status for Wales, for a start.'

'We've got the Welsh Office.'

'That's window dressing. The crucial thing was that it completely deprived the language of its status. From then on, from 1536, the language was to have no place in the courts or in government. And that's still the case today. That's not window dressing. That's official downgrading. It's the root cause of the position the language is in today.'

'So how do you account for the growth of the Welsh-medium schools, then?'

'There's no denying there's been some progress in the schools. There's also been a continuation of our literary tradition, a revival even in the present century. But the fact is that when Welsh people come face-to-face with authority, dealing with the government, with local government especially, and with the courts, the Welsh language has no place whatever.'

Owen picked up his coffee cup, took a sip and put it down again, trying to absorb what Rhiannon had said. She was plainly convinced, yet it didn't seem that straightforward to him.

'But Welsh is still a living language, even after all this time,' he said. 'How do you account for that? I mean when it's compared with the other Celtic languages, Irish or Gaelic?'

'That's mainly because the Welsh language was sustained by religion, and still is to some extent. In the churches and then the chapels, the language had its place, it had official status there, it was the official language of worship. But in Scotland and Ireland it was quite different. There the language of religion was English. In Wales, it was Welsh. But these days, with the decline of the religion, we can't rely on that.'

Owen thought for a moment. Rhiannon had an answer for everything.

'Cymdeithas has made the case for bilingual road signs. That's been agreed.'

'That's only a start,' she said.

'You've got to start somewhere.'

'Yes, but the basic thing is the lack of status for Welsh legally and in the government, where you're face-to-face with authority. That's led directly to the inferiority of the Welsh language in every other field, whether its education, commerce – wherever you look, in fact.'

Rhiannon put her elbow on the table and her chin on her hand, and smiled at Owen. 'He's obviously sympathetic,' she thought. 'But he doesn't get it. Why, when it's all so clear?' So she tried a different approach.

'Take the post office and getting a tax disc for your car. It may be a small thing, but it's symbolic isn't it? A bigger thing is television, which is why the campaign for a channel is so important. And if you want to pursue any kind of career, then English is essential.'

'I can't see that you'll ever change that.'

'Not if you're pursuing a career in England, I agree. But why should it have to be the case in Wales, in our own country? Anyway, it goes deeper than that even.'

'How do you mean?'

'J.R. Jones puts it best,' Rhiannon said. 'But I doubt if you've heard of him.'

'J.R. Jones?'

'Yes, he was professor of philosophy in Aberystwyth, and later in Swansea. His writings have had a big influence on Cymdeithas yr Iaith. The most important, I'd say, after Saunders Lewis.'

'I have heard of him, come to think of it. It was Cynog Dafis who quoted him to me, or rather at me, at the Plaid conference last year. That's where I saw you for the first time.'

Rhiannon blushed at the memory, but pressed on eagerly.

'Yes, Cynog thinks very highly of him. Quotes him a lot in the manifesto.'

'Manifesto?'

'*Maniffesto Cymdeithas yr Iaith.* Cynog wrote it.'

Rhiannon reached for the large handbag she had placed beside her on the seat and pulled out a bulging file. Leafing through a sheaf of papers, she lighted on one which Owen could see was heavily underlined.

'He points to the psychology of the whole thing. J. R. Jones, I mean. I've translated it. I was going to quote him yesterday, but I didn't have time. I wanted to make the point that the way the colonial system impacted on black writers operated in a similar fashion at home.'

Rhiannon placed the paper on the table between them and then read from it. 'It is but a short step from inferiority to servility, and but another short step to assimilation and *identification*.

'He's talking about the language,' she said, looking up. 'The inferior position the language has been placed in because of its loss of official status.' Then she read more from the passage she had translated.

> Because we feel that we are 'nobody' in the presence of an Englishman, because we admire and envy his superior identity, we identify ourselves with that which makes us feel pathetic and meaningless, and so heal the wound of our emptiness. And central to the pathology of this cowardice is shame for our language. Because we feel inarticulate and tongue-tied under the haughty official state of the 'natural mother tongue of this realm', we identify ourselves with the very language that breeds our inferiority. It may be that English has helped to 'unite' and 'civilise' large areas of the globe, but in Britain it is proof of the Welshman's inferiority. And therefore he adopts it, not so much because of its prestige and convenience as a lingua franca, but in the manner of one stealing a garment to hide his shame.

Owen's brow furrowed.

'Sounds a bit deep to me. I can't see how all that could apply to someone like me who has never had the language to start with, and that's most Welsh people these days.'

'I thought in a similar way until I began to read Frantz Fanon,' Rhiannon answered quickly. 'The whole question of négritude, and the colonial relationship between the superior whites and inferior blacks. There are extraordinary parallels with our linguistic situation in Wales it seems to me.'

'You were implying that yesterday I thought. About the way black poets took over the French language and used it for their own purposes.'

'That's right. And the fact, as Sartre says, that they write in poetry rather than in prose.'

'It made me think how many poets we've produced in Wales. I mean we've a lot more poets than we have novelists, don't we? Perhaps that's the reason.'

'You know I've never thought of that. Maybe it's not so obvious in Welsh language writing as it is in English.'

'Dylan Thomas, Idris Davies, R.S. Thomas, and all the other Anglo-Welsh poets.'

'Yes, though I don't like the term. Shouldn't we say Welsh writers in English?'

After that they spoke desultorily about more commonplace things until, after what seemed many hours, the train arrived at Shrewsbury. There they both alighted, Rhiannon to wait for a connection to Aberystwyth and Owen to join a train to Cardiff.

As he boarded and looked for a seat, Owen glanced through the window. And there, crossing an iron-trellised footbridge to a line on the other side, he saw Rhiannon. She strode across, her rucksack on one shoulder, her red hair flaring behind her in the breeze. Owen was struck by how fragile she looked, vulnerable even, but at the same time how strong, how purposeful, and ultimately for him, how unattainable.

Craswall
June 1974

It was a fine evening as Owen drove cautiously through narrow, high-hedged lanes in the Black Mountains close to the Welsh border. The single-track road curved to the right, then left which, together with the closeness of the hedgerows, reduced the visibility. Owen wasn't sure whether he was in Herefordshire or Wales. He judged he was probably just inside England because he was travelling north and the hill was to his left. It rose steeply, and the sun was about to disappear over its summit. To the right, the flatness of England merged with the sky. There had been showers earlier and the road was still wet. Droplets from the green overhanging branches splattered occasionally across his windscreen. Owen stopped the car to consult his map and felt a stillness descending.

'These roads are like some kind of maze,' he thought as he attempted to work out the direction he was travelling. He resolved to continue to the next junction where a signpost should give him a bearing. If he found himself approaching Hay-on-Wye, he would have gone too far.

Suddenly, as if from nowhere, the Craswall sign appeared, crushed into the hedge at the side of the road. 'You'll find the cottage a few hundred yards further on, on the left,' Raymond Williams had told him on the phone. 'You can't miss it.' But of course he did, and carried on for half-a-mile before turning and driving slowly back to catch sight of the two-storey cottage mounted high above the road. It was shielded from oncoming traffic by an abundance of green vegetation.

Raymond Williams had been an obvious choice to include in a series of articles Owen was putting together in the wake of the election. A leading figure on the intellectual left in England, in recent years Williams had been intent on re-engaging with his native Wales. He'd been brought up in Pandy, not far from Craswall, and had gone to the grammar school in Abergavenny. From there he had been given a scholarship to Cambridge in the late 1930s. Then his studies had been interrupted by the war. He had served as a tank commander in the Normandy landings, crossed France with the allied forces, passed through Paris, then into Belgium and on to Berlin.

After the war, a stream of influential books had flowed from his battered typewriter. He first received international attention with *Culture and Society*, a survey of English writing from 1780 to 1950. It traced a democratic notion of culture, from the industrial revolution onwards, that embraced the totality of human experience. But Owen was more interested in his novels. The first described how a boy who has grown up on the Welsh border leaves to achieve academic success in England. But he returns to discover his roots when his railwayman father is dying. As his fellow novelist Emyr Humphreys had put it, 'Not *Border Country* by Raymond Williams, but rather *Raymond Williams* by Border Country.'

* * *

Owen parked the car in a lay-by some way down the road and walked back to the cottage, mounting steep steps in a gap in the hedge to find a patio with an iron table and a few wooden kitchen chairs. A typewriter, together with books and papers, covered the table. Owen stood for a moment, taking in the tranquillity of the scene, before Williams suddenly appeared, bending slightly as he came through the cottage door. He was tall, stooped and his craggy face creased into a smile as he greeted Owen.

'You must be the man from the *Western Mail*. I think this is the first time our national newspaper has taken any interest in my work. Wait here and I'll bring us a pot of tea.'

Owen sat at the table wondering how he should begin their conversation. He was struck by how unlikely a figure Williams appeared. A large man, with a slow-moving gait, he was dressed in wide brown cord trousers and a checked woollen shirt open at the neck. He spoke with a soft burr that seemed to emanate from the Gloucestershire border. Altogether, he was more like a sheep farmer who had just walked off the Black Mountains than the Cambridge don Owen had imagined himself meeting.

When Williams returned bearing a tray with a teapot, a half-filled milk bottle and a couple of mugs, Owen ventured, 'How did you find this place?'

'Oh, that was quite a while ago, sometime in '68. The baker who delivered to the house told my mother about it. She still lives in Pandy about ten miles away. You must have come through it to get here. An elderly woman had lived here for many years and it was more or less in ruins when we found it. We've had to do it up from scratch. The roof was fallen in, even. But it's a great place to work, very quiet, you know, and the hills are on the doorstep.'

He got up and pointed to the slopes behind the cottage.

'We're on the eastern edge of the Black Mountains.'

'We're in England, then?'

'You could say so. England has the richer lowlands, Wales the hills. But historically the border has always been contested. These days it runs along the top of the ridge, the line of Offa's Dyke.'

Williams brought out his pipe, and as he lit it, Owen asked, 'You were brought up near here?'

'Not far. In Pandy, in fact, in the house where, as I say, my mother still lives. That's on the Welsh side of the border.'

'Were you aware of that when you were growing up? I mean being on the border?'

'Well, there was a sense, you know, that when we looked west we saw Wales and when we looked east we saw England.'

As he spoke Raymond gestured upwards to the hill rising above them, and then pointed to the lowlands in the opposite direction.

'This area was anglicised as long ago as the 1840s – the moment when mothers stop speaking with their children in Welsh, as it is said. In fact, of course, there was an intense and conscious pressure through the schools to eliminate the language.'

'The Welsh Not.'

'Much more than that. What I didn't realise when I was growing up, in the twenties and thirties, was that the grammar schools were implanted in the towns for the purpose of anglicisation. They imposed an English orientation, which cut you off from any sense of Welshness, cut you off completely.'

'Would the people in your village, your father for instance, would they say they were Welsh? Did they talk about that sort of thing?

Williams relit his pipe.

'They were very puzzled by it, as a matter of fact. I heard them talking about it. I think the sense of a *local* identity was much stronger.'

'It's much the same where I come from, in Pembrokeshire.'

'There are good historical reasons for it. Wales has never been a nation in a formal sense.'

'I'm not sure I follow.'

'It's had a cultural rather than a national existence, wouldn't you say? That's how it seems to me anyway. It was incorporated into England before it developed a really separate national identity, certainly in any political sense. So people would always ask what Wales actually was. This is how, in the end, I understood the question myself. I've found that virtually all Welshmen ask themselves what it is to be Welsh. It's a characteristic thing.'

'I suppose it is. Yes, you're right. We always ask where people are from, as if they can't just be from Wales. First they have to come from somewhere else, somewhere specifically in Wales.'

'That's true. Of course, growing up on the border was more problematic than in the north or west, say, in the still Welsh-speaking communities. They're that much further away from England. But for us there was a curious sense in which we could speak of both the Welsh and the English as foreigners, as not us. That may seem odd, but historically it reflects the fact that this was a frontier zone. It was the location of fighting for many centuries.'

'Did you ever consider yourself British?'

'That? No, not at all. Anyway, the term wasn't used much, except by people one distrusted. *British* was hardly ever used without *Empire* following, and for that nobody had any use at all.'

Raymond stood up and gathered his papers. 'It's getting a bit damp. We'd better go in.'

* * *

Owen followed him, carrying the typewriter. Inside there was a large room with an open plan stairway and a door leading to the kitchen. Tidy chaos reigned. Along one wall a large settee was covered with a few rugs. Owen placed the typewriter on a table in the middle of the room, pushing aside some books and papers to make space. Raymond had disappeared into the kitchen but re-emerged, carrying a bottle of Scotch and a few tumblers.

'You'll have one?'

'Oh yes, but with water please, an equal amount.'

Raymond Williams returned to the kitchen and Owen sat at the table, picking up a book. He saw it was about Euro-communism in Spain. When Raymond came back he changed the subject.

'I wanted to ask you about the political situation, how you see it in the wake of the election.'

'Well, it seems to me we went through the strangest political winter in Britain since the war, wouldn't you say? And against the odds, we've got a Labour government. To say that nobody quite understands it, or even yet quite believes it, would be an understatement.'

'I know what you mean. The result was quite a surprise to me as well. I fully expected the Tories to come back. The polls all indicated it. But I suppose none of us realised how well the Liberals would do.'

'That's right. Nonetheless, there was an important victory, you know. The Conservative government, with their deliberate prolongation of the wages dispute with the miners, had prepared the ground for a defeat of the organised working class. And at the beginning of the campaign it was made quite explicit. The militants, of all kinds, were going to be publicly defeated. "The miners have had their ballot, now we'll have ours," was how one minister put it.'

'Heath couldn't have put it clearer when he said it was about who governs Britain.'

'It was a nastier and much more class-conscious appeal than any that had been made for half a century.'

'Since the twenties, in the wake of the General Strike?'

'Yes.'

'But what exactly do we have now? We seem to be drifting.'

'Labour didn't exactly oppose the Conservatives, did they?

They didn't campaign for the rights of the organised working class. Some of us think they would have done better if they had.'

Raymond stood up and poured some more Scotch.

'Instead we've got this extraordinary fragmentation. In a large turnout, the votes of both Labour and Conservatives fell heavily. The Liberals advanced and there were gains as well for the nationalists in Scotland and here in Wales. In Northern Ireland, the Protestants swept the province. It's a strange situation. An election called in the midst of a bitter confrontation turned into a very quiet, very sober, deeply muddled set of decisions.'

'So what happens now?'

'Well, Labour is in office by default, really. And it can't last. Wilson is managing events quite well. He's good at that. But soon, and probably sooner than we think, he'll go to the country for another crisis management mandate.'

'Do you think he'll get it?'

'In the prevailing muddle there's considerable goodwill for any kind of conciliatory approach. But the underlying pressures – inflation, the trade deficit, balance of payments, the Common Market and the international oil companies – they're all still there and potentially explosive.'

'Listing those things, it feels there's a danger the government will simply be overwhelmed,' Owen said.

'Yes, you're right. It could be replaced by an extreme right-wing government, with a strong electoral majority. That's why I voted Labour in the election. I spoke at a few meetings for our candidate in Cambridge, a good local Labour candidate. There was an overwhelming need to defeat the Conservative political offensive which was supremely dangerous.'

'So the Labour victory, albeit narrow was a great relief, would you say?'

'As I put it in an article the other day, "Vote for them on

Thursday, fight them on Friday!" I said that in 1970 as well. But you know, when the opinion polls continued to indicate a Conservative victory, I felt, as so often in these last few years, that I no longer knew my own country.'

'The polls were extraordinarily misleading.'

'Thank goodness.'

'You said you felt you didn't know your own country?'

'It's a question that presses on me more and more. Wales, Scotland, the industrial North and Midlands, and London – this is the Britain from which I learned my political values. I feel its democratic and potentially socialist culture is still active.'

'And the rest?'

'Yes, the rest, in all of south-east and south-central England – the most populous and affluent regions – there is, in solid majority, a culture with which I have nothing in common. To me it's an alien society. The division is now right in the open and can't be ignored.'

Raymond poured a little more Scotch into their glasses and passed the water jug to Owen.

'This division you speak of, how is going to pan out, do you think?'

'Well, take Wales for example, it's very important there should be a nationalist party introducing another political tendency into the equation, to the left of anything the Labour Party has been since the war. At the same time, to the extent that Britain, as a member of the EEC, is integrated into a European electoral process, alternative alliances will have to be made – at the very least negotiations which are completely blocked in this country, between social democrats, socialists and communists.'

'You reckon all that is destabilising the system.'

'Absolutely. You could say we have two movements that are putting pressure on the system from opposite ends. There's the national movements in Wales and Scotland at one end, and the international movement towards an integrated Europe at the other.'

'I see.'

'I'm sure Tom Nairn is right. You know Nairn, the Scottish writer?'

'I've heard of him.'

'He's been publishing some interesting stuff. Anyway, I'm sure he's right to say that the nationalist movements pose a quite significant threat to the British capitalist state. They could precipitate a crisis in the Labour Party itself if they took away its traditional strongholds in Scotland and Wales.'

'But that's some way off, surely?'

'Maybe. The nationalists did quite well in the election.'

'But for the time being we've got a Labour government.'

'Yes, but a precarious one. There are dangers ahead, you know. I see great danger in the kind of crisis-management Labour government that's come in, but also with a right-wing government which may yet replace it. To hold that off, do I have to support the present government which is hollowing out all its conviction, all its ideals? It's the kind of Labour government that has regularly come in during times of extreme capitalist crisis. First it conciliates, and then it disarms working-class and radical movements.'

Raymond stopped for a moment, stood up from the table and stared at the floor. Then he picked up his glass.

'Some of us believed it would be easier to maintain the real momentum for change if we were facing a weakened right-wing government.'

He drank the small amount of Scotch that remained.

'But that's not the way it has gone.'

The Old College
September 1974

Inside the Gothic interior of the university's Old College, on the seafront in Aberystwyth, Professor Leopold Kohr blinked slightly nervously. Large numbers of students and academic staff were clambering into the serried layers of benches and desks rising in the lecture hall above him. The room was almost full, with well over three hundred people. He caught sight of Rhiannon and a number of his other students near the front row, nodded and smiled.

Seated alongside him was his great friend Alwyn Rees, director of the extra mural Department where he had worked since 1936. He had taken over as director in 1949, the year in which Leopold had first visited Wales. Since then he had come to regard its relationship with England as similar to that between his native Austria and Germany.

Rees leaned forward, touched Leopold's arm and, shuffling his papers, rose to the lectern.

'*Gyfeillion*,' he declared, clearing his throat while waiting for the audience to come to attention. 'Friends, we are indeed fortunate to have Professor Kohr as our lecturer this evening. Many of you will know him and his reputation for what one might say is an unconventional approach to economics.'

Leopold bent his head and reached for the aid attached to his right ear. His hearing had been damaged in Canada many years earlier in an explosion in the gold mine where he had worked. Since then he had grown increasingly deaf, so much so that his hearing aid was now attached to an amplifier device hanging from a cord around his neck. In small gatherings, he could point it towards whoever was speaking and hear what was being said. But this was not possible in a large lecture hall. He worried that he would be unable to decipher the questions following the lecture. Alwyn Rees had undertaken to repeat them to him. For now, pointing his amplifer directly towards Rees, his hearing was unimpeded.

'Leopold has a background that is as interesting and challenging as his views. He is an Austrian. He was educated at Salzburg and at the Universities of Vienna and Innsbruck, the Sorbonne and the London School of Economics. He has received doctorates in law and political science. He once told me that he had practised law only for a few months because he soon found that the best lawyers are those who get their guiltiest clients acquitted.'

As the anticipated laughter interrupted him Rees looked up, smiled and sipped some water from his glass.

'Leopold was a correspondent during the Spanish Civil War, working for the Agence Viator news agency in Paris. He shared an office in Barcelona with Ernest Hemingway, and was an acquaintance there of Eric Blair, better known as George Orwell.'

Some latecomers arrived noisily through the main door alongside the platform and climbed to the back of the lecture theatre. Rhiannon looked at them with an annoyed expression. Alwyn Rees allowed them to settle before continuing.

'Although his lecture this evening is entitled *Is Wales Viable?*, Professor Kohr would not claim to have the cultural and psychological attributes of a Welsh nationalist. Nevertheless, and I think I can say this without fear of contradiction, he sees in the condition of Wales a textbook illustration of a general truth – that provincial participation in the prosperity of a large political unit diminishes with the distance between the province and the centre of government.'

Leopold nodded enthusiastically as Rees, adjusting his spectacles, looked across to him.

'As another election advances rapidly towards us, Professor Kohr's thinking is more necessary than ever.'

* * *

With that, Rees sat down and motioned Leopold to take over at the microphone. However, when he stood before it he found it too high and spent a moment fumbling to lower it, before a student came to his aid.

'Alwyn, as ever you're too kind, too kind,' Kohr began, his thick Germanic accent combining curiously with a soft, melodious tone. The resultant sound provided a cadence to his words that was arresting. Then suddenly, with a theatrical move of his arm, he flung his papers on the desk behind him.

'There is another election on the horizon, as Alwyn has said. It seems to me that Harold Wilson and Edward Heath are in much the same position politically. It's as though they are joint captains of a boat, floating on the Niagara river.'

Leopold looked up at the lecture theatre rising above him and was gratified to see rows of expectant faces.

'The boat springs a leak which Heath's capitalist crew is unable to mend. So the boat is taken over by Wilson's socialist team and we find that their energy and fresh approach is able to repair the defect in no time at all.

'Now all that seems splendid. But, as I said, the boat is floating on the Niagara river. As a result, what has so efficiently been fixed causes the boat to be sucked into the roaring abyss of the giant falls much faster, precisely because it is so much fitter than it was with its capitalist leak.'

Leopold was rewarded by laughter that coursed through the lecture theatre and he noticed Rhiannon smiling at him. He smiled back before continuing, as though they might have been alone together at a tutorial in his office.

'The repair provides the same consolation to its occupants as a Welsh physician said of the well-medicated ever-jogging citizens of the United States. They arrive on their death bed in perfect shape.'

Encouraged by more laughter, Leopold pressed on.

'What the crew should have done is not repair the boat but to let it sink and then swim to the shore. That would have been the saving alternative, and not the attempt to repair the boat or, to pursue my analogy, fill it with a different ideology.'

More laughter went through the lecture hall but Leopold barely paused, continuing over the interruption with one of his favourite devices, a rhetorical question.

'But what is the saving alternative to those offered by right and left for overcoming the navigational difficulties that confront our age?'

He stopped and looked up once more into the depths of the lecture theatre, this time quizzically as though assessing how seriously his query was being taken.

'To give an answer, of which many are tendered, one must first have accurate knowledge of the question. What is the main problem of our age? Is it poverty? Is it hunger? Is it unemployment? Is it corruption, inflation, depression, juvenile delinquency? Is it the energy crisis? Is it war?'

He paused again, allowing the questions time to settle in the minds of his audience, before resorting to another of his favoured ploys, an analogy. He argued that the real problem was similar to the one besetting a mountain climber in the Himalayas. His heart aches, his lungs fail, his ears hurt, his eyes are blinded, his skin erupts, and yet no heart, lung, ear, eye, or skin specialist can help because there is nothing fundamentally wrong with any of his organs. His sole trouble is that he is too high up in the air. In short, he is suffering from altitude sickness. The answer was not to call in specialists but to bring him down to a lower level. Only if he was still in pain would it then make any sense to call in a physician.

Leopold's voice rose, his new tone punctuating his words.

'So it is with the social diseases of our age. It is not poverty that is our problem. It is the vast spread of poverty. It is not unemployment, but the dimension of unemployment which is the scandal. It is not hunger, but the terrifying number afflicted by it. It's not economic depression, but its world encircling magnitude. It's not war, but the atomic scale of war.'

Here Leopold stopped once more for dramatic effect before, moving to a conclusion, his voice gained a higher pitch.

'In other words, the real problem of our time is not material, but dimensional. It is one of scale, one of proportions, one of size.'

The sound of the last word rang in the air as Leopold reached for the papers he had flung on to the desk behind him. Adjusting his hearing aid, he turned back, staring once more at his audience. Then, in a more measured tone, he said, 'Which brings me to the main theme of my lecture.'

At this laughter swept through the hall.

* * *

Looking round Rhiannon could see that, by linking his theme with the immediacy of current events, her tutor had deftly captured his audience's interest. She turned to hear him speaking once more.

'Put simply, can Wales stand on her own feet? This, I have discovered is the most frequently asked question concerning an independent Wales. Can a country of such a small size live? Can it be economically viable?'

He went on to to say that his audience might as well ask whether other small countries such as Norway, Switzerland, Austria, Iceland, Costa Rica, Luxembourg or Denmark were economically viable. Whether they were or not, they certainly existed. Some did so at relatively poor levels, to be sure. But others had living standards that were among the richest in the world. The question followed whether these small states were endowed with more resources than Wales.

'We can ask what were the resources of the barren heights of Tibet which supported the Tibetans until their takeover by a poverty-stricken giant China? Or the frozen reaches of the Arctic which still support the Eskimos? Indeed, there is not a nation under the sun that does not have the resources it needs. Otherwise it would not have come into existence.'

Rhiannon sensed that Leopold's audience was with him, if somewhat sceptically.

'There is a further question, you will say. And that is whether in the twentieth century the Welsh would agree to an independence that, aside from the music of their language, could offer them no more than an Arctic cod-liver-oil or a Himalayan goat-cheese standard of living. Of course not. But neither would the Danes or the Swiss, whose resource-endowment in the conventional sense of the economic geographers is scarcely greater in relation to their populations than that of the Eskimos or the Tibetans.'

Leopold shifted his papers, but they were more of a prop than a prompt. He had delivered these lines many times before.

'But then, it is also said that unlike Wales, other small countries are able to overcome problems of their size and the scarcity of resources because of some very particular circumstances. Switzerland is the banker of the world. Liechtenstein lives on stamps. The Vatican exports theology. Venice, Genoa, and the Hanseatic city-states were the traders of the world, accumulating their riches by fleecing everybody else.'

Leopold looked up at his audience.

'Venice is a particular case in point. It disposes of practically no land area at all. Such is its pitiful resource base that a waiter at a Venetian restaurant once straightened me out when I patronisingly sought to order a local vegetable, by saying, *In Venice, the local vegetable is fish.*'

Laughter flooded the lecture hall once more.

Leopold waited for it to die away before launching into a paean of praise for the natural resources of Wales. They were bountiful in comparison with those enjoyed by Denmark or Switzerland. He extolled Wales's coalmines, slate quarries, steel and chemical industries, farmland and the beauty of her landscape. But Wales' main resource, he insisted, as with most countries, small or large, was the talent of her people.

As he came to the end of his lecture Leopold developed an argument that Wales lacked prosperity precisely because she was not independent. It was her dependence on major centres in England, especially London, and the resultant peripheral status of her economy, that was draining her resources.

'Wales is no more too poor to be economically viable than were the once similarly positioned colonies of America too poor to exist in separation from England. To the contrary, it was their separation that ultimately turned out to be an economic boon for both countries. Separation meant a contraction to more economically manageable proportions for both sides. The result created the foundation for a greater prosperity for England as well as the United States.'

*   *   *

Leopold sat down to applause, and a stamping of feet among his students in the front row. Several people raised their arms. Alwyn Rees pointed to a hand towards the rear of the lecture hall, and leant closely towards Leopold.

'He's asking how Wales can contemplate independence when

232

its economy is so weak. He's quoting statistics compiled by Edward Nevin, you know the economics professor at Swansea. It seems they show a large discrepancy in gross domestic product between England and Wales.'

Leopold stood, took hold of a sheet from his lecture notes and, with great theatricality, tore it up.

'I take professor Nevin's figures and rip them apart,' he declared, his accent pronouncing the word *feegures* having the effect of accentuating his dismissal.

'Let me tell you, the only figures that are completely unassailable are figures you invent! If you wish, I can invent a Welsh budget for you.'

With that he sat down, amidst a mixture of laughter and applause, looking somewhat self-satisfied.

'But Professor Kohr we have to live in the real world,' a woman nearer the front cried out involuntarily. 'Where would the money, the investment, come from if Wales were to go it alone?'

Leopold, having had the question repeated, stepped to the microphone. 'Let us go back to first principles.'

At this point he stopped, his countenance adopting an unusually stern look, as though it pained him to have to state the obvious.

'In the first place, things like roads, factories and power plants are not built with money, they are built with hands. Take for example the Mennonite communities in the United States. They are to this day not only among the most self-sufficient and independent communities in America, but also among the most affluent communities in the world. Indeed, they are world famous as pioneers of agriculture and in the making of tools of such outstanding functional design that many of them have found their way into museums of modern art.'

He went on to extol the fact that, nonetheless, the Mennonite people used no motor cars, petrol, telephones, indeed nothing that was normally associated with the making of wealth. But this did not mean they couldn't produce all they needed. However, all hands had to be employed to produce what was necessary.

At this point Leopold paused, searching out the woman who had put the question. Then, looking directly at her, he continued.

'And since all hands must be employed to secure for them such a high level of prosperity, they also reap the inestimable social bonus of Fritz Schumacher's intermediate technology. So they have no poverty, no crime, no juvenile delinquency, and no unemployment. They are no burden on the American state, and are exempt from the payment of social security taxes.'

Leopold stopped for another moment, as if surprised by his fluency, but almost immediately launched onwards.

'Now, I'm not suggesting that Wales should adopt the Mennonite way of life. What I am arguing is that we should learn the Mennonite lesson that it is labour, and especially unused labour, that is the source of wealth, and not money.'

He halted for a second, bowed his head, clasped his hands behind his back and then took a few steps to the front of the platform. For a moment his audience were left wondering whether he had anything more to say. But he was soon in full flow once more.

'In other words, as long as a country has unemployed labour, it is the same as if it had unused reserves of money lying idle in a bank. In the way Marx defined capital as congealed labour, we may define labour as liquid capital.'

He waited for a moment to let the point sink in.

'Of course, so long as we are trapped in conventional patterns of thought this kind of capital – I mean the unused labour that I've described as liquid capital – is somewhat difficult to withdraw from the bank. But imagine the unconventional circumstances that would arise if a group of unemployed workers on a welfare cruise were to find themselves trapped on a desert island. Discovered years later we would certainly not find them waiting in queues for their welfare cheques.'

A ripple of laughter accompanied this observation.

'No! What we would find is that the liquid monetary state of their labour would have been transformed into capital goods in the form of villages, ships, piers, churches, warehouses, shops, indeed all the requirements of a civilised life.'

'But Wales is not on a welfare cruise and it certainly isn't on a desert island,' objected the woman who had originally put the question.

'Madame, I'm merely asking you to consider the reality of what underlies our thinking about money and investment,' Leopold answered, before conceding that it was necessary to take into account the factors that persuade investors to invest in a country.

He said there were four. First was the opportunity to invest – much greater in a relatively under-developed country such as Wales. Second was stability, and of course Wales was a highly stable country. The third was that a government of a country should want investment, and certainly the government of an independent Wales would want investment. The fourth condition, Leopold said, was about incentives, to persuade investors to shift their money from one place to another, from England or America to Wales, rather than to India say, or Puerto Rico.

Mention of the last, where he had lived for many years, led Leopold to reflect that it had become the world's textbook example for rapid development. This was because it used exemption from taxes as a principal incentive for attracting investment. There were exemptions for ten years in relatively developed areas, and seventeen years in the most retarded regions.

But such initiatives were only available to a country if it were independent. Puerto Rico's government had wanted to develop the country as a tourist destination. However, no one thought it could be attractive to tourists. So the government itself built a hotel, hoping that someone would run it. No one would, except Conrad Hilton, Leopold said, and that was enough.

'Not only did the Caribe Hilton Hotel become the principal jewel in the crown of the Hilton hotel empire, it turned the beaches near San Juan into one of the most glamorous and sophisticated resort areas in the world.'

All this showed there was no reason to believe than an independent Wales would have difficulty in attracting investment. Rather it was the case that, without independence Wales did not have the essential means for doing so.

'Of the four conditions I have outlined as necessary only two of them pertain in Wales at present: under-development certainly and, arguably, stability. Only with independence will come the political will and the means to provide the necessary incentives.'

Alwyn Rees pointed to another questioner, and lent across to speak in Leopold's ear. 'He's asking whether an independent Wales could afford to import the things it cannot produce itself.'

Leopold rose once more.

'My dear young man, from time immemorial the so-called disadvantage of small national size has been overcome by international trade. In that way no country, however small, needs to be excluded from the economic benefits of specialisation and scale.'

Leopold hesitated, thinking over his answer.

'The only possible deficiency a small country could suffer from is a lack of talent amongst its people. Yet, as I've already suggested, talent is equally spread everywhere, as much in Liechtenstein, say, as in the United States. And if we wish to enlarge the base from which talent sprouts, we have the means for artificially stimulating the most barren of social environments with the fertiliser of education. And so far as education is concerned, does not Wales already have an enviable reputation in excelling?'

'But Professor Kohr, even if Wales had the best education system in the world it could not possibly afford to build Concorde,' one of his students in the front row objected.

'Concorde? Of course Wales is too small to build Concorde! But neither can an independent England or France. Instead they do so by pooling their resources. And so could an independent Wales, if it chose. But what sort of Welsh problem would Concorde solve? Could it get you from Aberystwyth to Cardiff faster than by car?'

Amidst the laughter that followed this reply, Alwyn Rees asked if there were any more questions. He pointed to a hand midway in the ranks of benches that led close to the ceiling at the back, and again spoke closely to Leopold.

'She's asking about the Common Market. Wouldn't Wales have to join in with the Common Market and wouldn't that limit her independence?'

Leopold rose again from his seat.

'I have calculated that at least forty international common markets have been negotiated since 1819. So the European Economic Community which Britain has just joined is nothing new. Indeed, a common market is almost never meant as a first step towards political union. On the contrary. When countries decide to set one up it is almost invariably for the purpose of *avoiding* a political union into which they might otherwise be driven.'

Leopold noticed that this last observation induced some puzzled expressions, so he offered his audience another analogy.

'It is comparable to a residential agreement in which the

owners of flats join in the common market of a lift, electricity, heating, water, garage, swimming pool, doorman for the whole building and so on. But is that to prepare themselves for a life in common, for some kind of commune? Certainly not. Instead, it is to strengthen the economic base for their continued existence in the sovereign separation of their separate flats.'

Alwyn Rees pointed to another hand, nearer the front. This time Leopold stepped forward, grasped the amplifier dangling from his neck and pointed it towards the questioner.

'Professor Kohr, it seems clear that, following your last answer, an independent Wales would certainly need to negotiate a common market with England. But what if England were to refuse?'

Leopold stared at his questioner quizzically for a moment.

'My dear young man, I think it was Lord Palmerston who once said *England has no friends she only has interests.*'

Laughter interrupted this observation, but Leopold spoke over it.

'That is true of any country. In their relations with each other all sovereign nations have no friends, only interests. And it would certainly be in the interests of a politically separated England to preserve her continued unimpeded access to the lopsidedly over-developed Welsh chemical and steel industries, and her electricity generation and water supplies, on which England is very much more dependent than Wales.'

Here Leopold ceased speaking and raised his eyes to the ceiling, as if seeking assistance from beyond the lecture theatre. When he continued, it was in a more reflective tone.

'Aside from all that, it is the case that England has never been known to be stingy in her relations with national communities that have decided to take their destiny in their own hands. On the contrary, she has unfailingly offered them the most generous assistance, including the advantages of free trade, common markets, preferential treatments, and even continued common citizenship, as is the case with Ireland. There is nothing in the character or the interests of England to suggest that she would be less co-operative with regard to Wales.'

'Professor Kohr, I don't follow your argument,' another questioner sitting in the front row alongside Rhiannon, interjected. 'On the one hand you say that Wales is presently suffering from her connection with England. But on the other you're arguing for an independent Wales to join in an economic union with England. What would be the difference?'

'The great difference is that Wales would be co-captain of the arrangement rather than the handyman. Not only that, the common market with England that I'm advocating would only be one part of Wales's wider economy. In particular, she would have control of her own separate internal economy.'

He paused again and then reached for another analogy, concerning tax systems.

'The simplest tax system draws from a single source, such as income or property. But the best tax system is the one that draws from a variety of sources, which makes it more productive. Similarly, the simplest arrangement between different communities may be total separation or total economic fusion. But the most fruitful is one that flexibly combines the best features of both.'

However, Leopold's questioner was not assuaged.

'It's difficult to imagine that Wales could be as prosperous as Switzerland as you've claimed. After all, as you said it's a base for a global banking system.'

Rhiannon began to fear for her tutor. She sensed that too many in the audience were discovering a restive scepticism. Leopold himself, however, was undeterred.

'You may think that Switzerland's affluence is a result of her role as one of the world's bankers. But, Switzerland is not prosperous because the banks are there. To the contrary, the banks are there because Switzerland is prosperous. In making that point I paraphrase the great eighteenth century English economist David Ricardo. I repeat, the prosperity of small countries like Switzerland is derived from the genius of their people and has nothing to do with their resources or any other innate advantages.'

At this point Alwyn Rees intervened from the podium.

'I think we should now draw this illuminating, and I think you'll all agree, highly entertaining session to a close... but perhaps there is time for one last question?'

Ioan Thomas, who was sitting alongside Rhiannon, rose to his feet.

'I've enjoyed your lecture immensely Professor Kohr. And I can see, as you say, that there are advantages to the small-scale. But Wales has to live in the real world, the world as it is. It seems to me that your recipe for our future resides in the world of romantic idealism. It would be nice but surely, we can't turn the clock back?'

'My dear young man, your analogy is as weak as your argument.'

His eyes twinkling Leopold advanced to the front of the stage, took his large pocket watch from his waistcoat and extending the chain so he held it in front of him, triumphantly turned back the hands.

'You see I turn my clock back! You say that smallness is just the irrational dream of a romantic. Of course it is romantic. But only to a romantic does life make sense. Starting from nothing and ending in nothing and costing a lot of money in between, in rational terms life is an indefensible loss proposition. Only a romantic can see glory and meaning in the rainbow spanning the two zero magnitudes at the beginning and the end.'

Leopold leant forward to judge whether Ioan had absorbed the import of his message.

'To put your question another way, it is also said that in this age of progress it makes no sense to step back. To which our great Welsh anthropologist and my great and dear friend Alwyn Rees here often replies, and I'm sure he won't mind if I quote him, "When one has reached the edge of the abyss, the progressive step is to take one backwards".'

* * *

As the audience flooded down the steps of the lecture hall and through the double doors that led to the quadrangle on the Old College's ground floor, Leopold was left on the stage talking animatedly to a group of people keen to continue the discussion. After a while Alwyn Rees intervened in an effort to bring the proceedings to a final close. As he did so, Leopold caught sight of Rhiannon.

'Alwyn's hosting a reception in a seminar room upstairs,' he told her. 'Why don't you join us?' Glancing at Ioan who was standing alongside he added with a chuckle, 'And bring along your charming young friend who asks such good questions.'

A short while later Rhiannon and Ioan, after helping themselves to a glass of white wine, were listening to a conversation about the forthcoming election.

'Of course, in Wales all eyes will be on Carmarthen where I'm sure Gwynfor must have an extremely good chance,' Alwyn Rees was saying.

Beside him a colleague added, 'I've lost count of the number of people in the constituency who believe, that, for whatever reason, it was their failure to vote that cost Gwynfor the seat in February.'

Another said, 'I know a family who were travelling back from

London and got stuck in traffic on the M4 the other side of the Severn bridge and didn't get back in time as a result. They reckon it was their three votes that lost the seat.'

Leopold, listened with his amplifier in one hand and a glass of wine in the other.

'But what a melodrama, a community so divided, so conflicted,' he exclaimed. 'It's like a communal form of schizophrenia.'

He turned to Alwyn Rees.

'I'm sure you're right, the three-vote margin will concentrate a lot of people's minds. It will make them determined to vote for Gwynfor this time. You know, Alwyn, I often think of you as the mind of Wales, but if you're the country's mind then Gwynfor is its soul.'

As he said this he saw Rhiannon in the background and, dropping his amplifier, grasped her elbow and pulled her towards him. 'Alwyn I'd like you to meet one of my students. She's reading for a Masters on the Algerian war of independence, making a special study of Frantz Fanon.'

'We've already met, at one if your soirées, as I recall,' Alwyn said. 'Fanon is an interesting case study. The whole period of decolonisation following the war has many lessons.'

Rhiannon was suddenly at a loss. Alwyn Rees was well-known to her but difficult to engage with in a conversation such as this. She knew he was highly regarded by her father, but for his editorship of *Barn*, the monthly magazine, rather than his ardent support of Cymdeithas yr Iaith.

Now he was saying, 'Have you come across the work of Ernest Gellner, a sociologist and anthropologist of some distinction, don't you think Leopold?'

'Of course, of course.'

Turning to Rhiannon, Rees continued, 'He has made a particularly interesting study of the Berbers in Morocco, which I imagine is also applicable to Algeria. It came out four or five years ago, *Saints of the Atlas*. It's a study of how holy men keep a fragile peace among the thousands of people who move each year with their sheep from the plains into the high pastures of the Atlas Mountains. In fact, the Berber people have maintained their independence over a couple of millennia by rejecting the authority of the Moroccan state. But I suppose that independence must be eroding these days.'

'I rather thought Gellner was a philosopher not an anthropologist,' Rhiannon said.

'Oh, he is that, too. He says, and I agree with him, that sociologists, anthropologists and philosophers need each other. All can benefit from clear thinking and elegant prose. Gellner is a philosopher who engages with the real world. Like Leopold here, he is among a remarkable group of refugees that came to the West from Russia and Central Europe in the 1930s. One thinks of Freud, Einstein, Hans Morgenthau, Herbert Marcuse, Eric Fromm, Friedrich Hayek, Karl Deutsch, Leo Strauss, Hannah Arendt, Isaiah Berlin… the list goes on. But I think Gellner is a philosopher who is especially important from a sociological point of view. His studies on nationalism bear some attention.'

At this point a woman arrived, carrying a baby and seeking her husband. The man, a colleague of Alwyn Rees, made his apologies as he prepared to leave, explaining it was his daughter's first birthday.

Leopold was delighted. He stepped forward to make the child's acquaintance and placed a finger into her small hand.

'You are one and I am sixty-five,' he told her. 'So I am sixty-five times older than you. But when you are five I shall be seventy, and I will only be fourteen times older than you. So, you see, as you get older I get younger!'

Pencader
October 1974

On a Saturday afternoon less than a week before the second general election of 1974, a cavalcade of cars halted on the outskirts of Pencader amidst the green hills of northern Carmarthenshire. The cars were plastered with stickers and photographs of Gwynfor Evans. Flags fluttered from radio aerials and poles protruded through rear windows.

Suddenly a loud speaker on the roof rack of the leading car crackled into life, emitting a loud Dafydd Iwan anthem. As the car set off into the village, followed by half the cavalcade, a voice rose over the music.

> 'Prynhawn da! Good afternoon! This is Plaid Cymru with Gwynfor Evans, Carmarthen's next MP! Come and meet Gwynfor!'

Clad in a grey suit and his favourite Eisteddfod tie, Gwynfor climbed out of one of the remaining cars and, accompanied by a posse of supporters, walked down the road towards the village. Owen James followed closely, impressed by the energy and organisation of the campaign.

All afternoon the pattern had been the same. A few cars would enter a village announcing Gwynfor's presence. Party workers would follow, putting leaflets through doors. There was no need to knock on them. The people came out on their own accord and lined the streets, waiting to shake Gwynfor's hand. In the past few hours they had been through Alltwalis, Dolgran, Gwyddgrug, and Llanfihangel-Ar-Arth.

Owen had covered election campaigns in constituencies across Wales, but he had never seen anything to match this.

People were standing in line waiting patiently to meet their candidate. 'It's more of a royal procession than canvassing,' he thought to himself, taking out his notebook.

'I confess I'm hopeless at remembering names,' Gwynfor had told Owen in the car earlier. 'I ask people about their families, their children. I tell them the election is an important chance to give Wales a step up.'

Owen watched Gwynfor crossing the street from side to side, shaking hands. Peter Hughes Griffiths, the campaign organiser, joined him. 'It's not like this everywhere, you know,' he said. 'The mining villages in the south are Labour territory, but we're making progress. I remember when we weren't given a hearing in those places. It's different now.'

Owen asked how he thought the vote would go.

'Labour's support is holding alright. Their vote will probably go up on the February result. They're attracting some Liberals, but I think we're getting more.'

By now they were walking at a brisk pace to keep up with the progress Gwynfor was making.

'Another indication is the postal vote, which is three thousand, up a thousand from February,' Hughes Griffiths said. 'We reckon that's down to students switching from wherever they're studying. Most of them are voting for us.'

'It's difficult for Plaid in a general election when all the attention is on the London parties,' Owen suggested.

'That's right. We don't get the television coverage that Labour does. But our organisation on the ground gives us an edge. During the campaign, and it's been going on since last February you know, we've had more than seven hundred people working for us. I'd say Labour have at most about two hundred.'

He had divided the constituency into twelve areas, each with a sub-agent in charge. These areas had been further divided into another three for the canvass. With such a large, rural constituency, the organisation had to be dispersed to be effective. Another crucial element was timing.

'In any campaign there's always a danger that you'll peak too early. We had that problem in February. If the vote had been held a few weeks earlier, I'm sure we would have won. But we peaked too soon and then we were beaten by a surge in the Liberal vote in the last week, driven by the media.'

'And you don't think that will happen again?'

'Not this time. The Liberal and Tory votes are crumbling. We've deliberately kept back until the last week the kind of campaigning we're doing here, with loudspeakers and Gwynfor walking through the villages. Until now it's been quieter, just door-to-door canvassing and leafleting. But we've always planned for this final push. We're organising an eve-of-poll rally in Carmarthen and reckon we'll get well over a thousand people in the Lyric Cinema. It should be the biggest political gathering anywhere in Wales.'

* * *

The morning had been spent in Carmarthen town, where Gwynfor met crowds of shoppers, deploying what had become known as the 'walkabout', with a candidate surrounded by a crush of television cameras. Observing, Owen felt the activity did not appeal to Gwynfor's retiring nature. His preference would have been to engage people individually for half-an-hour apiece. Instead he was forced to stop and sign his autograph twenty times within an hour. The campaign had created a magnetic aura around him.

The drama of February's close vote provided the backdrop, while the very names of the two main contestants added to the theatre. It was Gwynfor Evans against Labour's Gwynoro

Jones, Gwynfor versus Gwynoro, an alliteration the newspaper headline writers couldn't resist. Owen had already written the opening sentence of his own account, due to be published within a few days on the eve of the general election.*The Carmarthen election, which has now been under way for seven months and eight days, reaches its High Noon tomorrow.*

The consequence of such coverage had been to place a relentless squeeze on the Liberals and Conservatives in the constituency, the kind of squeeze that previously had left Plaid Cymru on the sidelines. It was shown in the rash of green and red posters in windows across the county. Never before had there been such an ostentatious demonstration of allegiance in what was normally a politically reserved community. There were very few yellow or blue posters, the Liberal and Conservative colours.

Carmarthen town was not Plaid's strongest territory. In the past it had won only about a third of the vote. As Gwynfor made his way through the crowd, his conversations reflected the division. One woman complained bitterly that a Labour poster in her garden had been pulled down. A little further on a man told Gwynfor he should be preparing to return to Westminster. 'I hope you've packed your bags,' he said.

Later they ventured into a council estate on a hillside above the town, reckoned to be a Labour stronghold. An excited group of small children followed them jeering. Nonetheless, Plaid Cymru posters could be seen in half-a-dozen windows.

'First time ever,' Gwynfor remarked.

They stopped for lunch at the Ivy Bush Hotel. Outside was a vintage Rolls Royce plastered in Plaid Cymru stickers. In the bar Gwynfor downed a ginger ale.

'Being teetotal doesn't do me any good at all,' he told Owen. 'People become uneasy when they're ordering pints while I have a soft drink. They think I'm disapproving. But I can hardly tell them, never mind me, go on drinking… that would make me more remote than ever. They even accused me once of being temperance in order to get the Nonconformist vote. Anyone who thinks that can't know the Welsh at all.'

It soon became clear that the main issues of the election elsewhere – inflation, Britain's role in Europe – were not high on his agenda. Instead, his main objective was to educate people in the idea of nationhood.

'In the past, our pride in ourselves has not gone much deeper than sentimentality,' Gwynfor said. 'We've not had a loyalty to the national community. That's what we need, first and foremost, above all else.'

Farming appeared to be one exception to his general avoidance of conventional policy questions. It quickly became evident, however, that even this was not really the case. In Gwynfor's mind, farming was closely aligned with national salvation. 'Our national community, its language and culture, stand or fall with the farmers,' he said. 'The family farm is the backbone of our Welsh identity.'

* * *

They ended the day in the small university town of Lampeter just over the Carmarthenshire border. Gwynfor was there to attend a rally in support of the Ceredigion candidate Clifford Davies, the party's rather cerebral director of policy and a teacher in Ysgol y Preseli in Crymych. Television cameras were on hand to record an item for BBC Wales. A respectable audience of about seventy people greeted them in the common room of the University College where they gathered for tea before the meeting. Owen was told that most were Plaid supporters if not members, some having travelled from as far as Aberystwyth.

Gwynfor made an unalloyed appeal to an audience he imagined might eventually see him on the news.

'In time, the nationalists will replace the Labour Party just as completely as Labour replaced the Liberals earlier this century,' he declared, deploying an optimism that was his hallmark. 'We alone have the policies and the philosophy required by the circumstances of our age.' Continuing in this vein, he was buoyed by a serenity arising from decades of simply ignoring what others would have regarded as pragmatic realities. 'As surely as the British Empire has vanished, so too the day of the huge centralist state is over.'

It was already dusk when they left Lampeter for Carmarthen. Owen had suggested he should bring his own car and give Gwynfor a lift. But Peter Hughes Griffiths told him in no uncertain terms that this would be impossible.

'Gwynfor can't stand being driven by anybody. Makes him physically sick. He always has to drive himself.'

As Gwynfor began negotiating the winding road towards Carmarthen, Owen remarked that it looked as though Plaid would win.

'Peter certainly thinks so. I've been dreading it for months.'

'Really?'

'Westminster nearly killed me last time. By the end I was very ill. I had an operation for gallstones, you know, just before the 1970 election. I hated it in London. The atmosphere in the House was poisonous. People like George Thomas and Leo Abse... it was a great relief when I lost. The defeat kept me alive.'

'This time you'll have the two Dafydds.'

'That's true, Dafydd El and Wigley will make a big difference.'

'And there's the SNP. Have you seen today's poll putting them in second place behind Labour in Scotland?'

'Yes, the SNP should do well. It's good that Winnie Ewing got back in February. And Douglas Crawford thinks he'll win in Perth this time which is extraordinary. The Tories had a majority there of more than 8,000 in February. If he does get in, we could have fifteen seats between us. With Labour and the Tories close to level pegging that would give us a lot of influence in the next parliament.'

'And the key will be delivering on devolution.'

'Absolutely. If Labour gets back in, we must push on it. They're willing to concede a legislative Assembly for Scotland, a parliament in all but name. Why not for Wales? If we are forced to accept executive devolution it will hold us back for years. People will say the Assembly must be given time to succeed or fail.'

'Might Wales get more out of a Conservative than a Labour minority government do you think?

'It's hard to say. Labour has come further, but only under pressure from us and the SNP. When it comes down to it the Tories are more pragmatic. I believe Edward Heath is a devolutionist. If anything, Labour is more centralist.

'But wouldn't it be more difficult to do a deal with the Tories? I'm thinking of the party in the Valleys and people like Phil Williams.'

'Yes, Phil... but you know I don't think of myself as a socialist. For me, socialism is the same as centralism and state control. In the end, state control means control by civil servants and that has been the fate of the nationalised industries.'

'So, if not a socialist?'

'I've been called everything in the past few weeks. The Tories have called me a communist. Labour has called me a Tory. The Liberals say I am a socialist, which is the worst sin in their book. But I'm none of those. I think of myself as a radical in the tradition of Lloyd George, Tom Ellis and Michael D. Jones.'

The car pulled up outside the Ivy Bush Hotel where Owen

was staying. 'I'm spending Monday with Gwynoro Jones,' he said as he got out. 'Good luck with the eve-of-poll rally.'

Gwynfor set off home to Llangadog. He had been campaigning non-stop for sixteen hours.

* * *

When the result of the general election was announced, Labour was returned but with a majority of only three over all the other parties. The nationalists had fourteen seats between them, eleven from Scotland and three from Wales. In Carmarthen Gwynfor's vote climbed from 17,162 in February to 23,325, the highest total achieved by any candidate in the history of Plaid Cymru. As Gwynfor himself observed, it was more than twice as many polled by the party across the whole of Wales in the general election of 1951. Moreover, it was the only seat that Labour lost in the election.

As Gwynfor headed back to Westminster, he was in a very different position to when he first entered Parliament following the Carmarthen by-election in 1966. He had allies in the form of the two other Plaid MPs and a phalanx of MPs from the Scottish National Party. The new Labour government's tiny majority gave the nationalists unparalleled influence. Gwynfor firmly believed that an Assembly for Wales was achievable within three years. Who could have guessed that his dream would so soon turn to ashes?

Dublin
November 1974

Rhiannon and Siobhan Cunninghame were leaning over the stern of the ferry from Holyhead to Dublin, watching its wake disappear into a darkening, choppy sea. The Welsh coast was just a smudge on the horizon, partially hidden by gathering clouds. The girls had come on deck after a spell below and were clinging to each other as the boat heaved against a rising swell. They were warmly wrapped in jumpers, scarves, and waterproof jackets which they pulled closer against a swirling wind and the first threatening drops of November rain.

Siobhan had suggested Rhiannon accompany her for a weekend in Dublin to attend a conference on the literature and politics of Ireland. She hoped she might be able to interview one of the speakers, the Ulster poet John Hewitt. Rhiannon needed little persuasion. She had always wanted to visit Dublin.

Now they were midway on their four-hour wintry crossing to Ireland. The previous day they had taken the bus from Aberystwyth to Bangor and, as usual, been met by Rhiannon's father. After spending the night in Llanddona, Penry had driven them to Holyhead. Rhiannon's mother had been delighted to meet Siobhan.

'Listening to you two talk I get more information about what's going on in Aberystwyth in an evening than if Rhiannon was staying here a whole month by herself.'

On the deck of the boat, mist turned to a blanket of rain that forced the two young women below. In the bar Rhiannon went for drinks while Siobhan sorted the papers she had been sent about the conference.

'I think it's going to be of as much of interest to you as me,' she said as Rhiannon returned with two glasses of lager. 'It's largely about the situation in the North as far as I can see. They've got Conor Cruise O'Brien speaking. He's a minister in the coalition from the Labour side. He used to be with the United Nations and was involved in the civil war in the Congo at the end of the 1950s. That'll interest you. There was a lot of controversy about it at the time. Later he became vice chancellor at the University of Ghana. And after that he was a professor of something – history I think, in New York. He returned to Ireland at the end of the 1960s.'

'They've given him the opening slot,' Rhiannon said, picking up the conference programme.

'They've more or less named the conference after his latest book.' Siobhan said reaching into her bag. 'I've got it here. *States of Ireland.* You should look at it sometime. It goes into the background of the civil rights movement and the Troubles. Actually, he takes quite a radical position. He says there are two Irelands, two different countries really, and until we accept that there won't be any solution.'

'Do you agree?'

'Not sure, but it bears thinking about. Look, this bit will interest you.'

Leafing through the book Siobhan came to a chapter headed 'Civil Rights: The Crossroads'.

'He's talking about a lecture he gave at Queen's University in '68 on civil disobedience. I was there, actually. In fact, only students were allowed in. You had to show your student's card. The vice chancellor had been urged by the powers that be, Stormont I suppose, to ban the meeting. There'd recently been riots in Derry. Anyway, the vice chancellor compromised by letting the meeting go ahead but excluding the press.'

Struggling to remove her cagoule that had got caught in her hair, Rhiannon could scarcely hear what Siobhan was saying.

'It's pretty fuggy down here.'

'Better than outside.'

Rhiannon reached for her lager.

'The civil rights movement began at Queen's didn't it?'

'Yes, all the leaders came from there. Eamonn McCann, Michael Farrell, Bernadette Devlin and the rest. They were all there.

'You knew them then.'

'Not really, more of at a distance, you could say. I was younger, of course. But the attempt to ban the lecture made it all the more exciting. There was a huge crowd.'

'We could do with a bit of that in Aberystwyth.'

'You should be careful what you wish for.'

'What did O'Brien have to say, anyway?'

'That civil disobedience, the protest movement, you know the whole thing that was starting up in Northern Ireland at that time, was going to be an effective lever for change.'

'No wonder they tried to ban the lecture.'

'He said civil disobedience only works in places where the authorities are sensitive to outside opinion.'

'You mean a system that's responsive to pressure?'

'I guess that's the nub of it. In places like South Africa, where the government pays no attention to outside opinion, civil disobedience doesn't work. On the other hand, in the southern states of America, the whites had only been able to oppress the blacks so long as they had the tacit consent of their state governments.'

'And only so long as the blacks themselves passively accepted their subordination,' Rhiannon added. 'When they resorted to civil disobedience, they were able to force the issue.'

'That's right. They exposed the contradictions at the heart of things, the reality of the conditions they were living under. Washington had to intervene and send troops to overrule the southern states.'

Rhiannon put her glass on the table and thought for a moment.

'So you could argue that for similar reasons civil disobedience is likely to work with the language campaign at home.'

'That's what I was coming to. I think you'll be interested in what Conor Cruise O'Brien has to say about the situation in Northern Ireland.'

*   *   *

Later that evening, after Rhiannon had been introduced to Siobhan's mother over supper at her home in Sandyford, the two women caught a bus into the city centre. They wandered down O'Connell Street, crossed the river Liffey and, passing Trinity College, found their way to Neary's Bar in Chatham Street. A traditional Victorian pub, its wide, dark interior exuded a plush elegance. A man in a white shirt and black bow tie served them and they retreated to a table away from the bustle of men standing at the bar.

'I do believe that's John Montague,' Siobhan whispered, lifting a pint of Guinness in the direction of a distinguished looking man engaged in a bantering conversation with a group of students. He was tall, good looking in the way of an actor, with a long straight nose and a mop of dark hair that he frequently pushed back across his head.

'What does he do?'

'He's a poet, a very good one, and a short story writer. Lectures at Cork University though he's from the North. Speaking at the conference tomorrow. Catholic, of course.'

'He's certainly handsome.'

'I'd like a chance to get chatting with him. He knows John Hewitt very well. In fact, he was responsible for negotiating the publication of his *Collected Poems*. Rescued him from obscurity, you might say. They went on a speaking tour of the North together a few years ago, a deliberate effort to bring the two traditions together, though it didn't do much good. *The Planter and The Gael* it was called.'

At that point one of the students talking with Montague glanced their way, saw Siobhan and advanced towards her grinning broadly.

'Well, if it's not Siobhan Cunninghame. What drags you away from Belfast to this heathen city? And who is your delightful companion?'

'I'm not in Belfast these days, Sean Maguire,' Siobhan responded primly. 'My ma's moved back to Dublin. Anyway, if you must know, I'm not in Ireland at all. I've migrated to Wales. I'm studying at Aberystwyth with Rhiannon here.'

'You don't say.'

'And would that be John Montague you're talking with?'

'The very same. Why don't you join us?'

Rhiannon and Siobhan rose, pints in hand, while Sean turned to Montague to introduce them.

'Pleased, I'm sure,' he said with a smile, clinking his glass of red wine against their pints. 'Would you be here for the conference?'

'Indeed, and I see you're leading a session.' Siobhan was a little breathless, anxious to engage but worried at appearing too forward.

Montague laughed.

'I wouldn't say leading. Just a few poems, with me and Hewitt giving a reprise to our double act.'

'That's why we're here.'

Siobhan explained her particular interest in John Hewitt.

'Yes, well he's an acquired taste all right, but you could say I've acquired him.'

Montague sipped his wine.

'All the same, he mellows as you get to know him, you know. It was his poem 'An Irishman in Coventry' that first caught my eye. He didn't say Ulsterman, you see. That was surprising. He even identified with his old Catholic neighbours...'

Montague paused, gazed towards the ceiling and proceeded to recite. '...*the whisky-tinctured breath, the pious buttons, called up by a people endlessly betrayed by our own weakness.* There's something we have in common I thought. The weakness that we own in common.'

'I went to one of your Planter and Gael sessions, the one in Belfast.'

'Did you now.'

'I remember Hewitt talking about your poem 'The Rough Field'. He said it did for the North what Hugh MacDiarmid's 'A Drunk Man Looks at the Thistle' has done for Scotland.'

'Yes, well, he was very nice about that. I amused him a lot, you know, especially my need for an injection of Dutch courage before our performances. I'm a bit of a stammerer and I needed to get to a pub before a reading. Still do.'

Montague laughed again.

'It's a kind of ritual. But John understood it.'

'Why were they called *The Planter and the Gael*?' Rhiannon spoke for the first time.

'We were making a gesture, trying to reach out to a common audience. We were both living abroad at the time, you see. John was still in England and I was in Paris. So we saw the tour as a return to our home territory in a way. But it was also a half-serious attempt at community relations. I guess we were over optimistic.'

'Why was that?'

Montague took Rhiannon's arm in a gesture that was familiar but not unwelcome.

'Well now, very few Planters came to hear us. But I don't

suppose you have this business of Catholics and Protestants in Wales.'

'Not really, we're mainly nonconformists. Dissenters if you like.'

'Well that would sum up John, I would say, a dissenter if ever there was one. After that tour, he wrote to me that he was considering moving back to Northern Ireland. But his trouble, he said, was that he stood between opposites. He was an interloper amongst us Gaels, with only four hundred years of Irish earth in his bones. And as for the Planters, he was a disaffected person to what he called the Stormont bullies. That's how he put it, anyway.'

* * *

Siobhan and Rhiannon arrived late at the conference the next morning. They had slept in and Siobhan had quarrelled with her mother for not waking them. Grabbing some toast, they had run for the bus. Now they were making their way into the large, crowded lecture theatre in Trinity College to find Conor Cruise O'Brien already speaking.

'The border makes us take leave of almost everything that is lovable about Ireland. The affection, the humour, the mutual concern, the courtesy and, yes, the peace that exists in abundance in our communities.'

Rhiannon missed what he said next as she edged along a row of people, a few of whom rose to let her and Siobhan pass. 'Sorry,' she whispered to a neighbour, leaning forward to give her full attention to O'Brien.

'Instead we must discuss the conditions of a multiple frontier. Not just the territorial border, but a very old psychological frontier area, full of suspicion, reserve, fear, boasting, resentment, Messianic illusions, bad history, rancorous commemorations and – today more than ever – murderous violence. Our frontier is now so disturbed that many of us fear we may be approaching the brink of full-scale civil war.'

'See what I mean,' Siobhan whispered.

O'Brien peered far into the recesses of the lecture theatre for so long that Rhiannon wondered if he was searching for her, to see if the import of his words had sunk in.

'When I'm abroad, especially in the States, I often get asked questions that are simple in themselves but to which there are no simple answers... Why do Irish Catholics and the Protestants hate one another so much? Is it a religious problem? A colonial problem? A racial problem? When is Ireland going to be united? What is the solution? It would take a book to answer these questions, and, indeed, I've written one.'

At this O'Brien held up the book in question and was rewarded by a ripple of laughter.

'I'm flattered that the title of this important conference makes reference to it.'

Placing the book on the lectern, O'Brien stepped away and paced across the stage before turning to face the audience.

'You see, these kind of questions lead on to others... After all, what does it mean to be a Catholic or a Protestant in Ireland? Does it mean the same in the North as in the South? Such questions lead to endless complications.'

He held up two fingers.

'The population of Northern Ireland consists of about two-thirds Protestants. That is one point from which we can start.'

Then he presented one finger. 'Two-thirds Protestants to one-third Catholics.'

He explained that Protestant fear and suspicion of Catholics in Northern Ireland did not correspond to these proportions. Rather they related to the proportions between Catholic and

Protestant *in the entire island of Ireland*. He paused again to allow the emphasis he gave the words to sink in.

'I repeat, in the *entire island* – in which Protestants are outnumbered by Catholics by more than three to one.'

Now he held up three fingers. 'And, just as significant, Catholics in Northern Ireland are also strongly conscious of this proportion, and to the rights they believe it implies.'

Returning to the rostrum O'Brien turned over his papers.

'It is important to understand, too, that arising from this, Ulster Protestants fear Catholicism in a way that Ulster Catholics do not fear Protestantism.'

Looking up he continued, 'Protestantism in Ireland has been on the defensive for more than a hundred years. In the south, it has just about gone under, conquered more effectively by Catholic marriage regulations than by any material force. Generally speaking, however, while Protestants might despise the Catholic community for its material weakness, there is still a strong element of fear in the relationship that they project on to the Catholic Church.'

Cruise O'Brien took a sip of water. Looking round the room he saw his audience was giving him their full attention.

'What of the Catholics?' he asked rhetorically, but provided his own answer.

'They may fear the material power of their Protestant neighbours, but they have no fear whatever of Protestantism. A Catholic in Ulster knows little about Protestantism and thinks little of it. There is simply no equivalent on his side to the Protestant brooding on the Pope of Rome. Indeed, his attitude to Protestantism – as distinct from his Protestant neighbours – is condescending. His youthful impression of Protestantism was that it was founded by Henry VIII in order to have eight wives. The impression may be somewhat refined in later years, in respect of Tudor marital statistics, at least – but there is no doubt that Protestantism as such is not to be taken seriously.'

O'Brien hesitated for a moment while he studied his audience closely.

'Of course, this is a kind of bigotry. But it is different to the Protestant kind. Contempt and fear enter into both forms but, from the Catholic side, the contempt is directed at the religion, and the fear to its followers. On the Protestant side, it is the other way round.'

He paused, before continuing more emphatically.

'What Catholics take seriously about Protestants are their material prosperity and power, their hostility towards Catholics, and their politics, which are the instrument of preserving their prosperity and power. That politics is Unionism.'

O'Brien paused once more, but quickly pressed on to raise the central question of his address.

'So is this a *religious* quarrel? I think the answer is yes, but with qualifications. It is not, after all, a *national* quarrel, as some might at first think. What would be the two nations that are supposedly at odds? Irish Catholics do not think in terms of an Irish Catholic nation, but of an Irish nation that includes both Catholics and Protestants.

'For their part, Ulster Protestants do not reject an Irish identity. Rather they think of themselves as Ulster folk, Irish but British as well, in the way that the Scots and Welsh are also British. They regard Irish Catholics as fellow Irishmen who refuse the common British bond. They regard Irish Catholics as wishing to impose a foreign status on them for remaining loyal to a British identity.

'So we are brought back, inescapably, to what so many people seek to deny.'

For a moment O'Brien stared at his audience as if challenging it to object to what he was about to say.

'And that is the rather obvious fact that this is a conflict between groups defined by religion. That does not mean it is a theological war. It would not be exact to say that it is a conflict between Catholics and Protestants. Rather it is a conflict between *Irish Catholics* and *Ulster Protestants*. More immediately, of course it is a conflict between *Ulster* Catholics and *Ulster* Protestants.'

* * *

At this point O'Brien laid his papers to one side, saying that the best use of his remaining time would be to take some questions. He pointed to a hand that rose near the front of the hall.

'One of the questions you posed Dr O'Brien, was about unity – would there ever be a united Ireland? Isn't that the only answer in the long run?'

'I don't believe that, at the moment, any of the main sections of the population in Ireland, whether North or South, actually wants unity. Ulster Protestants obviously do not. As for Ulster Catholics, they're interested in equality – especially in relation to jobs – rather than in unity, although it has to be said that their concept of equality does include the right to wave a tricolour whenever a Protestant waves a Union Jack.'

'What about the Irish constitution which claims sovereignty over the whole island of Ireland?' the questioner asked again.

'The constitution is unfortunate and will some day have to be amended, I hope sooner rather than later. In any event, in practice, when we in the South refer to "our country", invariably we mean the twenty-six-county state. Most of us are less than inconsolable about the rest of the island. Except, when we happen to think about it at all, we are uncomfortable and uncertain about it. And, of course, the events of the past few years have caused us to think about it much more, and with far greater inward discomfort, than at any time in our previous history.'

He pointed to another hand that was raised.

'Isn't the plight of the minority Catholic community in the North increasing the demand for unity?'

'To the contrary,' O'Brien cried, his eyes glittering. 'Forced for the first time to have a serious look at the problem, if only as it appears on our television screens, we are having second thoughts, even about the theoretical notion of incorporating the North. Only the other day one woman in my constituency here in Dublin said to me, "Northern Ireland? I wish someone would saw that place off."'

A murmur went around the hall, but despite it O'Brien pressed on.

'In theory, these strange, fierce people in the North are all one and the same as our easy-going selves. In practice they seem to be a bit different. The Protestants seem more determined, more numerous, and much more exceptional than we had thought about them before, if indeed we had thought about them at all. And as for those northern Catholics, well they look a tough lot as well. They should, indeed, get a fairer deal, so they should. So long as they stay up there.'

There was a release of laughter, a brief break in the nervous tension suffusing the room. But another questioner wanted to know, if not unity, then what might the solution be?

O'Brien was roused by his apparent failure to get his message across.

'Look, this is how it is. So long as Catholics generally think of unity as the solution – the only thinkable solution – so long will groups like the Provisional IRA draw their mandate and licence from that generally vague conviction.'

O'Brien stared challengingly at the lecture theatre in front of him.

'So long also will Ulster Protestants generally feel that the slightest concession to Catholics opens the way to Catholic power over Protestants. And so long, too, will some Protestants feel that Protestant murder-gangs are the only answer to Catholic murder-gangs. So long, in fact, will we have the conditions for sectarian civil war.'

At the lectern, O'Brien's hands shook slightly. His audience, Rhiannon and Siobhan among them, noticed a glistening of sweat on his brow. He wiped his forehead with a handkerchief as he signalled to another questioner. What did he think was the direction in which Ireland should move?

'I think we should listen to the ordinary people. What they're saying, what they're saying to me, is that our problem is not "how to get unity" but how to share an island in conditions of peace and reasonable fairness. Indeed, these ordinary people are well ahead of what we call public opinion, the opinions of the Dublin editorial writers who, to a man, are merchants of "inevitable unity".'

'But how different are you from the editorial writers?' another questioner asked accusingly. 'How can you claim to speak for ordinary people?'

'Well, sir, the fact is that some thousands of them in Dublin North East have elected me to speak for them. The empirical test of whether I am right in assessing their mood will come at the next election.'

*   *   *

This last reply brought the opening session to an end, prompting a surge towards the doors of the lecture theatre. Rhiannon and Siobhan found themselves trapped at the back of the hall, waiting in line.

'He made it pretty clear, didn't he, that he thinks there are two distinctive communities in Ireland,' Siobhan said.

'I thought he was really interesting about the different attitudes of Catholics and Protestants towards each other,' Rhiannon said. 'We've got our divisions in Wales, the language and so on. But nothing like the antagonisms you seem to have.'

Outside they made their way towards the refectory where they joined a queue for coffee. Throngs of people quickly filled the spaces between the counter and the small tables that filled much of the room. Seated at one was John Montague. As soon as he saw them he rose and, picking up his mug of coffee quickly joined them.

'What did you make of O'Brien?' he asked Rhiannon, but without waiting for a reply turned to Siobhan. 'I spoke with John earlier on and he said he'd be glad to meet with you, perhaps over lunch.'

'That's kind.'

'Think nothing of it. He was flattered that someone outside Ireland was studying him. I didn't tell him you were a Catholic from Belfast.'

'Actually Dublin these days.'

'Makes no difference, now does it, despite what Cruise O'Brien would have you think. Let's say we'll meet here at the end of the morning session and I'll introduce you.'

Which was how they found themselves sitting across a table from the bespectacled John Hewitt. He looked more of a bank manager than a poet. White hair and a neatly-trimmed moustache completed an air of unapproachable severity. However, he softened when he was introduced to Rhiannon.

'You've certainly caught the eye of young Montague,' he said, taking a pipe from his pocket.

Siobhan asked him to explain the way he thought Catholic

and Protestant writers felt about their common Ulster identity. Hewitt pursed his lips at the question and sighed.

'My people came to Ulster in the early seventeenth Century. My name is English, Hewitt. Nevertheless, we've been around for over three hundred years, which is long enough to make me feel that Ulster is my country, the place where I belong. But you have to remember, too, that there were no original inhabitants of Ireland, only succeeding generations of Planters. We Hewitts happen to be part of the last generation who came.'

Siobhan reached for a notebook and pen from the bag that was hanging at her shoulder.

'You said that Ulster was your country, but isn't it also part of Ireland?'

'Why, of course. I grew up in an Ireland of thirty-two counties. When I was born, in 1907, the Ulster we know today didn't exist. But it is true, as you suggest, that people of Planter stock often suffer from some crisis of identity, of not knowing where they belong. Some of us call ourselves British, some Irish, some Ulstermen. Usually it's with a degree of hesitation or mental fumbling, I suppose.'

'Which do you choose?'

'There is certainly a strand of me that is English, as I say. It would be false for me to deny that. Apart from the school curriculum, I've made my own way through English history and chanced upon people I liked. The Levellers, the Diggers, the Chartists, George Fox and William Cobbett, Tom Paine and William Morris – these were my brand of men. They were men with whom I shared much more than with any Irishman I have ever read about or known.'

'It's not clear from what you're saying whether it's Ireland, Ulster, Britain or even England that comes first,' Rhiannon said.

'I can see that it seems a bit complicated. I guess my emotional response, in terms of personal feeling that is – I mean

266

feeling for democracy and for dissent – is in the first instance a plain English Protestant tradition, but a Protestant tradition not a church-going tradition.'

'But Northern Ireland is nothing like England.'

'That's certainly true. But, still, based in Northern Ireland for centuries my family have strands tying us to the English radical tradition, as I say, but also to the Scottish popular tradition. So what is my nation? That's what you're asking, isn't it? Am I Irish? Am I English? Am I Scots? The truth is I'm a lot of all three of them. The question, I suppose, is whether this is just a special amalgam that is personal to me, or a more widely-held outlook.'

'Where does nationhood and nationality come into this?' Siobhan asked.

'Indeed! *What ish my nation?* says Shakespeare's only Irish character.'

Hewitt chuckled and nodded towards Rhiannon with a twinkle in his eye.

'As it happens Captain McMorris was answering a Welshman, Fluellen in *Henry V*. *What ish my nation? Ish a villain, and a bastard, and a knave, and a rascal.* Sums up Shakespeare's attitudes to the Irish, and the Welsh for that matter, don't you think?'

He laughed again, but then cut across himself.

'Seriously though, what makes a nation is the myth of a nation, with a capital N I should say. Every nation subsists on a fiction derived from folklore and history. If we think of Ireland, we think of the Irish myth – the Ireland of Cuchulain, Oisin and Columcille, St Patrick and Brigid, the Ireland of Strongbow, of Brian Boru, of Sarsfield. They all build up to the Irish myth. From it we get all the symbols – the Irish Wolfhound, the Harp, and the Round Tower, which was only dream't up in about 1845 – devised by Thomas Davis and his friends of the Young Ireland

Movement. So the notion of Irish nationalism was invented by intellectuals about a hundred and thirty years ago.'

'But it's no less powerful for all that it was invented, as you say,' Rhiannon said.

'Absolutely right! The myth of the Irish nation has had tremendous power, still does. One third of Ulster people subscribe to it. Then on my side – the Planter's side – we have our own mythology - the Plantation, the Apprentice Boys of Derry, the Boyne, the Ulster Covenant, the Gun-running, Carson, Colonel Fred Crawford and the rest.'

'But surely the Irish myth goes back further?'

'Yes, that's right, and our myth, the Protestant myth, is more vulnerable than the Irish myth as well. The Apprentice Boys, remembered for closing the gates of Derry against James II's Siege in 1689, were subsequently driven from their homes by rack-renting landlords. Meanwhile, the landlords remained to sit in the halls of power right up to the closing of Stormont a couple of years ago.'

'It makes for a kind of insecurity, don't you think?' Siobhan said.

'A dangerous insecurity, you might say, certainly. Thinking about this I came to the conclusion years ago that the best answer to these dilemmas was to think of Ulster as a region, not a nation. We need something we can attach ourselves to in Ulster, something that's between the nation and the family, something that can unite us. A region can give us that. I think there's hope for Ulster in that.'

'Hope for both sides?'

'Some of us felt we couldn't give our loyalty to a Republican government in Dublin. We would never surrender to that. But others felt they could never give their loyalty to an English state either. But I felt that both could give their loyalty to Ulster as a region. Decades ago I wrote an article and called it 'Regionalism: the last chance'. I still think that.'

'You seem to be saying that some form of federalism is the answer?'

'I suppose I am. A region must belong to something larger.'

'But that's the question, the problem really,' Siobhan said, an eagerness entering her voice. 'Which way do you go?'

'Where does our region belong? I've got what I call my personal hierarchy. I am an Ulsterman. I was born in the island of Ireland, before the partition of Ireland, so legally, and emotionally too, I am an Irishman. My native language is English – my literary loyalties and political enthusiasms are English. Therefore, I am Ulster, Irish, and British. Then again, in that I live in a region of an island in an archipelago off the shore of Europe, I am a European.'

* * *

The following day Rhiannon and Siobhan were once more on the Irish ferry, heading towards Holyhead in more clement weather. Although it was still overcast, the seas had subsided, and there was a following breeze rather than the battling wind that had accompanied their voyage the other way.

'I liked your John Hewitt,' Rhiannon said as they walked the deck, coming to a stop at the railings overlooking the foaming wake. 'I thought he was charming, and modest, really, for someone who has such a reputation.'

'I didn't tell you, but he was quoted in a speech the Taoiseach Jack Lynch made a few years ago,' Siobhan said. 'It was at an event in Dublin for the fiftieth anniversary of the truce between the English and Irish forces in the war of 1921. Lynch didn't agree with Conor Cruise O'Brien about two nations on that occasion. He said we Irish must settle our quarrel amongst ourselves.

Siobhan gripped the railings and stared for a moment at the wake receding behind them.

'The way he put it was that the national majority should examine their conscience – our consciences, you might say – in relation to the national minority. He quoted John Hewitt, his line that the national minority also had rights *drawn from the soil and sky*. He said those rights were as good as those held by any previous migrants into Ireland.'

'Drawn from the soil and sky,' Rhiannon repeated. 'That's a good way of putting it.'

'Yes, isn't it,' Siobhan answered. 'Comes from his poem 'The Colony', probably his best, I think.'

She gazed at the thin smudge of the Irish coast in the far distance, and from memory spoke its last lines.

> ...*this is our country also, nowhere else;*
> *and we shall not be outcast on the world.*

Eglwys Newydd
December 1974

Seated at the table in the living room of his father's bungalow, John Tripp was moodily chipping away at a few stanzas of verse. But he was failing to achieve his desired effect. It was past one o'clock in the morning and the last embers were dying in the grate. To his side, a cigarette was smouldering in a heavy glass ashtray. Newspapers were strewn on the floor. On the mantle-shelf was a half-drunk bottle of Sandeman's Port.

Tripp took a draught of cheap sherry and pulled his grey dressing gown tighter around layers of sweaters. He looked at the scraps of notes he had made on the inside of a cigarette packet. He had spelt out the few thoughts and phrases that appeared there while drinking a pint in the Three Elms on Whitchurch Common. Putting another sheet of paper into his typewriter, he began again.

'This is the real slog', he thought, 'the revising and polishing'. But the lines weren't working. John Ormond constantly told him his energy was misdirected. Too often he was pent up with anger or dismay. Ormond would say, 'Johnnie boy, stop bowling bouncers for a bit and give us some slow left-arm spinners, why don't you?'

Tripp was trying for those now, but their length wouldn't come. Instead, he found himself thinking about his dwindling resources. He'd already tapped his father that week and could no longer call on the benefactor he had come to rely on so much.

The previous year, at the beginning of January, Cyril Hodges had died. It was not altogether unexpected. He had been ill for a long time. But still, it had been an unpleasant shock. Tripp shuffled into his back bedroom and retrieved a large bulging envelope from the bottom of a chest of drawers that served as a makeshift filing cabinet. He picked out a sheaf of papers, among them some of the letters he had received from Cyril over the years. He glanced at one, and read it through.

Dear John

I'm very sorry to hear that you've been financially pushed. To be honest I am relatively in the same position, with very little liquid capital. But I am not yet so badly off that I cannot send you £100.

I am not exactly offended (this would be too strong a word) but surprised that you should speak of an I.O.U. between us. All I ask is that if one day you are driving your Bentley along Heol y Frenhines, and you see an old man selling matches by the kerbside, you should sling a bundle of twenty fivers to him, if that old man looks like me... because it probably will be!

The way things are going, only crusts are left in this bloody country, and we might as well help each other out as long as we have the crusts to share.

Don't worry a bit about the typing... I am in exactly the same position. I have not yet regained control of my fingers sufficiently to write by hand, except for my signature, and carefully printed words in capital letters.

After the last heart attack, I had to re-learn typing as well. My wife used to lie in bed at night, listening to the incredible slow taps of my fingers as they sought the correct keys, and the mind forced my hands to do the job. But I won out, John, in the end; and who the hell cares whether I can write by hand or not? But my wife cried her eyes out.

But to return to your own position, John… would it be better to seek a paid job, rather than depend on semi hack-journalism, which I always hated and despised in my inner heart, although I was forced to do it in the 1930s.

I always hated my job also; but I learned to separate myself from my job. And when I came home in the evening, I would write only what I wanted to write. Doubtless it took its toll, because I would write to 4am and then go to work again at 8am. But it gave a freedom for those nightly hours, which cannot exist if you are also worrying over getting an article out on time.

Hack-journalism seems to be dead, except for hack-journalists; and you can <u>never</u> descend to this level, John. I think, in the end, you will have to admit, as I have done, that first-class writing does not provide a living; and that it has to be stolen from our work-a-day world.

But these are matters for your own decision. Meanwhile, if we talk of debts… let us first decide who owes the most… myself, who took tremendous pleasure from your work; or yourself, who accepts a few miserable money orders. It would take a very unusual account to balance that, John.

The letter was signed *Cofion caredig, Cyril (Hodges)*. Three days later Cyril had sent the £100.

I enclose the promised amount. I refuse to define whether it's a loan or advance. If we jointly refuse to recognise its identity, there can be no future quarrel, can there? It could be a contribution towards your book... it could be anything. Can we leave it at that?

In friendship,

Cyril.

Lighting a cigarette, Tripp reflected that he knew surprisingly little about Cyril's background. Son of a Scottish mother and Cornish father he had been born in Cardiff during the First World War, which meant he must have been only in his fifties when he died. He had no formal education to speak of, but always wanted to be a writer, a poet. He began writing in the forties, adopting a pen name Cyril Hughes, and got a few poems in the second run of *Wales* and the *Welsh Review.* At the same time, he began reading the early Welsh poets in translation: Aneirin, Taliesin, and Dafydd ap Gwilym.

'He used to talk about them as though they were alive and well, and living outside Aberystwyth,' Tripp said to himself. 'I guess that was how he became a nationalist, all that reading. He used to say Anglo-Welsh poetry was the "rendering of Welsh poetry in an English tongue" and I suppose it is.' Tripp picked out another letter he had received.

Annwyl John

I don't care about keeping the lean fox from your door: it is more a question of keeping the fox from the lean John.

I cannot imagine from where you have obtained this image of me as a keen connoisseur of food and wine. Most of my life I have spent with home-prepared Irish stews, bread and cheese, porridges of various consistencies, and lentil soup. And wine was merely a word in the dictionary.

After I was married, and decided to start the

business, I had to manage by gardening one and a half acres of land on a 'hungry' hillside. The ground was good, but had to be fed with phosphates obtained from burned bracken, because I could not afford to buy ready-made materials.

And if I wanted potatoes for the winter I had to grow them; if we wanted vegetables for the spring, summer and autumn, I had to grow them also. For a season we had unlimited apples; for an even shorter season we had almost too many plums. All the rest was sheer back-breaking work.

Out of this background, John, I grew, and my family perforce had to share the same background, although the children were perhaps too young to understand our terrible anxieties.

Before I was married, I used to engage in a fever of hack-journalism, which gave me the illusion of a reasonable financial income (although it varied greatly from time to time). On average, however, it was enough to give me independence.

When I was married I could no longer sustain a family on casual earnings, and therefore I undertook this business venture. Very unfortunately, I didn't realise the magnitude of the task of building up a business, which put me out of writing circulation for seven long years.

My part in building up the business has come virtually to an end, and I have kept my original ideal bright and untarnished so far. I am not a businessman with a desultory, immature interest in poetry, but a poet with a very desultory interest in business.

I am not going to accept your light-hearted

evaluation of your own worth. You are a highly intelligent man, with a veneer of sophistication, and I'm certain there should be some job available to you (which you could do mechanically almost), leaving you free and untouched for the real job you have at heart.

John, I like your abrasive work very much. But please do not blunt your knife on casual journalism. I have tried it, and it thoroughly sickened me for life. Never would I turn to that again, unless direct necessity drove me to it.

Cofion gorau,
Cyril

'What was his business?' Tripp wondered. 'Some manufacturing concern making heating elements for engines,' he thought. 'But enough to make a reasonable living in the end.' He lived in a comfortable house in Sully and also owned a cottage somewhere in Breconshire. It was enough, too, to enable him to make surreptitious contributions to all manner of nationalist causes, usually with the proviso that they remain anonymous. Tripp recalled that such were his donations that someone wondered whether he was some obscure member of the Julian Hodge family, albeit untypical. He made substantial contributions to Plaid Cymru, paid off the legal costs of some Cymdeithas yr Iaith activists, and funded magazines like *Second Aeon* and Meic Stephens' *Triskel Press*. He took out subscriptions for a dozen copies of all the Anglo-Welsh periodicals, and sent them all over the world. He bought all the new books, turned up at every reading, treated young poets to meals in restaurants and gave or lent others cash, notably Tripp himself.

By the time he was fifty, with his children grown up and his business settled, he was able to devote more time to writing.

Then in the last two years, when he became seriously ill, his writing became compulsive. He spent long hours turning out a poem day.

'He was catching up on lost time.' Tripp reflected. 'I guess he realised he didn't have much time left.' He picked up another of Cyril's letters.

Annwyl John

Of course there doesn't seem to be much poetry in you these days. The reason is almost certainly temporarily retreating into yourself. It happens to every poet. It cannot always be summer, or spring. Then suddenly, for no apparent reason at all a need for expression will flow into you, and John Tripp will be alive again. It will not be the old John, because every retreat into our wintry seasons brings a little more wisdom, a little change. But you won't be essentially different, although you may alter manner and mode a trifle.

This is quite different from losing your grip, although I appreciate how you feel about this, because I have often felt the same. But it isn't true. And it isn't true with you.

These self-doubts are very common, and perhaps they do much good in a way. They stop us from becoming 'too satisfied' with ourselves, maybe. And anything which sharpens our inward ear, listening for the true voice, is good.

In a sense you are holding the front lines here in Glamorgan. This is the place where we can gain ground, and re-establish our Welsh tradition. While the enemy invades our empty Midlands, we can undermine his influence here in his initial stronghold, the supposedly thoroughly anglicised areas of Morgannwg and Mynwy.

The error was to assume that we were thoroughly anglicised. The Anglo-Welsh poets are a kind of turning point, where we realise our difference, but have to express the realisation in English for the moment, because that is what official education has forced upon us.

Wales is a collection of people centred on a tradition which is practically impossible to destroy (except by extermination), especially when they contain people like you and me. Politics is a mere portion of our life, although we cannot afford to ignore that portion. And people are much the same as they always were.

So don't worry about any of these aspects.

The first time I heard you (I think it was at the Grand Hotel, Caerdydd) declaiming your poetry I knew you were certainly not a phoney. Perhaps you are even better in prose that in poetry... I have no means of judging this... but your poetry is, and was, very good. It's flamboyant, but this is no fault. It is merely your vital essence forcing itself to the surface.

So there is no need for depression, no need for feeling that you have run yourself into the ground, which is patently not true.

Give yourself a little time, and the spark will break into flame again.

I mean well and I don't like to think of you at 'two in the morning, embers on the grate, sipping cheap sherry, that day's writing done or not done' (I am quoting your own words). You have a rough hard time ahead of you. If you face this knowing you have at least one friend behind you, the going may be a little easier.

Cofion gorau,
Cyril

Brussels
February 1975

Aneurin Rhys Hughes, an official with the European Commission's General Secretariat, was waiting at the Arrivals barrier in Brussels airport for the Plaid Cymru delegation to appear. It was a late Tuesday afternoon and the airport was a welcome haven of warmth. Bespectacled and almost bald, save for two sides of closely cropped hair, Aneurin's expression was normally one of a warm, amused and dark-eyed intelligence. At this moment, however, he looked distracted as he worried about the prospects for the next three days. Every effort had to be made to persuade this sceptical group that the European institutions in Brussels were not the hostile, centralising force most of them plainly thought them to be.

A month earlier he had been at Plaid's special conference in Aberystwyth where the European vision for which he was so ardently working had been overwhelmingly opposed. As far as he could see, only Dafydd Wigley, the party's Caernarfon MP, had a good word to say for it. Brought up in a Welsh-speaking, Plaid-supporting, Swansea Valley family, Aneurin had been taken aback by the hostility he had encountered in the bars and around the conference fringe. Vainly had he sought to argue that small nations such as Wales could expect a sympathetic hearing in Brussels. All he heard was that the emerging European capital would merely be a replica of London, only further away and worse because of that.

Now, as he waited, Aneurin glanced up at the large, black and white flickering message board and saw that Londres/London was only one of many European cities appearing there. It was preceded by Helsinki, Rome, Athens, Dusseldorf, and Madrid, and followed by Dublin, Turin, Oslo, Stuttgart, Edinburgh,

Venice, and eventually Cardiff. Not for the first time, this roll call and the atmosphere in the airport gave him a sudden and inadvertent thrill. It fortified his sense that he was at the centre of a movement, a current that was moving inexorably towards a common European destiny.

He was shaken out of this reverie by the sight of Gwynfor Evans appearing anxiously in the crowd emerging from the baggage claim area. Behind him were the two other Plaid MPs, Dafydd Elis-Thomas and Dafydd Wigley, and Vice President Phil Williams. Gwynfor was clutching a holdall. His eyes registered relief when he saw Aneurin coming towards him, hand outstretched.

'I was afraid we might miss you in this crowd.'

'*Croeso i Brifddinas Ewrop,*' Aneurin said. 'Come along, I have a taxi waiting.'

'You see we've brought our top brass,' Phil Williams said.

'And we're rolling out the red carpet. We're arranged a lunch with Sir Christopher Soames, vice president of the Commission, and drinks with Sir Michael Palliser, head of the UK Mission, and that's only for starters. You're dining at my place tonight.'

'You've got a bit of work to do, that's for sure,' Dafydd Elis-Thomas said, grinning mischievously. 'In the party back home, you're known as Nye the spy.'

'Really?'

'You made a big impact at the conference.'

'Well, anyway, I'm going to be in Wales pretty much full-time between now and the referendum. Another thing, I'm looking for premises to establish a European Office in Wales, in Cardiff.'

'That's very good news,' Gwynfor said emphatically.

'Assuming there's a Yes vote in the referendum, that is.'

* * *

The Plaid delegation checked into the Charlemagne Hotel in the centre of Brussels, a five-minute walk from the European's Commission's Berlaymont headquarters. Later in the evening another taxi delivered them to Aneurin's home on Avenue Marie Jean in the Rhode-St-Genèse district of Brussels where Hywel Ceri Jones and Gwyn Morgan were also waiting for them. They were two other Welshmen who had joined the Commission since Britain entered the Common Market in 1973.

All three had cut their teeth on student politics. Aneurin had become President of the Student Union in Aberystwyth before joining the Foreign Office and, from there, the Commission. Hywel Ceri Jones, originally from Pontardawe, had also been involved in student politics before pursuing a career in academic administration, ending up at Sussex University. He was head of the Commission's Department of Education and Youth Policy.

Gwyn Morgan, from Cwmdare in the Cynon Valley, had become president of the National Union of Students. This had opened doors to his appointment as international secretary of the Labour Party. In 1969, he became deputy general secretary, many thinking he was being groomed for the top job. However, when the post became vacant three years later, Gwyn's advance was halted. His application was rejected on the casting vote of the chairman of the National Executive, Tony Benn, who judged him too enthusiastic about Britain's membership of the Common Market.

Aneurin, Hywel and Gwyn formed a Welsh triumvirate inside the European Commission. They operated collectively as a kind of alternative Welsh embassy in Brussels. Like many exiles, their enthusiasm for all things Welsh, especially rugby, was infectious. Pressed with drinks the Plaid delegation was quickly won over by their warmth and conviviality. For much of the evening separate conversations took place around the table, mainly in Welsh. Towards the end of the second course, Aneurin tapped the glass in front of him with the side of a fork.

'Friends… and I think that despite our differences I can call you all that,' he said to laughter around the table. 'It gives me enormous pleasure to welcome you to Brussels. It is our intention to persuade you that the European Economic Community is not the centralist enemy that many in Wales appear to think it is. Rather, we believe it will increasingly lead us towards greater devolution of power throughout Europe.'

'That's all very well,' Phil Williams objected. 'We also see Europe as the arena in which Wales must seek her freedom. But we envisage a very different kind of Europe to the one being built here. Our vision is of a loose confederation, including the unrepresented nations of Brittany, Flanders, the Basque Country, Catalunya and the rest. We oppose the EEC because it is capitalist and centralist, unlike the English Left who oppose it because they believe it is eroding British sovereignty and reducing the power of Westminster.'

Opposite him, Hywel Ceri Jones leant forward eagerly.

'But on that basis, surely you should be supporting the EEC, precisely because it is about sharing sovereignty at the European level. The new institutions will make a space in which it will be easier for Wales to get a hearing. I was struck by that *Western Mail* editorial following your conference suggesting Plaid Cymru was in danger of becoming an isolationist party.'

'No, it said we *were* isolationist,' Dafydd Elis-Thomas said. 'And it's good to be attacked by the *Western Mail*. But we're not isolationist at all. Plaid has always been in favour of bringing Wales into the mainstream of international co-operation. But most of us regard the EEC as an embryonic, supra-national state in which Wales will become even more insignificant than we are now – in spite of vague promises about regional policies.'

Hywel Ceri Jones reached into into the inside pocket of his jacket and produced a newspaper cutting.

'Saunders Lewis doesn't agree with you. He sees Europe as undermining the power of the old nation states like France and Britain. You must have seen his letter in the *Western Mail* the other day.'

He waved the press cutting across the table. 'It's typically cryptic and terse, just like the old man himself.'

> The Plaid Cymru conference decision to vote against membership of the European Common Market is a very serious matter for Welsh Nationalists. The decision has two implications: (1) English nationalists like Mr Enoch Powell and Mr Jack Jones oppose Europe because it means a curtailment of the sovereignty of the Westminster government. But we see the Plaid Cymru conference voting for Westminster sovereignty and against Europe. (2) The referendum presupposes of necessity that there is only one nation and one state in Great Britain.

As Hywel Ceri read out the letter, he could see Dafydd Elis-Thomas becoming agitated. Just twenty-seven years old, with long hair that framed his face, he was younger than the others and highly fashion conscious, as much with the latest political trends as clothes. He was intellectual, impulsive, impatient with contrary views, attributes softened by his ready humour and quick wit. His was a restless, mercurial temperament.

He bristled as Hywel Ceri reached the letter's final sentence.

> The only thing consistent with the history and policy of Plaid Cymru would be to urge members to refuse

to vote or to destroy their voting papers. But no, Plaid Cymru's conference decided in favour of Britishness.

'But that's daft,' Elis-Thomas declared. 'For Saunders to suggest that our opposition to creating a centralised corporate state in Europe means we support Britishness is nothing short of ludicrous. Our efforts to promote Welsh interests, to assert Welsh sovereignty if you like, would be tremendously hindered if we were to be incorporated in a European state. The pressures on our language and culture as well as our economy would be far greater than they are now.'

There was a moment's silence, filled by Dafydd Wigley. Previously he had decided against entering the argument, but he could contain himself no longer.

'It's not as simple a choice as you're making out, Dafydd,' he said. 'Arguing that the Common Market is going to develop into some kind of super state just doesn't stack up.'

Gwyn Morgan intervened, 'There are simply too many differences between the countries that are coming together, for that to happen.'

'There are so many misconceptions,' Aneurin added. 'For instance, the Plaid conference called on the EEC to reject a military role. But it's simply not true that the EEC is seeking one. Nato and the EEC are quite separate.'

'That's true,' Wigley agreed, and turning to Gwynfor asked, 'Britain spends a far greater proportion of its budget on armaments than any of the other EEC countries, isn't that right?'

Gwynfor nodded.

'London is the great enemy of Wales, not Europe,' Wigley continued, looking directly at Dafydd Elis-Thomas.

Anxious to paper over the cracks that were opening up within the group, Phil Williams sought to change the subject. He held up a two-day old copy of the *Irish Times*.

'I've got my own press cutting. It's about the Breton nationalist leader Yann Fouéré.' Phil read it out.

> A leading member of the Breton movement, Mr Yann Fouéré, was banned by the EEC Commission from speaking at a meeting scheduled to take place here last night. Sources close to the Commission claim that Mr Fouéré could not be allowed to speak on Commission premises as he was persona non grata in France.

Gwynfor was listening intently.

'I hadn't heard about this. We've known, of course that Yann and the Bretons have their difficulties with the French authorities. But it seems extraordinary that he should be banned from speaking here.'

'Well, it happened,' Phil said. 'This is what the report says.' Phil read again.

> It appears that the Commission has been duped by malicious elements either working in the Commission or by sources close to the French government which has never disguised its hostility to the separatist movements in France.

He looked up from the press cutting in his hand.

'Ironically, it says that Fouéré was due to speak about his political objectives for European integration based on the regions – exactly our own objectives, as I was saying earlier. The meeting was being organised by the European Community's branch of the Union of European Federalists.'

'That's altogether rather embarrassing,' Aneurin admitted. 'Altiero Spinelli, the Italian commissioner in whose office you're having your first meeting tomorrow, is a member of its executive committee.'

'Yes, it says that in the *Irish Times*,' Phil said. 'The paper says the organisers of the Fouéré meeting are lodging a protest.'

'I knew Fouéré very well,' Gwynfor said. 'In fact, he and his family stayed with us in Llangadog after the war when he was on the run from the French authorities.'

'I don't imagine many people know that,' Gwyn Morgan said.

'It was in 1947. After the war, Yann was accused of collaborating with the Germans. It was quite untrue of course, but it was a technique the French government used to crush the nationalist movement in Brittany. Yann learned he was to receive a harsh sentence and so, while on bail fled to Paris, got himself a new identity and passport – he became Dr Moger, as I recall – and found his way to Wales.'

'Why Wales?'Gwyn wanted to know.

'Well, there were connections between our movements. Yann had some contacts himself, in particular John Dyfnallt Owen, who became Archdruid in the 1950s. He stayed first with D.J. Williams in Fishguard, then with Gwenallt in Aberystwyth, and later with us. His wife and family came as well. Mind you, it was as well he did. A French military tribunal sentenced him in absentia to penal servitude for life. He found work for a while teaching French at Swansea University.'

'How long did he stay with you?'

'Best part of a year. The French authorities knew very well where he was. They complained to the British government and his position became very difficult. Eventually, he and his family were forced to move to Ireland.'

'Neutral territory, I suppose,' Gwyn suggested.

'That's right. But then, by the 1950s the political situation was changing in France. Amnesties were offered to people who had been accused of collaboration. Even so, Yann insisted on appearing before a military tribunal in Paris to clear his name, in 1955 I think it was. He was completely exonerated. They had no evidence, you see. French citizenship was restored to him but by then he had settled in Ireland.'

'He's based in Ireland, but travels constantly to Brittany,' Phil said. 'In the 1950s he established the *Mouvement pour l'organisation de la Bretagne* which laid the foundation for the Breton national party. He once told me that it was the distance from Brittany that he experienced as a result of living in Ireland that enabled him to work for the Breton movement.'

'How come?' Gwyn asked.

'He said he stopped feeling the sense of inferiority that characterised so many nationalists in Brittany after the war.'

'We've had to get over that in Wales as well,' Gwynfor observed.

*   *   *

At nine the following morning, Aneurin met the Plaid delegation in the lobby of their hotel and led them the short distance to the Berlaymont building for their first meeting. He explained it would be with Riccardo Perissisch, chef de cabinet to the Industry Commissioner Altiero Spinelli.

'He's an interesting guy. Italian, of course, though his English is very good.'

'What's his background?' Phil asked.

'Well, he's a bit of an intellectual. He's an economist and was involved in industry after leaving college, but he soon gravitated towards research. For most of the sixties he was with the Italian Institute of International Affairs, a think tank that works out of Rome and Milan. He became its deputy director specialising in the European Community before being recruited to the Commission in 1970.'

On the fourth floor of the Berlaymont building they were ushered into a large office with a desk at one end and a low table surrounded by black leather settees at the other. In between was a trolley laden with a jug of coffee, cups, saucers and a dish containing what looked to be chocolate truffles. As Aneurin began pouring coffee, Riccardo Perissich appeared through a door at the back of the room and greeted him warmly, before shaking hands with each member of the Plaid delegation.

'Welcome, welcome. Take a seat. I have been looking forward to meeting Aneurin's friends from Wales.'

With a chuckle, Riccardo patted him on the back.

'He has told me a lot about you, about how you need to hear the reality of what we are trying to achieve in Brussels. Is that not correct Aneurin?'

'Now, now Riccardo. You must not reveal all our secrets.'

'Secrets? But we have no secrets in the Berlaymont, is that not true? But seriously…' He paused to draw up a chair to face his visitors.

Dafydd Wigley began. 'We're most interested to learn, from your perspective, the direction you think the Economic Community is likely to be heading in the next few years.' He paused then, and glancing round added, 'I think I speak for all of us?'

Acknowledging the query with a raised eyebrow, Perissich stirred his coffee before replying.

'You must realise that fundamentally what we are doing here is political. From the outside, and especially to you in the UK, I suspect, what we are doing must seem to be just about economics. But that really is secondary. What we are really about is creating a new basis for European relationships. The overriding purpose is to lock Germany into the system and create a political unit where it will be unthinkable for us to be involved again in a bloody European conflict.'

Gwynfor leant forward, cup and saucer in hand.

'For those of us who lived through the war, all that is logical. Admirable even. But for the younger generation, those born after the war, it's not so obvious.'

'I think it's clearer for the continental countries, those most immediately affected by the war. But I can see that for people in Britain it feels different. You've never been invaded. You've never been occupied. You won your wars, you still feel a great power.'

'They weren't our wars,' Phil interrupted. 'Wales is not, and never could be a great power.'

'I follow what you are saying. But not even the Second World War? The fight against fascism? Was that not your war also? Aneurin has brought you to the right place in the Commission, you know. Altiero Spinelli founded the *Movimento Federalista Europeo* during the war, and that laid the foundations for what we are doing here.'

'The European Federalist Movement,' Aneurin translated.

'Yes, quite so. It should appeal to you who are from Wales. It's about breaking with the past, to create a federal Europe in which the smaller countries can live on equal terms and tie the large ones so close together that war will be unthinkable.'

'But in the process, won't you just be creating another bloc to compete with Russia and America?' Phil questioned.

'We have to live in the world as it is. Europe needs to combine to become more effective. And we need to resist external threats. But this is not about creating a superpower. We are not envisaging the creation of institutions at the European level with the same degree of central control that is exerted over France by Paris, say, or over Britain by the government in London.'

'The question is the direction of travel,' Dafydd Elis-Thomas cut across him.

'Of course, there is a debate, about how loose or connected the relationships should be. Should we be creating an integrated federation where there are clear demarcations of responsibilities, competencies as we say, between levels of government? Or should we be thinking of a looser, more confederal system? The debate is about how far we need go to harmonise policies and regulations across our national borders. It is not easy to see which way it will end up. But we are moving towards creating a single market for most goods and services and for allowing the free flow of capital and labour.'

'That's all very well,' Phil countered. 'But what about the smaller countries that are trapped inside the old nation states?'

'As you know, there is a resurgence of devolutionary feeling across Europe.'

Riccardo turned to Phil to address him directly.

'The new European framework is encouraging it. Surely you can see that? Germany is itself a federation with its *Länder* regional governments. So is Belgium. Flanders and Wallonia are gaining more powers all the time. In Italy, we have our own regional system. France remains more centralised, I'll admit, but that can change. In the UK, you are having your debate.'

It was Wigley's turn to raise a question.

'But if you create a single market as you describe, won't that encourage centralisation of economic activity in the stronger parts of Europe and threaten the more outlying areas?'

'What you say is true,' Riccardo answered. 'We need a new set of policies for channelling resources to the under-developed parts of Europe, more intervention to protect the regions. Only then will more integration become possible.'

'But where does democracy fit into this project?' Dafydd Elis-Thomas demanded. 'I get no feel of a people's Europe in what you are describing, only a sense of bureaucratic structures.'

Riccardo responded eagerly, getting up to pour some more coffee as he did so.

'That is why the European Parliament should have more powers. How do we reconcile democracy and efficiency in these matters? Negotiations must allow latitude. But no decisions can follow from nine separate parliaments. A transnational debate is needed.'

'I don't see it happening,' Elis-Thomas said shortly.

'It is more complicated than introducing a Common Market, to be sure. There are political difficulties. At present only limited activity is allowed in the Treaty. But that will be changed, eventually. Of course, the oil crisis and the economic problems are making it difficult. And now everything is on hold because of the UK referendum.'

'How do you see these problems being resolved?' Wigley asked.

'Political union in Europe is no small undertaking. There are many difficulties. Not least, we Europeans tend to project on to Europe the experience of our own national systems. In other words, we instinctively believe that politics in Europe should work like our politics at home. But that is a very wrong assumption.'

'I'm not sure I follow.'

'Well, take the two main players in all this, France and Germany. Nowhere is difference in style and in substance bigger than between them. Despite their republican rhetoric, French politics still turn around the *power of the Prince*. It is he who must enjoy democratic legitimacy. In no other western country is the executive stronger and the parliament weaker than in France. Is that not so? Indeed, for French culture, the whole point of having a government is to expect it to shape events, to *make history.*'

After emphasising the last few words, Riccardo stopped, and looked round at his guests quizzically. Phil nodded encouragingly, so he continued.

'However, the reverse is true in Germany. Nowhere else is the central government weaker and the parliament stronger. Germany's federal system gives lots of power to the states — that is, the regions, the *Länder*, away from the centre. So while the French expect fast and decisive action from their politicians, the Germans are deeply suspicious of any form of discretionary power. They have an understandably difficult relationship with the notion of *making history*.'

'Yes, well, they tried that,' Phil said.

'The Germans believe that markets must be regulated. But they have as little appetite for French *dirigisme* as they have for Anglo-Saxon *laissez-faire*. They expect politicians to establish rules and to enforce them consistently with as little derogation as possible.'

'You make any agreement between France and Germany sound extremely difficult, even unlikely,' Gwynfor said.

'Ah, but do not underestimate the drive for unity. Continental Europeans will not give up on this new way of organising relationships. The lessons of history are too compelling, the vested interests too strong. And in the process European unification is redefining the problem of sovereignty.'

'That's the nub of it,' Elis-Thomas interrupted again, but Riccardo was not to be deflected.

'Naturally you are concerned about the problems of minorities within states. But Europe is changing the way we handle them. So, take the Tyrol in northern Italy, where there is a German minority. We have had that problem since 1918. Looked at from the traditional vantage point of the self-interest of Germany on the one hand and Italy on the other, it appears irresolvable. The EEC has not intervened directly but the existence of the EEC has had a beneficial effect.'

'I guess the same could be true for Northern Ireland,' Dafydd Wigley suggested.

'Exactly so,' Riccardo agreed enthusiastically. 'That is to say, if the UK votes to remain within the EEC. It was Jean Monnet, you know, who said that European solutions are only possible when national governments are trapped in unsolvable contradictions. That is why the European dimension could help with the Northern Ireland problem.'

At this point Aneurin rose, explaining it was time for their next appointment. Gwynfor shook their host's hand warmly, thanking him for a thoughtful exchange. But as they were leaving, Phil took Perissich aside.

'We are very concerned that the Commission stopped the meeting that was due to be held here with Yann Fouéré, organised by the European Federalist Union.'

Riccardo was momentarily discomforted. 'Yes, we are aware of that,' he said. 'I will convey your concerns to Altiero Spinelli.'

* * *

More meetings followed, with specialists in agriculture, the regions, social policy, energy, education and international co-operation until the delegation was incapable of absorbing any more information. They were given lunch by Sean Ronan, the Irish director general for information, in the oak-panelled and gilded restaurant of the Metropole Hotel, famous for being the Nazi headquarters in Belgium during the Second World War.

In the evening they attended a drinks reception in the office of the UK's newly established Permanent Representation. Later, following a dinner hosted by the Commission at the Berlaymont, the Plaid delegation walked back to their hotel.

Gwynfor immediately went to bed, but the rest wandered into the bar to continue the day's discussions over more drinks.

It was well past midnight when Phil Williams headed for his room. An insomniac, he found sleep as elusive as usual. Instead he began to sort through his notes in preparation for a press conference the delegation was due to give in the morning.

For a man of such intellectual accomplishment, his handwriting retained a childlike simplicity, his ink pen making exaggerated circles to the letters g and p in his lined notebook. Phil resolved that in a situation where the delegation was so conflicted about Europe, the safest course was to focus on the banning of Yann Fouéré. Reaching for his briefcase he found the *Irish Times* and opened it to the report about the Breton's cancelled meeting. He began to write.

* * *

The media briefing room on the ground of the Berlaymont building was encouragingly full as the Plaid group, led by Aneurin Rhys Hughes, filed in. He introduced the delegation and then invited Phil to make an opening statement.

'Cymru-Wales is one of the oldest nations in Europe,' he began. 'Our language and literature go back 2,000 years. Our laws were codified over a thousand years ago. However, today Wales is a submerged nation – a nation without its own government and without any official international recognition except in the field of sport.'

Alongside him Phil saw that Dafydd Elis-Thomas was shifting uneasily in his seat, but he pressed on regardless.

'Our delegation from Plaid Cymru – including three members of parliament – has come to Brussels to study the effect that membership of the EEC will have on the life of Wales. In doing this we are conscious of the other submerged nations of Europe, including Euskadi, Breizh, Catalunya, Occitania, Kernow and Scotland.'

Dafydd Wigley nodded encouragingly.

'In judging the effect of EEC membership, we decided in advance that our yardstick would be Breizh/Bretagne. The Bretons are our closest cousins on mainland Europe. Our languages are similar, and our personal contacts are very close. Moreover, we have both survived as nations under the rule of another powerful ex-imperial nation, and for both of us the future is uncertain.'

Phil took hold of the copy of the *Irish Times* he had brought and held it aloft, revealing the headline.

'It was therefore very unfortunate that the news that greeted us on arrival was that a meeting which was to be addressed by Yann Fouéré – a very old friend of Wales – had been banned by the EEC. It seemed clumsy, to say the least. At the very time when the Commission was providing us with every facility to question the operation of the EEC, a meeting arranged by a Committee which included representatives of Plaid Cymru had been forbidden by the very same Commission. It is sad that my first impression of the EEC was the suppression of free speech.'

There was a murmur among a group of officials who had gathered at the back of the room to watch the proceedings. Phil noted it with satisfaction.

'Our series of meetings with officials of the EEC continues today and tomorrow. But already our hopes, and our fears, are both confirmed. For example, in a discussion of industrial policy it was explained that steps were being taken to encourage transnational mergers and takeovers and to harmonise company law. This will ring alarm bells throughout Wales. We have suffered far too long from the branch factory syndrome where most of our factories are controlled from headquarters outside

Wales. Each merger seems to lead to the centre of power moving even further away.'

He stopped for a moment, to look defiantly around the room.

'We get the strong impression that in the EEC the first priority is economic growth, whatever the cost to the historic communities of Europe. To us, any economic plan should start with the aim of preserving communities – even at the cost of economic growth.'

Phil paused and folded his papers.

'It is noteworthy that in the EEC the word community is used so frequently. So it is ironic, don't you think, that this idea of community is the one concept that has so little bearing on the record of the EEC.'

With that flourish Phil finished. Aneurin signalled that the delegation was prepared to answer questions. The first was from a journalist with the *Financial Times*. He asked what Plaid Cymru's position was going to be in the forthcoming UK referendum.

'Shall I respond to that?' Gwynfor said.

'By all means,' Aneurin nodded.

'Our position is quite simply that we say Yes to Europe, but No to the EEC,' Gwynfor began, noting that his opening comment had the effect of making the journalists in front of him sit up.

'We believe in creating a European federation or, perhaps more accurately, a confederation. But it must be based on the older and generally smaller homelands of Europe, and not the more recent imperially inclined nation-states. We believe the day is coming when the peoples of Europe will feel more Breton than French, more Bavarian than German, more Tuscan than Italian and, indeed, more Welsh and Scottish than British.

'As Phil has said, we share this vision with Yann Fouéré. Each people in their homeland should be guaranteed the right to cultural and administrative self-government. In that way the problems of minorities, frontiers, and conflicts that have so plagued Europe for the best part of the last two centuries will be eliminated.'

Gwynfor broke off for a moment, pleased to see that some of the journalists were taking notes.

'For us the EEC threatens to take Europe in the wrong direction. Plaid Cymru is concerned in the first place to ensure a European order which will foster a European civilisation whose source is found, and found only, in the national traditions of Europe. Jean Jaurès put it well. "Destroy the nation," he said, "and you will sink back into barbarism".

'Attempting to create a successful European federation from among the British, the French, the Germans or the Italians will be very difficult. They have too much history of competition. But it would be much easier between peoples like the Basques, Bretons, Walloons, Alsatians, Catalans, Bavarians and, of course, the Welsh. We have never quarrelled over our frontiers. Our vision looks to Switzerland, which is a multi-lingual confederation made up of self-governing cantons.'

*　*　*

Following their visit to Brussels Plaid Cymru's leaders came up with a slogan that fully expressed the party's stance, *Europe Yes! EEC No!* But in the June referendum campaign itself, the slogan proved a disaster.

As Phil Williams wrote later, 'The EEC had already bought an effective copyright on the word *Europe* and had changed its meaning. Joining the EEC became *going into Europe*. To accept the Treaty of Rome was to be *pro-European*. And, as a double distortion of the language, a non-elected body with little power, representing just a third of the population, was referred to as the *European Parliament*.'

Cardiff
June 1975

Owen ran up the steps of the recently opened Oriel gallery in Charles Street near Cardiff's city centre and immediately met a wall of people clogging the entrance. Raymond Williams, billed as 'in conversation' with Carwyn James about his latest book, was popular. Owen was anxious that he would miss the beginning.

A hum of conversation greeted him together with an atmosphere heavy with smoke. He sidestepped to avoid a glass of red wine tipping down his jacket as he made his way up the stairs to the bookshop above. Waving to a few people he knew, he reached the first floor and gazed at a throng of people filling the spaces between the low-slung bookshelves, seeking out his friend Robin. He found him at the far end of the room close to a table littered with empty wine bottles, and plates with a few limp sandwiches.

'Help yourself to the dregs,' Robin greeted him.

Owen wiped a used glass with a paper napkin and poured a drink from a doubtful-looking bottle of Bulgarian red wine.

'I thought I'd be late.'

'We're still waiting for Carwyn. The main attraction if you ask me.'

'Yes, well that follows. Raymond's not exactly box office when you compare him with our obsession with rugby and all its works. Even Gwynfor says Carwyn's the most famous Welshman in the world.'

'He's a literary man as well, you know. He's most famous as a rugby personality, to be sure, the British Lions and all that. But for him rugby represents our potential, for what Wales could do in the world if we were only given the chance.'

'If you say so, but his rugby fame trumps Raymond's literary reputation when it comes to this crowd.'

'I guess you might be related to him.'

'Do you think so? It's possible I suppose. But no, I'm sure I'd know if I was. Definitely.'

Robin changed the subject. That morning Plaid Cymru had declared its response to the Common Market referendum held the previous week.

'What did you make of the press conference? I was surprised they'd worked out their policy so quickly.'

'Gwynfor's had it up his sleeve for quite a while, if you ask me.'

'He looked heartily pleased with the result, I thought,' Robin said.

'Exactly, he's a crafty old bird. Despite Plaid being against the Common Market, I think he was always secretly in favour.'

'He was always in favour of Europe. The Common Market was the problem. Anyhow, it seems we're now working for full national status within the European Community.'

'Sounds less alarming than independence don't you think? Or even self-government, or dominion status or whatever other formula Plaid has had in the past.'

'Gwynfor reckons the vote to stay in the Common Market demolishes the case against self-government. Anyway, that's what I'm saying in tomorrow's paper.'

'With a puff of smoke, Gwynfor gets rid of the argument about separatism.'

'If it were only that simple.'

'He says it's heads we win, tails we win.'

'There's Gwynfor for you.'

At that moment Peter Finch, the bookshop manager, appeared to announce that Carwyn James had arrived.

'I say, Peter, can I use your office phone?' Owen asked. 'I need to check something with the paper.'

'OK, but don't be long, we're starting soon.'

* * *

When Owen emerged from the office, he found the bookshop was deserted and everyone had crowded downstairs. People sitting on the stairs peered to get a glimpse of a small raised platform at the far end of the art gallery where Raymond Williams and Carwyn James were seated. Owen squeezed past and propped himself against a wall alongside rows of chairs containing most of the audience.

'I wanted to be very careful not to write in what had become identified as a Welsh style, that is to say, in England,' Raymond Williams was saying.

'Yes, it is extraordinarily spare, the very opposite of what you might call florid.' Carwyn James made his point with characteristic unobtrusiveness. Owen gathered they were talking about Raymond's first novel *Border Country.*

'It seems to me that you achieve your effect through the rhythms of spoken dialogue, rather than a more rhetorical flourish.'

'Yes, that's it. The Welsh style that had got recognition in England did, in fact, have certain relations to Joyce, in its extreme verbal exuberance. Dylan Thomas was the most notable example. It had the effect of turning Welsh people into the characters the style demanded – you know, garrulous eccentrics.'

Carwyn laughed.

'They do exist, of course.'

'The fact that it did represent observable forms made it all the more necessary to draw back. I admired it but I felt it necessary to get away from the perception of the Welsh that it presented to the outside world. It seemed to me that kind of language was a form of cultural subordination. It was as if this was the only way we could present ourselves to a London audience. At all events, I was determined to avoid that.'

'In one of your more famous essays you wrote that culture is ordinary. In fact, that was the title of one of your essays, wasn't it? It's a very simple but quite profound idea.'

Carwyn James leant forward eagerly as he said these words, his easy charm masking a shyness and complexity that was instantly attractive to the audience. Raymond responded by smiling approvingly.

'It's where we must start. We use the word culture in two senses, to mean the arts and learning of course, and then also a whole way of life. Some writers reserve the word for one or other of these senses. I insist on both.'

'And that, I think, is a product of your upbringing.'

'Why yes, I imagine that's right. I was brought up in Pandy, you know, and everything I had seen growing up there led me to towards that emphasis. To grow up in that country was to see the shape of a culture. I could stand on the mountains and look north and east to Herefordshire, the farms and the cathedral, or to the west and south to the smoke and the flare of the blast furnace making a second sunset. To grow up in that family was to see the shaping of minds, the learning of new skills, the shifting of relationships, the emergence of different ideas.'

'In the same essay you remark that when you arrived in Cambridge, straight from school, so to speak, you quite liked the place, the Tudor courts and chapels and so on. You weren't in any way daunted by it?'

'Not at all. I wasn't oppressed by Cambridge as you suggest. After all, I had come from a country that has twenty centuries of history written visibly into the earth. There is the joke that an upper-class Englishman says his family came over with the Normans, and we reply, "Are you liking it here?"'

Laughter greeted this response, which encouraged Carwyn to explore the issue further.

'It occurs to me that someone like yourself, if he'd come from a working-class background in a more urban environment, in England say, would have been unlikely to have had that sense of historical self-confidence?'

Raymond lent back in his chair. He was wearing a checked sports jacket and a round-necked sweatshirt, both a dark colour that emphasised the prominence of his craggy features.

'Maybe that's right, but it's also because the Welsh grammar schools are English implantations in Wales. It explains why obstacles of the kind you describe don't apply. Anyway, that's how it seems to me. Why didn't my headmaster send me to a university in Wales? That would have suited my life much better. It's no use going back over it, but it would have. But that's what he was there for – to find boys like me and send them to Oxford or Cambridge. I don't say this in any spirit of hostility to him, he thought he was doing the best thing for me.'

'Was there any way at all in which Cambridge jarred for you?'

Raymond Williams thought for a moment. He took his pipe from his jacket pocket, found some tobacco and struck a match.

'There's one occasion I can recall. It was later on when I returned to Cambridge after the war. I went to a talk by Lionel Knights on the meaning of neighbour in Shakespeare. When he said that these days nobody can understand Shakespeare's meaning of neighbour, for in a corrupt mechanical civilisation there are no neighbours, I got up. I said there were obviously different kinds of community, but coming from Wales I knew perfectly well what neighbour meant.'

'I imagine there wasn't much of a sympathetic response to that.'

'No. Someone attacked me for speaking sentimental nonsense. And there was F.R. Leavis you know, leaning against the wall at the back of the room, nodding approvingly while he was doing so.'

'And you didn't feel undermined?'

'Not at all. I had direct experience of neighbours, you see, when I was growing up, and later. When my father was dying one man came in and dug the garden. Someone loaded and delivered a lorry load of sleepers for firewood. Another came and chopped the sleepers into blocks. Another – I don't know who, it was never said –left a sack of potatoes at the back door. A woman came in and took away a basket of washing. That's what we mean by neighbourliness.'

'But they'd lost that sense in Cambridge.'

'Knights and Leavis had, certainly.'

Carwyn James shifted in his chair, seeking to change the conversation's direction.

'Moving on to the present day, can I ask your views on the Common Market debate we've been having? Which way did you vote in last week's referendum for instance?'

'To stay in, naturally. Since the early sixties I have been in favour of European integration, though at the same time against the Common Market in its limited form. International capitalism and its monetary system, including its British components, have now so thoroughly penetrated our economy and society that any *national* solution, even on the basis of the UK, is *politically* inconceivable.'

Raymond held his pipe half-raised while he was speaking, but now placed it in his mouth for a moment, reflecting.

Carwyn prompted him, 'So you think we must be involved.'

'Without doubt, but to go in passively would certainly be

wrong. At this late stage – we should have joined much earlier – we must go in actively, to work for a political presence in every area where decisions are still possible.'

'What kind of things do you have in mind?'

'Oh, an elected parliament, co-operative devolution and, above all, connecting the socialist and trade union movements across borders in Europe. It will be long and hard, but I believe it is now our only way.'

'So why do you think that so many on the Left were against?'

'Well, as I see it, the old Left, the Labourist Left, has always linked a social democratic ideology with the uniqueness of British society and its traditions. I know this because I grew up with it.'

'On the Welsh border?'

'Yes, people of that frame of mind speak of international capitalism as if British capitalists are simply not part of it. They speak of British freedoms as if we did not live in what is at best a capitalist democracy. After all, we have a manipulative electoral politics, with no proportionality in the voting system. And Britain is integrated substantially into the American military power structure.'

'And you see mainstream Labour as esentially collaborating with all of that?'

'Oh yes, the more the Labourist Left tries to avoid or cover up these contradictions, the more it becomes incredible.'

'You said you regard our elections as manipulative?'

'Absolutely. The classic way out of every crisis of English capitalism is to alternate the major parties. This process of replacement can defuse successive crises for years on end. Political coalitions are not built in this country. They arrive ready-made through the voting system. The two large parties do not really even have to negotiate their policies – they write a manifesto for the election, but once in power they do as they please.'

'So this will go on for years on end, as you put it?'

'It's my main reason for supporting the two movements which seem to me to be putting pressure on the system from opposite ends, so to speak – the national movements in Wales and Scotland, and the international movement towards an integrated Europe.'

'How optimistic are you that these problems can be resolved?'

'Well, now Britain is integrated into a European electoral process, there is some hope that alternative alliances can be made. At the very least, negotiations which are completely blocked in this country, between social democrats, socialists and communists can be opened up as a new perspective – that is to say, once we are beyond the confines of the British state with its curious electoral straitjacket.'

'You mean the first-past-the-post electoral system.'

'Indeed.'

'So you're in favour of electoral reform?'

'Proportional representation? Without a doubt, it's the one thing guaranteed to break the present stifling logjam in British politics.'

Sully Island

August 1975

When he mentioned he was going to Swansea, Mari said she would like to come as well.

'Why?' Owen asked before adding hurriedly, 'I mean, why do you want to go to Swansea?'

'It's not the ends of the earth, you know. In fact, it's a nice town, an ugly lovely town, as Dylan said. I like it better than Cardiff. It was my town when I was growing up. I've been meaning to spend some time at the Glynn Vivian.'

'Where?'

'The art gallery.'

'Never heard of it.'

'I don't suppose you've heard of Ceri Richards either.'

Owen looked at her blankly.

'You've got so much to learn,' she said.

* * *

A few days later Owen picked up Mari from her house in Penarth.

'So, where's Anna?' she asked brightly. 'Don't tell me she's working.'

Owen coloured.

'She's gone to stay with her parents.'

'In Grosmont?'

'Yes, hasn't seen them for a while.'

'Aren't they expecting you as well? It's the weekend, after all.'

'I'm working.'

'You're always working.'

'I don't go out to work, I go out to play,' Owen said, trying to lighten their exchange.

'*Ti'n fachgen drwg*, a bad boy.'

'I don't think so.'

'You wouldn't.'

Mari lit a cigarette and gazed through the window of the Volkswagen as they left the city and climbed the hill westwards towards Cowbridge.

'So what takes you to Swansea?' she asked eventually.

'Swansea Sound.'

'What?'

'The radio station. You know the commercial station they set up a year or so ago, first in Wales.'

'Oh, that.'

'I'm writing a piece on it, I'm told it's quite a success.'

'How do they know?'

'Well, the audience, for one thing. They reckon that to survive a local station needs to reach half-a-million people.'

'That's a lot more than Swansea.'

'Yes, the whole of Swansea Bay is not much more than 300,000. But it's getting well beyond that, into Dyfed and as far east as Aberdare, and even into England, apparently. They say it has an audience in Ilfracombe.'

'Straight across the sea.'

Owen laughed.

Mari wound down the window and threw out the stub of her cigarette. 'We're so close to England.'

'It's only pop records and chat. They probably like the Welsh accent.'

'All the same, do they have any Welsh on it?'

'A bit, I think. It's one of the things I want to find out.'

They drove through Bridgend and passed Porthcawl. When they reached Port Talbot Owen pointed to the smoke, steam and flares being emitted from the giant British Steel plant that spread for miles along the shoreline.

'It's all that'll be left by the end of the decade,' he said. 'And I suppose Llanwern if we're lucky.'

'What do you mean? Mari queried.

Owen glanced across at her.

'Reckon you've got a few things to learn too. Haven't you heard? There's going to be a huge shake-out in the steel industry. East Moors in Cardiff, Shotton in the north and Ebbw Vale are all going. Getting on for 30,000 jobs, that'll be. A thousand went at Newport's Tube works a year ago. Don't know how the economy's going to cope. It's about a tenth of the Welsh workforce we're talking about.'

'And that comes on top of all the coal mines closing.'

'That's right. Puts a lot of things into perspective.'

They crossed the Tawe at Briton Ferry and eventually reached the centre of Swansea and the Glynn Vivian gallery. As Owen gazed at the Edwardian splendour of its Bath stone columns, Mari lent across and kissed him on the cheek.

'Come and get me when you're ready,' she said opening the door. 'I can spend all day here.'

*　*　*

It was late-afternoon before Owen managed to return. The weather was warm. He took off his jacket and tie and threw them in the back of the car after parking a short distance from the gallery. Once inside, it was cooler. Owen was conscious of his shoes echoing as he walked through the marble-floored entrance. Ahead of him a broad stairway led upwards. Hesitating, he decided to climb to the top of the building and work his way down.

Once on the first floor he was bathed in a stream of light from the vaulting glass roof a few storeys above him. He climbed again to discover a mezzanine floor with shelves of pottery, plates and other artefacts. Glancing down through the opening at the floor below, he could see walls lined with heavily framed pictures. Suddenly he spotted her unmistakeable light green flowing dress. She was seated on a bench in the middle of the floor, her head bowed over a sketch book.

Owen decided to surprise her. He descended the stairs and slid his arms around her back.

'I already saw you,' she said.

Owen looked up at the painting she was sketching. The coiled naked body of a man was tumbling into a black void, legs and feet splaying upwards. Above him was some kind of bird flying past, bearing a white sheet in its beak.

'It's an owl,' Mari said, looking at Owen's mystified expression. 'I think Ceri meant the figure dropping out of the shroud, the falling man, to be Dylan. There is an earlier lithograph version in which the face is clearly Dylan's.'

'Dylan Thomas?'

'Yes, it's inspired by that line about the death of his father, you know, *Do not go gentle into that good night.*'

'Weird,' Owen said.

'But powerful, don't you think? Represents the futility of protest, Ceri said. But I think he also meant it to be a kind of affirmation, of the work we leave behind. Dylan's poetry, I suppose, and his own art.'

'A bit morbid, I'd say.'

Mari stood up and took his hand.

'Come on, I want to show you something else, something I think you'll like better.'

She led him to the far end of the room.

'Another by your…'

'Ceri Giraldus Richards, yes. It's one of my favourites.'

Mari stopped in front of a completely different picture.

'They're his two daughters,' she said.

Owen saw a strangely proportioned girl concentrating on playing a piano, an outstretched arm and large hand with ballooning fingers hovering over the keys. Another girl, seated in an armchair, looked on haughtily. Between them was an oddly-shaped piano. The composition was held together by contrasting colours and angles.

'This one makes a bit more sense,' he said after a while. 'Who was Ceri Richards, anyway?'

'He was brought up not far from here, in Dunvant.'

'On Gower?'

'Where Swansea merges into Gower, you could say. He left school just after the first war and started work as an electrical apprentice in a foundry. The firm went out of business, but he managed to enroll at the Swansea School of Art along the road from here.'

'That was a bit of luck.'

'He was encouraged by his family, his mother especially. She was a teacher before she married. They were a Welsh-speaking family, highly cultured as working-class people often were in those days, a lot of poetry and music in the house. Ceri learnt to play the piano when he was fifteen.'

'Hence this picture.'

'It's one of a series. But the great thing about him is the way he brings music, poetry and art together. Music especially. It's the colours, you see, the way they relate to music.'

'I don't follow.'

'Music is the ultimate teacher, was the way he put it.'

'I still don't see.'

'Kandinksy.'

'You've lost me completely now.'

'Kandinsky, the Russian painter, one of the early Post-Impressionists.'

'The what?'

'The movement that looked for the spiritual in art. Kandinsky had a big influence on Richards.'

As she spoke Mari opened her bag, pulled out a notebook and leafed through it.

'Here, this is something he said which Ceri quoted a lot. It's what I'm trying to get at myself.'

Mari read quietly at first, but then more firmly. 'Colour is the keyboard, the eyes are the hammers, the soul is the piano with many strings. The artist is the hand which plays, touching one key or another, to cause vibrations in the soul.'

'And you think that explains this picture, what Ceri Richards is up to.'

'I do. The artist envies the ease with which music expresses the inner life. So he applies the methods of music to his own art. It's all there, don't you see? Ceri gets his shapes from Picasso as well, and his colours from Matisse.'

'And makes them his own?'

'You're coming on, *cariad*.'

* * *

Later, driving towards Cardiff, Owen said they should stop for something to eat. He suggested a place near Penarth. It looked out on the Bristol Channel and Sully Island, a small strip of land not far from the shore, less than a mile long and fifty yards across.

Inside, Mari studied the menu.

'Why is the pub called the Captain's Wife?'

'They made it by knocking three old fishermen's cottages into one. One of them once belonged to a sea captain, and the story goes he took his wife with him on one of his voyages and during it she died. He brought her back and secretly buried her in a wood nearby. It's one reason why the pub is supposed to be haunted.'

'Do you believe in ghosts?'

'Not really.'

'I do, I believe they're all around us.'

'Good ones or bad ones?'

'Both, figuratively speaking anyway.'

Mari spoke seriously.

'It's why we're so fascinated by myths and stories. It's not a question of whether they're literally true, but the inner meaning that comes from them, the meanings behind the myths, you might say.'

'And you think it's the same with ghosts?'

'I do. It's the strong sense we have – I have anyway – that the past is always with us. Our ancestors are with us and living through us. They move through our heads and flow through our limbs.'

'That's just another way of saying that family ties are important, the world over.'

'But especially strong in Wales, don't you think?'

'Perhaps we like to think so.'

After they'd finished their meal they wandered outside and leant against the wall overlooking the strand of rocks, mud and seaweed that separated the shoreline from the island about four hundred yards away. The evening was drawing in, but they were reluctant for the day to end.

'Let's cross,' Mari said impulsively. 'You get a wonderful view down the channel.'

'The tide?'

'Oh, come on, it's miles out.'

Owen retrieved some jackets from the car and they set off. There was a gap in the wall and they had to step over some awkwardly jagged rocks before reaching the greasy wetness of the causeway that led to the island. Mari slipped and nearly fell before clinging on to Owen's arm. He felt the full weight of her ample body and stumbled himself. But eventually they reached the shingle-lined shore. Mari led the way through a muddy track lined with high rushes. In a short while they emerged to find a path along the grassy verge of a low cliff that overlooked the Channel. They followed it to a promontory that marked the island's highest point.

Mari held Owen's arm, leaning closely against him.

'Where we're standing was a Bronze Age barrow, and apparently it was a Saxon age fort as well. I come here quite a lot to sketch. 'You can feel the closeness of the sky to the water. It's another world.'

'It's a bit like being on a ship at sea. Except we're not moving.'

'Oh, but we are! The whole earth is moving. Being here makes you sense it. Sometimes the rushing tide makes me feel that the island is moving separately, like when you're sitting in a train in a station and another goes slowly past.'

They sat down and Owen pointed towards Flat Holm and Steep Holm between them and the English coast.

'They're quite far, maybe three or four miles, but they look a lot nearer.'

Steep Holm rose almost vertically out of a gathering mist, giving it a volcanic appearance. Owen rose to get a better view. Then he looked for a sandbank close to the island. A moment before it had seemed quite large. Now it had disappeared. He turned in search of the causeway and the gap between the island and the shore. But all he could see was water flowing strongly.

Urgently he pulled Mari to her feet.

'We're going to have to run. We could be cut off.'

Owen reached the shingle first. The causeway was still visible. He thought it could be crossed. But by the time Mari arrived, it was disappearing.

'I think we can make it.'

'I'm not sure.'

'I'll go first.'

Owen set out, but after about ten yards turned and saw that Mari wasn't following.

'It's no use. You go on.'

Owen returned and Mari laughed.

'How gallant.'

'Time and tide wait for no man.'

'Or woman. We'll just have to wait for the next low tide.'

'It's getting dark, and chilly.'

'So it is.'

*   *   *

Mari led the way back to the seaward side of the island.

'We'll have to find somewhere to hunker down. Go and find some driftwood. I'll light a fire.'

When he returned she had clambered down from the grass-edged cliff and made a bed of rushes and grass in an angle between two large rocks just above the tide line. She was lighting some twigs and paper she had torn from her notebook in a small circle of stones.

'Find some more wood before it gets really dark. We'll need all you can get.'

The fire was alight when he returned for a second time. Mari reached in her bag and pulled out a small bottle of Scotch.

'Emergency rations. I think we can call this an emergency, don't you?'

Inky water swirled in rapidly, covering the rocks just below them. The fire spluttered and sent some sparks into the air. Throwing some wood on it, Owen sat down and she passed him the bottle.

'Good job we didn't try and cross over,' he said.

'How long do you think we'll have to wait?'

'A good few hours.'

'It was clever of you to bring the jackets. I suppose this is Anna's.'

Owen grunted and they were quiet, watching the fire and the black water streaming past them up the Channel. The Devon coast fell away to the west. The rush of water gave the impression it was pushing uphill, against the curvature of the earth. It felt as though they were in a sphere of blackness, with the stars reflected against a mirror made by the water below.

Mari threw some more wood on the fire.

'I can't get my mind off this book I've been reading,' she said after a while. 'It's about Canada, Canadian culture I suppose, but it says a lot about us as well.'

'Canada?'

'It's by this writer Margaret Atwood, about how the Canadians live so close to the United States.'

'Ah, I see, you're talking about our being up against the English in the same kind of way.'

'There are parallels. She says countries have symbols that sum up who they are.'

'In what way?'

'They're generalisations, of course. For America it's *Frontier*. You know the unconquered spaces, the wild west, virgin territory and all that. For England, she says it's the *Island*, self-contained with the Queen in charge. The Englishman's home is his castle, an island unto itself.'

'Except England isn't an island. Though they act as if it is. What about Canada?'

'Oh, *Survival*. That's the title of her book. For the early explorers and settlers, it was a matter of carving out a place in a hostile landscape and simply keeping alive. She says that's stayed as the way Canadians think about themselves. Not only that, they're preoccupied with the obstacles to survival which they scarcely ever overcome. She says that whereas the Americans have a will to win, Canadians have a will to lose.'

'Sounds a bit sweeping.'

'It is, but it contains a kernel of truth don't you think? She talks about Canada being a victim culture, the result of being exploited.'

'A colony, you mean.'

'Which it was, to begin with anyway. But what's fascinating is the way she describes the response, what she calls victim positions.'

'Positions?'

'Yes, they can be the same whether you're a victimised individual, a minority group, even a country. Colonised people are victims, aren't they? They have a damaged psyche. Their confidence drains away, they lack a sense of empowerment.'

Interested, Owen sat up and leant against the rock that enclosed them.

'Go on.'

'She describes four positions. The first is simply to deny you're a victim. You pretend that obvious facts just don't exist. As a rule, it's an attitude taken by those in the victim group who are a bit better off than the rest.'

'Because they're afraid of losing what they've got, their status or whatever.'

'Exactly. And it's accompanied by anger. They say, "I made it, the rest of you are just lazy or stupid, so it's obvious we aren't victims."'

'And the second position?'

'You accept that you are a victim but explain it as an act of fate, the will of God, biology – in the case of women, for instance.' Mari laughed.

'Or what you think are the economic realities.'

'That's another one, anything that displaces the cause from

the real source of oppression. And in this victim position, the anger is directed against both fellow-victims and oneself.'

'And the third position?'

'This is where it gets interesting. You still acknowledge you're a victim, but you refuse to accept it's inevitable. You say, look at what's being done to me, but it's not an act of God, or fate or anything like that, so I can do something about it.'

'And your anger is directed at the real oppressors.'

'Right, and with a bit of luck it can be channelled into action.'

'So what about this writer's…'

'Margaret Atwood.'

'Yes, what about her fourth position?'

'Well, she says this is the one adopted by the creative non-victim. It makes creative activity possible.'

'It's what we should be aiming for then.'

'That's right. But it's a rare position, especially in societies like ours. It's a form of empowerment, after all. And artists have to feel empowered in order to work. We have to feel that the work we make is significant and important.'

'So artists and writers, people like Ceri Richards for instance, you'd say they're creative non-victims.'

'Absolutely.'

Owen stood up and kicked a large log closer to the fire where it blackened and glowed.

'You know you were talking about symbols earlier, that countries have certain ideas or words that sum them up.'

'Yes.'

'What would you say is ours?'

'Wales, you mean. I'm not sure, what would you say?'

Owen knelt down and found a stick to poke the fire.

'I don't know either. Maybe *Defeat*.'

Grosmont
August 1975

Lost in thought, Anna stared at the familiar fields and lines of the hills as the diesel train sped through the Usk valley towards Abergavenny. Early that Saturday she had come off the night shift and crept into bed, trying as usual not to wake Owen. He had murmured and moved, and then reached out, drawing her to his warmth. They had made love and then, eventually, she had slept. When she woke in the late morning Owen was long gone, away to some corner of Wales searching for a story for his newspaper.

Anna had a few days off and was spending a rare night at home with her parents. She rushed around the house tidying, and then went shopping. There was all too little time before catching the late afternoon train that would arrive, just over an hour later. Her father would be waiting at the station.

She had brought a book, a novel by George Eliot she was trying to read, but it lay unopened on her lap. Instead, the journey gave her a rare moment of stillness, to gaze unseeing through the train window, to think about the life she and Owen were sharing in their small terraced house.

'The thing is, what are we sharing?' she asked herself. 'These days we seem to see so little of each other. We have these odd hours. When I'm home, Owen is away. We don't seem like normal people. We don't even have the weekends most of the time.'

When had they last spoken at any length? Time seemed so short. 'If it wasn't for the Welsh classes,' she thought. 'If it wasn't for them, we might go days at a time without seeing each other.'

She decided something would have to change. In fact, she knew that change was coming. 'What will he think?' she wondered. 'What will he say?' She was reluctant to share her secret. Anyway, was she sure? In truth, she was frightened of

319

thinking about the future. For once her calm equanimity had deserted her.

* * *

She was relieved to see her father waiting in his distracted way on the platform. William was short-sighted and wore round thick glasses that his daughter thought always made him seem vulnerable. He held his squashed trilby in his hand. The draught from the slowing train caused his overlarge jacket to flap open, revealing a short-sleeved sweater and an awkwardly-fitting dog collar. Anna was amused to see that his baggy trousers were stuffed into wellington boots and held up by a rope. Jumping off the train, she ran to him and flung her arms around his neck.

'Just look at you, Dad, as rumpled as ever. How does Mam cope?'

'I've been gardening. And as for your Mam, she's got more important things to do than worry about me.'

They found his ancient, battered Land Rover behind the station and set off, along the narrow back roads out of the town, with Skirrid Fawr rearing to their left. Anna knew every twist and turn. She had been driven along these lanes every day she had attended secondary school in Abergavenny. All the same, it was a strange feeling to be making the journey again.

She glanced across to her father.

'What project have you on the go at the moment?'

'I've started working on a history.

'Oh, of what?

'How Grosmont got started, with the castle in the eleventh century, and then the building of the church. The town was of great strategic importance in those days, you know.'

'Village, you mean.'

'Well it was an important settlement and quite prosperous,

as big as Carmarthen or Abergavenny. It was the location you see. Plugged a gap in the border you might say.'

'I suppose the church is the main thing for you.'

'It's been pretty central down the years. I'm puzzling at the moment about the unknown warrior in the nave.'

'You mean that old block of stone that lies in the corner.'

'It goes back to the fourteenth century, maybe the thirteenth. I'm wondering if it might have some connection with Owain Glyndŵr.'

'You don't mean it could be him?'

'Well, one theory is that he ended his days in this part of the world. One of his daughters, Alys, married John Scudamore of Kentchurch Court. They lived not far from us, just over the border in the Golden Valley. It's said Glyndŵr went into hiding with them at the end of his revolt.'

'Owen would be interested in all that.'

'Yes, he would, wouldn't he.'

* * *

Later Anna helped her mother clearing up after their evening meal. It was a familiar, intimate task, one that had always drawn them together, prompting the kind of conversation that was now taking place. Anna dried while Sylvia washed the dishes.

'So tell me, how are you getting on in that little house of yours in Cardiff?'

'We're fine, we've been painting the kitchen. We're having a new washing machine put in next week.'

'That's good, a real blessing, they are. Wash days were difficult when you were small.'

'You mean the washboard in the sink, the tin baths for rinsing and the old mangle? What happened to the mangle?'

'It's in the back of the shed in the garden.'

Anna laughed.

'And the blue rinse for the sheets. Do you remember how you used to rub it on us when we fell in the stinging nettles?'

'Soothing, it was.'

Sylvia turned from the sink to pick up some more dishes from the kitchen table.

'And Owen, he couldn't come?'

'I told you on the phone, Mam, he's off working somewhere. Swansea, I think.'

'Always working, that one.'

'It's the job, he's got to be on hand.'

'Well, I don't know, you've got to live as well as work.'

'I think for Owen, work is his life.'

'That's all very well.'

'It's what newspapers are mam. Morning papers anyway. He doesn't get into work until mid-morning, but then it goes on. The busiest time is the evenings. Most days he doesn't get home until nine or ten o'clock at night.'

'Not much time for you, then.'

'Well, I'm working as well, shifts of course. But you're right, between the two of us it's hard to get much time together.'

Sylvia turned again, dishcloth in hand, and looked closely at her daughter.

'Remember, marriages are not made in heaven. I of all people should know that.'

'Oh, mam.'

Anna's eyes filled, but she checked herself.

'What do you mean you of all people?'

'Well, look at your dad. He's cuddly enough, especially to you, you're his favourite you know that, but he's the most exasperating person I know.'

Sylvia plunged a dinner plate in the washing bowl.

'Doesn't know where he is half the time. Head in the sky. All he thinks about is his books. If it wasn't for me, I don't know where this church would be.'

'Yes, but you've stuck together all these years haven't you?'

Sylvia looked closely at her daughter again.

'We're a different generation.'

*　*　*

Before she went to bed, Anna poked her head into her father's study. He was seated in his favourite armchair, surrounded by books and papers.

'Tomorrow's sermon?'

'That's right, but come in, come in.'

Anna curled up on the expansive arm of the chair, put her arm around his neck and her head on his chest.

'It's good to have you home,' William murmured, stroking her hair. 'We rattle around here, you know, with all of you gone. It's a big place just for the two of us. There's the upkeep, as well. There's talk of selling it and buying something smaller.'

Anna sat up.

'But that would be awful. They can't do that.'

William laughed.

'Well it's just talk at the moment.'

Anna thought of the years growing up in the place, with her two older brothers and her sister. It had been full of noise. She thought about the parties, when friends from school had come and stayed the night because of the impossibility of getting a bus home. The house had been full then, with mayhem into the small hours. She realised now how welcoming her parents had been. They had just left them to it, retreating to their bedroom and locking the door.

'Remember the parties?' she said now.

'Yes, well, we were the right size for those.'

He sat up in the chair, gathered some of his papers together and placed them in a Bible on the floor.

'Tell me about this Welsh course you're doing, you and Owen.'

'The Wlpan, you mean. It's a new thing. There've been adult classes for years, you know, along with all the other evening courses. But this is different, its intensive. It lasts for ten weeks, and we go every evening in the week for two hours, from seven o'clock. It means I can just make the night shift afterwards, when I'm on nights.'

'Wlpan, you say.'

'It's comes from a Hebrew word, means workshop or something like that. The whole thing is copied from Israel. In fact, it was Owen who started it off, in a way.'

'Really?'

'Yes, you remember, he had that trip to Israel for the paper about a year ago.'

'I do. It was a last-minute thing, wasn't it? Someone higher up who was meant to go was ill, so Owen stepped in.'

'That's right. It was in Jerusalem that he came across this Wlpan business.'

'I remember him telling me now. They're places where immigrants go when they first come to Israel, where they're taught about the country, learn a trade, that kind of thing.'

'But what's most important is that they're taught the language, Hebrew.'

'Just as you're learning Welsh, with your Wlpan in Cardiff.'

'Yes, and more are springing up around Wales, in the north as well. It's been a great success. Gwilym Roberts, our teacher, says it is anyway. He's been teaching classes for just one night a week for ages. But he says we learn more in a month than can be achieved in two years with the old method.'

'And, I suppose it's one thing the two of you get to do together.'

Anna laughed.

''You're right about that. Between everything we don't seem to get a lot of time.'

'Well, you should make the most of it.'

William stood up and gathered his papers and Bible. 'Time for bed. My big day tomorrow.'

* * *

Early the following morning, Anna repeated what she had often done as a child and crept into her parents' bedroom. Sylvia was already awake, sitting up and drinking a cup of tea William had brought her. He was upstairs, putting the finishing touches to his sermon. Anna climbed into the bed, pulled the covers over her and lay still, saying nothing. Eventually she turned over and rested her chin in her hands.

'Mam, I've something to tell you.'

'I know.'

'How?'

Sylvia put her cup and saucer on the table beside the bed, lay down and took Anna in her arms.

'Never mind, just tell me.'

'How did you know?'

'I just did. There's a darkness in your eyes, and look, your breasts are getting bigger.'

Anna giggled.

'I know.'

'What did Owen say?'

'I haven't told him yet.'

'But you must, and soon.'

'I'm afraid.'

'I know, but he'll be fine. Men are like that. They don't want to think about these things at first, but when it happens, well, they come round.'

* * *

Later that morning Anna found herself in her accustomed seat in church alongside her mother, gazing at her father standing in the raised stone pulpit with its set of candles to one side. It struck her again how authoritative he was when in church. He was a completely different man to the disarmingly vulnerable one she knew outside. 'Perhaps it's the cassock', she thought, as she had done innumerable times. He wore a simple single-breasted garment with a black buckled belt and the thirty-nine buttons signifying the Articles of Faith. It made him seem taller, a commanding figure.

His hands were spread out on the pulpit before him and he was speaking in his firm but friendly manner. However, Anna's thoughts drifted. She turned her head towards the stained glass window through which light was streaming. It illuminated the blue, red, purple and yellow figures participating in the Feeding of the Five Thousand. Anna thought how all the icons and images in the church seemed static, catching an ancient moment of time that was completely removed from present day meaning. Whenever she returned home, she slipped back into the comforting certainty of what they represented. When she was away, in what was now her normal life, she gave them no thought at all.

'But what is normal?' she asked herself once more, the question prompted by these thoughts. 'My life isn't normal, it's something completely different, or going to be completely different, but I have no idea what it will be like.'

In recent weeks she had found herself staring at mothers with young children. She looked particularly hard at babies in the hope that seeing them might clarify how she felt. She was disappointed that none of this affected her confused feelings. She told herself it was perfectly natural to feel this way. Why should other people's babies affect her? But Anna wanted certainty about her feelings and that was the one thing that eluded her.

Now it struck her how odd it was that she and Owen had never had a proper conversation about whether they should have children. It had somehow been assumed that it might happen, one day, but had never been really talked about. It had come up once, when they got into a discussion about the merits of Welsh schools and she had agreed that a Welsh-medium education would bring advantages. But that seemed disconnected from any immediate question of having a baby. And it was no answer to how he would respond when confronted with the reality of becoming a father.

* * *

Owen was standing on the platform of Cardiff station that evening when her train pulled in. It was clear that she hadn't seen him because she put her bag down, looking around amid the streaming people. Owen suddenly saw her anew, not as if for the first time, but more like it had been in the early days, and he suddenly felt a flood of protective affection.

He shouted, waved and ran towards her, and then she was in his arms, and he swung her around.

'I've missed you.'

Anna looked shyly at him.

'Have you?'

But soon they were making their way down the wide station steps to the concourse below, and pressed by the rush of people, out of the station. They found the car, parked close to the

Western Mail building, and Owen explained he had been in the office most of the afternoon.

At home he opened a bottle of wine while Anna prepared dinner. Afterwards they sat on their long settee, the main piece of furniture in their small living room at the front of the house and watched television. Owen started to doze, lack of sleep catching up with him. Anna lent against him and studied his face for a while. Suddenly she made up her mind, placed her glass of wine on the small table in front of them, reached forward and turned the television off. She pressed his arm.

'Owen,' she whispered urgently. 'Wake up, I've got something to tell you.'

He murmured and turned towards her.

'I think... I think I'm – I think we're going to have baby.'

Owen jerked awake.

'A baby?'

'Yes.'

'Are you sure?'

'I think I should know, don't you?'

'It's, er, well it's a bit of a shock.'

Owen was confounded, uncertain how to respond. Anna moved close to him and he put his arms around her.

'Oh, Owen.'

He realised she was crying.

'Don't Anna,' he said desperately. 'Why are you crying? It's wonderful.'

They held each other.

'Do you really think so?

'Why yes, of course.'

Owen took out a handkerchief and wiped her eyes. She smiled up at him, feeling a surge of optimism.

Crystal Palace
October 1975

Rhiannon was amazed at how easy it was to climb the mast. They had broken through the perimeter fence of the Crystal Palace television transmitter and were now scaling a built-in ladder that led to the first platform. Ahead of her were three other activists, her friend Branwen Thomas and Gruffudd and Alwen, from Crymych.

'It's like the bloody Eiffel Tower,' Branwen said when they arrived an hour before. Standing within the confines of the Crystal Palace Park and reaching nine hundred feet towards the sky, it was the tallest structure in London, sending television signals to the whole of south-east England. In the early hours of the morning, the small group had cautiously circled the complex to work out the best way to gain entry.

'We'll have to cut through the wire,' Branwen said firmly and reached into her rucksack for a long-handled wire cutter. Not for the first time, Rhiannon was impressed with the initiative and ingenuity of her new friend, a fellow student at Aberystwyth. She was small, little more than five-foot tall, with dark, closely cropped hair and a slash of red lipstick across her mouth. Her family were sheep farmers near Deiniolen on the slopes of Elidir Fawr overlooking Llanberis and Snowdon.

'We'll go through over there where the bushes are overhanging,' Gruffudd suggested. 'Give us some cover.'

Rhiannon had counted four lower gangways before the mast narrowed towards a circular platform near the top. There it became a single spire reaching high above them. The ladder climbed through the centre of the structure. They stopped for a moment when they reached the second ledge, uncertain as to their next move.

'We shouldn't go too high,' Alwen said. 'I've heard there's a risk of being radiated.'

Branwen led the way.

'We should make for the third gangway at least.'

'What do we do then?' Gruffudd asked.

'Stay as long as we can.'

They reached the third gangway and huddled down, squeezing against one another and pressing their feet against a low parapet. Rhiannon shivered and pulled her coat closer, wishing she had brought gloves as well as her woolly hat.

'It's freezing.'

'It's the wind chill,' Branwen said. 'Like on the mountain at home.'

Rhiannon closed her eyes. Her lower back ached where a policeman had punched her earlier in the day. 'Must be just above my left kidney,' she thought, shifting painfully. 'There'll be a huge bruise.'

* * *

They had gathered in Oxford Street in the middle of the afternoon. Twenty activists had travelled from different directions but arrived together at the appointed time. Chanting 'Sianel Gymraeg nawr!' they sat on the pavement, spilled on to the road and halted the traffic. Streams of bemused shoppers picked their way through them. A couple of youths unfolded a large banner. In bold red lettering it declared SIANEL GYMRAEG and below YR UNIG ATEB.

Rhiannon wondered what possible effect their demonstration could have, but then noticed a photographer on the pavement opposite. Soon the police began to arrive, wading into the demonstrators and dragging them away.

'Remember, just go limp,' Branwen hissed to Rhiannon

before she felt herself being grabbed from behind. She sagged. Her hair was wrenched, painfully, as she was pulled away. She was dragged along the pavement and then across the road, her heels hitting the kerb.

'Slags!' the police were shouting. 'Lesbians!'

'Good job I'm wearing my walking boots,' Rhiannon thought.

It was then she was punched. And after that she could recall little, except being bundled into the back of a police van, the door clanging loudly behind her. She was left winded on the floor. There were three boys and Branwen too, her face flushed.

'They've torn my coat,' she said angrily. 'My best coat.'

'Shouldn't have worn it,' one of the boys said.

'Only one I got.'

They were quiet after that, breathing shallowly, for what seemed an age.

Suddenly the doors were flung open and two more activists were hurled in. The van revved up, and they were off, siren wailing.

'Where're we going?'

'No idea.'

After about ten minutes, but which seemed much longer, the van lurched to a halt. The doors opened again, and two policemen appeared. Rhiannon was grabbed and pulled out, followed by Branwen.

'We don't want you,' one of the policeman said. 'Not this time, anyway.'

'Mind we don't see you again,' the other said. 'Get off back home wherever you come from.'

They sat on the kerb edge and watched the van disappear, turning left at a crossroads further up the street.

'Where are we?' Rhiannon asked eventually.

'Don't know, but we've got to get back to Victoria Station to pick up our things,' Branwen said, looking at her watch. 'We've got to get there and then find our way to Crystal Palace.'

*   *   *

Much later they were perched high in the sky with views far across London. The city was lit up against a cold, clear night sky. Rhiannon twisted painfully again, opened her eyes and nudged Branwen.

'How long have we been?'

'An hour, maybe.'

Suddenly, on the ladder below, a policeman appeared.

'We're from the Welsh Language Society, and we demand a Welsh television channel,' Branwen shouted at him.

'We've been told,' the policeman shouted back. 'But all I want to know, love, is when you're coming down.'

'We're staying here indefinitely.'

But that only proved to be another ten minutes.

'I'm dying for a pee,' Branwen confessed to the others. 'We'll have to go down.'

*   *   *

To get to London, Rhiannon and Branwen had hitch-hiked from Aberystwyth to Reading where Branwen's younger brother was in his second year at university. They spent the night in sleeping bags on the floor of his bedsit, a bleak room in a terraced house near the centre of town. Branwen had warned Rhiannon not to be put off by Emrys.

'He's very different to me. But you can't choose your brother, can you.'

He was welcoming enough, however, providing a meal of sausages, baked beans, mashed potatoes and mugs of tea, cooked on a stove on the first-floor landing outside his room. The one table was piled high with papers and books, so they sat cross-legged on the floor.

'What's happening in London?' Emrys asked as he offered the girls an extra helping of potato, scraping the bottom of a saucepan.

'We're going on a demo,' Rhiannon answered.

'What? CND?'

'Cymdeithas,' Branwen said.

'In London?'

'The English government are more likely to take notice if they see us in London than on the streets in Aberystwyth.'

'Or Cardiff, for that matter,' Rhiannon added.

'Can't see them taking much notice wherever you are.'

'An ounce of action is worth a ton of theory,' his sister said.

'I suppose some revolutionary like Karl Marx said that.'

Rhiannon laughed.

'I think it was Engels. Anyway, it's only since we started taking direct action that anyone's taken any notice.'

'Notice of what?'

'The television campaign, for a Welsh channel.'

'Oh that. Jac L. Williams says it would be disastrous for the language and I think I agree with him.'

'What do you mean?'

'He says it would drive the language into a ghetto.'

Rhiannon pictured Jac L. Williams, the professor of education at Aberystwyth. She had recently attended a talk he had given on Welsh-medium schools. She recalled an intimidating man, intense and uncompromising. He suffered from curvature of the spine and adopted a permanently stooped posture. His eyes glowered upwards from beneath dark bushy eyebrows and sweeping black hair. In his talk he had pointed to a precipitous decline in the number of children speaking Welsh, reduced to one in ten. The 1971 census had identified only about 10,000 three-to-four-year-olds able to speak the language.

'It is obvious that we can't rely any longer upon the homes of Wales to safeguard the national language and culture,' he had said. However, whereas in the past the schools had been responsible for the decline of Welsh, now they were the main hope of a revival. In anglicised areas such as Cardiff and Caerphilly, the number of Welsh speaking children had doubled in recent years.

'We know how to convert the young children of Wales into bilinguals with very little effort on their part. The typical child educated in Wales can be bilingual throughout the country by the end of the century, if the nation wishes it.'

Rhiannon had not realised that this powerful advocate of the language was also against the television campaign. But she could see he had influenced Emrys.

'All your channel will do will drive the language into a corner and away from the overwhelming majority of Welsh people,' she heard him saying.

Branwen disagreed.

'If we have our own channel, with Welsh language programmes shown at peak times, why wouldn't Welsh-speakers watch it?'

'Jac L. argues that it's all about Welsh programmes having a place on the mainstream channels and being scheduled to follow popular English programmes. I think he makes a lot of sense. This new channel where you want Welsh programmes to go...'

'The fourth channel,' Rhiannon said.

'That's right, Channel Four. It's bound to be a minority channel compared with BBC and HTV isn't it? The Welsh language would never be heard on television in 90 per cent of the homes of Wales. That's what Jac L. says, anyway.'

Emrys walked to his desk, picked up a copy of *Barn* and passed it to Branwen.

'Well, I think he's being defeatist,' she said defiantly, pushing the magazine away. 'Anyway, it's a matter of giving Welsh equality with English.'

'I don't see how that alters the way people watch television.'

'English is the language of broadcasting, isn't it? It's a constant presence coming into our homes and killing the language. It's destroying our sense of Welshness as well. It's forcing Welsh people to look at life through English eyes.'

'What about the Welsh programmes we've got? And we'll get more under Jac L.'s scheme.'

'Welsh programmes may increase as you say, but they'll always be seen as secondary and inferior to the English programmes. It'll just continue to demonstrate that Wales is a small, insignificant province of England.'

'Creating a separate channel just doesn't correspond to reality. We're only about half-a-million Welsh-speakers, after all. You might as well argue for a daily newspaper in Welsh.'

'Newspapers are different,' Rhiannon said. 'It would be good to have, of course it would. But newspapers operate in a commercial world, don't they? You can argue that it would be unrealistic for a daily Welsh language newspaper to make a profit. But broadcasting is different, it's a public service. And Welsh people have rights like everybody else.'

'Absolutely right,' Branwen said. 'Whether we're just half-a-million, as you say, is irrelevant. It's not about our being some kind of minority culture that has to be pandered to. That's not it at all. We're arguing for a fair broadcasting system for the Welsh people as a whole. In the first place, we need a

Broadcasting Authority for Wales. The people of Wales should have sovereignty over broadcasting.'

Her brother was puzzled. 'Sovereignty?'

'Yes, that's what Cymdeithas is arguing. An independent broadcasting authority would establish a Welsh language channel and an English language channel. Welsh-speakers and non-Welsh-speakers would receive a service in their own language.'

Emrys laughed.

'Can't see English-speakers going on the streets for a television channel.'

'That's not the point. The crucial thing is that we need a comprehensive service for all of the people, one that would look at Wales and the world through our own eyes, through Welsh eyes not English ones, and in both our languages.'

Emrys laughed again.

'So what you're saying, I suppose, is that English is a Welsh language.'

'Yes, of course it is! In Wales it is, anyway.'

*   *   *

After descending from the mast, Rhiannon and the others were arrested and spent the rest of the night in the cells in East Dulwich police station. Later that morning they appeared before Bow Street magistrates.

'This being your first offence, you're being bound over to keep the peace for twelve months,' the magistrate, a grey-haired woman with a bun at the back of her head, told Rhiannon.

'I refuse,' she answered, uttering the words Branwen had said she should be sure to say.

'Very well, I sentence you to five days' prison. Next.'

The journey to Holloway prison in south London was

disorientating. The prison vans were known as sweat boxes and with good reason, Rhiannon thought. She was already exhausted by the previous night and now became nauseous as well. She was fearful about how she would cope. The five days that stretched ahead seemed an eternity. Glancing towards the back of the van she saw Branwen who gave her a grin and a thumbs-up. Rhiannon smiled back wanly, wondering how her friend could remain so cheerful.

At the prison they were escorted through corridors that led to a room where they were searched, fingerprinted and then photographed. Holloway, with its 450 or so inmates, was the largest female prison in western Europe. Rhiannon's main impression was a labyrinth of corridors. Finally, she was pushed into a cell with a bed, chair and table, and a stinking slop bucket. She curled up on the bed and pulled a couple of rough blankets around her. She tried to block out the noises of doors clanging and women shouting. She shought of home on the shoreline in Anglesey, with the murmuring of the sea and occasional cries of gulls. Eventually she dozed, waking from time to time, to hear again the crashing of doors and the disturbed shrieks of women from somewhere below. Her cell was located above the asylum ward. The sounds mingled with those of the waves and gulls of her sleep.

*   *   *

In the late afternoon, a key turned in the door of her cell.

'Free association for an hour,' the warder muttered.

Rhiannon followed a line of women walking along the corridor to a large room where there were a few arm chairs and a table strewn with magazines. At the far end, a queue waited in front of a hatch where tea was being served. The women were smoking and chatting desultorily together.

'What you in for, love?' one said to Rhiannon.

'We were in a protest.'

'Against what?'

'About the language, the Welsh language?'

'What's that, then?'

'It's what we speak, in Wales?'

'Where's that?'

Rhiannon just smiled and drifted away. Then she caught sight of Branwen.

'Do you know what happened to the boys?'

Branwen shook her head and gestured at the groups of women around them.

'It's like a parallel world. I've spoken with a few of them. Kids, they are, in for drugs mainly, and shoplifting, petty crime really. A lot of them have been in care. Most seem to have been in before. One of them told me she even likes it here. Better than outside, she said. She gets fed, and is out of harm's way.'

'You could say the same about us,' Rhiannon smiled wryly.

'Not for long, though.'

'You're so optimistic, Branwen, so brave,' Rhiannon said with a sudden rush of affection intensified by the Welsh they were speaking in low tones together. 'Why are you so different from your brother? He's uncommitted, cynical even. What makes you? Where does it come from?'

'I don't know,' Branwen said, stopping to lift a mug of the bitter-tasting tea. 'I think getting involved with Cymdeithas was the start of it. The way we're treated. I mean, there's no difference is there? Men and women, there's no difference between us. We're all in it together.'

'It's more than that, surely.'

'I used to think that it was impossible to achieve the kind of things we want. I was conditioned to be a twenty-per-center I suppose. You know, the argument that only 20 per cent of the population speak Welsh, so what right have we to demand anything. But we're not twenty per cent at home, are we? Welsh isn't a minority language at home. Deiniolen isn't a twenty per cent village. It's a hundred per cent. I suppose it's the comradeship that keeps me going. What about you?'

'Me? It's the feeling that we're on the edge of oblivion if we don't do something, if we don't act. It's the system, isn't it? The average Welsh kid is brought up to be Welsh until the age of eleven. They're Welsh at home, in their village, when they're small. But as soon as they go to secondary school, they switch to English and their Welshness mysteriously disappears.'

'Unless they go to a Welsh-medium school.'

'There aren't many of those.'

'Not yet, anyway.'

'There's a kind of double think about the way we are. We're caught between the English we're taught to speak and think at school and nostalgic memories of childhood.'

'And we've got to break out of that.'

'Absolutely,' Rhiannon said. *'Rhaid i bopeth newid, os yw'r Gymraeg i fyw,* is what we say, isn't it? Everything must change, if the language is to live.'

Branwen stiffened, her voice sharpening.

'That's all very well. The trouble is, everything *is* changing, but in the wrong direction. The way I see it is this. In our society – in British society – even Welsh-speakers feel the language makes no sense.'

'No sense?'

'Well, it's inconvenient, it's not cost effective. It's troublesome. Our demands, for bilingual forms, road signs and all the rest, and especially for a television channel, are expensive and they can't see the point. Gets in the way of things. So, as I see it, the fight for the language is also the fight for a different kind of society, where market forces aren't the be-all and end-all.'

'You'll be saying it's the same as the fight for socialism next.'

'When you come to think of it, it's part and parcel of the same thing... don't you think?'

* * *

As evening fell, the sounds that receded into a background during the day became more pronounced. Rhiannon found herself overwhelmed by the crescendo of shouts, screams and clanging doors. Curled up on her bed, she stiffened. She gathered the blankets over her head and put her hands over her ears.

But after a while she said to herself, 'You mustn't cower, just ignore it, think of something else.'

She forced herself to relax, starting with her feet and slowly moving up her body. She sat up on the bed, then put her feet to the floor and stood up. Softly she started murmuring the words of a song she knew by heart from childhood, the well-known words and cadences that her mother Gertrude had sung to her when she was small.

Gradually she started to sing louder, then louder until the sound, gathering strength, seemed to overtake her whole body.

The melody, like Rhiannon's voice, had a sharp clarity that pierced the air around her and then the walls of the cell itself and beyond, throughout the immediate vicinity of the prison. And strangely, the other sounds that had previously been so dominant gradually fell away until they stopped altogether. They left a quivering emptiness that was only filled by Rhiannon's voice, a sound of such purity that it astonished those who were listening. It stopped them and held them still. Somehow conscious that she had an unknown audience, Rhiannon repeated the opening lines calling on a mother's baby to sleep. *Harm will not meet you in sleep,* were the words of the traditional lullaby, *hurt will always pass you by...*

When she came to an end there was a strange silence only eventually broken by a voice that called, 'Sing again, love, why don't you?'

'Sing in English this time!' another shouted.

'Let her sing how she likes,' the first voice said.

Rhiannon sang another haunting traditional song 'Dafydd y Garreg Wen', and this time she was joined by Branwen from a cell nearby. Together their voices blended, and Rhiannon let the full power of her voice pour into the melody. She felt a thrill of exhilaration, a feeling so powerful that it left her exhausted. At the end she slumped back on to the bed.

Each night after that, there were calls for Rhiannon and Branwen to sing. The five nights they were incarcerated were unusual in the experience of Holloway prison. Normally, after the locking of cell doors the prisoners screamed and shouted, kicking and scratching at the doors. But while the singing continued, there was silence as the sound of Welsh hymns and folk songs echoed through the building.

* * *

It was eight o'clock in the morning after their fifth night in prison when the two young women collected their possessions and emerged into the grey, damp daylight outside. On the opposite side of the road they were relieved to see Penry waiting beside his car.

Rhiannon ran across into her father's arms and breathlessly introduced Branwen.

'By the look of you both, something to eat would be in order,' Penry said after a moment.

'Oh, yes,' Branwen enthused causing Penry to laugh, more

in relief than any other emotion as he pulled Rhiannon's head to his chest. He removed his pipe from his mouth and tapped it against his hand.

They found a café a few miles away. Penry watched them devour platefuls of eggs, bacon, beans and toast while he drank a cup of coffee. He asked them how they had been treated, but received little response. In truth, they had yet to fully process the impact of the past few days.

Smiling at his daughter's friend, Penry searched for something to say.

'Well, at least your name suits this kind of thing.'

Branwen stopped eating and looked up in surprise, her fork poised halfway to her mouth. But before she could reply Rhiannon's laughter interrupted.

'He's talking about the Mabinogi.'

'The Mabinogi?'

'You know, the old Celtic tales.'

'Of course, but I'm not sure what your father has in mind.'

Rhiannon laughed again.

'It's where your name comes from. Branwen was the daughter of Llŷr, the high King of Britain. She was married to Matholwch, the king of Ireland. But he mistreated her – imprisoned her, in fact, which is why Dada mentioned it.'

'Oh, I see.' Branwen smiled.

'The story is that while in captivity Branwen reared a starling and taught it to speak,' Penry said. 'She sent the bird to her brother in Wales, Bendigeidfran the giant.'

'I've heard of him, at least.'

'He sailed across the Irish Sea to rescue her.'

'A bit like you coming to London to rescue us,' Rhiannon said wryly to her father.

'I hope it doesn't end up the same way,' Penry answered.

'What does he mean?' Branwen asked Rhiannon.

'Oh, there was a terrible battle,' she answered sipping her coffee. 'Bendigeidfran was killed. His head cut off and taken to be buried in London. Branwen returned to Wales – to Anglesey as a matter of fact, where she died of a broken heart.'

'Not a happy ending, then.'

'It's all myth, of course, but it's interesting that the bird was a starling, don't you think? Its song is like speech in a way, maybe a symbol of the power of language.'

'Birds are used in mythology to represent prophetic knowledge,' Penry said.

* * *

Later, during the long journey home when Branwen had fallen asleep alongside her in the back of the car, Rhiannon leant forward so that her head almost touched Penry's.

'How's Mam?'

'Fretting, as you might imagine, but she'll be alright once you're back.'

It began to rain and Penry turned on the windscreen wipers. They swished back and forth.

'You realise, don't you, that you have a record now? A criminal record I mean.'

'Well?'

'It means that if you get up to this kind of thing again, you can expect a much longer sentence than just a few days.'

'Our campaign is the only reason they'll do anything about the language.'

'That may be, but your campaign is about breaking the law and that ends up in violent confrontation.'

'Dada, you know we operate on the basis of non-violence.'

'But all the same, the law is the law. The alternative is anarchy.'

'Yes, but whose law? English law is almost totally based on property. They have a kind of sacred view about it. So when we attack their property, we are attacking the root of their way of thinking. But our way of thinking is different. We don't put the same stress on property, do we? It was Saunders who made the case that there's a moral law that is more important. You must agree with that, surely.'

'I don't go along with everything Saunders Lewis says. In fact, I don't go along with much of what he says at all.'

'The moral law recognises the family and the nation to be moral persons. That was how Saunders put it. By the law of God, the essential rights of the family and the nation, and especially their right to live, come before any rights of the government, of the state. The family and the nation have the qualities and natural rights of persons, he said. It's on the grounds of moral law that we have the right to damage property in order to prevent damage to the language.'

'Yes, that's all very well...' Penry's voice trailed off and he shook his head. 'But what are you actually campaigning *for*, at the end of the day?'

'We want the language to be treated normally, like the authorities treat English in England.'

'But what is normal?' Penry exclaimed.

Then, lowering his voice he reflected, 'We live so much of our lives through English, don't we? Certainly our working lives, even in the Welsh-speaking areas. We can't be insulated from the outside world.'

'No, but that doesn't mean we should abandon our fight for a stronger position for the language, and for its equal status in law.'

Penry glanced at Rhiannon, reaching to touch her hand.

'But how long can you go on making demands, asking for more concessions, more support?'

Rhiannon thought for a moment.

'I think in the end we'll have to have our own place where we can decide these things for ourselves. Otherwise we'll be dependent on others, forever. And, you're right, there's no future in that.'

Swansea
August to October 1975

Leo Abse idly flicked through transcripts of debates in Parliament that had been held during the previous few weeks. He sat in a reclining leather chair in the study of his London home. One wall was lined with bound volumes of Hansard covering the decades of his time at Westminster. After a few pages he caught sight of the beginning of a late evening debate at the end of July, prompted by the Scottish nationalists. Abse had left early that night, and he was glad he had since the debate had gone on until the early hours. Nevertheless, he glanced through the contributions with some interest. There were a lot of ill-tempered exchanges on abstruse Scottish matters, confirming the wisdom of his early departure.

Leafing through the pages, he saw that Plaid's Dafydd Wigley was called. Some way into his speech, Russell Fairgrieve, the Conservative MP for West Aberdeenshire, intervened. The Scottish National Party's aim was to take Scotland out of the United Kingdom. Was that also Plaid Cymru's policy?

'It is the policy of my party to give Wales the maximum possible degree of self-government,' Wigley answered. 'We need that self-government. It means going further than the devolution about which we are talking today. We have never tried to hide that.'

Abse smiled to himself and noted there was a further intervention, this time from Gerry Fowler, Minister of State in the Privy Council Office.

'Would the Hon. Gentleman define the maximum possible degree of self-government as what most of us would call independence?'

'I personally reject the term *independence*,' Wigley replied. 'I do not believe that any country today is totally independent.'

'Ah ha!' Abse exclaimed to himself. 'Dissembler.' But he continued reading.

'The United Kingdom is determined to have its own parliament and process for passing its own laws at Westminster. That does not mean that it cannot play a role in the international sphere at the United Nations or in such organisations as the EEC. That is not necessarily a separatist policy.'

Invited to give way again, Wigley refused.

'No, I will not. It is not a separatist policy. The United Kingdom is part of an economic unit called Europe. It is not economic separatism to retain a parliament in London. The same applies in the context of a fully self-governing Wales or Scotland. Those two countries can also be members of a greater economic unit. If Labour members cannot see that point, they have more thinking to do than they have done on this issue.'

Abse snorted.

'There's going to be a good deal more thinking, I'll see to that,' he muttered as he continued to look through the pages. He stopped short a little while later when he saw that the Swansea East MP Donald Anderson had intervened.

'Good, good', he murmured appreciatively, and then, 'Exactly so.'

He put the copy of Hansard down on his desk and thought for a while. Anderson would be a useful ally. He was far from a flamboyant figure, but all the better for that. It put him more in the mainstream. Brought up in Swansea, he had become a barrister, then a politics lecturer in the university in the town, and later a civil servant in the Foreign Office.

Abse rummaged in his drawer for his address book and thought again that Anderson brought a new dimension to the campaign he was beginning to mobilise. So far it had operated at the most basic and essential, emotional level. He was conscious that his arguments about the Welsh language hit home, certainly in the papers and on radio and television. But to convince his parliamentary colleagues he needed a subtler, more intellectual approach. He needed an argument that would appeal to their self-interest, and ideally this should not come from him. He was not the most popular of members. Donald Anderson was a far better candidate. He dialled the number and was gratified to have an immediate response.

'Ah Donald, delighted to find you. I'm ringing to congratulate you on your speech in the devolution debate the other night. Your points were well made, very well made indeed. I'm only sorry I wasn't there to hear.'

'Well, that's kind of you Leo. The implications of all this have yet to sink in.'

'Quite so, quite so. I was especially taken with your points about the impact on the House of Commons. If this thing goes through, there will be little left for us to do in our constituencies. If the Assembly takes over health and education, as it is bound to do and probably much else besides, then our constituency role, seeing people in our surgeries and so on, will be eroded.'

At the end of the line, Anderson cleared his throat.

'As you say, our welfare function, the things that really matter to people, will be removed. But at the same time much of economic and foreign policy may well flow to Brussels. Power will be taken away from us in two directions.'

'And in those circumstances, the case for keeping the present number of Welsh MPs in Westminster would disappear.'

'Precisely the point I made.'

'And we could say goodbye to the chances of a Labour majority,' Abse added. 'We'll have no chance without the full complement of our MPs from Wales and Scotland.'

'I know. This thing hasn't been thought through at all.'

'Donald, it was a late-night sitting and the debate got very little coverage. At any rate, I haven't seen anything beyond Hansard. I think your views need a wider circulation.'

'Well, if you think so, Leo.'

'I tell you what. I'll get hold of the *Western Mail*. I met the editor a month or so ago. New chap, a Yorkshireman, Duncan Gardiner. He's a bit soft on devolution, like the paper, but he's amenable enough. I'm sure I can get him to place an article. Stir things up a bit, don't you think?'

* * *

A few weeks later, two feature-length articles by Donald Anderson appeared. *Toothless in Westminster* was the *Western Mail*'s headline on the first day. *Let's look before we leap* the advice on the second. They struck an apocalyptic note, rudely disturbing the apparent unity of the Wales Labour Party.

'What role will remain for Welsh MPs as we continue blindly along the devolution path?' Anderson queried, going on to warn, 'There never was a more revolutionary situation in constitutional terms since Charles I lost his head'.

The articles provoked dissension at the monthly meeting of the Wales Labour Executive at Transport House in Cardiff.

'Where has Anderson been for the last decade or more?' cried Ray Powell, the Ogmore constituency secretary. 'He says the debate has yet to begin, but we've been passing resolutions for decades.'

'The policy has been approved by our annual conference more than once,' agreed Peggy England-Jones, chair of the Wales Regional Council of Labour and stalwart of the Swansea party.

Emrys Jones, the quietly spoken but steely secretary of the

Wales Labour Party, raised his hand to quell the murmurings of disquiet.

'It's unfortunate and likely to generate disunity. The articles betray a complete misunderstanding of our argument. The overburdening of Westminster and the growth of the undemocratic ad hoc bodies, already in effect a regional tier of government, is what makes devolution so necessary.'

'Oh, they understand alright,' George Wright, secretary of the Transport and General Workers Union, responded grimly. 'It's their own position they're most concerned about. Emrys, you must write to Anderson in the strongest terms on our behalf. Remind him that his first loyalty is to party policy and the government. This is a manifesto commitment, after all. And we should copy the letter to all Welsh Labour MPs.'

A few days later, Donald Anderson received a stern and recriminatory riposte. Emrys Jones complained that forty-four out of fifty-two column inches of his articles concerned the career possibilities of Welsh MPs at Westminster.

'There is no reference to the changes brought about by the enormous growth of functions at Westminster on the effectiveness of MPs to cope with those responsibilities,' he wrote. 'Lloyd George, as an MP to whom you refer, never had to deal with a fraction of the welfare questions which face MPs today. I find it odd, too, that in listing a selection of Welsh politicians, there was no reference to the late Jim Griffiths, whose contribution to the Labour Movement, and to the people of Wales, Britain and the wider world rank with those of any other Welshman. He argued consistently for responsibility to be devolved from Westminster and Whitehall on grounds of both democracy and efficiency.'

Emrys Jones didn't let up.

'I am also amazed to see from your articles that "a number of Welsh MPs insist that all the implications of devolution be argued before the people of Wales. The debate has not yet begun!" Where have you been this last ten years?'

As soon as he had read the letter, Anderson rang Leo Abse.

'I've already had a copy,' he said. 'This is exactly what I hoped would happen. It gives us our opportunity. We must defend the independence of MPs against the dictates of the party. You must reply, of course, and I will ensure that other colleagues do as well.'

'Could you draft something?'

'Let me reply first. Your response can come later. And I'll get other colleagues to chip in. But we shouldn't reply all at once. That would look like an orchestrated campaign.'

* * *

Emrys Jones received what at first appeared a conciliatory response from Abse. He began by agreeing that Donald Anderson had overstated his case in saying that the debate had not yet begun. Yet, equally, it was true to say that the debate had not yet concluded. Many MPs had only agreed to the party policy so long as there was no question that the Assembly should have any potential to acquire legislative powers. Many would be extremely hostile to a situation that could lead to a Welsh version of Northern Ireland's Stormont. That would result in a reduction in the number of Welsh MPs and lead to a situation where a Labour government could never get a majority in the House of Commons.

'I thought it right that I should not merely acknowledge the courtesy of your letter, but that I should make it clear where I stand on the matter as I fear that – although quite clearly it was not your intention – it may be thought that the letter is an attempt to stifle the discussions that must continue upon the issue of devolution.'

Donald Anderson delayed his own response until two weeks later. He complained that Emrys Jones had paid no attention to the substance of his articles. Devolution would radically alter the role of MPs. Moreover, the present structure of local government could not long survive the advent of an Assembly.

Anderson rounded off, 'A danger I did not mention is that of proportional representation being accepted for the Assembly and then leading to coalition politics at Westminster. Are we fully prepared to give priority to devolution this session, a subject irrelevant to the transfer of power to working people, at the expense of socialist priorities like nationalisation of the ports?'

Prompted by Abse, George Thomas wrote much more stringently, though privately since he was now Deputy Speaker. He said he agreed fully with the contents of Abse's letter, which had been circulated.

Some days earlier Owen James had revealed the contents of the Welsh Labour Executive's letter in the *Western Mail*. 'The letter and the Executive's lengthy debate on the issue at their last meeting reflect a growing anxiety that up to half of the Welsh Labour MPs are gearing themselves to sabotage the Welsh Assembly Bill.'

This only served to underline Emrys Jones' anxiety. It was accentuated when he received a further letter, this time from Bedwellty MP Neil Kinnock. He urged comradely respect for those who were opposing the policy.

Neither was Emrys reassured by an ambiguous editorial in the *Western Mail*, normally enthusiastic in its support for devolution. It said Donald Anderson's articles had articulated doubts and fears that were held, for the most part secretly, by an unknown number of Labour Members on the backbenches and within the government itself. It ended with an ominous warning.

More than a few Labour politicians are terrified of what they believe is going to happen. While we would not, in all probability, share their views, these people should not be coerced and intimidated into maintaining their silence. It is very nearly five minutes to midnight.

Corris
November 1975

Gerard Morgan-Grenville wrote to Rhiannon asking her to telephone him. In a short letter on his personal headed paper, he said he would be at Hascombe, his estate in Surrey, at 5pm for the next few days. It was not the first such letter she had received. An earlier one had resulted in their meeting for dinner when he was passing through Aberystwyth.

Making the call at the specified time, Rhiannon reversed the charges from a phone box behind the Old College near the Aberystwyth waterfront. Gerard responded in his clipped, military tone.

'Ah Rhiannon, wonderful to hear you. Now listen, the thing is I need a very special favour.'

He explained that he had persuaded the Duke of Edinburgh to visit the quarry in a few week's time. The occasion promised a good deal of favourable publicity. That was important since the project had provoked generally hostile criticism in the locality. It tended to be viewed as a hippy invasion. A Royal visit would do a lot to allay such sentiments. It would also be useful for fundraising.

However, the invitation to the Duke of Edinburgh had prompted great opposition amongst the volunteers who had flocked to the quarry. Many were either anarchists or republicans, or both, and regarded the monarchy with disdain. Only a handful were willing to staff the renewable energy exhibits that had so far been established. There was a danger the site would look deserted.

'Could you persuade some of your student friends to come and give the place a sense of bustle and atmosphere?' Gerard asked.

'They'll probably take a similar view to your volunteers.'

'But can't they see the wider picture? This isn't about politics.'

'Round here, the Royal family is intensely political.'

'We're taking a stand on the environmental crisis. It's what real internationalism is about, after all. Surely, students in your department would support that?'

'Well, I'll see what I can do,' Rhiannon said doubtfully, though buoyed by Gerard's enthusiasm.

'Wonderful! Call me in a few days. I'll arrange for the pick-up truck to fetch you. It's electric you know, runs on batteries.'

* * *

Rhiannon managed to persuade Siobhan and a few other students to accompany her to the quarry. In anticipation of the Royal visit, British Rail had painted Machynlleth's station in bright new colours. John Beaumont, who had leased the quarry to Gerard, was also mayor of the town and ensured that baskets of flowers hung along the main street.

Security men visited and poked around the few exhibits. One was a Cretan windmill with eight red cloth sails, of a type used for at least a thousand years. It had become the quarry's symbol and was displayed on all its publicity material. Erected on a high bluff, it produced enough electricity in a good wind to light a few light bulbs. Another exhibit featured a bicycle wheel with a dynamo-hub mounted on a pole. Occasionally it would turn in the wind and light a bicycle lamp. A large tank of water with a hand-operated paddle created waves whose energy caused a miniature lighthouse to flash.

'They're just symbolic of what's possible,' Gerard declared airily.

Prince Philip was due to inspect a 'house of the future' that Gerard had bought from the previous year's Ideal Homes

Exhibition in London. It had been rebuilt in the quarry and was fitted with insulation panels, double-glazing, a solar roof, and a methane digester. Gerard was also planning to use the occasion to unveil a new type of solar cell.

Ignoring Machynlleth's freshly-painted station, Philip arrived by helicopter. Gerard met him at the foot of the quarry, where the recently-donated electric pick-up truck was on hand to take him up a rough road to the main quarry workings. Philip sat in the passenger seat, grumbling that he was not at the wheel and doubting its ability to climb the steep slope. This proved an accurate judgement since, halfway up, the truck's main fuse blew.

'Told you so,' he exclaimed, scrambling out and striding onwards up the slope. Gerard was left struggling to prevent the truck from running backwards down the hill.

Waiting on the quarry's still-surviving rail track was a small narrow-gauge steam engine and carriage, loaned for the occasion. Its purpose was to demonstrate the superior energy efficiency of rail transport. It had been fired with straw briquettes, but they had given out insufficient heat for the engine to pull the carriage. In desperation, its demonstrator had put some coal in the firebox and more was stowed in the panniers behind, overlain with the straw fuel.

'It's another example of how we can make more sensible use of our resources,' Gerard said. Philip strode over to the panniers and dug his hand beneath the straw briquettes, and triumphantly held aloft a lump of coal.

'Thought so.'

Around him, newspaper cameramen delighted in the opportunity. Gerard hastily moved the entourage further up the quarry to where Rhiannon and Siobhan were using pickaxes to break up the slate covering the quarry floor in an effort to get to the soil beneath.

'What are you doing?' Philip asked.

Rhiannon gazed helplessly at Gerard.

'Oh, we're planning an organic garden to make us self-sufficient in vegetables,' he said quickly.

'Done this before, have you?' Philip asked again.

Rhiannon and Siobhan shook their heads.

'Best of luck with it anyway,' he said cheerily and the entourage swept by, the photographers pausing to take some close-up photographs of the two young women.

The light drizzle that had begun earlier in the day turned into a wetter, more enveloping mist and then rain. Rhiannon's group set about their task once more, but eventually leant on their spades and pickaxes, looked at one another and then to her.

'We think we've done our bit, don't you?' Siobhan said. 'Let's hitch a ride to Machynlleth, have a pint and get the bus back.'

'You go on, then,' Rhiannon said. 'I'll explain things to Gerard and follow you later.'

Siobhan smiled knowingly and went off with the others.

Rhiannon paused to survey the upper part of the deserted quarry. It suddenly seemed cold, dismal and unfriendly, an impossible place she thought to realise Gerard's dream. She tied her scarf more securely around her head and then, grasping the pickaxes and shovels, began to make her way gingerly down the slope. In the thickening mist, she missed the pathway. She found herself wading through a mass of bracken, becoming soaked before discovering more open ground. Eventually she saw some old caravans and the outline of the broken-down cottages that provided a primitive base for the volunteers. Inside a few were crouched around an open fire drinking tea, their backs to a gap in the wall that let in the rain.

A young woman passed Rhiannon carrying a chipped, steaming mug.

'I'm Diana, Diana Brass. And you?'

'I'm just helping out for the day.'

'Oh, one of Gerard's students.'

Rhiannon discovered that Diana Brass was the lynchpin of the quarry, holding the enterprise together. She kept the fires going in the cottages and provided meals. Indeed, she had been a cordon bleu chef, making her living by catering at parties for the well-off in southern England. It was at one of these that Gerard had met her, sitting cross-legged on a dining room floor. They fell into conversation and both realised that they had much in common. Later Gerard said it was her ideas that had steered him towards the path he eventually took.

Diana told Rhiannon the main challenge with the project was the constant rain. Set in the Snowdonia foothills the quarry had one of the highest rainfalls in Britain. Flash floods eroded the roadway and paths almost as quickly as they were repaired. The roofs of the buildings leaked and their walls were damp. It was impossible to keep dry.

Gerard emerged in the midst of their conversation and caught sight of Rhiannon.

'Why, you'll catch your death of cold if you stay here much longer.'

'Off you go then to your bolt hole,' Diana said distractedly, but without any rancour in her voice. 'Leave us to get on with things as usual.'

Gerard signalled to Rhiannon and she followed him out of the cottage into the streaming rain and vegetation that led another fifty yards down to the car park near the main road. There he held open the car door.

'I'll take you home, but first you need to get dry and I need something to eat.'

* * *

Driving out of the quarry, Gerard took a right turn and headed northwards.

'It's not far. We'll be there in a few minutes.'

'Where?'

'Oh, I have use of a place when I'm down. Makes life a lot more civilised.'

He explained it was a cottage that belonged to an acquaintance, Baroness Eirene White. She had been a minister in the Labour government in the 1960s, in the Welsh Office, but was now a member of the Royal Commission on Environmental Pollution.

'That's how I met her. It was at a seminar we organised in London when we set up the Centre for Environmental Improvement. I told her about the quarry, and when she realised it was just down the road from her own stamping ground she became interested. Since then she's been very supportive, in particular allowing me to use her cottage whenever I'm here.'

'You have a remarkable range of acquaintances, not least the Duke of Edinburgh.'

Gerard chuckled, and a few minutes later drove into Corris, a small slate-quarrying village. He slowed the car and turned off the main road into a lane that dropped down and across the valley. He drew to a stop outside a line of small terraced cottages. Inside, Gerard instructed her to go upstairs and have a hot shower.

'You'll find a dressing gown up there,' he called out as she climbed the stairs. 'Throw down your wet things and I'll put them to dry above the Aga.'

It was a luxurious bathroom, certainly by Rhiannon's standards. The shower was, indeed, as hot as Gerard had said it would be, and afterwards she found a hair dryer. She reflected on how, with Gerard, the most extraordinary things seemed so ordinary and commonplace. One minute she was in a wet, green wilderness, the next sitting in a bathroom that felt like being in a hotel. It was a world where visits from royalty or acquaintances in the House of Lords were everyday occurrences.

Coming down wrapped in a fluffy white dressing gown and matching slippers, Rhiannon found Gerard at the stove cooking spaghetti.

'I've opened a bottle of wine,' he said, looking over his shoulder. 'Help yourself, and you can pour me one as well.'

Sitting at the kitchen table, glass in hand, Rhiannon looked idly at a pile of papers. One was headed *Centre for Environmental Improvement*. Underneath were a list of Patrons: Lord Annan, provost of University College, London; Lord Robens, former chairman of the National Coal Board; Sir Bernard Waley-Cohen, former Lord Mayor of London; Roy Jenkins, Home Secretary…

'How do you know all these people?' she asked.

'What people?'

'These patrons on your letter.'

'I wrote to them, asking if they would help.'

'And they just said yes?'

'Roy Jenkins was the only one who actually asked to see me. So I presented myself at his office in the House of Commons. "You want me to lend credibility to your project?" he said, and I answered, "Your support would be immensely valuable. You are held in great esteem."'

Rhiannon laughed.

'What did he say to that?'

'Well, if I remember correctly, "It's nice of you to say so, but I doubt it. I see from your letterhead that you want to improve the environment. Sounds like a good idea but how exactly?" I ummed and ahhed and he interrupted, "Never mind. It's a good idea, probably impossible to describe. I'll happily be a patron if

I don't have to give money or time, especially the latter. Glad to have met you. Good luck. Goodbye."'

Rhiannon laughed again. 'You're obviously very persuasive.'

'It's a deliberate policy to involve people with a position in society.'

Gerard turned from the stove, spatula in hand, his voice becoming serious.

'A lot of people regard alternative technology as some sort of rationale for old-style anarchism. In fact, there are a large number of people out there, people who head industry, government, large organisations, and so on who are every bit as aware that something needs to be done.'

'Why don't they just do it, then?'

'They're sort of frozen, in a way, in their positions and they can't easily move. So right from the beginning we set out to establish a bridge which anyone could walk over. We deliberately set out to enlist the support of some of the wise men of our age. The people we have got on our letterhead are amongst the more effective, more intelligent people in various walks of life.'

'But doesn't it make you look like part of the Establishment, the government even...?'

Rhiannion's voice trailed off. She was afraid of sounding negative, but Gerard seemed not to notice.

'That is a danger. Some people think we have been deliberately created by the Establishment, or even that we're funded by the CIA, all sorts of funny ideas. Others think it means that we get huge hidden subsidies.'

'I can see that.'

'But you've got to realise that the people towards the top of the pyramid are vastly more effective in terms of what gets done than the people at the bottom. That seems obvious to me. If you can enlist the support of people at the top, you've got a chance of achieving really worthwhile things using conventional means.'

'And the people at the top obviously include the Duke of Edinburgh.'

'It would be naïve to think that someone like him isn't an incredibly powerful figure in the country. And his support is invaluable to the whole alternative technology movement. As you could see today, he is in the process of walking across this pretty delicate bridge that we're putting up.'

'He looked a bit sceptical to me.'

'But he came, didn't he? That's the important point.'

'So you think the day worked for you?'

'It begins to change our image, don't you think? The media deride us as scruffy hippies, environmental fanatics… middle-class visionaries even. They've made particular fun out of me, with my hyphenated name, Eton, the Army and all that. One journalist called me Mr Mournful-Windmill. That's why the visit today is so important. It means they have to start taking us seriously.'

*   *   *

Later, after they had made short work of Gerard's spaghetti bolognaise and drunk the best part of two bottles of 1968 Côte de Beaune, Gerard stood up and pulled Rhiannon to her feet. He lifted her in his arms and carried her towards the stairs. At first she was startled. But half way up she slid her arms around his neck.

Gabalfa
December 1975

Owen leant back in his chair and shifted his gaze from his typewriter to the office window. In the short gap that lay between him and the neighbouring building, he could see a patch of dark cloud. It added to the gloom of the late Friday afternoon. For once he had the weekend free and was thinking that if the weather held he might take off for the Brecon Beacons. He leant forward and pulled a sheaf of paper from the rolling return of the typewriter to consider how he could make a rather boring story more interesting. At that moment, his telephone sounded. He pulled up his chair and lifted the heavy black receiver.

'Owen?'

'Yes.'

'It's Dafydd, Dafydd Williams. Got a minute?'

Plaid Cymru's general secretary explained the party was due to give evidence to the Royal Commission on the Press. He had forgotten all about it and the deadline was Monday.

'It's looking at the independence and diversity of newspapers,' he said.

'And their editorial standards.'

'Yes, that too, but diversity is the main thing so far as we're concerned. Gwynfor thinks it's a peg on which we can hang something about the lack of an adequate press in Wales, especially for the Welsh language.'

'Don't tell me, he reckons it's made more pressing by the imminence of the Assembly.'

'Exactly. But apart from that, I can't think where to start. The Commission is also looking at the economics of newspaper production and the concentration of ownership as well. That affects us, I suppose. I was wondering, could you come up with something?'

* * *

After dinner with Anna that evening, Owen climbed the stairs of their small box-like home in Gabalfa and pulled down a loft ladder to his cramped study built into the low eaves of the house. Picking up a pen, he started jotting down some headings. There would have to be something about the current state of Welsh newpapers, and the changed circumstances that the Assembly would bring. As a first heading Owen put *Opportunities* and alongside *Responsibilities*. 'Devolution ought to require at least two competing daily papers covering the whole of Wales,' he thought.

Pulling his typewriter to the edge of the desk, he inserted some paper and began to list the problems that would arise when it came to reporting the Assembly. The first obstacle was the absence of a newspaper that circulated throughout the country.

Owen paused to consider. 'Well, why not?' he said to himself and began to type.

> There is a boundary line that runs roughly across the country east from Aberystwyth. North of this line the Liverpool-based *Daily Post* holds sway with a circulation for its Welsh edition of about 40,000. South of the line, the *Western Mail* has an indigenous daily monopoly with a circulation hovering on 100,000. The *Western Mail* used to circulate reasonably extensively in northern Wales and maintained an office, reporters and photographers in Bangor. But the costs of transport on inadequate roads from

south to north meant that the paper was losing a considerable amount on each copy sold in the north, up to 5p at today's prices. As a result, its north Wales operation has been cut back over the years until today it maintains just one reporter in Gwynedd and sells just 1,000 copies in the whole of the north on a break-even basis. In most of the north the *Western Mail* is unobtainable unless ordered, despite growing demand, particularly for the newspaper's sports and political coverage.

Owen stopped typing, chewed the end of his pen and reflected again how debilitating the lack of an effective press was for Welsh political aspirations. 'The *Post* is in an even worse state,' he thought as he continued writing.

The Liverpool *Daily Post* has never attempted to circulate south of the Aberystwyth line. Its penetration of north Wales, largely since World War II, has been the result of an effort to bolster its loss-making Liverpool city operation. For north Wales, the newspaper produces a special edition with a separate front page and internal northern news pages, together with the occasional feature. But it is far from being a complete Welsh newspaper. Welsh readers are faced with an excessive amount of, to them, largely irrelevant north-west England material, particularly in the paper's comment, general features and business news columns. There is a near total lack of an all-Wales perspective to the newspaper's outlook. As presently constituted, therefore, the *Daily Post* is not equipped to give adequate coverage to the Welsh Assembly, even just to its north Wales readers. And, if anything, coverage of the Welsh Assembly will be more important in the north than in the south because of the geographical distance and consequent threat of remoteness of north Wales from the Assembly, sited in Cardiff.

Having set out the realities of the Welsh daily newspaper scene, Owen thought the solution followed on pretty logically. He argued that subsidies should be introduced, to offset the losses to the *Western Mail* for selling its papers north of the line drawn from Aberystwyth, and to the *Daily Post* for any papers it sold south if it. For good measure, he added that to qualify for its subsidy, the *Daily Post* should be required to produce a completely separate Welsh edition.

On consideration, he further recommended that the subsidy should be administered by an arms-length independent Communications Commission and limited to five years to safeguard the independence of the Welsh press. He judged that this would give time for the new press operations to become self-supporting, though he admitted to himself that this was a somewhat heroic assumption. On the other hand, he felt he was far-sighted in suggesting that the coming of computer type-setting would reduce newspaper overheads, as was already the case in the United States.

At this point Owen glanced at his watch and saw it was well past midnight. Carefully climbing down the loft steps so as not to wake Anna – she had gone to bed hours earlier – he went to the kitchen and poured himself a Scotch. Despite the cold he opened the back door and walked into their small back yard.

It had been raining earlier, but the sky was clearing as rapidly moving clouds revealed a pale winter moon. Owen glanced up at their dark bedroom window. Anna was nearly six months pregnant and getting bigger by the week. She seemed to be taking things in her stride, but Owen felt they were becoming more distant from each other. To begin with he had tried to get home earlier from work but that was difficult. And anyway, Anna didn't seem to mind whether he was early or late, accepting it as part of his job.

Owen felt at a loss as to what he should be doing. In the end he decided the best thing was to carry on as normally as possible. He realised their life would be bound to change when the baby arrived, but couldn't imagine what it would be like. He didn't know what to think about the baby. 'What should I feel?' he asked himself, and suddenly realised that because he couldn't answer that question he was reticent about discussing things openly with Anna. 'Better just to keep things ticking over,' he told himself.

Inside the kitchen he poured some more Scotch and, adding water from the tap, his thoughts turned back to the paper he was writing. He realised that his proposal for a subsidy would be greeted with a good deal of scepticism. He decided it needed some further justification.

In his study he put a fresh sheet of paper into the typewriter. He stared over it, seeking the right form of words. The press should be free and independent of state control.

'That's all very well,' he thought.

Then, he wrote, 'The state should be obliged to ensure that the facilities of the press are not just available at the behest of the power of the purse.'

But he immediately realised that the two propositions would be seen to contradict one another. Any press subsidy was sure to be criticised as a form of patronage. So he continued, 'In a democracy, goodwill and tolerance must be presumed to exist, and the necessary administrative machinery is not beyond the resources of an advanced and truly democratic community.'

He rounded off this assertion with an optimistic flourish.

> We contend that the presumption we make at the end of the last paragraph is justified only in the context of a democracy such as could exist in Wales with her manageable population of just under three million people. Plaid Cymru is a decentralist party which believes that only by breaking government down into small units which correspond more closely to natural units will democracy and its corollary, a free press, survive in the United Kingdom. It is no coincidence that in most small Western European countries, like Switzerland, the Netherlands, Denmark, Sweden and Austria, newspaper ownership is decentralised across a wide range of organisations, sometimes commercial but as frequently non-commercial trusts, readers' co-operatives, political parties or trade unions. Such decentralisation encourages a diversity of opinion and an uninhibited approach to public debate.

* * *

Owen's premonition that his ideas for promoting a Welsh national press would generate controversy was amply confirmed the following week. Dafydd Williams received the paper with enthusiasm and readily agreed that Owen's authorship should be kept between the two of them and not shared even within the party. He added some proposals of his own to help the Welsh language weekly journals *Y Cymro* and *Y Faner*. Otherwise he left the paper untouched and submitted it immediately to the Royal Commission. He then arranged a press conference and persuaded Dafydd Elis-Thomas, Plaid's spokesman on cultural affairs, to attend.

The launch was held in the splendour of Cardiff's Angel Hotel. When he arriuved Owen saw that it had drawn an alarming attendance of journalists and film crews, some from outside Wales.

'There's been a great response,' Dafydd whispered to him before the formal presentations began. 'I've had calls from all over the place, from Scotland, even London.'

In his opening remarks Dafydd Elis-Thomas observed that the coming of the Welsh Assembly meant that the old-style pattern of newspaper coverage, with the London press predominating could no longer meet the needs of Wales.

'You cannot have devolution of power unless it is matched by devolution in the coverage of that power,' he said.

He went on to emphasise the importance of the party's evidence for the future of the Welsh language press. The difficulties facing all newspapers were compounded in the case of Welsh language titles by the relatively thin distribution of Welsh-speakers across Wales. The reality was that their circulation was to a great extent dependent on postal deliveries.

'That is why we believe the Royal Commission should examine the system operating in Norway where a state subsidy is available to reduce the cost to the press of its post and telecommunication links. We urge such a system to apply in the UK, and especially for the Welsh language press in Wales.'

'You're talking about another subsidy, Dafydd,' BBC Wales's industrial and political correspondent Patrick Hannan interrupted, clearly irritated. He looked as though he might one day step into a boxer's ring. He had previously worked on the *Western Mail* and now brought a healthy scepticism to Welsh broadcasting. He once described his role as being 'a lance corporal in the awkward squad.'

Now he said, 'Subsidies might be fine for Welsh language magazines, but when it comes to real newspapers – and the *Western Mail* is still a real newspaper I would say – a subsidy is a dangerous path to take, surely?'

Elis-Thomas bridled at the back-handed dismissal of the Welsh language press, but decided to answer the question head on.

'I know our proposals for a short-term sales-related subsidy to ensure national coverage during the first five years of the Assembly will raise concern amongst editors worried about their independence. But you have to ask yourself, is the press really independent anyway?'

'Newspapers jealously guard their independence,' Hannan said.

'But the press is run by commercial companies, and so they're inevitably linked with commercial interest groups.'

'Their editors are independent.'

'That depends on their personal integrity.'

'Do you have anyone in mind?' Hannan asked.

'Most newspapers have their own political commitments, regardless of which editors come and go,' Elis-Thomas said. 'The direct interference of newspaper owners in editorial policy varies from empire to empire, as we know.'

'That doesn't answer the question.'

'But it is no coincidence, is it, that the overwhelming majority of papers, even in a radical left-leaning country like Wales, have a right-wing political viewpoint.'

The exchanges continued in this vein for a while. Owen didn't ask any questions. He left as soon as the television crews started queuing up to interview Elis-Thomas.

*   *   *

When Owen reached the office, there was a message that the editor wanted to see him. Duncan Gardiner had not been at the newspaper long, but had already established a different, more relaxed regime from the one adopted by his predecessor John Giddings. A bluff Yorkshireman, he enjoyed a pint with his colleagues and preferred to talk about rugby more than politics. However, as Owen entered his office he saw that Gardiner had on his desk a copy of Plaid Cymru's evidence to the Royal Commission on the Press.

He raised his head from the document.

'Have you seen this latest ridiculous idea the nationalists have come up with?'

Owen looked askance.

'Of course you have. You're writing the story. Well I want you to write the leader as well. It's unbelievable that they could come up with government subsidies for the press. Smacks of Eastern Europe. They must be desperate for a headline, don't you think?'

'The idea's certainly causing a bit of a stir. I've just been to the press conference. Television is crawling all over it.'

'Yes, well they would.'

'Patrick Hannan was especially outraged, as you might imagine. But as far as I can see what they're proposing is not that different in principle from the BBC licence fee.'

Gardiner give Owen a quizzical glance.

'That's quite a different matter. Anyway, the sort of thing we should be saying is this.'

Owen began to take notes.

* * *

Sitting at his desk Owen resolved that before reiterating Gardiner's main arguments about press freedom he would at least compliment Plaid Cymru on its engagement with the issues. Looking at his notes he leant to his typewriter.

> The party's proposals are predicated on a number of assumptions: first there is a need in Wales for a healthy and diversified press; second that the establishment of a Welsh Assembly will impose new responsibilities on that press; and, third, that in this situation a combination of need (to get full coverage of Assembly affairs) and psychological change (the dynamic effect of devolution) will lead many more people to want to read an indigenous Welsh newspaper. It is the last of these assumptions that we would question. Even if we made the most immodest claims about our present performance we cannot dispute the fact that the existence of a new focus of political power in the Welsh capital will present us with onerous and costly responsibilities. The advent of these responsibilities may coincide with the advent of a new newspaper technology that will alter the economics of an already strong 'regional' press, so that we will be able fully to meet the challenge of new democratic institutions without resort to subsidies from public funds.

Owen then wrote as instructed:

> Wales is a small country where relationships between politicians and civil servants are much closer than between regional papers in England and any Whitehall department. The degree of pressure that can be brought to bear in this more intimate system is correspondingly greater. It has been and always

will be a pressure that will be strongly resisted but it is not right that it should be given any direct leverage against us.

A little later, as he walked through the office to deliver his draft editorial Owen thought, not for the first time, that perhaps he was sailing a little too close to the wind in his relationship with Plaid.

Paddington
March 1976

Shortly after ten o'clock at night, three months later, the *Western Mail's* first edition, destined for the north, rolled off the presses in the cavernous ground floor of Thomson House. And as was customary, members of the editorial team made their way to the RAF club on the first floor of the Royal Arcade off St Mary Street to discuss the fortunes of the day. The ancient lift with its trellised metal doors reminded Owen of a 1940s film, as did the club's dark and cramped interior. Its curving bar stretched the length of the back wall and left little space for the clientele who usually had no option but to lean against it. However, the club stayed open until the early hours, making it a natural gathering point for late night newspapermen.

On this occasion Owen arrived to find the paper's news editor John Humphries and assistant editor Geraint Talfan Davies engaged in an intense argument. Should the paper come down on the side of those who were calling for a referendum on the Assembly? Their dispute had been running for weeks and was beginning to fray tempers. Owen had heard it before and settled down at the bar to hear it once again. Labour opponents of devolution were calling for a referendum as a way of killing it off without directly attacking their party's policy. On the other hand, he acknowledged that opposing a referendum revealed a weakness in the democratic argument in favour of the Assembly.

Geraint was reiterating his view.

'If we come out for a referendum, we'll be reneging on the case we've been making for more than twenty years. We'll be going back on what we've said since the days we argued for the creation of the Welsh Office. It'll be a gift to our opponents.'

'It's democracy Geraint,' John Humphries hissed. 'The whole case we've been making for devolution is that it's about extending democracy. A referendum is a vote after all, a democratic vote.'

'We argued against a referendum on Europe last year. It would be inconsistent for the paper to change its stance now.'

'The genie's out of the bottle, you can't put it back.'

Humphries spoke fast with a Newport accent, a mix of West Country burr with a twang from the Gwent Valleys. It was higher pitched than the gentler tones of Cardiff. His style was manic and relentless. He worked a fifteen-hour day, arriving at the office from his home outside Caerleon at around 10am, in time for the first news conference of the day. He rarely left before 1am. He exuded tension, throwing his jacket over his chair and working with shirt-sleeves rolled up beyond his elbows. He spiked weak stories with a vehemence that struck terror into junior reporters. His constantly repeated instruction, when they approached him empty-handed after another fruitless inquiry, was, 'Ring 'em again!'

The illegitimate son of a sea captain, he had joined the *Western Mail's* Newport district office from school as a junior reporter and risen through the ranks. As such he was deeply resentful of anyone whose path he judged had been smoothed through life, especially university graduates and members of the establishment, above all members of the Welsh-language establishment. He placed Geraint Talfan Davies in all three categories. He was one of the first graduate intakes to join the *Western Mail*, from Oxford in the mid-1960s. His father had been head of programmes at BBC Wales and an uncle was chairman of HTV Wales. Humphries' burning ambition was to become the *Western Mail's* editor. He saw Talfan Davies as his main competitor.

Geraint was now attempting another tack.

'It goes beyond where the paper has stood in the past and whether we're being consistent. I agree your democracy argument has a certain logic. But we also need to take into account the consequences of having a referendum. I think you underestimate the impact on social and political harmony in Wales. A referendum campaign would be immensely divisive. We need to think about that.'

'I couldn't disagree more,' John cried, his voice rising. 'It would be more divisive if we try to force this change on people against their will. In a country with half-a-million Welsh-speakers, some of them desperately worried about the threat to their Celtic heritage, and two million mongrel and monoglot but no less cultured English-speakers, there's always potential for a clash of interests. You can see it before your eyes with the antics of the Welsh Language Society.'

'A referendum would stir up those antagonisms even more.'

'No, no, we should be arguing that we need the Assembly to provide an arena in which the different cultures in Wales can flourish alongside each other. But don't you see, that can only happen if the majority of English-speakers volunteer their co-operation. They must feel party to the contract. A referendum is the only way it can be demonstrated.'

'John, how many times do I have to tell you that devolution is not about the language, about the differences you see between Welsh- and English-speakers?'

Owen left the bar fearing that Humphries was winning the argument.

*   *   *

It continued in the office the following morning. Duncan Gardiner had been features editor of the *Western Mail* in the 1960s before working for a spell with the *Sunday Times*. He was no stranger to Welsh disputes, but failed to engage with the passion of his colleagues. Indeed, he found their quarrels wearisome. Even more trying was the pressure he was coming under from the management on the third floor. They were hostile to devolution. They saw the paper's support for it as anti-Conservative, a destabilising influence and, worst of all, potentially harmful to advertising revenues.

Gazing pensively through his window to the street below, Gardiner reflected on the decided opinion of his Irish wife who declared a natural affinity with the Welsh, whom she termed her 'Celtic cousins'. Their aspirations for more autonomy were perfectly understandable, she insisted. In any event, he was reluctant to reverse the paper's long-standing commitment. First it had been to the creation of the Welsh Office, then more powers for it, and now a measure of democratic accountability. He didn't agree with the third floor that it was simply pandering to nationalism. But this question of a referendum was more perplexing. Gardiner swung his chair around from the window towards his two colleagues who were still arguing.

'This debate is really just an internal Labour Party quarrel between pro- and anti-devolutionists,' Geraint was saying. 'We shouldn't get drawn into it. It doesn't reflect a groundswell of opinion.'

'Our opinion polls have shown strong support, around 75 per cent.'

'But polls invariably give support to a referendum, whatever the issue.'

'You can't just ignore the polls. Especially ones we've paid for.'

Geraint turned to the editor, almost pleading.

'Duncan, there's a deeper, more fundamental issue underlying all of this. If we reverse our position, I believe that in the long run we'll be opening the door to an attack on the integrity of the union itself, not by us but eventually by Scotland. Allowing a referendum on devolution will open the door some time in the future to a referendum on independence.'

'If it comes to that, you can't stop the democratic will of the Scottish or even the Welsh people by refusing a referendum, even one on independence,' Humphries cried.

'If we reverse our position, then large numbers of our readers will think that we've just surrendered to pressure,' Geraint answered bitterly. 'They'll say we're going cold on devolution.'

'Our support for devolution and whether we're for or against a referendum are quite separate.'

'That's not how the world out there sees it.'

Reluctantly Duncan Gardiner realised that he was going to have to choose sides. He was also conscious that the following week the paper's political editor had arranged a dinner at Westminster for him to meet with a group of Welsh Labour MPs.

'Look,' he said finally. 'We're going to have to decide on this one way or another. Why don't you each prepare a memorandum for me on it, setting out the pros and cons. I'm going to London next Tuesday. Let me have them by then.'

* * *

The next day, worn down by the late-night arguments, Geraint succumbed to a throat infection and stayed at home. But this did not prevent him from composing his memorandum. Sitting up in bed with a portable typewriter on a tray balanced on his knees he started constructing his case. He summoned the editorial secretary Madelaine Morris to his bedside with files of cuttings from the newspaper's library.

After she left Geraint continued typing. He conceded that there was a natural predisposition to referendums. Although the

Western Mail had no illusions about the growing strength of the demand, it had already argued against them in two leaders. It had stated that whatever the attractions, there were difficulties and dangers inherent in a referendum on devolution that could pose a greater threat to the unity of the United Kingdom than anything the government had proposed.

Downstairs Geraint's wife Elizabeth heard the clattering of typewriter keys.

> Thus the *Western Mail* has refused to concede the issue of principle both in the European and devolution contexts. It has refused to concede that a referendum is right even on an unprecedented constitutional issue such as the EEC. Secondly, it has explicitly argued that whatever the rights and wrongs of referendums in principle, there are grave objections to the holding of a referendum on this issue in that it would imperil that very unity of the United Kingdom that we are unshakeably pledged to defend. It is against this publicly declared unequivocal opposition to referendums that we are now considering a volte-face.

That afternoon, back in the office Madelaine Morris whispered to the deputy editor that though ill, Geraint was typing away furiously. His submission was already running to many pages carefully setting out the arguments. When finished it came to 5,000 words.

Immediately Humphries realised he had the upper hand. Newspapermen do not read, they scan. Typically, their attention span is little more than three-hundred words, after which there is a law of diminishing returns. This was certainly the case with

Duncan Gardiner. Humphries decided he would confine his submission to one side of a single sheet of paper.

*   *   *

In London the following week, Gardiner found himself the guest of Leo Abse. Together with fellow Welsh MPs Donald Anderson, Ifor Davies, Fred Evans, and Ioan Evans – all opposed to devolution – he had organised a dinner in a small committee room in the House of Commons. Abse was at his most charming, congratulating Gardiner on opening his pages to the opponents of devolution. Not long after the appearance of Swansea East MP Don Anderson's articles the previous September, Abse had contributed an article himself. This claimed the Assembly would result in a Welsh-speaking bureaucracy ruling Cathays Park.

He had written in his typically pugnacious style. 'With a totally untried assembly, with local authorities butchered, and the influence of elected MPs eroded, the one certain consequence of the constitutional changes would be that the real masters of Wales would be a Welsh-speaking bureaucratic élite.'

Now, over dinner, Abse quickly turned the conversation to the referendum.

'We're confident that we're going to get a majority for it in the House. But we want to persuade you on the merits of the case.'

Don Anderson leant across the table.

'The most powerful argument is the fact that we had one on the Common Market last year. That set the precedent, really. We're arguing that from now on, whenever there is an important constitutional question to be settled, a referendum is inescapable. There's strong support for that here, across the parties.'

From the end of the table Gower MP Ifor Davies said he doubted there would be a majority for devolution, but it needed to be tested.

'How can we justify imposing such a massive constitutional change on the people of Wales if it cannot be demonstrated that they support it?'

The following morning, Duncan Gardiner woke early in his hotel adjoining Paddington station. He walked out on the platform and picked up the London edition of the *Western Mail* from a newstand. Then, after a leisurely breakfast he telephoned Madelaine Morris in Cardiff and dictated a memo to be given to John Humphries and Geraint Talfan Davies.

'I have decided there should be a referendum. I will explain my reasons when I return.'

* * *

Owen typed the heading he had been instructed to give the Editorial and examined it: *Devolution: Let the people have a say.* In his notes he had underlined a point that Gardiner had particularly emphasised, that the Assembly should not have legislative powers.

'He's really been got at by the MPs,' Owen thought, as he began to write.

> For more than a decade the *Western Mail* has been firmly in favour of devolution – the decentralisation of powers from Westminster. Initially, we sought the formation of a strong, constructive and influential Welsh Office. We have watched it grow both in strength and influence.

'Influence?' Owen asked himself. 'It's just a Whitehall post box.' However, he pressed on.

> In more recent years we have advocated the need for a Welsh Assembly with non-legislative powers to ensure that the people of Wales have considerably more say in their own affairs and more power to run those affairs. We still seek this.

'This is where the *but* comes in,' Owen muttered to himself, as he continued typing.

> Increasingly we have become aware of the quite considerable groundswell of serious opinion from all parts of the political spectrum that seeks to discover through a referendum what are the aspirations of the people of Wales. The *Western Mail* has been hostile to the idea of referendums – over, for example, the Common Market – and we still believe that the vast majority of decisions should be taken by elected representatives. But we now believe that it is right that the government should discover whether its proposals are in line with a fair percentage of public opinion. We now believe, in short, that there should be a referendum.

Owen paused to glance once more at his notes, saying to himself, 'Duncan always has to have on the one hand this, on the other hand that.' So he added the required qualification.

> The fact that we have taken this different view of the balance of advantage in holding such a referendum

does not mean that any or all of the dangers inherent
in such a course evaporate.

At that moment Geraint looked into Owen's new office that he
shared with the farming correspondent.

'I see you've been given the short straw.'

'It's not easy to soften the blow.'

'I tried to persuade him that if we were going to change our
line then we should advocate a multi-choice referendum. At least
that would reveal the range of people's views and underline that
a referendum can only be consultative so far as the Commons is
concerned. But, of course, he wouldn't wear that.'

Owen suddenly became animated.

'But that's the essence of it Geraint. A referendum can't be
just consultative, can it? By its very nature it hands sovereignty
to the people. It destroys the so-called sovereignty of Parliament.
That's what the referendum on the Common Market did last
year. This one on devolution will do the same.'

'I bet Duncan doesn't want you to say that in his leader.'

'Of course not, but that's what it will do. And in the long
run there will be all sorts of consequences that we can barely
foresee. It will galvanise Welsh politics, for one thing.'

'I'm not so sure about that. Anyway, the longer run is all very
well. In the long run, we're all dead. You seem to be warming to
a referendum. But it's going to kill off devolution, probably in
Scotland too.'

'Yes, I guess you're right about that, for now. But somewhere
down the line people are going to be persuaded. That's what I
think. The key thing about the referendum is that the decision
will be made in Wales.'

'I don't see your point.'

'Well, there's an argument that since devolution affects the
whole of the United Kingdom, then England should be involved

as well. MPs like Eric Heffer are saying that. They're arguing the English should have a vote as well as the Welsh and the Scots. But at least Abse, Kinnock and the rest are campaigning for a Welsh referendum for the Welsh.'

'And that's what they're going to get, as now seems inevitable with our supporting them. And we'll kill off the Assembly in the process.'

'But Geraint, regardless of the result, it'll be an affirmation of Wales as a political nation,' Owen answered, his voice rising. 'That's the important thing at the end of the day, don't you see? We'll have our own voice, our own sovereignty.'

'It makes me think, Owen that you're a bit of an independence man at heart.'

Maerdy
May 1976

'You're interested in revolutions in the third world, so you should be in those closer to home as well,' Ioan said. He was pressing Rhiannon to come to a conference at the Polytechnic of Wales in Treforest to mark the fiftieth anniversary of the 1926 General Strike.

'It was hardly a successful revolution,' she said.

'In Wales, we specialise in unsuccessful revolutions.'

'You mean we take pride in being defeated.'

Rhiannon agreed to go, partly because of this exchange. She had become interested in the era between the wars in Wales that Ioan was studying, and was intrigued to learn more. They set out from Aberysytwyth on a Friday afternoon in his ancient Ford Cortina, driving eastwards through Ponterwyd. The incline made the car labour and wheeze as they crossed the Pumlumon range with Eisteddfa Gurig rising to their left.

Rhiannon laughed.

'Do you think your old banger will get us there?'

'Don't tempt providence.'

'I'm looking forward to it now. I've never been to the Valleys.'

'You haven't lived.'

'You haven't been to north Wales either.'

'I've been climbing in Snowdonia.'

'That's just mountains. You haven't been to Anglesey or, for that matter, Bangor or Llandudno.'

'Aberystwyth's enough.'

'I went down to Cardiff once, when I was teenager. We went on the train to stay with a friend of Dada's. It was the rugby. Dada had some tickets and he took me. I must have been fifteen or sixteen. It was quite a famous match, I think, because some newcomer scored a lot of tries.'

'You must mean Keith Jarrett from Newport,' Ioan said excitedly.

'Yes, that was it. I remember coming out of the stands at the end and Dada buying the *Football Echo*. It was pink and already had a description of the game with the score and everything. I thought it was amazing to get a paper out so quickly.'

'It's the game against England in 1967 you're talking about. I was there too. Jarrett was only eighteen and it was his first cap. He was selected as full-back despite never playing in that position in senior rugby before.'

'All I can remember is struggling in the crowd to see anything. Dada brought a biscuit tin wrapped up in brown paper which he stood on, to get a view.'

'Jarrett scored this amazing try.'

Ioan glanced across at Rhiannon and thought again how striking she looked.

'England won a lineout in their own twenty-five. They passed down the centres and kicked towards the halfway line. The ball bounced once and looked as though it was going into touch. I thought it was, I was standing a few yards away. But, instead Jarrett runs onto the ball and takes it without breaking his stride. Incredible. He sprinted down the touchline, outflanking the whole of the England defence and scored in the left corner.'

'I didn't realise you were such a rugby fan.'

'Couldn't be anything else from the Valleys, could I? Jarrett converted his own try from just inside the touchline. On top of that he kicked two penalty goals and five conversions for a total of nineteen points. Amazing.'

'Ah, the Valleys. Why do we spell the word with a capital V?'

'You'll see.'

'*How Green Was My Valley*. Have you read it?'

'No, but it's a load of old tosh.'

'How can you say that if you haven't read it?'

'Miners were never paid in gold sovereigns, the very idea.'

'You've got to allow some artistic licence. I loved the book. Reminded me of Steinbeck's *The Grapes of Wrath*, same kind of family saga.'

'I've seen the film anyway. Sentimental rubbish and nothing like the reality of miners' lives. No one speaks like they do in that film.'

'But don't you think it creates a myth, or reflects a myth that we like or want to believe, or need in some way?'

'My nan saw the film when it first came out at the beginning of the War, in Pontypridd. She told me there was a banner outside the cinema saying, *Come and see yourselves as others see you.*'

Rhiannon laughed.

'That's good.'

'Talking about myths, do you know why it was filmed in black and white?'

'All the films were then, weren't they?'

'No, not at all, they already had colour, but the war was on, you see. The plan was to film it in colour in Wales, but they couldn't get across the Atlantic because of the U-boats. So they filmed it in Hollywood, in the Malibu desert of all places. Not much greenery there.'

'I suppose not.'

'That's why they filmed it in black and white. And they made a special set for the pit village. But they put the winding gear on the top of the hill, with the miners singing as they walked up it to work. Bloody nonsense, it was.'

'Wasn't nonsense. It explored the mythology, as I say, our Welsh mythology.'

'Maybe.'

*   *   *

The next morning Rhiannon accompanied Ioan down the steep hill on which the college campus was built. They entered a large, low-slung concrete building where the conference was being held. The room was full of men. Ioan explained they were mostly activists in the miners' union, the South Wales NUM. The conference was organised by Llafur, the Welsh Labour History Society, which had been created by Labour-supporting historians together with the miners' union. Looking around, Rhiannon could see the occasional woman, whom she judged to be academics. Ioan told her there were contingents from more than twenty universities across Britain.

'Llafur's unique, you know,' he said. 'The way it brings trade unionists and academics together. Nothing like it anywhere else. The English Labour history society only has academics.'

Through a window Rhiannon could see more miners climbing out of a minibus.

The previous evening there had been an introductory lecture on the background to the strike by an academic from the University of Strathclyde. He had described how the urgent demand for coal during the First World War had depleted the richer seams so that less coal was being exported. South Wales was hard hit as demand for its steam coal that had powered the world's fleets collapsed. Coal was being rapidly replaced by oil. And the industry was out of date. Most of the miners still wielded pickaxes.

Coal production fell from about 250 tons per man before the war to less than 200 tons in the years leading up to 1926. The mine owners responded by cutting wages and increasing working hours. By the time of the strike, wages had fallen from £6 a week to £3.90 in the space of seven years.

'It'll be more interesting today,' Ioan assured her as they found a seat among the narrow wooden benches that spread in front of a raised platform. 'There'll be more about the communities and what happened during the lockout.'

At this point a stocky man in a creased suit that barely contained his bulging frame, stepped on to the platform. He removed his glasses and swept his hand through a brush of flowing white hair.

'Comrades, before we start I'm going to ask Emlyn to say a few words.'

'That's Dai Francis, the general secretary,' Ioan whispered.

'General secretary?'

'Of the South Wales NUM. Known as Dai Unanimous.'

Rhiannon cast him a questioning look.

'Because that's the way he invariably describes votes in meetings. 'He says, "That'll be unanimous, then."'

'And who's Emlyn?'

'Emlyn Williams, he's president of the South Wales Area, known as Rommel.'

'Rommel?'

'Fought in the Western Desert in the war.'

While Ioan and Rhiannon were whispering, Emlyn Williams rose to his feet. A stocky pugnacious-looking man, his gravelly voice seemed to ricochet off the ceiling. He threw out sentences that merged together, unconnected by punctuation.

'Fundamentally, although we are commemorating the 1926 period, of the history of the working-class movement, I believe that by doing so we are learning the mistakes, the successes, the tactics that will serve young people in the struggles they will have to face ahead in the trade union movement, I believe that by knowing what took place in 1926 and in the depression days of the thirties, and reading and finding out, we were able in the leadership to combat certain innovations that were being projected by so-called socialists in our movement.'

'What on earth does he mean?' Rhiannon asked in a low whisper.

'Oh, he's talking about the incomes policy the Labour government is trying to impose. The Social Contract and all that.'

Until this point Emlyn seemed to be following a formula, as though reading minutes from a meeting. But suddenly he came alive, slamming a large fist into the palm of his hand.

'Why should men who risk their lives through injuries and disease, who work physically hard, who produce a commodity which is essential to British industry, not be paid accordingly?'

Rousing applause and whistles caused Emlyn Williams to raise his voice.

'If the answer is that society can't afford it, then my reply is that society must be changed so it can afford it.'

More applaused accompanied Emlyn stepping down from the platform. He was replaced by a younger, intense-looking man bearing a large tape recorder.

'Who's this?' Rhiannon whispered again.

'Oh, that's Hywel, Dai's son,' Ioan said. 'Works in the extra mural department at Swansea. Doing some interesting research on the coalfield.'

As Hywel Francis began to speak, Rhiannon leant forward listening hard to his soft voice. He spoke in a quiet, but insistent manner.

'The nine days of the General Strike, and more especially the seven-month lockout revealed an alternative cultural pattern which had no comparable equivalent in the other British coalfields. The totality of commitment to the miners' cause was a form of class consciousness which translated itself into a community consciousness, so overwhelming were the miners in numbers and influence.'

Rhiannon sensed he was a Welsh-speaker and said so, glancing at Ioan.

'Yes, he's from Onllwyn in the anthracite part of the coalfield, in the Dulais Valley. They're a different breed over there.'

Rhiannon looked up to see Francis in full flow.

'The trade union and political experience of the miners in south Wales was unique, relatively homogeneous and sophisticated. The South Wales Miners' Federation was a single union operating in single industry community. It was the largest regional union in Britain at that time. The Fed, as it was known, was the focal point of the community and, by its very nature, the lodge, the union branch, was vested with considerable independence. This encouraged a healthy anarcho-syndicalist rank-and-file outlook towards industrial and political problems.'

'Anarcho-syndicalist?' Rhiannon queried again.

'Workers taking control with direct action,' Ioan whispered as the speaker continued.

'Allied to this, was the building of over one hundred miners' institute libraries between 1890 and 1920 which stocked many socialist texts. The existence of this phenomenon on such a universal scale was peculiar to the South Wales coalfield. There was no comparable educational institution generated almost entirely by a proletarian culture anywhere else in the world.'

Francis leant over the tape recorder on the desk beside him switching it on.

'This is Jim Evans of Abercrave. We interviewed him a couple of years ago. He explains how the experience of the strike distorted the nature of traditional society.'

Francis pressed a button, the large tape-reels began turning and from the loudspeaker emerged a Welsh voice. Thinned by age it was distant, but still firm.

I saw two grown men in their thirties, fighting each other to the point of unconsciousness over two marbles, because we had to get something for currency, and with marbles you could sell thirty for a penny.

Francis pressed another button, stopping the tape-recorder. He adjusted his glasses and examined his notes. He described how the communal kitchen was the cement that held miners and their families together. In some cases, local Boards of Guardians issued relief notes in place of cash. However, shopkeepers could not exchange them immediately and so wholesalers were not prepared to supply them. Food ran short, sometimes with tragic consequences.

Francis started the tape recorder again. 'This is an interview we did last year with Ned Gittens.'

We had a daughter, so it was a family of three then, existing on thirteen-and-six a week relief. The child was born in November 1926 and of course it died as a result of malnutrition. The wife suffered from meningitis, and the doctor reckoned it was due to the fact she carried the baby through the strike.

'This is D. C. Davies, another miner involved in the lockout,' Hywel said.

My mother died of pernicious anaemia which is a polite name for starvation due to the awful conditions in 1926 and just after.

Francis consulted his notes.

'If food was the most pressing issue, footwear was the

most humiliating. In October 1926, a hundred and forty-one Glyncorrwg children attended school barefoot whilst ninety-one were absent owing to lack of boots. The situation would have been a lot worse without the miners' co-operative boot centres. Ynysbwl alone repaired seven hundred and eighty-two children's boots and three hundred and forty-seven adults' shoes in three weeks.'

At the end of the talk, questions were invited. The first queried Francis's claim that the strike and the nine-month lockout was experienced differently in south Wales.

'What distinguished the south Wales miners from those in the other coalfields was the manner and intensity of the resistance. I think the most profound impact of the strike on the coalfield was the way in which it began to clarify and then polarise class loyalties, a development which deepened irrevocably during the lock-out.'

'Wasn't the whole thing in the end just a dreadful defeat?' another questioner asked. 'After all, the south Wales coalfield didn't recover for years afterwards, not until the war really.'

'You're right, the lockout was a catastrophe,' Francis answered. 'But something could be claimed from the wreckage. For one thing, it taught us to know our enemies, as they say. The political consciousness that was lacking during the Nine Days of the Strike began to evolve in the coalfield during the lockout. What emerged was in the manner of an alternative culture with its own moral code and political tradition. It was a society within a society.'

At this point Francis stopped speaking, reflecting on his own words. Then, putting his notes on the table he turned off the tape recorder and looked out at his audience.

'On the face of it the defeat in the lockout was catalytic in turning many miners towards conventional Labour Party politics and away from the quasi-syndicalism of industrial action. It was a hard lesson. But the Labour Party strengthened its support in the Valleys as a result. In the debacle of the 1931 general election, whilst the party was decimated everywhere else, south Wales was the only big coalfield to hold all its mining seats. Four candidates were returned unopposed.'

*   *   *

Rhiannon was surprised to discover that after lunch the conference was embarking on a bus tour of some of the Valley towns that played a prominent role in the strike. Four coaches were laid on and they set off in a convoy on the winding road northwards.

They passed through Cilfynydd and then, when they reached Treharris, instead of heading directly towards Aberfan and Merthyr, they took a right turn for Bedlinog. The narrow roads were more like country lanes and the buses made their way with difficulty. They passed through Trelewis and then into the neighbouring valley from where the Bargoed Taf flowed into the main Taf river. The mountain sides were so close to the valley floor that the road and railway were forced to run along lines carved into the hillside above.

'I've never heard of these places,' Rhiannon said to Ioan who was sitting alongside her.

'You'd be unlikely to come through here unless you were making for Bedlinog itself. The village wouldn't be there but for the mine. But it was famous in the Strike, you know.'

He glanced towards the front of the bus.

'There's Edgar Evans down there. I'll go and have a chat.'

'Who's Edgar Evans?' Rhiannon asked when he returned.

'Oh, he's been an activist up here for years, joined the Communist Party the year of the strike. A councillor for a long time as well. He was imprisoned in the thirties on jumped-up charges. *Incitement to riot* they called it. That was during the Taff-Merthyr dispute over the company union when miners across the coalfield had their famous stay-down strikes. Edgar served nine months and got a hero's welcome when he came out. Amazing fellow. I've persuaded him he should say a few words.'

Not long afterwards, Evans struggled to his feet, a microphone in one hand while he held on to the luggage rack above with the other.

'The bus has got loudspeakers for the guides when it goes on tour,' Ioan said.

'So what's this tour exactly?'

'A bit of a history tour, I suppose you could say.'

Despite his seventy-six years, Edgar Evans had plenty of energy. He was heavily built with a lined craggy face, a sweep of white hair and black bushy eyebrows.

'I've been asked to say something about what happened in Bedlinog in '26.'

As he began to speak, Evans' face broke into an amused smile.

'Well, I was twenty-six-years-old then and I'd been running the ironmonger's shop in the village since just after the war. I came into shopkeeping by accident really. I would have gone down the mines like most of my brothers but myself... I was the weakling in our family. We were twelve children brought up in Garnant. I was a sickly child, in a sanatorium for a year when I was eight.'

He paused, as if gazing into the past, but then shook himself.

'Anyway, my uncle, who was running an ironmonger's in Bedlinog, said to my mother that I could come and work with him. So I did, just as the war was starting. I was fourteen then. After the war, my uncle moved to run a shop in Bournemouth and it was agreed that I should take over in Bedlinog.'

As he spoke the coach swung its way up the narrow hillside

and then down into Bedlinog itself, and stopped for a moment in the village square. Edgar Evans bent to peer through the window and upwards at the mountainside. Then he straightened and spoke once more through the microphone.

'There were five shops in the village in those days, most of them run by people who were either communists or in the Independent Labour Party. Hector Bolwel, for instance, he was a former miner who had been victimised after an earlier strike. He ran the grocery store. Eddie Ingram who ran the boot and shoe shop was a party member as well.

'We formed a branch of the Communist Party in the village in 1924, and most of the shopkeepers joined. In fact, we got together in the Bedlinog Chamber of Trade. Arthur Horner was always going on about the role of the Bedlinog Chamber of Trade. In those days, Maerdy was regarded as the pinnacle of the revolutionary struggle. But Arthur would often say, "In Bedlinog they even run the Chamber of Trade."'

A ripple of laughter through the coach interrupted him and Evans joined in, chuckling to himself.

'Aye, well, that's what he said. Now when the strike was called, the first thing we did was to transform the Trades Council into a Council of Action and we ran the whole thing through that. So, for instance, the butcher supplied the soup kitchen with meat at cost price. The soup kitchen kept the whole thing together.'

'What about the politics, Edgar?' a man from near the back of the bus called out.

'That was a question of having contact with the movement outside. I had a chat about it with Harry Morgan who ran the fish and chip shop. Our ironmonger's shop was a do-it-yourself. We kept everything you know, from camera films to cement and timber, even those old vinyl records. But we also had a motor bike in the shop – a new one, a Royal Enfield bike, two-

and-three-quarter it was. And I thought it would be a good idea if we licensed it and put it on the road. I had a chat with Harry, as I say, and he said "Right-oh, we'll go fifty-fifty with it". So we decided to license the bike, tax it, and we had three people who were prepared to be couriers or despatch riders.'

Edgar stopped for a moment to give himself a breath.

'So with the bike, we had contact with Maerdy almost every day of the week. Now Maerdy had become the centre more or less of the Movement in south Wales I'd say. Anyway we used to bring piles of literature from there for distribution, in the Bedlinog, Trelewis and Treharris areas. We'd distribute everything to do with the Strike, to build it up, expand it and get the whole thing solid.'

Edgar hesitated while the bus took a particularly sharp turn, pressing him hard against the luggage rack he was clinging to.

'In fact, we were able to reproduce a lot of the stuff we were bringing back from Maerdy ourselves. We had a typewriter – I was not very efficient on that – and we had one of those Gestetner duplicating machines. We produced quite a lot. We also distributed the *Daily Worker* door-to-door.'

Edgar stopped again while the bus turned, but then raised the microphone.

'So you ask about the politics. The fact was, we were very well-informed right from the beginning.'

'I love listening to people like Edgar lewis,' Rhiannon said as the bus climbed the steep road out of Bedlinog. 'Brings it all alive somehow. He's a lovely man, too.'

'Seems harmless here, right enough,' Ioan said. 'But according to the police, he was a menace to the youth of Bedlinog. They brought a court case against him in the thirties.'

They were approaching Fochriw, a small mining community held in a fold of the hills at the head of the Rhymney Valley. The bus turned and within a few miles they were in sight of Merthyr

Tydfil, crucible of the industrial revolution. They would track westwards, Ioan explained, along the Heads of the Valleys road to Hirwaun before turning south to Aberdare and then cross over the mountain to the Rhondda Fach and Maerdy.

'The place Edgar Evans has been talking about,' Rhiannon said.

'Yes, we're more or less following the route of his motor bike despatch riders.'

*　*　*

In Maerdy the coaches stopped alongside the Workmen's Institute, a grim-looking, black-stoned building capped with a green copper roof. Inside the visitors were ushered to the first floor where there was a large room with a stage at one end, used for social functions as well as a cinema. Ioan led Rhiannon up the stairs.

'It's known as the Rainbow Room because the central light casts rainbows around it,' he said.

Alongside one wall were trestle tables with tea, biscuits and Welsh cakes. Members of the Institute's committee and the NUM Maerdy Lodge were among the welcoming party. Hanging at the back of the hall was a vivid red and gold banner which excited a good deal of interest. A member of the Institute's committee, cup of tea in hand, cut through the hum of conversation by tapping the edge of his saucer with a teaspoon.

'We'd just like to welcome you all to the Institute,' he said. 'We based the Strike Committee here in 1926. The original Institute was built in 1905 but burned down in 1922. Within three years the miners had raised enough money – £35,000 in fact, which was a lot in those days – to replace it with the hall you're standing in today.'

Ioan explained the speaker was Wil Picton.

'He was part of the Strike Committee in 1926. I think he's going to be talking to Hywel Francis.' Ioan pointed to the stage where two chairs and a table had been set.

On cue Hywel Francis led Picton on to the stage and they sat in front of a microphone.

'We'd like to thank you Wil and the Institute Committee for your welcome today,' Hywel said. 'And I'm glad to see the banner hanging there.'

Ioan bent towards Rhiannon.

'A. J. Cook was given it in Moscow during the lockout,' he whispered. 'He was there to acknowledge the money the Russians had given the miners, more than a million pounds.'

'A.J. Cook?'

'Arthur James Cook, secretary of the Miners' Federation of Great Britain during the Strike.' As they spoke they drifted to the back of the gathering to take a closer look at the banner and its slogan.

> *Proletarians of all countries unite!*
> *To the fighting British Miners and the British Miners*
> *Wives*
> *From the Working Women of Krasnaya Presna June 3,*
> *1926 Moscow*

'Cook said it ought to be kept in the place which was at the heart of the struggle,' Ioan said. 'Hywel found it a few years ago.'

'Really? Where?'

'Well, it got lost. It was used in the twenties and thirties to drape the coffins of communists and socialists but it disappeared after the 1939 funeral of Lewis Jones – you know, the novelist, leader of the unemployed in the Rhondda. Hywel found it years later in the attic of the offices of the Communist Party in Cardiff.'

Francis tapped the microphone which crackled.

'Wil, could we start by asking you to recall some of the early days of the Strike?'

'Well, we had some exciting times. You see, there were too many people in Maerdy for the police to handle. One occasion was just when the strike started. We had a packed meeting in the hall here. There was a lot of coal due to the workers in Maerdy that hadn't been delivered, you know the concessionary coal. And, of course, the sidings were full of coal.'

Wil Picton shifted in his chair, and rubbed his chin with his hand.

'That was at the very beginning of the strike. Somebody came in to say there was two engines down by the station just going to start to take the coal out. Down the siding we had a discussion with the drivers. There were two foremen and two drivers, and they said, "Fair enough, boys, all right with us".

'So they unhitched the engines and off they went. The next thing we did was to knock all the doors out of the trucks. We formed a committee and everybody was getting their ration out of the wagons. It was carried all over, by night as well, and distributed so much for every person. Everybody had a share.'

He paused, allowing Hywel to ask, 'What was it like afterwards, after the lockout?'

'After the Strike? Everyone one of us in Maerdy who were active in that period were victimised, you know. People were unemployed for years after, until the war broke out in 1939 in most cases. There was a deliberate attempt to crush the militancy of Maerdy. It was tragic. The place was so depressed, so poverty-stricken that people suffered from malnutrition. Some people committed suicide, some were taken into the mental home.

Maerdy had to be adopted by people in Warwickshire who sent clothes, shoes and other things to help the unemployed.'

'What happened to you?'

'I was unemployed myself after 1926, until 1938 in fact. On the dole I was getting twenty-eight shillings for me, my wife and the child. My role was the organising of demonstrations of the unemployed, leading them against the police, representing the claims of the unemployed, inside the Court of Referees and Tribunal Boards.'

'You said there was a deliberate attempt to crush the militancy of the place.'

'Aye, there was, but despite that we made some progress. Maerdy's collieries were closed then, and today there are only two collieries left working in the whole of the Rhondda Fach. But they didn't crush our spirit. No. It's gratifying to find that the militancy that was adopted during that period has been transferred into the minds of the leadership of the Maerdy colliery today. It's a progressive lodge, of which I'm very proud.'

'What happened when the mines were nationalised?'

'I remember after the war the secretary of the Lodge, Charlie Jones, brought one of the Big Shots from the Coal Board to have a look at the Institute and he said to me, "What do you think about nationalisation, Mr Picton?" I always remember it. I said, "Nothing." "Oh, I'm surprised by that, I thought you were a socialist," he said. "I am," I said. "But this is not socialism, you've only changed the name from coal owners to nationalisation. The same buggers are running it. The same manager and the same overman."

'And another thing I said, "You may have a consultative committee, but the man in the chair has got to be the manager." "Oh well", he said. "It'll work out. It's just like in Russia, a form of nationalisation." But I said, "Don't compare it with Russia. Over there production is for consumption, here it's for profit."'

'How did Maerdy become known as Little Moscow?' Hywel asked him.

'It was in 1926 that they started calling the place that. The *Western Mail* started it off, and then the *Daily Express*. It was all propaganda. It wasn't a question of calling it Little Moscow because there were so many communists here, it was to put a slur on the place. And it proved itself when many of the unemployed were going looking for jobs. "Where do you come from? Oh, Little Moscow... get out, get off the premises!" That was widespread. So it had its effect.'

'So it wasn't a matter of pride, then?'

'Oh no. It was resented in Maerdy. But you see it had its effect, it served its purpose, especially when you were looking for a job. I remember one time going up to Bradford, to a Conference of Unemployed, in 1932 it was. And the voucher then from Cardiff was a green voucher like that for a return. It wasn't a ticket. You just showed it at the gate. So I was coming out of this gate in Bradford and I handed the voucher over, and the two blokes there gave me a look, and as I was going down one said to the other, "That's a bloke from Little Moscow."'

Wil Picton stopped what he was saying for a moment, and frowned.

'There was Maerdy on the voucher you see, it said Maerdy to Bradford.'

* * *

'Where next?' Rhiannon asked as they settled into their coach lined up at the back of the Institute.

'We're heading down the Rhondda Fach and stopping off at the Lewis Merthyr Institute in Porth,' Ioan said picking up the conference programme. 'Looks like there's going to be a social evening, with a buffet, and they're showing a film.'

'Film?'

'An extract from the series that went on the BBC last year. Didn't you see it? It was about what happened in the years leading to the Strike. *Days of Hope* it was called.'

'I don't watch much television.'

'It was really good, directed by Ken Loach. A.J. Cook features in the last episode, on the Strike. It says here that Dai Coity Davies is talking about it. In fact, Dai plays A.J. Cook in the film.'

'Dai Coity Davies?'

'Yes, Dai Davies, he's compensation secretary with the South Wales NUM, quite a character I can tell you. Coity's the place he comes from, a village near Bridgend.'

'Bit odd, isn't it for someone like him to act in a film?'

'That's how Ken Loach works. He gets real people so to speak, to appear in his films. Dai Francis was very keen on the idea. Arranged for him to have time off.'

At the Taff Merthyr Institute, another imposing building similar to the one in Maerdy, Rhiannon and Ioan managed to get seats in the main hall close to the front of the stage. A screen had been lowered from the ceiling. There was a projector at the back of the hall that threw a still picture of a gaunt-looking man with a hooked nose and moustache leaning over a balcony gesticulating to a large crowd beneath him. *Unity is Strength* declared a banner fixed to the balcony.

Suddenly, the man in the picture strode on to the stage.

'That's Dai,' Ioan whispered.

'Comrades, it's an honour to welcome you to the Rhondda where A. J. Cook was the miner's agent in the years leading up to the strike. And it's been a great honour for me to play the man in Ken Loach's great film.'

There was a round of applause, but Dai Coity Davies held up his hands to quell the sound.

'I was only just eight-years-old when the Strike started, but I can remember my father being involved. He was beaten up, set upon by the Devon Police he was, and they'd only just come to our village. He was set upon with no accusations, nothing said, just beaten up and frog-marched through the village to show the young militants exactly what would happen to them if they didn't curtail their activities. They brought him home, dumped him on the couch we had inside the door, and then left. He wasn't accused of anything. His only crime, of course, was that he was on strike and not working.'

Raising his hand to shield his eyes from the glare of the light from the projector, Davies stared at the audience.

'Comrades, to my mind what we've been through in the last few years, in the 1972 and 1974 strikes, is payback for what happened in 1926.'

Applause interrupted him, but he raised his hands again to quieten the audience.

'So, as I say, it was a privilege for me to be asked to play the part of A. J. Cook, the greatest leader the miners have ever produced. He mixed revolutionary fervour with religious revivalism. No doubt he picked that up from his days as a Baptist lay preacher. He was a mirror image of every miner's frustrations and yearnings.'

Davies reached into the inside pocket of his jacket and pulled out some sheaves of paper.

'Now, when I was thinking about how I should try and portray him I did some research. I came across a number of accounts which give you an idea of what he was like. Arthur Horner spoke with him at countless meetings up and down the country. He said that Cook always had the better reception and for a long time he couldn't understand why. And then it came to him. He realised that at the meetings he was speaking *to* the people whereas Cook was always speaking *for* them.'

Davies stopped for a moment to allow time for the point to settle, then he continued.

'Mind you, not everything I researched was that complimentary. Beatrice Webb, for instance, viewed him with a mixture of middle-class fascination and distaste. Typical of the Fabians of those days I would say.'

Davies unfolded a pair of glasses and picked up a book from a table alongside him.

'But here is a recollection I am especially fond of, from Idris Davies' epic poem 'The Angry Summer'. I reckon he would have seen A.J. Cook on the stump during the Strike. In fact, I'm sure he would have.'

Putting on his glasses Davies read the words:

> *Here is Arthur J. Cook, a red rose in his lapel,*
> *Astride on a wall, arousing his people,*
> *Now with his fist in the air, now a slap to the knee,*
> *Almost burning his way to victory!*

Llanrwst
May 1976

'I'm afraid there's not much enthusiasm for your Assembly in these parts,' John Môn Hughes said, standing to carve a generous joint of lamb.

Expertly, he ran his knife across a steel.

'The truth is, folk up here view people in the south with a lot of suspicion, Valleys people especially.'

Mari uttered a peal of laughter.

'So that's what you thought when you ran into me, is it?'

'Absolutely, never trusted you from the start.'

John smiled at his twin teenage daughters who were giggling across the table. 'Never trust those people in the south,' he told them. 'They talk too much, for a start.'

At the end of the table Owen was discomfited. Wondering again how the evening would turn out, he felt he should respond in some way.

'Isn't it rather a question of country people feeling that people in the towns don't understand them?'

'Well, that's true, of course, but there's more to it than that, especially when it comes down to politics.'

'Don't take any notice of him, Owen,' Mari said. 'John's just a sounding board for the county set.'

'That may be, but I'm sure what I'm saying reflects a general view across north Wales.'

'Which is?' Owen asked.

'It's quite simple. We just think it's inevitable that in any Cardiff Assembly, our views will be subordinated to those people crowded between Swansea and Newport.'

Hearing that Owen was spending the best part of a weekend in Llandudno covering the annual conference of the Welsh

Counties Committee, Mari demanded he must be sure to call at Plas-y-Bryn.

'It's half-term and the twins will be home, so I'll be there,' she said. 'Do come.'

'Won't John think it a bit odd?'

'Oh, no, not at all, we have people staying all the time. He's quite sociable, really. One reason I like him.'

Which is why at the end of the meeting, Owen had driven southwards from Llandudno through Llanrwst to find Plas-y-Bryn on the slopes of the Conwy Valley. The driveway led to an imposing Victorian house with a verandah and a large front door flanked by two life-like stone dogs.

Owen was met by the twins, alarming fourteen-year-old girls who dragged him into the kitchen at the back of the house crying, 'Mummy look what we've found!'

Mari showed him to a bedroom and told him to settle in.

Owen took stock of his surroundings. The room was large, almost as big as the ground floor of his house in Cardiff. A double-bed, a wardrobe and bookcase occupied some of the space, but there was still plenty of room to walk about. Owen went to the window and pulled aside the heavy curtains. Beyond the courtyard and outbuildings were fields that fell gently to the plain below. Hills rose in the distance. Owen could make out the river and the railway close together on the far side of the valley.

After a while he descended the wide stairs to find John Môn Hughes stretched out in an armchair in the drawing room reading a newspaper. He jumped up immediately he saw Owen, shook his hand warmly and gestured to the drinks table. Owen judged him to be in his late fifties, a good fifteen years older than Mari. He was tall, ruddy-featured, with a ring of untidy hair streaked with grey. He'd been to public school in England

and had a career in the army before leaving in his forties to run the farm and business.

He told Owen that the family had made its money a few generations before, mining for copper and lead in the Gwydyr Forest in the hills on the other side of the valley. All he had done was divert some of it into farming at Plas-y-Bryn and a building suppliers in Llanrwst. 'You could say I've had it easy,' he said. 'But running a business these days, keeping your head above water, well… it's challenging, to say the least.'

Their conversation turned to devolution after John had asked about the local government conference. Owen said the counties feared another reorganisation once the Assembly was in place.

'But we've only just had one.'

'Yes but Labour think the eight new counties are too big. They see them as a Tory fix, in the south anyway. They want a new set up of around twenty, perhaps twenty-five authorities.'

'Every time they change, it just costs more money.'

*   *   *

They were interrupted by Mari calling them into the dining room. Once there, John renewed the exchange.

'And the Assembly itself is going to cost, isn't it? How many Assembly members are we supposed to have?'

'Eighty, two for each of the parliamentary constituencies,' Owen told him.

'There we are. They're all going to have to be paid, and their offices and staff. We'll have yet more civil servants, an extra thousand I've heard. What's all that going to cost?'

'About £12 million a year, but it's democracy. Worth paying for, I say.'

'That's right, Owen,' Mari said, laughing. 'You tell him.'

'It's just another tier of government which we simply don't need.'

It was Owen's turn to be exercised.

'We've already got the tier of government you're talking about, all the appointed bodies, the Welsh Development Agency, Wales Tourist Board, Health Board, Water Authority, Arts Council and the rest.'

John went to the sideboard to open a bottle of wine, turning to Owen as he did so.

'But we're still going to have to keep them, aren't we? They're not going to be run directly by the Assembly, surely? We're not going to disband the National Museum or the National Library.'

'No, but they'll be accountable to the Assembly. It'll be more democratic.'

'You'll never convince him,' Mari said. 'Not worth bothering.'

'What really annoys me is why they're doing it,' John said over her. 'You can see their heart isn't really in it? They're doing it because Plaid Cymru won a few by-elections in the 1960s.'

'There's some truth in that,' Owen conceded.

'Nationalism is at the root of it. People like Gwynfor Evans reject the idea that they're British. I respect their right to do so. I have to, with Mari in the house.'

'You don't really,' Mari said.

'I do, but I don't admire them for it. I'm just as Welsh as they are —more Welsh in many ways, if one is talking about ancestry. But tens of thousands of Welshmen fought in the two world wars. Tell *them* that there is no such thing as being British and you place a bitter wreath on a lot of hallowed graves. We're British, you know, as well as Welsh.'

After that, Mari was careful to steer the conversation towards lighter subjects. They spoke about the farm, the children, a holiday in Italy, and a Kyffin Williams exhibition in the Mostyn Gallery in Llandudno. Then they moved into the drawing room and John, restored to his genial self, plied Owen with drinks until nearly midnight.

* * *

In the large bedroom, Owen was unable to sleep. Instead, he turned on the light, fetched a glass of water from the adjoining bathroom, and tried to read. But that also proved impossible. He had enjoyed much of the evening, but there had been moments when he had felt the incongruity of his situation. He knew he ought to be at home. Before leaving Llandudno he had telephoned Anna from a call box. She had been bright but brittle and he'd heard a catch in her voice. It was hardly surprising. Angharad was barely a month old.

Owen was at a loss when thinking about the child. She stirred something surprisingly profound in him. Her presence was making him think about his life in a completely different way. The future was suddenly more important, for one thing. And his failure to anticipate the impact of Angharad's arrival made his unease that much greater. The manner of her birth had been the start. He had been completely unprepared for what had taken place.

He and Anna had been left alone in a windowless room in the hospital for what seemed endless amounts of time. Occasionally a nurse would come in, busy herself with various tasks and tell Anna she was doing fine, which hardly seemed the case. Owen handled sponges and towels but mainly sat mute, holding Anna's hand, feeling useless. At one point he went off in search of tea. Time seemed to hang still.

Eventually a nurse and doctor appeared and decided Anna needed to be moved to another room. Here, they attached her to monitors. Owen was told to keep an eye on one. Its waves and bleeps were a response to Anna and the baby's heartbeats. Time crept slowly by. Anna's contractions intensified. She told him later that the onset of pain was like the disturbing of tectonic plates deep inside her. They shifted and scraped into a hot, searing rumble before reaching a crescendo that lasted minutes before retreating. Owen could only gaze helplessly. More hours passed.

He must have dozed because suddenly he was jerked awake to hear a continuous bleep and see a line on the monitor track horizontally. He hurried to the door and ran out into the corridor. There was no one to be seen. He ran blindly, turning a corner and then into another corridor. He caught sight of some figures in the distance. He shouted and waved.

They came towards him and he ran back to the room. Suddenly it was full of people and bright lights. Anna moaned and then cried out. Someone leant forward, spoke to her and placed a mask over her face.

'We'll have to use forceps,' another voice said.

Owen backed away, panic rising in his throat. All he could see was a wall of bodies.

Anna gave a great cry.

The bodies parted, and Owen caught sight of the baby. He was amazed at how long it looked. He had an inexplicable feeling of hostility to this being that was causing so much pain.

But then he heard Anna sobbing and saw she was holding the babe to her breast. Then he was with her himself, holding her and also crying. All of this happened as though in slow motion.

They were moved on to a ward, and later Anna slept with the baby in a small cot beside her. After standing watching them for a while, Owen went home to fetch some things. As he walked into the house he felt the ordinariness of the day almost impossible to bear. It was late afternoon. They had set off for the hospital about nine o'clock the previous evening. Owen poured a Scotch and walked into weak sunshine in the yard outside.

* * *

Anna felt she was wading through a miasma of tiredness. The baby needed constant feeding, especially at night. Angharad would wake, it seemed, every hour. Sometimes she would doze for just fifteen or twenty minutes before clamping herself once more to the breast. She was less demanding during the day, but still required feeding every two to three hours.

Anna had ceased thinking clearly. Sometimes she felt as if she was hallucinating. The most straightforward tasks took an age to accomplish. She needed more than an hour to get everything ready to go out. She'd cut her long hair short to save time washing it.

Sylvia had stayed for the first few weeks and had been a great help. Anna had felt a surge of tenderness towards her mother. But that had been complicated by feelings of awkwardness whenever Owen was around. There was a tension between the two of them.

Anna thought back to when they had first brought Angharad home. She had collapsed with the baby in their bedroom at the back of the house. Owen had gone downstairs. A little while later Anna heard voices through the open window. Owen was in the garden talking over the wall to their neighbour who was hanging out some washing.

'It all sounds so normal,' Anna thought desperately. 'But nothing is as it was. How can he be talking in such a matter of fact way when everything has changed? Everything is different. Why doesn't he know?'

She'd started sobbing then and couldn't stop. Owen came into the house and hearing the sound, rushed upstairs.

'Whatever's the matter?' he asked. But Anna couldn't explain.

Now in a rare moment with Angharad asleep in her cot Anna leant across feeling again an overwhelming connectedness. It was as though she was melting into this creature and Angharad into her. She wondered if this small thing was really a separate being. She reached out and touched Angharad. Of course she was! She smelled differently, for one thing. But looking at her now, sleeping on her tummy, in a corner of the cot with her legs drawn under her nappy, Anna wondered if she would ever grow apart from her.

'What does Owen think?' Anna asked herself. 'He seems to be affected by her, of course he does. The way he holds her, looking delighted. But how can he bear to be parted from her, for days at a time?'

Anna thought irritably how Owen's life seemed to be continuing as though nothing had happened.

'He has his work that is nothing to do with us,' she thought. 'He just sleeps through Angharad crying. He carries on in his own world. He can think of little else but the paper and his writing. But what does it amount to? He is so preoccupied all the time. Why is Wales so important? After all, it's just a theoretical thing. How can it compare with home? How can his world compare with us? How can it come before Angharad and me?'

*   *   *

Morning came and Owen woke. He got out of bed, went to the window and drew back the curtains. Light was streaming over the fields. Across the valley a wreath-like mist was spiralling above the Conwy river. Despite the brightness of the day Owen felt something leaden inside him. 'That malt whisky, I must be a bit hungover,' he thought. He resolved that he would have to say something to Mari, but was uncertain about the words he should use.

When he came downstairs there was only Mari in the kitchen, making coffee. Her hair was tied up and she wore a flowing silk dressing gown. She explained that John was already out on the farm and the girls were still asleep.

Owen sat at the table and began to speak, but his words trailed.

'Shush.'

Mari came across and put a finger on his lips.

'I know.'

'What?'

'It's Angharad, isn't it?'

Later, after breakfast, when Owen had collected his things and was standing at the door of his car, Mari followed him out of the house.

'Drive safely.'

She reached a hand to his head, drew him to her and kissed him warmly.

'We can still be friends, after all.'

Treforest
May 1976

They had returned to the Glamorgan Polytechnic after their bus tour and Ioan and Rhiannon found their way to the student bar. It was filled with a crowd of mainly young people who were also attending the conference. Ioan fetched a round of drinks to their table.

'Well, what did you think of Dai Coity Davies?'

'He was very good, but the film was depressing.'

'In what way?'

'It just revealed how chaotic their whole organisation was. That banner, for a start. *Unity is Strength* it said, which is quite right. But they were all over the place, or at least their leadership was.'

'Hard to get different unions to work together.'

'Hard to get one union to work together, more like.'

'You've got to remember that in those days there were different wage scales in different regions. Even in south Wales there were different going rates according to the seams and the difficulty of getting the coal out. It made unified action all but impossible.'

'But I thought there was unity in the south Wales coalfield. After all, the strike was solid here.'

'A lot of that was down to the Communist Party. But at the same time at the national level, in London, there was a good deal of tension, especially between Labour and the communists. There was in Cardiff, too, for that matter. You saw in the film how Ramsay MacDonald was really against the whole idea of a General Strike. What did they have him say in the film? "I have nothing to do with discussion of general strikes, Bolshevism and all that kind of thing". He was about respecting the constitution.

That pretty much reflects what the Labour Party was about and has been ever since.'

'That's inevitable, isn't it, for a party working through Parliament?'

'Yes, but it creates a tension. Labour's always been against industrial action, especially when it's in government. That's the situation today as well. Emlyn Williams made the point this morning.'

Ioan looked towards the other side of the bar where a group seated round a couple of tables had starting singing. The soft harmony of male voices drifted across the room. Rhiannon had picked up a guitar leaning against the wall and was plucking at it idly, trying to get it into tune.

'Come on, Rhi, why don't you give us a song?'

'No, no. it's getting late.'

'Go on, mun.'

Rhiannon lowered her head and her long red hair fell across her face. She strummed the guitar more strongly, finding some chords and silencing the hum of conversation that flooded the bar. And into the space, between the rhythmic sound of the guitar her voice, piercingly translucent, began an anthem with the words borne along a strong melodic current.

> As we go marching, marching, in the beauty of the day
> A million darkened kitchens, a thousand mill lofts gray
> Are touched with all the radiance that a sudden sun
>   discloses
> For the people hear us singing, bread and roses, bread
>   and roses.

Rhiannon's voice died away although she kept a low rhythm with the guitar, and the break in sound was filled with clapping and whistles, causing her to blush.

'I don't think the song was sung during the '26 strike, though it could have been.'

'Speak up, love,' came a voice from the back.

'It was written in the States a bit earlier, in 1912 I think, after a textile strike by women who carried a banner, *We want bread and Roses too.*'

'Aye, that's it. That's what all workers want,' someone agreed.

Rhiannon resumed, the guitar sounding more strongly.

As she finished there was a momentary silence before the bar filled once again with conversations. After a few more drinks, Rhiannon and Ioan made their way across the campus. Eventually they came to their newly-built student resident block with its featureless corridors and communal bathrooms.

Rhiannon rose on her toes and kissed Ioan lightly at the foot of a flight of concrete steps.

'*Nos da.*'

She left him then and made her way to her room. Inside she pulled the curtains and switched on the strip lighting. There was a narrow bed, a desk and a chair. A cork noticeboard on the wall above the bed had been hurriedly stripped, leaving behind drawing pins holding the odd jagged edges of photographs and pieces of paper.

Rhiannon leant back on the bed, and thought about the day and the faces of the old miners who had spoken. How distant those times seemed, so long ago, and yet how urgently present in the memories of those men.

'And they were men, all of them,' Rhiannon thought. 'It's the men who we hear about. It's the men who make history. Where are the women? They're invisible, though not in that song I was singing...'

Suddenly, there was a muted but urgent knocking.

Opening the door, Rhiannon found Ioan. She sighed, and let him in.

*   *   *

After breakfast in the refectory they made their way early to the conference hall. It was already quite full. Rhiannon caught sight of a man sitting in the front row. She knew he must be Raymond Williams from photographs she had seen. According to the programme, he was the opening speaker. Most people were sitting expectantly, except for a few organisers huddled on the stage. They were grouped around the chairman, Ieuan Gwynedd Jones, a professor of history at Aberystwyth. A kindly figure encased in a suit that seemed a little big for him, he was gazing over his spectacles and holding out his hands in a gesture of ignorance. Rhiannon realised they had yet to meet their speaker.

There was a hiatus until, smiling a little hesitantly, Raymond joined the organisers on the stage to make himself known. An awkward shaking of hands took place. Then Ieuan Gwynedd Jones cleared his throat and began the morning's proceedings.

Raymond sat on the platform gazing abstractedly at the ceiling. When he realised his moment had come he advanced to the lectern and grasped it with both hands. A microphone was connected by a cord to a tape recorder placed on the floor. This, combined with a realisation that he would be speaking without notes, gave Rhiannon a sudden feeling of nervousness on his behalf.

But his delivery was even and calm.

'I came down this morning from a village above Abergavenny, travelling the quite short distance to this centre of the mining Valleys, and travelling also, in memories, the connections and the distance between one kind of country and another.'

Raymond stopped and strayed a hand across his brow. He looked up and a fleeting smile broke across his craggy features.

'In 1926, in that village, my father was one of three signalmen in the old Great Western Railway box. He was an ardent participant in the General Strike. So was one of the other two signalmen, and the stationmaster, who was subsequently victimised. So, too, were the platelayers. One of the signalmen was not.

'In the discussions and arguments that took place during those critical days, among a small group of men in a very specific social situation, some of the most important themes of the social significance of 1926 became apparent. They were often recalled in later years. I heard them throughout my childhood, and I went through them again, consciously, with my father, when I was preparing to write the General Strike sequence in *Border Country*.'

Listening to Raymond speak, Rhiannon felt there was a hypnotic quality to his voice. His measured tone was understated but nevertheless unhesitating. He spoke about the connection between railwaymen and the miners, the links between coal and its transportation, and the difficulties of achieving solidarity between different groups of workers. In deciding to commit to action, in the realities of the circumstances in which they found themselves, men and groups of men had been forced to cross a line in their minds. Even though the General Strike had been generally written off as anything between a disaster to a mistake that led to the moderation and reforms of the labour movement, Raymond insisted that important advances were made.

'The part of the history that most needs emphasis, and that was actually very evident in that country station in Pandy, and in thousands of other places up and down the country, was the growth of consciousness during the action itself.'

He paused, lifting his hands from the lectern in an

unconscious movement, as though to gather his thoughts. Then he resumed, finding a new, more optimistic note.

'As the strike progressed, the confidence, vigour and self-reliance among the men grew. This was not just the spirit created in a fight. It was a steady and remarkable self-realisation of the capacity of a class, in its own sufficient social relations and in its potentially positive social and economic power. This meant that at the very moment of the strike's collapse at the centre, after nine days, the momentum among the striking workers themselves was at a high point. There were more men out on the day after the action was called off, than during it.'

Raymond left the lectern and stepped across the stage as if to physically shift the attention of his audience to the changes that had taken place in the half century since the strike.

'In 1926 the mining villages were modern communities. Our village, even with the railway through it, was an older type. Today we have to deal with a special and physical distribution in which mixed communities not centred on single industries are much more characteristic. The special struggle for class consciousness has now to be waged on this more open, more socially neutral ground.'

Williams stopped for a moment, looking up as though to acknowledge his audience.

'I still find it impossible, whenever I come to the mining Valleys to understand, at first, why there is not yet socialism in Britain – the need and the spirit have been evidenced so often in these proud places. But then I remember all the other places, so hard to understand from this singular experience.'

Rhiannon leant forward, her elbows on the bench rail in front with her chin held in her hands, and marvelled at the fluency with which Raymond Williams was setting out the connections between 1926 and the present day. Reaching the end of what he had come to say, his craggy face broke into another smile.

'A child of five, as I was then, can gain from a father who had experienced that complex struggle for consciousness – a spirit and a perspective that have lasted, often under pressure, in the radically different places where I have since worked and lived.'

* * *

A few hours later Rhiannon and Ioan were heading north once again, up the Taff Valley, through Merthyr's winding streets, on through Cefn-Coed-y-Cymmer and finally across the moorland slopes of the Brecon Beacons. For the first part of the journey they were quiet, each absorbed in what they had experienced over the past few days. As they were passing Storey Arms and beginning the long, winding descent into Brecon, Ioan broke the silence.

'So what did you think of it, Rhi?'

'What do I think? I don't know. So much was packed into a few days.' She looked across at him with a smile. 'You got yourself into it somewhere, I seem to remember.'

'No, but seriously, what did you make of it?'

'Well I suppose the point of it was to draw out the lessons, wasn't it? I mean what the 1926 strike tells us about things today and all that. But it's difficult for me. I know nothing about the Valleys, about mining, about the communities Raymond Williams was talking about.'

'I think its vital we know about our history, our own past,' Ioan said with a sudden vehemence. 'What was it Faulkner wrote? *The past is never dead. It's not even past.*'

Rhiannon laughed.

'That's certainly true if this weekend is anything to go by. All those old guys reliving their memories. *And we shall remember 1926 until our blood is dry.* Idris Davies had it right.'

'Aye, *The great dream and the swift disaster.*'

'*The summer my country died.* That was how Harri Webb put it.'

They were silent again for a while until Rhiannon spoke.

'That Dai Davies character.'

'You mean Dai Coity Davies, the one who introduced the film.'

'Yes. I was struck by what he said about the strikes in '72 and '74 being a kind of payback for what happened in 1926. Do you think he was right?'

'It's one way of looking at it.'

Ioan furrowed his brow and thought for a moment.

'But you see, the circumstances are very different these days. There are a lot fewer miners for a start. They were the first national stoppages since 1926, and were over pay. Not a pay reduction, mind, but a pay rise. The miners were demanding a forty-three per cent increase and the Tory government offered eight per cent.'

'Not much meeting of minds there, then.'

'No. Anyway we were much better organised than in 1926. Scargill's flying pickets had a huge impact and the Welsh miners took a full part in them. Coal stocks had run down and it was a bad winter.'

'There was the three-day week,' I remember.

'Aye, Heath was forced to the negotiating table.'

'Then he called the general election.'

'And that didn't work for him, did it? But a lot of other things helped us as well, things that are unlikely to last.'

'What things?'

'Well, the Middle East oil crisis in the autumn of '73 for a start. It put a premium on all energy sources, including coal.

That created an entirely new situation. Then there'd been very few pit closures in the years leading up to the strikes. The miners weren't so worried that if they came out it would only mean more closures. In the 1960s, it felt as if a pit was being closed virtually every week in south Wales. In 1959 there were about 93,000 men working in the coalfield. A decade later there were only 30,000. But between 1970 and 1974 only two collieries closed in Wales.'

On the front seat beside him Rhiannon had drawn her knees up to her chest and held her arms tightly around them. She studied the road while trying to take in what Ioan was saying.

'And then there was something else, the National Power Loading Agreement.'

'What on earth was that?'

'A single-wages structure. It was the National Coal Board that introduced it, as a matter of fact. It meant that miners all over Britain were getting the same rates of pay, or they were getting close to it by 1972. That had the effect of creating a unity across the coalfields. We were all in it together.'

Ioan changed gear as they reached the outskirts of Brecon. He glanced across at Rhiannon who was looking away from him, out of the window. He thought again how slender she was, frail even, but how self-contained and resolute.

'Not only that, we were well organised, you know. In the strike in '72 we really went on the attack. It was like a military campaign.'

Now Rhiannon turned her face towards him and smiled.

'But do you think the solidarity you speak of can last?'

They came to a stop at some traffic lights in the middle of Brecon.

'I don't really know,' Ioan said, looking thoughtfully across at Rhiannon. Then, as they set off once more he stared at the road ahead for a while before heaving a sigh.

'But it's difficult to see how it can.'

'Why is that?'

'The NCB will wise up and introduce productivity schemes that will benefit miners in the pits that produce more, in the Midlands and other places in England.'

'It's all terribly complicated.'

'Aye, I suppose it is.'

Tenby
July 1976

As John Tripp approached fifty, he felt a growing fretfulness. A male version of the menopause was the way he put it. 'It's a change of life going on inside the skull,' he would say. 'It's the over-45 churn-up.' His friends, many of them fellow-poets, were conspicuously getting older. He'd recently met one at a cocktail party, perfectly sober but spilling gin on the carpet. 'What's the matter?' Tripp asked.

'The wobblies, boy,' the poet replied. 'The fifth decade wobblies.'

Tripp's own anxiety took the form of a vague unease verging on depression that resulted in bouts of insomnia. Trying to get back to sleep, he would recall characters from the novels of Henry James. He had a talent for inventing unusual, memorable names: Henrietta Stackpole, Guy Domville, Owen Wingrave, Densher, Croy, Stant, Quint, Theale, Verver, Monteith, the list went on. To combat the onset of despair Tripp made a conscious effort to develop a sense of humour at life's absurdities. 'Where there's a scrap of gaiety, there's an indestructible piece of battered hope,' he told himself.

Lately these efforts had been assisted by his relationship with Jean, or Jeannie as he called her. She was unusual in that she was close to his own age. Previously he had favoured younger women in what were destined to be casual and fleeting liaisons.

But Jean was different. It was partly because she reminded him of his mother, who had died ten years earlier. She had been addicted to respectability, against which Tripp now admitted he had rebelled. His mother had sought to escape from the family's working-class origins by attending coffee mornings in the more genteel corners of Cardiff, and voting Conservative.

Jean herself was a Conservative councillor and lived alone in a bungalow in Pentyrch to the north of the city. There she had won support by leading a campaign against open-cast mining which threatened the equanimity of the middle-class ward she reprepresented. She had survived a number of difficult relationships, one of which had brought her close to ruin. She was hardened to the world of men, especially those who seemed feckless. Altogether, their's was an unlikely relationship, but somehow it had blossomed, perhaps because of its contradictary nature.

They met on a late train from London to Cardiff. Tripp had performed at a poetry reading, after which he had signed five copies of his latest collection and consumed twice that number of glasses of tepid white wine. He had noticed her in the first-class restaurant car while swaying towards the bar. She had medium blond hair and blue eyes, wide apart. Her figure comfortably filled a red-white-and-blue dress that was zipped to her neck. She was attacking a plate of lamb chops, new potatoes and broccoli spears. Alongside was half-a-bottle of red wine.

'That's the woman for me,' Tripp thought.

At the bar he drank two cans of lager and on his way back, on an impulse, sat in the comfortable leather seat opposite her.

'Where are you going?' he asked.

'Away from the emotional cement mixer,' she said, laughing. She took a sip of wine and wiped her lips with a white cloth table napkin.

'And you, where are you going?'

'Oh, I'm on my way to a haven for the mediocre,' Tripp replied and then they both laughed, breaking a tension that hardly existed.

She explained she had been representing Taff-Ely council at a meeting of the Local Government Association in London.

'Don't we have one of our own?' Tripp complained.

'How so?'

'A Welsh one.'

'Well, yes, there's the Welsh association, but it's a branch of the London one, where the real decisions are taken.'

'I see.'

A waiter passed and Jean ordered another whole bottle of red wine as their conversation turned to the more congenial topic of Tripp's poetry.

'I'm a late developer,' he told her. 'I'm not like those lyric poets who start early. I belong to the band who have to live first and then ransack their experience to write.'

'Late developers are best,' Jean said.

When they reached Cardiff she offered Tripp a lift in the taxi she was taking.

'It'll go through Whitchurch,' she said.

But halfway there Tripp leaned against her, sighed and went to sleep. Jean adjusted her arm, placed it round his head and on his shoulder, and decided to take him home.

* * *

John Tripp's relationship with women was, to put it at its kindest, under-developed. He liked and needed them, and as often as not they found him attractive. But as he once put it in an unusual moment of self-awareness, he had never entered the kind of relationship where two people set out on the journey of custom and habit. Nevertheless, he possessed a strain of romanticism and went out of his way to cultivate connections.

'We try to preserve what we cherish, but the sift of time dissolves it,' he wrote.

His cast of mind about women had been formed in the repressed period of his youth and by his experiences in the army. These days he lived in a permanent state of dissonance between the enticing freedoms of the sixties and perplexity about the strange formations of the emerging women's movement.

> *I bet you think I'm shocking,' she says,*
> *Stroking my grey hair in the refectory*
> *As I smile with pleasure*
> *As she drinks her pint*
> *And puffs on a thin cigar.*
> *'On the contrary,' I reply;*
> *'Where have you been hiding for centuries?'*

Recently he had been exchanging letters with a friend, a fellow poet, a bit younger with an actor's expansive temperament. For different reasons – his friend had recently been divorced – they shared similar feelings of sexual frustration. Their exchange had left Tripp feeling dismayed at the contrast between what men and women appeared to want.

'I have no idea what to say to you about your sexual problems,' his friend had written. 'Because you seem to want companionship, kindness, support, and my problem is different: I just want sex, and they can keep their kindness (and still more, their need for it) to themselves.'

Tripp suspected that underneath it all he shared much the same outlook. He liked to think that his own history of trysts with women had been conducted between equals. In reality, he knew that all too often they provided him with an opportunity to vent his frustrations and sourness at his failures in life. These, he acknowledged, were his lack of a formal education, the absence of steady reward from secure employment, and his avoidance of the responsibility of a family, much as he was fond of small children. In drink, all these failures welled to the surface and became the objects of destructive fury.

What was it a former girlfriend Jacqueline had written him as he was finally leaving London at the end of the sixties?

> My criticism of your self-neglect must have come across to you as something different from the concern intended. You turned on me as if you had to use every weapon at your disposal, taunting me about my own self-doubt – given you in the confidence of shared feelings and getting-to-know-you talk. The change in you as night and drink took over made me feel that I was witnessing a pattern played before, painfully often. The tenderness of earlier in the day was usurped and I have no way of knowing how completely. But if I were not remembering the tenderness, I should not be writing this.

Then there was Paula. He had kept some of her letters, too. In one she had written out a quotation from Virginia Woolfe which, she said, might help him understand her better.

> It is fatal to be a man or woman pure and simple, one must be woman-manly or man-womanly. It is fatal for a woman to lay the least stress on any grievance; to plead even with justice any cause; in any way to speak consciously as a woman. And fatal is no figure of speech, for anything written with that conscious bias is doomed to death. It ceases to be fertilised... Some collaboration has to take place in the mind between the woman and the man before the act of creation can be accomplished. Some marriage of opposites has to be consummated. The whole of the mind must lie wide open if we are to get the sense

that the writer is communicating his experience with
perfect fullness.

Tripp reflected on these words from time to time, but they left
him puzzled. He just felt like a man as far as he could see. Paula's
last letter, now several years old, was more agreeable.

You are a lovely, sensitive, <u>kindly</u> man with an excellent
brain and the perception of a true poet. Despite your
rather bilious view of life, I couldn't help but be fond of
a man who actually likes intelligence in women.

Soon after he returned to Cardiff, he met Faye at a poetry
reading in Swansea. He was forty-two and she twenty-three, a
secretary who worked in Cardiff and lived in a flat not far away
from him in Whitchurch. Despite the age gap they fell deeply
in love. At one point it seemed they might marry. Tripp never
moved from his father's bungalow, but would stay in her flat for
days at a time, writing there while she was at work. Then, one
day, he visited the National Museum in Cathays Park to look
at the Impressionists and he saw her. She had her arm linked
through another man's as they climbed the wide stairs to the
first floor. He wrote afterwards, 'She was wearing her best dress
and her hair was like flame.'

*   *   *

Not long after they met, Tripp and Jean Henderson decided to
spend a few days in Tenby.

'Do us good to get out for a bit,' she said. 'Somewhere down
west. Why not?'

Tripp suggested Tenby. Some years earlier he'd been
commissioned to write an article about the monks on Caldey

Island, a few miles off shore. Mischievously, he told Jean they should go to the town to pay homage to Robert Recorde.

'Who was he?'

'A mathematician. He was born in Tenby, during Henry VIII's time. He invented the equals sign. Rather Welsh that, don't you think, giving us ideas about equality?'

They drove down in Jean's Mini and stayed in a guest house inside the town walls. Walking along the cliffs, high above the beaches where the light of the western end of Wales illuminated the yellow sands, they enjoyed the sea air. But Tripp complained about the seediness of the town itself, with its steamy cafes, run-down pubs, and gift shops full of junk aimed at tourists from the English Midlands.

'There's a dangerous smell of boredom in the air,' he muttered as they walked the streets. 'You'd expect it somewhere like Southend, but I never thought I'd feel it in respectable Tenby.'

The impression was confirmed the next day over breakfast of bacon and eggs, black pudding, tomato and mushrooms when they fell into a conversation with the landlady. She confirmed there had been a decline in the quality of the clientèle.

'They've no courtesy. A lot of them stay in caravans. Caravan people they are.'

'You seem pretty busy, though,' Jean said.

'Oh yes, we've no complaints on that score. But there's no fun in them, is there, not like the old crowd, the old class of people we used to get. A higher class came then, with their nannies and dogs and children. But these today, I don't know what to make of them. They're quite depressing, they never seem to smile or enjoy themselves. And they watch television half the time, wet or fine. You'd think they'd get enough of that at home. They're clean enough, but they're sort of dead.'

That evening they decided to make an occasion of dinner and discovered a mock Tudor cellar above the South beach. Here

Tenby's elegance of previous days made a fleeting reappearance in the form of snails, French onion soup, roast Lincolnshire duckling in orange sauce flavoured with Cointreau, crème caramel with fresh farm cream, Turkish coffee and a good Burgundy.

Jean interrogated Tripp about his visit to the Caldey Island monastery. He said it had been established in the sixth century by the Benedictine order. They had survived until 1929 when they surrendered it to the Cistercians.

'I'd heard they lived on potatoes, parsnips, swedes and cabbage while they meditated and made their perfume,' he said. 'In fact, a local grocer who supplied them told me the brothers order red meat and plenty of fruit.'

'What are they like?'

'They live in silence most of the time. But they've had their moments. I looked into a bit of the history. Pyr was the first abbot. He fell into a well in his cups and drowned. St. Samson took over, but he found the rule was so lax and the monks so ungovernable he resigned in disgust.'

'What happened to him?'

'Went to Stackpole, by all accounts. Lived as a hermit in an isolated cave.'

'Not a lot of fun then.'

'Well, it's odd, you could write the Great Welsh Novel there in perfect peace.'

'So you quite liked it.'

'In a way I did. Apart from the article I was commissioned to write, one of my better poems came out of it.'

Tripp moved his plate to one side and, lifting his glass with one hand, cupped his chin in the other and leant on his elbow across the table.

'You see, Jeannie love, I'm not a Romantic poet, I'm too much of a realist for that.'

He thought back to his time on the island, how it had made him yearn for the possibility of belief in something good and eternal. He had written a few lines expressing what he felt.

> *Undernourished on stale puritan crust,*
> *I still ferret for a method of praise*
> *to celebrate something.*

All the same it eluded him. Instead, he wrote that the only thing he could feel was *the splinter of ice at the heart of things*. But when, after his last meal in the monastery one of the monks took his plate and said, 'I hope you have the story you came for', Tripp realised that in a strange way his visit had given him a melancholy satisfaction.

> *The kind monk escorts me to the slip;*
> *I tell him not to linger in the drizzle.*
> *Waiting for a boat*
> *to the mainland, I am one sodden scrivener*
> *again – hatless, hopeless, in the rain...*

Now, turning to Jean, he said, 'My work these days is hard, steely. I want to see it as it is. We've got to get away from this awful, phoney Welsh sentimentality, this treacle, marzipan and marmalade. Tell it like it is, our doubts and dilemmas, the human predicament.'

'A bit grim.'

'You can have compassion and pity. But you've got to cut through the crap. I think I've got better as I've got older, as a poet anyway. What's been happening in Wales these last years, what I came home to write about, it'll all go, it'll all become history.'

Tripp poured them both a last glass of Burgundy.

'I think I'll sink or swim with half-a-dozen of my latest poems. That's not bad. They're not about Wales at all actually. But I'll settle for that.'

PART III

Westminster
November to December 1976

When Dan Jones, the MP for Burnley, ventured into Leo Abse's office in the House of Commons, he was not his usual self. Rather he was anxious and cowed, fearful that he was about to be enveloped in a scandal. The whips had insisted he speak with Abse, the criminal lawyer they turned to on such occasions.

In normal circumstances, Jones would never have approached the Pontypool MP for whom he bore a grudge that went back to 1958. In that year, Abse had beaten him for the Labour nomination when a by-election occurred in the constituency. As a native of the Rhondda and a trade union official, Dan Jones felt he had a prior claim, certainly well above that of a lawyer from Cardiff. Instead he had been forced to seek a parliamentary seat beyond Wales and uproot his family in the process.

He was selected for Burnley and entered the Commons in the 1959 general election. Though an assiduous constituency MP, he was not at home in Lancashire. By now his natural habitat was the tearoom in the House of Commons, forever whiling away his time in gossip with like-minded MPs, especially at the Welsh members' table.

Dan Jones had lobbied Burnley council for swift, unimpeded planning approval on behalf of the developers of a prime site in the town centre. There were suggestions, already surfacing in *Private Eye,* of financial kickbacks. A tentacle of involvement was crawling towards the MP's door. He told Abse there was no basis for the allegations. He had been merely seeking to promote jobs. Nevertheless, it was clear to the seasoned lawyer that the MP's self-justifying manner betrayed the hallmarks of a guilty man. His demeanour was worsened by his religious fundamentalism. Abse warned him that the police were sure to come calling. And he insisted that he must present when that occurred, fearful that Jones might blurt out his guilt in a fatal confession.

The police questioned Jones twice. On both occasions Abse was at his side, monitoring the answers he gave and carefully crafting the statements he signed. In the end, the police gave up and concentrated on others more closely linked to the affair. But Dan Jones was not out of the woods. He was threatened with blackmail and lurid stories appeared in the local press. When they did, Abse was ever at hand, negotiating his path with more carefully guarded statements. Eventually, after months of anxiety, the issue died away.

All this had occurred a year earlier, but Dan Jones remained embarrassingly grateful, constantly seeking Abse out to ask if there was anything he could do for him. Now, with the government's Scotland and Wales Devolution Bill due to reach its Second Reading, the moment had come to call in the debt. As a result of by-election defeats, the government had lost the majority of three it had won at the October 1974 general election. It had become reliant on support from the Liberals and the Nationalists which, in turn, was dependent on the government continuing with its devolution policy.

Its opponents decided that the only way the Welsh Assembly could be stopped was by a referendum. Accordingly, Abse placed an amendment to the Bill's Second Reading requiring one to be held before the legislation could go ahead. However, such amendments were rarely called, especially when placed by a backbencher against a major piece of government legislation. Whether they made it to the floor of the Commons was within the discretion of the Speaker.

The only way for Abse's amendment to have any chance would be if it attracted substantial support. That would embolden the Speaker, George Thomas, to find a way of letting it through.

Thomas hated the nationalists and would be sympathetic. Abse also had a number of friends inside the Cabinet who would be more than amenable. They were, as he put it, his fifth column.

Though a Welsh speaker, Dan Jones was as implacably opposed to Welsh nationalism as Abse himself. He eagerly agreed to gather signatures supporting the referendum. Abse was determined to have a hundred, with at least half from Labour members. This presented an onerous task since they would be seen to be opposing their own government's policy.

Nonetheless, Jones set to with great enthusiasm, circulating among his fellow backbenchers, cajoling, and scoffing at any notion that each signature was a nail in the government's coffin. He was much better at the task than Abse who had never gone out of his way to cultivate his fellow MPs. Dan Jones' quiet banter and engaging manner, accompanied by flattery and persistence, generally led to success. Each night in the weeks leading up to the vote he would call in Abse's office, triumphantly bearing the latest signatures. On the eve of the debate these had reached ninety, of which seventy were Labour and the rest Conservative.

* * *

On the Monday the Second Reading debate was due to begin, Owen James caught an early train to London. He had persuaded the editor that the occasion justified coverage over and above that provided by the regular parliamentary team. The debate would last four days and he would be able to write a number of background features and contribute to the paper's diary column.

He had an additional reason for going – an invitation from John Mackintosh to a dinner in the Commons. They had struck up a correspondence following the Edinburgh seminar Owen had attended. The dinner was for a group Mackintosh was bringing together with a view to producing a special devolution edition of *Political Quarterly* of which he was an editor. Some of those attending Owen had come across as a student. There was Birkbeck professor of politics Bernard Crick, who Owen had met when he had visited Bristol as a guest lecturer. He recalled they had had a heated argument about nationalism. Then there was Samuel Finer, an Oxford professor, and Sir Kenneth Wheare, another famous political scientist who Owen knew as an expert on federalism. Also present would be Enoch Powell and the Liberal leader David Steel. Owen was flattered that he had been invited to such a prestigious gathering.

In the Commons David Rosser, the *Western Mail*'s political editor, took him to lunch.

'I don't know why you need to be here,' he complained. 'I told Duncan as much. But there you are, these days the paper is more interested in gossip than real news.'

Owen asked how he thought the vote on the Second Reading would go.

'They'll get their Bill in principle. They always do. The fun comes later at the Committee stage.'

'But what about the campaign for a referendum that Abse is running? Won't that put a spanner in the works?'

'Don't underestimate the power of the whips when push comes to shove. I spoke with John Morris this morning. He's confident they can see the rebels off.'

Owen was dubious about this assessment. His anxiety was heightened when he made his way to see Gwynfor Evans in the office he shared with Dafydd Elis-Thomas. He was preoccupied with his speech.

'I'm likely to be called this afternoon,' he explained. 'I reckon George Thomas wants to get me out of the way early in the debate.'

Owen asked about the pressure building for a referendum.

'Dafydd El can give you the best information on that, he gets on well with quite a few Labour members. But I see he's gone out. He tells me there's a lot of support. Of course, we'll have no choice but to support it too.'

'But why?'

'We can't be seen opposing a democratic vote offered to the people of Wales.'

A shadow passed Gwynfor's face but then, typically, he brightened.

'All the same, this is an historic occasion. Whatever its shortcomings we've got a devolution Bill to a Second Reading. I had a meeting with Michael Foot at the end of last week and they're allowing at least thirty days for the Committee stage, perhaps forty days. It's the first time Wales has been centre stage here for well over a generation, you could say since the days of Lloyd George, Tom Ellis and Cymru Fydd. It's a remarkable achievement. Whatever happens in the short run, our progress is unstoppable.'

* * *

Owen left Gwynfor and made his way to the press gallery, high above the Commons debating chamber. Looking down it struck him again how intimate it was, like a small theatre. As he found a seat in the front row he saw the Secretary of State for Energy Tony Benn rise answering questions about a leak of radioactive waste at the Windscale nuclear power station in Cumbria. Hardly looking at his notes, he swept away a range of hostile attacks with calm, steady responses that demonstrated total confidence in himself and his brief.

By now the chamber was filling up in anticipation of the start of the main debate. It was nearly four o'clock. Owen saw the Prime Minister James Callaghan take his seat. John Morris, the Secretary of State for Wales, and Michael Foot, the President of the Council with overall responsibility for the devolution Bill, were on either side of him.

There was a pause in proceedings until the Speaker George Thomas, gathering his black gown around him, began intoning his plans for the forthcoming four-day debate. He was barely into his stride when Leo Abse jumped up, two rows behind the Prime Minister.

'I have on the Order Paper a reasoned amendment calling for a referendum before the Bill comes into effect, an amendment signed by at least seventy of my Hon. Friends and twenty Opposition Members. I should be obliged if the House could be told whether the amendment will be called.'

George took off his spectacles, glanced around the chamber and then looked pointedly at Abse.

'I am still giving consideration to the question of the amendments on the Order Paper. I shall in due course indicate to the House my decision. The Hon. Gentleman may be well assured that I have been watching the Order Paper very carefully.'

Abse sat back in his seat satisfied that he had drawn attention to his cause before the start of the debate. There had been no need for him to be a supplicant behind the Chair asking the Speaker for his favour or to take tea with him in his rooms in an attempt to influence him. There was a tacit understanding. George's reply, though seemingly equivocal, was in such terms that Abse was sure the whips would decipher its meaning.

George Thomas would have no compunction in frustrating the objectives of the Prime Minister, his fellow Cardiff MP James Callaghan. Abse had known both men since before he entered the Commons. As chairman of the Cardiff Labour Party in the early 1950s he had often struggled to persuade them to co-operate. In the run-up to the 1945 election, although an outsider, Callaghan had beaten George for the nomination in Cardiff South. At the selection meeting he had worn his Navy uniform, silently underlining the point that George had failed to serve in the armed forces during the war.

Moreover, George harboured a more recent grudge. Following the February 1974 election, Callaghan had prevented his appointment as Secretary of State for Wales. He feared that Thomas's attacks on the Welsh language were creating disharmony and persuaded Harold Wilson to promote John Morris instead. Unlike Thomas, he was a Welsh-speaker and a strong devolutionist. Bitterly disappointed, George had to make do with the role of Deputy Speaker. Although this had led rapidly to his elevation as Speaker, Abse knew that Callaghan would understand that he could expect no favour from Thomas over the referendum amendment.

Now, in his opening presentation of the Bill, the Prime Minister was addressing the question directly, acknowledging there was an impressive amount of support for a referendum. Neil Kinnock intervened to ask when a decision would be made. Callaghan suggested that it might be as early as the Christmas recess. He then outlined three principles that lay behind the Bill. Owen noted them. Respect for the distinctive traditions of Scotland and Wales had to be balanced with a need to ensure the unity of the United Kingdom. Second was continuance of the sovereignty of Parliament. Finally, there was a need to maintain a fair distribution of resources across the whole of the United Kingdom.

'Hardly a ringing endorsement,' Owen thought to himself, as he scribbled his own version of shorthand into his notebook. 'More like a series of hurdles that have to be overcome.' Then he noticed that Steve Thomas, a Press Association reporter he knew, was leaving the gallery, and quickly followed him into the corridor outside.

'Fancy a cup of tea?'

'OK, but I haven't got long.'

They found their way to a cafeteria situated alongside the Commons chamber. Owen set a tray with a teapot, two mugs and a couple of currant buns on a secluded table.

'What do you make of this push for a referendum?'

'Dunno, really. Government side don't like it, of course. It's messy and gets in the way. John Morris hates it. Foot says it undermines the authority of Parliament, though he wasn't against the one on the Common Market. But they may have no choice. We're calling them the Gang of Six up here.'

'Who exactly?'

'You know the MPs that Abse has corralled, including himself obviously, to oppose the whole thing. They're out to wreck it really.'

'Not a bad line,' Owen said, taking out his notebook. 'Who are they, again?'

* * *

Later as he slipped back into his seat in the press gallery Owen picked up some order papers from the bench alongside him, and turned them over to reveal plain white sheets. He began writing, 'The Gang of Six Assembly wreckers is the label being used to link the Welsh Labour rebels in the House of Commons who are on a mission to defeat their own side.'

Looking at his notebook he studied the list with the constituencies he'd placed in brackets alongside them - Ifor Davies (Gower), Donald Anderson (Swansea East), Ioan Evans (Aberdare), Neil Kinnock (Bedwellty), Fred Evans (Caerphilly), and, last but not least, Leo Abse (Pontypool). Absorbed in his work Owen lost track of the debate taking place below him.

Suddenly, however, he noticed that Gwynfor Evans was on his feet and he stopped to listen. It was just gone six o'clock.

'The Bill would not be before the House but for the growth of Scottish and Welsh national consciousness,' Gwynfor was saying. 'I hope that Members realise that they are dealing with two nations, two of the oldest in Europe. About three-and-a-half centuries ago, in a play performed before the Council of Wales, John Milton wrote of Wales that she was *an ancient nation, proud in arms*. At that time, the magnificent literature of Wales had an unbroken history of a thousand years. Welsh was the language of government and the law in Wales when French was the language of government and the law here. The House is dealing not with two regions, two parts of the country, two colonies, but with two old national communities.'

At this point an exasperated Leo Abse intervened.

'As half the people in industrial South Wales are descended from Englishmen and Irishmen who came there in the nineteenth century, by what presumption does the Gentleman state that those people, English-speaking Welshmen as they describe themselves now, fall into the medieval category that he is describing, so insulting more than half the people of Wales?'

Gwynfor stared over his papers at Abse for a moment.

'I hope that the House will agree that nationhood is not a medieval category but a factor that is very much alive and very important in the world today. The power of nationalism is probably the strongest moral power in the world.'

He was immediately interrupted by Percy Grieve, a Conservative barrister with Scottish roots who had worked with De Gaulle and the Free French during the war.

'I take the Gentleman's point that the Scots and Welsh are ancient peoples with roots deep in history, but does he not appreciate that over the centuries we have created a British people, in which the blood and names of all the British races run together? We have achieved greatness as the British people, and it is for the British people that many of us are here to speak.'

Gwynfor, who had taken to his seat while yielding to this question, stood up, straightened and stared directly at Grieve.

'What has been created is a British State. Whenever Members speak of the nation, they mean the state. They confuse nation and state. There is not just one nation on this island, there are at least three, and Wales is one of them. Do Members acknowledge Wales and Scotland to be nations? If they do, do they acknowledge that Wales and Scotland have a right to live as nations and to act as nations? That is behind our policies as national parties in both countries.'

Donald Anderson rose.

'The Gentleman has often spoken about the identification of nation and state. Will he confirm his view of the future of Wales as a self-contained state, with all the panoply of a state, including separate armed services?'

'I shall come later to my idea of what Wales should be. The Establishment parties had thought, as many of their members still do, that Welsh nationalism would fade away. They must face the fact that once nationalism is as deeply rooted as it is now in Wales and Scotland it will not go away.'

Ioan Evans attempted to intervene but Gwynfor swept him aside.

'As the people of Wales increase in self-confidence and their sense of loyalty to their nation, in their capacity to accept responsibility, so will Welsh nationalism grow until it becomes irresistible. That is the history of nationalism, and the House must face it. No one can afford to ignore the dynamic in the power of nationalism, least of all those who do not want to repeat the mistake made in Ireland at the end of the last century.'

Gwynfor then proceeded with a favourite topic, an examination of Labour's early history when it had supported

Home Rule. Turning to the contemporary debate he said that it was about centralism versus decentralism, the need for human scale and dispersal of power to underpin democracy, themes that were common in states across Europe. He extolled the economic benefits that accrued to the smaller countries of Europe.

'I find it extraordinary that so many people think that Scotland and Wales are best governed as peripheral regions in a huge unitary centralist structure, especially when the advantages of decentralisation are to be seen in West Germany and the advantages of small size are to be seen in the five Scandinavian states, whose total combined population is only half that of England.'

He accused his opponents of wishing Whitehall to continue with its monopoly control of Welsh institutions, denying the Welsh people the chance to develop their own sense of self-reliance and responsibility. MPs were restive most of the time he was speaking, but there was silence as he reached his peroration, which was an answer to the question Donald Anderson had posed. Those who were against autonomy had no faith in their country, Gwynfor said. On the other hand, the number supporting it were growing.

'Those who see the great possibilities of their nation – a nation whose people are as gifted, as talented and as well able to govern themselves as any – are on the increase. They believe that their little land, which is no bigger than Israel, has all the conditions necessary to becoming a social laboratory which will have positive value for Europe and the world. They see Wales in the future as a member under the Crown of a closely-knit partnership of nations in no way subordinate one to the other in any aspect of their domestic or external affairs, but freely co-operating as members of a Britannic confederation.'

It was nearly seven o'clock when Gwynfor sat down. At ten

o'clock the debate was adjourned but a motion proposing it be continued was immediately agreed. It then carried on for a further two hours.

* * *

The following evening Owen found himself at John Mackintosh's dinner, at a long table in a plush gilded room somewhere in the Commons he had not been to before. Seated immediately opposite him was Enoch Powell. Owen introduced himself as a journalist from the *Western Mail*.

'I imagine, therefore, you must be in favour of the proposals we're debating.'

'Why yes, broadly speaking. Devolution would certainly give Wales a voice, put us on the map, so to speak.'

'Devolution?'

Powell barked the question and glared at Owen across the table.

'One-wheel carriage, I say!'

'Oh, come on Enoch,' John Mackintosh butted in lightly from the head of the table. 'Devolution is certainly a compromise between extremes, but that's what politics is about, after all.'

'Well, now then John, a Parliament for Wales, which is what this young man undoubtedly wants.'

Powell pointed at Owen.

'That's not some kind of local or even regional democracy, no no, not at all. If it came about, it would be a watershed, the parting of the ways, the sign that a separate nation had been consciously, deliberately and, irrevocably and once and for all admitted to be there. It would be an admission that the House of Commons no longer served the whole of the United Kingdom. It would be a declaration that one nation no longer existed.'

Powell appeared to rear up during this tirade, but as he

finished he subsided into his seat, continuing to make barely audible, grumbling sounds while still glaring round the table. David Steel took the opportunity to intervene.

'There are only three tenable positions in all of this that have some logic to them.'

Leaning forward he put his elbows on the table and placed his hands together.

'The first is simply to do nothing, to follow those who might favour continued administrative devolution, of the kind we have now with the Scottish Office and so on but say, as Enoch does, that Parliament should remain in total control of everything that goes on in Scotland and Wales. I do not agree with that position, but it has a certain logic.'

Enoch Powell grunted affirmatively and Steel looked around the table to confirm he had caught everybody's attention.

'Then there's the position of the nationalists, of Plaid Cymru and the SNP. They argue the case for a total secession from the United Kingdom and the creation of separate sovereign states. I do not agree with that concept, but again as an argument it has a certain logic and consistency.'

'So what is your third proposition?' Powell asked.

'If one does not accept either position, one is forced to argue a federal case,' Steel replied. 'That says there must be a clear division of powers between this Parliament and devolved Assemblies for Scotland and Wales acceptable to the majority of public opinion in those countries.'

'What in essence is the difference between that and what the government is proposing?' John Mackintosh wanted to know.

'My quarrel with the government's devolution Bill is that it does not set out such a clear division of powers. It muddies the water at almost every stage. You're right, Enoch, to say it's a one-wheel carriage. The Bill's in a mess because it proceeds from no discernible principle.'

He had hardly finished speaking before Powell picked up on his remarks, as though receiving a baton that had been handed across the table.

'You're correct to say that a federal solution and the legal separation of powers it entails would be a logical solution. Certainly, it would be intellectually coherent. It works in countries like Canada and Australia, West Germany even. But it wouldn't work in Britain.'

'And why is that?' Steel interrupted. 'I suppose you're going to say, like the Commission on the Constitution, that it is because England is too large.'

'No, no, not at all. There are disparities between the states of the United States and between the component parts of many federations. The objection to a federal system for the United Kingdom is far simpler and deeper than that.'

Powell paused, to glare around the room once more.

'It's simply that England does not want it, and neither do the people of Great Britain as a whole for that matter. They do not want a federation. They are incapable of conceiving the destruction of the political system they already have and which they understand.'

Owen listened closely to the cut and thrust of the discussion around him. He felt he should be taking notes, but it was clear it was not that kind of occasion. Instead he concentrated on the main course that had been wheeled in on a trolley. The menu card he picked up described it as Beef Wellington, fillet steak covered with pâté and wrapped in puff pastry. It was accompanied by a Mâcon Supérieur burgundy, which Owen thought the best wine he had drunk, and followed by strawberries with a crème mousse meringue, cheese, coffee and brandy.

Towards the end of the evening, with the dinner over, the men rose from the table, glasses in hand, and the conversation turned to more intimate exchanges. After a few moments John Mackintosh came alongside Owen.

'I thought that was a striking suggestion Gwynfor Evans made in the debate yesterday, his reference to a Britannic confederation. Seemed to come out of nowhere. Did you hear him say that?'

'Yes, I did. It's one of his hobby horses. Answers the separatist charge I suppose, but the idea has quite a bit of history.'

'Go on.'

'In the fifties Plaid collaborated with the SNP and the Commonwealth Party to produce a booklet *Our Three Nations.* Essentially it was about how they could work together as self-governing entities. They developed the notion of Britain as a confraternity.'

'How interesting. The Commonwealth Party you say, I thought that died out during the war.'

'It did to a large extent. By the end of the war it only had a few MPs and they switched to Labour. Even so it carried on as pressure group. Gwynfor has become particularly interested in the Swiss confederation as a model, you know its cantonal system. One of Plaid's thinkers wrote a book on it a few years back.'

Listening intently, Mackintosh took out a notebook and fountain pen from his inside pocket, as Owen continued.

'Ioan Bowen Rees, works with the Gwynedd local authority, quite high up. His book, *Government by Community,* puts it very well I think. Anyway, Gwynfor thinks a lot of him. They're looking at the Nordic Council which brings together the Scandinavian countries in a co-operative grouping.'

'Well, well.' Mackintosh waved to one of his guests who was leaving. He then turned back to Owen.

'What do you think of Leo Abse? I can't understand why he's

so exercised by this whole business. Quite vituperative. Got the bit between his teeth hasn't he? Implacable.'

'He's obsessed by nationalism.'

'Yes, but it's the nationalism that says, "We are better than others and, because we are superior, we must dominate them". I can see he's against that. So am I. That sort of thinking led to the war. But surely we must also recognise that in many respects nationalism is a constructive, not to say liberating force which can lead to greater understanding of people's backgrounds. There is a great difference between that and the kind of chauvinism that Leo is against.'

'He wouldn't see it in those terms.'

Mackintosh laughed.

'I suppose not. Seems to me that he would be a great defender of the Austro-Hungarian Empire. You know he once told me, confidentially I should say, that his origins were Phoenician. Many who defended the Austro-Hungarian Empire were Phoenician. They cast aside their nationality and defended the curious amalgam of people in that empire on the basis that they shared nothing in common.'

It was Owen's turn to laugh, but Mackintosh interrupted him.

'I suppose in that way they felt their solidarity could be based on something other than a nationalist impulse.'

'But what else is the impetus behind an empire? Owen asked.

'Yes, quite. Seriously though, in most ways Leo's a good social democrat, pro-Europe and so on. I rather liked his book.'

'*Private Member*?'

'Yes, that's the one.'

Mackintosh chuckled.

'Stirred up quite a few people here, I can tell you. But he doesn't mind making enemies.'

'That's certainly true. I've heard him say that in politics it's possible to choose your enemies, but not your friends.'

* * *

By the time of the fourth and last day of the Second Reading of the Scotland and Wales Bill, Leo Abse's referendum amendment had attracted 150 signatures. Before the debate itself began, just after half-past three in the afternoon, the Speaker George Thomas told the House that he had decided not to call any amendments. Nonetheless, he had been busy behind the scenes. Earlier in the day he had communicated through the back channels of the Government's Whips' office to inquire whether there would be a positive response to the growing demand for a referendum. He made it plain that if there was not he was minded to allow Abse's amendment to be placed.

But now Abse was on his feet on a point of order, demanding to know why there would be no debate on his amendment.

'If I had selected it and it had been carried, it would have had the effect of defeating the Bill, but without the House ever having voted upon the Bill,' George Thomas told him.

This prompted Tam Dalyell, the West Lothian MP and another implacable opponent of devolution, to ask why carrying the referendum amendment would defeat the Bill.

'If carried, the amendment would have superseded the Question on the Second Reading,' George Thomas answered, indicating to the Minister of State to the Privy Council John Smith that he should move to open the debate.

Immediately Smith, a quiet but determined Scottish lawyer, jumped to his feet and placed his hands on the despatch box in front of him. Then, to gasps around the chamber, he announced that the government conceded that referendums should be held in Scotland and Wales.

There was uproar, with members waving their order papers and seeking to catch the Speaker's eye. There were innumerable queries about how the referendums should be conducted. What question or questions should be asked? Why were they were to be confined to Scotland and Wales, so excluding England?

Leo Abse sat back in his seat and placed his hands together. To the very end he had doubted that his stratagem would work. If his amendment had been called and succeeded there was a danger the government would fall. Certainly it would have had to be followed by a vote of confidence, one that the government, with its non-existent majority could not risk.

Abse had no genuine belief that the Labour signatories to his amendment, most of whom were traditional loyalists, would have dared go into the lobby to vote with him when they saw the full consequences of what would arise. But he also reflected that his prior judgement was correct. Callaghan, for whom the first priority was the continuation of his premiership, would simply not take the risk.

'Jim's not the man to play poker with me when the stake is his premiership,' Abse thought to himself. 'That's not the type of courage he possesses.'

Knighton
January 1977

Owen had taken most of the short winter day to drive north from Cardiff through the Taff valley, over the Brecon Beacons, and then to Builth and Llandrindod. Now he was travelling eastwards, passing through unfamiliar country towards the border. His destination was Knighton, a small market town that straddled Offa's Dyke. It was the first day of 1977 and, despite stopping for lunch and drinking copious water, Owen still felt the effects of the previous night's New Year excess. The road was climbing once more, traversing moorland that felt strangely forbidding. The windscreen wipers deflected an onrush of snowflakes that turned to sleet on the glass as Owen stared ahead at the whitening landscape.

A few days earlier a telephone call from Gwynfor Evans had prompted his journey. Could he come to a special meeting of Plaid's National Council? It was being held to discuss the progress of the devolution legislation through the House of Commons. Gwynfor explained that when the committee stage of the Scotland and Wales Bill resumed early in the New Year the Conservatives intended moving an amendment that would have the effect of removing Wales completely from the legislation.

'They can't do that, can they?'

'Oh, they most certainly can. We got wind of it during the Second Reading debate. Dafydd Wigley raised it in his speech on the last day. Now we've heard it's certain they will press an amendment to delete Wales at the start of the committee stage in a couple of week's time.'

'Delete Wales,' Owen repeated. 'What an idea!'

'Exactly, it's bound to provoke consternation and I hope

opposition. But we need to mount a campaign if we are to turn it to our advantage. That's why I want you to come. We need to drum up support from people outside the party, influential people. Do you think the *Western Mail* could help?'

Plaid's National Council met three or four times a year. Generally, its deliberations were closed to the press. Owen had easily persuaded the news desk it was worth the journey to Knighton, but he was worried about how his presence would be greeted by the constituency and branch delegates.

Gwynfor had dismissed his concerns.

'It's not unusual to have outside people come along. Dafydd Williams will make it clear I've invited you.'

* * *

The light was fading when Owen caught a first glimpse of Knighton through a gap in the hills. He saw the roofs of the small town in the valley below but quickly had to turn his attention to the road, grown slippery by falling snow turning to slush. As he drove through the outskirts he was glad he would be staying overnight at the Norton Arms, a sixteenth century inn near the centre of the town. The main meeting was taking place there the following day, but Gwynfor had explained the most important discussions would be held that evening.

As Owen pushed his way through the heavy double doors of the hotel entrance he saw they were already underway. Gwynfor was seated at a table in a corner of the bar not far from a warming log fire. Alongside him were the party's chairman Eurfyl ap Gwilym, Dafydd Wigley, and Dafydd Williams. On the other side of the table Phil Williams was holding forth in his usual, animated way. Gwynfor caught sight of Owen and beckoned him over.

'It's a trap,' Phil was saying, pausing only to nod as Owen

pulled up a chair beside him. 'We're being led into a trap, can't you see?'

He turned to Owen.

'I've been saying that it's been obvious for some time, and certainly since the Second Reading debate, that Labour have no intention of establishing an Assembly.'

'I can't see how that follows.'

'Well, if Labour were committed to a Welsh Assembly why haven't the rebels – Abse, Kinnock, and so on – why haven't they received any reprimand from the Whips' Office?'

'If that really were the case why would they be going through the motions at all?' Dafydd Williams asked.

'They've got Scotland to think about. But more importantly, they're concerned about their small majority. That's our only leverage. The real purpose of the Scotland and Wales Bill is to keep us on board. They need our fourteen votes until there's a favourable opening for them to call an election.'

'The real threat to Labour is in Scotland,' Dafydd Wigley said. 'The SNP are breathing down their necks in a swathe of their seats. They have to deliver devolution for Scotland. So long as we can keep Wales in the Bill we're in with a chance.'

'The truth is Dafydd that Wales doesn't matter to them,' Phil said. 'I come back to my question. Why haven't they disciplined Fred Evans, Ioan Evans or any of the MPs who are causing them so much trouble?'

There was a hiatus in the conversation, prompting Phil to continue.

'Look, in my scientific work there is one lesson I try to pass on to all my students. If there is a question you have failed to answer don't ignore it. It won't go away and if you are not careful some day it will rise up and thump you.'

Gwynfor sighed.

'I don't see we have any real choice.'

'There's always a choice,' Phil said.

Gwynfor turned to him. 'Of course, the Assembly they're offering is inadequate, it's not what we want, it's not our policy. But you can't deny it's a step forward. It will be elected which is the main thing. And it's bound to influence the decisions of government. More fundamentally, it will constitute the raw material of a future Welsh state. We have to start somewhere. So we must campaign for it energetically, as the SNP will be doing in Scotland.'

Dafydd Wigley looked at Gwynfor.

'We've two choices, it seems to me. We can opt for gradual progress to self-government or try and achieve it by the kind of revolution that Phil is arguing for.'

Then he turned to Phil. 'I wish I could agree with you, but the fact of the matter is we don't have a revolutionary situation in Wales.'

'That's true. But we're still walking into a trap.'

*   *   *

The National Council met the next day in the Norton Arms' Great Hall, an imposing banqueting room with large wooden beams that rose through two storeys. About fifty activists from the four corners of Wales had gathered to debate how their party should position itself in the referendum, expected before the end of the year.

Some argued that they should demand two questions on the ballot paper, one being Labour's Assembly proposals and the other full self-government. Others pointed out that a two-question referendum was unlikely. If the party followed its instincts, campaigned vigorously for full self-government and distanced itself from Labour's proposals, it might de-motivate its grassroots activists when the referendum came. On the other hand, a strong Plaid campaign in favour of the Assembly would play into the hands of Labour MPs like Neil Kinnock and Leo Abse. They would say Plaid's stance demonstrated that devolution was but a step on the road to an independent Wales.

Most agreed that there would be little appetite amongst Labour activists to campaign in favour. In many areas, and especially the Valleys, only Plaid would provide the necessary commitment. Yet a Yes vote was unlikely to succeed if Plaid was seen to be too obviously taking the lead.

These were dilemmas to which no one had a clear answer, apart from Phil Williams. He argued that in the House of Commons Plaid should simply oppose the government's plans. But others said they could not avoid the fact that most party members enthusiastically supported Labour's proposed Assembly. They simply wouldn't understand Plaid opposing it.

Outside snow was continuing to fall, and it was obvious there would be little chance of leaving Knighton that day. Surrounded by hills it was a remote settlement. Llandrindod, the nearest town to the west was nineteen miles away while Ludlow, the nearest in England, was sixteen miles.

Over lunch Owen questioned Dafydd Wigley about the progress of the Scotland and Wales Bill through the Commons.

'It's going to be painfully slow,' Wigley told him. 'I reckon there will be more than three hundred amendments. We've put down forty ourselves.'

'What about?'

'Oh, constructive things, to give the Assembly primary lawmaking powers, proportional representation, establishing overseas offices, that kind of thing. But others are putting down amendments that would effectively wreck it.'

'In what way?'

'Well, for instance, Abse is demanding all kinds of impossibilities. Like there should be no discrimination against non Welsh-speakers. Who's suggesting there would be? But he's saying that if someone fails to get appointed as an Assembly official and feels he's been discriminated against because he doesn't speak Welsh, then he should be able to take the Assembly to the High Court. It's a ridiculous scenario, a political ploy. Abse's using it as a way of raking up the language issue.'

'With so many amendments how will they be able to get the Bill through?'

'They'll have to bring forward a guillotine motion.'

'The government you mean, to timetable the debate.'

'Yes, exactly, to get it through. That'll be the crunch vote. But before we get to that, we've got this Tory attempt to remove Wales from the Bill altogether.'

Owen phoned through a story based on this conversation.

* * *

An hour before dinner Owen saw Phil Williams sitting alone in the bar staring gloomily into an empty glass and offered him a refill. When he returned a few moments later bearing two pints Phil brightened.

'You know, we had one of our few victories near here.'

'What do you mean?'

'It was in Owain Glyndŵr's time, one of his most important, the Battle of Bryn Glas.'

'What, here in Knighton?'

'Not far, it was fought near Pilleth, a few miles away, in 1402. Owain had encamped there. Edmund Mortimer advanced towards him from Hereford where he had estates.'

'So, what happened?'

'Mortimer's supposed to have had about 4,000 men, and Owain only about half that. But the Welsh occupied the high ground. And Owain hid some of his troops in woodland lower down. Anyway, when Edmund advanced up the hill our archers had the height advantage and fired first, causing havoc. Then Owain's men in the woodland hit Edmund's flank. Some of Edmund's own archers, said to be Welsh, turned against him. It was a rout, a bloodbath. Edmund was captured.'

By now Phil had fully recovered his usual sunny disposition. Owen could see that just telling the story had cheered him up.

'The thing is there's no point our fighting that kind of pitched battle these days, he continued. 'Owain rarely did anyway. Normally he carried out hit and run raids. He was an early exponent of guerrilla warfare, perhaps the first.'

'I thought it was the Chinese.'

'Whatever. You could say that today's equivalent to a pitched battle is playing Labour's game at Westminster.'

'But the way things are we don't have much choice.'

'We need goals we can achieve, goals that can lead to further victories. It's no good aspiring to the unattainable. It's even worse to lose a battle that totally cuts off all prospect of final victory. That's what we look like doing with this devolution business. It could set us back years.'

'The Second Reading got through.'

'But that was only after they conceded the referendum. One thing is as certain as night follows day. We'll never win if we copy the tactics and strategies of our enemies. That's a lesson I learned as a little boy playing chess against my father. I thought that if I copied every move he made the game would be a draw. At first I couldn't understand why he always won. But then I learned that the only way I could win was by playing an unexpected move.'

'So what would that be now?'

'It certainly won't be playing the Westminster game. We copy the tactics and strategies of Labour at Westminster – and then we complain when we lose.'

* * *

After dinner the bar became crowded. At the end of the room Owen saw Rhiannon sitting at a table with Ioan and moved through the crowd to join them. He had noticed them earlier but hadn't had a chance to speak with them before.

'Surprised to see you here,' he said, sitting opposite Rhiannon.

'Ioan persuaded me to come, though he said it would be just for the day,' she answered, laughing.

'I'm not in charge of the weather,' Ioan said gruffly and then, looking at Owen, he added, 'We were surprised to see you as well. Can't remember a journalist being at National Council before.'

'Gwynfor invited me.'

'Oh.'

Owen coloured slightly as he felt the scepticism in Ioan's voice.

'I'm doing a piece on him.'

'I see.'

Sensing Owen's embarrassment, Rhiannon changed the subject.

'We nearly didn't get here actually. Ioan's car slithered in the snow halfway down the hill coming into Knighton. Quite frightening it was.'

'The weather's getting worse I reckon,' Ioan said. 'I heard Dafydd El didn't make it this morning.'

'I was wondering why he wasn't here,' Owen said.

'He ran into snow drifts, somewhere on the A470 between Dolgellau and Dinas Mawddwy, and had to turn back.'

'Probably Bwlch yr Oerddrws,' Rhiannon said. 'Cold Door Pass,' she translated, turning to Owen.

'Anyway, what did you make of the debate we've had?'

'You mean about the Tory plans to delete Wales?'

'Yes, that would be terrible, don't you think? Taking Wales out of the picture, not allowing us a voice.'

'I'm not at all sure that's right,' Ioan said. 'I think I agree with what Phil is arguing, that we're just playing Labour's game by trying to rescue the Bill. As he says, we're walking into a trap.'

'I don't see how we can avoid supporting the Assembly,' Rhiannon persisted. 'Gwynfor's right on that, surely? Our people – ordinary party members I mean, not activists like you, and I suppose me as well – well, they just wouldn't understand it.'

'You mean they'd think Plaid wasn't supporting the Assembly,' Owen said.

'Exactly,' Rhiannon said.

'It's a dilemma, I'll admit,' Ioan said.

'Plaid has to be in favour of the Assembly, surely?' Rhiannon exclaimed, and Owen was intrigued to see that she was becoming animated. Before this moment he had assumed she was only interested in language politics.

'As a political party in Parliament, Plaid has no choice but to follow the constitutional route,' she said firmly. 'That's what Gwynfor is saying. The other stuff he's leaving to us, to Cymdeithas yr Iaith.'

'The other stuff?' Owen queried.

'Protests, direct action, that kind of thing. Plaid does the politics, we do the campaigning.'

'I'm not sure you can separate the two,' Ioan said.

'I think we need another drink,' Owen said, collecting their glasses and making for the bar. When he returned the conversation had turned to other things.

Owen passed Rhiannon her drink and smiled at her.

'Do you think there'll be any singing tonight?'

She blushed.

'Not by me.'

Cathedral Road
January 1977

The next day Owen had first to head east to Leominster on his drive back to Cardiff. As he moved into lowland England the roads became progressively easier and were clear before he reached Hereford. After that it was a straightforward run through Abergavenny, a route that avoided the snowbound Brecon Beacons. Even so it was well into the afternoon before he reached the newsroom to find a message that Geraint Talfan Davies wanted to see him.

He was reading that day's paper in his windowless office.

'I see you've been spending the weekend with Gwynfor and his crew. Are they right to be worried about this Tory amendment?'

'Well, this is how Wigley sees it.'

With difficulty Owen took a seat across from the desk that almost filled the cramped room.

'The government starts with the forty-five majority it won at the second reading. But that was built on five Conservatives who voted for the Bill and thirty-two more who abstained.'

'And they'll vote against this time.'

'Yes, they won't want to defy their whips twice in a row. So that brings the government's majority down to about eight. However, Wigley reckons it's likely that the Ulster Unionists who voted against the Second Reading, will vote this time to keep Wales in the Bill.'

'They'll think it will be easier for them to argue for the re-introduction of Stormont if Wales is left in.'

'That's right. Anyway, if they do, the government's majority would climb to about twenty, according to Wigley's figures.'

'That sounds pretty comfortable.'

'On the face of it, yes.'

Owen flicked open his notebook.

'But everything would then depend on the government's own backbenchers. At the end of the Second Reading ten of them voted against and another twenty-nine abstained, including the Gang of Six. That's thirty-four dissident MPs.

'And if enough of them vote to delete Wales, the government could lose.'

'Wigley reckons they could lose by upwards of a dozen votes.'

While they were speaking Talfan Davies jotted notes on a large, biro-stained leather-framed sheet of blotting paper in front of him.

'We should do a leader on this. Have you got any other stories to keep the thing going?'

'We can do leaders and stories, Geraint, but what difference will they make?'

Owen pulled his chair a fraction towards the desk.

'There's less than two weeks to the vote. We need something more, to make an impact.'

'And you've got something in mind?'

'I've been thinking. We need to demonstrate that there's real support out there for the Assembly. The MPs need to understand that if they delete Wales there'll be a backlash. What about getting up a petition? I don't know, get a thousand prominent people on board. Wouldn't that make them sit up?'

Talfan Davies pursed his lips.

'There's not a lot of time. It would have to be well away from the office, we couldn't do it here.'

'We couldn't do it by ourselves, either.'

'I tell you what, I'll give Gwyn Morgan a ring. As a matter of fact, I was talking to him before Christmas and he said that with this referendum coming up we'd need to organise a cross-party campaign.'

A year before, following Britain's vote to stay in the Common Market, Gwyn Morgan had been despatched from Brussels to open a European Community Office in Cardiff. Since then he had been busy establishing its presence, travelling the length of Wales and accepting every offer to speak: to councils, farmers' organisations, Merched y Wawr, trade union branches, student unions, Soroptimist clubs, anyone who would give him a hearing about how Wales could take advantage of membership of the European Community.

He was ideally suited to the task. Brought up in Cwmdare the son of a miner, he had a mischievous, easy-going nature and rich sense of humour. He ran like warm oil through the machinery of an emerging Welsh civil society. A natural politician he seemed on everybody's side. For many working in the branch offices of England and Wales institutions, the new European dimension was exotic and comfortably liberating. More to the point was the promise of grant aid for all manner of projects. Gwyn's postbag was full of invitations.

In Brussels he had been responsible for helping establish the European Regional Fund and was convinced that an elected Assembly would give Wales an edge in taking advantage of it. So he was increasingly alarmed at the difficulty the Labour government was having in getting its devolution policy through. When Geraint rang him, it was Gwyn who suggested that instead of a petition they should take out a full-page advertisement in the *Western Mail*. They should collect a thousand signatures certainly, but place them beneath a declaration demanding that Wales be kept in the Bill.

They arranged to meet the next evening in Gwyn's office in Cathedral Road, not far from the *Western Mail*. Geraint would persuade his uncle, Sir Alun Talfan Davies, a barrister and member of the Commission on the Constitution to come along. Owen would do the same with George Wright, secretary of the

Transport and General Workers' Union and the Wales TUC, and also Barry Jones a politics lecturer and Labour supporter. Gwyn would ensure the attendance of Jack Brooks, Callaghan's agent and the leader of South Glamorgan county council.

'Between us we should be able to conjure up enough names,' Gwyn chuckled on the phone to Geraint.

* * *

Owen met with George Wright in his Transport and General Workers' Union office at the bottom of Cathedral Road. A substantial, purpose-built five-story building, it also housed the Wales TUC and the Wales Labour Party.

Owen found George Wright unsettling. It was not so much that he was English, or so relatively young to be holding such a commanding position. Partly it was because of his background in the Midlands car industry, a territory and industry entirely outside Owen's experience. But what he found most disconcerting was Wright's assured arrogance. He felt he would trample on anyone or anything to get his way. At the same time, he was sharp and energetic, and a powerful ally in the devolution debate who needed to be cultivated.

The middle child of nine Wright had started work at the Austin Longbridge car plant in Birmingham in 1955 when he was nineteen. Within a year was on the picket line amidst violent clashes in an industrial dispute. It was then he met Jack Jones, the Midlands Secretary of the Transport and General Workers' Union, who recognised his leadership potential. Wright's career as a union official took off. He rose rapidly through the ranks, honing his skills as a reader of men and tough negotiator.

He arrived in Wales in 1972, in the wake of a merger of the north and south regions of the TGWU to create a Welsh national entity. It gave Wright the platform he needed. He knocked heads together amongst other unions, formed an alliance with Dai Francis, secretary of the South Wales NUM, and in defiance of the TUC in London, set about creating a Wales TUC.

The notion had been debated for more than twenty years, always foundering on disunity between north and south, on different interests between unions, and on suspicions of nationalism. Wright had no truck with any of this.

'As an Englishman I recognise that Wales is geographically separated,' he said. 'It has a separate culture, a separate people, and a separate language, and it has special problems. We intend to defend Wales against the economic and social neglect of the last fifty years.'

Owen covered the Wales TUC's inaugural conference at Llandrindod in February 1973. He had also been at a follow-up conference three months later when the organisation voted overwhelmingly in favour of establishing a Welsh Assembly with legislative powers. He interviewed Wright at the time.

'If we want something done in Wales the instinct is to buy a ticket to London and ask their permission,' he said. 'In Birmingham we don't ask, we just do it.'

Now, sitting in Wright's expansive office on the top floor of the TGWU building, Owen had little difficulty in persuading him to throw his weight behind stopping Wales being deleted from the devolution Bill.

*　*　*

When they met the following evening in Gwyn Morgan's office in Cathedral Road, the dominant figure was Sir Alun. He was regarded with some suspicion by George Wright and Jack Brooks because he had been a Liberal parliamentary candidate in the 1960s, in Carmarthen and Denbigh. Tall and white-haired he exuded wealth and confidence, attributes from which they also recoiled. But he also extended charm. Meanwhile, Gwyn Morgan was at his best in delivering bonhomie along with a plentiful supply of drinks from a well-stocked cupboard that filled one side of the room. Owen sipped a Scotch from a heavy glass and passed around a draft he had prepared of the declaration.

Sir Alun pushed it to one side.

'Before we get to that, how are we going to pay for this? Geraint, how much to you reckon the advertisement will cost?'

'If we're thinking of a page, and I think we are, it would be around £1,000.'

'We should also consider north Wales, the *Daily Post*.'

'I'm not so sure how much that would cost, but perhaps £500. It's a tabloid format.'

'Well then, we're talking £1,500, more if we took in the *Swansea Post*. We should ask for contributions, of course, a minimum of a pound per signature perhaps, but in the time we've got...'

Sir Alun looked around the table positioned in the middle of Gwyn's large office. The Welsh and European flags stood against a wall on either side of a large desk.

'We have a week at most,' Geraint said. 'Owen and I have agreed we can take two or three days off to bring together a list of names.'

'But we'd need to book the space in advance I imagine,' Alun said, looking at Geraint who nodded.

'We'd need a guarantee,' he said.

There was a pause before George Wright spoke for the first time.

'We could put £750 on the table. The unions, that is.'

'Then we're in business. Splendid! A very handsome offer, if I may say.'

Sir Alun effortlessly adopted the role of chairman. A discussion followed on the wording of the draft declaration, during which he pulled out a fountain pen, found a scrap of paper and dashed off a note of his own.

A few of us are endeavouring at very short notice to assemble a substantial list of signatories for publication on Thursday of next week immediately prior to the crucial debate on devolution which takes place in the Commons that day. As you are probably aware there is a strong move afoot to delete the Welsh clauses from the present Bill. If this takes place, then all our efforts in the past decade to establish a Welsh Assembly will be frustrated. I would be extremely pleased if you would add your name to the signatories and if possible assist by obtaining the permission of some others to do likewise. We propose to publish the list in the three main daily papers circulating in Wales and this will cost £3,000. If you could make a donation towards this expense it would be greatly appreciated although this should not deter you from adding your name if you are unable to subscribe.

I am enclosing a stamped addressed envelope and if I could receive a reply by Monday morning it would greatly assist the small number who are endeavouring to do three months' work in three days. If you think it is unlikely that a letter would reach me by then I would be grateful if you could phone me on Cardiff 701341. Were it not for the fact that it is essential that this should be done I would not trouble you. We must make it plain that the people of Wales generally are as anxious about their future as the people of Scotland are about theirs.

The meeting continued for more than an hour. As they rose to leave Sir Alun took Owen to one side.

'Ben is in town, Ben Bowen Thomas that is. He was on the Commission with me. He's staying at the Angel. Why don't you go and see him? Tell him what we're up to. If the two of us put out a statement it would make a story, I would think. Move things along a bit.'

*   *   *

Over the next few days Owen and Geraint worked feverishly in the European Community office, occupying a small room alongside Gwyn Morgan's more luxurious quarters. They started with their own contacts, ringing people they knew and compiling a long list of anyone who might wield influence. Jack Brooks supplied the names of councillors across Wales.

George Wright came up with fifty trade unionists. 'No need to contact them. I'll let them know they're signing.'

Gwyn Morgan supplied a list of his own, together with reams of paper, envelopes and stamps. 'Powers that be will be impressed at my workload.'

Owen rang Dafydd Williams to requisition Plaid Cymru's Gestetner machine, together with the help of the party's administrator Gwerfyl Arthur. The machine rolled out a thousand copies of Sir Alun's letter and the same evening he called in to sign them.

Sitting at Gwyn Morgan's desk he wielded his pen, now and then grumbling to himself. He looked up as Owen came entered the room.

"I suppose you agree with the line the nationalists are taking on all this.'

'They're not that united, you know. Phil Williams, for one, he thinks we're just walking into a trap.'

'Phil Williams? He's a deeply dangerous man.'

*   *   *

Owen met Sir Ben Bowen Thomas over coffee in the lounge of the Angel Hotel. He found an avuncular figure, well into his seventies, who gazed at him with the calm assurance of one who has no anxiety left to assuage. 'I follow you in the *Western Mail*,' he said, with a twinkle in his eye.

He was one of Wales's most accomplished mandarins, highly influential but ever in the background. For nearly twenty years after the war he had been the permanent secretary at the Welsh department of the Ministry of Education in Whitehall. He had used this position assiduously to advance the growth of Welsh-medium schools. After that he had become president of the university at Aberystwyth.

They talked a good deal about the progress of the Assembly proposals. Owen confessed he was worried that the referendum would prove fatal to the devolution cause.

'Maybe, maybe, but only in the short run. It's bound to come eventually.'

Owen asked why he was so confident.

'It's a matter of determination. Those of us who want Wales to have the institutions she needs are more determined than those who are opposed to us.'

Later Owen rang Sir Alun to report on the conversation.

'So what did he say?'

Owen studied his notes, which he read over the phone, 'This attempt to delete Wales is a real insult. It should be a single straight issue on the government's proposals as debated and approved by Parliament that should be put in a referendum. I am gravely disappointed in those who are perpetrating the attempt to remove Wales, especially people like Mr Wyn Roberts who is my own MP in Conwy.'

'That's very good. Now I'll give you my response. Are you ready?'

In the next day's *Western Mail* Owen reported that Sir Alun Talfan Davies and Sir Ben Bowen Thomas were leading a campaign to keep Wales in the Bill. *Tory 'humbug' attacked by Kilbrandon Commissioners* ran the headline across the top of the front page.

'We have been provoked by this attempt to delete Wales which would effectively deny the people of Wales the right to decide the issue for themselves,' declared Sir Alun. 'The Conservatives have been clamouring for a referendum. To try and deny one now is a negation of everything democratic. It is political humbug and hypocrisy of the worst kind, bordering on the dishonourable.'

Within six months Sir Ben Bowen Thomas was dead. But Owen never forgot the confident assurance he had given him.

Westminster

February – March 1977

Signatures poured into the European Communities Welsh office in Cathedral Road. Many came by return of post, others were delivered by hand. The phone rang continuously with pledges of support. By the time the advertisement went to press seven hundred and eighty signatures had been collected. It was arranged that six hundred and twenty-five individually wrapped copies of the paper, one for each MP in the House of Commons, would be picked up from the *Western Mail* in the early hours of the morning of the debate. In the event it was decided that Barry Jones should collect thirty-six copies, one for each of the Welsh MPs, before catching the early train to London to deliver them to the House of Commons. The others were sent by post.

The Commons debate that day did not get as far as the Tory amendment to delete Wales. Instead, hours were spent on arguments over procedures and points of order, with opponents of the Bill intent on talking the measure out. The amendment was reached when the Committee resumed five days later, and then only after questions were raised with the Speaker about the propriety of members receiving copies of the *Western Mail* in House of Commons envelopes that had been given to Barry Jones by a friendly MP.

The advertisement was referred to many times during the long debate that followed. Neil Kinnock devoted a large passage of his speech to a detailed line-by-line analysis of the declaration to which the signatories had put their names.

We, the undersigned, believe that an unanswerable case exists for a real extension of democracy and responsibility to the people of Wales within Britain.

'If there is anyone in Parliament who disagrees with that I should be truly amazed,' Kinnock said. 'We are all in favour of an extension of democracy and responsibility to the people of Wales within Britain, just as we are all in favour of motherhood, sunshine, love and — as my Friend the Member for Swansea East who is under the American influence, suggests — apple pie. But I do not know what that has to do with the proposals of the Bill. The idea that the Bill extends democracy — when in fact we are having just a multiplication of the deficiencies of the House of Commons without significant changes in the rights and responsibilities of people anywhere in Britain, including Scotland and Wales — defeats me.'

Present arrangements for the accountability of the existing governmental administration in Wales are wholly unsatisfactory.

'And so say all of us, too. Present arrangements for accountability of existing governmental administration everywhere in Britain, in all departments, are unsatisfactory. Of course, nobody has defined the meaning of *unsatisfactory*. But any Member who has sat in the House of Commons for longer than a week will understand that our arrangements, both in the House of Commons and at other levels, leave much to be desired. I do not know what all this has to do with the Bill. I do not know how the Bill would expand the scrutinising powers of elected representatives of the people.

'The advertisement says, *As Parliament grapples with the increasing volume and complexity of European legislation, it is unrealistic to expect it to devote more time to Welsh affairs.*

'Parliament has never devoted a great deal of time to Welsh affairs. One may hold British membership of the Common Market culpable for many crimes against the British people, but less time for Welsh affairs in the House of Commons is not one of them. The shortage of time results from the way that we approach the whole question of European legislation, as well as many other matters of interest to the House of Commons. It is not the Common Market that has spoiled things for Wales, or Wales that has spoiled things for the Common Market, but the inadequate, outdated procedures of the House.

'The declaration says further, *Welsh economic and social problems, as well as the problem of accountability, cannot be met through any reform of procedures of one central parliament.* I think I said that first, so I can only agree.

'It goes on, *That the situation in Wales, therefore* — and I ask everybody to note that *therefore* — *demands the establishment of a directly elected Welsh Assembly, answerable to the people of Wales.* This assertion and conclusion directly follows the suggestion that Welsh economic and social problems cannot be met through reform of the House of Commons. We are led to believe that it can be met by the creation of a directly elected Welsh assembly. This is the central misrepresentation of the whole devolution case – the idea that more houses can be built, more jobs found, more happiness manufactured, more security and more unity exist, if only we have an Assembly. Once that central idea of devolution is shot through by practical examination, the whole case crumples. Unless the changes proposed by the government can deliver more resources to the people of Wales — and I mean more, not just better, because they are our first demand as an impoverished country — the proposition that our condition in Wales can be substantially improved, let alone transformed as some devolutionists would have us think, is totally rejected.

'*The need for a directly elected Welsh Assembly, and the expectation that has been built up over the last ten years, has reached a point where any frustration of the aspiration would dangerously threaten social harmony in Wales and relationships in Britain as a whole.*

'I was once involved in a building strike — in fact, I have been involved in more than one building strike — that took place at a school. The employers' representative had been particularly unforthcoming in his reactions to our request for a little more recompense for our labours. In fact, he had been very cheeky about the whole matter and had disregarded democratic procedures. I remember a shop steward standing in front of the school, which had great plate glass windows, addressing the assembled building workers, and saying, "We do not want any violence in this dispute, so I want you to ignore completely that pile of bricks behind you."

'I am sorry that, in the name of expanding democracy, people have given legitimacy, succour and significance to lunatics in Wales — and there is a tiny minority which seeks the violent road to what is called *freedom* for Wales — that they have never had from responsible politicians of any party in Wales or from the Welsh people.

'The idea is being spread that, if one does not vote "Yes" in the referendum, one will dangerously threaten social harmony in Wales and relationships in Britain as a whole. Fear and democracy cannot travel together, and fear cannot produce democracy. Those who, in the name of democracy, use the threat that others may disrupt, disharmonise and destroy, are doing themselves an immense disservice and ruining the core of their argument.'

Despite this speech Neil Kinnock voted to keep Wales in the Bill, along with three other members of the Gang of Six – Ifor Davies, Donald Anderson, and Ioan Evans. They did so to ensure that the referendum would go ahead so that, as Kinnock put it in his speech, 'the whole nonsense of devolution will be buried for ever in Wales'. Leo Abse and Fred Evans abstained.

The government won by two hundred and eighty-seven to two hundred and sixty-three votes. But that was nearly half the margin of forty-five votes they'd mustered at the second reading. And still to come was the guillotine vote, to timetable the discussion of the large number of amendments that had been tabled and were being added to on a daily basis. That would be much more difficult.

* * *

During the next six weeks the Bill was debated on ten occasions before the guillotine motion was tabled. In that time just three of its one hundred and sixteen clauses were discussed and there was a concerted effort to talk it out by filibustering. Eight anti-devolution MPs, including Leo Abse and Neil Kinnock, together made a total of seventy speeches, fifty-seven points of order and two hundred and fifty-seven interruptions.

On the morning of the guillotine vote, a delegation from the Wales Labour Party and the Wales TUC made their way to Westminster for a meeting with the Welsh Parliamentary Labour Party. It was an ill-tempered affair. Leo Abse set the tone. He asked the chair, Caerphilly MP Fred Evans, whether it was in order for people other than members of the Labour Party to be present.

'You'll be referring to Ivor here,' George Wright, the Wales TUC secretary, said pointing to Ivor Davies sitting alongside him who was a member of the Communist Party.

'Ivor was elected chairman of the Wales TUC this year. In our constitution we elect our chairman from among the Trades Councils every third year.'

Ivor Davies then spoke on his own account.

'The Trades Councils make up a third of the Wales TUC. Most towns in Wales have a Trades Council and there are county federations. I'm chairman of the Glamorgan federation.'

'We all belong to the Labour movement,' George Wright added.

'The unhappy fact remains that the Wales TUC's policies

coincide with the views of the Welsh Communist Party,' Abse objected. 'And, of course, they're constantly welcomed by the nationalists.'

'We should press on,' Fred Evans said. 'I think Emrys has some opening remarks.'

Emrys Jones, secretary of the Wales Labour Party and usually a mild man, was on this occasion supressing a good deal of anger. He shuffled his papers, cleared his throat, and looked meaningfully around the room.

'We all know why we're here. It's because of the vote this evening, a crucial vote for the government I think we can all agree. We're here to remind you of the decisions that have been democratically arrived at by the party. And, moreover what was included in our manifesto at the last election.'

He then set out the dates when Labour's devolution policy had been agreed, including a meeting of the Welsh Labour Parliamentary Group in November 1973. Final approval had been reached at the party's special devolution conference, at Llandrindod the following June.

'It's a pity that some of our MPs do not feel it important enough to attend our conferences,' he added. 'It might make meetings such as this unnecessary.'

Leo Abse immediately swung into attack.

'We're well aware of party policy. But we have a duty to our constituents as well. When people say that it was in the manifesto and was sold as such to the electorate of Wales, I am reminded of the cheap huckster who goes to the door and, having presented a contract for sale, carefully conceals the small print. The fact of the matter is that the proposals that have come forward in the Bill are not those that were agreed before the election.'

There was a murmur of agreement across the room.

'For instance, there was a firm pledge, it was in the White Paper, that the Welsh Development Agency would be under the control of Parliament. But now it seems it is going to be transferred to the Assembly.'

'That's a detail,' interjected Ray Powell, chairman of the Wales Labour Party. 'It is my view that members who do not accept what has been democratically arrived at as party policy should resign.'

'It is certainly more than a detail,' Abse retorted. 'It undermines the powers and position of the Secretary of State for Wales and so, again, the role of this Parliament.'

'What we find deeply damaging is the cynical use that is being made of the Welsh language,' Jack Brooks, a member of the Welsh Executive said. 'I for one, and I think my colleagues agree, deplore the extreme views being put by fanatics on both sides of the language divide. To suggest that a democratically elected Assembly in which English-speakers are inevitably going to be in a majority, will discriminate against that majority is to stand truth and probability on its head.'

Abse bridled.

'You're right, the majority of Assembly men will be able to speak only English. But that is no argument. Anxiety pervades Wales because people know the belligerent attitude adopted by so many in Plaid Cymru and the Welsh Language Society. They fear they will pursue their campaign more aggressively once the Assembly is established.'

'The Wales TUC provides clear evidence of the advantages devolution will bring,' George Wright told him. 'Before we were set up we had to fight dire warnings that we would be dominated by Welsh-speakers and nationalists, and that would lead to a fragmentation of the Labour movement.'

There were murmurs of agreement among many of the MPs in the room, but George Wright's voice rose above them.

'The reality is there is not a single member of the nationalist party out of the forty-five men on our general council.'

He paused until the murmuring ceased. Then he banged a fist on the table.

'In fact, we have become one of the most influential voices speaking on behalf of Wales. In fact, we are one of the most rapidly developing trade union organisations in the whole of Western Europe.'

Wright gazed scornfully at the Welsh Labour MPs assembled in front of him.

'Not only that, we have led to the decentralisation of the TUC structure in England.'

There were more murmurs, interrupted this time by Neil Kinnock, keen to move the discussion towards more advantageous territory.

'We have solid evidence that we are more closely representing the views of our constituency parties and, as Leo has said, our constituents.'

'The constituency parties have had every chance to put their views across,' Emrys Jones said. 'And we've had strong majorities on each occasion.'

'That's the union block vote, not the constituency parties,' Donald Anderson muttered.

'There's strong support in the country, too. For instance, that advert in the *Western Mail*,' Emrys Jones answered.

'That was organised by people I can only call leading lights in the Welsh Establishment,' Anderson retorted. 'It's an Establishment that has been wrong on most issues affecting Wales for generations.'

The Cardiff delegation continued to press its case, accusing the rebels of filibustering and undermining the government's authority. But they received no support from the other MPs present who notionally supported devolution.

* * *

Later that evening, when the guillotine motion was put, the government lost by thirty-five votes, and the Bill fell. Leo Abse and Fred Evans voted against, while the other four Welsh rebels abstained. However, the government had not reckoned on a large number of Labour MPs from the north of England who voted against. They were fearful that the Scottish and Welsh Assemblies would gain powers and finances at the expense of their region.

The government also lost the support of most of the Liberal MPs, frustrated about the lack of consultation they had received on what they thought was an unwieldy measure. But mainly they believed that the Bill's collapse would force closer co-operation between them and the Labour Party that, in turn, might open the door to some form of coalition.

Wild scenes as anti-Assembly MPs cheer the 312-283 vote declared the *Western Mail*'s front page the next day.

Westminster
January 1978

Within weeks of the collapse of the Scotland and Wales Bill, the Labour government's slim majority eroded to such an extent that Margaret Thatcher, the new Conservative leader, tabled a motion of no confidence. This provided Liberal leader David Steel with the opening he wanted. He entered into talks with the Prime Minister about an arrangement to keep the government in office for the remainder of the parliamentary session. There were three main strands to what became known as the Lib Lab Pact: control of inflation through an incomes policy, direct elections to the European Parliament, and the revival of the devolution legislation with separate Bills for Scotland and Wales.

Yet, when they were presented to the Commons in the autumn, the separate Bills were indistinguishable from the previous measure that had tied them together. In particular, the commitment to referendums, reluctantly conceded by the government and opposed at the time by the Liberals, was retained. Even so this failed to assuage the Labour rebels. Throughout the autumn of 1977 and into the New Year, they sought amendments to undermine the legislation. They could not kill the Bills outright, but they could undermine them. As George Cunningham, Labour's MP for Islington South, said, 'It was in the ground of the government's fatal concession of a referendum that we planted the delayed-action bomb that blew up devolution.'

These were the circumstances that brought Owen James to a committee debate on the Scotland Bill on 25 January 1978, a date that coincided with Burns Night. An amendment tabled by George Cunningham provided for a threshold requiring forty per cent of the electorate to vote Yes in the referendum before the Scottish Assembly could be established. This was his 'delayed action bomb'. Although MP for a London seat George Cunningham was Scottish by birth, if decidedly British by inclination. He might have been persuaded there could be a federal solution to Britain's territorial problems but not one that only considered part of the state. He was dismayed at the thought of an autonomous Scotland undermining Britain. While he regarded himself as British, he certainly couldn't claim to be English.

When he arrived in the Commons, Owen immediately sought out his friend and former colleague Steve Thomas of the Press Association in the cafeteria alongside the chamber.

'There must be trouble at mill if you're around,' Thomas mumbled, taking a bite of buttered muffin. 'What brings you? Scotland's on the agenda today, not Wales.'

'Whatever they decide is likely to find its way into the Wales Bill, wouldn't you say?'

'Suppose so. It's a bit up in the air at the moment.'

'What do you reckon?'

'Well, its complicated. There are at least three amendments, all calling for different thresholds for the number voting Yes, or rather the proportion of the electorate voting Yes in the referendum, before the Scottish Assembly can go ahead.'

'Sounds a bit of a gerrymander to me.'

'That's what the SNP are saying.'

'Will it get through?'

'The government whips reckon they're on top of it, but I don't know. Might come down to the way it's chaired.'

'George Thomas isn't any friend of devolution.'

'He's not in the chair, it's the deputy speaker Sir Myer Galpern.'

'Don't know anything about him.'

'He's been here forever, since the fifties anyway, Glasgow Labour.'

'A loyalist, then?'

'Not on devolution he isn't. I once heard him say he'd like to throw the Scotland and Wales Bill in the Clyde. But then he said, on second thoughts he wouldn't because it would pollute the river.'

* * *

Later Owen made his way to Gwynfor Evans' room where he found him in a gloomy mood.

'We've come to the crunch. This debate is a test of whether the government's serious about the whole thing. If any of these amendments go through then the Scottish Assembly is finished.'

'And the Welsh Assembly as well.'

'Absolutely. I was optimistic before Christmas. Callaghan and John Morris told us they were going to make devolution a confidence issue. I thought Michael Foot was splendid in the way he steered the Scotland Bill through its first stages in November. He sat through all the debates and was obviously committed. Indeed, I wrote to him saying how much I admired his work. But now...'

'What's changed?'

'Well it's obvious that opposition is mounting across the Labour Party.'

'That's certainly true. We did a survey a few weeks ago. Virtually the whole of the government's backbenchers in Wales, those who are not on the payroll, can be counted against. At least thirty, I would say.'

'We might have expected Labour support in Dyfed at least. But I hear the Aberystwyth Labour branch voted twenty to one against an Assembly and the Ceredigion constituency Labour

Party fourteen to nine against. The Labour agent of my own Carmarthen constituency has come out strongly against, as has the Labour-controlled Dinefŵr council, even the Brynamman branch. I haven't heard anything from Llanelli. In fact, there has been complete silence in recent weeks from Labour's pro-devolution people across the country. No one has spoken up in favour, either from the party or the unions.'

Pushing his chair away from his desk, Gwynfor stood and crossed his spacious office to gaze through the window at the Thames flowing below.

'This forty per cent threshold that George Cunningham is pushing is the last straw. It's completely undemocratic. It means that if, for whatever reason the weather say, only forty per cent of the electorate vote, then every one of them would have to vote Yes for the Assembly to succeed. Even on a reasonable turnout of seventy per cent, fifty-eight per cent would have to vote Yes.'

'I suppose the argument is that a big constitutional change requires a substantial majority.'

'They didn't demand forty per cent for the Common Market referendum. That was an even bigger change, surely? Parliament was handing some of its power to Brussels. A majority of one was thought enough then.'

'That's true.'

'Very few governments if any would have been elected this century if they had had to command the support of forty per cent of the electorate.'

'The SNP are saying it means that those who don't vote will be counted as No voters.'

'Exactly, the electoral register will be out of date. So the dead will also be counted as No voters. There are some ludicrous anomalies. George Reid was telling me the other day that because his house has two doors on different streets he is registered to vote at two different addresses. So his front door vote would be cancelled by his not appearing to cast his back door vote.'

* * *

As always when it was considering the committee stage of a constitutional bill, that evening the House of Commons sat as a whole. Owen found himself a place in the press gallery of the Commons alongside Steve Thomas. The debate on the referendum amendments to the Scotland Bill began shortly after six o'clock.

'Bruce Douglas-Mann's amendment is being tabled first,' Steve said. 'He's Labour, but represents an English seat, Mitcham and Morden I think. He wants a threshold of a third of the electorate. George Cunningham is amending it to call for forty per cent.'

Owen opened his notebook as Douglas-Mann began speaking.

'I regard this amendment as absolutely central to the support I give to the Bill,' he was saying. 'I abstained on Second Reading of the Scotland and Wales Bill and I voted against the timetable motion for that Bill. By the end of the summer, I had come to the conclusion that if — and it is a large if — a substantial majority of the people of Scotland were determined on this measure, it was not for English Members to defeat it.' He was not against the forty per cent threshold, he said, but thought there might be a greater chance of a consensus for a third.

Owen laid down his pen as the MP became sidetracked into procedural issues, carrying on for what seemed an interminable length of time. Eventually he sat down and Owen's interest quickened as Alick Buchanan-Smith rose to his feet.

'He's one of the few pro-devolution Tories,' Steve Thomas muttered. 'He resigned from Thatcher's shadow cabinet a couple of years ago when she abandoned Heath's support for an Assembly.' Buchanan-Smith said he was against a referendum in principle, as undermining the power of Parliament.

George Cunningham then rose to argue that referendums were justifiable on constitutional questions when the parties were divided internally, as they were on devolution and entering the European Economic Community. Setting up a Scottish Assembly would be an irrevocable step. His proposal for a forty per cent threshold was merely a response to the claim by the government and the SNP that the people of Scotland supported devolution.

'If they overwhelmingly want devolution, far more than forty per cent will presumably vote for it,' he said. 'I am not asking that the overwhelming majority, or even that the majority of the electorate should vote for it, but only that forty per cent should be prepared to go out and do so.'

As the debate droned on, Owen realised that no one from the government side was speaking against the amendments. Opposition came from Gordon Wilson for the SNP and Jim Sillars, leader of the breakaway Scottish Labour Party. Otherwise, a succession of Tory MPs and Labour dissidents spoke in support.

The only Welsh MP to take part in the debate, Aberdare's Ioan Evans, said forty per cent was too low and instead should be fifty per cent.

It was ten o'clock before John Smith, for the government, began his winding-up speech and another half-an-hour before the voting began.

'We could be in for a bit of melodrama in the next few minutes,' Steve Thomas told Owen.

It took the best part of a quarter-of-an-hour for the MPs to pass through the lobbies to vote on George Cunningham's amendment. It was passed by 166 votes to 151 despite the

Conservative front bench abstaining and four Conservative backbenchers, led by Edward Heath, voting against. Many Labour backbenchers abstained, refusing to vote it down.

Commentators later judged the vote to be the most important backbench rebellion in British politics since 1945.

But the voting was not yet over. As the last members emerged from the lobbies, a Conservative MP demanded of the Deputy Speaker, 'On a point of order Sir Myer, I am told — and I have seen this — that there are Members in the "No" Lobby who are sitting down and not being counted.'

'Cheating!' other members cried.

'What happens in the Division Lobbies is not a matter for me,' the Deputy Speaker replied. 'I shall ask the Sergeant-at-Arms to find out what's happening.'

Owen turned to Steve Thomas.

'What's going on?'

'The Labour whips are trying to delay the voting to make the overall vote null and void,' he explained. 'Voting on all the amendments has to be completed by eleven o'clock, otherwise they all fall. It's getting awfully close to the deadline.'

As he spoke, a Labour Scottish back-bencher, Willie Hamilton, jumped to his feet.

'I inform you, Sir Myer, that I have seen Members in the Lobby—there are at least five of them—flatly refusing to come out.'

'Cheat!' other Members cried once more.

But the Sergeant-at-Arms had done his work.

It later transpired that, learning of the lost vote on the forty per cent amendment, Government whips had rushed into the lobby to delay the final vote until past eleven o'clock. They almost succeeded. However, the Sergeant-at-Arms pinned the chief whip Michael Cocks against the wall, demanding the errant MPs leave immediately.

The final vote, on an amendment about the status of the Shetland Isles if devolution went ahead, was announced just as Big Ben was striking eleven.

'A Burns Night massacre,' Steve Thomas said as they left the press gallery above the chamber.

*   *   *

A short time later Owen found Gwynfor Evans in his room preparing to leave the Commons. They walked out of his office and down the corridor.

'You still have the option of voting against the Bill because of the forty per cent threshold,' Owen suggested. 'It's bound to be seen as a gerrymander.'

'I don't see how we can. The people of Wales wouldn't understand it. And the government could easily blame us for defeating it. Nothing would please them more.'

'But they've made the referendum unwinnable.'

'We must see the campaign as an opportunity to deepen national consciousness,' Gwynfor said. 'Somehow we've got to get our people to dedicate themselves to the work. Everything we've been involved in has been like this. The Parliament for Wales campaign in the fifties, even Tryweryn...'

They turned into another corridor and their conversation tailed off as, in the distance they saw a woman advancing unsteadily towards them. Owen recognised Winnie Ewing, the Scottish Nationalist MP. He had first seen her a decade before, on the stage at the first Plaid conference he had attended, at Dolgellau. He remembered she had come on to the platform carrying a bowl of white heather. He had been totally caught up with the rapturous applause as she spoke about the forthcoming by-election in Hamilton where she was the candidate.

She told Gwynfor, 'Before the blooms on this heather

fade, I'll be sitting beside you in Westminster to speak up for Scotland as you do for Wales.'

But it was a very different Winnie Ewing tonight. Her hair was awry, the mascara on her eyelashes was smudged, and her high heels wobbled as stumbled along the corridor.

Suddenly, she realised who was standing in front of her.

'Oh Gwynfor!' she cried with a sob.

She rushed forward and flung her arms around his neck.

Astonished, Gwynfor dropped the brief case and coat he was carrying and placed an arm around Winnie's heaving shoulders.

Pontypool
April to May 1978

Owen waited, clipboard in hand, after knocking at the front door of the pebble-dashed semi-detached house. A man in a vest appeared.

'I'm from the *Western Mail*. We're doing a property survey. Would you be able to tell me whether this house is freehold or leasehold?'

'No idea mate, what do you mean exactly?'

'The ownership.'

'Oh yeah, we own it alright.'

'But is it freehold or leasehold?'

The man turned and called out.

'Mavis! There's a fellow here wants to know about the house.'

A woman joined him, her head swaddled in a towel. 'What does he want to know?'

'We're inquiring whether it's leasehold or freehold, for a survey.'

'It's leasehold I think, isn't it George? All the houses round here are, but we own it mind.'

'You wouldn't happen to know who owns the leasehold?'

'Dunno, wouldn't know where to look.'

'Well, thanks anyway.' Owen retreated down the path.

It was a Saturday afternoon and he had spent the best part of the day knocking the doors of houses in a number of small privately-owned estates in Pontypool. He'd begun in the morning in Lansdowne and Clarewain in the Sebastopol district. There were a hundred-and-twenty-eight houses in the first estate and sixty-two in the second. All were small box-like structures built in the early 1960s. Now he was in the the Jerusalem Lane estate in New Inn on the other side of the main

Newport road that cut Pontypool in half. Here he counted ninety-four houses. There was one further estate nearby to examine, Ruth Road, where he reckoned would be a further two hundred homes.

The response he had just received was typical. Very few knew whether their house was leasehold or freehold, though none had so far claimed they were freehold. In fact, Owen was sure that they were all leasehold and that the leases were owned by Leo Abse and Cohen, the Cardiff firm of solicitors.

His quest had begun a few weeks before as a result of a conversation with Steve Thomas in the House of Commons. They had been discussing Abse.

'They say he's not short of a bob or two,' Owen said.

'And the rest. I'm told he's made a pile in the property business.'

'Really?'

'Owns the leaseholds of a good chunk of his constituency. And that's despite him being one of the main authors of the Leasehold Reform Act. You should look into it.'

'Where did you hear that?'

Steve Thomas tapped his nose.

'Go on.'

'Well, if you must know, I've been talking to Roy Hughes.'

'The Newport MP?'

'Yes, he's from Pontllanfraith so he has his ear to the ground in Pontypool. No friend of Abse's either. They hate each other as a matter of fact. Started with Leo's legislation on homosexuals. Roy's got no time for them. Now they've fallen out over devolution.'

'Hughes is in favour, isn't he?'

'That's right.'

Back in his office in Cardiff, Owen called a Plaid Cymru councillor he knew well. Aneurin Richards was the leader of the party's small group on Islwyn borough council which bordered Pontypool. He had recently also won a seat on Gwent county council in a by-election.

'I was wondering if you had any contacts in the county planning department who would know the history of housing developments in Abse's constituency.'

'I see what you're after,' chuckled Richards, a dark-bearded mining engineer. 'I'll see what I can do.'

A few days later he rang back.

'I think you're on to something. There are four estates that fit your description. My man thinks they could be leasehold properties which is unusual for recent developments. It's being phased out, as you know. Unpopular with purchasers, for obvious reasons.'

In the course of his day in Pontypool Owen found three householders who were willing to give him the information he was seeking, all of them women. One in the Clarewain estate told him immediately. 'Twenty pounds a year,' she said. Earlier in the Lansdowne estate another woman invited him in and gave him a cup of tea while she rummaged amongst files in a small metal container. Eventually she pulled out a piece of paper.

'Here it is. The ground rent is twelve pounds a year, payable to Dealry Investments Ltd.'

'Is there an address?'

'Yes, here it is, a Post Office Box in Cardiff.'

'That's a bit odd, don't you think?'

'Well, I don't know really.'

Owen reckoned that the average ground rent on the five hundred Pontypool leaseholds across the four estates was £15 a year. Together they made £7,500. Over ninety-nine years it would amount to nearly £750,000.

That evening he rang Aneurin Richards.

'I've been in Pontypool today. It could well be that Leo Abse and Cohen own all the leaseholds on those estates. Could you get your man in the planning department to dig around a bit more?'

* * *

At eight o'clock in the morning a week later, Owen boarded a train for London. Chartered by Friends of the Earth, it was one of three that were heading from different parts of Britain for a demonstration in London. The protest was against the building of a nuclear waste reprocessing plant at Windscale in Cumbria.

Owen had picked up a Friends of the Earth leaflet advertising the demonstration.

> If the Windscale plant is built, then large quantities of plutonium will be produced and transported, and a future decision on the plutonium-fuelled fast breeder reactor will be loaded in favour of expansion. The dangers of long-lived wastes, leakages, thieving of plutonium, or weapons proliferation, pose not only safety risks. They are also a threat to civil liberties and trade union rights through much increased security activity.

Owen agreed with these sentiments and was planning to write a piece about the day. But he was also intrigued that Leo Abse was billed as one of the speakers at the mass rally in Trafalgar Square.

The train had started its journey much earlier, in Haverfordwest. It had stopped to pick up demonstrators in Carmarthen, Swansea, Neath, Port Talbot and Bridgend. And it would be picking up more as it travelled through England, calling at Bristol, Swindon, Reading, and other points in between. There was a carnival atmosphere in the carriages. Jokes and banter abounded. Children were put to work colouring in posters and banners on the tables, between the seats and on the floor, wherever space was available.

Owen found a seat in the restaurant car and settled down with a coffee and Abse's memoir *Private Member*. It was an intriguing mix of autobiography, accounts of his various campaigns, political gossip, and dissections of the personalities of his fellow MPs. Owen was amused to see that as well as his wife and children, Tobias and Bathsheba, the book was dedicated *to the Electors of the Eastern Valley of Monmouthshire in gratitude for their forbearance.*

'I doubt they know exactly what they're forbearing,' Owen thought to himself as he scanned Abse's study.

The note on the flyleaf was clear about his intention. 'Political decisions can have fateful consequences,' it declared. 'Elected politicians cannot claim the same rights of privacy as those afforded to their electors.' On every page it seemed there was a reference to the author. Owen's eye was caught by a passage describing how Abse had established his legal practice in Cardiff in the early 1950s. He was joined by 'a pure young man of considerable skill, Isaac Cohen, who determinedly chose me as a partner'.

> He possessed a detached, academic interest in money and, taking complete control of the finances of the practice, and indeed of my own, he freed me for law and politics.

Sipping his coffee, Owen was fascinated.

> I have never been interested in money. It is true that I have, out of whim, whilst in the House of

Commons been prepared to devote just sufficient time to money-making to ensure that I earn each year at least as much as the Prime Minister; but that no doubt is a little private game which I play in order to ensure complete immunity from the temptations of pelf and place at Westminster.

Owen could see why the MP wanted to keep his game, as he put it, to himself.

As soon as the train reached Paddington the demonstrators streamed on to the platform to make their way to the designated meeting point in Hyde Park. Owen followed them on to the Tube's Circle line, changing after one stop for the Central line connection to Marble Arch.

Walking up the steps, Owen emerged into crowds of demonstrators, many wearing PVC protective clothing and gas masks. A group of men clung on to ropes tied to a large balloon floating high above them shaped like a mushroom cloud. Others clutched cylinders emitting red smoke. Posters proclaimed *No Nukes is Good Nukes!* and *Hell no, we won't glow!*

On the street opposite were rows of policemen. But the atmosphere was far from confrontational. People were smiling and the police were joking. Eventually the demonstrators set off, on a straggling march through Oxford Street. The police walked alongside them. Owen was behind a group carrying a box with *Nuclear waste – do not open 'till the year 200,078!* emblazoned on its side.

Saturday afternoon shoppers stared, mystified by the banners and slogans. *Fish and chips today, Chips and Fission tomorrow,* declared one attempting a gruesome humour. *Safe? So was the Titanic!* announced another.

'What a way to spend a Saturday afternoon,' a shopper shouted at Owen as the column turned into Regent Street.

'Have you got any kids?' one of the men carrying the nuclear waste box shouted back.

'What's that got to do with it?'

'Windscale No! No! No!' they chanted as they tramped down Haymarket, their shouts echoing against the tall buildings. They spilled into Trafalgar Square where thousands of demonstrators jostled for position. The steps in front of the National Gallery were a mass of people. A rough wooden platform had been raised in front of Nelson's Column and the crowd were cheering a singer strumming on a guitar, straining against a crackling sound system that jumbled his words.

Owen pressed forward to gain a position closer to the platform. Eventually he gave up and retreated to find a space on the wall surrounding the fountain at the centre of the square. Loud applause greeted the first speaker, a French campaigner hot from a victory in Le Havre. The day before they had won a court order to halt a nuclear development.

Three trade union leaders took their turn at the microphone, one of them Arthur Scargill of the Yorkshire Miners. He insisted there was enough coal beneath the earth to tide Britain's energy needs over the period while alternative energy sources from wind, wave and solar power were developed. Actress Janet Suzman of the Royal Shakespeare Company read out a declaration rejecting a report by Lord Justice Parker on the Windscale expansion.

After a gap in the proceedings, Leo Abse advanced to speak. Owen was struck by the politician's small stature. He was introduced as the leading figure of the campaign in Parliament and stood passively for a moment while the microphone was lowered to accommodate him. Gazing at the massed crowd of faces he savoured their youth, exuberance and humour. They reminded him of when he was young in the optimistic days after 1945.

'You are a new generation. Quite rightly you reject the values of your parents. Their concerns are all too easily confined to getting on in the world, to the next car, the new house. I sense you are not so preoccupied with such materialism. You know that increased happiness cannot be equated with increased wealth.'

This declaration prompted loud applause, whistles and cheering.

As he scribbled a note, Owen marvelled at Abse's effrontery, chutzpah even. Now, to more applause, he was urging that many more such rallies should be held. Nuclear weapons were the greatest threat to mankind. The reprocessing of nuclear fuel and production of plutonium would inevitably result in their spreading.

Abse spoke more quietly as the applause died down, though his words, carried by the sound system, still echoed across the square.

'The Parker report makes the absurdly unconvincing argument that we should expand our reprocessing plant and provide facilities and plutonium to others because otherwise other countries will go ahead and do it themselves.'

Abse pulled a handkerchief from the top pocket of his jacket, wiped his brow and surveyed his momentarily quietened audience. Owen could see that he had their complete attention.

'But that argument was heard when the slave trade was being conducted,' he suddenly cried, grasping the stem of the microphone with both hands.

'It was said that if we did not do it, others would. That was the argument used then to justify our involvement in the slave trade. And it is being used now to justify our being involved in the exporting of plutonium.'

He stopped for a moment once more, allowing a silence to descend as if to accentuate the meaning of his words. Owen sensed the skill of the seasoned orator.

'If we go ahead with this plan, we confirm to the world our role as nuclear hawks. We destroy our credibility as a nation genuinely concerned to make the attempt to arrest nuclear proliferation.'

Abse allowed another moment of silence to be filled by a tense feeling of expectation amongst his listeners

'I will use emotive language. The atomic salesmen are like pimps peddling a diseased harlotry, eager for profits, ready to put into world circulation cancer and death. Cool language will not distance us from the awesome consequences of allowing plutonium to fall into the hands of the Amins, the Gadaffis, the PLO and the Red Guards.'

At this there was applause and loud cheers of agreement.

'I am a man of sixty years of age. It is a time for all people of my age to contemplate death. That must come to us all. However, for the first time in human history man has to contemplate the possibility of the destruction of the human species. It is the first time that man has had that capacity. I do not say that we alone as a nation can prevent that catastrophe. But I do know that we can make a contribution towards its prevention.'

* * *

A few days later, back in Cardiff, Owen was researching Abse's role in the leasehold reform debate that had taken place a decade before. In the 1960s a higher percentage of the population of Glamorgan and Monmouthshire owned their own homes than any other part of Britain. However, very few owned the leasehold. These were held with small ground rents and had been granted for ninety-nine years by the coal owners and landlords at the time of industrial expansion some eighty years before. Inevitably, as their expiry date approached, anxiety mounted. This was made clear in Leo Abse's account in his memoir.

The leaseholders were certainly not reconciled to the argument that they knew, when they had purchased or inherited the home, that the tenure was not an indefinite one; and they were no less contemptuous of the argument that the sanctity of contracts had to be maintained and that it would be a breach of the rule of law if, ninety-nine years after the contract had been entered into, the landlord should not now be able to obtain his agreed pound of flesh.

Once again Owen was taken aback by the MP's ability to separate his political utterances from his actions. In his memoir, Abse celebrated his role in the leasehold reform movement of the 1960s. At the time the Whitehall housing department was overstretched and for decades its officials had placed obstacles in the way of change. Accordingly, the Housing Minister Richard Crossman called on the services of two legal minds on his backbenches, Leo Abse and Sam Silkin, a Queen's Counsel whose Dulwich constituency was also plagued with leasehold problems. Abse's memoir related how over many months they created a departmental brief upon which the Leasehold Reform Act of 1967 was, as he put it, 'slavishly drawn'.

Owen next turned to Hansard. Eventually he found what he was looking for, a debate in June 1966 on the White Paper that was tabled in advance of the Leasehold Reform Bill. Owen noted that at the outset of his contribution Abse declared an interest, as was customary.

May I follow practically all other Welsh Members and declare my interest in leasehold? So pervading is the effect of leasehold in Wales that it would be exceedingly difficult for any householder, business or professional man not to declare such an interest.

'That's not far short of dissembling,' Owen thought to himself. But as he scanned through Abse's speech he saw that the Cardiff North Conservative MP Donald Box intervened. He pointed out that when Abse had declared an interest he had not said what it was. In his reply the MP was somewhat more illuminating.

> I will certainly declare my interest. I have a leasehold property and I also have shares in a company which owns leasehold property.

Shortly after he noted this, Owen's office telephone rang. It was Aneurin Richards.

'We've made a bit of progress. My man in the planning department has been looking through the records.'

'And?'

'That first estate you mentioned.'

'The Lansdowne estate in Sebastopol.'

'Yes, well it was originally owned by Sir Richard Hanbury-Tenison.'

'The High Sheriff of Gwent?'

'That's the one, a big landowner in the county. Anyway, he sold the land, twelve acres altogether, to a company called Dealry Investments in February 1962 for £14,000.'

'Dealry Investments you said?'

'That's right. But the shares in the company were split between Leo Abse, Isaac Cohen, David Shepherd, who is Abse's uncle, and someone called Susan Freeman, the daughter of the Cardiff industrialist Ferdinand Kraus who we think is a neighbour of Cohen.'

'So effectively the company is run by Leo Abse and Cohen.'

'Yes. And not long after they bought the land, they sold it to the Cardiff building firm F.B. Beavis for £19,500. They then obtained the detailed planning to build the estate in January 1963.'

Owen made a quick calculation.

'So they made £5,400 profit on the land.'

'Yes, and of course they also kept ownership of the leasehold on the houses that were built.'

Owen whistled softly.

'What about the other estates?'

'Similar story. Leo Abse and Cohen set up various companies to buy land in Pontypool. It seems that as an MP Abse had a close connection with Hanbury-Tenison, which helped oil the wheels, you might say. Altogether my man reckons Leo Abse and Cohen's companies spent £111,426 buying the land for the four estates, but sold them to the building firm for £232,000.'

'That more than 100 per cent profit.'

'Yes. It was an ingenious scheme. The deals were designed to give Leo Abse and Cohen the lion's share of the profit with virtually no financial risk. Unlike most property speculators who buy land at agricultural prices and then have to obtain planning permission before selling it on, they bought land which already had outline planning.'

'And then they charged the builders a premium for being allowed to build the houses.'

'Exactly. In the case of the Clarewain estate the builders had to pay a premium of £400 for each house they built.'

Owen made another calculation.

'That's £24,800 for the 62 houses.'

'Right. They originally paid £9,216 for the land. So overall they made £15,584 on the transaction, kept the ownership of the leaseholds of course, and, as I say, for no financial risk.'

'And all above board.'

'Well, that's for you to say.'

* * *

Owen realised that he would have to give Leo Abse and Isaac Cohen a chance to respond to the story. First he rang the firm of solicitors. Eventually, after insisting he would speak to no one else, he was put through to Cohen and explained he was investigating the firm's leasehold transactions.

'I don't want to discuss my business with you. I do not give interviews. I never have and I never will.'

With that Isaac Cohen put the phone down.

Owen decided he would have to tackle Leo Abse directly and looked around for a suitable opportunity. He discovered that a few days later the MP was speaking at an event organised by the United Nations Association in Pontypool.

The meeting was held on Friday evening at the Settlement Community Centre near the middle of the town. Owen arrived early and made himself inconspicuous at the back of the hall. Banners along the wall revealed that nuclear power was the subject matter. At a table near the door, students from the town's St Albans High School were organising a petition. There was a surge of people as the meeting was due to start and an air of anticipation. Ten minutes past the appointed time Abse arrived, accompanied by two men Owen judged to be local party officials. Abse himself looked tired and slightly crushed as he sat at the table at the front, idly shifting a few papers he had taken from the shoulder bag he was carrying.

But then, after a short introduction he was on his feet, suddenly animated, pugnacious and indignant at the forces he was confronting. His audience, most of them campaigners, needed no convincing. He began by pointing out that the people of Pontypool lived within a radius of fifty miles of one of the largest concentrations of nuclear reactors in the world. Eight Magnox or advanced gas-cooled reactors were already in operation, and two more were planned nearby at Portskewett and Oldbury. All were producing nuclear waste.

So far people had learned to live with the danger. But now misgivings were growing as it was well known that the Central Electricity Generating Board had established a list of possible sites for new fast breeder reactors. Many would require a remote coastal location and the geography of Wales had obvious attractions.

Abse moved to the front of the table and leaning with his back against it, adopted a more confiding stance, his voice becoming conversational. If Britain moved to the new generation of fast breeder reactors so much plutonium would be produced that the present security arrangements overseeing its storage would be totally inadequate. Nuclear reactors currently producing electricity didn't use plutonium. Irrevocably, however, if the Windscale plant was approved Britain would be transformed into a plutonium economy.

Abse's voice heightened.

'Plutonium is one of the most dangerous substances known to man. A handful would be sufficient to build a device that could destroy an entire city. We must realise that the construction of a nuclear bomb would not be much more elaborate than that already used by criminal gangs engaged in the illicit manufacture of heroin. There are terrorist groups so alienated and estranged from society that they seek every means to attack us. It is a phenomenon known throughout Europe and a constant danger to our security.'

Reverting to a conversational tone, Abse explained that because of these dangers Parliament had approved the creation of an atomic police force. They had special powers and were not answerable to the Home Secretary, but only to the Atomic Energy Authority.

'By the nature of their secret work, we know all too little of the way they operate. At the moment their operation is small, but moving into a plutonium economy will inevitably increase their size and threaten our democracy.

'Workers would have to be vetted before they went into a plant and when they came out. So would their families. Even the threat of someone saying they had a handful of plutonium could be enough to terrorise a community.'

Abse paused, before continuing.

'The truth is, if they are approved, the fast breeder nuclear reactors will put our civil liberties at the mercy of an extended armed constabulary with sweeping powers of general arrest, answerable to no elected body, and of a secret service effectively answerable to no one.'

He stopped again, to give time for his message to be absorbed.

'The test of a civilisation is its concern not only for itself but the next generation,' he said finally. 'Out of concern for ourselves and those who come after us, are we prepared to take this massive gamble which may mean the next generation could be our last?'

Abse left the question hanging in the air as he sat down to applause. After a moment there were questions, mainly about the campaign and his view on the likelihood of Windscale being approved. Eventually the chairman signalled the meeting should wind up. Abse's minders quickly rose, anxious to move on. Owen stepped forward through the crush and managed to catch the MP's attention as he left the room.

'James, isn't it?' Abse raised an eyebrow. 'Owen James, *Western Mail*? Well, well, surprised, but glad all the same, to see you here.'

'I was in London at the weekend, at Trafalgar Square.'

'Were you indeed, a great demonstration. They say over ten thousand people were there. And this…' Abse gestured back at the room. 'It's unusual to get fifty or sixty people to turn out in

Pontypool on a spring evening, I can tell you. My third meeting this week, the campaign is gaining momentum.'

'Mr Abse, I need a chance to talk with you.'

'Yes, yes, of course, any time. Give my office a ring, arrange an appointment.'

And with that, swept along by his entourage, Abse was through the door and gone.

* * *

Late the following Monday Owen was standing in the anteroom to the editor's office waiting for the meeting he had been called to attend. In front of him one wall was taken up with a giant blown-up photograph of rugby hero Gareth Edwards. He was rising from the try-line, his face and shirt covered in mud.

Eventually, Duncan Gardiner appeared and beckoned Owen in. The large office was bathed in a subdued light. A vibration and low hum emanated from the printing presses in the depths of the building. Gardiner walked behind his large desk and lowered his heavy frame into his chair. Owen sat opposite.

Gardiner picked up a sheaf of copy paper in front of him.

'You've certainly been digging around. Interesting piece, well written. Never ceases to amaze me, what these MPs get up to.'

Owen leant forward, encouraged.

'So, what do you think?'

Gardiner grunted and leant back in his chair.

'As it is, what you've got, it's fine as far as it goes but I don't think we can run it.'

Owen frowned.

'Strictly speaking, they've done nothing wrong have they? Gardiner said. 'It's all within the law.'

Owen hesitated.

'Yes, but the exploitation. Abse's been making money out of his own constituents.'

'That's certainly the case. This planning chap in Gwent county council, I don't suppose he'd go on the record.'

'I don't think so, but I could go back.'

'More than his job's worth probably. Have you had any reaction from Abse?'

'No, but I approached the firm. Said they wouldn't comment, never give interviews. I can arrange to see Abse himself, but first I thought I should run it past you.'

'You'll get the same response from him, except he'll threaten us. Litigious bastard.'

Owen stood up, agitated.

'But the hypocrisy of it,' he cried. 'Abse is perpetuating the system he's been involved in reforming.'

'You're right, no doubt. But charges of hypocrisy won't get you very far in court.'

'The galling thing is that he's exploiting his own constituents.'

'I know. That's the story, essentially. But if we run it, we'd be accused of having a go at him because of devolution.'

'Because he's leading the campaign against the Assembly.'

'That's right. We're in deep enough water there as it is. And that's quite apart from the legal risk. Hang on to the story, though. You never know what'll come out in the wash.'

A few weeks later the House of Commons gave its approval to the reprocessing of nuclear waste and the production of plutonium at Windscale power station. Leo Abse described the decision as a staging post on the road to Armageddon.

Risley
April to June 1978

Rhiannon stared at her father through the cloudy glass panel, reaching out to touch it. Maybe it was plastic. She noticed there was an ashtray on the shelf on the other side but even so the wood was blackened with stains left by stubbed out cigarettes. She saw with a pang that her father looked worn. The button of his dog collar was coming loose at his throat, a sure sign of tiredness.

'*Sut wyt ti, cariad?*' Penry began, concern entering his voice.

But before he could say anything more a prison officer standing behind Rhiannon stepped forward, and lent over the partition between them.

'None of that, now. You'll speak English or nothing at all. We don't want any of that Urdu nonsense.'

'I was speaking in Welsh.'

'Makes no difference.'

There was a silence, until eventually the officer stepped back and allowed his attention to be drawn to some of the other inmates sitting alongside Rhiannon.

'How's Mam?'

'She's thinking about you all the time. She wanted to come, but in the end couldn't bring herself.'

'Oh Dada, it won't be long. You can get used to anything, they say.'

'I brought you a radio, so you could listen to Radio Cymru, but they wouldn't let me give it to you.'

Penry shifted in his seat and searched for some opening that would ease their usual flow of conversation. He had rarely spoken to his daughter in English, only when there were non-Welsh-speakers present and then with a sense of embarrassment.

'It's odd, isn't it,' Rhiannon said.

'Yes, it's extraordinary. It's as though we were strangers.'

'You can see why they call it the thin language.'

'Oh Rhiannon, is all this really necessary, all this sacrifice? It's hard for us to understand. Your mam was saying only last night, about your campaign for a channel, what difference will it make? We don't even have a television.'

'For you, things are caught up in books, in one book especially. But for a lot of people out there…'

Rhiannon faltered but then waved her hand upwards.

'For most people out there, well they watch television all the time, children especially. The language may as well not exist if they don't hear it on television.'

'Yes, I know the arguments and, of course, I can see the force in them. But where we live…'

'Of course, where we live it seems fine. People live their lives through the language. It's spoken everywhere, in the shops, in the pubs, and in chapel. But that's only where we live. In most of Wales it isn't anything like that. If we don't do something the language will die out in a few generations. Why can't people see that? That's why we have to act. We have to wake people up, the authorities, the government.'

'But you've important things to do in college, you've got your studies. You could become a teacher, maybe a Welsh teacher, wouldn't that be more important? We're afraid that all of this…'

'You're afraid that it'll somehow prevent me doing well, getting a job.'

'Of course.'

'Dada, of all people you should know the importance of our language and culture.'

'But why does it have to be a burden, like chains around our feet?'

* * *

A few weeks earlier Rhiannon and three other activists had hitch-hiked in pairs from Aberystwyth and met in Bolton. Their target, the Winter Hill Transmitting Station, was situated on the moors high above the town. When dusk fell they climbed to the outer perimeter, forced their way through and approached the buildings. As they did so a watchman appeared, took one look and fled.

Rhiannon and the others ran in the opposite direction. This brought them to the other side of the buildings that surrounded the tall transmitting mast. There they found a door that was unlocked. They went inside and along a corridor until they came to a room that contained an operating board. It had a large number of dials and switches. They turned all the switches off. For a brief period, no television programmes were transmitted from the Winter Hill Transmitter that served around six million people in the north-west of England.

Later that night the four were arrested and held in Bolton police station. They were fingerprinted, photographed, searched for explosives and closely questioned about connections with Ireland and the IRA. Appearing before magistrates a few days later they explained they were members of Cymdeithas yr Iaith Gymraeg and were campaigning for a Welsh television channel.

The magistrate's bench had never heard of the Welsh Language Society, let alone its curious campaign. They were sentenced to six months. For three of them that was suspended for two years. However, because of her previous conviction Rhiannon was sent to Risley Remand Centre located on the edge of Warrington, midway between Liverpool and Manchester. Its inmates knew it as Grisly Risley.

The prison comprised two and three-storey squat buildings crammed within rectangular-shaped high walls set amid fields just outside the town. There was very little outside space. The women's section comprised forty-two cells designed for one person, a dormitory for a further twelve, and thirty-one hospital places. Invariably there were more women than the available spaces, requiring most of the single cells to be shared.

Rhiannon's cellmate, Kathryn, was a Liverpool girl of similar age who had been convicted of multiple drugs and shoplifting offences. Metal bunk beds with thin wasted-looking mattresses and minimal bedding filled most of the space. Kathryn was lying on the lower bunk when Rhiannon was pushed into the cell. There was a small table with a couple of mugs and, high above, a small glass window, with one pane broken. It took Rhiannon a week to get used to the smell from a slop bucket in the corner.

'What you in for?'

'Fighting for the Welsh language.'

'What's that?'

Rhiannon spoke a few words in Welsh.

'That's funny, that is,' Kathryn said. 'Can't understand a word of it.'

'You wouldn't, it's another language.'

'Yeah, but I understand Pakis talking, and Afro girls. You're different.'

There was silence until Kathryn said, 'Any kids?'

'No, no, I'm not married or anything.'

'It'll be easy for you then.'

* * *

As Rhiannon discovered, routine dulls anxiety and the senses. The prisoners got up at eight o'clock, or, if they were going to court, were woken at six. Breakfast was porridge or cereal in the cell. There was bacon and chips for lunch and sausage and chips for supper. Prisoners spent most of the time in the cells sleeping or reading magazines. Their cells were unlocked for what was called association between ten-thirty and noon, one-thirty to five-fifteen in the afternoon, and then between six and seven in the evening.

Rhiannon spent all the time she could and most afternoons in the prison Education Room where there were a few shelves of books and magazines. She read them in the first week. She started to work some mornings in the prison gardens. Because of the time she spent in the Education Room most of the other prisoners assumed she was remedial and needed to learn to read, an impression reinforced by her accent. They deduced she was unable to speak fluently either.

One afternoon, some time during her third week, a warder advanced towards Rhiannon in the Education Room bearing a large carboard box.

'You've got friends in high places, you have,' she said dropping it on the table. 'Came in a special delivery from London it did, full of books and papers. Governor says you can do whatever you want with 'em in the Education Room. But you must hand 'em back at the end of the day. You can take 'em with you when you've done your time, of course.'

Rhiannon looked at the contents in astonishment. They were all from her bedsit in Aberystwyth. There were books, notebooks, course readers, her complete collection of the works of Frantz Fanon, reams of paper, a dictionary, even her pencil case.

'How on earth!'

'Yes, well, as I say you've got some friends somewhere.'

Rhiannon leafed through the books, feeling strangely unsettled. The sudden appearance of these familiar things, as though from an alien world, rudely disturbed her equilibrium. She realised that the only person who could have put them together was Siobhan. Only she would have known what Rhiannon was studying and also had access to her bedsit.

Rhiannon had given her a spare key before she left Aberystwyth and asked her to keep an eye on things. But she couldn't imagine how Siobhan had managed to get the box to Risley.

The books and papers drew her back to what now seemed a previous life, one that oddly was far more demanding than her present existence. Here she had no responsibilities or pressures, other than to conform with the routines and order of the prison. Rhiannon began to wonder how people in Aberystwyth were thinking about what had happened, what she had done – the college authorities, her tutors, Professor Kohr. Her mind turned to the campaign, which seemed never-ending. How long could they keep on protesting, climbing up television masts and breaking into television studios, in some kind of circular process of defiance? Surely the impact must fade?

They were such a pitifully small group. How long could they sustain their campaign? Rhiannon understood why the decision had been made to embark on the course that had brought her to Risley. It had happened years before, in the late 1960s. They had faced a fork in the road. The movement could adopt more conventional methods in the hope of gaining broader, and more widespread support. It was agreed that such a course would be unlikely to achieve a great deal. Anyway, Plaid Cymru was already carrying out that role. Alternatively, it would have to use more extreme methods, and accept it would remain a small minority. This was the route taken. There was no real alternative.

All the same, it felt like living through a kind of nightmare. Examined objectively, rationally even, the decline of the language and all the culture it carried with it, seemed inevitable.

'There's nothing we can do to stop it,' Rhiannon thought to herself. 'What's the point of being here in this wretched place?'

But now, looking at the bundle of books and papers she realised she had been handed a lifeline. There was at least a chance of some kind of control, choices she could make. She knew she must grasp the opportunity. And suddenly she rediscovered a sense of purpose, one that had been slipping away inside prison. Rhiannon felt the glow of optimism that invariably accompanies the recovery of hope.

* * *

The prison was filled with continual sounds, odd shouts and bangs, some of them seemingly far in the distance. But there wasn't much conversation.

'I'm in prison for the language but there's hardly any language here,' Rhiannon thought to herself on more than one occasion. At the same time, she also felt cut off from the complications of the outside world. In some ways it was like being on a retreat, perhaps in a monastery.

Sometimes she thought about Ioan and wondered where their relationship might lead. But increasingly it felt as if she was living her life in separate, insulated compartments. And being in prison was the most insulated compartment of all.

She looked again at the bundle of books and papers, noticing for the first time there were a few titles in Welsh, in particular *Dail Pren*, a slim volume of poetry by Waldo Williams. Reaching for it, she recalled one of her last conversations with Siobhan who had been interested in the books that lined her shelves.

'Do you have many political poets writing in Welsh?'

'They all are, to an extent. The ones you can see there are, anyway – Gwenallt, Saunders Lewis, and Waldo Williams. Waldo is particularly special I think.'

'In what way?'

'You could say Waldo's our poet, the poet of the movement, the language movement that is. Gets quoted all the time. You could say he's our national poet.'

'National… you mean nationalist, supporting Plaid Cymru?'

'Well he stood for the party, back in 1959 I think it was, in Pembrokeshire where he was from, but I don't mean national in that party sense.'

'In what sense, then?'

'Well, he conveys a deep sense of the unity of Wales for one thing. One part of his family came from the north and another from the south. He was always conscious of that. So much fuss is made about the differences between the north and south of Wales, but Waldo always stressed the unity. Then I suppose we like him because, despite everything, he's so optimistic, about the essential goodness of people I suppose. He talks about the essential brotherhood of mankind, that sort of thing.

'And womankind.'

Rhiannon laughed.

'That too, but Waldo never referred to it in those terms. They didn't in those days did they?'

Now, looking at the book in her hand Rhiannon let it fall open and the pages slid through her fingers until she stopped at some of her favourite lines.

> *Beth yw byw? Cael neuadd fawr*
> *Rhwng cyfyng furiau.*

She remembered she had translated the poem's title *Pa Beth yw Dyn?* to 'What is man?' and then read the lines to Siobhan, translating them afterwards. 'What is living? It's having a great hall between cramped walls,' she had suggested, following the words literally. Now she wondered whether they could be translated as finding a hall inside a prison cell. And she remembered that Waldo himself had been imprisoned several times, in Swansea jail. He'd refused to pay his taxes in protest against military conscription following the Korean War.

Each stanza of Waldo's poem began with a question. Rhiannon was always struck by the one that asked the meaning of singing. *Beth yw canu?* And the response: *Cael o'r creu / Ei hen athrylith.* 'Singing, what is it?' she murmured to herself now, in English, and translated Waldo's answer, 'The ancient genius of the creation'. Perhaps it might be, 'Winning back the first breath of creation'.

Rhiannon thought, too, that with such poetry it was surely unbelievable that the Welsh language could be in the slightest danger of extinction. She glanced at another stanza, and read, mouthing the words to herself again, this time in Welsh, savouring them:

> *Beth yw bod yn genedl? Dawn*
> *Yn nwfn y galon.*
> *Beth yw gwladgarwch? Cadw tŷ*
> *Mewn cwmwl tystion.*

She reached for another volume Siobhan had included in the bundle, *Ac Onide* by the philosopher J.R. Jones. Rhiannon turned to a page of text she had marked with a green highlighter pen. It was a line-by-line analysis of the poem she had just been reading. 'Being a nation, what is it?' was Waldo's question, and his answer, *Cadw tŷ / Mewn cwmwl tystion* – 'Keeping house in a cloud of witnesses.' Rhiannon re-read J.R. Jones' commentary.

> In this phrase I see a clear picture of the kind of thing I mean when I speak of being aware of the past and of the relationship of the past to life as we are living it. *Cadw tŷ* – this means daily life, housekeeping, earning our daily bread –that is what the whole of mankind has in common, the necessity of a working

life. How then can our life claim to have a unique and separate national quality? How do we follow our routine daily tasks in the secure knowledge that what we do is part of the life flow of our particular nation? No doubt our allotted space gives part of the answer – the theatre of our effort. On this territory, on the earth of our country, together we keep house.

'On the earth of our country,' Rhiannon mused. 'Yes, that's where you start, the familiar landscapes.' And she recalled the sight of the mountains of Snowdonia rising steeply, as if from the ocean floor, when they reached the top of the hill above their cottage at Llanddona. Yet there was more to what Waldo was saying. She read on.

But the past must also be an integral part of the answer. You are keeping house surrounded by a cloud of witnesses, not witnesses of flesh and blood, but a cloud of witnesses – witnesses in the mind, in the language you speak, witnesses from the past.

'That's right,' Rhiannon thought. 'It's the language that makes the connection.'

We know of course where Waldo picked up that phrase. After the roll-call of the great figures of the nation's past, Abraham, Isaac, Jacob, Moses, the author of the Letter to the Hebrews addresses those who remain, 'Wherefore, seeing we also are compassed about with so great a cloud of witnesses, let us lay aside every weight, and the sin which doth so easily beset us, and let us run with patience the race that is set before us.' The cloud of witnesses of a nation are the generations of her history.

*   *   *

Some weeks later Rhiannon found herself waiting in the corridor outside the office of the prison governor. 'Always waiting,' she thought. 'Standing around in queues, wasting time, doing nothing, achieving nothing, a cramped, airless, pointless existence.' And it was a build-up of frustration due to endless, listless, queuing and waiting that had resulted in Rhiannon waiting yet again, this time outside the governor's door.

Rhiannon had run. And running in prison is an offence.

One late afternoon she had been waiting once more, in a line in front of the servery at the end of her corridor to get a piece of bread and a cup of tea. Suddenly something inside Rhiannon's head gave way, snapped. And she set off.

She ran. She ran faster and faster. She ran along the corridor. Climbed the next landing. Ran back in the opposite direction. As she ran she untied her hair. It loosened and streamed behind her. Astonished inmates backed away.

Rhiannon realised she hadn't run for weeks. The experience was liberating. Exhilarating even. She gasped for breath. But she kept going. It was a kind of freedom. It *was* freedom.

'*Dwi'n rhydd, rhydd, rhydd!*' Rhiannon hissed loudly as she raced on. She just ran, without any thought of direction or destination. 'I'm free, free, free!'

Eventually, one of the prison warders grabbed her. They whirled around in a macabre dance. They slithered down the corridor. Bumped into the wall on one side, the landing railings on the other.

'Hold on girl,' the warder cried. 'Where do you think you're going?'

Rhiannon panted.

'I'm just running.'

'Not here you're not, lass.'

Back in her cell, her heart thumping, Rhiannon slumped, first against the wall, and then against the iron-framed bunk bed.

'I was free, for a moment, for just one instant,' she thought. 'That's what it will be like.'

When she found herself in front of the governor, she imagined she would say all manner of things. 'Yes, madam, of course I ran. I gained a small measure of freedom. You can never take that away. It made me think of home. How one day we might gain a small measure of freedom.'

Instead, when she was asked to plead whether she was guilty or not guilty to the offence, Rhiannon merely murmured 'guilty', as she had been advised.

The prison governor raised her head from the papers in front of her and wearily removed her spectacles.

'Look, my girl, you need to be sensible. With good behaviour you can be out of here within little more than a month. I'm going to ignore this incident, this time. But if you come in front of me again, it will be a different matter.'

*　*　*

Hours went by, hours that turned into days and then weeks. Rhiannon spent as much time as she could in the Education Room. She read, and then re-read the works by Fanon, including a biography. Now she was drafting a series of notes setting out the themes she wanted to cover in her thesis.

Shortly after the bundle of books and papers had arrived Rhiannon received a letter from Siobhan.

'I got a message through the department from your friend Gerard Morgan-Grenville. He said I was to ring him, reversing the charges, and gave me a number and a time. So I did of course. He told me he would be passing through Aberystwyth and asked to meet. He suggested the Belle Vue and said I should collect any books and papers I thought you might find useful to work on while you're inside. When we met he said he would arrange for you to be sent them. I asked him how and he referred vaguely to contacts he has in the Home Office in London. He's really quite an extraordinary man, isn't he? I mean at one level he's so posh, upper class even. But then again he seems to sympathise with people like us.'

Rhiannon and Siobhan fell into a regular correspondence after this. Rhiannon received a large number of letters from supporters in and around Cymdeithas yr Iaith, and from her parents. She even had a few from Ioan, penned awkwardly, revealing that he found it difficult to imagine, let alone identify with the situation she was in. But it was Siobhan's letters she looked forward to most. They were a link with what she missed above all, her work at the university.

Since being in prison, Rhiannon's thoughts on Fanon had taken a new turn. She had originally been attracted to him because of the controversy over his views on the use and inevitability of violence in the Algerian conflict. She was interested in trying to make a comparison with the situation faced by Cymdeithas yr Iaith and its debates over the uses and categories of violence. But soon she realised that little was to be gained from comparing the repression and murderous use of force by the French in Algeria with the response of the authorities to language campaigners in Wales.

Fanon declared decolonisation to be an inevitably violent

phenomenon. But Rhiannon was not at all sure whether decolonisation could be applied to the Welsh situation. Could Wales be described as a colony in the same way as Algeria? In any event she disagreed with some of Fanon's critics who accused him of writing as if violence itself, detached from its objectives, its political goals, was in some way necessary, a kind of cleansing process for revolutionaries. She thought that, for him, the struggle and the violence it entailed was only justified so long as it was directed towards political ends.

Instead of all this, Rhiannon had become more interested in Fanon's analysis of the connections between the revolution in Algeria and the country's cultural identity. She had become fascinated by his observations on how cultural activity was changed and enhanced by the experience of the revolution. He described how the role of storytellers had been transformed. In the past the stories and songs of the people had been static, set in the long ago and merely repeated from one generation to the next. But now they were much more energised, introducing contemporary events and modern heroes. In a letter to Siobhan, Rhiannon quoted Fanon.

> From 1952-3 on in Algeria, the storytellers, who were before that time stereotyped and tedious to listen to, completely overturned their traditional methods of storytelling and the contents of their tales. Their public, which was formerly scattered, became compact. The epic, with its typified categories, reappeared; it became an authentic form of entertainment which took on once more a cultural value. Colonialism made no mistake when from 1955 on it proceeded to arrest these storytellers systematically.

Rhiannon added how Fanon wrote that this kind of development was repeated through all the art forms of the people, from music to handicrafts, ceramics and pottery. They all changed and began to reflect an awakening of national consciousness.

> The nation is not only the condition of culture, its fruitfulness, its continual renewal, and its deepening. It is also a necessity. It is the fight for national existence which sets culture moving and opens to it the doors of creation.

'What I've decided to do is to follow these ideas through in the Welsh situation,' Rhiannon wrote. 'It would be interesting to see if we can identify whether in our art forms – especially writing, painting and music – we can detect a similar awakening.'

> The struggle for freedom does not give back to the national culture its former value and shapes; this struggle which aims at a fundamentally different set of relations between men, cannot leave intact either the form or the content of the people's culture. After the conflict there is not only the disappearance of colonialism but also the disappearance of the colonised man.

Rhiannon wrote to Siobhan, 'I think placing these ideas alongside today's situation in Wales could make a good comparative study.'

* * *

Rhiannon served three months of her six-month sentence. Early one June morning, clutching a large plastic bag containing her books and papers and a smaller one of sparse personal belongings, she stepped out of the narrow prison gate. The air was cool and clear. It seemed an extraordinary moment.

Across the road she saw Siobhan standing alongside her father who, as usual, was holding his pipe. Rhiannon ran to Penry and buried her head in his chest, inhaling the familiar tobacco aroma.

'*Cariad.*' He stroked her hair.

Looking up, she noticed an expression of alarm and concern in his eyes.

'Don't worry, Dada,' she said, speaking in Welsh. 'I'm still me. I haven't really changed.'

But Rhiannon had changed. She emerged from prison far more determined than she had been before her incarceration.

Penglais
July 1978

As always when driving to Aberystwyth Owen faced a choice. One route ran westward, passing Swansea, through Carmarthen, Llandysul, Synod Inn, and then north along the coast. The alternative was to head over the Beacons to Builth, Rhaedr and Llangurig before turning to cross the Cambrian Mountains. Influenced by the fine day he chose the mountain route. All the same, it had taken more than four hours that Friday morning. He arrived at the seminar in the Hugh Owen building on the university campus in time for lunch.

It was the second meeting of a new branch of the Political Studies Association, the work group on UK politics. Comprising an increasingly wide range of scholars studying devolution, there were contingents from Wales, Scotland and Ireland, but as yet only a small number from England. That was destined to continue, with academics from English universities reluctant to concede there was a discussion to be had, let alone to engage with it. Richard Rose, an entrepreneurial professor of politics at Strathclyde University, had established the group in Glasgow the previous year. Hailing from St Louis in Missouri he explained to Owen that his interest stemmed from the border state's involvement in the Civil War. His specialism was Northern Ireland but that had led him to consider politics in the British Isles as a whole.

Owen was particularly struck by an assertion Rose once made about British unity, 'It is likely that the only time at which the population of British Isles formed a reasonably homogeneous category was prior to the Roman invasion, when it was heavily Celtic.'

The presentation following lunch was by James Kellas, a

sallow-complexioned specialist in Scottish politics at Glasgow University. Owen had met him at the first seminar there the year before and he had been struck by his dour humour and apparent detachment from Scottish aspirations. In fact, Owen found it impossible to tell what his allegiances were.

Kellas was arguing now that since the Treaty of Union between Scotland and England in 1707 the United Kingdom had been a 'quasi-federal' state. The Treaty had set up constitutional guarantees for Scotland, which were to stand *in all time coming*. No amending process was provided for, and there was no system of judicial review. 'Which court was to decide,' Kellas asked, 'Scottish or English?' The Westminster Parliament appeared to bind its successors, or at least that was what the Scots thought.

The Government of Ireland Act, which had established Stormont in 1920, did not tie the hands of future parliaments but even so it resembled the 1707 Treaty. Stormont would determine the destiny of Protestant Northern Ireland.

Kellas then turned to consider Wales, and Owen leant forward, listening intently.

'Wales seems to resemble Québec,' Kellas said. 'A linguistic sovereignty is perhaps the most separatist of all. It effectively excludes the outsider from education, jobs, government positions. Even if this sovereignty is exercised by or on behalf of a minority – 21 per cent – in Wales, it is the hallmark of the whole Welsh position in the UK. Top this up with a Welsh referendum on devolution, and you have the makings of federalism in Wales. Whether devolution is added in the immediate future is almost irrelevant. Wales lives, and it is sovereign within its sphere.'

Kellas's argument was that the present-day starting point for the UK was not a centralised, unitary system, as was commonly assumed. The precedents were already set for indirect rule from London over Scotland, Ireland and Wales. However, he acknowledged that this left the question of England.

'Whitehall's rule over England is very direct indeed, and to hive off the English component of the UK would require the Establishment to change into another animal. How does one rule oneself indirectly? One answer is for the English Establishment to divide. One part will look to Europe and elsewhere for power, as did the old Imperial Establishment, and the other part will be domestic and English. Scots have divided thus for centuries, and Scottish MPs are easily classified on that basis. Can one doubt that such a division is inevitable, after the Scots, the Welsh and the Northern Irish have their own governments?'

Owen started taking notes when Kellas insisted that it was this that led to the inevitability of federalism, the title of his paper – that is to say, some system of two-tiered government. And he predicted that it would happen before the end of the century. The tiers would, of course, be the UK government and those of the territorial governments of Wales, Scotland, and Northern Ireland. The position of England remained uncertain. But then Kellas went on to make a prediction.

'I am prepared to stake a lot on English nationalism and the weight of history and institutions, which all point to an English dimension and English institutions,' he said. 'Regional fragmentation in England – or consolidation if viewed from local government – may also come, but that is not federalism. The UK federation is inevitably national in character, unlike the US or Germany, but like Canada or Yugoslavia or Switzerland.'

Kellas focused a lot of his attention on England, which Owen found interesting since most debates on these questions tended to concentrate on the preoccupations of the Celtic periphery.

'It might be asked what England would gain from setting up a federation. There are three obvious answers. First is the security of most oil powers and revenues. Second an assured domestic market. Third is the retention of international confidence.'

He conceded that London institutions would lose some of their power. However, with 83 per cent of the UK population and superior resources behind it, the English Establishment would soon recover.

'The new UK game would be played along EEC intergovernmental and bureaucratic lines, but that is increasingly familiar to Whitehall. Indeed, one might draw parallels between the inevitability of future patterns of political behaviour in the EEC and the patterns of behaviour within the UK. In each case, bargaining between states or regions replaces intra-governmental decision-making.'

Owen was struck by the confidence and panache with which James Kellas offered his predictions on the future shape of the UK. He felt strangely comforted at the assumption that Wales would inevitably be part of the new arrangements. At the same time, he thought the predictions contained large assumptions that airily swept aside difficulties.

Over tea in the common room, Owen approached Kellas who gave him a sardonic smile of recognition.

'I much enjoyed your presentation.'

Kellas raised an eyebrow.

'But it seems to me that there are some obvious difficulties.'

'And what are they?'

'Well, the Irish precedent for one thing. You seem to think that the English, or the English Establishment in Whitehall as you put it, will easily come to terms with a new kind of federal relationship. But they didn't with Ireland, did they? There was the suppression in 1916, and then the Black and Tans after the war and all that. The English Establishment fought before they were willing to let Ireland go, and then they ensured that Northern Ireland remained.'

'You're right, of course, but I'm certain they won't want to repeat that experience or, rather, that mistake. They will regard federalism as a compromise that is infinitely preferable to inflexibility and then a descent into coercion. That is not the British way.'

'What about the nationalist parties, the SNP anyway? Aren't they going to insist on independence and separation, if they get the chance?'

'Ah, you underestimate what I see as the essential conservatism of the peripheral nations. If offered a federal solution, which would grant them sovereignty over most of their domestic concerns, I am sure they would opt for that rather than the uncertainty and risks of separation. My whole argument is based on what I see as the bargaining, pluralist nature of the UK. It holds together because it provides an underpinning of the key conditions of social harmony, whether that's economic or territorial.'

'Can't you foresee any circumstances where that might break down?'

'No, not really. But even if parts of the UK were to separate or be coerced – and you're right, of course to point to the Irish Republic as a precedent – they would come together again, as if by nature.'

'You see that as inevitable?'

'Yes, inevitable in the sense that Scotland and Wales will be in close proximity with England, and in close interdependence whatever the future holds. As I say, their inevitable governmental relationship is one of federalism.'

* * *

Phil Williams was the guest speaker that evening. Owen observed him in animated conversation with the Work Group's co-convener, Peter Madgwick, an urbane Englishman and politics lecturer at Aberystwyth. They were discussing the role Welsh speakers would play in the Assembly.

'I agree that Leo Abse is completely over the top,' Madgwick was saying. 'It's illogical to think that a body elected by a dominant Anglophone community could be manipulated by a minority of Welsh-speakers in the way he tries to argue. But all the same you have to admit that it's not healthy the way language policy is so influenced by Welsh-speaking élites. They may have achieved gains, but they hardly advance the language cause by operating behind closed doors.'

'But that's exactly the point,' Phil replied excitedly, waving an arm that nearly overturned his glass of red wine. 'With the Assembly, you can't have closed doors. It'll all be in the open.'

Madgwick smiled at him benignly.

'And in those circumstances the language advocates may not get as much as they do now. The reality is they'll be in a minority. They'll have to fight their corner with other Welshmen more interested in the health service or education or building a dual carriageway somewhere rather than spending money on things like a television channel.'

'Tell that to Abse.'

At which point Peter Madgwick rose to his feet. He waited a moment to allow the conversations around him to die away.

'Friends, may I first welcome you all to Aberystwyth and our university on the hill. Facing westwards out to sea is a bracing cure for any inward-looking navel gazing is what I always say.'

He waited for the laughter he was accustomed to hearing in response to this remark.

'These are hardly formal occasions but we thought it would be interesting for our visitors to have the benefit of the thoughts of a rather unique person who is a colleague of ours here. Not, I hasten to add, within our discipline.'

He looked to his side.

'Phil, I should say Professor Phil Williams is a scientist and a rather exotic one at that. Something to do with astrophysics and the ozone layer I believe. But he is also, as chairman of Plaid Cymru...'

'Vice president,' Phil interjected.

'I must keep up. As well as being a leading scientist on the world stage Phil is a practising Welsh politician, and very much at the fulcrum of the devolution debate in this part of the world. He is also, as I am sure we shall hear, a highly original thinker and, more to the point, an entertaining speaker.'

As he rose to speak Phil took hold of a book on the table in front of him and held it aloft.

'Most of you, I'm sure, will be familiar with this. It came out a couple of years ago. *Internal Colonialism – The Celtic Fringe in British national development 1536-1966,* by the American sociologist Michael Hechter. I have a bit of a quarrel with the title and its assertion, by implication anyway, that Britain is a nation. But at least Hechter has got his dates right. Henry VIII's so-called Act of Union incorporated Wales into England in 1536. And 1966 was the year that Gwynfor Evans won Carmarthen, initiating the modern era of Welsh politics and, of course, the unravelling of Henry's Act.'

Here Phil allowed himself a sip of his red wine.

'But it's the colonial idea I want to explore this evening, or rather Hechter's idea of Wales as an internal colony. Of course, he did not invent the notion. He says himself that it was Lenin who was first to define it. And several years later, Gramsci discussed the Italian south in similar terms. But for me the story begins on the Metro in Paris. It was sometime in 1971 and *Le Monde* was running a series of articles on *La révolution régionaliste.'*

He stopped to take another sip of wine from his glass, as if toasting the idea.

'In any event, in the article on Brittany I read an evocative phrase, *To speak Breton is a revolutionary act!* I kept repeating it to myself for weeks after that, but adapting it to our own situation.'

At this point Phil lowered his paper and raised his voice.

'To speak *Welsh* is a revolutionary act!'

There was a titter of laughter across the room, but Phil ignored it.

'Perhaps for the first time I had a clear idea of why it is necessary to restore Welsh. Not because it is one of the oldest languages in Europe. Not even because it is our own language, a badge of our identity... No, the main reason is because it is a weapon we had let slip from our grasp.'

Phil placed his glass back on the table.

'I tried to trace the source of the quotation. None of my Breton friends could help. Then one evening I called on the poet Harri Webb, and while he was making coffee I rummaged through a pile of magazines and came across the Basque journal *Zutic*. I scanned through it, as I had never before seen the Basque language, Euzkerra, in print. At the back the articles were repeated in Spanish, and among them was a piece by Jean-Paul Sartre on the Burgos trials. And in it he says, *For a Basque to speak his own language is a revolutionary act.*'

Phil now looked defiantly around the room.

'I well remember the protests against the Burgos trials. After driving down from Aberystwyth to an evening meeting in Cwmbran I went on to Cardiff to spend a cold night with a dozen or so others outside the Spanish Consulate. The Spanish Consul whom the protestors were accusing of being an "agent of fascism" was, in fact, an extremely courteous, elderly gentleman who had lived in Wales for thirty years. He was, of course, Basque.'

The revelation was greeted with a few chuckles.

'At half-past six I went to a café for breakfast and, blow me, while I was away the BBC turned up with a prominent member of the Welsh Communist Party in tow. He then gave an interview on why *we* were staging an all-night vigil. The cheek of it. But at least I learned something about the way the media works.'

There was another murmur of amusement and Phil lifted his glass, continuing to speak as he did so.

'Sartre took his argument about the revolutionary character of the Basque language much further than just being a political slogan. Harri Webb's translated the article in *Planet* magazine and, as a result Sartre's message became widely known in Wales.'

Phil glanced up before quoting.

> Most people could protest against the Franco régime.
> But then they had to support the accused who said,
> *We are not only against Franco, we are first and*
> *foremost against Spain.*

He left a moment for the point to sink in, before pressing on.

'The Burgos trials drew attention to the rebirth throughout Europe of what centralist governments call *separatism*. All imperial and ex-imperial states contain internal colonies within frontiers they themselves have drawn. In France, Spain, Britain and Italy, provinces declare themselves nations and claim the status of nations. It becomes clear that the present frontiers between states correspond to the interests of the dominant classes and not to popular aspiration. It becomes clear as well that the unity of which the great powers are so proud is a cloak for the suppression of peoples.'

Phil stopped for a moment, partly for effect. Picking up his glass he looked around the room, then continued.

'Sartre suggested two reasons for the rebirth of nationalism. First, was the atomic revolution at the end of the war. Morvan Lebesque, the great Breton writer and nationalist, tells of one of his countrymen who, hearing the news of Hiroshima, cried out *At last the Breton problem exists!*

'What he meant, of course, was that the atomic bomb had signalled the beginning of the end of the large nation-states. At any rate, if we are to survive they must be superseded by new structures in which our small nations will have a pre-eminent role.

'But I digress. Sartre's second reason for the rebirth of nationalism, related to the first, is the worldwide process of decolonisation. He imagines a young man from Finistère doing National Service in Algeria who is informed that Algeria must always remain a Départment of France. But a few years later Algeria is recognised as a sovereign nation. So he realizes that *departments* are only abstract divisions, serving to disguise conquest by force and subsequent colonisation.'

As he said this, Phil's voice took on a note of indignation.

'But why shouldn't this be the same both sides of the Mediterranean? He learns that as a Frenchman he has the same rights as the inhabitant of any other province. But as a Breton he cannot raise a finger, much less fight against the central power which can annihilate him effortlessly. Yet in Vietnam poor peasants drive the French – and later the Americans – into the sea. The realm of possibilities is suddenly enlarged.'

Phil picked up another piece of paper with some scribbled notes in his childlike hand.

'So the anticolonial struggle moves nearer the metropolitan

heart and we must ask – is Euzkadi a colony of Spain? Is Breizh a colony of France? Is Cymru a colony of England?'

He left these queries hanging in the air for a moment.

'The questions are important.' Phil looked searchingly around the room, seeking to persuade. For a moment Owen felt his eyes were just on him, but then realised they were on everyone else as well.

'You see, it is in the colonies that the class struggle and the national struggle merge. Under the colonial system the colonies supply cheap raw materials and food products for the industrial metropolis and at the same time the workers in the colony are underpaid. This is certainly the economic history of Western Europe, and it is essentially true whether they are under-developed, as in the French provinces of Euzkerra, in Breizh, or in the rural areas of Cymru.'

Phil paused again for effect.

'Or, indeed, whether they are over-industrialised, as in Biscay in the Basque Country, the central belt of Scotland, or in the Valleys of Glamorgan and Gwent. In every case we have the three essential factors of classical colonialism.'

He stopped once more.

'Do I need to rehearse them? They are, first economic exploitation of the colonised country to meet the needs of the metropolis. Then there's super-exploitation of the workers. And thirdly – following from the first two – there's the rhythm of emigration and immigration used as a technique of social destruction.'

Phil hesitated, as if wondering whether he needed to elaborate, but carried on nevertheless.

'Of course, there's more to the exploitation than even this. Colonisation is a slippery business. The exploitation always occurs with the complicity of the large employers in the colony. They cut themselves off from the community of the nation and play the role of *comprador*, seeking to identify themselves with the imperial power. It is this that establishes the identification of the class struggle with the national movement.

'This is common to all colonies, whether they're external or internal. The special paradox of internal colonialism is that the imperial power will exploit an internal colony without ever conceding that is exists as a distinct unit.'

As a practised speaker Phil realised he was straying into complexity. He gave his audience a moment to catch up before continuing.

'Sartre puts it well. *Spain super-exploits the Basques because they are Basques. Without ever officially admitting it, they are convinced that the Basques are distinct ethnically and culturally.*

'On the one hand there is the official denial that the problem exists. It is still common for educated French people to refer to Occitan, Brezonek, and even Euzkerra as primitive dialects of French, which are in any case almost extinct.

'A recent statement by the International Socialists refers to the *six thousand people who still speak Welsh*. I tell you, just six thousand! There are as many imperialists on the Left as the Right...'

Laughter rippled through the room, but Phil spoke over it.

'This refusal to admit that an alternative culture *exists* even, is combined with a systematic and ruthless campaign to humiliate that culture on every possible occasion. The language is officially prohibited, excluded from public affairs, ignored in the mass media. Children are punished for speaking the language in schools. To the normal pattern of economic exploitation is added a subtle cultural humiliation. Together they represent the super-exploitation of the internal colonies.'

Phil allowed Peter Madgwick to reach over and refill his glass. But he was almost finished.

'However, by the inexorable force of the dialectic, exploited men negate the contradictions that are enforced upon them. Thus the Basque must be the negation of the Spaniard, the Cymry the negation of the imperial English. In this way, centralisation and super-exploitation are resulting in the maintenance and strengthening of our claim to independence by the very forces used to suppress it.'

Phil looked around the room for a last time.

'The lesson drawn by Sartre is clear. This is what he said. *The fight for socialism and the fight for independence must be the same fight.*'

* * *

Later, in the bar, much of the conversation turned on Phil's speech. Many questioned the idea of colonialism being applied to Wales and Scotland.

Owen overheard one say, 'Look, a theory like this has to hang together logically, and it's got to be compatible with the empirical facts – with reality if you like. I don't think either tests work when you apply them to the Welsh situation.'

'But you can't deny the relative poverty and under-development of Wales compared with England,' someone objected.

'No, no, but colonialism implies that one part of the state, what Hechter describes as the core, the English south-east in this case, is actively or consciously exploiting the periphery and that's much harder to prove, it's much more subjective.'

'It applies just as much to the north of England, it seems to me,' another said.

'But when you come to Wales you've got the cultural element to contend with, the language and so on,' said a third person.

'Uneven development, of the kind Hechter relies on, is inherent in capitalist systems,' said the first speaker. 'It's misleading to describe it as colonialism, though I admit it's pretty convenient for the nationalists to do so.'

At this point Phil Williams himself approached the group, pint in hand.

'You've stirred things up a bit amongst this lot,' Owen told him.

'It seems I've ruffled a few feathers.' Phil grinned, but then resumed a more serious expression. 'I was just saying to a group over there, the key thing for us is that economic exploitation is tied together with cultural differences. The whole thing is dramatised by the language. And it's that which presents us with our opportunity.'

'How exactly?' Owen asked.

'Why, it's then that we assert that our own culture is equal to the exploiter. It's then we make the connection with independence. That's what distinguishes us from the North of England which some might argue is equally exploited.'

'But where's the evidence that what you describe is really happening?' one of the group that had now gathered around Phil countered. 'Plaid Cymru is very much a minority in Wales, much more so than the SNP in Scotland for instance. Overwhelmingly people vote Labour in Wales. For that matter even the Conservatives do better than Plaid. If you were correct shouldn't you be mobilising a tide of opinion in your favour?'

'Yes, well that is a weakness,' Phil conceded. 'In our case, we have to contend with far more internal divisions than in Scotland, not least over the language. At the same time in both the Labour and the Conservative parties you can identify obvious signs of politicians reacting to our colonial status.'

As was often the case, Phil's mind was racing ahead of what he was saying.

'As I see it, three categories of political leaders typically emerge within cultures that can be categorised as internal colonies.'

'And what might they be?' It was Owen again who put the question.

'Well, it's pretty straightforward when you analyse it in these terms,' Phil replied, speaking now as though he was in a tutorial.

'In the first category, you have a group of ambitious individuals who identify almost entirely with the English political system. In Wales you've only got to look at politicians like Roy Jenkins, Michael Heseltine, John Silkin or Geoffrey Howe to recognise what I'm talking about. Take Roy Jenkins for instance. When someone suggested to Aneurin Bevan that Jenkins was lazy he replied, "To have been born in Abersychan, the son of a Welsh miner, and to have developed that *accent* means that the man can't be lazy."'

Laughter greeted this anecdote. Owen moved to the bar to deposit his empty glass, returning in time to hear Phil continue with the analysis he had begun earlier.

'The second category of politicians attempt to strengthen their position by acting as brokers between Wales and England. In effect they're ethnic leaders who seek to narrow the differences between the core and the periphery, by appealing to aspirations established by the core.'

'Who do you mean now?' Owen asked.

'Well, I'm talking about most Welsh politicians, as a matter of fact. Just think of Lloyd George, Jim Griffiths, Cledwyn Hughes, George Thomas, even Don Anderson and Leo Abse in their way. All of them have adopted a Welsh role, but they insist that they must work in the UK context to win a better deal for Wales.'

'That's certainly true.'

'Lloyd George secured jobs at the top of the English establishment for his Welsh friends. He would have assumed –

correctly, of course – that this represented the highest of their ambitions. The dismal chain of Welsh secretaries of state have all claimed that, given a few more years, government policy will solve our economic and social problems.'

'How do you fit Don Anderson and Abse into your picture?' Owen asked again.

'Both believe that Wales could not survive unless it is represented at Westminster by men of their calibre. Well, let us judge them by their results. It's only if they achieve economic integration will they undermine the basis for Welsh nationalism. I mean, only if they get us to a point where the average incomes and unemployment levels are the same in Gwynedd or the Valleys as the south-east of England.'

'So your third category of politician is nationalist, I suppose.'

'Of course. The reality is that the gap between the economic performance of South East England and Wales is widening. Meanwhile, politicians like Abse and Anderson are only feeding Welsh aspirations for improvement. Every day they're demonstrating the contradictions of their position. That's the basis for our advance, for the creation of a radical group that, as I say, combines the dynamic of socialism with nationalism.'

'But there's not much sign of the forces of nationalism and socialism collaborating,' Owen objected. 'Plaid and Labour take every opportunity to knock lumps out of each other.'

'That's true, for the immediate future at any rate. But in the longer run, the contradictions in the system will give us our chance.'

'How do you mean?'

'If we play our cards right, nationalism will give us the opportunity to bring together a wide range of classes in Wales, in a way that is simply unavailable to socialist parties elsewhere, like in the North of England for instance.'

'So you're saying that politically we're different,' Owen said.

'Yes. Because as a people, as a nation, we're a vehicle for social change.'

He furrowed his brow for a moment.

What was it that Sartre said? Yes, this was how he put it, *There exists a Basque people, and a Breton people, but today there are only French masses.*'

Phil gave those around him a knowing look.

'Why shouldn't that apply equally to Wales?'

Pentwyn

August 1978

'We want at least 25 hours a week.'

'And enough money to make it work.'

'Your costings are completely inadequate!'

The Secretary of State for Wales John Morris had only just begun his speech as President of the Day at the National Eisteddfod when the shouting started.

Owen was sitting a few rows behind the hecklers in the gloomy expanse of the Pavilion. Hundreds of people turned in their seats. Owen strained to make out the Welsh that was being hurled at the platform. But most of all he was struck by how calm the protesters appeared. One stood nonchalantly, keeping a hand in his pocket as he pointed a finger with the other. He lectured John Morris as if he was in a seminar room.

'What you're offering is too little, too late.'

Then about thirty young people seated around him began chanting and stamping their feet.

'*Chwarae teg i'r sianel!*'

They unfurled a large banner containing the same words: 'Fair play for the channel!'

On the Eisteddfod stage John Morris stepped back from the microphone, spread out his hands and smiled.

Owen noticed Rhiannon Jones-Davies among the demonstrators, her flowing red hair unmistakable. The interruptions continued as stewards gathered around. The protestors rose to their feet and began filing out, still chanting. As they left applause broke out from some sections across the Pavilion.

John Morris waited patiently. Then, as the last of the young people left and the closing doors blocked out the harsh sunlight that had cast a beam across the auditorium, he won a round of applause of his own.

'They have made their point. Perhaps I can make mine. They're knocking at a door that is already open. I have the honour of opening that door.'

He reminded the audience that in its Broadcasting White Paper published a few weeks earlier the government had agreed to the fourth channel being used in Wales for an enhanced Welsh language service. He mentioned twenty hours a week at a cost of £3.8m a year, with setting up costs of £2.5m.

Listening through the translation service and making notes, Owen mentally contrasted these figures with the recommendations made by the Welsh Office's advisory committee on setting up the channel. They were twenty-five hours a week as a start, with running costs of £8.5m and setting up costs of £14m. This, he thought, would be his story in the next day's paper, together with an account of the demonstration.

But now John Morris was returning to his prepared speech. His department was putting forward legislation to enable specific grants to be made towards the costs of bilingual education in Wales.

'If the Welsh language is to survive the key to its survival is in our schools,' he declared, to more applause.

*   *   *

Outside, Anna was wheeling Angharad in her pushchair through the crowds on the *Maes*, in search of Owen. She'd reached the main entrance to the Pavilion when she was accosted by her Welsh teacher Gwilym Roberts. He beamed delightedly and bent down to clutch Angharad's fingers.

'How old is she?'

In confident Welsh Anna replied that Angharad had turned three at the end of June.

'It'll soon be time for her to attend *ysgol feithrin* then.'

'Yes, we're thinking about that.'

At this point they were joined by Owen, who shook Gwilym Roberts' hand. Angharad squealed at her father and he reached down, undid the straps of the pushchair and swung her up on to his shoulders. In a mixture of Welsh and English, he described the Cymdeithas yr Iaith demonstration he had just witnessed.

A cloud passed across Roberts' face. He worried that the renewal of the campaign on the fourth channel was alienating people at just the time the Eisteddfod's presence in Cardiff was proving a boost for the language.

'Their campaign is important in keeping up the pressure,' Owen said, causing Anna to smile at his halting use of the language.

But Roberts interrupted him, first to correct what he was saying and then, turning to Anna, spoke so fast that Owen completely lost track. Eventually he stopped, looked at his watch and sped off, saying he was late for a meeting.

'What was he saying?' Owen asked.

'Didn't you hear? He was talking about the demonstration against the British Rail stand at the beginning of the week.'

'They were plain stupid, having all their displays in English.'

'Yes, but did they really need to smash up the stand? Gwilym said they caused a £1,000 worth of damage.'

'I suppose there is a risk they'll put people off. Gives a weapon to the other side. Some people in the office are already calling Cymdeithas yr Iaith fascists would you believe.'

They turned a corner and entered a narrow roadway lined with tents and stalls on either side. Suddenly they were confronted by John Tripp.

'Ah, Owen, good to see you. And this must be your daughter.'

Angharad leaned over Owen's head and grabbed at Tripp's moustache.

Anna was apologetic.

'I don't think she's seen one before.'

Owen introduced his wife.

'Charmed, I'm sure. Well, this is a great event, don't you think? Let those English scriveners, with nothing much left to believe in, snidely chuckle as we give them a show of quality, sensitivity, and intellect, and all of it laced with gaiety, panache, arrogance and strut. Where else in the world would you find a land that honours its language and its bards so magnificently?'

'Found anything for *Nails*?' Owen asked.

'Not really, but I met a cub reporter from one of those posh country periodicals earlier on. *Horse and Hound* was it? *Country Life* perhaps. Anyway she was quite bemused. Some sadistic editor has sent her from the calm of Berkshire to do a piece. She couldn't have looked more lost if she'd been dumped in the middle of Outer Mongolia. I felt so sorry for her I bought her a cup of tea. She was surprised to learn that the Pavilion is a moveable structure that does heavy duty anywhere from Chester to Penarth.'

* * *

Later they ran into Aneurin Rhys Hughes. His bald head gleamed in the sun and his face broke into a mischievous smile.

'Aneurin represents the European Commission,' Owen explained as he introduced Anna.

'Yes that, but my important role today is leading *Cymry ar Wasgar.*'

'The Welsh overseas,' Anna translated.

'That's right, I'm leading them on to the stage this afternoon, a great honour.'

'But you're not really an overseas Welshman,' Owen objected. 'You're still from Swansea, I'd say.'

Aneurin's eyes twinkled.

'Brussels these days, but have you heard? There's a move afoot to declare England and Scotland overseas territories so Welsh people there can join Wales international and take part in the ceremony.'

'They're hardly overseas,' Anna said.

'Well, foreign then, whatever.'

'But their numbers would swamp everyone else,' Owen said. 'Instead of having three hundred on the stage you'd have more than double that.'

'The idea is to have representatives, people who are members of Welsh societies across England.'

Owen changed tack.

'I'm sorry I missed your press conference.'

Anna looked puzzled, causing Aneurin to laugh.

'He's talking about the other hat I wear. We were announcing there's to be a Welsh delegation to Brussels next month to meet the German commissioner, Herr Brunner. He's responsible for culture.'

'Will the Commission really give the financial support to the Eisteddfod you mentioned?' Owen asked. '£200,000 wasn't it? Rather optimistic I thought.'

'Well, you're right, it's ambitious, but we're keen to demonstrate that we're interested in cultural welfare as much as the economy.'

* * *

A while later they passed the stand promoting Plaid Cymru's Welsh language newspaper *Y Ddraig Goch*. Owen explained that although political parties were not allowed on the field,

Plaid used the stand to promote itself, much to the annoyance of Labour, Liberals and the Tories. He saw that Gwynfor Evans was inside the tent and made to go and meet him, but Gwynfor came out instead, greeting Anna warmly.

'So this is little Angharad.'

He reached up to her, still perched on Owen's shoulders.

'I've heard a lot about you. I expect you would like an ice cream.'

He beckoned and they followed him along the roadway until they came to a stall bearing soft drinks, strawberries and ice cream. He handed Angharad a cone which she grabbed eagerly.

Anna laughed.

'Do you know, it's her first one.'

'I hope she remembers it.'

They walked on chatting, but were constantly stopped by people anxious to shake Gwynfor's hand and exchange a few words. Eventually they found a secluded spot with bales of hay in the shade of a tree and sat down. Owen asked about the growing speculation that there would be an early election.

'There's a lot of pressure on Callaghan, it's true, and he's going to have to make some kind of announcement soon, one way or another. But I don't think he's keen to go early.'

'What makes you say that?'

'Well, he's an instinctively cautious man for one thing. Not only that, why would he be courting us so assiduously if he was intent on an early election.'

'Go on.'

Gwynfor smiled, and looked across to Anna.

'Can't leave his reporter's mission behind for long can he?'

'You should know,' Anna replied.

'Well, now then, this is in absolute confidence. If anything of this were to get out it would be of no help to us at all.'

He explained that the three Plaid MPs had had a number

of meetings with the Deputy Prime Minister Michael Foot to discuss the basis on which the party might support the government. The latest had been nearby a few days earlier at the Cardiff home of Brecon and Radnor MP Caerwyn Roderick, Foot's parliamentary private secretary.

'Caerwyn is such a congenial man, not your run of the mill Labour MP, not in the least,' Gwynfor said. 'A Welsh-speaker, too, from Ystradgynlais. Do you know why he continues to live in Cardiff?'

'I've often wondered,' Owen said.

'It's because one of his children is disabled, so being in Cardiff means he can get home from Westminster during the week as well as weekends. Anyway, as I was saying, we've been having these discussions.'

Gwynfor paused for a moment, while Anna leaned across to wipe some ice cream from around her daughter's mouth.

'You see, the Lib-Lab pact is coming to an end, any day soon as a matter of fact. So the government are desperate for support from wherever they can get it. They're talking to the Ulster Unionists as well as us. I think they're hoping we can persuade the SNP to come on board, but that's tricky.'

'So what's the deal?'

'In the first place we're looking for a firm date for the referendum and that the government will throw its weight behind the Yes campaign. It was encouraging that Callaghan spoke so strongly in favour of devolution in his speech here on the *Maes* on the eve of the Eisteddfod don't you think?'

'And what else?'

'We've already got the commitment on the fourth channel. Then we're looking for help for the north Wales quarrymen who suffer from pneumoconiosis. They're fully entitled to compensation. That's particularly important for us in Arfon and Meirionnydd obviously. And we want more money to alleviate the effects of unemployment, training grants for teachers, that kind of thing.'

'Quite a list.'

'But there's nothing on it that Labour should object to. They're simply extensions of policies already being pursued by the government. In fact, we're embarrassing them by asking for things they know they should be doing.'

They continued walking. Gwynfor remarked on an article Owen had written the previous week, about the pressure for devolution that was mounting in the north of England.

'I was interested in the debate within the Campaign for the North on what constitutes English identity.'

'You mean their dismissal of the notion of an English parliament.'

'Yes, on the grounds, apparently, that England is not a nation in the way Wales and Scotland are. I don't think they're right about that. England's a nation alright.'

'Well, they're keen to establish the credentials of the North.'

'But which north? Are they talking about the huge region from the Mersey and the Humber to the Scottish border? That would contain about seventeen million people. Or would they divide it into the north-west, the north-east and Yorkshire and Humberside?'

'That's a debate they're having. It's unresolved.'

'I was taken by the comment you quoted from Douglas Houghton.'

Owen explained to Anna that Gwynfor was referring to the former Yorshire Labour MP who had been a member of the Commission on the Constitution.

'That's the one. He said the experience of Wales and Scotland proved that it was only when their national movements had become strong enough to frighten the main British parties that devolution had come on the agenda. He said, in effect, that the north needs its own nationalist party if it is to exert any pressure.'

'Not much chance of that,' Owen said.

Anna looked at the two men as they spoke and it struck her again how at ease Owen was when talking with the people they had met. She was amazed at the effortless way he seemed able to persuade them to confide in him, to reveal matters that were private, confidential even.

'This is his world,' she thought, looking round the Eisteddfod field. Then with a rush of intuition she suddenly knew that if her family was to survive, somehow it would have to become her world as well.

Sant Miquel de Cuixà
August 1978

Rhiannon walked slowly through the trees feeling the heat of the night air. The ground was wet from the thunder storm. But through gaps in the branches she could see the sky had cleared. Grass brushed against her bare legs and twigs snapped under her feet. A mist drifted along the scrubland floor and a scent of moss and herbs rose intoxicatingly in the dampness. Cicadas chattered incessantly. A breeze from the sea made Rhiannon's shirt cling to her body but it still felt warm. She followed the wind until she came to a path leading through tall bamboos to sand and an opening to the ocean beyond. Light glowed from a myriad of stars. They lit up the dunes that rolled southwards around the bay. Inland they picked out the looming dark shapes of the mountain range. Rhiannon wandered along the shoreline. On the silent, slowly moving sea the stars were reflected in a maze of dancing shimmering streams.

She and Ioan had spent most of the previous week driving the length of France and only hours before had reached the Mediterranean where the Pyrenees meet the sea. After driving through Perpignan they had headed directly for the coast looking for a campsite. Then it started to rain heavily. Lightning flashed, followed by thunder. The road became a single track and quickly flooded. Ioan had put the headlights on and peered between the sweeping wiper blades at the low-lying land around them.

Eventually the track petered out into what was evidently a picnic site surrounded by trees. There were a few stone tables and a residue of burnt-out fires and barbecues in the grassy scrubland. Ioan stopped the car and the dying of the engine emphasised the sound of the rain drumming on the roof.

'Do you think we can camp here?' Rhiannon asked.

'Don't see why not. We're well off the beaten track.'

Dusk was gathering and there was no sign of a let-up in the rain. The sky lit up again and there was a loud crack of thunder.

Ioan stripped off his shirt. 'Only one thing for it.'

Rhiannon giggled.

'You're not going out in this?'

In nothing but his underpants Ioan jumped out of the car and slammed the door. The beating rain drenched him immediately. Through the misted-up windows Rhiannon caught sight of his hair being flattened. Water glistened on his back. He opened the boot and pulled out their tent, an ex-US Army two-man bivouac that his father had brought back from the war. Rhiannon was laughing now as he slipped and struggled to pitch it. Nonetheless she was impressed by his fortitude and humour.

'If we can survive camping together we can survive most things,' he'd said when she hesitantly agreed to make the journey to the Spanish border. Ioan suggested the idea when Rhiannon told him she had been asked to represent Cymdeithas yr Iaith at a summer school organised by a Catalan nationalist group near Prades on the French side of the Pyrenees.

'We could make a holiday of it,' he said. 'Drive through France and camp. Be great.'

'Are you sure your old banger would make it?' Rhiannon asked dubiously.

So far it had transported them without incident. It was Rhiannon's first time on the Continent and she revelled in the particularity of France, its wide horizons and skies, its towns and villages of orange brick and rickety wooden buildings and cobbled streets, its empty poplar-lined roads. Rhiannon had never seen rivers of such width as the Loire and Dordogne. At the Loire Ioan turned off the road and drove a little way alongside the river bank before finding a place to stop. Immediately he jumped out, found his swimming trunks and plunged into the flowing stream. When they reached the Dordogne Rhiannon followed him, marvelling at the silky flow of the water on her skin.

They followed the river eastwards almost to its source, driving deep into the heart of France. Each day they would break camp and be off by eight, stopping an hour later for coffee and a croissant. They would buy bread, cheese and wine and break again at about two o'clock for lunch near the roadside. In the late afternoon they would drive on for a further three hours. Camping was easy since each small town had its municipal site. In the evenings they survived on more French bread and a store of canned stew that Ioan had thrown in the back of the car along with a Primus stove.

The further south they drove, the warmer it became. Rhiannon spent hours leaning into the wind that rushed through the open windows of the car, flowing through her hair. The colours of the landscape enchanted her, the lines of vines and olive trees and the yellow sunflower fields. And always the cicadas, the trill sound of their rattling tails adding to the atmosphere of heat and haze.

* * *

Ioan soon fell asleep after the exertions of pitching the tent, unloading their things and cooking supper. But Rhiannon lay awake for a long time, listening to the rain against the canvas. Eventually she dozed but woke some hours later, hot inside her sleeping bag. She slid out and realised the rain had stopped. Carefully so as not to wake Ioan she undid the string that held the tent flaps closed and stepped outside.

Now she was slowly walking along the shore, luxuriating in the warm night air that was blowing from the sea. On an impulse she took off her shirt, kicked away her sandals and waded into the water leaving a florescent bubbling wake behind her. If anything it was warmer in than out. Rhiannon swam with a strong stroke into the current before stopping to make sure she was not out of her depth. Her foot touched the sea floor. Then she turned on her back, floated and stared at the night sky far above. It was a great luminous arc curving from the inland mountain range and then outwards over the bay. The darkness of the land and the sea only served to magnify the brightness of the stars that glittered in their infinite distance. Contemplating the huge emptiness, for once Rhiannon had no thoughts or questions, no agony at the prospect of a ruptured future that so often preoccupied her. Instead she just drifted, living inside the moment.

* * *

Soon after first light they broke camp and left what they discovered was the Mas Larrieu nature reserve and drove a few miles south to Argelès-sur-Mer where they found a café overlooking the sea. After breakfast they headed inland, into the foothills of the Pyrenees looking for Sant Miquel de Cuixà, a Benedictine monastery where the summer school was being held.

Their first sight of the abbey was its four-storey bell tower faced with pink marble stone rising amidst the hills leading to Mount Canigou.

'It's the largest preserved pre-Romanesque church in France,' Rhiannon said, studying a guidebook.

'I thought it was supposed to be Catalan.'

'Well it was, still is really. Depends whose side you're on, I suppose. It says here it was founded in 878 and for centuries was in the control of the Counts of Barcelona. It only passed over to France in 1659 as part of the Treaty of the Pyrenees.'

'So it's French then.'

'This is a part of Catalunya that's in France you could say, what they call Roussillon. But it's still Catalunya culturally speaking. Catalan is still spoken.'

'A bit like the northern Basque Country which is this side of the Pyrenees, in France.'

'Yes, all these frontiers are artificial really.'

'But as you say, it depends which side you're on.'

* * *

When they arrived, the monastery courtyard was bustling with young people making their way into a refectory where a long trestle table was set up with benches on either side. They were in time for lunch.

For a while the visitors stood uncertainly in the courtyard by their car until a dark-haired, heavily featured woman approached them.

'You must be Rhiannon,' she said pointing at the car's number plate, her face lightening as she smiled. 'I am Marta Pessarrodona, your translator.'

Holding out a hand she continued, 'Very few people here speak English. It's Catalan, French, Italian, Spanish, but no English. But me? I studied in England. I love England, Stratford and your Shakespeare, and Germany, too, especially Berlin.'

'You speak German as well?' Ioan queried.

'Yes, but not very well.'

She explained she lived in Barcelona where she was a teacher.

'But really I am a poet. That is my vocation.'

In the refectory they queued for a bowl of thick pea and ham broth, bread and cheese. The conference was being organised by the Escarré Centre for Ethnic Minorities and Nationalities based in Barcelona.

'Who was Escarré?' Ioan asked.

'Aureli Maria Escarré was the abbot of Montserrat which is near Barcelona,' Marta told him. 'He was abbot during the civil war and fled to Italy for a while. But he returned and made Montserrat the beacon for Catalan hopes. For the most part he remained on good terms with the régime, even with Franco himself. After all, they supported the church. But that changed when, famously he gave the interview to *Le Monde*, in 1963 I think it was.'

'What did he say?' Rhiannon asked.

'Oh, nothing you would think so remarkable these days. That Catalunya is a nation among the Spanish nationalities, that we have our own personality, that kind of thing. But he did say that Catalan should be allowed in our schools and in the media. Because that was forbidden, he said Spain was a state that didn't obey the principles of Christianity. He said that when a language is lost, religion tends to be lost as well.'

'I can't see Franco liking that much,' Ioan said, breaking off a piece of bread.

'No, especially as the ideology of the Franco's regime was National Catholicism. They immediately closed the Omnium Cultural down.'

'Omnium Cultural?' Rhiannon asked.

'How do you say? It was an organisation established by Catalan business people to teach Catalan. In a way it was an alternative to a political party in Franco's time. Anyway, they made it illegal. Then in 1965 Escarré was forced into exile, to a monastery near Milan. And in 1968 they made him resign as abbot as well and not long afterwards, he died. As he used to say, *Spain despises everything it ignores.* He was quoting the poet Antonio Machado.'

At that point a mild-looking man of about forty in a white open-necked shirt and slacks appeared at their table. He rested one hand on Marta Pessarrodona's shoulder and stretched his other to Rhiannon and Ioan in greeting.

'This is Aureli,' Marta said. 'Aureli Argemí, the director of CIEMEN.'

'CIEMEN,' Ioan repeated.

'Yes, the Escarré Centre.'

'You are most welcome,' Argemí said but broke off, smiling again. 'My English…' He turned, spoke rapidly to Marta, and then with another wave of his hand disappeared.

'He organises everything,' Marta explained without waiting for a question. 'He founded CIEMEN about four years ago, in 1974. He is a monk but CIEMEN is his main task now. He was Escarré's secretary at Montserrat and went with him into exile. When Escarré died Aureli came here to Cuixà. Then after Franco's death three years ago he was able to return to Montserrat.'

The conference was to be opened with a speech by Aureli himself. Rhiannon and Ioan followed Marta and found seats at the back of the large central church. It was an impressive airy space. Bare stone walls reared upwards and then soared into horseshoe-shaped arches.

'Despite it being so old the place has excellent acoustics,' Marta whispered. 'Pablo Casals often played concerts here. After the civil war he lived close by, in Prades.'

Wooden benches placed in wide circles around a central dais were soon filled up by scores of excited young people, talking and laughing. They were dressed as if they were going to the beach. Argemí soon appeared and approached a rostrum on the platform. He raised his hands for silence and began to speak in a quiet, measured way. His words effortlessly carried to the four corners of the church, seemingly borne aloft by the stone arches above.

'He's saying that in our sessions over the coming week we shall be hearing from speakers from Euskadi...'

'The Basque Country,' Rhiannon whispered to Ioan.

'Yes, and from Friuli. That's an autonomous region in northern Italy. And from the Flemish, and the Jura.'

Ioan looked puzzled.

'Jura's a Canton in Switzerland,' Rhiannon whispered again.

'From Yugoslavia, from Québec, from Valencia, the Balearic Islands and of course Catalunya itself...' Marta paused and strained forward to listen. 'And now he's talking about you,' she said smiling.

'What's he saying?' Ioan asked.

'I'll tell you later. Now he's going on to talk about the need to protect linguistic diversity, but not he says within – how do you say? – not within a framework of cultural rights. Languages don't have rights he says. It is individuals who have rights. It is for that reason that we distinguish between languages and cultures. It is individuals and societies that have the linguistic rights, not the cultures themselves. That's why linguistic diversity needs to be protected within the framework of human rights. That's what he's saying.'

*   *   *

At dinner that evening Rhiannon and Ioan found themselves placed next to Miquel Strubell, a lecturer in socio-linguistics at the University of Barcelona, the only other fluent English-speaker in the gathering. Indeed, his English was so good Ioan told him he thought he was English.

'You even look like an Englishman,' he said.

'It's true I am half-English,' Strubell conceded. 'My father is

English, though my mother is Catalan. I was born in Oxford and we moved to Catalunya when I was eight years old in 1957. Later I studied in Oxford. So in some ways you might say I am English, but I am mainly Catalan I think. Half-and-half perhaps.'

'Catalunya and England, a good alliance,' Rhiannon said.

'Well it is true, our countries have often been allies, not least in the Napoleonic wars.'

Ioan said he found the range of languages among the people at the gathering extraordinary.

'It's normal,' Strubell said. 'Apart from Catalan and English I can speak Spanish of course, but also French and Italian.'

'Do you use Catalan every day, at work and so on?' Rhiannon asked.

'Oh yes, in the university in Barcelona, and in Palamós a little up the coast where we have a place we go to at weekends, not too far from here as a matter of fact. And that is despite use of the language not being permitted in schools until the Franco regime came to an end three years ago. Only very rarely do I come across someone who doesn't understand me. A couple of months ago, a young Chinese man in a bar, for instance. I imagine he'd only just moved to Catalunya.'

'I've heard that nearly half of the population was born outside the region,' Ioan said.

'Country,' Rhiannon corrected him.

'He's right,' Miquel said. 'Catalunya is one of the most industrial parts of Spain and for that reason has long attracted workers from elsewhere, especially Andalusia. But since the end of the civil war it's been the Spanish government's policy to encourage immigration. Over the past twenty years perhaps a million people have come in.'

'That must have caused big problems,' Rhiannon said.

'Indeed. It's been on such a huge scale that at times we've

been incapable of housing all the new arrivals. Shanty towns mushroomed around Barcelona for a while, though most of them have now disappeared. Still, hundreds of thousands of non-Catalan workers live in what used to be quiet little towns around Barcelona, places like Terrassa, Sabadell, Badalonas, and L'Hospitalet. They're packed with Castilian speakers.'

'Leaving Catalans in a minority?'

'A recent study showed that in these places only about thirty per cent of primary school-children speak Catalan at home. They are cultural ghettoes where Catalan is not the everyday language of most of the people.'

'Something similar happened in our industrial Valleys,' Ioan said. 'The opening up of coal mines led to a massive inflow of people from England.'

'You can't really compare the two places, though,' Rhiannon said.

'It's true there are differences,' Miquel agreed. 'In comparison with Welsh it seems to me the Catalan language enjoys considerable prestige amongst the bulk of the population. And it remains strong because of that. But still, what happened to Welsh should be a warning for us. That link between land and language, which in our case has lasted for a thousand years, that link is in danger of being broken.'

'The link between land and language,' Rhiannon repeated. 'You're right, that's the essence of it. I'm planning to talk about the same thing.'

'But you get the impression that Catalan is in a strong position, certainly when compared with other minority languages around Europe,' Ioan said.

'You can't really describe Catalan as a minority language,' Miquel objected. 'More people speak Catalan than speak Danish, Norwegian or Finnish. It's spoken by around seven million people. And generally, the tendency is for incomers who speak only Spanish to become absorbed, certainly by the second generation.'

'That is certainly different from the situation in Wales,' Rhiannon said.

'As I say, Catalan enjoys a high status. It's the language of the well-off and the boss, and therefore looks desirable to the incomer. Working-class immigration has pushed Catalans up the social ladder. It has enhanced the social status of our language and culture.'

'And not because of any intrinsic merit, would you say?' Ioan asked mischievously.

'Well, you're right about that. But the reality is that a large majority of immigrants want their children to grow up speaking Catalan. And until quite recently the only way they could was in the playground or in the street. Catalan was banned from the schools, and virtually everywhere else, the mass media, public events and so on, until only a few years ago.'

'Until Franco died in 1975,' Rhiannon said.

'That's right.'

'I wonder if the Welsh language would be in a stronger position if it had been banned?'

'The main thing is not to lose heart,' Miquel told her. 'I always think of what one of our greatest historians wrote years ago.'

'Who?'

'Jaume Vicens Vives.' Miquel paused and cast his eyes upwards. 'Can I recall what he said?'

Then he spoke from memory.

> Ancient peoples have tough and deep roots. Many years may pass without any flowers appearing on branches broken by wind and frost. But under the ground, like a plant, they continue to work

and accumulate reserves. Despite the appearance of death, they are alive and one day their vital force will begin to flow again.

'That fits us Catalans very well, I think, and perhaps you Welsh also.'

* * *

A few days later, as the conference resumed for a morning session it was time for Rhiannon's contribution. Aureli Argemí was already standing at the lectern when she entered the church. He motioned that she should join him on the platform. She wore a burgundy red dress, purposely brought for the occasion, which perfectly set off her hair. Reaching to her feet, the dress gave her a striking presence.

As the church filled up Argemí began speaking in fast-flowing Catalan and Rhiannon realised he was introducing her. She caught the name of Frantz Fanon and a reference to the Algerian revolution. 'He must be talking about my research,' she thought. In fact, he was referring back to his message at the opening session about human rights. The French relationship with Algeria had been a classic case of human rights being framed in a way that ignored a community's national identity. The Algerians would be allowed their human rights only to the extent that they spoke the French language and adopted French citizenship.

But then Rhiannon sensed Aureli was speaking once more directly about herself. Suddenly, to her surprise the conference erupted into a long round of applause. She lent forward, puzzlement filling her face. Argemí smiled, took a step and embraced her, kissing her expansively on both cheeks.

This provoked more applause, much to Rhiannon's acute embarrassment. Later she was told that he had been explaining that she had only recently been released from prison.

She had resolved to talk about Cymdeithas yr Iaith's campaign. Why else would they have invited her? She spoke of the literary tradition and how it stretched far back to the sixth century. Saunders Lewis, who she described as the greatest living Welsh writer, judged Welsh literature to be among the most important in Europe during the Middle Ages. He claimed the language had an aristocratic lineage, sharing with French, Spanish and Italian a close relationship with Latin. But first she complimented her hosts for inviting a representative from Wales.

'We are becoming increasingly aware of the importance of establishing international links,' she said. 'One recent event, if I may call it that, was the publication by one of our writers Meic Stephens, of his book *Linguistic Minorities in Western Europe*. It describes the cultural and political situation of more than fifty linguistic minorities in sixteen states across Western Europe.'

But then she checked herself and added, to laughter when it was translated, 'Of course, I've learnt since I've been here, indeed I've been told in no uncertain terms, that you cannot describe Catalan as a minority language.'

The laughter allowed Rhiannon a moment to gather her thoughts. She was standing directly beneath the ancient church's high Romanesque arches. The wooden benches were packed with young people but even so her voice echoed against the stone walls of the nave. More disconcerting was having to stop every few minutes to allow her words to be translated. It put her off her stride and made what she had to say feel disjointed. Speaking in English in public did not come naturally either.

She had placed her notes on the lectern in front of her. But she had read them over so many times that she knew them off by heart. While she was speaking, Rhiannon could hear murmured whispers through the church, but these hushed as soon as Marta Pessarrodona began translating. Marta spoke Catalan in low, husky tones that all the same sounded mesmerising.

Rhiannon explained how Welsh had retreated as a community language through the twentieth century until it was a normal part of daily life in just the rural areas of the north and west. Nevertheless, these areas were fundamental to the future. Only where the language was used on a day-to-day basis could it retain its energy and inventiveness, could it adapt and change. Its continuance as a living language in these areas was essential to encourage those outside to want to learn it. It was the base from where it could be possible to reach out and re-establish Welsh over the whole land of Wales.

Rhiannon stopped again to let the translator do her work, and then plunged into what she thought her most important message, one she hoped would resonate with her audience. This was the bond between land and language, for her the very root of Welsh identity.

'A people achieve their connection with the land through the language they use in their daily lives,' she declared.

She paused, to allow the translator to intervene.

'The same is true, I know, of the relationship between land, people and language in Catalunya, of life lived through the language on the land over generations.'

There were murmurs of affirmation. Emboldened, Rhiannon pressed on, now referring to the Welsh philosopher J.R. Jones.

'In Wales, the remains of this bond I am talking about are in those districts where Welsh is still in this sense the language of the land. It is because of this living language in the restricted foothold that remains to it, that we are a *people*. Every inch of it is beyond price.'

She explained that J.R. Jones had insisted that the language was of just as much importance to non-Welsh-speakers because it was one of the structural ties that bound all Welsh people together. In its connection with the land the Welsh language shaped a spiritual unity of the people as a whole.

'J.R. Jones tells us that the importance of the Welsh language is not so much as a means of communication, but as the vessel in which the tradition of our inheritance is held. It has been enriched by accumulation over the centuries. All the past culture of the people is stored up in the language. It is the core of our separate Welsh identity, this bond between the Welsh language and our space of earth between England and the Irish Sea.'

As Rhiannon stopped in mid-flow to allow her words to be translated, she could see that she had her audience's rapt attention.

'In present-day Wales, English is now performing many of the functional roles of a language – in commerce, in education, in broadcasting, and in public life generally. This reality leads us to understand what is the one essential role of the Welsh language. Its essential task, one that no other language can do, is no less than to save the separate identity of the Welsh as a *people*.'

Leaving another moment for the translator, Rhiannon brought her message to a close.

'It is for these reasons that we cannot think of our language as just a matter of choice. We cannot think of it as some kind of optional thing to have. We cannot say it is something that might be worth keeping up. No! There is no way that the Welsh nation can survive and keep its distinctive, separate identity without the language.'

Rhiannon stood silently for a moment, fighting back an emotion that was gathering at the back of her throat.

'Our standpoint is simply this,' she cried finally, her voice gaining a passionate edge. 'There would be no reality to a self-governing Wales, even one possessed of every possible political institution, if we did not also have the Welsh language.'

With this she sat back on the bench alongside Argemí who, she saw, was smiling warmly as Marta Pessarrodona reached the final few sentences of the translation. He then stood up to speak but was interrupted by a wave of applause, whistles and cheers as Rhiannon's audience spontaneously rose to their feet.

*　*　*

That evening after dinner, the young people surged along the colonnades into the Abbey's grassy central square where they sat in groups talking quietly as dusk fell. Rather than cooling, the coming of the darkness brought an enveloping warmth with a breeze that flowed gently but constantly up the hillsides from the sea.

Rhiannon and Ioan, with Marta Pessarrodona alongside, found themselves in a small group with Aureli Argemí at its centre. He took Rhiannon's arm and, signalling to Marta as he did so, spoke quietly but insistently.

'Aureli is saying how much he appreciated your talk this morning,' Marta told her. 'He says, I think one could put it like this, he says you captured the spirit of CIEMEN.'

Rhiannon smiled. 'Ask him to tell us about it, how it came about.'

Marta and Argemí spoke for some time.

'He says it was founded in Italy, in Milan, where he had been in exile with Escarré,' Marta translated. 'After a few years Aureli moved the office to Sant Miquel de Cuixà. The Monastery had been re-established in the mid-sixties by monks from Montserrat, so it was natural while Franco was alive that CIEMEN should make its home here. This summer school is the third that's been held, it's one of the Centre's most important initiatives.'

By this time another group of young people, one of them carrying a guitar, had joined them and they started singing quietly. After a while the singing stopped and the young person with the guitar started to play a slow, plaintive but penetrating melody that echoed against the walls above. It caused the other groups to quieten and listen.

Rhiannon was captivated by the sound and looked questioningly at Marta. '*El Cant dels Ocells*,' she said. '"The Song of the Birds", a traditional Catalan lullaby. Casals made it famous. He played it at all his concerts, in front of the General Assembly of the United Nations in New York and in the White House. He said it was the soul of Catalonia.'

There was silence as the last notes died away. Aureli looked at the young people gathered round him and spoke a few words. 'He's quoting Casals,' Marta whispered. 'He used to say, we are leaves on a tree and the tree is all humanity. A musician, as every man, must take part in the movement of the world.'

By now the guitar was being passed from hand to hand, with some playing the odd chords, until eventually, it came to rest with Rhiannon. She fingered the strings quietly, pausing to tune it.

'Give them a song Rhi,' Ioan urged.

Quietly at first she started a rhythm on the guitar, began to hum and eventually broke into song. It was very different to the Catalan lullaby, more strident and defiant, a declaration made more emphatic by Rhiannon's flushed face and tangled, wind-blown hair. She was confident now, in full flight, oblivious to those listening, just caught in the melody's ebb and flow and the rhythm that her fingers were driving forward on the guitar.

'*Don't ask your stupid questions*,' Rhiannon sang when she

came to the chorus. '*I know what freedom is, I know what the truth is, I know what love is...*'

And as she was singing, the thought went through her mind that music was so much easier and clearer in conveying the meaning of things. It enforced simplicity. 'That's where the genius lies,' she thought. 'Music tells you what's in the soul. You only have to feel to understand. But if you try and put it into words, it just becomes complicated.'

*   *   *

Early the next day, before dawn, Rhiannon woke in the dormitory she was sharing with about a dozen other young women in the abbey. She lay on top of a bunk bed trying but failing to get back to sleep. After a while she climbed carefully down the ladder and crept outside, taking a linen shawl and drawing it round her shoulders.

The air was still warm. Rhiannon walked in bare feet down a corridor to a door that led outside. She opened it. The moon cast shadows behind the pillars that lined the colonnade. In the distance she heard the sound of an owl. Eventually she came to the courtyard where they had gathered the previous evening.

Sitting on a low wall Rhiannon gazed across at the mountains. They encircled the monastery, their tall ridges sharp against the moonlit sky. The stars were less bright than when she had been swimming a few nights earlier, but appeared larger and more luminous. 'It must be because they seem closer to the land here,' Rhiannon thought, drawing her knees to her chest and wrapping her arms around them.

She thought of the past few days, and the people she had met. 'How can you compare their lives with people living at home?' she wondered. 'The Catalans with their suffering and oppression under Franco, and ourselves who are just left alone? No wonder we're apathetic.'

Rhiannon considered the passion and commitment of the Catalans. How could you arouse such resistance in the Welsh people who, by comparison, failed to realise how much they had to lose?

'The Welsh people have lost their memory, that's the trouble,' Rhiannon decided. 'It's only if we keep our memory that we can find meaning. We must have a rootedness in space and time.'

Gazing across at the mountains and the stars enveloping them in a soft, shimmering light, Rhiannon continued to wrestle with these ideas.

'We need a sense of time that is greater than our own lives,' she thought. 'We stand in a flood of time, in a track that spans the ages. That's what give things their meaning, their purpose.'

As she dwelt on these notions the apparent nearness of the heavens and their myriad stars gave added weight and substance to a conviction that was settling in her mind. For Rhiannon at that moment the stars seemed to illuminate a truth that she felt to be at the very core of her being.

The Black Hill
October 1978

During a dinner at Jesus, his Cambridge college, Raymond
Williams had a heart attack. Or rather it was a tremor, a
harbinger of what was to come. It was a sickening feeling, a
sweatiness, a long constriction of breath, and then a rising
heavy pulse through his neck and shoulders. He hunched and
sat stiffly, clenched his hands and waited for the feeling to pass.
Mercifully it did, almost as quickly as it had come. But it was
enough to make him retreat to his room and lie back in his chair
for a long while, stretching away from his desk.

He saw his doctor the next day and was referred to hospital
for tests. Afterwards he said he felt fine but was recommended
moderate exercise, a change in his diet, and above all, urged to cut
down on smoking. He recalled how his father had been similarly
stricken, but made light of it, and resumed his normal routine.

Later in the year Raymond realised the attack might have
been the trigger for the quite exceptional levels of anxiety he
was feeling. He couldn't at all understand his state of mind.
At times it felt like a form of mental paralysis. His normal
discipline fell away. He struggled with day-to-day work. About
the only productive thing he could do was garden. After thirty-
odd years of writing, on a daily basis most of the time, he was
left feeling strange and worried.

He realised, too, that the lengthy series of interviews about
his work he was undertaking with the editors of *New Left
Review*, friends really, had been destabilising. The process
had forced him to reconsider his life. It had stirred sediments
in his memory that floated to the surface. For the first time
he felt his confidence, his habitual slow and steady certainty,
was wavering.

In one interview, Perry Anderson, the Review's editor, had asked a question about his soon-to-be-published novel *The Fight for Manod*. He had taken Raymond to task for what he felt was the book's fatalism.

'It seems to give an undercurrent of sadness to the book that is unlike its predecessors,' Anderson had said.

'A certain sadness, yes, but there's no term for it, really,' he'd answered. 'It's not nostalgia. Indeed, it's the opposite of that and distinctly different from the confidence in the future many of us have had, and that I've often written to try to restore.'

He'd called such confidence 'crucial', but in truth such a thing, once lost, was not easily regained. For Wales, it meant passing through the devastating experiences of war and depression, of the disintegration of a previously unproblematic labour movement. For Raymond himself, it was all of that, compounded by his own sense of a more personal erosion.

He'd referred to the experience of ageing. 'I don't so much mean myself,' he had said, 'though I've felt it at times, but in a few people I know very well and deeply respect, who have fought and fought and quite clearly expected in their lifetime, their active lifetime even, that there would be decisive breaks to the future.'

The interviewers had also asked about his earlier work, particularly his first novel. In it Raymond had portrayed his father at the time of his last illness. And now he recalled his sense of bewilderment on seeing his father, who he had always thought of as strong and confident, suddenly weaken, his interest in the world around him retreating.

Raymond had written all this tellingly at the time, but with a sense of detachment. It was as though he was observing a scene in which he was not directly involved. But now it hit him with a sense of finality. His account of his father's decline was intimately about himself. That, he thought, was the source of his anxiety. Might he be prevented from going on, from completing his work? Might he lose the inner sense of urgency that had always impelled him forward?

Haunting him, as well, was a feeling that he was destined always to be on the losing side. Solidarity, mutuality, fight, opposition, and equal shares in difficulty were his essential values. He had internalised them from his father and the small, isolated community of his upbringing. He had always believed that over the long cycle of the generations they would come through. He still did. But the evidence was discouraging.

*   *   *

'You'd better borrow some walking boots,' Raymond told Owen, fishing out a pair from a box in the porch at the back of the cottage in Craswall. 'It's pretty boggy up there. And you'll need a waterproof as well.'

It was late October when Owen had come to interview him about his forthcoming novel, the third in what was being called his Welsh trilogy. Raymond had suggested they climb the hill above his cottage. They could talk as they walked, he said, adding with a smile that Owen would just have to remember their conversation.

They took Owen's car a few miles south, and left it where the walk started on the southern slope overlooking the Olchon valley. At first the going was steep, but eventually the path levelled out into a series of rocky ledges like giant steps leading to the summit. On the first of these they stopped and looked out at the landscape spreading away towards Hereford.

Raymond took out his pipe, knocked it against the palm of his hand and began filling it with tobacco.

'All this is a world away from Cambridge,' Owen said. 'What was it like when you first went there? I was struck by what you said at that meeting where you were interviewed in Cardiff, that you weren't at all overawed by it.'

'It wasn't that easy at first you know. In fact, I was wholly unprepared. I knew nothing about it, you see. I was pretty isolated among the rest of my age group. They'd been geared up from birth, their boarding schools and so on.'

Raymond stopped and sucked at his pipe, and then removed it as he exhaled the smoke.

'My father went on ahead to sort out my lodgings. At Trinity the porter asked whether my name was already down. "Yes", my father said, "since last autumn." "Last autumn," the porter replied. "Many of them, you know, are put down at birth." I remember sitting on the benches in Hall, surrounded by those people and wishing they *had* been put down at birth.'

Owen laughed.

'But all the same you stayed. When you were talking with Carwyn James it seemed as if you were a bit seduced by the place.'

'Not really. Not at all, as a matter of fact. When I went there first, it was winter and that wasn't particularly seductive, especially if you've grown up in this more climatically civilised part of the country. Those east winds blowing off the fens, you know. But, I came to realise that Cambridge offered something that was intellectually important. That's why I stayed. The arguments and the contestation I'm interested in happens in places like Cambridge.'

'And after all, it is attractive, isn't it? I mean it's a beautiful place.'

'It's more naturally beautiful here, I always think. It's obvious isn't it, that places like Cambridge that have accumulated so much capital are bound to have beautiful things. But very little of it is natural. It's the result of wealth being poured in, generation after generation. All those fine buildings and fine gardens.'

'You can't ignore them.'

'But I always have mixed feelings about it, like I do when I'm looking at castles here in Wales. I mean you can see they're beautiful castles, but you also remember what they were put here for.'

They walked on and upwards until they reached the rock-strewn heights of the ridge which narrowed and then broadened out, the land to the north slowly rising towards the horizon in the far distance.

'It's extraordinary to think that this is the highest point in the whole of southern England,' Raymond said.

Owen looked down into the narrow Olchon valley where a thin single track connected isolated farm buildings. Turning, he gazed eastwards into the widening English lowlands, the fields becoming larger as they receded towards the Malvern Hills. It felt like standing at the central compass point of a hemisphere, while the outer arm scanned the horizon from the north, swinging round to the south and revealing the glittering line of the Bristol Channel.

'In Welsh the hill's known as Twyn Llech,' Raymond said. 'Hill of stone or, perhaps more accurately, hill of slate I suppose you could say. The ridge we're traversing is Crib y Gath, what the English call the Cat's Back, because from a distance that's exactly what it looks like, a bristling arch.'

Turning again Owen's saw a steep ridge extending far to the south. It rose like a military rampart against the land below. The moorland descended steeply from the glacier-carved mountain edge until about halfway down it reached the farms, where the grass fought for space with the bracken.

'That's Hatterall Ridge,' Raymond said, following Owen's

eye. 'Along the crest is Offa's Dyke path and the Welsh border. That's where we're heading.'

They pressed on until the hill widened and flattened, and the land became boggy, with heather interspersed by pools of brackish water. They skirted the curved top of the Olchon valley and struck upwards and directly westwards to join Hatterall Ridge. Raymond led the way, through broken ground with only the odd sheep track to guide them. Eventually they reached the top, marked by the well-trodden Offa's Dyke path, and set out on it, now heading northwards. Great waves of open moorland hilltops stretched into Wales as far as they could see. Owen thought they looked like the backs of great whales.

'Beyond are the Brecon Beacons,' Raymond said 'On a clearer day you can see Pen-y-Fan.' He pointed downwards. 'That's the Vale of Ewyas leading to Capel-y-Ffin and Llanthony. Giraldus Cambrensis wrote that it was encircled on all sides by lofty mountains, but only an arrowshot broad. The road you can see there, leading over the mountain to Hay, is the highest in Wales. It's known as Gospel Pass.'

'Why is that?'

'It depends on who you believe. One version is that it comes from St Paul who was brought to the pass by the daughter of Caradog whom he had previously met in Rome. Another is that it derives from the twelfth century and the passage of Crusaders through here, preaching and fundraising.'

They followed the path as it descended about a hundred feet over rocks that Raymond explained were called Llech y Lladron. 'It means the Robber's Stone, though why it's called that I've no idea, except to surmise that some skulduggery went on here.'

They went on further until they reached Hay Bluff, a high outcrop overlooking the Wye Valley that provided views far to the north and west. The height they had reached meant that the landscape had widened to a full circle. Above them the light came from the sky with a new intensity. In the far distance, the horizon merged with a thin line of clouds.

Here they sat against a large triangulation point that offered a backrest. Raymond took off a small rucksack and reached inside for bread and cheese wrapped in greaseproof paper. He offered some to Owen. For a while they were silent until, eventually, Raymond placed his right hand palm down on the ground between them, raised his hand and spread his thumb and fingers.

'I think of my hand as representing the Black Mountains, the fingers pointing south. The hand is the plateau. The thumb is the Black Hill and the Cat's Back we walked earlier.'

Owen listened closely against a blustering wind as he spoke.

'Six rivers rise from my wrist. The first, Mynwy, flows at the outside edge of my thumb. The Olchon flows between my thumb and first finger to join the Mynwy. The third, the Honddu, flows between my first and second fingers and then curves to join the Mynwy as well. The fourth river, the Grwyne Fawr, flows between my second and third finger and then curves the other way, south, to join the fifth river, the Grwyne Fechan, that has been flowing between my third and little finger.'

'And the sixth river?'

'That's the Rhiangoll that flows at the outside edge of my little finger to join the Usk.'

'And your fingers are the whaleback ridges we can see.'

'Yes. I like to think of this region as being held in an all-encompassing hand, through which the generations have flowed in a timeless sequence. I'm thinking of it as a setting for a long-running novel, one that will trace the history of the different peoples who have inhabited this place since the earliest times.'

'Your long revolution stretches very far back.'

'But that's exactly the point, don't you think?'

Raymond leant forward and plucked a few blades of grass with his fingers.

'The very survival of people in a place like this means there must be hope for the future.'

'You mean the sense of place that binds people to the land.'

'It's more than that. It's the way we relate to place, with our sense of the presence of the past.'

'And the future?'

'Yes, the future. Well, the depth of our past gives us hope for the future anyway, optimism even, and the way we make that future, now, here, today. It came to me strongly earlier this year when I was working on a lecture about the writers who emerged in the mining Valleys in the twenties and thirties.'

'People like Lewis Jones and Jack Jones.'

'Those, but it was Gwyn Thomas I was thinking of especially.'

'But didn't that period just lead us into a dead end? The General Strike and then the months of the lockout and after that the long years of depression. How can all that be connected with any sense of optimism?'

'It's true that the defeat became fused with a more general sadness of a ravaged, subordinated and depressed Wales. That's reflected in the novels, of course. But there was also the intense consciousness of the struggle – the militancy and the fidelity – and that inheritance continues.'

'But I don't see where you find any sense of hope for the future in what, after all, was still a defeat.'

'I think it's there in the novels if you look hard enough. You find it in the sense of place, ultimately the sense of Wales, the distinctive physical character of Wales as a whole.'

Raymond paused, reflecting.

'Of course, the immediate landscape in the era of steam and coal was almost invariably dark and smoke-ridden. In the mines those general qualities were intensified. The darkness, the running grime, the sense of a huddled enclosure.'

'There's not much hope in that, surely?'

'But don't you see, for the miners coming back up from the pit, to the daylight there was the profoundly different yet immediately accessible landscape of open hills and the sky above them, of a rising light and of clear expansion. It seems to me that those experiences of the hills above us are effective in so much Welsh feeling and thought.'

'Perhaps you're right.'

'And in the specific environment of these Welsh valleys, they have a further particular effect. There are sheep on the hills, often straying down into the streets of the settlements.'

Owen laughed.

'Those sheep aren't always popular, you know, what they get up to.'

'Yes, but they're evidence of the pastoral life, not just in the past but also in the present and the future. As I say, they combine with that sense of the hills and the skyline that can be seen from the streets and the pit-tops – a presence that manifests itself not only in a consciousness of history but in aspirations and possibilities for the future as well. That's what I think, anyway.'

*   *   *

They gathered their things. Raymond donned his rucksack, and they began to retrace their steps. They walked for a while without speaking, until Owen broke the silence.

'I wanted to ask you about your new novel.'

'*The Fight for Manod.*'

'Yes. It seems to me your most strongly felt piece of Welsh writing that you've produced. To what extent would you say it reflects the way your thinking about Wales has changed?'

Raymond stopped, took his pipe from his mouth and began refilling it with some tobacco he found in his pocket.

'Well, yes you're right, a big change started to happen from the late sixties. There was a continuity, of course, in a quite overwhelming feeling about the land of Wales, as I've been saying.'

'I can see that.'

'And then I began having many more contacts with Welsh writers and intellectuals, all highly political in the best tradition of the culture, and I found this curious effect.'

They continued walking, with Owen keeping closely alongside, anxious that he might miss something.

'You say a curious effect.'

'Suddenly England, bourgeois England, wasn't my point of reference any more. I was a Welsh European, and both levels felt different.'

Owen hesitated for a moment, before asking, 'In what way were they different?'

'I can hardly describe the difference of relating now with writers and political comrades in Wales. Of course, we're are all hard up against it. From outside the situation here is seen as an expression of a remarkable vitality, and so objectively it is.'

'I don't see it like that."

'You're right, of course, from your perspective. From the inside, we're living through a hard, fierce, disputacious and bitterly contested time.'

'I can recognise that alright.'

'It's where I'm placed as well, and where I can now see that in the truest sense I'm from.'

They continued walking again for a while, until Owen said, 'I suppose by the bitterly contested time you mean the politics, the arguments we're having over the language, devolution…'

Raymond stopped, mulling over what Owen had said. He

gazed thoughtfully at the horizon, then took his pipe in his hand, exhaling a trail of smoke.

'Well, now then. Through the intricacies of the politics, and they are intricate, aren't they? You should know. Anyhow, through the intricacies I want the Welsh people to defeat, override or bypass bourgeois England. After all, we're still a radical and cultured people.'

'You're envisaging something completely different, then, to make that possible?'

'Yes, it follows from the intricacies. It connects for me with the sense in my work that I am now necessarily European, that the people to the left and on the left of the French and Italian communist parties, the German and Scandinavian comrades, the communist dissidents from the East like Bahro, they're my kind of people, the people I come from and belong to.'

'But how exactly does Wales fit into all these relationships you speak of?'

Raymond looked back from where they had come and then turned to look at Owen. He placed a hand on his shoulder.

'This is how I feel it. My more conscious Welshness is my way of learning these connections. It comes across strongly to me, for instance, when Welsh-speaking nationalists tell me how thoroughly Welsh *Border Country* and the social thinking are. I used not to realise that, you know.'

'It's always seemed Welsh to me.'

'There you are. The same is true when they offer recognition of the whole range of my work, which literally none of my English colleagues has seen a chance of making sense of.'

Raymond paused to re-light his pipe. He struck a match, shielding the flame with his hand against the wind, and smiled at Owen.

'Then I'm in a culture where I can breathe,' he said.

Epynt
January to March 1979

As the date of the referendum approached, Leo Abse found himself in great demand at meetings across Wales. Weekends were fully taken up and he was required to venture out of London during the week as well. His rousing style and inflammatory language caught the headlines and projected him as the leading voice of the No campaign.

'The fear of English-speaking Wales is that a Welsh-speaking bureaucratic élite will be the new masters of Wales,' he declared on platform after platform. 'Sooner a Home Counties Oxbridge permanent secretary in Whitehall than the man from Machynlleth in Cardiff.'

Abse's leadership of the No campaign prompted Duncan Gardiner, the *Western Mail*'s editor, to instruct Owen to produce a profile of him. 'We've got to be seen to be giving an equal shout to both sides,' he said. 'Anyhow, it'll be a chance to probe him a bit more, don't you think?'

They met on a Sunday morning at Abse's home in Cyncoed in the northern suburbs of Cardiff. It was an affluent setting, befitting the successful solicitor and MP. The red-brick Edwardian house was set well back from a tree-lined road that led towards the hills encircling the city.

As he advanced up the drive towards the house, standing splendidly in its well-tended gardens, Owen reflected ruefully on the origins of the MP's wealth. An outer door to a large, glass-covered porch was open and Owen stepped inside. He waited for a while after pulling a cord attached to a loud bell. He was somewhat disconcerted by the warmth of Abse's greeting as the main door opened. There was an expansive hallway and Owen was directed into a large, book-lined study alongside.

'You'll have coffee?' Abse asked, and without waiting for an answer disappeared into the kitchen. He was alone in the house and would be driving back to London later in the day. He had spoken at three meetings the previous evening, in Bedwellty and Caerphilly, and in his own Pontypool constituency.

After a while he brought in a tray and gestured Owen to take a seat on a low settee along one wall. He sat himself in a leather chair that he pulled away from his desk. Between them a gas fire hissed quietly.

'I imagine we won't see eye to eye on what you want to talk about,' he said. 'But all the same I'm glad of the chance to have an airing in the *Western Mail*.'

Owen took out his notebook.

'Do you have any sympathy at all with the *concept* of devolution?' he began. 'It seems to me to be essentially about spreading out power in a more democratic way.'

'Yes, certainly, if what you are talking about is decentralisation. But if you speak in terms of economic devolution, what links my constituency in any way with Anglesey?'

Abse began in reasoned tones but as he warmed to this theme his voice took on a higher pitch.

'I can see that Welshness of a certain type is common to my constituency and to Anglesey. But economically, I find it ludicrous to put Anglesey and Pontypool together. The fact is that Gwent's future is tied to London and Bristol far more than it can ever possibly be with Anglesey. And in the same way with north Wales as a whole, it is quite clear that it's going to have its linkage with Merseyside and Manchester.'

Abse stopped to pour the coffee, but then, still standing, became even more animated.

'So certainly, I'm not opposed to the *principle* of decentralisation. There would be great advantages in that at a time when the anonymity of large units is causing increasing alienation within society, and especially a society like Wales.'

'But isn't that exactly what the devolution proposals are seeking to address?'

Owen's voice contained a tinge of exasperation, which was immediately matched by Abse himself.

'What I am opposed to is that we should attempt it on the basis of artificial and sometimes racial theories. Because in fact, all you are trying to do is use much-needed decentralisation as an excuse for what you are really trying to get, and that is tribalisation.'

Abse spat out the last word with a vehemence that resulted in him spilling some of his coffee into his saucer.

Owen forced himself to respond mildly.

'I would have thought that most people are *for* the concept of decentralisation and totally *against* what you call tribalisation.'

'I'm sure they are, but I don't think they see the way the winds will blow.'

'You seem to be saying that anyone who seeks the strengthening of Welsh institutions – and, I would say, that includes Welsh culture and language – that that sort of person is, by definition, inward-looking and that he tends to lose sight of the wider world. But surely, one can have very strong – nationalist, if you like – feelings about one's own country, without that excluding a commitment to international concerns, Europe for instance?'

Abse pondered for a moment, choosing his words.

'Well, seriously, I think the corollary to excessive pride in race, language or nation – the corollary of that, and we've seen it in my lifetime – is xenophobia. And you see how excessive nationalism and over-pride in one's particular ethnic group have fed some of the xenophobic attitudes that lead to war. That is an appalling risk to be taking in an atom-bomb age – that is to say, to be creating institutions which are likely to incite xenophobic beliefs.'

'But why do you have to use words like xenophobic?'

'Because when you talk, for example, about the language, what I have witnessed is it becoming a political football. We are seeing increasing alienation in constituencies like mine to the aggressive stance of the language militants.'

'The so-called militants you speak of are just a tiny minority.'

Abse swivelled in his chair and placed his cup and saucer on the desk behind him. Then he swivelled back, studying Owen closely.

'You need to know your history. I was born during the first war. My father was at the front. I took part myself in the last war. We were the fortunate ones. We came back. When I look at my children, your generation in fact, I am aware that the next generation could be the last. There have been wars involving Europe and the United States every eighteen-and-a-half years, on average, since the end of the eighteenth century.'

'Yes, but surely all that's in the past, it's just history.'

'It may just be history as you put it, but the next war could be the last. It is because we should never underestimate the risks that I say this movement for devolution will inflame and encourage the menace of nationalism.'

Abse stood up, and placed his hands on his hips.

'It is an irrational, insatiable passion that can never be assuaged.'

* * *

The phone rang just as John Tripp was trying to feed a new spool of ribbon into his typewriter. Depending on how it was adjusted, it allowed you to type with black or red letters. Tripp's typewriter had defaulted to half-black and half-red. On the phone was the editor of a magazine he occasionally contributed to asking him to write a piece on the views of ordinary people about devolution.

'What do you mean by ordinary people?'

'Oh, you know, the man in the street.'

'The man in the street is a myth.'

'What we want is an impression of what people generally are thinking.'

'About devolution?'

'You might be surprised at how strongly they feel about it.'

Inspired more by the thought of a cheque than any great enthusiasm for the subject matter, Tripp set forth to encounter some ordinary people in a few pubs across Wales. He borrowed a Philips Memo tape recorder and retrieved an unused 1975 diary from a drawer in his desk to make notes, despite the difficulty he knew he would have in reading back his abbreviated long-hand.

His first stop was the Halfway in Pontcanna, a working-class pub containing a fair number of blunt customers. Tripp got into a conversation with one of them, a bricklayer, who after they'd chatted for a while asked, 'What's the name of that chap who rabbits on a lot on the telly?'

'Malcolm Muggeridge?'

'No, this was a Welsh bloke.'

'Gwyn Thomas?'

'That's him. He was right in what he said, something about shrinking horizons. He said we'd be losing connection with England and all that. We'd be too weak. Only he said it better than I can, you know the way he talks. Mind the promised land doesn't become paradise lost, he said.'

'You can have a shot at paradise, can't you?'

'It's not on, kid. There's no promised land, either.'

Tripp pulled a newspaper cutting out of his wallet.

'I'll tell you what Gwyn Thomas wrote in the *Western Mail*.

> The Anglicised philistine valleys of the Welsh south-
> east are to be the new Patagonia for the thrusting
> graduates of the north and west. We poor, raffish,
> backsliding lot are to be brought back to linguistic
> and political grace.

'Sounds like him.'

'Do you agree with it?'

'Yes.'

'Why?'

'He sounds as if he knows what he's talking about. He's chopsy, but he's clever.'

Tripp turned to a man, obviously a companion in the building trade, who was standing alongside.

'What do you think?'

'I don't know what it's all about. It'll make no bloody difference to me one way or the other. I hear some of them speaking Welsh in the other bar and it means nothing to me. They're foreigners as far as I'm concerned.'

'Where are you from?'

'Cardiff, Ely.'

'Look, Wales isn't just Cardiff and the Rhondda Valley. And Welsh isn't a foreign language.'

'Who cares, I'm British.'

At that point Tripp gave up and retreated to one of his many locals, the Mason's Arms in Whitchurch. But there it was much the same. Nobody seemed to have an opinion worth recording. Most of the men were studying the racing pages with the concentration of generals poring over battle maps. Others were playing the jukebox or the one-armed bandit. The only one politically minded was a Tory who, ignoring Tripp's question, launched into a rant about shipping all immigrants back to where they belonged.

A fresh pint in one hand and clutching his tape recorder in the other, Tripp recognised a regular, a full-time punter who he had learned to avoid. Feeling thwarted, he declared to the assembled company, 'My life and my poetry have been dedicated to one end – the breaking of England's grip on Wales.'

'Bollocks,' the man said.

Despite this, Tripp's intervention stirred a bit of interest. Another regular, a lorry driver, thought that Lloyd George and Bevan wouldn't have gone along with devolution because it was too narrow.

'What's that got to do with it?' another drinker said. 'They're both dead.'

A week later, in Swansea Tripp ventured into the Bush Hotel in the High Street, a Georgian hostelry said to be the last pub in which Dylan Thomas drank before heading for his final ill-fated journey to America. Here he encountered a woman worried about being cut off from England.

'We'll be out in the cold,' she said.

'That's what disgusts me,' Tripp responded bitterly, shaking off any pretence at journalistic inquiry. 'I'll never forget an Irishman who referred to us as *England's little butty* when Ireland was fighting for her life during the Troubles in the twenties.'

'I don't know anything about that,' the woman replied, her voice trailing off. 'In fact, I don't understand anything much what they're all talking about.'

Tripp could see she was a decent woman, but without any feeling or instinct that Wales should stand on its own dignity. It was useless informing her about her disinheritance from Welsh tradition and culture. Years of living in a Welfare State, alternating between Labour and Conservative governments that shared the same theories of materialistic paternalism, had left their mark. Devolution, or whatever she understood by it, looked a wild irresponsible misadventure to her, dreamed up by mad Welsh radicals.

Tripp began to realise that if the people he had spoken with were any kind of a cross-section, then the aspirations of the devolutionists were sunk. It was one thing to read sophisticated accounts of devolution by experts. It was quite another to move among people in pubs and cafes and listen to the extent of their indifference and apathy, if not hostility. Tripp reminded himself of an essay E.M. Forster had written, entitled 'Two Cheers for Democracy'. He couldn't give it three because it wasn't perfect. The most Tripp could hope for was that one day the people of Wales might give at least one cheer for devolution.

'One cheer enough,' he jotted down.

Some time later he found himself in the Duke of Wellington in Cowbridge where he met a teacher of mathematics. He was surprised to discover a man after his own heart.

'You know what being British means, don't you?' the teacher said.

'What's that?'

'It's sending Welshmen off to get killed in two world wars.'

'Like Hedd Wyn.'

'Who?'

'A dead poet. He won the Chair at the Eisteddfod in 1917, but he couldn't be there to sit in it because he was dead in France.'

'Ah, what was the *murder machine* exactly, do you know?'

'It was the English educational system in Ireland. Patrick Pearse called it that because it destroyed the Gaelic language and culture, or at least it tried to. The same applied to Wales.'

'I read in *The Guardian* about what someone called the Irish miracle. Gwynfor Evans mentioned it in a speech. They're doing all right now over there, economically speaking. That's a real community for you.'

'They've been doing all right for a long time. All that turbulence wasn't for nothing. They're free.'

'Well, I know who I'm voting for on March the first.'

'Good boy,' Tripp said, buying the teacher a pint. 'That's the spirit.'

*   *   *

The St David's Day referendum took place at the worst of times for the Yes campaigners. Heavy snow had fallen throughout February. In the Valleys, it rose more than three feet and had to be shovelled from paths and doorsteps. On the roads, melting snow turned to slush and then froze to be overlain by more treacherous snow.

It became known as the Winter of Discontent. Faced with a balance of payments deficit and high inflation, Callaghan's government attempted to impose a wages freeze. There were widespread strikes. Buses and trains stopped running. Schools closed. Piles of rubbish were left uncollected on the streets. Even the dead went unburied in some areas. Ghoulish newspaper headlines dramatised the unpopularity of the government. In truth, any government would have been unpopular.

'Get the government off your back', was the constant refrain of the new Leader of the Opposition, Margaret Thatcher. Pro-devolutionists struggled to make the case for what their opponents easily labelled as more and more expensive government.

Despite these circumstances few anticipated the defeat would be so overwhelming. The count did not take place until the day after the vote, so there were no late-night vigils. Instead, Owen paced the floor of the *Western Mail* newsroom during long daytime hours waiting for the outcome. The polls had forecast the No vote, but as the results for each of the eight counties came through he could scarcely believe the four-to-one rout. Overall just twelve per cent said Yes. Even in Gwynedd, the nationalist heartland, the vote barely rose to twenty-two per cent. In Gwent it was a paltry seven per cent. It felt like a blow to the solar plexus.

Reaching for his coat, Owen stumbled out of the office into the darkening Cardiff streets to try and gather his thoughts for the commentary he had to write. How was he to explain what had happened? An hour earlier he had watched an Oxford academic authoritatively explain to his television audience that those pressing the Assembly cause had argued Wales needed a distinctive voice to speak on its behalf. But that hardly seemed necessary when Westminster was already packed with Welshmen. Merlyn Rees was at the Home Office, David Owen was Foreign Secretary, George Thomas was Speaker of the House of Commons and Lord Chancellor Sir Elwyn Jones presided over the House of Lords. And although they were English, Prime Minister James Callaghan and his deputy Michael Foot both represented Welsh seats.

'It must appear to the casual observer that Britain is run by the Welsh,' the academic said.

Owen recognised the argument. He had written about it himself. Yet deeper reasons were needed to explain so crushing a defeat. After all, Scotland shared much of the same circumstances as Wales. The weather and the strikes were the same. Dominated like Wales by the Labour party, Scotland could scarcely say it was unrepresented by a Labour government in London. If anything, the Labour movement in Scotland was even more divided about devolution than in Wales. After all, it had spawned a separate Scottish Labour Party. And yet, despite all this, the Scots had voted in favour, if only narrowly.

Over the previous two weeks Owen had written a series of articles outlining the positions of the Yes and No campaigns. He covered arguments about costs, bureaucracy, funding, and competing claims about the impact on the economy. He addressed the so-called slippery slope to separatism, and the role of the Welsh language. The articles had been accompanied by drawings of a puzzled dragon, variously clutching a megaphone or school slate, and depending on the point of view, wearing a cloth cap or bowler hat.

Yet despite column inches running to thousands of words, something was missing. Owen realised he had failed to tap into the mixture of sullen hostility and incomprehension that lay behind these debates. He had failed to put his finger on the dislocation that separated his own enthusiasm from the harsh dismissal he felt resonated across the rest of the media, especially at the BBC.

The key to understanding what was going on had to be the language. How else could you explain how Abse had so effortlessly deployed his grotesque arguments? In his one intervention in the campaign, in Swansea, Prime Minister Callaghan had delivered a speech in support of his government's policy. But even he had been forced to confront Abse's claims that Welsh-speakers would dominate.

'I believe the Assembly by its very composition will put a stop to any such tendency,' he had said. 'It is inconceivable that a body representing all parts of Wales should, or could discriminate against the vast majority of the electorate in Wales.'

But such protestations seemed only to consolidate the prejudices of those to whom they were addressed.

Owen concluded that what all this confirmed was an underlying distrust between communities across Wales. It was not just attitudes towards the language. In the north, he had picked up a good deal of resentment about the south. What was it that Wyn Roberts, the Conservative MP for Conwy, had said about what he called the new bureaucracy that would be created in Cardiff?

> It is like putting the Irish mail train on the Snowdon railway. The small scale is tailor-made for the cosy Labour Party caucus in south Wales.

And then there was that woman, Gwen Mostyn Lewis, chair of the Clwyd No campaign. What had she said?

> People in south Wales are very charming, but as a crowd they are loud and coarse. We do not want to be governed by Cardiff. The Assembly will be permanently dominated by Labour. It will be a dictatorship.

Owen decided he would have to highlight the depth of the divisions that so evidently existed across Wales. He would also have to try and predict the implications for the future and the probability of an early general election.

Returning to the office he hung up his coat, sat in his swivel chair and pulled his typewriter towards him. Glancing across his desk he noticed he had left a folded edition of the paper from a few days earlier open at the editorial page. Picking it up his eye was drawn to the letters column and a brief contribution he had underlined in blue biro. It was from Saunders Lewis, in what was to be his last intervention in Welsh politics.

> We are asked to tell the government on St David's Day whether we want a Welsh Assembly or not. The implied question is: 'Are you a nation or not?'

May I point out the probable consequences of a No majority. There will follow a general election. There may be a change of government. The first task of the Westminster Parliament will be to reduce and master inflation. In Wales there are coal mines that work at a loss; there are steelworks that are judged to be superfluous; there are valleys convenient for submersion. And there will be no Welsh defence.

* * *

A few weeks later, after a poetry reading with Nigel Jenkins in Swansea, John Tripp accompanied him to his place on Gower. He often stayed with him in his Nissen hut on a farm at Pennard when he ventured west. Nigel lit a fire and opened a bottle of his home-brewed beer, pouring two foaming glasses.

'Ah, the usual Jenkins' Thump, I see.'

'Reckon there's enough here to see us out 'til tomorrow.'

'Not much else to look forward to.'

'Bit morose, aren't you? Wasn't such a bad night.'

'Our writers are lost in myths and legends. Most of us are far too careful. There's too many deacons and lay preachers at it. It's up to your generation to do something.'

'Got to be outward-looking.'

'Yes, that's it. I want Wales to stand free, to be part of Europe, to be proud in its own way. I can't stand the narrowness of the chapel. The Anglo-Welsh are bedevilled with this pew-and-deacons thing, my generation is anyway. You must be modern, you've got to make it new. I'm an anti-sentimentalist. What I see all around me in Wales is third-rate, down-market sentimentality. I want hardness, steeliness, compassion and pity. I don't want phoneyness, all this stuff and nonsense, the chapel hangover.'

'Writers can make some sense of it all,' Nigel suggested.

'It's true a poet can bring people back to essentials. All the time he must hammer away at a few things. *What's happening to Wales? Why don't we love each other?* It's the one thing I can do. Justifies even one's outrageous behaviour. You pay a price for it, of course, to have this liberty.'

'But you wrote once that poems make nothing happen.'

'I said that? Well, yes, I did. So did Auden. I don't think poets make much happen in a general sense, do they? We don't have any feedback, we don't get any evidence back. I hardly think so.'

'Especially after March the first, bit of a flattener that.'

'It flattened me. I've got to be frank about it. I've written nothing much since. The Assembly was obviously inadequate. But the fact that we couldn't even make the first step... It was rather appalling. Four-to-one against. I shall write about something else instead, like R.S. Thomas.'

'You've finished with Wales then?'

Tripp drank some more beer.

'Finished with the politics, yes. Those dreams kept me bolt upright for years. How easily it's gone, all that care and thought and love for a country. All the poems written about it, gone in one night – through the Gang of Six, the Abses and the dreadful Kinnocks of this world. You can ask so much of your poets. It's a tragedy, what happened on March the first.'

'Harri Webb says it was only a hiccup in the long run of history.'

Tripp considered the point, taking another long pull of Nigel's heavy, sedimented beer. With the wine he had drunk earlier he could feel himself edging towards inebriation.

'It's more important than that, much more. It was awful, what happened that day, and you can't expect your poets to be the same again. You spend ten or twelve years of your life working up to something, you know, with all the irony and cynicism, and with all the beating of breasts, you've had these great hopes for your country.'

* * *

A week later Owen James was in Aberystwyth covering a meeting of local authorities. It started early so he had driven up the evening before and stayed at the Marine Hotel. Anxious to mull over the referendum result he had arranged to meet Phil Williams for a drink in the Cŵps.

'You're looking cheerful,' Owen greeted him when he entered the bar.

'There's more to life than politics, you know. I've just had some good news.'

'Oh, what's that?'

'I've got a secondment with EISCAT. I'm going to be associate director of science at Kiruna.'

'Hang on, what's EISCAT and where's Kiruna?'

'It's the European Incoherent Scatter Scientific Association. One of its receivers, sub-receivers actually – you'd call it a giant telescope – is in Kiruna in northern Sweden. We're studying the interaction between the sun and the earth by looking at disturbances in the ionosphere and the magnetosphere.'

'Fascinating.'

'But I guess you want to talk about the referendum.'

'Well, yes.'

'It wasn't as if I didn't warn them. We walked right into it. It was like a car crash you could see coming, years in advance if you see what I mean.'

'But the thing now is, how do we pick up the pieces?'

'Up to a point, but there's no virtue in picking up the pieces if we just put them back together in the same old way. If you keep on fighting your battles like that you tend to get the same results.'

Owen turned to the bar to pick up his pint.

'It seems to me the referendum told us that what divides us in Wales is more important than what unites us. Don't you think so? There's such a level of distrust, especially between the north and the south...'

'And I suppose you're going to tell me that it all comes down to the language.'

'You've got admit that Abse had a field day.'

'And we let him, didn't we? Encouraged him even.'

'How do you mean?'

'If there's one thing above all else which tells you what I mean, it's that poster we put out after the October election in '74.'

'The one with the three MPs, Gwynfor and the two Dafydds.'

'That's it. In one piece of paper we told the people of Wales that Plaid is a political party which represents Welsh-speaking areas and gives its highest priority to Westminster.'

'We could hardly ignore the success of the three MPs.'

'But how much better it would have been if the photograph had shown the leaders of the Plaid groups controlling Caerphilly, Merthyr and Dwyfor.'

'Surely Plaid has to support the language?'

Becoming agitated Phil placed his pint on the bar.

'That's not it at all. I'm not arguing against that, of course not. But as a national party, we have to be seen as supporting and representing the whole of the country, not just the Welsh-speaking part.'

'No one would argue with that.'

'They wouldn't, but what do they do about it? Look, in the 1960s Cymdeithas yr Iaith took up the main responsibility for the language and that left us free to concentrate on other issues, the politics.'

'So?'

'The result was we grew rapidly in the non-Welsh speaking areas. I did an analysis of our election results in 1970. It showed that by far and away the most important factor deciding our share of the vote in seats across Wales was the number of times we had fought them before. Once that factor was removed there was very little difference between the Welsh-speaking and non-Welsh-speaking constituencies. In seats like Neath, Aberdare and Caerphilly the results were similar to those in Meirionnydd, Caernarfon and Sir Fôn.'

'And you reckon that's changed.'

'I'm sure of it. You'll see in the forthcoming election the main correlation in where the Plaid vote holds up will be the number of Welsh-speakers in a constituency. The opinion polls are already telling us that. Support for Plaid is increasing amongst Welsh-speakers, but sharply decreasing among non-Welsh-speakers.'

'Why is that happening then?'

'It's obvious. To me, anyway.'

'Go on.'

'First of all, our enemies, people like Abse, made the Welsh language a major issue in the referendum campaign. But even more important, we ourselves have given far more emphasis to the language in recent years compared with the 1960s.'

'So we need to give more attention to English-speaking Wales.'

'In a word, yes. If you listen to Gwynfor you'd think that it's the Welsh language alone that carries our history, culture and traditions. It's important, of course, but it's not the only part of our heritage. Take Robert Owen, for instance, the most significant Welshman in the history of political thought. He coined the word *socialist* after all. He wrote all his books in English. And take Raymond Williams today. He's the only living Welshman to be making a major contribution to political thought. He's very conscious of his Welsh heritage, but all his books are in English.'

Phil stood up and finished his drink.

'I've got to go. But we should continue this conversation. The next few years are going to be difficult. You know it was the Scottish scientist Alexander Bell…'

'The inventor of the telephone?'

'That's the one. He famously said that when one door closes, another opens. But he also said that we often look so long and so regretfully at the closed door that we fail to see the one opening for us.'

*　*　*

When Phil had gone Owen thought for a while about he had said. Knowing Plaid Cymru, and knowing Gwynfor in particular, he found it hard to think what would persuade them to take his advice. He reflected on the result of the Scottish referendum. Faced with much the same circumstances as Wales, the Scottish people had still said yes. Their political voice had registered. Not loud enough to produce immediate progress to be sure, but their strange victory-defeat would make an advance towards a Scottish Assembly inevitable sooner or later.

'But here we're still stuck in the politics of the 1960s or maybe even the 1950s,' Owen thought. At which point he glanced up and noticed Ioan Thomas coming into the bar with Rhiannon. Their eyes met, she smiled and advanced towards him.

'What brings you to Aberystwyth?'

'Oh, you know, meetings.'

Ioan followed her.

'Our man from the *Western Mail*. Will you have a drink?'

'Why yes, thanks. Half of bitter will do. I'm setting off soon, back to Cardiff.'

'I suppose you were disappointed by the referendum,' Rhiannon said as Ioan went to the bar.

'Of course, weren't you?'

'It was terrible. Can't stop thinking about it, even now. I wasn't that optimistic to begin with, but to lose so heavily… even in Gwynedd.'

'There was an argument to make, an economic case for the Assembly.'

'I never heard it.'

'It never had a chance because the debate got stuck around nationalism and the language.'

Ioan brought their drinks.

'You're on about this wretched devolution business. I blame Labour, likes of Kinnock and the others. Damn traitors, if you ask me. In some parts of Wales Plaid was left distributing Labour leaflets. Did you know that? And even then, a lot of them mysteriously disappeared from Labour offices before Plaid could get their hands on them. Dai Francis said it was organised sabotage.'

'It isn't just a matter of the Labour Party,' Owen told him. 'It goes deeper than that. You've got to ask yourself why the Scots voted so differently.'

'Why did they, then?'

'Because they've got a stronger sense of who they are, of citizenship if you like.'

'You mean they think of themselves as being citizens of Scotland,' Rhiannon said.

'Yes, they've got their own institutions.'

The Welsh are just Brits at heart,' Ioan said bitterly.

'We've got to develop our own institutions,' Owen answered.

'We need a sense of solidarity around them. We need a new campaign.'

'But we've just been smashed,' Ioan said.

'When is there a better time?'

Owen laughed, but he saw Rhiannon's eyes widening.

*   *   *

He got to his car as dusk was falling. The skies were clear and he reckoned he could make it to Cardiff not long after midnight. These days he felt a need to return home whenever and as soon as possible. He headed east through Cwm Ystwyth with the snow-covered slopes rising on either side. Then he was driving through Llangurig and Rhaeadr.

It was approaching ten o'clock when he switched on the car radio and tuned in to Radio Wales. He thought he caught the voice of Gwyn A. Williams. Owen was interested in the professor of history at Cardiff University. He leant forward, turned up the volume and gently moved the tuning button to find a better reception. He was aware of his reputation as a radical interpreter of the country's past. Now the sound of his distinctive Merthyr voice, sharp and lifting, filled the car. He was talking about how the Welsh had developed their identity over the centuries always in relation to their neighbours.

'What defined the Welsh in the end were the English,' Gwyn Alf, as he was generally known, said. His voice stammered over the E of the English. Yet, rather than interfering with his message the hesitation impelled the listener to concentrate. Owen did so intently as in a few minutes the historian covered centuries spanning the life of Wales from Roman times to the coming of the Normans. It was they who had ripped half the country apart into a rich hybrid Welsh-European civilisation. They had projected Welsh culture into Europe, thrust European modes into the semi-independent west and north, and dragged the Welsh out of the Celtic-Scandinavian world into the Latin.

Owen listened transfixed. Gwyn Alf galloped through the next centuries, past the eras of Owain Glyndŵr and the Tudors, relating a story of continual disruption. The Welsh lurched from crisis to crisis. They barely survived as they were thrown in one direction and then another by the grinding maw of events.

Driving through Builth, Owen decided to take the mountain road, over Mynydd Epynt through Upper Chapel to Brecon. It was single-track in places, but more direct and the late hour meant there would be little traffic. The mountains were covered with thick snow, but the roads were clear. As the car laboured up the hill, Owen's attention drifted away from the radio and he gazed at the mountain landscape around him, etched clearly by a nearly full moon.

He wound down the window as he always did when passing this way, in a conscious effort to sense the ghosts of the past. In the early years of the Second World War, four hundred people from twenty-four farms were forcibly evicted to make way for the army firing range that still occupied the land. In the process, the boundary of Welsh-speaking Wales was pushed twelve miles westwards.

Owen recalled how in 1940 a museum curator had made several visits to Mynydd Epynt to survey the disruption and take photographs. On his last visit near the end of June, Iorwerth Peate found a few people were still moving from their homes. He passed a family with their furniture on a cart coming through a mountain gate.

Later he met a woman in her eighties outside a farmhouse expecting to leave that day. She had dragged an old chair to the furthest end of the yard and was sitting there motionless, gazing towards the mountain with tears streaming down her cheeks.

'Get back to Cardiff,' she said. 'It's the end of the world here.'

As he neared the top of the mountain, Owen sensed a familiar overwhelming feeling, a combination of frustration, helplessness and anger. The people had gone. They would never return. Then his attention was drawn back to the radio. Near the top of the hill he stopped at the side of the road. He turned the volume up. Gwyn Alf was speaking about the decades around the turn of the twentieth century when immigration into south Wales was only second in intensity to immigration into the USA.

> And after a Klondike climax to this new American Wales in the First World War, the terrible Depression of the 1920s and 1930s burned through this complex and contradictory Wales like radioactive fall-out from a distant holocaust.

The Depression played the same role in Welsh history as the Famine in Irish, Williams said. It unhinged Wales, devastated its communities, and dispersed a quarter of its people. It thrust the survivors, struggling to rebuild consensus in a precarious post-war prosperity, into the crises of identity that was plaguing them to this day.

> In such a people with such a history, the problem of identity has been desperate from the beginning. In recent centuries we have progressively lost our grip on our own past. Our history has been a history to induce schizophrenia and to enforce the loss of memory. Professional history, history as a craft, is even more recent a phenomenon in Wales than in England. Half-memories, folklore, traditions, myths, fantasy are rampant. We are a people with plenty of traditions but no historical memory. We have no

historical autonomy. We live in the interstices of other people's history.

Owen switched off the radio and sat for a moment.

'Don't get angry,' he reminded himself. 'Get even.'

He started the car and began to move off. Then, on an impulse, he stopped at the brow of the hill. Getting out he walked forward a few paces. The headlights of the car cast his silhouette on the slush and snow in front of him. Far in the distance, illuminated by the bright moon he could see the sharply drawn, snow-covered outlines of Crybyn and Pen-y-Fan of the Brecon Beacons. They rose up clear against the dark azure blue of the sky. The white escarpment of the Black Mountains curved away eastwards. And always above, the great arc of the heavens, where ten million stars were burning.

Author's note

This book tells how the Welsh people struggled to came to terms with their identity during the last quarter of the twentieth century. Specifically, it deals with the years between 1973 and 1997, dates which frame the devolution debate of that era. This first volume takes the story to the first referendum that was held in 1979. A second volume will deal with the 1980s, the traumatic years defined by the miners' strike of 1984-5. A third volume addresses the subsequent period that led to the second devolution referendum in 1997.

I found the best way I could explore the complexities of the events and arguments that took place during these times was through the form of a documentary novel, rather than a more conventional historical approach. Hence, most of the people in the book actually took part in the episodes that are described. The words they use have been taken from contemporaneous records of the period, either from their own recorded or written accounts, often to be found in archives, contemporaneous interviews, or from third party observations, such as newspaper reports. Exceptions include two fictional characters who carry much of the narrative, Rhiannon Jones-Davies and Owen James and their immediate families and friends. However, in both cases they are amalgams of people who lived through the period and many of their experiences actually took place.

The quarter of a century dealt with in these volumes has been one of the most formative in the life of my country. Indeed, the very survival of Wales as a distinctive nation was at stake at this time. This has been true of many periods in our long history, stretching back to the Roman era. A common experience of the Welsh has been disruption and defeat, and we have become practised in the arts of survival. I think, however, that in September 1997 a defeat in the second referendum would have been especially difficult. It might have proved insurmountable set against the intensity of the dislocation and absorption of peoples and languages that were taking place across the globe, and which is continuing in the twenty-first century.

In the event we experienced a rare, if extremely narrow victory, just eighteen years after the crushing defeat of 1979. We are now living with the problems of shouldering the responsibilities that have accompanied that success. I am sure, however, that they are easier, and certainly more pleasurable, than coping with the alternative. This is the measure of the achievement of my generation in Wales.

A word about the documentary novel, a genre that emerged in the United States in the mid-twentieth century. I am conscious that all historical accounts are partial, and inevitably a reflection of the attitudes and prejudices not only of their authors but also of the era in which they are written. As Conor Cruise O'Brien, who appears in these pages, put it in his book *States of Ireland,* in 1972, 'Most history is tribal history: written, that is to say, in terms generated by, and acceptable to, a given tribe or nation.'

It can be argued, too, that a certain type of truth is much more difficult to relay in non-fiction than in fiction. That is my justification for choosing this form. And it was Raymond Williams who judged fiction to be the most complete sort of history. In what must have been one of his last interviews, in late 1987, he remarked, 'There is a sense, I would say, in which history, which is both recorded and unrecorded, can only find its way through to personal substance if it then becomes a novel, becomes a story.'

Acknowledgments

My first thanks go to Ashley Owen, my editor with Gomer, who from the outset had an intuitive grasp of what I was trying to accomplish and pointed me in directions I needed to go.

Peter Finch, Cynog Dafis, Rhys David, Ceri Black, Rosanne Reeves and Peter Stead read drafts of the manuscript at different stages and I am grateful to them for their many helpful suggestions. One challenge was to find ways of weaving the lives of the fictional characters through the real events and people of the period. In this respect, and others, Ned Thomas provided much valued guidance. Any errors and deficiencies are, of course, my own.

Libraries and archives across Wales proved invaluable for my research. I am grateful to Rob Phillips and his colleagues at the Welsh Political Archive in the National Library of Wales, Aberystwyth; to Siân Williams, Librarian at the South Wales Miners' Library in Swansea; to Rob Davis and his colleagues at Cardiff Central Library and Cathays; and to the Gwent Archive in Ebbw Vale.

During the weeks I spent working at the National Library in Aberystwyth, I benefited hugely from the convivial hospitality of Sue and Denis Balsom and Llinos and Cynog Dafis. Diolch o galon.

The whole undertaking would have been impossible save for Ceri's patience, support, and love.

John Osmond
Penarth

Biographical Notes

Donald Anderson (1939 –) was Labour MP for Monmouth from 1966 to 1970, and Swansea East, from October 1974 to 2005. In the 1970s he opposed the Labour government's devolution policy, becoming known as a member of the 'Gang of Six'. In 2005 he was created a Life Peer as Baron Anderson of Swansea.

Perry Anderson (1938 –), professor of history and sociology at the University of California, Los Angeles, was editor of *New Left Review* from 1962-1982 and from 2000 to 2003. He is the author of many books that have applied novel Marxist theories to historical development, in particular the peculiarities of English nationalism.

Aureli Argemí (1936 –) is the founder and president emeritus of the Escarré International Center for Ethnic Minorities and Nations (CIEMEN). He lived in the Abbey of Montserrat between 1946 and 1968. He was secretary to Aureli Escarré the abbot of Montserrat Aureli Escarré, accompanying him when the Franco regime forced him to exile. When Escarré died in 1968 Argemí settled at the Abbey de Cuixà near Prades where he founded CIEMEN in 1974. In 1981 he was one of the promoters of the Call for Solidarity in Defense of the Catalan Language, Culture and Nation. In 1988 he promoted the creation of the Conference of Nations Without a State in Europe, and in 1996 he was one of the promoters of the Universal Declaration of Linguistic Rights. He runs the magazine *Europa de las Naciones* and the digital newspaper *Nationalia* and is also the director of the Center Mercator Derecho e Legislación Lingüística.

Margaret Atwood (1939 –) is a Canadian poet, novelist, literary critic, and environmental activist. She was awarded the Welsh Arts Council's International Writer's Prize in 1982.

W.H. Auden (1907–1973) was an English-American poet, taking up American citizenship in 1946. He was a prolific writer of prose essays and reviews on literary, political, psychological and religious subjects.

Rudolph Bahro (1935–1997) was a leader of the dissident movement in Communist East Germany in the 1960s and 1970s. His key work in this period *The Alternative in Eastern Europe* was first published in English in 1978. He became a leader of the Green movement in West Germany. Later he became disenchanted with formal politics and instead turned to exploring spiritual approaches to sustainability.

Aneurin Bevan (1897–1960) was Labour MP for Ebbw Vale from 1929 to 1960. He was Minister of Health during Clement Attlee's 1945-50 government when he was responsible for the creation of the National Health Service.

Roderic Bowen (1913–2001) was Liberal MP for Cardigan from 1945-1966. A barrister he chaired a governmental committee (1971-2) which recommended the introduction of bilingual road signs in Wales.

Jack Brooks (1927 – 2016) was Labour secretary to the Cardiff South East constituency and agent to James Callaghan MP from 1966 to 1984. He was appointed to the House of Lords as Lord Brooks of Tremorfa in 1979. He was a Cardiff councillor during these years and became leader of South Glamorgan Council during the 1980s, a period when he was also deputy chairman of the Cardiff Bay Development Corporation.

Donald Box (1917 – 1993) was Conservative MP for Cardiff North from 1959 to 1966.

Giraldus Cambrensis (Gerald of Wales, 1146 – c.1223), of mixed Norman and Welsh descent was a historian and also archdeacon of Brecon. He was nominated for several bishoprics but turned them down in the hope of becoming Bishop of St Davids. Among his many publications those on the history and geography of Wales stand out, in particular *Desciptio Cambriae 1193* ('Description of Wales'), a meditation on the nature of Wales and its people and their cultural relationship with the English.

Rachel Carson (1907 – 1964) was an American marine biologist and conservationist, especially concerned about the spread of synthetic pesticides. Her book *Silent Spring* (1962) led to the creation of the US Environmental Protection Agency and the banning of pesticides such as DDT.

Pablo Casals (1876 – 1973) was a cellist, composer and conductor from Catalunya, generally regarded internationally as the pre-eminent cellist of the first half of the twentieth century. He was an ardent supporter of the Republican government during the Spanish Civil War in the 1930s After its defeat he vowed not to return to Spain until democracy was restored.

Barry Commoner (1917 – 2012) was professor of Plant Physiology at Washington University, St Louis, and one of the founders of the modern ecology and environmental movements. His bestselling book *Closing Circle* (1971) was among the first to advance the idea of sustainable development. He ran in the 1980 US presidential election on behalf of the Citizen's Party.

A.J. Cook (1883 – 1931) was general secretary of the Miners' Federation of Great Britain from 1924 to 1931. He was born in Somerset but moved to Wales to find work as a miner, first in the Rhondda and later in Merthyr where he was also a lay preacher in the Baptist chapel. He first came to prominence in the Cambrian Coal dispute in 1910 and was involved in the Miners' Unofficial Reform Committee which published the syndicalist pamphlet *The Miners' Next Step* in 1912. It argued for workers' management and ownership of industry and that the left should organise at the grassroots to gain control of the union. Cook was elected general secretary of the South Wales Miners' Federation in 1921.

Michael Cocks (1929 – 2001) was Labour MP for Bristol South from 1970 to 1987 when he was deselected and replaced by Dawn Primaralo. He was the Labour's chief whip between 1976 and 1985.

Douglas Crawford (1939 – 2002) was SNP MP for Perth and East Perthshire between October 1974 and 1979. A former journalist he was the SNP director of communications and adviser to **Winnie Ewing** MP in the late 1960s.

Bernard Crick (1929 – 2008) taught politics at Sheffield University, the London School of Economics and founded the Department of Politics at Birkbeck College in 1972. He settled in Scotland in the 1980s and became an ardent advocate of a Scottish Parliament.

Richard Crossman (1907 – 1974) was Labour MP for Coventry East from 1945 to 1974. He was Minister of Housing and Local Government between 1964 and 1966, Leader of the House of Commons from 1966 to 1968, and Secretary of State for Health and Social Services from 1968 to 1970.

Sir Geoffrey Crowther (1907 – 1972) was an economist, businessman, journalist and editor of *The Economist* from 1938 to 1956. He became a knight in 1957 and was awarded a life peerage in 1968, when he became Baron Crowther. He was chairman of the Commission on the Constitution from April 1969 until his death in February 1972, when he was succeeded by the Scottish peer Lord Kilbrandon.

George Cunningham (1931–) was Labour MP for Islington South West in 1970, and for Islington South and Finsbury in the February 1974 election. Strongly opposed to Scottish devolution he proposed the 40 per cent amendment to the 1978 Scotland Act. This meant that a majority voting Yes in the referendum would have to constitute at least 40 per cent of the electorate. In November 1981 he resigned from the Labour Party and sat as an independent MP before joining those who established the new Social Democratic Party. He lost his seat at the 1983 general election.

Tam Dalyell (1932 – 2017) was MP for West Lothian from 1962 to 1983 and then Linlithgow from 1983 to 2005. Strongly opposed to a Scottish Parliament he became identified with what became known as the 'West Lothian Question', named after his constituency. This was the conundrum over whether Scottish, Welsh and Northern Irish MPs should be able to vote on English-only matters after devolution.

Sir Alun Talfan Davies (1913 – 2000) was a Welsh judge, publisher and Liberal politician. In the 1930s he was a member of Plaid Cymru but later joined the Liberals and stood for the party on three occasions, in Carmarthen in 1959 and 1964, and in Denbigh in 1966. He was a member of the Royal Commission on the Constitution 1969-73. Knighted in 1976 he was chairman of the Welsh board of HTV from 1967 to 1973.

Dai Coity Davies (2017 – 1980) was an underground worker in the Wern Tarw pit, at Pencoed near Bridgend. In 1955 he was elected to the Area Executive of the South Wales NUM, becoming Compensation Secretary, a position he held until his death.

Idris Davies (1905 – 53) was a poet born in Rhymney where he left school aged 14 to work as a miner until the General Strike of 1926. He then trained as a teacher in England and taught in primary schools there, mainly in London, until he returned home, finding a post in his native valley in 1947. He published three volumes of verse: *Gwalia Deserta* (1938), *The Angry Summer* (1943) about the 1926 General Strike, and *Tonypandy and Other Poems* (1943). Most of his poetry deals with the mining Valleys during the depression of the inter-war years. Early judgements of his work criticised what was seen as his narrow range. However, he has become regarded as a voice of great sophistication and humanity.

Ifor Davies (1910 – 1982) was Labour MP for Gower from 1959 to 1982. He was a junior minister at the Welsh Office in the 1960s, defied the whip to vote in favour of entry into the EEC in 1971, and was a member of the 'Gang of Six' Labour MPs who opposed Labour's devolution policy in the 1970s.

Tom Davies (1941 –) was brought up in Pontypridd, and sailed as a merchant seaman on ships to Australia and Africa, drove a bus through Europe and India, served as a social worker on the lower East Side of New York, and as a teacher with VSO in Indonesia. In the mid-1960s he became a journalist with the *Western Mail* and later the *Sunday Telegraph,* the *Sunday Times,* and *The Observer,* before becoming a full-time writer and novelist.

Thomas Davis (1814 – 1845) was an organiser of the Young Ireland movement in the first half of the nineteenth Century, giving voice to the foundation of modern Irish nationalism. A Protestant he stood for the unity of all the people of Ireland, regardless of their religion.

Bernadette Devlin (1947 –) is an Irish civil rights leader. She became MP for Mid Ulster in a by-election in 1969, rejecting the Irish Republican policy of refusing to sit at Westminster. She held the seat until 1974.

Desmond Donnelly (1920 – 1974) was Labour MP for Pembroke from 1950 to 1968 when he resigned the Labour whip and was expelled from the party. He sat as a member of his newly formed Democratic Party for a further two years until he lost the seat at the 1970 election, to the Conservatives.

Sir Gareth Edwards (1947 –) played rugby for Wales as scrum half, winning his first cap in 1967. He is widely regarded as the finest player to don a Welsh jersey.

Huw T. Edwards (1892 – 1970) was a leading figure with the Transport and General Workers Union and the Wales Labour Party, initially in north Wales. In 1949 he was appointed the first chair of the Council for Wales and Monmouthshire. In that role he oversaw the production of a number of reports calling for the creation of a Welsh Office and the position of Secretary of State for Wales. Frustration with the lack of a positive response from the Conservative government led him to resign from the Council in 1958. In 1959 he left the Labour Party and joined Plaid Cymru, though he returned to the Labour fold in 1965. In 1956 he bought the Welsh language periodical *Y Faner* to save it from liquidation. In the early 1960s he became the first president of Cymdeithas yr Iaith Gymraeg, the Welsh Language Society.

Ness Edwards (1897 – 1968) was Labour MP for Caerphilly from 1939 to 1968 and a strong opponent of the creation of the Welsh Office in 1964.

Nicholas Edwards (1934 –) was Conservative MP for Pembroke from 1970 to 1987. From 1975 to 1979 he was Shadow Secretary of State for Wales. He was Secretary of State for Wales in the Thatcher government from 1979 to 1987, when he was made a life peer as Lord Crickhowell. As Secretary of State he instigated the Cardiff Bay Development Corporation.

Wil Edwards (1938 – 2007) was Labour MP for Merioneth from 1966 to February 1974. He was an outgoing solicitor who was often critical of the party line, especially on entry into the European Community of which he was a passionate exponent. In 1981 he was selected to fight Ynys Môn, but withdrew shortly before the 1983 general election in protest at Labour's policies for withdrawal from the EEC, unilateral nuclear disarmament, and closure of US military bases in the UK.

George Eliot (1819 – 1880) was a leading writer of the Victorian period, author of seven novels including *The Mill on the Floss* and *Middlemarch*.

Tom Ellis (1924 – 2010) was MP for Wrexham from 1970 to 1983, first as a Labour member, before defecting to the SDP in 1981. He was an ardent pro-European and supporter of devolution seeing both movements as complementary. He served as a nominated member of the European Parliament in the late 1970s.

Thomas Edward Ellis (1859 – 1899) was Liberal MP for Merioneth from 1886 to 1899. He was a leader of *Cymru Fydd*, the Welsh

Home Rule movement, in the 1880s and early 1890s. In 1892 when Gladstone formed a new administration Ellis accepted the post of second whip, which meant that he had to withdraw from the movement, whose leadership was taken over by Lloyd George.

Friedrich Engels (1820 – 1895) was a German philosopher, journalist and businessman. He was a close associate of **Karl Marx** with whom he co-authored *The Communist Manifesto* in 1848.

Edgar Evans (1900 – 1993) was an ironmonger in Bedlinog. He joined the Communist Party in 1926 at the time of the General Strike and was a member of its Welsh Committee from 1933 to 1957. In 1934 he was elected as a Communist to a seat on the Gelligaer Urban District Council. In 1936 he was charged with 'incitement to riot' due to his involvement in the Taff Merthyr Dispute and was imprisoned for nine months. On his release he was deprived of his civil liberties for ten years, entailing his removal from his role as a councillor. He regained his seat in 1947.

Fred Evans (1914 – 1987) was Labour MP for Caerphilly from 1968 to 1979. During the 1970s he opposed the Labour government's devolution policy, becoming known as a member of the 'Gang of Six' Welsh Labour MPs.

Ioan Evans (1927 – 1984) was Labour MP for Yardley (Birmingham) from 1964 to 1970, and then for Aberdare from February 1974 to 1983. During the 1970s he opposed the Labour government's devolution policy, becoming a member of the 'Gang of Six' Welsh Labour MPs.

Winnie Ewing (1929 –) was SNP MP for Hamilton from the by-election in 1967 to 1970, and then SNP MP for Moray and Nairn from 1974 to 1979. She was a Member of the European Parliament for the Highlands and Islands from 1975 to 1999, and a Member of the Scottish Parliament for the Highlands and Islands from 1999 to 2001. She was the President of the SNP from 1987 to 2005.

Sir Russell Fairgrieve (1924 – 1999) was Conservative MP for Aberdeenshire West from February 1974 to 1983. He was an outspoken politician fro a business background who combined staunch Toryism with a strong commitment to devolution for Scotland.

Michael Farrell (1944 –) is an Irish civil rights activist and was a leader of the People's Democracy movement in Northern Ireland from 1968 into the 1970s. He was a member of the Irish Human Rights Commission from 2001 to 2011.

Peter Finch (1947 –) is a poet and writer, known for his development of experimental forms and his extrovert poetry readings. Between 1975 and 1998 he ran the Arts Council of Wales's Oriel Bookshop in Cardiff. He then became chief fxecutive of Academi, and its successor body Literature Wales, until 2012. He is the editor of the *Real* psychogeographic memoirs, being the author himself of four Cardiff volumes in the series.

Samuel Finer (1915 – 1993) was a political scientist and historian who taught at Balliol College, Oxford, Keele University, Manchester University, eventually becoming Gladstone Professor of Government at All Souls, Oxford.

Michael Foot (1913 – 2005) was a politician, journalist, and biographer of Aneurin Bevan. He was Labour MP for Plymouth Devonport 1945-55, and Ebbw Vale 1960-92. He was Leader of the Labour Party between 1980 and 1983.

E.M Forster (1879 – 1970) was an English writer, with Anglo-Irish and Welsh roots, whose novels – including *Howard's End* and *A Passage to India* - examined class differences and hypocrisy.

Yann Fouéré (1910 – 2011) was a Breton nationalist and a European federalist. He spent part of the Second World War in exile in Wales living with the Welsh nationalist leader **Gwynfor Evans**. After the war he was accused of collaborating with the Nazis, fled France and eventually became an Irish citizen. He returned voluntarily to France in 1955 to face trial and was exonerated.

Ffred Ffransis (1948 –) is a prominent member of Cymdeithas yr Iaith Gymraeg and has served many jail sentences for taking part in non-violent direct action on behalf of the language. In his defence statement in the Crown Court at Mold in 1971 Ffransis set out the principles of non-violent-direct action which Cymdeithas yr Iaith subsequently followed. These were that other non-violent means should already have been used, and that it was certain that no harm or danger would be caused to life. Following that trial Ffransis was given a two-year prison sentence for entering Granada Television studios in Manchester and causing damage. Ffransis was also responsible for developing an ideology for Cymdeithas yr Iaith known as *Cymdeithasiaeth* (community socialism). He is married to Meinir, a fellow activist with Cymdeithas yr Iaith and daughter of **Gwynfor Evans**.

Gerry Fowler (1935 – 1993) was Labour MP for the marginal seat of The Wrekin from 1966 to 1970, and from February 1974 to 1979. He was Minister of State at the Privy Council Office from 1974 to 1976 during which time he was responsible for the development of the government's devolution policy.

Dai Francis (1911 – 81) was a member of the Welsh Communist Party and general secretary of the South Wales Miners from 1963 to 1976. He led the campaign to establish the Wales TUC – a 'Workers' Parliament for Wales', as he put it – and was elected its inaugural chairman in 1974. In the 1979 referendum he chaired the pro-Assembly campaign in South Glamorgan.

Hywel Francis (1946 –) was Labour MP for Aberavon between 2001 and 2015. Previously he was professor of Adult Continuing Education at Swansea University where he founded the South Wales Miners Library. Earlier he was a founder of Llafur, the Welsh Labour History Society. During the 1984-5 Miners Strike he chaired the Wales Congress in Support of Mining Communities. His publications include *The Fed: A History of the South Wales Miners in the 20th Century* (1980, co-author Dai Smith); *Miners Against Fascism: Wales and the Spanish Civil War* (1984); and *History on Our Side: Wales and the 1984-85 Miners' Strike* (2009).

Ernest Gellner (1925 – 1995) was professor of anthropology at Cambridge University and later head the Centre for the Study of Nationalism at the Central European University in Prague. He was born in Paris but brought up inPrague and London. He was a renowned philosopher and social anthropologist who fought consistently against what he regarded as closed systems of thought, including communism, psychoanalysis, and relativism. He wrote or edited more than twenty books, including *Nations and Nationalism* (1983).

Eric Gill (1882 – 1940) was an English sculptor, typeface designer, stonecutter and printmaker associated with the Arts and Crafts movement. After the First World War he founded The Guild of St Joseph and St Dominic, a Roman Catholic art colony, at Ditchling in Sussex, where his pupils included **David Jones** who began a short-lived relationship with Gill's daughter, Petra. In 1924, Gill moved to Capel-y-Ffin on the Welsh border, where he established a new workshop.

Edward Goldsmith (1928 – 2009) was an Anglo-French environmentalist who was a founder of *The Ecologist* magazine in 1969. In 1972 he co-authored, with James Allen, *A Blueprint for Survival* which advocated a decentralised, de-industrialised society. Selling more than a million copies it became a key environmental text and inspiration behind the emergence of the Green Party.

Antonio Gramsci (1891 – 1937) was an Italian neo-Marxist philosopher and politican. He was founder of the Italian Communist Party and imprisoned by Mussolini's Fascist regime from 1926 until his death. Gramsci was brought up in Sardinia whose distinctive identity informed his thinking. During his imprisonment he wrote more than thirty Notebooks and their eventual publication made him one of the most influential political thinkers of the twentieth century. He is best known for his theories on cultural hegemony which analyse how the state and capitalist class utilise cultural institutions to consolidate their power.

Percy Grieve (1915 – 1998) was Conservative MP for Solihull from 1964 to 1983.

James Griffiths (1890 – 1975) was Labour MP for Llanelli from 1936 to 1970. Following Labour's victory at the 1945 election he was made Minister for National Insurance and, along with Aneurin Bevan, was an architect of the welfare state. He was spokesman for Welsh Affairs in opposition between 1955-9 and used his relationship with the Labour leader Hugh Gaitskell to commit the party to the creation of the Welsh Office and Secretary of State for Wales with a seat in the Cabinet. He became the first occupier of the post between 1964 and 1966.

Peter Hughes Griffiths (1940–) was agent and Plaid Cymru organiser in the Carmarthen constituency between 1972 and 1984. He was the organiser when Gwynfor Evans stood in the constituency in the February and October 1974 general elections. He was four times mayor of Carmarthen Town Council and became a county councillor for the Carmarthen North ward in 2004.

Eurfyl ap Gwilym (1944 –) is an economic adviser to Plaid Cymru. He was the party's chairman between 1976 and 1980 and stood in Merthyr Tydil in the 1979 general election. He is a director of a number of companies and deputy chairman of the Principality Building Society.

Gwenallt (1899 – 1968) was the bardic name of David James Jones. A poet and novelist from Cwm Tawe he was a conscious objector during the First World War and later a lecturer in Welsh at Aberystwyth. His work and outlook was the result of a unique combination of Marxism, Christianity and Welsh nationalism.

Willie Hamilton (1917 – 2000) was Labour MP for constituencies in Fife, Scotland, between 1950 and 1987. He was anti-devolution but best known for his republican, anti-Royalist views.

Sir Richard Hanbury-Tenison (1925 – 2017) was a soldier and diplomat, and a Gwent landowner who was appointed High Sheriff of the county in 1977 and Lord Lieutenant in 1979, serving for 21 years. He lived at the Clytha Park country estate near Abergavenny which he restored following wartime neglect. Of Irish County Monaghan stock the Hanburys had mined iron ore and developed forges and the first rolling mills around Pontypool in the the late sixteenth century, the foundation of the family wealth.

Patrick Hannan (1941 – 2009) was a Welsh industrial and political journalist, author, television and radio presenter, and commentator. He began his career with the *Western Mail* in the 1960s, then from the 1970s to the 1990s worked in various roles for *BBC Wales*, including as political editor, and later as a freelance. For the best part of fifty years he provided a sustained analysis of developments in Welsh current affairs.

Keir Hardie (1856 – 1915) was a Scottish socialist and trade unionist and founder of the Labour Party in 1900. He was elected in Merthyr Tydfil in 1900 and remained an MP for the seat until his death.

Seamus Heaney (1939 – 2013) was an Irish poet who won the Nobel Prize for Literature in 1995. Brought up near Bellaghy in Northern Ireland he attended Queen's University in Belfast, later becoming a lecturer at St Joseph's College in the city. He held various academic positions, including at Oxford and Harvard. He lived in Dublin from 1976 until his death.

Sir Edward Heath (1916 – 2005) was Conservative Prime Minister from 1970 to 1974. He led the negotiations that resulted in the United Kingdom's entry into the European Economic Community on 1 January 1973. The Miners' strikes, in 1972 and at the start of 1974, led to the Three-Day Week to conserve energy. Heath then called a general election in February 1974, seeking a mandate to face down the Miners' wage demands. However, this led to a hung Parliament and a Labour government.

Michael Hechter (1943 –) is professor of political science at Arizona State University and professor of sociology at the University of Copenhagen. He is the author of numerous books, including *Internal Colonialism: The Celtic Fringe in British National Development, 1536-1966* (1975).

Eric Heffer (1922 – 91) was Labour MP for Liverpool Walton from 1964 to his death. He was a strong critic of devolution for both Scotland and Wales. He was first a supporter, but later an opponent of Britain's membership of the EEC.

Michael Heseltine (1933 –) was born in Swansea and was Conservative MP for Tavistock from 1966 to 1974 and for Henley from 1974 to 2001. In Margaret Thatcher's government in the 1980s he was successfully Secretary of State for the Environment and later for Defence. In John Major's government in the 1990s he was President of the Board of Trade and then Deputy Prime Minister.

John Hewitt (1907 – 1987) was the most significant Northern Ireland poet to emerge before the 1960s generation of Seamus Heaney, Derek Mahon, and Michael Longley. He was attached to the dissenting tradition rather than mainstream Protestantism, and drawn to a regional identity for Ulster within the context of the island of Ireland.

Sir Julian Hodge (1904 – 2004) was an entrepreneur and banker who founded the Commercial Bank of Wales in 1971. It was denied the title 'Bank of Wales' because the Bank of England objected that the title would give the impression it was a Central Bank. However, the title was eventually bestowed in 1986, the year ironically when it was taken over by the Bank of Scotland. It ceased trading as a Welsh brand in 2002. Julian Hodge was born in London but moved with his family to Pontllanfraith when he was five. He left school at 13, worked as an assistant in a chemist shop, and later joined the Great Western Railway as a clerk. He trained in accountancy in his spare time and went into business for himself as an accountant in 1934. When he died his fortune was estimated at £48 million.

Arthur Horner (1894 – 1968) was a Welsh trade union leader and communist. Born in Merthyr Tydfil he became president of the South Wales Miners Federation in 1936 and later, in 1946, general secretary of the National Union of Mineworkers. He played a leading role in the ten-month lockout following the 1926 General Strike.

Douglas Houghton (1889 – 1996), MP for the Yorkshire constituency of Sowerby from 1949-1974, was chairman of the Labour Party 1967-74. He was a member of the Commission on the Constitution, but resigned in January 1973 when it became clear that its report would advocate separate Assemblies for Wales and Scotland.

Sir Geoffrey Howe (1926 – 2015) was born in Port Talbot and was Conservative MP for Bebington 1964-66, for Reigate 1970-74, and for East Surrey 1974-92. During the 1980s he was Margaret Thatcher's longest serving Minister successively holding the posts of Chancellor of the Exchequer, Foreign Secretary, Leader of the Commons, Deputy Prime Minister and Lord President of the Council.

Geraint Howells (1925 – 2004) was Liberal MP for Cardigan from February 1974 to 1983 and for Ceredigion and Pembroke North from 1983 to 1992. He was a strong devolutionist, playing an active role in the 1979 referendum campaign. He was a sheep farmer at Ponterwyd, and as part of the Lib-Lab pact in 1978 secured recognition for the Farmers Union of Wales as one of the official unions for government negotiations, along with the NFU. He was made a life peer after losing his seat to Plaid Cymru in 1992.

Aneurin Rhys Hughes (1937 –) was a British diplomat and later career civil servant with the European Commission. From 1973 to 1976 he was head of the Division for Internal Coordination of the

European Commission in Brussels; and from 1977 to 1980 adviser to the Director General for Information. In 1981 be became chef de cabinet to Ivor Richard, a member of the Commission, and later represented the European Union in Norway and Australia and New Zealand.

Emyr Humphreys (1919 –) is a novelist, poet and dramatist. He was born in Prestatyn and educated at the University of Wales, Aberystwyth where he read history and became a nationalist. Fe first worked as a teacher, but then joined BBC Wales as a drama producer. Later he became a lecturer in Drama at the University College of Wales, Bangor, before becoming a full-time writer in 1972. Among the best known of his works is a sextet collectively entitled *Land of the Living*.

Cledwyn Hughes (1916 – 2002) was MP for Anglesey from 1951 to 1979 when he became a life peer as Baron Cledwyn of Penrhos. He followed **James Griffiths** as Secretary of State for Wales between 1966 to 1968 and during this period attempted to create an all-Wales tier of democratic government as part of a projected local government reorganisation. However, this was opposed from within the Cabinet. Between 1970-72 he was Minister for Agriculture, but was sacked by Prime Minister Harold Wilson for defying the Labour whip and voting for Britain to enter the EEC. Later he became chairman of the Parliamentary Labour Party.

Roy Hughes (1925 – 2003) was Labour MP for Newport from 1966 to 1983 and for Newport East from 1983 to 1997 when he was appointed to the House of Lords as Lord Islwyn. He was strongly pro-devolution. In 1994 he was one of six Labour MPs who voted against any reduction in the age of consent for homosexuals which at that time was 21.

Carwyn James (1929 – 83) was a Welsh rugby international but more famously a coach for the British Lions against the All Blacks in 1971, and also for his own club Llanelli which he inspired to a famous victory over the All Blacks the following year. He was a deeply cultured man with an abiding love of Welsh literature.

Keith Jarrett (1948 –) played his first rugby international for Wales in 1967 when he scored 19 points, including a famous try. He went on to be selected for the British Lions tour of South Africa in 1968, but illness forced him to retire from sport in 1973.

Jean Jaurès (1859–1914) was an early social democrat who became leader in 1902 of the French Socialist Party.

Nigel Jenkins (1949 – 2014) was a poet, journalist and editor. Brought up on a farm on Gower, he worked for a travelling circus in the United States and studied at the University of Essex, before working as a journalist on newspapers in the Midlands. In the 1970s he settled in Swansea as a freelance writer and editor, later becoming a lecturer with Swansea University's Creative and Media Writing programme.

Roy Jenkins (1920 – 2003) was Labour MP for Southwark Central from 1948 to 1950 and then for Birmingham Stechford from 1950 to 1977. He was Home Secretary and then Chancellor of the Exchequer in Harold Wilson's governments between 1964 and 70. He became President of the European Commission between 1977 to 1981 after which he returned to Britain to lead the Social Democratic Party. He was SDP MP for Hillhead in Glasgow from the 1982 by election until 1987 when he entered the House of Lords.

Norman St John-Stevas (1929 – 2012) was Conservative MP for Chelmsford from 1964 to 1987 when he was made a life peer. He was minister for the Arts in Edward Heath's government between 1973-4 and Leader of the House of Commons in Margaret Thatcher's government from 1979 to 1981.

James Joyce (1882 – 1941) was an Irish novelist, short story writer and poet, best known for his novel *Ulysses*, centred on Dublin, in which he deploys a modernist-style stream of consciousness.

J. Barry Jones (1938 – 2015) was a political scientist and Welsh Labour activist who strongly supported the devolution cause. He was the main author of the Welsh Labour Party's submission to the Commission on the Constitution in 1970. In the 1979 referendum campaign he was secretary to the Yes for Wales Campaign. In 1997 he founded the Wales Governance Centre at Cardiff University.

Bobi Jones (1929 – 2017) was a poet, novelist, short story writer and literary critic. So prolific was his writing that he published under two names: Bobi Jones for his poetry and fiction; and R.M. Jones for his academic work. Brought up in Cardiff he learnt Welsh and took a degree in the language at University College, Cardiff. Later he become the first Welsh learner to be appointed a professor of Welsh, at the University of Wales, Aberystwyth. A Welsh nationalist and republican, he gained some notoriety when he taught Prince Charles Welsh during his time at the University of Wales, Aberystwyth, in the summer of 1969.

Dan Jones (1908-1985) was brought up in the Rhondda and was Labour MP for Burnley from 1959 to 1983.

David Jones (1895-1974) was a painter and one of the first generation of British modernist poets. As a painter he worked chiefly in watercolour, painting portraits and landscapes, and animal, legendary and religious subjects. He was also a wood-engraver and designer of inscriptions. As a writer he was considered by T.S. Eliot to be of major importance, especially his *In Parenthesis* (1937), which he described as 'a work of genius'. Jones' *The Anathemata* (1952) was considered by **W.H. Auden** to be the best long poem written in English in the twentieth century. His Christian beliefs and Welsh heritage were a strong influence on his work.

Sir Elwyn Jones (1909 – 1989) was born in Llanelli and educated at Aberystwyth and Cambridge. He became a barrister and Labour MP for Plaistow (east London) from 1945 to 1950, and for West Ham South from 1950 to 1974. He was appointed Attorney General in

1964, a post he held until 1970. In 1974 he was made a life peer and served as Lord Chancellor until 1979.

Emrys Jones (1914 – 1991) was secretary and organiser of the Welsh Labour Party from 1965 to 1979. A close associate of **James Griffiths**, he oversaw the development of Labour's devolution policies in the 1960s and 1970s and was also a strong advocate of a Welsh language television channel.

Glyn Jones (1905 – 1995) was a novelist, poet and literary historian. He served as both chairman and president of the English language section of the Welsh Academy, now Literature Wales. His study, *The Dragon Has Two Tongues* (1968) discusses ways in which the period between the World Wars affected his generation of Welsh writers.

Gwynoro Jones (1942 –) was Labour MP for Carmarthen from 1970 to October 1974, in the latter election losing the seat to **Gwynfor Evans**. In 1981 he was a founding member of the Social Democratic Party in Wales.

Hywel Ceri Jones (1937 –) was a leading figure in the European Commission administration from 1973 to 1998. He was successively director for Education, Training and Youth Policy, and Director of the Commission's Task Force for Human Resources, Education, Training and Youth where he was responsible for the development and management of the Erasmus and other EU programmes. Between 1993 and 1998 he was director general of Employment, Social Policy and Industrial Relations.

Ieuan Gwynedd Jones (1920 –) was the Sir John Williams professor of Welsh History at Aberystwyth from 1969 until his retirement in 1984. A specialist in Victorian Wales he exerted great influence over successive generations of Welsh historians during the latter part of the twentieth century. He was the first President of Llafur, the Welsh Labour History Society that was founded in 1970.

Jack Jones (1884 – 1970) born in Merthyr Tydfil was a novelist who chronicled life in the southern Valleys, notably in *Black Parade* (1935), *Rhondda Roundabout* (1934), and *Off to Philadelphia in the Morning* (1947).

Jack Jones (1913 – 2009) rose to become general secretary of the Transport and General Workers Union during the 1970s when he was a powerful influence on the Labour government. Behind the scenes he was an influential supporter of the creation of the Wales TUC in 1973.

Lewis Jones (1897 – 1939) born in Clydach Vale was a novelist of the Valley communities in which he lived. His works included *Cwmardy* (1937) and its sequel *We Live* (1939). In the 1926 General Strike he was imprisoned in Swansea jail for three months for his trade union activities. In the 1930s he was Welsh organiser for the National Unemployed Workers Movement, leading hunger marches to London in 1932, 1934 and 1936. In 1936 he was one of two Communist members elected on to Glamorgan County Council. He died in January 1939 at the end of a day in which he addressed more than thirty meetings in support of the republican side in the Spanish Civil War.

Michael D. Jones (1822 – 98) was a Congregationalist minister, widely regarded as being the leading early thinker of modern Welsh nationalism and the inspiration behind the foundation of the Welsh colony in Patagonia.

J.R. Jones (1911 – 1970) was born in Pwllheli and educated at University College, Aberystwyth and Balliol College, Oxford. He became a lecturer in philosophy at Aberystwyth in 1938 and professor of philosophy at University College, Swansea in 1952. His main philosophical interests were the nature of the self and other selves, religious belief, and the nation. Key works included *Prydeindod* (1966), an examination of the concept of Britishness, and *Ac Onide* (1970), a collection of essays on the crisis of Wales in the twentieth Century, his most substantial work.

Wassily Kandinsky (1866 – 1964) was a Russian painter and art theorist, credited with painting one of the first purely abstract works. His major influence was to emphasise the importance of artists expressing their inner lives in their work, articulated in his book *The Spiritual in Art*, first published in translation in English in 1914.

James Kellas (1936 – 2015) was professor of politics at Glasgow University and a penetrating analyst of the political sociology of Scotland.

Neil Kinnock (1942 –) was Labour MP from 1970 to 1995, first for Bedwellty and then Islwyn (from 1983). During the 1970s, along with Leo Abse, he was a leading member of the group of Welsh MPs opposing the Labour government's devolution policy, known as the 'Gang of Six'. He was leader of the Labour Party from 1983 to 1992 and a European Commissioner from 1995 to 2004. He was created a life peer as Baron Kinnock in 2005.

Lionel Charles Knights (1906 – 1997) was professor of English Literature at the University of Cambridge from 1965 to 1973 and an authority on Shakespeare.

Frank Raymond (F.R.) Leavis, (1895 –1978), was a literary critic who taught for much of his career at Downing College, Cambridge, and was an important influence on **Raymond Williams**.

Morvan Lebesque (1911 – 1970) was a Breton journalist and nationalist activist. He was involved with the Breton Autonomist Party in his home town of Nantes but in 1931 helped found the more extreme Breiz da Zont. During the Second World War he worked for the collaborationist newspaper *L'Heure Breton* and for various journals in Paris where he met **Jean-Paul Sartre** and Simone de Beauvioir.

Vladimir Lenin (1870 – 1924) was a Russian Communist revolutionary who served as head of government of Soviet Russia from 1917 to 1922 and the Soviet Union from 1922 to 1924.

Saunders Lewis (1893-1985), dramatist, poet, and literary critic, was one of the founders of Plaid Cymru in 1925. In 1936, along with Lewis Valentine and **D. J. Williams**, he committed arson against a RAF Bombing School in the Llŷn for which he was sentenced to a year's imprisonment. In February 1962 he delivered the BBC Wales radio lecture *Tynged yr Iaith* ('Fate of the Language') which led to the formation of Cymdeithas yr Iaith Gymraeg.

Emyr Llewelyn (1941 –) was a political activist and leading figure in Cymdeithas yr Iaith. He was also a founder of Mudiad Adfer (Restoration Movement), a breakaway group that advocated the creation of a monoglot heartland, Y Fro Gymraeg, in the west of Wales. His ideas are well summarised in his speech 'Adfer' published in his collection *Areithiau* (Y Lolfa, 1970).

Margo MacDonald (1943-2014) was an SNP MP for Govan 1973-4 and also served as an SNP and later independent member of the Scottish Parliament 1999-2014. She was deputy leader of the SNP 1974-79, but lost that role after becoming a leading figure in the 79 Group within the party that argued it should move in a more socialist direction.

Ramsay MacDonald (1866 – 1937) was the first Labour leader to become Prime Minister, leading minority governments in 1924 and 1929 to 1931. With **Keir Hardie** and Arthur Henderson he was a founder of the Labour Party. He headed a National Government from 1931 to 1935, supported by only a few Labour members, and was expelled from the party for doing so. Among the many parliamentary seats he represented was Aberavon between 1922 and 1929.

Antonio Machado (1875 – 1939) was a Spanish poet and one of the leading figures in the literary movement known as Generation of '98. This was a group of writers who reacted to the moral and political in Spain produced by the loss of its colonies of Cuba, Puerto Rico, the Philippines and Guam after its defeat in the Spanish-American War.

John Mackintosh (1929 – 1978) was Labour MP for Berwick and East Lothian from 1966 to February 1974 and from October 1974 to 1978. He was also professor of politics at the University of Strathclyde and later at Edinburgh. He was an early advocate of devolution publishing *The Devolution of Power* in 1966.

Eamonn McCann (1943 –) is an Irish journalist and politician. He was involved in organising the first civil rights marches in Northern Ireland in the late 1960s. He was elected as a People Before Profit Alliance member for the Foyle constituency in the 2016 Northern Ireland Assembly election, but lost his seat when it was abolished in 2017.

Peter Madgwick (1924 –) was a lecturer and later reader in politics at the University of Wales, Aberystwyth, from 1964 until 1981. Later he became a professor of politics at Oxford Brookes University.

Karl Marx (1818 – 1893) was a German philosopher, economist, and revolutionary socialist, best known for his pamphlet *The Communist Manifesto* (1848) and his three-volume *Das Kapital* (1867, 1885, and 1894) which analysed the capitalist process of production.

Henri Matisse (1869 – 1954) was a French artist known for his fluid use of colour and flowing draughtmanship. Along with **Pablo Picasso**, he is regarded as one of the artists who defined the revolutionary developments in the visual arts throughout the opening decades of the twentieth century.

Stephen Maxwell (1942 – 2012) was a Scottish nationalist politician, academic and intellectual and, from the 1980s, a leading figure in the Scottish voluntary sector. During the 1970s he was the SNP's press officer and one of its most articulate spokesmen. In 1979 he directed the party's campaign during the referendum and later in the year, along with Alex Salmond and others, was a leading figure in the '79 Group within the party which urged that it should take a more left-wing stance.

Jean Monnet (1888 – 1979) was a French economist and diplomat. He was a key mover behind the founding of the European Coal and Steel Community in 1951, a precursor of the present day European Union.

John Montague (1929 – 2016) was a prolific poet who interwove personal and family themes with Irish history. He was born in New York and spent his student days in the United States, returning to Ireland in the 1960s. He eventually becoming Ireland's first professor of poetry, dividing his time between Queen's University Belfast and Trinity College Dublin.

Barry Moore (1944 – 1988) was agent to Neil Kinnock MP from 1974 to 1987. Brought up in Blackwood he left school at fifteen but later attended Coleg Harlech. He succeeded Neil Kinnock as a WEA lecturer in south-east Wales in 1970.

Elystan Morgan (1932 –) was Labour MP for Ceredigion from 1966 to February 1974 and under-secretary at the Home Office between 1968-70. In that position he was influential in persuading the Home Secretary James Callaghan to establish the Commission on the Constitution. In his early political career, he was an leading figure in Plaid Cymru, contesting Wrexham three times, at the by-election in 1955, and at the general elections in 1955 and in 1959. He also contested Merioneth at the general election in 1964. He was created a life peer as Baron Elystan-Morgan in 1981.

Gwyn Morgan (1934 – 2010) became assistant general secretary of the Labour Party in 1969 and in that capacity gave evidence to the Kilbrandon Commission on the Constitution in January 1970. Many thought he was being groomed for the top position. However, when it became vacant in 1972 he narrowly failed to be elected, after a deadlock and three successive ballots and on the casting vote of Tony Benn. Subsequently he became chef de cabinet to George Thomson, one of Britain's first European Commissioners, from 1973 to 1975. From 1976 to 1979 he was head of the the Commission's Office in

Wales. Later he filled a variety of diplomatic posts for the EU, in Israel and the Far East.

John Morris (1931 –) was MP for Aberavon,1959 to 2001, and Secretary of State for Wales, 1974 to 1979. He became Lord Morris of Aberavon in 2001.

Malcolm Muggeridge (1903 – 1990) was a journalist, author and satirist. He had left-wing sympathies in his youth but later, after working as a Moscow correspondent for the *Guardian* in the 1930s, became strongly anti-communist. He was a soldier and spy during the Second World War. In later life he became preoccupied with religious and moral issues.

Paul Murphy (1948 –) was MP for Torfaen from 1987 to 2015. He was appointed Secretary of State for Wales twice, between 1999 to 2002 and 2008-09. He was Secretary of State for Northern Ireland from 2002 to 2005, and made a life peer in 2015.

Tom Nairn (1932 –) is a Scottish political theorist of nationalism. During the 1960s and 1970s he contributed many articles to *New Left Review*, some of which were collected together with other essays in an influential book *The Break-Up of Britain – Crisis and Neo-Nationalism* (1977).

Conor Cruise O'Brien (1917 – 2008) was an Irish politician, writer, historian and academic. He was elected to Ireland's Parliament for the Irish Labour Party in 1969 and became a Minister between 1973 and 1977. During the 1970s, in response to the outbreak of the Troubles in the north of Ireland, he came to see the opposing nationalist and unionist traditions as irreconcilable and switched from a nationalist to a unionist view of Irish politics and history.

John Ormond (1923 – 1990), was a poet and documentary film-maker. Born at Dunvant near Swansea he began his journalistic career with *Picture Post* in London in 1945, returning to Swansea in 1949 to work as a sub-editor. He worked with BBC Wales from

1957 as a director and producer of documentary films including studies of Welsh writers and painters such as Ceri Richards, Dylan Thomas, Alun Lewis and R.S. Thomas. His poetry collections include *Requiem and Celebration* (1969) and *Definitions of a Waterfall* (1973).

François-Xavier Ortoli (1925 – 2007) was a French politician who served as the fifth President of the European Commission from 1973 to 1977.

Dafydd Orwig (1928 – 1996) was a teacher in Blaenau Ffestiniog and Bethesda before becoming a lecturer at Bangor Normal College. He was an active language campaigner and an influential Plaid Cymru councillor and organiser in Gwynedd.

David Owen (1938 –) was Foreign Secretary in James Callaghan's Labour government between 1977 and 1979. In 1981 he was one of the 'Gang of Four' who left Labour to form the Social Democratic Party, which he led from 1983 to 1987. He was made a life peer in 1992.

John Dyfnallt Owen (1873 – 1956) was a poet, writer and journalist. He was Congregational (*Annibynwr*) minister at Trawsfynydd (1898 and 1902), Deiniolen (1902-05), Sardis, Pontypridd (1905-10), and at Lammas Street, Carmarthen, from 1910 to his retirement in 1947. He won the Crown at the Swansea National Eisteddfod in 1907 and was elected Archdruid of Wales at the Rhyl Eisteddfod in 1954. After the Second World War he gave refuge in his home in Carmarthen to the Breton writer Ropaz Hemon who had escaped before his trial in Brittany.

Glyn Owen (1932 – 2013) was a Plaid Cymru member of the Aberdare Urban District Council, the Cynon Valley Borough Council, and Mid Glamorgan County Council over 15 years during the 1960s and 1970s. He was the party's parliamentary candidate in the Cynon Valley at the two 1974 general elections.

Sir Michael Palliser (1922 – 2012) was a British diplomat and Permanent Representative to the European Economic Community in Brussels between 1973 and 1975.

Sir Roger Parker (1923 – 2011) was a Lord Justiceof Appeal from 1983 to 1992 and Chairman of the Bar in the early 1970s. As a High Court judge, he chaired the hundred-day public inquiry in 1977 into the building of a reprocessing plant for atomic waste at Windscale, later Sellafield. His unequivocal advice that the new THORP plant should be built without delay to obviate storage and disposal problems and 'keep the nuclear industry alive' was strongly endorsed by James Callaghan's Labour government.

R. Williams Parry (1884-1956) born at Tal-y-Sarn, Dyffryn Nantlle, was one of the twentieth century's great lyric Welsh language poets.

Patrick Pearse (1879 – 1916) was an Irish poet, teacher and one of the leaders of the Easter Rising in Dublin in 1916. He was among those responsible for the drafting of the Proclamation of the Irish Republic which he read outside the Post Office, the headquarters of the Rising. Following the surrender, he was one of fifteen leaders of the Rising court-martialled and executed by firing squad.

Iorwerth Peate (1901 – 1982), was a poet and scholar as well as founder and first curator of the Welsh Folk Museum (now the National History Museum) at St Fagans between 1948 and 1971.

Riccardo Perissich (1942 –) headed research between 1966 and 1970 into the European Community at the Italian Institute of International Affairs in Rome that was founded by **Altiero Spinelli**. In 1970 he followed Spinelli to Brussels and began a 25-year career with the European Commission, first becoming Spinelli's chef de cabinet and then continuing in that role with three other Commissioners. Later he became deputy general manager for the Commission for the internal market and general manager for industry.

Marta Pessarrodona (1941–) is a Catalan poet and literary critic. Her poetry combines medititation and memory with a feminist commitment. She has co-ordinated the International Commission for the Dissemination of Catalan Culture, part of the Department of Culture of the Generalitat de Catalunya.

Pablo Picasso (1881 – 1973) was a Spanish painter and one of the most influential artists of the twentieth century. He was founder of the cubist movement, co-inventor of collage, and developer of a wide range of other styles.

Enoch Powell (1912 – 1998) was a Conservative MP for Wolverhampton South West from 1950 to October 1974, and an Ulster Unionist MP for South Down from October 1974 to 1987. An ardent opponent of devolution he had a unique outlook on identity, believing Wales and England to be conjoined since before Roman times. In 1978 he declared, 'The English are the Welsh who have lost their language', adding: 'If any should ask me what I am, I would reply, "I am, Sir, an Englishman. That is to say, Sir, I am a Welshman. If you enquire more particularly, Sir, I believe I am a Cornovian - you will find me especially at home around the upper waters of the Severn and the Wye."'

Sir Ray Powell (1928 – 2001) was a leading member of the Welsh Labour Executive in the 1970s and MP for Ogmore from 1979 to 2001. He was knighted in 1996.

Gwilym Prys-Davies (1923 – 2017) was an early advocate of devolution within the Welsh Labour Party. His pamphlet *A Central Welsh Council,* commissioned by **James Griffiths**, was published in 1962. He was Labour's candidate in the 1966 Carmarthen by-election which was won by Gwynfor Evans. He was chairman of the Welsh Hospital Board between 1968 and 1974, and an advisor to the Secretary of State for Wales John Morris between 1974 and 1979. He was appointed a life peer as Lord Gwilym Prys-Davies of Llanegryn in 1982.

Robert Recorde (1512 – 1558) was a physician and mathematician who invented the 'equals' = sign. He was born in Tenby, attended Oxford University where he was elected a Fellow of All Souls College.

George Reid (1939 –) was SNP MP for Clackmannan and East Stirlingshire from 1974-1979.

Alwyn D. Rees (1911 – 1974) was director of the extramural department at the University of Wales, Aberystwyth from 1949 to 1974. He was editor of *Barn* ('Opinion') from 1966 to 1974 and published a ground-breaking anthropological study into *Life in the Welsh Countryside* in 1950.

Ioan Bowen Rees (1929 – 1999) was chief executive of Gwynedd County Council from 1974-91. An advocate of localism and decentralization, he authored *Government by Community* (1971) which drew inspiration from the Swiss cantonal approach to governance. He was a strong advocate of improving the environment, especially in relation to the national parks.

Merlyn Rees (1920 – 2006) was MP for Leeds South from 1963 to 1983, and for Morley and Leeds South from 1983 to 1992. Born in Cilfynydd, near Pontypridd, he was Secretary of State for Northern Ireland between 1974 and 1976, and Home Secretary from 1976 to 1979. He was made a life peer as Baron Merlyn-Rees in 1992 and became the first chancellor of the University of Glamorgan, between 1994 and 2002.

David Ricardo (1772 – 1823) was an influential English classical economist, advancing the *labour theory of value* (that the economic value of a good or service is determined by the amount of labour invested in it) in his *Principles of Political Economy and Taxation* (1817).

Aneurin Richards (1923 – 2016) was a Plaid Cymru councilor on Islwyn Borough Council from 1973 to 1996 and a Gwent county councillor from 1977 to 1981. He was Plaid's candidate for Abertillery in both the 1974 general elections and for Islwyn in 1983 and 1987.

Ceri Richards (1903 – 1971), brought up at Dunvant near Swansea was one of the most important Welsh painters of the twentieth century, much influenced by the surrealist movement. Among his most notable works are a series of paintings connected with the poetry of Dylan Thomas and Vernon Watkins.

Emrys Roberts (19312 –) was organising secretary for Plaid Cymru from 1957 and then in 1960, became its general secretary, serving for four years. In 1964, Roberts left politics to become press officer with the Welsh Hospital Board, but he quit this in 1972 to stand as the party's candidate in the Merthyr Tydfil by-election. He came second with 37 per cent of the vote, providing hope for the party that they would gain seats in the next general election. He stood again in the seat in the February and October 1974 general elections gradually losing vote share. However, he was elected to Merthyr District Council where he led the group of Plaid councillors. Under his leadership Plaid took control of the council in 1976, the first authority it had ever run. They retained control until 1979. In that year Roberts was elected as vice president of Plaid Cymru, serving until 1981.

Goronwy Roberts (1913 – 1981) was Labour MP for Caernarfon from 1945 to February 1974. He was strongly in favour of devolution and a leader of the Parliament for Wales campaign in the 1950s. He was Minister of State at the Welsh Office 1964-66. He was created a Life Peer as Baron Goronwy-Roberts in 1974, after losing Caernarfon to Plaid's Dafydd Wigley. He then served as Minister of State for Foreign and Commonwealth Affairs 1975-79.

Sir Wyn Roberts (1930 – 2013) was Conservative MP for Conwy from 1970 to 1997. He was Under Secretary of State at the Welsh Office from 1979 to 1987, and Minister of State from 1987 to 1994. He was made a life peer in 1997.

Caerwyn Roderick (1927 – 2011) was Labour MP for Brecon and Radnor from 1970 to 1979 and strongly in favour of devolution. He was parliamentary private secretary to Michael Foot from 1975 to 1979.

Sean Ronan (1924 – 2000) was an Irish career diplomat and director general for information for the European Commission between 1973 and 1977. In this role he stressed that the EEC was not about amalgamating national identies and should demonstrate there was a true European community and not just, as he put it, a 'community of merchants'.

Richard Rose (1933 –) is director of the Centre for the Study of Public Policy and professsor of politics at the University of Strathclyde.

Jean-Paul Sartre (1905 –1980) was a French philosopher, novelist, and political activist. He was on of the key figures in twentieth century political thought, challenging oppressive conformity (*mauvais foi* – literally 'bad faith') with an authentic way of being. His system of thought known as existentialism can be summed up by his phrase 'man is condemned to be free'. As an anti-colonialist, Sartre took a prominent role in the struggle against French rule in Algeria. He was also a supporter of movements struggling in internal colonial situations, such as the Basques and Bretons.

Arthur Scargill (1938 –) was president of the National Union of Mineworkers from 1981 to 2002. He was a key organiser during the strikes of 1972 and 1974, the latter of which helped bring about the end of the Heath Conservative government. However, his leadership during the 1984-5 Miners' Strike contributed to its failure.

Fritz Schumacher (1911 – 1977) was a German-born economist best known for his advocacy of small-scale, intermediate technologies. He settled in England in the 1930s and studied at Oxford and Columbia universities. In the 1950s he travelled to Burma as a consultant and developed a set of principles he called 'Buddhist economics'. His influential *Small is Beautiful: a study of economics as if people mattered* was published in 1973.

John Seymour (1914 – 2004) was a prolific author in the self sufficiency movement, based from 1964 at a smallholding in the Preseli hills.

Jim Sillars (1937 –) was elected Labour MP for South Ayrshire at a by-election in 1970. In the 1960s he had been a powerful opponent of devolution but changed his views and in 1976 led a group of Scottish MPs to found the breakaway Scottish Labour Party. However, this foundered at the 1979 election when Sillars lost his seat. In the early 1980s he joined the SNP and in 1988 was returned to Parliament at the Glasgow Govan by-election, holding it until 1992. He became deputy leader of the SNP but did not stand against Alex Salmond for the leadership in 1980.

John Silkin (1923 – 1987) was Labour MP for Deptford from 1963 to 1974 and for Lewisham Deptford from 1974 to 1987. He was Chief Whip between 1966-69, and served as Minister for Planning and Local Government 1974-76, and Minister for Agriculture, Fisheries and Food 1976-79.

Sam Silkin (1918 – 1988) was Labour MP for Dulwich from from 1964 to 1983. He served as Attorney General from 1974 to 1979.

Sir Christopher Soames (1920 – 1987) was MP for Bedford between 1950 to 1966. He was Vice President of the European Commission between 1973 and 1976, and created a life peer in 1978.

Donald Soper (1903 – 1998) was a leading Methodist minister, socialist and pacifist, famous for preaching in the open air at Speakers' Corner in Hyde Park, London, until well into his nineties. He was made a life peer in 1965 and was active in the Campaign for Nuclear Disarmament from its beginnings.

Altiero Spinelli (1907 – 1986) was an Italian Communist politician, political theorist, and European federalist. He was European Commissioner for industrial policy between 1970 and 1976.

Imprisoned by Mussolini, in 1941 he co-authored the Ventotene Manifesto, eventually entitled *Per un'Europa libera e unita* ('For a free and united Europe').

Paul-Henri Spaak (1889 – 1972) was a Belgian socialist politician and statesman and a founding father of the European Union. He played an influential role in preparing the 1957 Treaty of Rome which established the European Economic Community.

David Steel (1938–) was Liberal MP for Roxburgh, Selkirk and Peebles from the 1965 by-election to 1983, and then for Tweedale, Ettrick and Lauderdale (a new seat covering much the same territory) until 1997 when he was appointed a life peer. He served as leader of the Liberal Party from 1976 until its merger with the Social Democratic Party in 1988 to form the Liberal Democrats. He was a member of the Scottish Parliament from 1999 to 2003 where he was its Presiding Officer.

Gertrude Stein (1874 – 1946) was an American novelist, poet, playwright and art collectoir. In 1903 she moved to Paris where she hosted a salon attended by leading moderoist figures in literarure and art, including **Pablo Picasso**, Ernest Hemingway, F. Scott Fitzgerald, Ezra Pound, and **Henri Matisse**.

Meic Stephens (1935 –) is a poet, editor, and prolific writer. In 1967 he was appointed literature director at the Welsh Arts Council, an influential role he occupied through the 1970s into the 1980s. In the 1990s he worked as an academic at the University of Glamorgan. He founded the *Triskel Press* in the early 1960s and later the magazine *Poetry Wales*. He compiled and edited *The Oxford Companion to the Literature of Wales* (1986).

Miquel Strubell (1949 –) is a sociolinguist and was professor of linguistics at the Autonomous University of Barcelona and later director of the Humanitis Programme at the Open University of Catalunya. He has produced reports on the lesser used languages of applicant states to the European Union for the European Parliament. He was a campaigner for Catalan independence during the referendums in 2014 and 2017.

Janet Suzman (1939 –) is a South African-born actress who had a successful early career with the Royal Shakespeare Company, later becoming famous for many roles in film and television.

Sir Ben Bowen Thomas (1899 – 1977) was permanent secretary to the Welsh Department of the Ministry of Education from 1945 to 1963, and president of the University of Wales, Aberystwyth from 1964 to 1975. Born in Ystrad, Rhondda, and educated at Jesus College Oxford he became the first warden of Coleg Harlech between 1927-40. He was a member of the Royal Commission on the Constitution 1969-73.

Dylan Thomas (1914 – 1953) was one of the most important and popular Welsh poets and writers of the twentieth century. He was known for his original and rhythmic use of words and imagery, notably in his play for voices, *Under Milk Wood.*

George Thomas (1909 – 1997) was Labour MP for Cardiff Central from 1945 to 1950 and for Cardiff West from 1950 to 1983. He was Secretary of State for Wales from 1968 to 1970 and was elected Speaker of the House of Commons in 1976. He became Viscount Tonypandy in 1983. He was president of the 'Just Say No' campaign in the devolution referendum held in 1997. In the general election in the same year he endorsed Sir James Goldsmith's Referendum Party, believing that the European Union was compromising the sovereignty of Parliament.

Gwyn Thomas (1913 – 81) was a novelist and playwright born in the Rhondda who dwelt on the humorous absurdities of working-class life in the Valleys during the inter-war depression. His characters speak in an idiom that relies on wit and hyperbole. Among his publications are *The Dark Philosphers* (1946), *All Things Betray Thee* (1949), and the play *Gazooka* (1957).

Wynford Vaughan-Thomas (1908 – 1987) was a journalist, author and radio and television broadcaster. He made his name as a correspondent during the Second World War, most memorably broadcasting from a Lancaster bomber over Berlin. In 1967, after leaving the BBC he was one of the founders of HTV.

Jeremy Thorpe (1929 – 2014) was Liberal MP for North Devon from 1959 to 1979 and leader of the Liberal Party between 1967 and 1976.

Pierre Trudeau (1919 – 2000) was Liberal Prime Minister of Canada between 1968 and 1979 and 1980 to 1984. He was a lawyer and activist in Québec politics and opponent of the province's movement for autonomy, the Parti Québécois. In pursuit of Canadian unity, he sought to introduce official bilingualism across the whole of the country and to re-write the constitution, initiatives in which he was only partially successful. However, he was successful in opposing the referendum on Québec sovereignty in May 1980.

Aled Vaughan (1920 – 1989) was a journalist and radio producer in London in the 1950s, later becoming a television director and producer for the BBC in Cardiff during the 1960s. In 1967 he helped establish HTV where he became programme controller. He was also a novelist and short story writer.

Jaume Vicens Vives (1910 – 1960) was one of the most influential Catalan historians of the twentieth century. Although suffering from the purges of the Franco régime following the Spanish Civil War in the 1930s, he became successively professor of modern history at the University of Zaragoza in 1947, and modern and contemporary history at the University of Barcelona in 1948. Among his many books was *Notícia de Catalunya* ('News of Catalunya') published in 1954. His early death was felt as a tragic loss amongst the Catalan cultural community.

Barbara Ward (1914 – 1981) was a writer and economist and an early advocate of sustainable development. She was co-author, with René Dubos, of *Only One Earth: The Care and Maintenance of a*

Small Planet commissioned for the 1972 UN Stockholm conference on the Human Environment.

Vernon Watkins (1906 – 1967) was a poet who lived on Gower near Swansea and was a close associate of Dylan Thomas.

Beatrice Webb (1858 – 1943) was an economist, labour historian and social reformer. Together with her husband Sidney Webb, whom she married in 1992, and other collaborators she was responsible for founding the Fabian Society, the London School of Economics and the *New Statesman*.

Harri Webb (1920 – 94) was a nationalist poet born in Swansea and educated at Oxford. He served in the navy during the Second World War and afterwards worked as a librarian at Dowlais and later Mountain Ash. He joined the Welsh Republicans in the late 1940s and subsequently Plaid Cymru in 1960. He published four volumes of verse between 1969 and 1983, notably *The Green Desert,* his collected poems 1950 to 1969.

John Wheatley (1869 – 1930) was born in Ireland but emigrated to Scotland aged seven, and was Independent Labour MP for Glasgow Shettleston between 1922 and 1930. Along with his friend John Maxton he was a leader of the Red Clydesiders. He began work as a miner, aged 14, but later, after studying at night school, became successively a publican, grocer, and journalist with the *Glasgow Catholic Observer.* He was a leading Glasgow councillor and Minister of Housing in the first 1924 Labour government.

Kenneth Wheare (1907 – 1979) was an Australian academic who was appointed Gladstone Professor of Government at All Souls College, Oxford, in 1946, later becoming Rector of Exeter College.

Eirene White (1909 – 1999) was MP for East Flint from 1950 to 1970 when she was appointed to the House of Lords as Baroness White of Rhymney. She was a Minister in the Colonial and Foreign Office between 1964 and 1966, and Minister of State in the Welsh Office between 1967 and 1970. She was chairman of the Land Authority for Wales 1976 to 1980 and was a member of the Royal Commission on the Environmental Pollution 1974 to 1981. Later she became a governor of the National Library of Wales and president of Coleg Harlech.

D. J. Williams (1885 – 1970) was a writer and an early member of Plaid Cymru. Along with **Saunders Lewis** and Lewis Valentine he participated in the burning of the Penyberth Bombing School in 1936, for which he received a nine-month prison sentence in Wormwood Scrubs.

Emlyn Williams (1921 – 1995) was elected to the executive of the South Wales area of the NUM in 1955, vice-president in 1966, and president in 1973. His time as president was marked by a series of strikes: the UK-wide strike of 1974, the South Wales strike against pit closures in 1981, and the further UK-wide strike of 1984-5. Born in Aberdare he began work aged fourteen at the Nantmelyn colliery. After war service that lasted until 1947 he returned to mining, first at Nantmelyn, and then Bwllfa and Maerdy, at both of which he became chairman of the Lodge.

Gwyn A. Williams (1925 – 1995) was professor of history at University of Wales College, Cardiff, from 1974 to 1983. A compelling communicator he made a number of influential television programmes, including the 13-part history of Wales, with fellow presenter **Wynford Vaughan-Thomas**, *The Dragon Has Two Tongues*, broadcast in 1985. A committed Marxist he became disillusioned with Communism and eventually joined Plaid Cymru in 1983. Among many publications was his history *When Was Wales?* (1985).

Jac L. Williams (1918 – 1977) was professor of education and vice principal at the University College of Wales, Aberystwyth. He was an expert on bilingualism and campaigned successfully for the teaching of Welsh to pre-school children, demonstrating that they could absorb the language effortlessly at that age.

Kyffin Williams (1918 – 2006) is widely regarded as one of the defining Welsh landscape painters of the twentieth[h] Century. He lived near Llanfairpwll on Anglesey. He was knighted in 1999.

Waldo Williams (1904 – 1971) was a leading Welsh language poet of the twentieth Century, an anti-war campaigner, Quaker, nationalist, and an inspiration for the campaigns of Cymdeithas yr Iaith Gymraeg. His most notable publication was *Dail Pren* ('Leaves of the Tree', 1956).

Virginia Woolfe (1882 – 1942) was an English writer novelist, a leading figure in literary modernism and an originator of the stream of consciousness as a narrative device. She was an inspiration for the feminist movement in the 1970s.

George Wright (1936 –) was the first general secretary of the Wales TUC when it was founded, in the face of opposition from the British TUC, in February 1973. As a trade union official he began his career in the Midlands car industry, arriving in Wales in 1972 to head the Wales area of the Transport and General Workers Union. He brought a new dynamic to trade unionism in Wales, one that was more used to private than public sector bargaining and less inclined to rely on leadership from London. He forged a relationship between the TGWU and the NUM and built the Wales TUC on that foundation.

Hedd Wyn (1887 – 1917) was a poet from Trawsfynnydd where he worked as a shepherd on his family's sheep farm. He was killed on the first day of the Battle of Passchendaele during the First World War and posthumously awarded the Chair at the 1917 National Eisteddfod at Birkenhead. Born Ellis Humphrey Evans he took Hedd Wyn as his bardic name after winning several chairs at eisteddfodau in his native Meirionnydd.

Page Notes

Page 30 *Cymdeithas yr Iaith Gymraeg*

The Welsh Language Society, founded in August 1962 during Plaid Cymru's annual conference in Pontarddulais. Its formation was prompted by an impassioned BBC radio lecture, *Tynged yr Iaith* ('Fate of the Language') delivered by Saunders Lewis in February 1962. He warned that unless a new campaign was initiated, Welsh would cease to be a living community language by the end of the twentieth Century.

Page 30-31 The biography Rhiannon is reading is *Fanon – The Revolutionary as Prophet* by Peter Geismar, first published in the United States in 1969.

Page 37 *Yr Wyddgrug*, the Welsh name for Mold in north-east Wales.

Page 42 *Ynni Niwclear NA!* – Nuclear Power NO!

Page 56 *the Yom Kippur war*

The Yom Kippur war was fought by a coalition of Arab states, led by Egypt and Syria, against Israel from 6 to 25 October, 1973. It was launched as a surprise attack on Israel on Yom Kippur, the holiest day in Judaism.

Page 72 *…the death of Llywelyn ap Gruffudd, Owain Glyndŵr …. The Act of Union, Penyberth.*

Llywelyn ap Gruffudd (1223-82), also known as Llywelyn the Last (*Llywelyn Ein Llyw Olaf*), was the last sovereign prince before the conquest. He was Prince of Wales from 1258 until his death on 11 December 1282 at Cilmeri, near Builth, killed by a band of Edward I's army.

Owain Glyndŵr (1359 - c.1415) led the revolt against English rule in Wales between 1400-15.

The Act of Union – the Laws of Wales Acts of 1535 and 1542, or the Acts of Incorporation – annexed Wales by extending the laws of England to the country.

Penyberth was a farmhouse at Penrhos, on the Llŷn Peninsula near Pwllheli, which had been the home to generations of patrons of poets, and also a way-station for pilgrims travelling to Bardsey Island. However, it was destroyed in 1936 in order to build a training camp and aerodrome for the RAF. This provoked the protest, led by Saunders Lewis, in which he, D.J. Williams and Lewis Valentine set fire to the buildings. It was a defining moment in the growth of Plaid Cymru and became known as *Tân yn Llŷn* (Fire in Llŷn).

Page 104 *Tryweryn*

The Tryweryn Valley near Bala in north Wales was the site of a proposal, made by Liverpool City council in 1955, to develop a water reservoir that would entail the flooding of the Capel Celyn community. The next year the council sponsored a private Bill in Parliament. By obtaining authority via an Act of Parliament, the council would not require planning consent from the relevant Welsh local authorities. This, together with the fact that the village was one of the last Welsh-speaking communities, ensured that the proposals became deeply controversial. Thirty-five out of thirty-six Welsh MPs opposed the bill (the other did not vote), but in 1957 it was passed. The members of the community waged an eight-year effort, ultimately unsuccessful, to prevent the destruction of their homes. Nonetheless, the episode entered Welsh political folklore and has remained a source of mobilisation ever since, in particular stimulating the growth of Plaid Cymru and Cymdeithas yr Iaith Gymraeg in the 1960s and 1970s.

Page 134 Nigel Jenkins is reading from his poem 'Yr Iaith', published in his *Acts of Union – Selected Poems 1974-1989* (1990).

Page 135 Peter Finch is reading from his poem 'A Welsh Wordscape', published in his *Selected Poems* (1983).

Page 136 John Tripp's poem 'Mission' is taken from his *Collected Poems 1958-78* (1978)

Page 138 *Bevin Boy*
Named after Ernest Bevin, Minister of Labour in the Second World War coalition government, they were conscripted to work in the coalmines between December 1943 and March 1948. They were chosen by lot as ten per cent of all male conscripts aged 18–25, with some volunteering as an alternative to military conscription. Nearly 48,000 Bevin Boys performed important but largely unrecognised service in the mines. Many were not released from service until well over two years after hostilities ended.

Page 142 *Landsker*
Refers to the linguistic boundary between Welsh-speaking northern Pembrokeshire and the English-speaking territory colonised by the Normans to the south. It starts at Newgale on St Brides Bay in the west and follows an irregular course, westwards to Laugharne. During the eleventh and twelfth centuries both invaders and defenders built more than fifty castles to mark the line in a complex period of conflict.

Page 151 Siobhan is reading from Seamus Heaney's poem 'The Other Side' in his volume *Wintering Out*, published by Faber in 1972.

Page 188 John Tripp is reading from his poem 'Anglo-Welsh Testimony', published in his *The Province of Belief: Selected Poems 1965-1970* (1971); and from his poem 'Caradoc Evans Revisited' published in his *Collected Poems 1958-1978* (1978).

Page 190 Rhiannon is reading from Frantz Fanon's *Black Skin, White Masks*, originally published in French in 1952, and later translated into English and published in 1967.

Page 199 *Cumberland* refers to Prince William, Duke of Cumberland (1721 – 1765), the third and youngest son of George II, best known for his role in putting down the Jacobite Rising at the Battle of Culloden in 1746.

Page 201 *The Upper Clyde campaign*

The loss-making Upper Clyde Shipbuilders, a consortium created in 1968 by the amalgamation of five large shipbuilders, went into liquidation in 1971 amidst much controversy. Instead of striking the workers organised a 'work-in' campaign, led by Jimmy Reid and other Communist shop stewards. This strategy attracted a good deal of public support, including many demonstrations in Glasgow. One march was attended by 80,000 people. The outcome was that the Heath government relented and restructured the yards aroud two new companies, Govan and Yarrow Shipbuilders.

Page 202 Rhiannon is quoting again from Frantz Fanon's *Black Skin, White Masks*.

Page 203 Here Rhiannon is quoting from *Black Orpheus*, an essay written by Jean-Paul Sartre in 1948 and published as a preface to *Anthologie de la nouvelle poésie nègre et malgache* ('Anthology of New Negro and Malagasy Poetry'), edited by Léopold Senghor, the Senegalese poet.

Page 204-5 The interview with Aimé Césaire was originally published as *Discours sur le colonialism* ('Discourse on colonialism') by Editions Presence Africaine in 1955, and translated and re-published by the Monthly Review Press (New York) in 1972.

Page 208 *...such Anglo-Scottish figures as Macaulay, Carlyle and Ruskin*

Baron Thomas Macaulay (1800 – 1859) was an historian and Whig politician who held office as Secretary at War between

1839 and 1841, and Paymaster General between 1846 and 1848. He was born in Leicestershire, the son of a Scottish highlander. Among the seats he represented in Parliament was Edinbugh between 1838 and 1847. His historical works included *Lays of Ancient Rome* and *History of England from the Accession of James II*. He divided the world into civilised nations and barbarism, with Britain representing the high point of civilisation.

Thomas Carlyle (1795 – 1881) was a Scottish philosopher, essayist, and historian. Among his most influential works was *The French Revolution: A History* in which he expounds his theory that history comprises the actions of great men. A polemicist he coined the term 'the dismal science' for economics.

John Ruskin (1819 – 1900) wasthe leading art critic of the Victorian period, as well as an art patron,drauightsman watercolourist, a prominent social thinker and philanthropist. He thought of himself as English though his forbears were Scottish.

Page 209 *political kailyarders … Königswinter*
Kailyard is derived from the Scots for small cabbage patch or kitchen garden.It was used to describe a school of Scottish fiction that developed in the last decades of the nineteenth Century. It was popular in its time but later provoked a reaction from writers such as George Douglas Brown and Hugh MacDiarmid who viewed it as projecting a sentimental, provincialised and unreal picture of Scottish life.

Königswinter is a city in North Rhine Westphalia which has given its name to an annual German-British political and academic conference which was founded there in 1960.

Page 211 *ysgol feithrin*
Welsh-medium playgroup for two to five-year-olds where

many children from English-speaking backgrounds effortlessly absorb the language. There are about 500 groups throughout Wales.

Page 220 *The Welsh Not*

This was a punishment used in some schools in the nineteenth Century to dissuade children from speaking Welsh. It was a piece of wood, inscribed with the letters 'WN', that was hung around the necks of children who spoke Welsh during the school day. The 'Not' was given to any child overheard speaking Welsh, who could pass it to a different child if they were also overheard speaking Welsh. At the end of the school day, the child left wearing the 'Not' would be punished.

Page 243 *One thinks of Freud, Einstein, Hans Morgenthau, Herbert Marcuse, Eric Fromm, Friedrich Hayek, Karl Deutsch, Leo Strauss, Hannah Arendt, Isaiah Berlin...*

Sigmund Freud (1856 – 1939) was an Austrian neurologist and founder of psychoanalysis.

Albert Einstein (1879 – 1955) was a German-born physicist who developed the theory of relativitity.

Hans Morgenthau (1904 – 1980) was brought up in Germany and became a major figure in the study of international politics in the United States.

Herbert Marcuse (1898 – 1979) was born and educated in Berlin and became a prominent philosopher and political theorist in the United States.

Eric Fromm (1900- 1980) was born in Frankfurt, where he began his studies, and was a psychoanalyst and humanistic philosopher, settling in the mid-1930s in New York.

Friedrich Hayek (1899 - 1992) was born in Austria-Hungary, settled in Britain in the 1930s, and was an economist best known for his defence of classical liberalism.

Karl Deutsch (1912 – 1992) was born in Prague when the city was part of the Austro-Hungarian Empire and settled in the United States in 1938 where he became a social and political scientist.

Leo Strauss (1899 -1973) was brought up in Germany and in the 1930s found refuge in England and then the United States where he became a famous political philosopher.

Hannah Arendt (1906 – 1975) was a German-born political theorist who settled in America becoming known for her work on totalitarianism.

Isaiah Berlin (1909 – 1997) was born in Latvia and brought up there and in Russia, moving with his family as a child to England where he became a noted political philosopher and historian of ideas.

Page 266 *The Levellers, the Diggers, the Chartists, George Fox and William Cobbett, Tom Paine and William Morris*

The Levellers were a political movement during the English Civil War (1642 -1651) that emphasised popular sovereignty, extended voting rights, and religious tolerance.

The Diggers were an offshoot from the Levellers. In 1649 they described themselves as the 'true' Levellers, advocating the creation of small egalitarian rural communities.

The Chartists were a working class movement for manhood suffrage that was active between 1838 and 1857. They were particularly strong in the south Wales Valleys and in the north of England.

George Fox (1624 – 1691) was an English Dissenter and founder of the Religious Society of Friends, generally known as the Quakers.

William Cobbett (1763 – 1835) was a farmer, journalist and MP, elected in 1832 for the newly franchised borough of Oldham. He campaigned for the reform of Parliament and Catholic emancipation. His best known publication *Rural Rides* (1830) is still in print.

Tom Paine (1737 –1809) was an English-born American political activist, philosopher, and revolutionary. He wrote a number of influential pamphlets, including *Common Sense*, that inspired the 1776 American Declaration of Independence. He spent most of the 1790s in France where he wrote *The Rights of Man* (1791), in part a defence of the French Revolution against its critics.

William Morris (1834 -1896) was a textile designer, novelist and socialist activist, one of the most significant cultural figures of Victorian Britain.

Page 267 *…the Ireland of Cuchulain, Oisin and Columcille, St Patrick and Brigid, the Ireland of Strongbow, of Brian Boru, of Sarsfield…*

Cuchulain is the central figure of the Ulster Cycle, a series of tales revolving around the heroes of the kingdom of Ulster in the early first Century.

Osian, was regarded in legend as the greatest poet of Ireland, and is a warrior of the fianna in the Ossianic or Fenian Cycle of Irish mythology.

Columcille, also known as Columba, was was an Irish Abbot and missionary credited with spreading Christianity in what is today Scotland. Aroud 563 he crossed to Argyll, before

settling in Iona (then part of Ulster) where he founded a
new abbey.

St Patrick was a fifth-century Romano-British Christian
missionary and bishop in Ireland. Known as the 'Apostle of
Ireland', he is one of the patron saints of Ireland, along with
saints *Brigid* of Kildare and Columba.

Strongbow was the name given to a Norman lord of the
twelfth century, Richard Fitzgilbert de Clare, who came
from England to Ireland at the urging of Diarmaid Mac
Murchadha. Diarmaid was the King of Leinster who had fled
to Britain because he backed the losing contender for the high
kingship of Ireland. Strongbow married Diarmaid's daughter
Aoife and restored his kingdom.

Brian Boru (c 941 – 1014) became High King of Ireland and
founded the O'Brien dynasty.

Patrick *Sarsfield* was an Irish landowner and soldier in the
seventeenth century, noted for his role in the Irish confederate
wars in which Catholic Ireland rose up against the English
Parliament and sided with King Charles I, during the time of
the English Civil War.

Page 268 *...the Plantation, the Apprentice Boys of Derry, the Boyne,
the Ulster Covenant, the Gun-running, Carson, Colonel Fred
Crawford...*

Plantations in sixteenth and seventeenth century Ireland
involved the confiscation of land by the English crown and its
colonisation with settlers from the island of Britain.

The *Apprentice Boys* are a Protestant fraternal society with
a worldwide membership of more than 10,000. Founded in
1814 the society commemorates the 1689 Siege of Derry when

Catholic James II of England laid siege to the walled city, at the time a Protestant stronghold.

The *Boyne* refers to the Battle of the Boyne which was fought in July 1690 between Catholic James II and Protestant William of Orange. The battle took place across the river Boyne near the town of Drogheda in the east of Ireland and resulted in a crushing victory for William. It turned the tide in James' attempt toregain the English throne and led to the foundation of the Orange Order in Northern Ireland.

The *Ulster Covenant*, was signed by nearly 500,000 people in September 1912, in protest against the Third Home Rule for Ireland Bill introduced at Westminster earlier that year. Signatories pledged to resist Home Rule with 'all means necessary'.

Gun-running refers to a gun smuggling operation involving some 25,000 guns from Germany into Larne, organisd in April 1914 by the Ulster Unionist Council to equip the Ulster Volunteer Force.

Sir Edward *Carson* (1854 – 1935) was an Irish unionist politician who led the resistance to Home Rule for Ireland in the early twentieth century, being the first signatory to the Ulster Covenant.

Colonel *Fred Crawford* (1861 – 1952) was a staunch Ulster Loyalist most notable for organising the Larne gun-running operation.

Page 272 *Heol y Frenhines* – Queen Street, a main shopping street in the centre of Cardiff.

Page 274 *Wales* and the *Welsh Review... Aneirin, Taliesin, and Dafydd ap Gwilym*

The magazine *Wales* was published by Keidrych Rhys in three intermittent series between 1937 and 1960.

The *Welsh Review*, published by Gwyn Jones, first in 1939 and then between 1944 and 1948.

Aneirin was a poet of the late sixth Century who is believed to have lived in the 'Old North', now southern Scotland. His best known work is the *Gododdin*, a series of elegies to six hundred warriors from the Kingdom of Gododdin who fell in battle against the Angles at Catraeth (Catterick, North Yorkshire) in about 600.

Taliesin was another poet of the late sixth Century who, along with Aneirin, is named in a famous passage of Nennius's *Historica Brittanica* as one of the poets who flourished in the 'Old North'. Other scholars have argued that he was a native of Powys. In the *Book of Taliesin* there is a group of twelve poems believed to be his work. He appears in many legendary accounts. Saunders Lewis identified him with the praise tradition in Welsh literature, a theme elaborated by the novelist Emyr Humphreys in his *The Taliesin Tradition* (1983).

Dafydd ap Gwilym, said to have been born near Llanbadarn Fawr, lived around the middle of the fourteenth Century. He is regarded as the greatest poet of that period, perhaps the greatest Welsh poet of all time, with more than five hundred poems attributed to him.

Page 276 *Second Aeon ... Triskel Press*

Second Aeon was edited by Peter Finch with occasional help in the review section from John Tripp. It began in 1966 and ran for twenty-one issues until the mid-seventies. Originally established as a small mimeographed vehicle for the experimental work of a small circle, *Second Aeon* soon became a major outlet for the poetry revolution of the period.

With financial aid from the Welsh Arts Council and the arts patron Cyril Hodges it grew to become a fully printed magazine of several hundred pages.

The *Triskel Press* was founded in the early 1960s by the poet and editor Meic Stephens. From the mid-1960s it also published *Poetry Wales*.

Page 278 *Morgannwg and Mynwy* –Glamorgan and Monmouth.

Page 330 *Sianel Gymraeg nawr!* – Welsh Channel now! *YR UNIG ATEB* – THE ONLY ANSWER.

Page 341 *Harm will not meet you in sleep*
Rhiannon is singing *Suo Gan* ('Cradle Song'), a traditional Welsh lullaby written by an anonymous composer which first appeared in print around 1800. The lyrics were by the Welsh folklorist Robert Bryan (1858–1920).

Page 341 *Dafydd y Garreg Wen*
Translated 'David of the White Rock', this is a traditional folk tune written by David Owen, a harpist and composer, during the first half of the eighteenth century. He was known as *Dafydd y Garreg Wen*, after the name of his farm near Porthmadog in Caernarfonshire. The words of the song were added by the poet John Ceiriog Hughes nearly a century later.

Page 368 *Y Faner* and *Y Cymro*
Y Faner (The Flag) was founded in Denbigh in 1843 by Thomas Gee as a Welsh-language weekly, liberal newspaper. It merged with *Amserau Cymru* ('Welsh Times') published in Liverpool in 1859, to create *Baner ac Amserau Cymru* ('Welsh Banner and Times'). By the late nineteenth century it achieved a weekly circulation approaching 50,000 and exerted a powerful influence. Its circulation declined during the twentieth century and the paper went through many changes of ownership. Most notably it was bought by Kate Roberts

and her husband in 1935. During the Second World War *Y Faner* was avidly read for its column *Cwrs y Byd* in which Saunders Lewis wrote about world affairs. From the late 1970s it received Welsh Arts Council funding but eventually folded in 1992. In 1997 *Y Faner Newydd* ('The New Flag') was launchedby Emyr Llewelyn and Ieuan Wyn.

Y Cymro ('The Welshman') was founded as a weekly newspaper in Wrexham in 1932, succeeding other titles of the same name during the nineteenth and early twentieth centuries. It was the last national newspaper in the Welsh language, eventually folding in 2017, by which time it was being published by North Wales Newspapers. In November 2017 it was announced that a campaign group had received funding from the Welsh Books Council to assist a relaunch of *Y Cymro* as a monthly newspaper.

Page 391 *Anarcho-syndicalism*
A theory of anarchism which views revolutionary industrial unionism as a method for workers in capitalist society to gain control of the economy and use that control to influence broader society.

Page 416 *Bread and Roses*
This is a phrase attributed to Rose Schneiderman (1882-1972) an American trade union leader, socialist and feminist. It inspired the title of a poem by James Oppenheim. It was first published in *The American Magazine* in December 2011 and became associated with a successful textile strike in Lawrence, Massachussets, during January to March 2012. On a march during the strike some women carried a banner inscribed 'We want Bread, and Roses too'. Rhiannon is singing a version set to music in 1974 by Mimi Farina, a singer-songwriter and younger sister of Joan Baez.

Page 421 *The past is never dead. It's not even past.* – Ioan is quoting from William Faulkner's *Requiem for a Nun* (1951).

And we shall remember 1926 until our blood is dry –
Rhiannon is quoting from Idris Davies' *Gwalia Deserta*
(1938).

The great dream and swift disaster – Ioan is also quoting from
Idris Davies' *Gwalia Deserta* (1938).

The summer my country died – Rhiannon is quoting from the
Harri Webb poem 'That Summer', contained in his collection
A Crown for Branwen (1974).

Page 428 The lines beginning *I bet you think I'm shocking, she
says* are taken from John Tripp's poem 'Mrs Pankhurst's
granddaughter', in his collection *Passing Through* (1984).

Page 429 Paula is quoting from Virginia Woolf's *A Room of One's
Own* (1929).

Page 433 John Tripp is quoting from his poem 'Stop on a Journey'
from his *Collected Poems 1858-78*.

Page 440 *Cymru Fydd*
Literally, 'Young Wales', this was founded in 1886 in London
by a group of Liberal sympathisers including J.E. Lloyd
and O.M. Edwards. Its leader was T.E. Ellis, Liberal MP
for Meirioneth (1886-1999). Its main objective was to gain
self-government for Wales, in the context of seeking equal
participation for the country with England within the
Empire. The movement lost some of its impetus following
the withdrawal of T. E. Ellis to join the government as Chief
Whip in 1892. The leadership of Cymru Fydd was then taken
over by Lloyd George. It had an initial period of success
in 1894-5, when it merged with the North Wales Liberal
Federation to form the Welsh National Federation. However,
it met with fierce opposition from the South Wales Liberal
Federation, led by its President, David Alfred Thomas (MP
for Merthyr Tydfil 1889-1910). In January 1896, a proposal

to merge the South Wales Liberal Federation with the Welsh National Federation was put to the AGM of the South Wales Liberal Federation, held at Newport. After Robert Bird, a senior Cardiff alderman declared his determination to resist 'the domination of Welsh ideas', Lloyd George was howled down and refused permission to speak. Cymru Fydd collapsed soon afterwards.

Page 465 *Merched y Wawr*

Literally, 'Daughters of the Dawn', this is a Welsh women's organisation, similar to the Womens' Institute, whose activities are conducted through the medium of the Welsh language. It was established in 1967 when the WI insisted that English should be the official language of the movement. It has around 5,000 members.

Page 472 *Kilbrandon Commissioners*

Refers to the Scottish peer Lord Kilbrandon (1906-1989) who chaired the Commission on the Constitution from 1972-73, following the death of its first chairman Lord Crowther. Subsequently the Commission became known by his name.

Page 487 *the breakaway Scottish Labour Party*

The Scottish Labour Party (SLP) was founded in January 1976 by a group of Labour politicians led by Jim Sillars, then MP for South Ayrshire, together with sympathetic journalists. Pro-nationalist with a small 'n', it was set up as a response to their view that the Labour government's had failed to produce more robust devolution legislation, and also as a competing force to the SNP from the Left. Initially, the party achieved some success, gaining nine hundred members in its first year. However, it was subject to entryism by Trotskyist groups which caused fissures and disputes. None of the three MPs who formed the party retained their seats at the 1979 election and it was disbanded soon afterwards.

Page 489 even *Tryweryn* - see note to page 82.

Page 499 *the Amins, the Gadaffis, the PLO, and the Red Guards*
the Amins refers to Idi Amin, the military officer who was President of Uganda from 1971 to 1979. His rule was characterised by human rights abuses, repression and corruption.

the Gadaffis refers to Colonel Muammar Gadaffi who ruled Libya as a dictator from 1969 to 2011.

the PLO is the Palestine Liberation Organisation, founded in 1964, with the poupose of freeing Palestine through armed struggle.

the Red Guards were a student paramilitary social mobilised by Mao Zedong in 1966 and 1967, during the Chinese Cultural Revolution.

Page 509 ...*like chains around our feet.*

In this phrase Penry is referring to the novel by Kate Roberts *Traed mewn Cyffion* ('Chains around my Feet'), first published in 1936.

Page 516 *Being a nation, what is it? A gift*
In the depths of the heart.
Patriotism, what's that? Keeping house
In a cloud of witnesses.

This stanza, from Waldo Williams' poem *Pa Beth Yw Dyn?* ('What is Man?') is translated by Anthony Conran in his *The Peacemakers* (1997).

Page 521-22 Rhiannon is quoting from Frantz Fanon's *The Wretched of the Earth*, first published in France in 1961, and then translated and published in Britain in 1965. The passage

she is highlighting is taken from Fanon's speech to the Second
Congress of Black Artists and Writers, held in Rome in 1959.

Page 531 *The Burgos Trials*

Held between December 1970 and January 1971, these
occurred following the assassination by members of ETA
(Euskadi Ta Askatasuna/Basque Country and Freedom) of
Melitón Manzanas, a notorious police torturer. This provoked
a reaction by the Spanish authorities in which the sixteen
accused at the trial were selected at random from a group
of previously arrested ETA leaders. They were sentenced
to death but, following widespread international pleas for
clemency, the sentences were commuted. The trial had the
effect of bringing the Basque question to the forefront of
international attention. The Jean-Paul Sartre article quoted by
Phil Williams is from the Basque magazine *Zutic No. 61* and
is translated by Harri Webb in *Planet No 9*, December 1971/
January 1972.

Page 567 Rhiannon is singing a song written by Dafydd Iwan in
1971, *Pam Fod Eira yn Wyn*? ('Why is the Snow White?'). At
the time Iwan was chairman of Cymdeithas yr Iaith and had
recently served three weeks of a three-month prison sentence
for refusing to pay a fine for defacing English road signs.

Page 589 *...a separate Scottish Labour Party* - see note to Page 382.

SAFE?
WAS THE
TANIC!

SIANEL
GYMRAEG

'WE WANT
BREAD AND
ROSES TOO.'

PROLETARIAN
OF ALL
COUNTRIES
UNITE!

IPS
ON
W

SAFE?
SO WAS THE
TITANIC!

SIANEL
GYMRAEG

YR UNIG
ATEB

SH AND CHIPS
TODAY,
HIPS & FISSION
TOMORROW

SA
SO W
TITA

SA
SO V
TITA

8/5/18

AR
—
'TILL
,078!

'WE WANT
BREAD AND
ROSES TOO.'

ANEL
RAEG

NUCLEAR
WASTE —
DO NOT OPEN 'TILL
THE YEAR 200,078!

FISH

CHIP
TO

SIAN
GYMRA

RAE
I'R
EL!'

NUCLEAR
WASTE —
DO NOT OPEN 'TILL
THE YEAR 200,078!

FISH AND CHIPS
TODAY,
CHIPS & FISSION
TOMORROW

SAFE?
SO WAS THE
TITANIC!

'CHWARAE
TEG I'R
SIANEL!'

NUCLEAR
WASTE —
DO NOT OPEN 'TILL
THE YEAR 200,078!

YR UNIG
ATEB

SAF
SO WAS
TITAN